CARROLL & GRAF

More Black Magic

MORE BLACK MAGIC

ANONYMOUS

CARROLL & GRAF PUBLISHERS, INC.
NEW YORK

This collection copyright © 1998 by Carroll and Graf Publishers, Inc.

First Carroll & Graf edition of *Leda in Black on White* 1993
First Carroll & Graf edition of *Angelica* 1986

All rights reserved

Carroll & Graf Publishers, Inc.
19 West 21st Street
New York, NY 10010

ISBN 0-7867-0548-5

Manufactured in the United States of America

LEDA IN BLACK ON WHITE

LEDA IN BLACK ON WHITE

Chapter 1

Even a freshman sexologist would have no difficulty establishing the link between my mother's traumatizing example, my own childless marriage to a voyeur, and the unprecedented sexual adventure I have been living since our arrival in West Africa.

I met my husband when I was seventeen and we were married a year later, that is to say as soon as I reached the age of consent and my father could no longer legally oppose a marriage he disapproved. It has been much more than a physical love-match in the restricted sense of the term, as during the ten years that have elapsed my sex life has become phenomenally intense, owing to my husband's imaginative and perverted sensuality and my own sensitivity to almost all forms of stimulus, as well as a lack of modesty or inhibition. However, we could not continue fuelling our erotic appetites without the pressure reaching a point where the dam of civilized appearances had to burst, sweeping us away in a torrent of inter-racial fornication.

I was born Leda Swanhurst in Highfield, Mass. on June 21 1947. My surname was of course an open invitation to the given name of Leda, the Greek princess who was loved by Zeus in the form of a swan, and my literary-minded mother just could not resist the temptation, little realizing the almost prophetic nature of her impulse.

My father, who was fifteen years her senior, had risen to partnership in a Boston law firm, a position involving him in frequent overnight stays in town, as the forty-mile drive to Highfield could prove formidable in winter after a dinner with clients. It was during one of these paternal absences that I was to live the traumatic experience whose influence on my future behavior would prove decisive.

My mother had been born in England of parents who were both professors in a provincial university, where she herself majored in English literature — the subject that her father professed — and played tennis for the county. At the tender age of two I was to discover England myself, as my father was appointed to his firm's London office, where he remained for eight years, during which we rented a furnished house in Bloomsbury, near the college that had offered my mother a temporary post of tutor.

She was a distant, strikingly handsome, blond woman of Junoesque proportions, about whose everyday life I remember surprisingly little, apart from her obsession with my English and English studies. She hoped I would follow in her father's footsteps, and was openly disappointed by my preference for rhythmic gymnastics and dancing. She would no doubt have compelled me to go to college and major in English had my father not insisted I be allowed follow my own inclinations, little knowing where they would lead! However, her efforts cannot have been entirely vain, as sixteen years later these diaries are proof of my taste for the written word, as well as for other much less respectable interests!

I should perhaps mention, in brackets, that as part of her pipe-dream for my future academic career in England, and for as long as she had a say in the matter of my education, my mother made me use English rather than American spelling. At the age of thirteen I switched completely to American, although my English teachers, in a school mainly dedicated to other forms of study, were unmethodical in their correction of my deviation, with the result that my writings are a hopeless mix of the two systems, with English coming out more and more frequently on top as I grow older.

During our stay in London, I can clearly recall that when my father was away at the office our house seemed to be permanently overrun with handsome black students, who would take me on their knees and play with me while waiting for their tutorial. I would often wonder why there was such a hard lump in their pants, and why my mother locked the door of her study when receiving one or more students, and why she would cry out excitedly when she was in there alone with them, and why she would emerge flushed and trembling at the end of tuition.

I was to discover the answers to all these whys on one father-in-Boston evening, during a summer vacation some years after our return to the States. I had been invited to a party on the far side of town with a batch of other twelve year olds, and was due to stay overnight, as the hostess's daughter was my best friend at the time. Owing to some problem, another girl had to have the only spare bed, and I was driven back to the house and deposited at the end of the drive, protesting energetically that I was quite old enough to walk the last fifty yards unescorted.

Letting myself in with the emergency key that was in its usual, obvious hiding-place, I would have sneaked upstairs to avoid disturbing my mother, imagining her asleep in bed, had it not been for my ears being assailed by an avalanche of sound from the half open lounge door, which gave the impression of coming from darkest Africa rather than suburban New England, as it consisted of roll upon roll of tribal drums.

I walked over to the door thinking quite naturally that she must be looking at some exotic, late-night programme, and was about to push it wide open when something strange about the color of the light filtering through the crack made me suddenly wary. I eased the door a little further to peer into the room, and was confronted with a spectacle that made me flush to the roots of my hair, while producing a strangely exciting sensation in the pit of my loins — a sensation I had never experienced before, but which was ultimately to become the mainspring of my whole existence.

A space had been cleared in front of the closely drawn curtains of the French windows that gave onto the garden at the back of the house, which was illuminated by a single, red spotlight that must have been brought in specially for the occasion. On the couch, which had been turned to face the window, two black men — whom I recognized as the team of the local sanitation service that removed our trash — were lounging back entirely naked and drinking large quantities of my father's Bourbon, while they played almost nonchalantly with their penises, which were in a state of rampant erection.

I should perhaps add that my description of this incident is that of an adult woman of twenty seven, as at the time I was quite incapable of understanding what was happening, although every minute detail of the scene has remained indelibly engraved on my memory over the years, and until my dying-day it is certain that none will ever be effaced.

The two speakers of the hi-fi system were blaring at near maximum volume, but the real shock came from the sight of my mother, stark naked on the improvised stage, dancing convulsively to the sound of the drums, running her hands lecherously over her shapely body, particularly her vulva, buttocks and breasts, which swung and bounced heavily to the primitive rhythm.

The heat given off by the spot added to the exertion of the dance had bathed her body in a sea of sweat, and she must also have been drinking, as otherwise the abandon and immodesty of her gestures would have been unthinkable; or so I thought at the time. She frequently executed a figure known in the world of striptease as the 'bumps and grinds', consisting of rotating her hips — which she thrust repeatedly in the direction of the two men, giving them a grand stand view of the flared-out lips of her closely shaved sex — while joining her hands behind her neck to raise her heavy breasts, to which she imparted a rotating movement. This gesture drew a welter of obscene comment from the spectators, who would grab at the swinging orbs, pulling and kneading them roughly with their calloused hands, to her evident enjoyment, as she would push them at the men even harder, while sticking out her tongue in a lewdly suggestive manner.

I was paralyzed by a mixture of horror at what I saw and fear of being discovered, although I soon realized there was no risk of this happening if I remained where I was, as the three actors were entirely engrossed in their debauch. As unhealthy curiosity soon overcame initial disgust, I decided to stay on and watch the show in silent but excited dismay.

At one point my mother approached the sofa and, positioning herself between the two men with her back towards them and her inward-pointing feet some distance apart, bent down to grasp her ankles, presenting her audience with a panoramic view of her widely-splayed vulva and anus. The men lent forward to fondle the delicacies which were within such easy reach with an eagerness that belied their previous lethargy, a surprising number of horny, black fingers being thrust in and out of the proffered holes, whose owner responded to the treatment with a shameless volley of sow-like grunts.

The hole-prodding routine must have continued for at least five minutes, until both cavities were distended and swimming with secretion, when the brawnier of the two men said to his partner: "Look man, you take it lying down tonight, I feel like a piece of real ass for a change!" His companion dutifully lay down on the floor with an organ standing up like a cathedral spire, and my mother straddled him, facing his head, kneeling down with her legs on either side of his body to impale herself with her usual neatness. Gasping breathlessly, she reached back to pull her rear-cheeks as far apart as possible, whereupon the other man knelt down behind her and, pointing his rampant member straight at her heaving rosebud — as his companion was already giving her some pretty thrustful treatment out front — slid it into her rectum until the encounter of thigh and buttock put an end to deeper penetration.

Leaning forward, my mother arched her back and started a carefully orchestrated body-ballet, pressing downwards and forwards onto the sex that was reaming her slit, which then withdrew as she seesawed upwards and backwards onto the ass-pummeling parallel, which thrust forward until buffered by her buttocks. Once this alternating routine was locked into place, the protagonists speeded up considerably to an accompaniment of farmyard noises, and I was horrified to hear my mother mouthing the most revolting expletives, until her sodomizer reduced her to silence by grabbing her hair, wrenching round her head and jamming his tongue into her mouth, while her frontal lover greedily gobbled her juddering breasts.

Up till then sex had been a closed book. I was intrigued by the noises that emanated at night from my parents' adjoining bedroom, muffled by the partition wall, but in the state of total innocence in which I was then enveloped I presumed they were having a friendly chat and gave the matter no further thought, life being full of so many more interesting things, such as gym and dancing. In my presence my mother and father had never shown any form of affection for each other which might have put ideas into my head, and up till then I had always fought shy of school-girl confidences and insinuations with the result that my sexual awareness was completely retarded. I would soon catch up at recklessly high speed, as the effect of what I was witnessing was not only traumatizing for a child of my age, but would liberate my sexual impulses virtually overnight.

Finally the spectacle of my mother's black, double-barrelled adultery became too much, particularly when I discovered I had a hand deep inside my jeans busily tittilating a nascent but highly responsive clitoris. Forgetting the unfinished live-show in the neighboring room, I fled upstairs to my bedroom where I was violently sick in the wash basin.

The following morning my mother walked blithely into my bedroom on some every-day household errand, clearly expecting to find an empty bed, and stopped dead in her tracks when she saw me lying there, her eyes filling with an expression of panic I will never forget. I burst into tears, leaving no doubt as to what I had seen, but instead of trying to comfort me and somehow endeavor to bridge the terrible gap, she turned on her heel and ran out of the room. Looking back on that unreal incident I recognize that my mother did the only thing possible in view of her introverted nature, as there was no way she could conceivably have explained the inexplicable or repaired the irreparable.

A few months later, at school, I was to learn that my father had started divorce proceedings on the discreetly convenient grounds of incompatibility, but had little difficulty in divining the true reason, particularly as my mother meekly accepted immediate seperation without any form of alimony or even visiting rights where I was concerned. I vaguely understood there was something in her she could not control, and for my part I felt only a strange indifference, tinged with relief, when she left the house, our formal, embarrassed words of farewell being devoid of any real emotion. I somehow knew we would never meet again, and was not shocked or even surprised to learn, many years later, that she had worked for some time in a colored brothel in New Orleans before disappearing entirely from the record.

Now that I myself am addicted to as much inter-racial sex as I can get, I can understand what happened, but illogically can never forgive, let alone forget.

Chapter 2

Whatever the effect of this shattering experience may have been on my adult libido, the immediate outcome was to shut off any desire for normal, sexual relations with boys. I was happy in my boarding school in one of the neighboring states, as its specialization in various forms of physical training, sport and dancing coincided with my adolescent tastes and ambitions, which led, when I was fourteen, to victories in junior, rhythmic gymnastics championships.

My incipient, sexual appetite was, to start with, entirely self-centered and I became a frequent and imaginative masturbater, my bodily suppleness, which was enhanced by a certain degree of double-jointedness, enabling me to discover methods and positions involving contortions which were well beyond the capabilities of most girls. When I was thirteen these tastes and skills led naturally to my first totally uninhibited lesbian love for a passionate, sixteen year-old red head, a certain Victoria Henley-Nebbitt — nicknamed Queen Victoria because of her regally commanding habits — the daughter of pretentious local socialites. She was also an adept of rhythmic gymnastics and was to be the first of a long line of lesbian lovers and mistresses, both fellow students and teachers, with whom I alternated the male and female roles, displaying a shameless abandon that made me the most sought-after of partners. Without ever having made love to a man my virginity evaporated as if it had never existed, as a result of the wide variety of devices, gadgets, vegetables, fruit and heaven knows what else, not to mention innumerable fingers, that we all used to further the pursuit of forbidden love.

However, I was only a circumstantial and never a dedicated lesbian, as an increasing desire for contact with men was to reveal once the psychological shock of my mother's example wore off, although for several years I led an exclusively Sapphic existence that gave me a great deal of pleasure and even ecstasy, while temporarily satisfying an appetite which it would have been unwise to unleash completely at such a tender age.

By the time of my marriage I had blossomed physically to a degree that precluded continuation in training as a rhythmic gymnast hopeful of attaining Olympic standards. On my eighteenth birthday, I stood five feet ten and weighed 130 pounds, with vital statistics of 38-22-32, dimensions that ruled out any further progress in a field which favors the slightly built, and has in any case become the preserve of much younger girls. I might add that my impressive bust measurement was due to breasts that stood straight out from the thorax in an arrogantly, self-supporting attitude which added at least two inches to the statistic, causing my husband, during the early years of our marriage, to refer to them jocularly as my "jutters". As for my facial appearance, he would say laughingly that he married me as the cheapest way of acquiring a Boticelli Venus. This was misleading, as the almost disconcerting symmetry of my features has little in common with those of any of the Florentine master's stunning model, particularly my nose which is absolutely straight and fine-boned. In repose my face still radiates an aura of purity and innocence which is cruelly at variance with the facts.

My physique, which was and still is beautifully muscled and proportioned, with breathtakingly lovely legs, was made even more striking by a flaring mane of luxuriantly thick and wavy hair I had allowed to grow until it could be drawn between my buttocks and thighs. When platted, with a brush-like end, it was a formidable instrument of titillation, for either female partners or myself. This profusion of hair continued in my pubic regions where it grew in krinkly, chestnut-colored abundance, welling out from between loins and buttocks, as well as from my armpits. The latter was in defiance of my mother's systematic depilation of these regions, including her sex, although I will never know whether this was to please herself, her black boy friends or my father. My legs and buttocks and forearms were — and still are — adorned with an almost imperceptible gossamer sheen of the finest blond hair which has never been removed.

I was to meet my future husband in the Boston apartment of my father's younger sister, to whom I had been entrusted following my mother's departure and the sale of the house in Highfield. At the time, she was herself a childless widow in her late thirties, having lost her husband in a road accident two years earlier, since when she had led an irreproachable existence, divided between the golf course, bridge evenings and a large greenhouse, where she cultivated cloying tropical plants and flowers which frequently won prizes in horticultural shows, more through their rarity and a general lack of competition than for any inherent beauty.

She was a subtly feline brunette in whom, as my own lesbian

experience developed, I detected a fellow-feeling which I rapidly converted into something more sexually tangible, as her small but beautifully built body was compellingly erotic, with a suggestion of boyishness that was an inducement to specifically anal fun and games.

I was then fourteen and, for some time past, had noticed the more than familial interest she took in my body when undressed. The more I sensed her attention, the more I would walk round the apartment in the nude, with the fairly respectable excuse she was my aunt and there was no reason why I should hide myself from her. My intentions were, however, far from pure, as I had decided that the nights of the summer vacation were really rather long and lonely, and there was no reason why we should not pass them together doing all sorts of horrid things.

I would therefore always rub against her when our paths crossed, prodding her gently with my breasts, whose surprisingly mature nipples just happened to be erect at that moment. When I felt her eyes watching me from behind, I would find a reason for bending down with my feet apart, or when she was seated I would slump down in a chair opposite, crossing my legs in such a way as to provide her with uninterrupted views.

Returning from the gymnasium one evening I invented a story about having pulled a muscle on the inside of the upper thigh, and asked her to rub in some embrocation to relieve the pain. Stripping off I lay down on the bed on my back, indicating the supposed seat of the trouble, having timed my initiative to coincide with a moment when she was herself only wearing a bath-robe.

As she started to massage me gently at an exasperating distance from the target area, I sat up and transferred her hand forcibly to my groin, burying the tips of her fingers in the abundant pubic hair. When our eyes met conspiratorially I said: "You must be terribly hot in that bath robe", and without waiting for a reply,

I slid it off her shoulders, passing my arm behind her neck and pulling her lips down onto mine.

I made it clear it was not a normal 'niecey' kiss by thrusting my tongue between her lips while grasping one of her taught nipples and tweaking it so hard she winced with pain. Falling back onto the bed, I spun over onto my front and jackknifed the cleft of my buttocks up against her mouth, which had not moved, snapping: "Lick my bloody ass!" inexplicably using language at total variance with my normal verbal primness. She recoiled in amazement, more because of the unaccustomed obscenity than the shamelessness of the gesture, stammering somewhat illogically: "How dare you — you shameless trollop!" but her tone lacked any real conviction.

"Well", I rapped out, leaping agiley off the bed, "If you won't lick my bloody ass I'll lick yours!" So saying I moved quickly round behind her, levered her buttocks apart and buried my mouth in her anal cleft to lap away happily. To start with she protested, but was physically no match for her athletic niece, and her opposition became feebler and feebler as my tonguing produced its first effects.

She nevertheless continued to babble conventional, middle class recrimination, while taking great care not to impede my progress, gasping with undisguised pleasure and arching her back so I could dig my darting tongue deeper into her back door. Any semblance of resistance soon disappeared, to be replaced by an ascending scale of moans and groans which left little doubt as to the decline of her moral standards. She even agreed to help me when I asked her, between licks, to hold her butttocks apart so I could use my own hands to better effect on the glistening oval of her sex.

Since the prising apart of her hemispheres, she was as pretty as a dirty picture in her bottoms-up pose with rearing half-moons and a perfect central ellipse. I needed no encouragement to go to work with a will, licking her neat little sphincter, thumbing her rigid clitty and deep-fingering her yawning slit, which was as beautifully shaped as an exotic shell.

I did not have to wait for my reward, as her sound track soon rose to a hysterical pitch and she came profusely, inundating the counterpain and rinsing my face with a colorless, salty fluid that, in my inexperience, I took to be urine.

"You filthy bitch!" I shouted in mock anger, "You've wet my bed!" Take that, and that, and that!" Cupping my hand I landed a resounding salvo of slaps on her right buttock, producing reports like pistol shots as well as a delicious shade of pink. I repeated the dose on the left side, and then alternated, becoming more and more expert with practice. Far from provoking any form of protest, my ministrations resulted in even more volume and further fluxes of liquid as Laura traded-in her remaining principles for a king-sized climax. "Oh yes! You sexy little whore! Give it to me harder! Give me more fingers! Stick them all in there! Ah! Ah! The thumb as well! Do you hear me? I said all! Ah! Ah!

Strange though it may seem, I had not only got all the fingers of one hand into her poke, but even the knuckles as well, followed rapidly by the rest of the hand up to the wrist. With elbow bent and bicep flexed I pounded her insides as if they were a punch ball. The more I pistoned, the more she moaned and leaked, until, in a final spasm of ecstasy she cried out: "I'm coming! Oh my god I'm coming buckets!" and wet the bed for the third time before collapsing in a deep swoon.

When I broke the news to Queen Victoria, we were fingering each other in one of the gymnasium toilets after a strenuous work out with the Judo class, followed by cold showers that had left our nipples standing up on end.

"Wow!" she exalted, letting the extremity of my breast slide out of her mouth, are we going to have lots of nice clean fun! I can't wait to get my fingers up her!" So saying, she thrust my nipple back into her mouth and continued to roll it expertly between her incisors by sliding her lower jaw first one way and then the other. This torture monopolized most of my attention, being accompanied, as it was, by a systematic pinching of my already prominent clitty, but I could not help thinking, between gasps, that there really were times when Vicky was quite gratuitously coarse. It was one thing to use rude words when self-control was obliterated by a rousing climax, but quite another to employ such vulgar language on normal occasions.

I showed my displeasure by jabbing a middle finger into her anus, but to no avail, as she just arched her back so I could get it in further, sighed with satisfaction and said: That's it my pet, shove it up my shit-hole — as far as you like!" It is a mystery why my middle class upbringing should often have asserted itself when I was behaving like a rutty little slut myself, but that is the way things were until the absurdity of such an attitude was finally brought home to me by a shattering sexual experience.

Two other friends who were also delighted by the news, and with whom my lesbian relationship was almost as intense as with Vicky, were the twins, Ingrid and Mara, the daughters of first generation Swedish immigrants to Canada, where they had founded a large timber business. The twins, who were indentical and a year younger than Vicky, were of the purest Scandinavian stock with startlingly blue eyes, flaxen blond hair and long, athletic limbs. But there was nothing pure at all about their sexual behavior, which, unlike Vicky's spontaneous immorality, was cold bloodedly lecherous.

From earliest puberty they had cultivated mastery of mutual masturbation, to such a degree that when locked together in a soixante-neuf embrace — with the thumb and forefinger of the right hand plugged into the other's greedy little holes, the tongue busily activating the sisterly clitoris and the left hand exciting her maidenly nipples — they were able, through an uncanny understanding of their intimate reflexes, to come continuously, with love juice trickling down their darting fingers until the tension built up to a point where the loser could take no more and had to let go.

They adapted this technique to intercourse with outside partners, whom they would suck completely high and dry, producing palpitations that could take several minutes to subside. The first twin, lying underneath, would adopt a conventional 69 position with the outsider on top, while the second would devote herself entirely to the third party's anus, licking and fingering to such effect that, after a few minutes, the sphincter would be so distended she could insert the first three of her long and shapely fingers right up to the knuckles.

The next stage would be to push them in and out until the muscle lost all resilience, enabling her to fit her lips inside the gaping rim for a suck and blow job that drove the recipient crazy with pleasure. Whatever the state of their victim's emotions they would cling to her like two lovely limpets who refused to be shaken loose, racking her with one orgasm after another until she either fainted or became hysterical.

I can remember how I would plead for mercy as my orgasms piled up, one behind the other, jostling each other for enough ero-space to survive, while the remorseless and unshedable twins kept pumping away with an unhealthy and libidinous glee, greeting my sexquakes with squeels of cruel delight and redoubled effort. In their mid-teens, with still pubescent, button-nippled breasts and close-cropped hair, they were only distinguishable from beautifully buggerable boys by the absence of the famous appendage.

After our evening of mutual discovery Laura worshipped me

unconditionally, pandering to my every wish and whim and using any excuse to establish physical contact between our bodies, her hands permanently groping for one of my recesses or rotundities. Of course, I was the dominant male and master and she the submissive female.

The greatest moment in Laura's world of sex was my sixteenth birthday party. I had refused her offer of a larger celebration, preferring a more intimate dinner in her apartment, to which only my closest friends or accomplices were invited, that is to say Vicky and the twins, my father being unable come as he was absent in Europe attending a legal congress. My guests had been well primed as to my intentions, which were to give Aunty Laura the time of her lesbian life, and Vicky promised to bring along her impressive collection of sexual appliances.

She arrived dressed in a skin-tight denim outfit consisting of a micro skirt and a sleeveless waistcoat-corsage with a plunging V neck that showed a lot of inner breast. The twins wore red parkas cut to bare their adorable midriffs, as well as navel-exposing white leather mini skirts. Needless to say there was not a trace of bra or panties between the three of them, the slightest movement or lowering of an angle of vision being enough to reveal the most heavenly perspectives.

Vicky was carrying a fashionable brief case containing her penis substitutes and the like, neatly housed in plastic foam niches of appropriate shapes and sizes. I wore a halter-necked, backless, white mini-dress in a body-clinging material that silhouetted my already aggressive nipples, and was cut so low behind that it exposed the top of my other cleft. In the presence of all this tempting young flesh Laura's austerely elegant black silk chiffon skirt and jacket seemed almost provocative.

Despite her moments of unbridled lechery during the course of our 'husband and wife' existence, my Aunt clung to the appearances of conventional morality, and had not as yet been exposed to the rough and tumble of lesbian group sex, her contacts with my other partners in lechery having been purely social.

She had therefore never seen them dressed for action, with the result that her first reflex was one of hypocritical disapproval. Deciding to put an end to that sort of silliness immediately, I turned my back to her, raised my dimunitive skirt to above the level of my buttocks and said brutally: "Laura darling, would you like to show my friends how sloppily you lick my little bull's eye?" She blushed deep scarlet and, having taught her a lesson, I restored my hemline to its normal position. "Now my angel", I said, taking her head in my hands and planting a very wet and tonguey kiss between her lips, "Let's have something to eat and drink to satisfy our more respectable appetites before starting in on the other ones!"

Thoroughly discountenanced, she relapsed into an embarrassed silence, leaving the four of us to indulge in an outpouring of girlish phantasms and confidences that would have made any normally constituted headmistress take a running jump onto the nearest psychiatric couch.

Vicky, who had failed to graduate the previous summer, was in what was to prove to be her last semester at school. She was a planturous eighteen and madly in love with the new basket ball coach, a splendid, six-foot black girl called Hatty, who had been a reserve for the national Olympic team the year before. One could not open a lavatory door without finding them frigging like mad, and Vicky must really have wanted to find out what Laura was all about to abandon that beautiful dusky body for a whole evening. It may have been that the idea of debauching a personable and beautiful woman almost twice her own age appealed to her innate sense of wickedness.

We were about to start on the dessert which, like the rest of the delicious meal, had been supplied by one of Boston's leading caterers, when I saw Vicky take advantage of Laura's temporary absence in the kitchen, to empty the contents of a small sachet into our hostess's glass of wine.

The effect of the potion, which I learned later was a relatively innocuous form of Spanish Fly, was almost immediate. From a distant and disapproving duena Laura was transformed, in a matter of minutes, into an uninhibited harlot who promptly became the ring leader in indecency, goading us on to more and more scandalous conduct, to such a point that it was our turn to look like paragons of all the moral virtues.

Her first initiative, completely out of the blue, was to seize Vicky by the midriff, as she passed by on the way to fetch another bottle of wine, and pull her down onto her lap, where she slid a hand into the inviting decolleté and jerked out a deliciously freckled tit, whose rapidly stiffening nipple was thrust between her teeth and given an energetic nibbling that produced an appreciative yelp of pain.

"There you are you randy, red-headed whore!" Auntie Laura exclaimed in a blurry voice, "Now I'm going to gobble your dirty little cunt!".

We all looked uneasy, as the change was too radical for comfort, and there was always the risk of impure ingredients having been used in the preparation of the stimulant. In any case, the cunt in question was always irreproachably clean and sweet-smelling. Vicky, however, was in at least a seventh lesbian heaven, as Aunty Laura had spun her round so she was straddling her knees, placing her hands under the girl's exposed buttocks to lift her vulva up to her mouth, fulfilling the promise to give it a good gluttonizing, after having released the grazed nipple, which in any case needed a rest.

Vicky positively writhed with delight, groaning and gasping with an intensity of pleasure which showed what a good pupil Laura had been with her lapping lessons, burrowing away with her head between the red head's thighs until the girl became quite hysterical, dribbling rivulets down her benefactor's chin and onto the silk chiffon skirt.

This was the sign for a general free for all, and in a trice the twins were as naked as the day they were born and busy unbuttoning Vicky's corsage, whose removal completely liberated her firm but generous breasts. Aunty Laura was prevailed upon to let go of her victim's inner lips for long enough to lay her across a low table, with her thighs widespread at one end and her head hanging down at the other. Laura got back to work on her sex, the twins latched on to her nipples for the big suck, while I hitched up the skirt of my dress around my waist, squatting down with my back to the group, my furry cleft poised over Vicky's mouth for an upside-down cunnilingus. During the darting of her tongue I compounded my ecstasy by fingering my clitty until it stood to rubbery attention, while drops of my love-drip pearled off onto Miss Henley-Nebbitt's freckled forehead.

We were soon all racked by series of spasms. The twins and Aunty Laura, although mainly concerned with the dispensing of pleasure, had not overlooked their own requirements, and all three were using free hands to explore the endless possibilities of self-abuse, Laura all by herself, and Ingrid and Mara reciprocally, Vicky using her fingers, which could not quite reach the twins' genitals, to fondle their little boy breasts, which reacted pointingly to the treatment.

After a breathing space during which we finished off the long-neglected dessert, I suggested that we transfer to the velvety Ispahan carpet in front of the empty fireplace, where Auntie Laura was rapidly divested of her haute couture. Once naked she was submitted to reactivation by the twins, with greedy lips producing the usual delirious effects, whose verbal expression was somewhat stifled by the fact that Laura's mouth was full of Ingrid's blond and curly muff, to which she gave as good as she was getting elsewhere.

While this exchange was taking place, a still breathless Vicky, who had wiped my come off her brow, was busy assembling a formidable looking weapon consisting of a double diljo whose parallel branches were of equal length, being spring-loaded in such a way as to squeeze the two component parts together against the membrane seperating the vaginal and anal channels, once the apparatus had been introduced into the respective holes. A third branch, stubbier than the others and facing in the opposite direction at an oblique angle, was the stay which was planted in the sex of the dominant partner.

Vicky gingerly inserted this protruberance in her vagina, squirming pleasurably as she did so, and then picked up a strange-looking harness composed of two adjustable straps attached at one end to a rubber ring and at the other to two paper-clip devices. The surfaces of the straps, where they came together, just above the ring, were convex and coated with an abrasive substance. She momentarily withdrew the stay to secure the ring around it, before returning it to her loins, wincing with pain as she fixed the two clips to her nipples. Then, bending her back slightly, she shortened the straps so that when she straightened up again they pulled her teats downwards with a jerking movement that was obviously painful.

The operation of this ingenious mechanism was quite simple. All the wearer had to do, on the in-stroke, was to straighten her back, making the straps tauten and pull cruelly at the nipple-clips, producing a masochistic sensation whose intensity was in direct proportion to the uprightness of the spinal column. At the same time the rounded section of the rubber strap would drag over her clitty with equally beneficial results.

I had always admired Vicky for the inventiveness she brought to the design of sexual hardware. I myself am quite incapable of creating artificial aids to better sex, although I have a natural gift for ad-libbing with all available props to the best possible effect. I felt like asking her for a trial run, but as my anus was still virginal I thought it would be better to wait for a more appropriate occasion, little knowing it was imminent.

At a sign from Vicky the twins obediently gave up their assault on Laura's loins, which were now so moist and open that when she knelt down with her buttocks raised receptively, the red head had no difficulty sliding in the two branches to skin-against-skin, without any apparent resistance other than a violent bucking of buttocks as the owner of the holes writhed in rapture at the size and the suddenness of the duality, before groaning with renewed pleasure when she felt the converging pressure of the spring.

On the second stroke the redhead straightened her back, making it her turn to gasp in delighted agony as the clips clawed at her teats and the strap scraped her sex. The twins locked themselves into position on Laura's breasts, fondling her clitoris with the hands that were not already hard at work on their own unsated slits. While all this was happening I could find nothing better to do than stick a well manicured finger nail into Vicky's rubicund anus, planting another one firmly in my own.

Our improvised quintet played the score with increasing harmony and fervor, Vicky withdrawing and reinserting her instruments to the point of maximum sensation for the half swooning Laura, who could no longer find noises or words to express her coming. At the end of an inning Vicky would straighten up, snarling with pain as the clips chewed her nipples and the asperities on the straps savaged her long-suffering clit.

The twins energetically sucked and fingered, appearing at times to have most of Laura's neat little breasts in their mouths, and it was evident afterwards, from a series of teeth marks — some of which had even drawn blood — that not only had they given Laura a lot of rough treatment, but that she had enjoyed every minute, as at no stage had anyone heard the slightest whisper of complaint.

Finally, under the centrifugal force of incessant orgasm, the group disintergrated, all four participants being dispersed around the carpet's central medallion like a scattered bouquet of exotic flowers. I alone, having had my finger wrenched out of Vicky's anus, retained a certain degree of composure, which was largely due to not having removed my thoroughly indecent dress, as so far there had been no real call to do so.

After recovering their breath and baptising the bidet I had forced Aunty Laura to install, Vicky and Laura tenderly massaged each other's breasts with a pain-killing and cicatrizing gel, whose chilling properties produced a spectacular tit-stiffening side effect. Despite soreness and sensitivity they began to develop an unhealthy interest in their abnormally swollen nipples, the massaging movements becoming less and less therapeutic and more and more indecent. They were soon interspersed with episodes of teat-tweaking, followed by a slobbery kiss and, before you could say cunt, they were fork-fucking on the floor, grinding their groins together in a noisy quest for clitoral fulfilment.

They would no doubt have gone on like that for ages had I not pushed a big toe in to Aunty Laura's rectal cleft and snapped: "When do I get a share of the action? Don't forget it's my birthday not yours!"

With the twins assistance I prised their interlocking limbs apart, the seperation of their vaginal lips producing a sucking sound as what must have been an air-lock was liberated. Pulling a somewhat dazed Vicky to her feet, I suggested it was about time we got round to the matter of the birthday surprise I had been promised.

"You're quite right", she said, "I had almost forgotten; we have a very special present for you". Crossing over again to the famous briefcase she took out a wickedly curved diljo connected by a flexible pipe to a transparent reservoir equipped with a plunger. This made it possible to expel its liquid content under high pressure through the artificial penis and out of the hole at the tip of the glans.

I thought for a minute she was going to give it to me. She was, but not in the way I expected, as she marched off with her nipples still protruding naughtily under the effect of the gel, declaring: "I must prepare and heat the mixture, as it is important to get it just right".

We all trooped into the kitchen behind her, and while Ingrid and Mara, bottom to bottom, played obscene games with the rolling pin, sliding it, back and forwards through the opening at the top of their thighs after having smeared it with butter, Vicky seperated the whites of three eggs from the yokes, took two pints of full cream milk from the ice box and whipped them up together until the mixture had the glutinous consistency of human sperm. It then passed a minute in the sauce pan to reach the right temperature, making due allowance for cooling during the period that would elapse before it was actually ejaculated.

We were ready for action, and by now I had understood I would not be receiving the diljo gift-wrapped, but where it would do me most good. I felt the adrenalin start to pump as we paraded back into the lounge, realizing I was about to pass an important milestone on my highway of sex.

Vicky carefully checked the connecting pipe between the brimming reservoir and the awe-inspiring phallus, before buckling on the harness with a between-the-thighs strap secured by a stubby diljo covered with jagged excrescences. This accounted for the care with which she inserted it and the quantity of vaseline applied. It took her some time to press it the whole way home, as its thickness alone made introduction problematical, and the asperities created a further resistance that my darling only overcame at the price of a genuine suffering confirmed by the crying and the sobbing which accompanied the implant.

At one stage I even thought she was going to give up, as tears of pain ran down her cheeks, but she finally made it, and from the shudder that racked her body, and the long gasp which issued from her contorted mouth, I knew she had come.

"Now you vicious little slut", she panted, turning to face me, "Although you don't deserve it, as a special treat for your sixteenth birthday we are going to ravish your anal virginity! Remove your dress and kneel down on the carpet with your knees apart, your head down and your rump well up in the air. The twins will prepare you for the supreme sacrifice, which may hurt a little, as I have chosen a weapon worthy of such a memorable defloration!"

At last the moment I had been looking forward to and dreading at the same time had come. Lucidly I did not want it to happen, and yet I knew deep down inside that it would prove to be the key to my sexual fulfilment.

Trembling with suppressed anxiety, I obeyed my executioner's orders and the twins went to work on my poor, condemned rose-bud, licking and fondling until they were able to introduce one finger, then two, then two on either side, working away until the muscle relaxed completely to frame a wide-open cavity that was ready to contain Vicky's terrible gadget. She rounded off the preparations by annointing my aperture with the same perfumed vaseline she had just used to solve her own problem, pushing whole wads of the stuff into my rectum.

There had been much giggling and gasping going on behind me during this softening-up period, which I vaguely realized was due to Vicky kneeling behind the twins and rubbing the end of the diljo up and down their slits. As the slightest movement of the weapon produced a corresponding effect of torsion at the end buried in the red-head, she was also contributing noisily to the sound-effects.

Finally the twins announced that all was ready, and moved aside to allow Vicky to approach the target. I felt her kneel between my legs and place her hands on the sides of my buttocks, lining up the glans with my yawning sphincter. All she needed to do was lean forward and the evil-looking device slid easily and effortlessly into my most intimate recess, the curved shape exercising a heavenly upward pressure against the roof of the rectum.

It was as if a miracle had taken place, as I could hear the bells pealing while the organ played; not a real live organ this time, but a divine substitute that left me in no doubt as to my true vocation: I had been born to be buggered. Just as some people are born to be lawyers or doctors or artists, I, from the womb, had been predestined to sodomy. My whole being was suffused with a delicious warmth which was both tense and lethargic. I could not possibly describe the feeling, any more than anyone has succeeded in describing orgasm; it just felt so vibrantly and giddily good, as if I had started to melt. As I had not yet even begun to come, what was it going to be like when I had a full rectal orgasm, not to mention an anal climax?

Vicky was taken totally by surprise. She was expecting sobs of suffering and cries for mercy. Instead she discovered that in destroying my anal maidenhead she had transfigured me with a sexual joy of an intensity beyond her comprehension. At least she got the message I was ready for a great deal more, and throwing caution to the winds started to sock it to me for all she was worth.

The first orgasm came more rapidly than I would have thought possible, and in any case a great deal sooner than would have been the case with the neighboring hole. However, it was not just the speed that took me by surprise, but the raging intensity. It felt as if my bowels were cavernously empty and yet extravagantly full; that they were searingly hot yet icily cold; that they were exploding at the same time as imploding, and that they were doing everything I could not possibly hope to understand let alone explain, but that felt good to the point where the comparatives end and the issimos begin.

I dug my nails deeply into the carpet's silky pile and even tried to get my teeth into its weft. Then suddenly the unthinkable happened: I, whose language had always been so measured and prim — no doubt a heritage of my mother's up-tight literary aspirations — started to mouth a stream of unbelievable obscenities: "Come on you ass-fucking bitch! What are you waiting for? Get that black jack up my shit-hole! Ah! Ah! Bugger me! Bugger me! Ass-fuck me deeper! Harder than that you rutty cow! Push damn it! Push it further in! Ram it! damn it! Ah! Ah! Oh! Haven't you got anything bigger? What about a wine bottle? That's it — a wine bottle! Ah! Ah! faster you shitty bung-fucker!"

There ensued a moment of consternation even more stunned then when Aunty Laura had let fly, as the other participants wondered where such unspeakable words could possibly have come from. Vicky was so astounded she stopped what she was doing, and they all froze into the immobility and silence of a waxwork's tableau. I broke the magic spell by firing off another salvo of the vilest expletives, wrenching them back to the world of the unwholesome. Like an amateur movie in an old projector that had been stopped and then re-started, the action resumed in flickering slow motion, before gradually reaching a normal and then an excessive speed.

This was because the comparatively sedate rhythm of the initial phase had now been replaced by a frenzied to and fro, as Vicky, who had finally been galvanized into action by my verbal encouragement, threw everything she had into my birthday treat, withdrawing to the limit of the sphincter before ramming the blissful bludgeon back into my entrails, banging the harness against flattened buttocks with each stroke. For our further enjoyment I imparted a rotating movement to my backside, producing a double torsion effect, as the diljo strained against the edges of my alimentary tract, while the stubby stay ground around Vicky's vagina.

As my partner's in and out movement accelerated, one of the twins (I was too far gone to recognize which) slid her head under mine and took my mouth in hers, thereby almost interrupting my stream of oral filth, without, however, silencing me entirely, as half-muffled obscenities continued to escape whenever a gap opened up between our lips. The other twin somehow managed to pass a hand between my thighs and jab a forefinger into my dribbling slit, wickedly thumbnailing my rampant clitty in the process.

It was obviously much too good to last, particularly as Vicky had shifted her knees to outside mine, pressing inwards to generate the maximum possible friction. I had been coming incessantly for at least five minutes, and could no longer stave off a terminal climax. The red-head was also in a state of chronic orgasm, as the excrescences on the stay were playing havoc with her vaginal walls. By mutual consent we decided to ring down the curtain, and she hit the plunger, injecting a quart of warm, artificial semen into my seething bowels, triggering a climax during which they all had to hold me down, as I reared so violently my ginger lover was completely unseated.

Subsiding twitchingly into a fetal position on the carpet, I still needed it enough to reach back and clasp Vicky's buttocks with my hands to retain the device in my rectum until the last traces of orgasmic eruption had billowed out of my loins. When I finally shuddered to a halt, she slumped down beside me, the displacement of her body causing the diljo to slip out of me with an unseemly sound.

Suddenly all chaos was let loose as the terrible realization dawned that I had just been administered an outsize enema, and had two seconds flat in which to reach the nearest john. Running as if Olympic selection was at stake, propelled onwards by the thrust of a Vicky-mix that spouted from behind like the solidified vapor trail of a jet aircraft in a clear sky, I made it. Luck had fortunately been on my side, but as I sat there sheepishly after the storm had passed, I had time to reflect on the secondary risks of unpremeditated sodomy.

Chapter 3

My conversion to heterosexuality came as naturally as falling off a dyke, a tumble made all the easier by the fact that for some time I had subconsciously felt the need for more in the way of satisfaction than my girlies and gadgets could provide.

I met my future husband just after my seventeenth birthday, when my father, who had been invited to an informal and respectable dinner party by his sister — as he of course remained in total ignorance of our scandalous liaison — asked if he could bring along a new French client who had come to see him unexpectedly.

The new French client turned out to be Etienne. I was immediately attracted to him by the instinctive realization I was in the presence of an 'Homme à Femmes' who, without being overtly macho, quite clearly not only knew everything there was to know about the sexual mechanics of the human female, but had attained a libidinous dimension that transcended a simple mastery of feminine plumbing, a limitation frequently encountered with the basic, bread and butter stud. He was a man who would obviously be able to take me a long way down the road to erotic discovery, although neither of us could have imagined how far that would be.

From the outset he was clearly fascinated, as beneath the surface of a conversation ostensibly devoted to socially permissible subjects ran an intensely sensual undercurrent, whose presence was acknowledged by exchanges of furtive glances that only a father lost in a legal labrynth could possibly have failed to detect.

It was in fact my father who unwittingly supplied the opportunity we both eagerly sought, when he suggested that his sister show Etienne, who had expressed an interest in painting, round the Museum of Fine Arts the following morning, before he caught the midday flight back to Paris. It it was of course child's play for me to tag on to such an emminently respectable outing.

By that time I was fully grown and developed, and my body tan had benefitted from two months of an exceptionally sunny summer. As I was determined that Etienne should not have to strain his imagination to visualize the physical assets that were his for the takeover, I dressed — or more accurately undressed — in a minute, denim micro-skirt that barely concealed the rise of my buttocks, with a white, sleeveless, debardeur top which had shrunk in the wash and gave a three-dimensional reading of my aggressively jutting breasts. My fabulous legs — arguably the first among my many beautiful physical features — were set off by a pair of white leather ballerinas that emphasized the finesse of my ankles and the perfect muscular swell of my calves. With such a scanty skirt I could hardly not wear panties, as all I posessed would have been on public display every time I moved, but I rationed myself to the smallest string-style pair I could find, pulling them up tightly into my cleft, a process that forced luxuriant tufts of pubic vegetation out into the open.

The next gambit in my plan of campagne was Laura, who was going to have to understand that this was the end of the exclusively lesbian line. There could be no question of jealousy or exercise of authority, as the time had come for me to get myself well and truly laid. Not only would she have to resign herself to this change, but I needed her active collaboration to bring my plan to fruition, so when she reached for my vulva upon waking the following morning, I frigged her into a state of quaking submission in which she was quite incapable of refusing my ultimatum. She even surprised me by making only one request — to be allowed to watch!

The deal was struck on the spot and the contract sealed by supple lips on my clitty which sucked me the whole way to my breakfast orgasm, while my hands, cupping the sides of her head, adjusted the degree of contact with voluptuous precision.

As agreed, we met Etienne at the ticket counter. He greeted me with a thin, enigmatic smile as his eyes visually lifted the hem of my micro and removed my panties, which, as planned, left him in no doubt as to my aspirations. The only unknown factor was where and when, as his flight took off at 12.30 pm, meaning we had to leave the museum at the latest by 10.45 to allow for the vagaries of Boston traffic, and it was already 9.30.

My past experience came to our assistance, as two years earlier my age-group at school had visited the museum, and an experience had taken place that had been a milestone in my education, while providing me with a knowledge of the vast building's geography which was to stand me in good stead on this important occasion.

The milestone was the discovery of the origins of my given name, as for the first time I was to become aware of the significance of the Leda legend, when confronted with a remarkable copy of Correggio's erotic masterpiece, Leda and the Swan, thought to be by the hand of the master's most gifted pupil, the sublime Parmeggianino, hence the place of honor accorded in the museum's main gallery. I stood rooted to the spot with my eyes rivetted on the central group of the elegant white swan reclining suggestively between the naked princess's open thighs, only being jolted back to reality and dire embarrassment by the peals of laughter that followed the mistress's reference to the painting and its title. I blushed several colors of red at having been caught in the act of obviously admiring my namesake's bestial behavior rather than the genius of the artist.

The rest of the group moved on, with the exception of the terrible twins who had sensed there was something sinful in the air. They were quite right, as the image of the young woman copulating with the divine swan had thoroughly aroused my libido, and I was quivering with sexual excitement.

I whispered the plan I had improvised on the spot into their randily receptive ears, and with a subdued squeal of delight they joined me in slipping away from the group unobserved, in the direction of a toilet I had just used on the same floor. The individual lavatories were of a 19th century capaciousness that provided ample space for us to act out our own version of another Leda's bit of obscene fun, until we were noisily expelled by the elderly latrine attendant, who had become suspicious when we failed to reappear.

On the morning of Etienne's visit my plan of action was quite simple: pay a courtesy call on the divine Leda, as I longed to see what my future lover's reaction would be to the provocative masterpiece, and then make a bee-line for the first floor toilets, where there was enough room for us to make love and for Auntie Laura to watch.

Etienne required no further stimulus, as the mere sight of me in such scanty clothing had been enough to produce an impressive bulge in his pants he tried to hide from the ticket controller by turning his back to her and walking sideways like a crab. Once through the turnstyle we hastened up to the first floor and along the corridor to the great gallery, where we stopped opposite the famous painting.

The Frenchman gazed at it almost incredulously, no longer making any attempt to hide the state of his erection, which was so rampant it stretched the expensive worsted material of his elegantly tailored trousers. We stood side by side in front of the mythical couple, I stroking his prominent bulge and he fondling my left nipple through the debardeur, until suddenly and spontaneously we were running down the gallery in the direction of the providential public convenience, followed by a breathless Laura.

On the way, the rigid prominence of my bouncing nipples, which had both risen to three-dimensional heights under the flimsy material, shocked a couple of old ladies, to whom we gave no time to express an opinion on the shameless exhibitionism of the younger generation, disappearing through onto the landing without even slowing to take the corner.

As we arrived at the door to the toilets, I stopped Etienne — to whom I had already whispered Laura's price of compliance — by laying a hand on his virile bulge to say: "Give me a $50 bill for the attendant". He understood the position with admirable rapidity, and as we entered, the old crone made as if to tell Etienne to leave, but when her eyes saw the banknote they lit up with comprehending avarice, and pushing it into the folds of her bodice, she turned her back in an eloquent gesture of assent.

No sooner had the door closed behind the three of us than Etienne and I came together in an impassioned embrace, our mouths locked in greedy, tooth-jarring contact. The debardeur and micro-skirt seemed to evaporate of their own free will, only the panties recalling their ingloriously brief existence by a feeble ripping sound, while Etienne's fly and belt self-destructed, and I had my first fleeting vision of the rampant male organ that was to procure me so much pleasure in the years to come.

It was only the briefest of glances, as he spun me round with my back to him and my humidity pressed against the tip of his member. And then, without any foreplay, and before I even had time to bend down to facilitate entry, he was inside me, right up to the pubics and thrashing to and fro as if survival depended on instant ejaculation. In any case, that is what we got, and for the first time I felt myself brimming with genuine sperm. As several days must have passed since the last call on his capacity, the surplus semen my maidenly tightness was unable to contain seeped out between his member and my inner lips to trickle down my sun-tanned thighs.

Shuddering violently I came, and then recame and reshuddered, ushering in a new era. Turning my head, I gasped in a raucus voice: "For God's sake stay inside me, stay right there inside my body, don't even move!" as I was suddenly panic stricken at the idea he might withdraw. I need not have worried as, bending forward to take my mouth in his, munching my lips gently and exploring me with a strong and assertive tongue, he took me again with long, sweeping strokes that stopped just short of complete withdrawal. His bloated glans came to rest briefly against my lesser lips at the end of each seperation, before plunging back in as far as my undeveloped condition would allow. Sighing with deep delight I reached behind me to grasp his fully clothed buttocks and pull, revelling in the thudding impact of the glans against something a long way up.

I soon stopped counting my blessings as they merged together in a continuous stream of sex, our juices mingling to coat inner surfaces with a glistening sheen of come. Our mouths fought a salivering battle as opposing tongues struggled for mastery, and I felt an overflow of spittle run down onto rigid breasts which were being kneaded and pinched as the speed of our reciprocating movement increased, making me brace myself instinctively for his second spasm.

Just as we were on the point of climax he completely withdrew, causing an accute surge of frustration, but it was only to rub his glans across my clitty, making me wince with pleasure. For a moment I thought he would take the plunge of my anus, as my bent-over position made it yawn invitingly, but he ignored the impatient little orifice and thrust his member back into my sex, no doubt considering I was too young and inexperienced to be treated to a rousing round of sodomy. This was an illusion I was to correct almost immediately, as there could be no question of my first male lover being allowed to neglect the most sensitive of my erogenous apertures.

Etienne redoubled the already lively pace of his drubbing, and my last vision, before being submerged in a tide of climax, was Auntie Laura masturbating frantically in her neutral corner, without missing any of our moves. Finally, overcome by the strength of new sensations, I sank to my knees in a swoon just as Etienne released his second salvo of sperm.

I must have recovered almost immediately, as when I looked round I discovered my lover's penis in such a state of erection that it stood up against his shirt, and would obviously require further consideration before resuming proportions compatible with its owner appearing in public.

Brushing aside the melting Laura, who was wedged against a triangular wash basin, I sat on it with my back to the corner. Holding on to an antiquated bracket that stuck out beside my head, I spread my legs as far as the walls would allow to enable Etienne to penetrate me again. After a few strokes he slipped his hands under my buttocks to help me place my ankles on his shoulders and take some of the strain off the museum's fixtures. In this position he continued to ream me with unabated virility, rotating his hips through an angle of 90° between each stroke to produce maximum internal torsion, to which I replied by constricting my vaginal passage around his seesawing member, helping him to come again at least three times while I quietly blew my gasket.

Mouth to gobbling mouth we continued to copulate and ejaculate without another thought in the world other than how to ring the last drop of desire from our all-obliterating intimacy, and it was a quaking Laura, crouching in her corner and worn out by self-abuse, who brought us back to the reality of airline timetables.

Etienne was still as stiff as a concrete flagstaff, despite at least six orgasms to my fifteen, but somehow or other he managed to jam his undaunted organ back into sperm-soaked trousers and rip the zipper over a bulge of Herculean proportions. As for the remains of my panties, they had fallen into the john where I abandoned them to their fate. It was in this condition that we beat a hasty and disorderly retreat to Laura's large and luxurious coupe in the car park, with Etienne in front, doubled over to hide the indecency of his fly, followed by a visibly bare-bottomed Leda, with a dishevelled but more or less respectable Laura bringing up the rear.

We tumbled into the car with undisguised relief, Laura behind the wheel and Etienne on the front passenger seat. I perched myself on his knees, where an insistant presssure brought the realization that his hard-on was still intact and pressing against my nether nudity through soiled and crumpled trousers. As the car glided smoothly away from the pay gate, my hand glided just as smoothly down to the overworked zip, which was the only obstacle between the irrepressible member and further bliss. Such was the thrust of the erection that it took me some time and a broken finger nail to liberate the straining shaft, which promptly stood to rigid attention with its angry, bulging head only an inch away from the nearest of my holes, which happened to be the one that had not already seen service in the museum toilet.

We looked into each other's eyes for a second and I nodded my agreement to the unspoken question, underlining my consent by reaching down to spoon back a little overflow to where it was most needed. Etienne took hold of the sides of my buttocks, displacing them gently until his glans came into contact with my cringing sphincter, and when I felt the ramrod right on target I let go of the grab handle with which I had been supporting my weight, sitting down with a thump on my lover's thighs and sundering myself anally on the bulging helmet.

I let out an elated cry of triumph as my rectum was raped by the outsize object, surprising the driver of the van in the adjoining lane, who, from his raised position had a bird's eye view of a lot of bare leg and bottom, and swerved dangerously as our routes diverged when he took the exit on the right. I waived to him happily and bared my right breast in a gesture of erotic farewell that horrified Auntie Laura.

Etienne slid up his hands to take over the proffered breast and its neighbor, while Laura reached over to pull down the debardeur to at least hide what what going on at that level, but there was still a lot of bulgy fumbling under the light material. It was now my turn to make the running further down, there being little Etienne could do in his sitting position other than manhandle my breasts whose nipples responded in three-dimensional relief. With one hand on the central console and the other on the grab handle, I raised and lowered my bottom, sliding the member to and fro, allowing the jumbo-glans to pop out at the end of each stroke prior to sitting down suddenly to force it back in as far and as quickly as possible, before rising again inch by inch, as slowly as my muscles could manage.

However, the nearer we got to the airport the faster I had to transfix, abandoning the luxury of sensual slowness for a high speed in-and-out until my future husband produced his farewell ejaculation, squeezing a few reluctant drops from his overtaxed testacles while I came again and again, as I had been coming every five or six hundred yards since the start of the journey. Then suddenly and providentially his mizzen mast went slack, as if the wind had been taken out of its sails, the limp and dejected remains being oozily evinced by the vigorous pressure of my young and resilient sphincter.

How we managed to get his zipper shut, his flight bag out of the trunk and Etienne into the toilet to change his defiled trousers — whose revealing stains were half hidden under a famous financial newspaper — would be a tale too long to tell; but he made it!

A year passed before he came back for me for keeps, although we had some wonderful week ends in between. In the meantime I lived a more and more frustrated existence, as now only a man could satisfy me and I frequently had to live for weeks without real sex. Girls were alright as far as they went, but for self-evident physiological reasons that was not far enough, and a few, fumbling experiences with clammy-handed youths were no substitute for the resources of the mature male.

The first years of our life together were characterized by a high degree of fidelity on my part, as my husband was an assiduous and imaginative lover, and my adulterous interludes were of the 'sudden impulse' variety. Although I enjoyed fondling and sucking strange members in exposed places where we were likely to be found out — and often were — none of them had the ability to make me come like Etienne. It was only when I was twenty eight that I was to undergo the first of a series of sexual experiences that a psychiatrist would no doubt describe as being symptomatic of a chronic form of nymphomania. I dislike the implication of frustration inherent in this term, as I am not and never have been in any way hung up, but am driven on to a deeper exploration of the world of innovative sex by an unquenchable thirst for new and exhilirating experience. If that's nymphomania — I'm your woman!

Chapter 4

Our house in the Loire Valley consisted unoriginally but charmingly of a hamlet of 18th century farm buildings upon which my husband had lavished the architectural skills frustrated by his full time activity as a real estate dealer.

Situated at a certain distance from the sub-prefecture that was the nearest town of any standing, it was equipped with all the conventional amenities, among which a large pool with a pool-house transformation from an old cottage. These installations were protected from the prying eyes of passers-by, using the public footpath that ran behind the boundary fence, by a well groomed privet hedge which had lost two of its bushes during the exceptionally cold spell of the preceding winter. Following a misunderstanding with the local nurseries, these had been replaced by immature specimens that made it possible — as I was to find out — for someone using the footpath to glimpse the sun pad through the wide-meshed wire grill of the seven foot fence.

On that July afternoon, after Judo practice at the keep-fit club I had opened in town and ran with two women associates — not out of financial necessity but through a need for some form of distraction and as a means of keeping my body in perfect trim — I decided to go down to the pool for a nude sunbathe in the sweltering sun. However much I expose myself my skin never goes darker than a fascinating shade of gold, and, using various color tones I dye my hair, both normal and pubic, a matching tint, going to endless trouble, in front of a full length mirror, to obtain complete uniformity of coloration, including lipstick, nail varnish and eye make-up. This turns me into an authentic golden girl whose overall appearance, from a certain distance, gives the impression of having been fashioned entirely from the precious metal.

While covering myself with a thick and heavily-scented oil from some remote Pacific island, which had the quality of being impervious to the dissolving effects of water, I became conscious of the sounds of some form of manual labor from the direction of the path. It was as if someone was shovelling earth, but the ardent rays of the midsummer sun on my body were already starting to lull me into a torpor peopled with erotic visions, and I gave the noises off no further thought.

Turning to face the sun, I spread my thighs to allow the heat to penetrate my loins, which I stimulated by sliding an inquisitive finger down onto my vulva, where it teased the rubbery clitoris into a state of assertive tumescence. With the fingers of my free hand I stroked and pinched the nipples of my now ample breasts into inch-long erection, making them stand out prominently from their angry red halos. They owed their surprising maturity — in the absence of any children — not only to a predisposing heredity on my mother's side, but to an extra-uteral pregnancy during the first year of our marriage that had, of necessity, been surgically terminated, involving the removal of organs that put an end to any hope of motherhood.

The only other noticeable side-effect had been a rise of milk at the end of what would have been the normal term, that my lasciviously minded husband had encouraged and developed by avidly sucking the nipples for what seemed like hours on end — I would frequently fall asleep while he was suckling contentedly — or by milking my breasts manually to drain off the creamy fluid, which was then used for immoral games.

Rather than allow such a providential source of pleasure to dry up, Etienne had sought out a lactogenic hormone that activated the mammary glands, with the result that at regular intervals, or sometimes during moments of intense sexual excitement, my already generous breasts would swell even further and require milking in one way or another, if only to avoid medical complications. As they are almost as sexually sensitive as my anus, I was delighted with a state of affairs that furbished yet another weapon for my already formidable arsenal of lust.

My adult body, in the fullness of its maturity, was even more perfect than its adolescent predecessor, as I was determined to keep my twenty-three inch waistline, and in addition to my work-outs at the fitness club, I would swim at least twenty lengths a day. Following in my mother's footsteps I had become a rated tennis player and even reached the quarter-finals of the regional championships.

I still obstinately refused to bow to the dictates of hair-dressing fashion, and my tresses continued to fall down to my knees, except when done up in one of the old fashioned styles I favored, whose basis was one form or another of platting. When I was seventeen I had shaved my armpits and trimmed my pubic hair to take part in my one and only beauty competition — that of Miss North East — which I won from fourteen other finalists without the jury even withdrawing to deliberate. The chestnut curls had sprouted again even more abundantly, encouraged by systematic pruning, with the result that my appearance on beaches or in sleeveless dresses could and did cause raised eyebrows, shocked expressions and, of course, lecherous leers.

The sun beat down on my oil and sweat-soaked nudity, driving up the temperature inside my sex, which was brimming with tepid love-juice from the fondling it had received. The time had come to damp down the furnace in a way that ensured immediate orgasm, consisting of pushing ice cubes from a purpose-filled thermos into my steaming sex. The fire went out and I came in, gasping with pleasure and masturbating convulsively for a minute or more before lying back to let the sun bring me up to the boil again for another joy-ride.

On the third occasion I was stupefied to hear a gutteral voice calling out: "White lady like nice black meat! You look big cock!"

I blenched under my sun-tan at the realization my interlude of self-abuse had not gone unobserved, and sat up with a jolt to stare in the direction of the utterance, which coincided with the two undersize privets. I was faced with the astounding and primitively exciting spectacle, on the other side of the wire, of a sculptural black giant in a diminutive pair of light blue shorts, that he had pulled down to display the object of his recommendation, which must indeed have been the finest ebony column in the Loire Valley.

"Lady come!", he exclaimed ingenuously, "You come play black banana; you like; lady look!". So saying he began to jack himself off energetically, pointing his thing at me and pushing it through the mesh of the wire.

I was so stunned by the sheer, bestial vulgarity of the gesture, I hid my breasts with my hands in a movement of misplaced modesty, which lasted until I realized that what I had taken for a reflex of bourgeois respectability — which would have pleased Auntie Laura — was no more than a brief prelude to acquiescence, as I was quaking with a wilder and more uncontrollable excitement than I had ever known before. Although I did not recognize it at the time, this reaction, mingled with blurred recollections of my mother's black double-up, was the first sign of a craving for African virility that would soon deprive me of any sense of the social decencies, precipitating me into a wonderful new universe of inter-racial abandon.

"Yes!" I felt like shouting, "I want to play with your big blacky! I want to suck it and fuck it and stuff it up my ass!" But the words got stuck in my throat, and all I did was transfer my hands to underneath my breasts to point the nipples at him, squeezing them obscenely while meaningfully pushing out my tongue.

Seeing my eloquent if silent response to his offer, my dream boat parted his lips in a broad grin, running his enormous member to and fro through the wire mesh, which was just wide enough to allow him to do so without the contact being painful. This strange gestual dialogue went on for at least a minute, until I could contain my shameless impatience no longer, and ran round the pool to jump agiley over the bushes and fall to my knees in front of the fence and the beautiful black object, which I took tenderly in my hands, reverently kissing the glans before sliding as much of it into my mouth as was initially possible.

I then relaxed my throat muscles — which was not all that easy, as the monstrous weapon was stretching the corners of my lips — and pushed my face forwards until my nose touched the wire, feeling the glans crush my epiglottis as it surged right through to the end of the line. Fortunately, after amateurish beginnings, I had been well schooled in the art of fellation by a call-girl my husband sometimes invited to make up a threesome when we stayed overnight in Paris. She had taught me the importance of the breath control without which, when deep-throating, it is quite possible to choke on a really big penis.

Her lessons stood me in good stead with the African laborer, who had never had it so deep, as I was able to take all the eleven inches that were on my side of the wire, curling the point of my tongue, when I moved my head backwards, to dig it into the V shaped recess on the underside of the glans.

To reduce the effort of my to and fro, I raised myself onto my haunches and, spreading my thighs into a splits position, was able, by grasping the wire with both hands, to force my body up against the fence, doing away with the need to bend forward. My new stance meant that my breasts were pressing against the mesh, with their rigid nipples poking through to the other side; a tacit invitation my black Hercules hastened to accept, reaching down on either side of his thighs to take hold of the angry looking teats. For a few minutes we continued on our respective ways, I sucking and sliding and he rolling and pinching. His handling of my nipples became progressively rougher, as after squeezing brutally to see what my reaction would be (it was a sigh of pleasure), he pulled so hard that a good third of the breasts themselves was forced through the wire and compressed like two oily golden sausages.

I snorted delightedly, longing to feel the asperity of his hands on the rest of my body, but seven feet of fencing were a formidable obstacle. Yet they did not stop my partner making the most of the parts he he could reach, and he continued to manhandle my dairies until they glistened with milk. As my vulva was already rubbing against the wire, I added to my pleasure by rotating my buttocks, dragging my clitty over the metal links to induce a self contained orgasm while my mouth was busy elsewhere.

All this fellation finally produced the inevitable result, and I felt the towering member jerk convulsively, while the Titanic testacles heaved in their sack on the other side of the wire, flooding my throat with a torrent of seething sperm I was physically incapable of swallowing outright. As there was no way the liquid could escape round the tightly fitting sides of the stem, the back pressure forced the mighty, spouting nozzle out of my mouth, leaving it free to spray my face and hair with an abnormal quantity of come. For his part, my lover accompanied his ejaculation with an even more violent kneading of my breasts, extracting a gurgle of gratitude in place of a cry of contented pain, so full was my mouth of the unassimilated remains of his discharge.

Through the mists of my excitement I became conscious of the fact that the navvy was trying to tell me something. As his basic French was unequal to the challenge, he had reverted to an African dialect which was so incomprehensible that even with the help of sign-language it took me some time to decode his message. This was that his organ had swollen under the effect of my oral caress to the point where it was completely trapped in the wire, making it impossible for him to move it other than within the limits of the sheath.

What he expected me to do about it I do not know, but the sight of my lewdly exposed nakedness, coupled with the stimulus of an intensely erotic situation, was obviously not going to help him deflate. It did not take me long to figure out the potential of the set-up, which was a unique opportunity to make love to the most virile of black stallions while retaining complete control, as if I were the male and he the most supine of females, it being impossible for him to disengage without painful injury to his mammouth member. Provided he remained totally erect — and I was there to see to it he stayed that way — I would be able do what I wanted with and to him. He was the man in the iron fence and could do nothing to challenge my supremacy.

If this almost comic situation had not arisen, I imagine I would have returned to the pool house, slipped on a bath robe, and gone round the wire, like a bitch on heat, via the normal entrance, to join the object of my unbridled lust and get myself brutally laid somewhere on the ground in the neighboring wood, whose stones, twigs and other protruberances would have left their imprint on my flesh, pressed against their asperities by the weight of my lover's pummelling body.

But he was caught in the snare of his own lechery, and I intended to ring every possible drop of pleasure from the situation. Casting round for a solution, I pensively took the beautiful bludgeon between my fingers and rubbed the wicked looking glans over my navel, which was at just the right height, exasperated by the sexual superfluousness of the elegant little orifice. By standing on tip-toe, as my laborer must have been six foot six, I managed to get my lips up to a level at which we could exchange a cannibalistic kiss. The grill was supported at the top by a thicker strand stretched tautly between the supporting posts, and by grasping it in the palms of my hands I even managed to pull myself up far enough for him to gobble my nipples as they pressed through the mesh, but I had to let go just as the milk was starting to flow, as the wire was cutting into my hands.

The problem I had to solve was how to bridge the nine inch difference in height between my genitals and the gleaming black penis, as once this obstacle had been surmounted I could have myself the screw of the season. What was needed was some form of base on which I could stand, as there was no way my African could bring his enmeshed phallus down to the level of my sex.

I gestured towards my feet and in the direction of the pool, trying to explain that I was going to look for a solution, and tenderly planted a last kiss on the bulging helmet before making off as fast as my legs would carry me. As luck would have it, in a compartment at the back of the pool house I found a stout wooden box, but as this would not have been quite high enough, I took a sun mattress as well, and fled back to the answer to a vulva's prayer, half afraid he had only been a mirage which would have dissolved by the time I returned.

I need not have worried. When I got back to the fence the

splendid object was still pointing the way through the wire like a signpost to sex. As my plan depended on the African staying where he was and being unable to move, I crouched down, taking both breasts in my hands to rub them over and around the black torpedo, which responded by jerking up and down as if nodding its head in approval, increasing its angle of erection by at least ten degrees.

When I felt certain there was no risk of detumescence, I stopped massaging, not wanting to go too far and provoke another ejaculation, as his balls were starting to heave and his breathing to become more labored. Picking up the wooden box I placed it against the fence under the protruding member and climbed up, turning my back to the navvy. I knew immediately it was too low, as even with my feet well apart the tip of his member prodded my rear cleft just above the anus. Getting down from my perch I folded the beach mattress in two, placed it on top of the box and remounted the improvised rostrum. This time it was exactly right, as the glans fitted neatly between my inner lips.

All I had to do to initiate the first stage was to reach behind me with both hands and take a firm grip on the wire, arch my back, lean slightly forward from the hips and pull myself slowly backwards, forcing the eleven inches which were on my side of the wire as far as they would go into my innards. I should perhaps add that when I returned to the pool house I had smeared my holes with Polynesian sun oil, and was very glad to have done so, as despite the lubricant and my state of rapturous readiness, I was groaning with pain by the time the first eight inches had disappeared out of sight, as it was not just a question of length, but of truly prodigious width, making my tunnel of love feel as if it was splitting at the seams.

With my legs straight, I only needed to push back against the fence with my arms, for my hips to be thrust forwards and for the giant ramrod to slide out of my distended tunnel, although I did not release it entirely, as reinsertion at the start of each run might have been a problem until my sex adapted itself to the width of the intruder. Taking it slowly, I repeated the in-out maneuver, once, then twice, then an increasing number of times, accelerating gradually as my sheath widened to accommodate the huge organ, and even grew in length, as by pulling back when I felt the glans bump against my uterus I somehow managed to gain another inch and a half.

The muscular strain involved, combined with the heat of the midsummer sun, made me stream with sweat, and the searing sensation in the loins, due to the increasingly rapid to and fro of the column of black flesh, made me gasp and groan as I started to build up a head of pressure, imposing a considerable effort of will not to let go of the wire. I must have had to work for at least ten minutes on the last inch, as apart from the pain, which was becoming a significant factor, I was half silly with orgasmic pleasure. But I kept going relentlessly, and was finally rewarded by the feel of the wire against my buttocks and a glow of pride at the thought of having upped my first eleven incher: I was a big girl now!

Allowing the glans to pop out, making a noise like the cork of a champagne bottle whose contents had gone slightly flat, I lined myself up for phase two. This consisted of repeating the dose, but with the other orifice, meaning I would have to lower my buttocks, which I did by flexing my knees until I could feel the glans prodding my butt. Taking a deep breath and clenching my teeth, I pulled back on the wire, and after a moment of hesitation, when I felt the shaft bend ever so slightly, my sphincter burst open and the massive piston lunged in deeply. I cried out in pain, as it had entered me more rapidly and profoundly than had been the case further down, my asshole clearly having a better handling capacity for the big ones. Although there was a certain symbolic resistance, I was soon able to speed up, slowly expelling the greasey pole until its tip was half way out, when I would ram it back in until the wire thudded against my buttocks, leaving its lozenge-shaped imprint on their sun-tanned skin.

"Bugger me you black bastard! Ass-fuck my bloody bung! Ooh! Ooh! That's it! Get it right in! I want all of it in my shit-hole! Push harder! Give me your pisser in the bowels! Ooh! Ooh! Harder! Stiff it to me! Ah! Ah! Ah!"

Apart from its gratuitous obscenity, most of this was arrant nonsense, as I was doing everything and the laborer could hardly move. I could be partly excused on the grounds of being delirious, as not only was I starting to come continuously, but was in danger of a full climax, which, if allowed to occur, would diminish me for the third and final phase. I therefore let the big black phallus slip out with a farewell squelch, and concentrated on the most difficult part of the operation, as, having thoroughly prepared both my holes, I was going to try for alternating penetration, one in the regular and the next one in the other; a feat requiring perfect timing and muscular control.

I took the first thrust in my sex very gently indeed, as I was afraid it would have reverted to its normal size. But all was well, as it was still distended and I managed to push in the first nine inches without any real effort or pain. When I switched to the anus, the first thrust bounced clumsily off the rim, but the second was a bull's eye, and thereafter I became a better and better shot, and could speed things up. The effect on my senses was of course even more elecrifying than before, as each stroke involved complete withdrawal and reinsertion in the neighboring channel, and I will never know how my muscles stood the strain, or how I managed to keep going when the orgasms started to march up and down my vulva in hobnailed boots.

When the full climax began to roar at me like an angry lion I went over the edge, shuddering, shouting and grinding my teeth, while pulling convulsively at the wire to hold the African as far in as possible, not wishing to loose a drop of his precious torrent, which filled me so utterly I felt as fat and inflated as if fully expectant.

Once the shock waves of orgasm, rippling away from the epicenter of sex had disappeared over the edge of exhaustion, my pulse-count slowed to a feasible pace and a tide of tiredness swept over my satiated body, forcing me forwards away from the massive black stake on which I was anally impaled.

Normally it should have been easy for me to slump down on my knees, but something had gone wrong with the release mechanism and I was unable to move. Instead of sliding out easily as I started my forward movement, the giant member remained firmly embedded in my backside, as my much-abused sphincter, having up to then accepted and even revelled in the ill-treatment to which it had been subjected, suddenly decided to rebel at the last moment. It showed its dissatisfaction, or possibly its resentment at having to part with such a rapturous injection by closing round the invading column with a vice-like grip that not only prevented our seperation, but provided a powerful stimulus which maintained the African's magnificent penis in a state of unyielding rigidity.

We were in fact stuck together like a pair of copulating mongrels whose mating instinct had brought them together in a public place. This was not serious in itself, and had a problem not arisen would have continued to be quite sublime, as I defy any normally constituted woman who has overcome the taboos of civilized behavior to want to part with such a heavenly insertion. It seemed to be part of me, as if my anus had been purpose-moulded around it, rather than receiving the monstrous intrusion as an invader from outer space.

My desire was on the point of rekindling, and with it my energy, when I realized, to my stunned surprise, that we were no longer alone. During the period in which we had been lost to the world in our vortex of lust a small crowd had gathered on the footpath, comprising a couple of boy scouts from a nearby summer camp — who were busily fingering the bulges in each other's shorts — sundry other spectators of both sexes, who made no secret of their interest in our performance, my new Algerian maid, Yasmina, who was on her knees behind my partner, doing something to him with her mouth while one of her hands was busy between her legs, and — horror of horrors — our next-door neighbor, the bigotted wife of a senior civil servant, whose face was purple with outrage.

Initially I was so embarrassed I just did not know what to do, flushing several shades of burning scarlet as I hung there helplessly suspended from the rock-hard penis, as however much I squirmed and strained there was no way I could persuade my sphincter to relinquish its grip of iron. In the end my contortions produced a pleasing sensation, and instead of trying to disengage I found myself rotating my buttocks, almost but not quite involuntarily, imparting a circular motion to the staff of flesh that bisected my entrails.

As the purpose of movement changed from seperation to orgasm, the realization dawned I was no longer ashamed or humiliated, but elated and excited by the idea of being watched by an attentive audience of voyeurs. This was to be the day's second revelation, the first having been the irresistible attraction of blackness, now followed by the discovery that I adored making love before the largest possible number of spectators, whether motivated by lechery or disapproval; the latter being arguably an even stronger incentive than the former! To scandalize my horrified neighbor even further, I took my breasts in my hands and, sticking out my tongue, turned in her direction, as far as my transfixed situation would allow, and began licking my nipples, breaking off for an instant to call out: "How would you like a nice black ass-fuck Madame Landrel?"

As if a hidden operator had suddenly turned on an unflattering spot her complexion turned from purple to grey: "How nauseating Madame Calavent! How utterly revolting!" she spluttered, "You must be mad! You really must be completely insane!" So saying she stumped off up the path in the direction of her villa, leaving me with the feeling that a latent regret at being deprived of the unthinkable spectacle outweighed her indignation. Her departure was the sign for the rest of the audience to disband, with the exception of Yasmina. The latter's references had given the impression she was a paragon of virtue, but her conduct behind the laborer dispelled any such illusion, as I could hear her lapping away devotedly, and although I could not see what was actually happening, an infallible guess required little imagination.

With an effort of will I forced my mind to concentrate on realities, as however ecstatic the rectal feeling of a black bonanza, the next people to appear on the path might well be the local gendarmes, who frequently made rounds to satisfy the security cravings of influential residents. Despite my inclination to stay sex-locked with my dusky Atlas until the next spasm, I forced myself to appeal to Yasmina for assistance, just as a series of excited cries announced the successful conclusion of the efforts of the hand with which she had been sawing away at her gap.

"Yasmina!" I gasped, as I was perilously near to coming again myself, "Run round the fence quickly and fetch a bucket of cold water from the well". As with all self-respecting farm house conversions, the well of the original group of buildings had been retained for decorative purposes after having been suitably restored, and although no longer in every day use still produced water of remarkable purity at a low temperature.

I had to repeat the order a second time in a more menacing tone before she unwillingly stopped her nasty little games.

walking off sulkily to fetch the only solution to our problem I had been able to devise — the age-old method of seperating copulating dogs.

Yasmina returned five minutes later, when I was on the verge of another climax, as we had passed the intervening period perfecting the rotating technique, achieving a degree of expertise that enabled me to use the great penis like a giant ladle to stir my seething innards around the cauldron of my crotch.

Reluctantly I bent down until I could grasp my ankles, making it possible for the Algerian girl to position the bucket directly above my hairy furrow and then incline it to send a stream of ice-cold water over the point of inter-penetration of our sweat-soaked bodies. We both bucked violently under the effect of the glacial liquid, and as it trickled around the phallus and over my vulva I was rewarded with the climax on which I had been working for the past ten minutes.

It ended in a violent shuddering and chattering of teeth, until, without warning, the dam burst and muscular tension was suddenly replaced by relaxation. As the once proud penis accepted expulsion, I heralded the collapse of my self control with a long drawn-out fart that echoed down the path, followed, to my dire but secretly delighted dismay, by the contents of my bladder, which splashed off the dusky scrotum before trickling down thighs and wire to dribble off onto calves and feet.

At last I could sink down in a faint, being only dimly conscious of a straining Yasmina carrying me back to the pool house, where she stripped off her rudimentary dress, exhibiting a pair of juttingly purple nipples. Busying herself about my body, she greedily licked away the coagulated traces of sperm, sweat, milk, urine and dust which coated my skin, while her eager fingers plucked angrily at her upstanding clit, or joined together to form a wedge which she thrust repeatedly into her major recess.

Before losing consciousness I can remember thinking vaguely

that I would have to have a word with her on the question of sexual hygiene, although I was so glad she had turned out to be such a rutty little slut.

Chapter 5

When I came to I was lying on my back in bed, where I had been transported by Etienne the previous evening. As consciousness returned I became aware of a warm and pleasant feeling, and opened my eyes to find myself staring into Yasmina's dark brown pupils, which were veiled with the excitement of sex.

For some time I lay drowsily between sleep and wakefulness, without trying to find out what she was doing, or why her body was being jolted to and fro. When I finally shook off the lethargy of sleep, I raised my head to survey the scene and discovered that I owed the pleasant sensation to the kneeling Yasmina, who, astride my hips, was rubbing her swaying nipples against mine. The movement of her body was due to my husband, who was standing behind her at the edge of the bed methodically plumbing her ass.

I lay back again, breathing in the pungency of hairy armpits and spreading my thighs hospitably. Etienne willingly answered the call of marital duty, withdrawing his glans from my maid's distended rectum, which must already have seen extensive service despite her tender years, to thrust it manfully into my netherness, which was still unctuous from the African's visit. Yasmina grasped one of my breasts in each of her hands and squeezed until the milk started to trickle from the nipples, which she then licked and sucked eagerly. Notwithstanding the vigor of my husband's sodomy, as he was ramming me as if meting out some form of corporal punishment, an irresistible sleepiness returned and I floated off, leaving my two partners to do as they wished with my supine body.

I only woke completely at ten the following morning, to discover the spectacle of an indefatigable Yasmina busily sucking Etienne's half-tumescent penis, which, despite the skill and vitality she was dispensing obstinately refused to rise to the occasion, presumably owing to the number of times it had been solicited during my hours of sleep. The girl was kneeling with her bottom towards me, and it was evident from the state of her anus, which was yawning wearily as a result of frequent abuse, that they had not passed the night in the innocence of sleep.

Fascinated by the aperture in its undergrowth of curly black hair, which contrasted with the clean-shaven nudity of Algerian custom that characterized her frontal appearance, I propped myself up on one elbow and started to finger the promising crevasse. This was obviously just what its owner wanted, as she thrust back at me until it was right under my nose, assailing my sense of smell with a composite odor I would prefer not to describe. Although there are few things more exciting than the fragrance of an irreproachably clean vagina that has just been a vessel of orgasm, the same being true of a recently unwashed armpit heated by the stresses of sex, I resolutely draw the line at an accumulation of superimposed layers of organic grime.

I therefore gave the offending bottom a resounding slap, prompting the girl to relinquish Etienne's member and turn her head with a smile which showed she would have liked me to continue. But that was not my purpose, and I took her firmly by the hand to propel her towards the nearest bidet. The lesson in downstairs hygiene which followed soon degenerated into a petting party, as the soapy fingers I pushed into her distant corners rekindled desire, and once her own ablutions were over she stood up and pushed me down to render me an identical service, which, it must be admitted, I probably needed almost as badly.

After she had spent a few minutes with one hand soaping my clitoris and the other my sphincter, I turned to pull her down onto my thighs, and we were just warming to a game of 'taste a tongue and pinch a tit' when Etienne appeared at the bathroom door. After watching us slyly for a minute or two he told the Algerian girl to leave, as he wanted to talk to me before his departure for the office.

I sat apprehensively on the edge of the bed to listen to what he had to say. Although his attitude during the night we had just spent with Yasmina suggested an unsuspected degree of tolerance and even connivance, Etienne had a secretive side to his nature which made it difficult to foresee how he would react, and I did not know how much, if anything, Yasmina had told him of my demented episode with the African navvy.

I need not have worried, as he sat down beside me, and after planting a moist kiss on my right nipple exclaimed: " Well, well! So my randy, little wife has just found out she likes big black cocks, and, what is more, she likes them in public where everyone can see her rutting! Well, if that's what she wants, that's what she'll get! Providing her dear husband can watch!"

I almost jumped with elation at the last part of his remark, as the price of his compliance could not have pleased me more, completing as it did the cycle of my new-found sexual fulfilment. Throwing my arms around his neck I gave him an almost sisterly kiss of gratitude: "Oh you darling voyeur! and when I think I never even suspected you might be like that! Don't worry, I will give you the most lecherous sex shows anyone has ever seen, that you can look at, film, record and take part in with anyone or anything you care to invite!"

To show my appreciation I started to feel under his bath robe, forgetting his extenuating night with Yasmina. He removed my hand gently and said: "You can save that for our next door neighbor. We have to fix his cow of a wife before she broadcasts the details of your inter-racial saga throughout the center of France! Listen, I have a plan that has the advantage of enabling you to put on your first show, even if it is only for an impotent old pervert and not a magnificent black stallion — don't worry, there will be plenty of those later!"

There would indeed be plenty of those to come in both senses of the word, but how many no one could have foretold! In the meantime he explained the details of his scheme to put Madame Landrel out of action.

Monsieur Landrel, apart from being fat, had always been blatantly and unashamedly fascinated by my body, and whenever we met at receptions or dinners, he would place himself so he had the best possible view of my decolleté or legs. Etienne laughed at this obsession, and even incited me to wear revealing clothes when he knew Landrel was going to be present, telling me to provide him with a eyeful of my charms, as he was influential in the important field of building permits.

I really believe that if Landrel had made it a condition for granting a permit for a large project, Etienne would have told me to go to bed with him, but the question had never arisen, as it had been enough for me to parade my thinly veiled body under his gaze to obtain the desired result. This time we would however have to go a step further, as Etienne's plan to neutralize Madame Landrel, before it was too late, consisted of compromising her husband with his own wife.

The same evening he rang Landrel and invited him round to discuss the possible repercussions of my disgraceful behavior, discreetly implying I would be personally available to make amends in any way he chose. Our neighbor jumped at the opportunity of seeing his fallen goddess with even fewer clothes than during our normal, social encounters, and it was agreed that he would call in the following morning on the way to the office.

Etienne told me to put on my most revealing dress and wait in the study until he arrived with our guest, to whom he would already have explained that I wished to talk to him, in private, to try and explain my extraordinary behavior and seek his indulgence. Once Landrel was in my presence, Etienne would leave, and it would be up to me to attract my guest over to the chintz sofa facing the East window, which, at that time of day, was normally an ideal source of light for a photographic frame-up.

What I did not know was that the large, built-in mirror in the center of the bookcase was two-way from the other side when the decorative panel screwed onto the wall behind it, in the adjoining dining room, was removed, giving a perfect view of everything happening in the study.

The discovery of this device came as an intriguing surprise, as I had once made love on the sofa in the study with the swimming instructor from the municipal pool. Etienne confirmed my suspicions by producing an attractively bound album containing color enlargements of his naked wife offering all her holes to the superbly built athlete, whose phallic development was worthy of the prophetic bulge in his trunks that had attracted my interest. I had never invited any other passing lover back to the house, but had taken the incredible risk just once with my aquatic playmate, having grown tired of clandestine fast fucks in cubicles and wet costumes which were just sufficiently removed to let his splendid object out of one and into the other. Using the feeble excuse of needing advice on a modification to our pool, I had spent an afternoon eating him raw without ever dreaming that my lechery was being recorded for posterity.

Despite our pact I flushed dark red at having already been caught in the act, and was therefore quite flabbergasted when Etienne laughed and said: "I expect you to do better than that with Monsieur Landrel; at least I won't have to pay for his services!" So that was it! It had been a put-up job! I who had thought I was blithely cuckolding my husband with a super stud, had in fact been enjoying no more liberty than a performing seal! If that was how things were, my wiley Etienne would soon see what his loving wife could provide in the way of erotic entertainment!

The following morning I chose a red, bare-shouldered, mid-thigh length beach dress. Yasmina — who was an accomplished needle-woman — lowered the décolleté to a point where the slightest inclination of the bust bared at least one nipple, which she had to be restrained from taking in her mouth as our important visitor was due to arrive from one moment to the next.

He was in fact ominously punctual, and after a brief conversation with my husband in the entrance hall, entered the study followed by Etienne, kissing my hand with a solemnity belied by the fixedness with which he stared into my upper divide and at the segment of purple halo that peeped over the top of the bodice.

"I think you will find Monsieur Landrel is prepared to understand the position and adopt a lenient attitude, providing he is satisfied you were the involuntary victim of some sort of seizure", Etienne remarked, "I leave you with him to justify your conduct".

So saying he withdrew and I was left on my own with our unappetizing neighbor. In his early sixties, he was a parody of the ideal lover, as not only was he fat and bald, but his features were ugly and he was sweating profusely despite the morning mildness.

M. Landrel", I said, "Please excuse my informal dress, but I intend to spend most of the day down at the pool, and it is so easy to slip off for a spell of nude sun bathing".

His piggy eyes gleamed with lecherous glee, and it was evident I would have no trouble providing action photos which would have compromised even the most notorious of sinners, as I was his dream of adultery come true. I sat down and crossed my superlative legs a long way up, gesturing to him to join me on the settee.

"What can I say about that terrible incident the other day except that I was not in my right mind?" I ran an impeccably manicured hand along the top of my right thigh, moving back the hem of my already diminutive skirt by a good five inches to reveal a luxuriant tuft of pubic hair: "I must have had some sort of attack". I bent forward in his direction, making sure the left nipple peaked over the top of the bodice and ran my mouth provocatively up the inside of my arm: "I really don't know what came over me; normally I'm only attracted to mature men of your type".

All this was of course unbelievably crude but effective, as it was what he wanted to believe more than anything in the world. His eyes were rivetted to the nipple, which I stiffened nonchalantly between finger and thumb as if it was the most commonplace of social gestures, clinching the matter by uncrossing my legs revealingly to give him a plunging view onto my mons veneris.

"Just feel how my heart is beating", I murmured, taking hold of his hand and placing it over the protruding tit, rising as I did so and helping him to follow my example. We stood there facing each other incongruously, as I was the taller by at least four inches, meaning my breasts were on a level with his mouth, which was what I intended. Reaching behind I unzipped the dress, whose disappearance revealed total nudity, and thrust the right sphere forwards, encouraging him to take it in the other pudgy hand.

His face crimson with excitement, he pushed first one and then the other nipple into his thin-lipped mouth, squeezing the breasts uncouthly. After a few moments of untidy suckling, his face registered stupefection when he realized that milk was starting to flow. His manipulation became more and more energetic as he kneaded away, initially extracting only a few isolated drops, which were licked off greedily. Practice making perfect he soon became skilled, and with each downward pulling movement fine jets of sparkling fluid would spurt into his mouth which, from time to time, closed posessively over a nipple.

Finally the excitement became more than he could bear, and pushing me down on the sofa, with his elephantine legs astride my body, he unzipped his fly to liberate a fat and floppy penis which he stuffed rather than slid into the valley of my breasts, after having lubricated it with three or four more squirts of home-made cream. Taking my right nipple in his right hand and my left one in his left, he pulled at them diagonally, stretching one breast over the top of the other to envelop an organ which had grown to a plausible size without losing its unhealthy color.

He then ran his member to and fro in the improvised tunnel, speeding up the movement as he pulled harder and harder on the nipples to tighten the skin around his flailing phallus. As the sperm welled up he grunted like an excited pig, letting go with his hands to direct a surprisingly copious ejaculation over my breasts, snorting spasmodically and rubbing in his outflow, which was beginning to trickle out of my valley and spill over onto the couch. Sliding down my body to lick off the remains of the mixture, he lapped away happily, with an occasional pause every now and then to savor the mayonnaise before swallowing it with evident relish.

It was a thoroughly revolting exhibition of impotent perversion, and I was therefore surprised to discover that not only was I starting to enjoy it, but was becoming positively excited. No doubt stimulated by the knowledge that my husband was busy behind the mirror with his camera, I took hold of a breast and squeezed out a further driblet to replenish the pool he had licked almost dry.

I was just starting to come myself when his boarish grunting was interrupted by a series of agonized groans, followed by a sinister rattle in the back of his throat, before he slumped forward over my body and rolled heavily off the couch onto the floor. In a flash Etienne was in the room, still holding his camera, and falling to his knees he grasped my late lover's wrist to have his worst fears confirmed by a complete absence of pulse.

Fortunately there were the photos, as without them we might have been in serious trouble, but a glance at the prints was enough to transform Madame Landrel from an avenging fury into a self-effacing widow, and our version that her husband had died of a heart attack while discussing official matters with Etienne was accepted gratefully by all concerned.

Whatever the effectiveness of the cover-up story, quite a few people had actually seen me copulating with the navvy, making our departure from the region a necessity. In view of my newly acquired addiction to blackness, the obvious choice was Africa, which happened to be a good idea professionally, as my husband had been invited to master-mind the construction of a series of tourist facilities on the Gulf of Guinea, and was considering the offer when my inter-racial freak-out brought matters to a head.

Inevitably, a certain amount of time was needed to wind up his real estate operations in the center of France, and while these arrangements were being made, Yasmina, who was to accompany us in her dual capacity of lady's maid and sex-toy, asked our permission to lodge her younger brother in her room during a three week visit he was due to make to France. We agreed reluctantly, as we were concerned that his intrusion might involve us in having to hide or interrupt our sexual relations with his sister.

Houari, as he was called, duly arrived and turned out to be a strapping adolescent with an athletic physique and pronounced Arab features, which would have been handsome had it not been for a pockmarked complexion. A bed was installed for him in his sister's room in the loft, and she was told to pass on the message that Casbah standards of hygiene were not acceptable and that a shower a day was part of the basic routine.

That Houari was sexually wide-awake was evident from the intensity with which he stared at the exposed parts of my body whenever we chanced to meet in the house or garden. When I went down to the pool for one of my sun bathing sessions, he would creep up stealthily and hide behind the famous hedge to feast his eyes on my body. I knew he was there, as although his approach was a model of silent stalking, the sight of my nudity excited him so much he had to masturbate, and his heavy breathing gave him away. I would exacerbate his desire even further by turning towards the hedge and fondling my genitals with my thighs asplay to let him admire every detail of my femininity. As I never let on I knew he was there, our relations, for some time, remained those of an unsuspecting voyeur and a knowing exhibitionist.

I was to discover rapidly that his sexual activities were not limited to self-abuse and lusting after the apparently unattainable, as one evening after dinner, when Yasmina and her younger brother had retired to their room to watch television, I realized I had forgotten to give her instructions for the following morning. I therefore climbed the narrow stairway to their room to repair the omission before going to bed.

I was on the point of knocking at the door, which was ajar, when familiar gasping sounds that were clearly audible over the din of the box, stopped my hand in mid-air. Putting an eye to the opening, I was treated to the spectacle of a naked Yasmina kneeling in front of the screen with her elbows on the top of the set, while her equally naked brother, who was kneeling behind her with his legs between hers, humped her at the speed of a jack rabbit who had been deprived of sex for six months, his taught buttocks shuttling to and fro so rapidly that their outline was blurred. The girl's ass-cheeks were covered in come, as every minute or so the boy would withdraw in what looked like an attempt to prevent ejaculation, but to no avail, as in the second following the removal of his penis from the sisterly slit, a jet of sperm would splash onto her backside.

Without even stopping for breath he would force his member back down to an angle suitable for the repenetration of whatever hole happened to be the most accessible. On the next occasion it was the girl's anus that hosted the fraternal phallus, as it happened to be in the right place when he lunged blindly for the sixth or seventh time, and managed to score a direct hit, sliding right in up to the short hairs and rabbiting away as hard as he could.

Yasmina was clearly delighted with the family feeling, as was confirmed by a string of Arabic imprecations which were self-evidently intended to spur her kid-brother on to greater efforts, which he enthusiastically supplied, his thighs thumping her slippery buttocks with such force that the slapping sound could be heard above the noise of the set and the caterwauling of his sister. To drag him into her more forcibly she reached back between her thighs and took hold of his scrotum, using it as a handle to pull him bodily against the resiliant buffer of her bottom, while the forefinger and thumb of her free hand aggressed her upstanding clitty as if it was a personal enemy.

All this was much too good to miss, and shrugging off my bath robe I burst into the room just as naked as the two protagonists, and in three strides was kneeling behind Houari, whose buttocks

I parted to apply my tongue to his anal opening. This was a difficult maneuver, owing to the speed of his thrashing, but I somehow managed to find the aperture and stuck onto it like a leach. His reaction was instantaneous. Jerking his member out of the incestuous asshole he spun round to face me, his upright cock flat against his belly, and as I reached for it to bring it down to my lips, he grabbed my plait and wrenched me round to face the other way, with the cheeks of my ass directly opposite his loins, forcing me to remain in a bent over position by pressing forwards and downwards on the nape of my neck.

In fact I needed no coercion, as I wanted nothing more eagerly than his incredibly rigid young cock in whichever hole he could occupy soonest. I had come on trickle at the mere thought of being transpierced by his youthful stiffness, and was seething with impatience to get myself spiked, even if such precipitation meant a few painful exploratory jabs in the wrong places.

He only needed three stabs to embed his dagger in my regular opening, and I sighed with lecherous relief when I felt him pick up speed, until he was buck-rabbiting me at what must have been a rate of at least three hundred strokes a minute. I was to learn later, from Yasmina, that although he suffered from premature ejaculation — which was hardly surprising at the speed at which he drove — his adolescent virility was so boundless that the intensity of his erection was never in doubt, only the output of his two overgrown testacles diminishing as spurt followed spurt. Even then there still seemed to be enough to make a showing, however many orgasms he notched up, as it was commonplace for him to come between fifteen and twenty times during a given bout of loving.

The only limiting factor to the duration of his performance seemed to be muscular exhaustion, as the time inevitably came when fatigue supplanted his ability to maintain the ultra-rapid coital movement, and he would finally keel over and pass out, leaving his orgasm-racked partner drained of erotic capacity and feeling as if she had been reamed by a combined harvester. The increase in distance covered due to the speed of his action was such that in terms of penis-travel she had probably received six times as much linear fucking as with a normally cadenced stallion.

All this was abnormal and even a trifle sinister, as in his trance-like state he was capable of the most violent behavior, his partner being no more than an animal means to his own ends, and the fact that he should propel her into paradise was merely an unintentional by-product. As it was, I myself experienced the roughness of his reactions when he suspected I was on the point of taking the initiative and preventing him from doing exactly what he wanted. I attempted to modify my position to obtain what I thought would be a better angle of penetration, and my move was greeted with a slap on the right buttock of such savagery that a pistol like detonation echoed round the room, leaving me with a delicious stinging sensation that lasted all of five minutes. Although I could have sent him spinning with my mastery of unarmed combat, I enjoyed the pain too much, providing he stuck to the fleshy parts with the flat of the hand. After one or two scuffles, when he tried to hit me with a clenched fist, we reached a working agreement: I got my resounding smacks where I liked them most and he was left with his macho feelings intact.

In any case, on this occasion I was rewarded when, of his own volition, he changed the position of his legs from inside to outside mine, enabling him to exercise an inward pressure that tightened the lips of my sex round his member. The result was an ecstasy I celebrated with a solo of groans and gasps, gradually developing into a chorus of whoops and wails loud enough to be heard in our bedroom suite. Involuntarily I had made certain Etienne would be left in no doubt as to what was happening upstairs when Houari, withdrawing from my vagina, let go of my pigtail, which he had been holding to keep me under control, and, using his hands to part my buttocks, aimed his driving force at my asshole, which he penetrated at the first attempt, but only after bouncing painfully off the unlubricated rim.

The burning sensation was so intense I let out a piercing scream, without in any way interfering with what he was doing, as although it may have hurt like all hell I did not want to stop, as it was the first time I had enjoyed the combination of bone-dry cock and arid ass. For at least a minute I thought the heat would set something on fire, even if it was only the chestnut curls that adorned my rectal furrow. Whatever my sufferring it made no difference to Houari, as in his lunatic world of high speed sex nothing really mattered except getting in and out as fast as possible, and I really think that if his penis had caught fire and burnt out he would only have noticed the following morning. By pushing fingers into to my vaginal gap, which was as seepy as usual, I managed to spoon enough juice onto his pistoning member to ease the situation, allowing me to revel in his runaway ramming of my favorite entry.

Once I felt the anal to and fro I lost all civilized restraint and shouted strings of obscenities at the top of my voice: "Ass fuck me you little shit! Shit fuck me you little ass! Ah I can feel you in my pantry! I can feel you in my food! Ah! Ah! Ooh! You're really bigging me now! Ooh! that's it! Bang my bung-hole! Go on then, butt-fuck me faster! Bugger me harder! Ah! Ah!"

My bowels were a burning fiery furnace into which Houari continued to pour molten drops of liquid flame, his member jerking convulsively every two minutes to advertize yet another orgasm. Little by little I learned how to make my own delirious spasms coincide, greeting them with outbursts of Anglo-French verbal filth proclaiming the emancipation of my rectal libido.

As we were both soaring through one of our now well-orchestrated crescendos to a joint orgasmic climax, the door was thrown wide open to reveal my naked husband in a state of advanced tumescence, his rigid member coated with a layer of gleaming vaseline that left little doubt as to the anal nature of his ambitions or, for that matter, the identity of his intended partner. He rarely used vaseline on me or Yasmina, as usually our assholes were equal to his unlubricated challenge, and the fact that he should have taken such a precaution before coming upstairs had to mean he was thinking in terms of another butt.

The only other one available was of course Houari's tight little rosebud, which was still moving to and fro at high speed, like the counterpart of his lightning penis, which was lashing in and out of my rear at the speed of sound. Etienne climbed onto the bed and knelt down behind him so we were lined up in a row, the first two already joined in the throes of supersonic sodomy, while the third adjusted his position with great care in order to penetrate the Algerian at the moment his buttocks attained the limit of their backward travel. His aim had to be perfect, as Houari's legs were squeezing mine together, with the result that his own ass cheeks were not spread receptively, meaning the incoming glans would simply bounce off in the absence of a direct hit.

He lunged forward at just the right moment to impale Houari on the whole his manhood, which, although mainly famous for the size of its glans, was nevertheless a good eight inches in length. The youth's yell was at least as piercing as my own earlier shriek of pain, and, for an instant, I thought he would buck Etienne off his backside, as he reared away from me, and it was only my husband's forward pressure, coupled with my own fierce determination to stay speared that stopped him bailing-out.

Little by little his resistance waned, and after two or three minutes of holding on we were able to restore some semblance of order to our club sandwich. To our surprise, Houari even began to cooperate, and it became possible to synchronize our movements so that we all benefited equally, Houari moving his bottom backwards to withdraw from me and be penetrated by Etienne and vice-versa.

Yasmina — who had been wiling away the time with an

absurdly large cucumber, which she had somehow managed to force into her painfully distended slot and was rotating to an accompaniment of squeels of suffering — had been left out of our picture. As I did not want her to feel we were discriminating in any way, I told her to move over and kneel in front of me in a position in which I could lick her backstage while helping with the vegetable.

Any misgivings the boy may have felt as to the advantages of double-decker buggery had by now been dispelled, and he was thrusting back at Etienne, who was having difficulty adapting himself to the rapidity of the rhythm. I was in fact to learn from Yasmina that Houari was an old hand at the game, as his elder brothers had already laid first claim to his anal virginity. His present experience with his sister was in fact his first taste of heterosexuality, although it did not change his conviction that women were no better than reproductive cattle and incapable of the noble sexual relations possible between men.

All four of us were nearing our terminal climax, and Houari and I could no longer remember the number of orgasms we had piled up since I entered the room, and even Yasmina was coming more and more often as her ecological diljo came to terms with the space available. When the fateful moment drew near the racket was indescribable, as if a monkey house had been merged with an exotic pig sty to produce the most bestial of sound effects, and it was against a background of grunts and hoots and screams and verbal obscenities that Etienne inundated the adolescent rectum, that Houari squeezed his last pathetic drops into my anus, that I peed on the counterpain and that Yasmina fainted as the whole of the cucumber disappeared out of sight.

As I lay in bed the following morning everything seemed unreal. Ten days earlier I had been a provincial housewife living contentedly with her husband, with only the occasional adventure to alleviate the boredom of a certain life style, rather than to satisfy any systematic craving for extra-marital sex.

Paradoxically, my escapade with the late and unlamented Monsieur Landrel played a more important role in opening my eyes to the murkiness of the depths of my libido than my surrender to the African road laborer. With the latter I at least had the excuse of lusting after a magnificent animal, but the fact of having been excited by the humiliating obscenity of our neighbor's perverted lechery, was a revelation of the levels to which I might now sink to satisfy my new-found depravity. It was evident that in Etienne I had unexpectedly found the ideal accomplice, who could be relied upon to stage-manage situations which would enable me to wallow publicly in the mire of every conceivable excess.

A strange by-product of the events of the last ten days was my release from the last inhibitions in the use of language. Looking through the pages I have written recently I have been struck by my increasing willingness to use expressions I would previously have shunned on the grounds of their coarseness. In other words I am now prepared to call a fuck a fuck and a cunt a cunt, at least when the excitement of circumstance seems to warrant a less formal approach!

Chapter 6

When late in November the day of departure finally came, I was bursting with impatience to plumb the depths of the inter-racial debauch I knew was waiting for me in Africa. I had just about exhausted the inventive possibilities of Yasmina and Houari, Etienne having insisted I avoid outside sexual contact, as he did not want his disengagement to be complicated by a new scandal. Now I had seen the light there was no knowing what I might get up to; the genie had been let out of the bottle in a big way!

How the four of us managed to fit into the car with all the goods and chattels that were not following by boat I will never know, as even with a large luggage rack on the roof, we still had to pile suitcases and bags on the back seat, with the result there was only one place behind.

Seizing the opportunity of passing the boring drive up the

motorway to Paris doing what I liked most, I said I would sit on Houari's lap in the back, and we installed ourselves on this basis, Etienne turning the driving mirror to get a good view of what we were doing. I was wearing a U necked, knitted-wool, mini-dress with matching scarf and stockings and nothing else, apart from a smart pair of expensive Italian tennis shoes. Once we had sorted ourselves out, and I had extracted Houari's ever-erect member from the fly of his jeans, all I had to do was pull my dress up over my hips and sit down on the gristly spike to enjoy the ideal travelling position for our three-hour drive to Roissy Airport.

Houari ran his hands up under my dress to fondle my breasts while gnawing gently at the back of my neck, and started an up and down movement that was slowed by his position and the weight of my body, which I alleviated by supporting myself with the passenger grab handle. It was the first time I had made love in a car since the famous rush from the museum in Boston to the airport all those years ago, but this time there was no need to hurry. I even managed to convince Houari to ditch his rabbit habbit and stay still, allowing me to do most of the fucking by lifting myself to a height where his glans was on the point of bursting free from between the lips of my sex, before lowering myself as slowly as I could.

Not to be outdone, Etienne opened his fly to let Yasmina give him the go down. We played a little game of 'coming together', consisting of both delaying and controlling our orgasms until we could have them at the same time, the one who could finally hold on no longer giving the finishing signal, whereupon I would come and he would ejaculate. Once the girl had syphoned off the last drops she would turn round to give me an oral transfer of husband. During most of the trip I kept my eyes on Etienne's reflexion in the driving mirror, except when the tremors of a particularly strong sensation or orgasm disturbed my self-control, making me lose sight of him for a while, although I would return to the rear-view mirror with a guilty smirk as soon as I recovered my composure.

From time to time I would rest my arm muscles and allow Houari to take over with all my weight resting on his lap. Sometimes, to make a change for Etienne, I would pull my dress up over my breasts to let him see the Algerian boy's hands at work, kneading and pinching and twisting and tweaking while, with necks turned at right angles, we exchanged long and sticky kisses. Every now and then, squatting with my feet on the boy's thighs I would allow the glans to slide out and use my free hand to guide it into the other hole, before resuming my pull-ups on the handle, accompanying the resultant sodomy with my usual stream of filth.

We all thoroughly enjoyed the drive, only unplugging when the car drew up in a parking bay on one of the upper floors of the famous camembert-shaped air terminal, by which time Yasmina was in any case having a problem maintaining her employer erect, let alone ringing a few symbolic drops from his depleted testacles.

Things had been going too smoothly, as we were to discover at the desk that the night flight to Abidjan had been cancelled following crash damage to the runway at the airport of destination, necessitating the suspension of all services for twenty four hours. We were given complimentary accommodation at one of the airport hotels, and after an initial outburst of ill humor, decided to make the best of a bad job and spend the night out on the town. A collective perusal of an entertainment guide produced agreement we should visit the sex-industry area of the Rue Saint-Denis to see whether we could glean any information or experience that might prove useful where we were going.

After walking up and down the street to see what was on the menu, we started in a promising looking sex-shop equipped with movie viewing cabins, Etienne sharing one with Yasmina, leaving Houari and me to pursue our experiments in the neighboring cubicle. We had chosen, without knowing it, one of the great classics of black and white porn, shot in an amateurish way by the husband of the woman who was subsequently to become the porno queen Angelica Longstaff, starring his lovely young wife and their Doberman hound.

The dog, after much licking, sniffing and failure to penetrate, finally succeeded in accidentally plunging its slimey stem into its naked mistress's asshole, which had obviously not been as carefully prepared as her other entry, her intitial expression of pained surprise being as genuinely unfeigned as her subsequent gasps of pleasure. It was the first time I had witnessed any form of bestiality, and I was so excited with adrenalin working overtime, I made myself a secret promise that one day I would find out what it felt like to carry sex a stage further than was possible with a human partner.

If the effect of the film on me was electrifying, Houari's reaction was even more spectacular. The cabin was furnished with a single chair covered with a black, synthetic material, on whose back I was leaning so he would find it easy to enter me if he managed to recover in time from the trip. It seemed to take him longer to realize what was happening on the screen, as my juices were already atrickle when I felt him suddenly stand bolt upright, rip open his fly and lunge at my loins, which I only succeeded in baring in the nick of time.

However, he made no effort to penetrate me normally, as to do so he would have had to force his member down from its usual vertical position. Instead he placed his feet outside mine, which he pushed together, and simply ran his archi-rigid penis up and down the furrow formed by my vulva and the cleft of my buttocks, spreading secretion from one end of my valley to the other.

The main beneficiary of this treatment was my clit, which responded by standing out at right angles from its niche, improving contact with the shuttling organ, particularly as Houari's glans had a deep V shaped recess on the underside, which caught on the rubbery protrusion on each downward run, bending it over with a notchiness that had me squirming with delight. As the film drew to an end, and the Doberman dragged itself further up the young woman's shapely back with its front paws scraping down her sides — the pentration of her anus being made clearly visible by a helping husbandly hand which reached out from alongside the lens to grasp the animal's tail and lift its rear clear of the focal point — I felt I just had to join in myself and reached round behind my buttocks to press Houari's prick down to the right angle to stuff it up my ass.

His speed picked up again to its giddy maximum, and I climaxed at the same time as the adorable Angelica, although as her partner was a dog, she had the usual post-coital canine problem, and I saw her try to disengage as I had with my African laborer and fail for a different reason. Looking panic-stricken, she said something to the man behind the camera, who obviously told her to continue until the dog's detumescence, as she resumed her love making, starting to rotate her buttocks as I had to extract maximum pleasure from the unusual situation. Unfortunately, the film came to a flickering end a minute later, and I was left with a frantically excited Houari banging away at my bottom.

As usual, when being sodomized, I mouthed every vile obscenity in the book of buggery, and it was therefore hardly surprising that the attendant, a Vietnamese hunchback, should have opened the door to see what was happening, as for all he knew Houari might well have been murdering me. When he saw what we were really doing, he threatened us with just about every form of retribution, including the police, for a variety of reasons none of which made as much sense as the eloquent bulge in the left leg of his pants.

Summing up the situation in a flash, I broke free of Houari's penetrating link and passed my hand behind the attendant to shut the cabin door. I then whisked my wool dress over my head and, standing naked in front of him with the exception of my long woollen stockings, I pulled down his zipper, which opened onto the base of a penis I tried to extract, thinking its other end would appear. I was therefore horrified to discover that the long, thin, blue-veined member continued right on down to his knees, and could only be liberated by removing the pants, a disrobing that unveiled a twisted, yellow hosepipe writhing into an amazing eighteen inch erection — by far the longest and the ugliest I had ever seen.

I gazed helplessly at Houari, hoping he would find me a way out of the dilemma, as I may have perverted tastes, but there are limits to what I am prepared to do for a thrill, and the Vietnamese freak was one of them. However, all the Algerian boy did was smile a cruel little smile and make it transparently clear that not only had he no intention of helping me out of my potentially mutilating fix, but even intended to have a good look at whatever might happen, propping himself up against the door to stop me making a run for it.

Left without any support, I could find nothing better to say than: "I cannot make love tonight as I have my menses, which was why I was protesting when my friend here tried to penetrate me, but I would love you to fuck my breasts, as they are very sensitive and I adore having a man run his prick up and down between them and then come in my mouth!" I gave him a winning smile and taking my globes in my hands, I fondled and pressed them together making their cleft even more pronounced than when they hung normally. Pinching the nipples back into a state of prominence I pointed them at him and said: "Why don't you try them for size?"

Cupping their undersides in my palms I squeezed deliberately, making the nipples glisten with milk, which was the sign for the attendant to wrench them out of my hands and push them excitedly between his lips, one after the other, sucking vigorously as he did so. It looked as if my ruse had worked, and before he had time to change his mind I dropped to my knees, pulling the teats forcibly out of his mouth and, taking hold of the long, revolting object, which was now at the same height as my two beauties, I leaned over backwards so that the angle of my body was just right for him to slide his nauseating thing up and down between them.

To get it over with I pressed my chin down onto the base of my neck, as this way I could take the glans and an inch or two of stem in my mouth at the end of each stroke, clamping my lips round them to give him the strongest possible sensation on withdrawal. Holding onto my breasts he forced them together around his obscenity, the effect of these caresses raising his excitement to a pitch where he could no longer hold on, discharging considerably into the back of my throat. To my surprise I found myself swallowing unashamedly, and even pulling his mouth down onto mine for a wet and juicy I made last as long as possible.

My loins were a steaming sauce-pan of lust and, lost to all sense of shame, I would no doubt have forced his abnormality as far into me as it would go, had there been anything left of his erection. But only a flaccid and useless sausage remained, and it was Houari who came to the rescue by jamming three tightly bunched fingers into my sex as I knelt on the floor of the cabin, begging for release from the tension that was racking my slit, finishing me off with a series of brutal jabs into which he put all the strength of his elbow.

We emerged from the cubicle at the same time as Etienne and Yasmina, the latter visibly flushed with an excitement that had made her forget to remove a tell-tale smear from the corner of her mouth. I took her in my arms and lovingly licked off the trace of conjugal misconduct, our contact developing into a tongue-twister which would surely have led to further dykery, as our hands had already started to grope, had Etienne not exclaimed sternly: "Enough of that! We still have a lot more to see!"

The street at that point was a side-by-side series of sex stores proposing wide ranges of erotic attire and gadgetry, porno movies, peep and live shows. We entered a super peep and live show bazar, supplied ourselves with a stock of coins at the counter and went towards the two cabins whose numbers had been growled out by the receptionist. This time the girls stayed together, leaving the man and boy tandem to amuse themselves in the other cubicle.

The cabins were evidently only intended to accommodate a single spectator, who was presumbaly supposed to indulge in the solitary joys of self-abuse while feasting his or her eyes on the spectacle being enacted on the other side of a glass panel, where a revolving, octagonal stage provided the setting for the usually listless copulation of lesbian or hetero couples. Yasmina and I installed ourselves on the arms of yet another black plastic chair and inserted our first coin in the slot, activating the mechanism that raised the blind over the viewing window.

We were in luck, at least insofar as the physique of the first of the participants was concerned, as the female was a splendid, naked black girl with a an electrifying Afro hair style. Her body looked as if it had been purpose-designed as a love machine, as all those parts that had a sexual connotation, while being beautifully made, were just a shade larger than life, from her protruding rump, which was a personal invitation to sodomy, to her bulging, big nippled breasts that were a retarded suckler's dream of breakfast in bed.

When she started to sway her hips to the rhythm of jungle drums, it also became apparent that the girl was a professional dancer, probably from one of the experimental, modern companies in which Paris abounds, but which fail to provide anything like a decent living for their members, who often have to find other less respectable ways of making ends meet, from striptease, to live-showing, to casual prostitution.

The swaying movement gradually became one of rotation of the hips coupled with a to and fro pelvic thrust, developing into the basic figures of a dance derived from the positions of love, which were mimed with a vivid and intensely erotic realism. Her only form of adornment, as she was not even wearing any costume jewellry, was a large white feather planted upright at the back of her hair. At one stage she solemnly withdrew it and, squatting down on her haunches, with thighs well asplay, titillated her nipples and clitty with the end of the vane. Yasmina and I, who had long since thumb-nailed our own buttons into a state of dire tumescence, were both wildly excited by the sensual elegance of the spectacle, and slid our slippery vulvas to and fro over our plastic perches.

Under the caress of the feather the girl's already aggressive nipples slanted diagonally upwards, her clitoris burgeoned to the size of a cigarette filter, and from her obviously unsimulated facial expressions and authentically raucous breathing, it was clear she liked the job and took the sensible view that if you have to do something to earn a living and can enjoy it, so much the better.

The stage door then opened to admit an equally naked Indonesian youth, who, in his own way, was just as striking as the girl. Stockily built, his body was nonetheless a poem of muscular developement and he moved with the ease and assurance of an experienced dancer. His already rigid penis had been anointed with an oily substance that must have been mixed with some sort of golden pigment, as it gleamed opulently in the orange lighting. He had timed his entry to coincide with the precise moment when his partner's buttocks were lined up with the axis of the door, meaning he only had to take three short steps to bisect her vulva from the back, as if anything she was slightly taller then he, and was bending forward at the moment of impact to facilitate entry.

The pas de deux which ensued was as technically perfect as anything I have ever seen on the international ballet stage, as not only was it evident, from the way they caressed each other, that the couple were in love, but also that they revelled in copulating to music in public. Carried away on the wings of both dance and desire, the two bodies melted into each other with a lascivious grace that somehow enhanced the intensely erotic nature of the spectacle, without detracting from its beauty. The two sexes came together and seperated as the dance progressed in such a natural manner, it was tempting to conclude that this was the most normal and certainly the most aesthetic way of making love.

It was only towards the end of their number that a pornographic note crept in, and even then it was a matter of impression rather than intent. It started when the youth sank onto his haunches with widespread knees and the girl, without missing the beat for even an instant, knelt with her back to him, her thighs tightly pressed together and her feet apart to slide them under her partner's shins, guiding his member into her sex with an ethereal gesture that conveyed an impression of absence of physical contact, despite the visible evidence of the organ shuttling between their groins like the fleeting messenger of a carnal communion.

The Indonesian boy retained his balance, which was highly precarious, by reaching round in front of the girl to hold on to her nipples, upsetting the lovely sweep of her breasts when he had to steady himself with a movement that was somehow much more immoral than all their explicitly sexual contacts.

After they had made love for some time in this position, she rolled over onto her back, and the youth momentarily released the captive teats, before taking hold of them again as the girl passed her legs behind his neck. Supporting her weight on her forearms, she threaded herself back onto the golden member without the boy having changed position. Their routine became less and less composed as the climax drew near, the man pulling harder at the nipples to retain both momentum and balance, distorting the shape of the exquisite globes until they both cried out in unison, the Indonesian withdrawing suddenly to cover her breasts with with his liquid of love, which the girl spread over them suggestively before bending her supple neck to lick it with a gesture whose shamelessness contrasted with the strange purity of their earlier convergence.

Yasmina and I had by now reached a stage of near hysterical excitement and were masturbating each other convulsively. I was not however too far gone to notice that the Indonesian youth, whose partner was lovingly sucking the last drops from his still rigid penis, was staring at me through the glass panel. To start with I thought he was looking at his own reflection, but then I saw him make a remark which did not appear to be addressed to the girl. An instant later a loudspeaker announced that the occupants of our cabin had won a 'Spécial' — whatever that might be — with the 'Man with the Golden Groin' and his partner.

Laughing at the aptly chosen title, we nervously agreed to accept our mysterious prize and were shown into a salon, a room some fifteen feet by ten, furnished with fitted carpet and an arm chair in the same, monotonous moisture-proof material, which was set against one of the end walls. The side walls consisted of mirrors along the whole of their length and a white ceiling reflected red, indirect lighting.

No sooner was I seated — as Yasmina quite naturally conceded me this right — the door, which was in the other end wall, opened to admit the couple. The girl entered first leading the youth by his still rampant penis, which she was obviously intent on maintaining in its rigid condition, as from time to time she would move back against him and rub the glans up and down the cleft of her buttocks. Leading him across the room, she stood aside so he could press his shins against the front of my chair, after I had obeyed the girl's injunction to seperate my knees. She then removed her guiding hand from the youth's sex, which pointed at my face like the barrel of a golden gun ready to shoot me down at point blank range.

I needed no prompting, as the shining phallus was not just an invitation to fellation, but an irresitible temptation to kiss and lick and suck for hours on end. Without further ado I slid forward to the edge of the cushion and, opening my mouth and throat at the same time, slipped the heavenly genital between my widely parted lips until my nose was burrowing into the pubic hair at the base of his stomach. Taking his firmly muscled buttocks in my hands, I imparted a movement to his pelvis that slid the glowing member back from the bottom of my gullet to the limit of my lips, which glided lovingly over the softly stretched skin of the sheath, releasing the glans for a second to dart the point of my tongue into the opening of the urethra, which was large with flared-out edges. Then I replunged the whole organ as far as it would go down my obedient throat, before repeating the process.

When we had achieved synchronization, and his buttocks required no further guidance as to rhythm or direction, I used one hand to dandle his testacles in their velvety scrotum, which I hoped still contained enough semen to drown my erotic sorrows, and the other to slide the distended sheath up and down his stem in time with the speed of my sucking.

Without a word, but with an instinctive feeling for the subordinate but essential nature of their roles, like neophytes preparing a high priestess for some sacred ritual, Yasmina and the black girl lovingly undressed my yearning body, without disturbing my ecstatic mouthing of the saliva-slicked penis, which gleamed wierdly in the reddish afterglow of reflected light. My stockings were silently withdrawn from my parted legs, and my dress pulled down over my shoulders, slipped round my thighs and under my buttocks before being discreetly removed from around one ankle after the other, all this being done so skilfully that I did not have to remove the glans from my mouth and the spell remained unbroken.

All was silence apart from the muted lapping that accompanied my oral ministrations, or the intermittent squelching of my sex, that the girl was reaming with her lovely fingers, having passed her arm under my right thigh. Yasmina had stretched out over the opposite leg to reach my clitty, which jutted upwards in great expectation. With their free hands both girls titillated my nipples, making them aggressively erect.

The erotic tension increased until it had to turn into a copulative reality, and it was the most naturally in the world that I ended my deep-throating of a member quivering with readiness. A glance at his face was enough to tell me the moment of magic had come for both of us, and he sank almost reverentially to his knees to penetrate me profoundly without any other form of contact. I placed my elbows behind me on the cushion to push forward to meet his thrusts, using the muscles of my buttocks to impart a slight rotation to my slit, my lover contributing a classic to and fro movement, handling it with such precision that his glans withdrew completely at the end of each stroke before plunging again into my innermost being.

Our lips met in an embrace that would have been almost chaste had it not been for the feeling my mouth had disappeared into his and his into mine. My two attendants gently disengaged my breasts to either side of his torso and started to suck them, relieving their ache at the moment I was racked by a vaginal orgasm of such impact that it forced my shoulders against the back of the chair, without dislodging my limpets, who remained attached to the precious orbs, dragging them momentarily out of shape. My lover's mouth also followed me down, and I raised my legs to cross them behind his back, obtaining a purchase enabling me to increase the pressure of his thrusts by pulling his body into mine. In turn, he passed his hands under my buttocks to reciprocate, and our combined movements resulted in a series of hammer-blow penetrations which had me riding the crests of one heady spasm after another. Then the room started to spin and the giant hand of climax wrenched at my loins, sending shock waves the whole way up my spine.

"I want to eat your seed!" I cried emphatically, releasing his mouth as his member began to heave. He withdrew just in time to allow my lips to close round his gleaming stem and garner its harvest, which I did not swallow immediately, allowing some of it to trickle onto my fingers, which I then used to rub the creamy fluid between the legs of the African girl and Yasmina, massaging it tenderly into their slits.

I must have fallen into one of my sex-swoons, as when I revived, the mirror side walls, which were two-way, had became plain, transparent glass panels, behind which crowded a throng of spectators, like aquarium visitors gazing at an exhibit. I recognized Etienne's features in the foreground and the realization dawned I had been the main attraction in an improvised sex show, whose spectators had no doubt paid a substantial price for their tickets without my even having had the thrill of knowing they were watching me.

Before they were able to disperse, I spun round onto widely seperated knees, splaying my buttocks as invitingly as possible and lubricating my sphincter with the sperm which remained in my mouth. I then quickly felt around behind my back for the golden groin, but was mortified to encounter only a slimey little slug, as after a working day that probably involved at least eight hours copulation, the Indonesian had nothing left to offer.

I cried out in frustration, fearful I would miss the incomparable thrill of being sodomized for the first time in front of an audience I knew to be there and could feel their eyes boring into my most intimate privities. I was reckoning without my darling husband, as he suddenly burst into the room holding an athletically built black youth by the elbow.

"He was jerking himself off in front of the window", he shouted, "Will he do?" "You bet he will!" I rejoined, gloating over the astonished teen-ager. Leaving Etienne to undress him more or less forcibly — as masturbating when looking at a peep show is one thing, but taking an active public part another — I knelt down on the seat, presenting my anus for all to see, and for the youth to posess. It was only when Etienne lined him up behind me, and I passed my hand back between my thighs, that I realized he was hung like a horse. I hesitated for a moment because of the sheer size of the problem, as he was, if anything, even better endowed than the African navvy of my original negroid sin.

As there was nothing for it but to take the plunge or pass the night in a state of exhibitionist anticlimax, I chose the plunge. Grasping his monument I placed it carefully opposite the entrance to my ass, with the intention of feeding it in as slowly as possible, but at that very moment Etienne, who was standing behind the boy, gave his buttocks a violent shove, causing the huge column to literally rape my rectum.

I reacted so noisily that some of the spectators started to leave out of fear the police might be attracted by the volume of my hysterics, which made the boy grab me by the hips, as rape or no rape, he had never had a white or any other ass like this one before. With no consideration for my pleasure or pain, both of which he in any case supplied in ample quantities without even trying, he rammed me as fast as he could, interested only in ejaculating before someone told him to stop.

He need not have worried, as once the initial agony subsided I adjusted to the required diameter, and began to thrust back at him with a verve and dedication that made his eyes open in wide amazement. This increased when he heard the torrent of verbal filth which poured from my mouth, just as he began to inject the contents of his ram-sized balls into my bouncing butt, triggering an orgasm that again shook me to the core. As I turned from the waist to push my tongue gratefully between his thick and rubbery lips, I became aware that the armchair, on which I was still kneeling, was surrounded my men of all types and ages who were masturbating with their members pointing at my body.

I hardly had time to realize what was happening before one of the cocks ejaculated, splashing sperm over the side of my left thigh, followed by another and another and yet another, on different parts of my body. As each prick came its owner would withdraw from the vicinity of the armchair to be replaced by yet another masturbater who, in turn, would discharge the contents of his testacles, hardly a second passing without a squirting of sperm falling on me somewhere, until very nearly every man in the audience had emptied his quiver of come over my trembling nudity.

There were yellow pricks and white pricks and black ones, there were big and little splashes, there were those who finished themselves off in my still distended asshole and those who preferred to come in my hair. Like a scene from a B series graveyard take the zombies shuffled up to my body in the blood red light, crouchingly completing the fitful gestures needed to produce their viscid share of my baptism of lust.

Standing up when the last of them had emptied his final drop, I soaped myself with semen, rubbing it over my skin with a caressing, circular movement, carefully spreading the white fluid across every square inch of my body, helped by the two girls who massaged it in until their was nothing left on the surface.

Then they poured me into the woollen dress, stockings and tennis shoes before bundling me down to the car for the return journey to the airport.

Chapter 7

I spent the following day asleep at the airport hotel, only waking when Etienne gently shook my shoulder to tell me the time had come to dress, as the AUA night flight to Abidjan was due to take off on schedule in two hours time.

I addressed the problem of what to wear when boarding a flight in Europe with a ground temperature of 30°F, knowing that the following morning I would be landing in Africa in a temperature of around 100°. No difficulty would have arisen had it not been for the new clothing rules drawn up by my husband which forbade any form of pants, jeans or underwear. The reason for this was that to fulfil my new function of exhibitionist-sex-toy, I had to wear clothes which were revealing and did not impede access to my body, so as to be able to benefit rapidly from any interesting situation which might develop.

Etienne's requirements in the field of dress created secondary problems, of which the most important were the adaption of such clothing to normal social circumstances — as I could hardly go to the vicar's tea party dressed like Irma la Douce — and the availability of such a specialized wardrobe, as over-revealing styles are not normally stocked by retailers. I overcame these difficulties by having almost all my clothes hand-made by a modiste who had just retired from one of the leading French fashion houses, necessitating frequent and amusing visits to Paris for fittings during the months preceding our emmigration to Africa

My technique consisted of searching out a dress or outfit in the mode mags and having it copied with more revealing decolletés, barer arms and shorter skirts. I would then choose the accessories, some of which were also hand made, whose purpose was to hide what could not be normally exhibited, foulardes being in great demand to camouflage plunging neck lines, visible underskirts for lowering bum-freezing hemlines, capes and jackets for hiding overbare tops and so forth. In a matter of minutes, in a restaurant toilet, I could strip down to near nudity or revert to elegant respectability according to the requirements of the moment.

In fact, my Paris-Abidjan flight attire needed no more than a few seconds thought, and consisted, for boarding, of a white cashmir cape over a sleeveless, smock style, button fronted, blue shantung silk dress, whose skirt stopped three inches above the knee. Its vertiginous decolleté was hidden from sight by a silk scarf from the Faubourg Saint-Honoré. Underneath I wore the shearest, nylon, self supporting stockings and nothing else apart from an elegant pair of matching ballerinas.

My preference for ballerina-type shoes stems from the fact that just as high heals flatter indifferent legs, so shoes without heals do justice to a beautiful leg by underlining authentic perfection unimpaired by unnatural muscular effort, which also has detrimental effects on the overall carriage. For me personally they also have the added advantage of compensating for my height when in my husband's presence, as I would otherwise tower over him.

When the time came we boarded and were shown to our seats on the main deck, but after reconnoitering the upper cabin, whose temporary configuration had been installed for a charter by a multinational flying buyers to an overseas convention, involving its transformation into a luxurious executive suite, we decided to take up our quarters there for the whole flight. The handsome, black steward served us drinks, allowing his eyes to linger meaningfully on my purpose-crossed legs, which were shown off to advantage by the lowness of the pullman seat and the shortness of the skirt. I lifted my right knee to improve his field of focus, and after staring at what he saw nestling at the end of the nylon tunnel he lifted his eyes to mine with a comprehending smile of complicity: we knew what was in store, it was just a matter of where and when.

We had chosen the two seats facing forwards on the right side of the cabin, whose lay out, apart from the usual bar at the back, consisted of a cluster of four pullman seats on either side of the central aisle, with a low, oblong table in the middle of each group. While finishing our drinks Etienne, who had noticed my exchange with the steward, said: "Leda darling, I know you simply cannot wait to get your shapely hands on our dusky friend's three piece service, but I don't want any invisible Emmannuelle-style nonsense in the toilet. Besides, the other passenger might like to join in the fun, not to mention me; in any case there's plenty of room up here for you to do your rutting where everyone can use you!"

Smiling a demure little smile I replied: "Whatever you say my sweetheart, I wouldn't want you to miss a thing", underlining my remark by wetting my finger with my tongue, swivelling my seat in his direction and lazily caressing my clitoris after having uncrossed and opened my legs.

At that moment the other passenger, who was already in his seat on the main deck when we boarded, put in an appearance at the bar. He turned out to be a fat and fortyish black businessman in a remarkably ill-fitting and crumpled suit. With a drink in his hand he slumped down on one of the seats facing us diagonally on the other side of the aisle, just as I recrossed my legs.

Without even waiting for take off I looked at Etienne dreamily and said: "Now we're all here, don't you think you should warm me up a little, as we can't expect these gentlemen to do everything, can we?" Matching word to gesture I hitched my skirt up over my hips and adopted a squatting position with my feet on the cushion and my knees well apart, providing him with a panorama obstructed only by the luxuriant undergrowth that overgrew my loins.

While I was kicking off my ballerinas and removing the silk foularde, revealing the deepness of my decolleté, my husband opened his briefcase to extract a shining aluminum cylinder of the type used for storing rolled plans and similar documents, which must have been about a foot long with a diameter of two inches.

I could feel the tension rising behind me as the effect of what was happening produced the expected repercussions on the spectators, the steward having left the bar for a better vantage point behind my chair. After recovering from their initial astonishment, both of them released swelling penises from the confinement of pants with a quiet deliberation that augured well for my future satisfaction, starting to masturbate slowly while awaiting the further developements which would involve them more directly in the proceedings.

Etienne, holding the cylinder in his right hand, as if it had been a sword, applied one of its blunt and rounded extremities to the lips of my sex, which had been prepared for the insertion by a flickering caress of fingers. This produced the usual ample secretion of a genital fluid whose clean but pungent smell and bitter flavor are much sought-after by connoisseurs, although why I should be so prolific remains a biological mystery.

Putting the weight of his forearm behind the gleaming object, while I stretched my inner lips to accommodate the inconvenient shape of the improvised diljo, Etienne watched it disappear into my depths, rotating it to the right and then to the left as it sank into obscurity, thrusting implaccably until the end came to rest against something solid. I groaned with contentment as he initiated the to and fro movement which was what I had been waiting for, continuing to twist the cylinder with his wrist and then speed up to the point where I was gasping with pleasure, crying out in elation as the first orgasm clawed at my cavity.

Without waiting to be invited, the steward lent over the back of the seat and plunged both hands into my corsage, manhandling me with a roughness that ripped two buttons off the front of the dress. Leaning head-down over my shoulder he stuffed my nipples into his mouth, one after the other, sucking them noisily after a certain initial nibbling. In the meantime Fatty — as I had immediately baptized the other passenger — after undoing his zip and stepping out of his badly creased trousers, which he carefully laid over the back of a chair in a long overdue gesture of respect for their appearance, leaned against the arm of my seat to thrust his massive penis in the direction of my mouth, at an angle that made it impossible for me to swallow more than the first few inches.

By now the cylinder was pistoning in and out at such a speed that Etienne had given up any pretence of trying to turn it at the same time. He compromised by keeping up the pace and modifying the angle of penetration every few strokes so that the pressure on the vaginal walls was constantly changing, to my much-publicised delight in the form of an ecstatic gasping and groaning, accompanied by a steady but silent dribble. I joined in by using one of my hands to pinch and fondle my clitty, taking part of the below-the-belt workload off my husband.

While this was happening the steward had discovered, with the usual signs of stupefaction, that by a minimum of sucking and squashing my breasts could be made to produce a plentiful supply of stickiness. In his enthusiasm for my hidden assets he overdid the squeezing, with the result we had difficulty stopping the outflow, and although he lapped as hard as he could, there was a lot of wastage, quite a pool forming on my stomach which had been bared by the capitulation of the remaining buttons.

Fatty was fucking my mouth as if it were the last aperture on earth, but the angle of my head stopped him going the whole way, and I had to concentrate more on contact than travel. He had just about the largest foreskin I have ever encountered, bunched up in the deep ridge behind the helmet, which I teased out of the furrow, running it back over the glans and then taking the end between my teeth to stretch the hood like a piece of loose elastic, shaking my head like an angry terrier before allowing it to snap back into the groove.

He also boasted a pair of Gargantuan balls in a huge black sack of a scrotum proportionate to the size of his foreskin. As soon as I saw them dangling in the background, half hidden by the cock in my mouth, I took them in my free hand and distinctly remember thinking: "I hope they haven't been used for days!" My wish was to be granted in full as, feeling them start to heave, I removed the glans from between my lips, pointed it at my breasts, and was rewarded by a cataract of come the like of which I had never seen before — at least from the balls of any one man.

The steward received part of the discharge on his cheek, and hastily got out of the line of fire to let the main salvo splash onto my bosom, as I turned my torso to the left to receive it gratefully on both breasts, which were by now as hard as if they had been artificially inflated, with dark red nipples standing out from their halos in diagonal excitment. As my body quaked in the throes of a vaginal climax, that I acknowledged loudly enough to be heard on the main deck, the three men eagerly massaged the mixture of milk and sperm into the skin of my breasts and stomach.

When they had finished, I swivelled my chair to face the table and, taking the two black members in my hands, rubbed their glans over my nipples, as the massage, apart from the usual hardening effect, had left them in a state of hyper receptivity to stimulus, and I was reluctant to allow the men to concentrate their attention on the other parts of my body until I had rung the last drop of pleasure out of my breasts.

As it was evident, from the state of his erection, that the steward could wait no longer, I resigned myself to making the next move, withdrawing Etienne's cylinder from my pussy to leave the seat and lie down across the low table, sliding off the remains of my dress as I did so. It made sense to give the steward the first full fuck, as his reserves of sperm were still untapped and deserving of my urgent attention if they were not to be squandered in the wrong place.

When he realized his turn had come, he was down on his knees in a trice, and after rubbing his glans up and down my almond until it glistened with output, sank into me right up to the pubis, initiating a regular banging which made it clear he had come to stay and would stay to come, and that I could rely on his scraper for the big runaround.

Resting my calves on his shoulders, I settled down to a nice, old-fashioned fuck with no frills and plenty of good, solid screwing. He had a simply divine way of withdrawing very slowly until the tip of his glans emerged completely, and then, holding onto my thighs to steady his aim, he would slam it back in to the very bottom of beyond without ever missing dead center on the return journey.

At that rate I soon started to crescendo, simpering and sighing with lecherous joy. Etienne and Fatty came round either side of the table to allow me to reach their members and jack them off in a leisurely but affectionate manner, using almost all wrist and no arm because of my position; but it was very effective. I rightly prided myself on my masturbatory talents, and they soon gave unmistakable signs of oncoming orgasm. I therefore eased the pace with the intention of making all three of them come as one, but not yet, as there was still a lot of erotic milage left to put on the clock.

The two men at my sides kneaded my breasts, wringing out the occasional drop, as my reserves were running low, although the nipples remained surprisingly stiff. One of them — I cannot remember who — was fondling my clitty and making a very good job of it, as it was standing right up to erotic attention, and contributed greatly to the final intensity of my fireworks.

Sensing that the steward was ready to go into orbit, I told him to speed up the action and bring me to the boil, while I accelerated the jerk off, masterminding all four of us to a simultaneous climax that filled the cabin with animal crackers, flooding me, both inside and out, with the contents of three bumper pairs of balls. This time all my admirers, under the loving supervision of my husband, set about massaging their output into the skin of my breasts until the last traces of the most effective of beauty creams had been completely absorbed.

Neither of the two black bean poles appeared to be in the least put out by their exertions, and continued to protrude at right angles or even better from their respective launching pads of crinkly pubic hair. As it was evident that both Fatty and the steward were ready and even rearing for another visit to my happy hunting grounds, I decided to offer them the only other hole available for such grown up games.

Clad only in my flesh-colored, self-supporting stockings,

which a strange reflex of neatness made me smooth and straighten, I knelt down on the table, asking Etienne — who was busy taking his 16mm camera out of a hold-all to record his young wife's first essay in the field of aerial buggery — to prepare me for the ordeal. He was only to pleased to oblige, parting my buttocks almost reverentially to be able to lick, suck, finger and even blow into my strawberry, whose innocently puckered appearance when undistended gave little idea of the size of the objects, whether animal, vegetable or mineral it could accommodate when called upon to do so.

Once he had finished, and I could feel my anus glowing in pleasurable anticipation, Fatty lined himself up behind and, with a commendable, no-nonsense approach, thrust his member straight into my butt, using my breasts as handles to pull my torso upright into a vertical position, which had the mutually beneficial effect of tightening the grip of my sphincter. While he continued to give my bottom a real bruiser of a basting, I slipped my arms behind his neck, turning my head so he could give my lips a lecherous chewing with plenty of wet and rubbery tongue in support.

The steward was staring in astonishment at my hairy armpits, as although such a handsome black boy must already have had an impressive number of white women in the crew toilet on the lower deck and elsewhere, it was clearly the first time he had seen an unshaved Aryan, and his mouth hastened to explore the two luxuriant depressions, tugging with his teeth at the curly tufts while sniffing excitedly at the beads of sweat which had risen to the surface.

Fatty was treating me to an unexpected bonus, as his balls, swinging like some obscene pendulum, were banging my clitty at the end of each arrival, making it jump for joy. His sodomy was starting to become more and more agitated, his breathing more and more raucus and his kneading of my breasts more and more aggressive, until he finally topped me up to the rectal brim. I hardly had time to realize he had withdrawn before the steward took over and, with virtually no interruption, went on with the good work.

It was in my regular orifice, to which he paid frequent visits, that he finally decided to deposit his second instalment, prompting Etienne to abandon amateur photography and drop to his knees to sniff me feverishly, before removing almost all the traces of other people's enjoyment with his tongue, ejaculating spontaneously on the deep-piled AUA carpet in the process.

We must have spent five minutes recovering our breath, whereafter Fatty suggested that we drink a toast to my wifely obedience, and the steward, after having dressed hastily, disappeared behind the bar to fetch a bottle of vintage champagne and four glasses. Still only wearing a wedding ring and a pair of badly laddered nylons I flopped down onto one of the pullmans, fingering myself nostalgically. This somehow gave my husband a bright idea, as he motioned to the youth not to open the bottle immediately, adding: "I am sure my wife will not deny us the pleasure of mixing our last drink in her own inimitable way".

He then whispered the unthinkable in my ear and, understanding what was required, I smiled slyly and moved into the center of the aisle, where I waited for the steward to produce the bedpan specified by Etienne. Visibly surprised, he nevertheless managed to find one in his medical cupboard and placed it on the floor behind me. I squatted down over it with my knees as far apart as they would go, and Etienne, after shaking the bottle of champagne with scant respect for vintage or label, whipped the cork out with an expert twist and jammed the neck straight into my opening, making the contents surge round my reproductivity with a force that almost upset my balance.

As the liquid was sadly overchilled for such a good brand, the combined effect of iciness and effervescence made me blow my cork. Letting out a shriek of delight I came, adding a good measure of steward sperm and genital juice to the luxury produce of France, which, after having bubbled through my loins under pressure and failed to find another exit, flushed itself noisily into the bedpan. Picking up the unseemly receptacle, Etienne made a good job of pouring its cloudy contents into the glasses, and having passed them round proposed a toast: "Gentlemen, my wife and I would like to drink to your virility — long may it last — but before emptying your glasses I would ask you to follow my example".

So saying he grasped my left breast, which he had to knead for some time before a pearly jet of milk spouted neatly into his glass. Unfortunately the Africans did not have his experience, and were not helped by the fact there was precious little left to extract. To assist them, I went down on my hands and knees in the hope that the dangle angle would make it easier to aim the drippings into their glasses, but it was only after much lewd pulling and pumping that they managed to produce a few squirts and join us in the toast.

While they had been playing at milkmaids, Etienne and I had invented a new game with the cylinder, which consisted of pushing it almost the whole way into my asshole, whereupon I would squeeze it out again in an unladylike manner which produced gusts of bawdy laughter. Unfortunately Etienne overdid things, thrusting it in so far that it disappeared entirely, necessitating the salvage expertise of all three men, with much licking and fingering, to relax me sufficiently to enable the steward to slide it out squeezily.

We all agreed my champagne cocktail had an acrid taste more suited to an Italian apéritif, and that cock and tail would have been a better name. While sipping it thoughtfully, I remained on all fours, allowing my guests to take it in turn to push and pull the cylinder in and out of my sex — as a frontal insertion was fraught with fewer risks of disappearance — while palm-smacking my buttocks with their other hand. I was rewarded with a terminal orgasm as a going away present, before Fatty rounded off our evening by taking a marker pen and printing 'Happy' on my left lower cheek and 'Landings' on the right one.

Our African saga was off to an auspicious start, even if at Abidjan airport I had to walk down the steps from the plane clad only in shoes and the white cashmir cape, which I had to clutch around my nudity, as it was only held together by a single clasp at the neck.

Chapter 8

Our life pattern in Africa had to reconcile the apparently conflicting requirements of Etienne's professional activity, necessitating his presence in Abidjan three or four times a week, and my burning desire to be sired several times a day by the finest African stallions. My recent experience had proved the truth of the French adage 'L'appétit vient en mangeant' (The more you eat the hungrier you get), and although there was presumably some limit to the amount of black cock I could handle, it was evident that if I tried to satisfy my cravings in too noticeable a manner — as would inevitably be the case if we lived in Abidjan — my promiscuous behavior might involve my husband in situations that could be prejudicial to his business interests.

For this reason we decided to rent a villa sufficiently near to the capital to enable Etienne to see to his affairs, while at the same time far enough away to avoid the type of complication I have just described.

On his third preparatory trip to Abidjan he stumbled across the perfect solution to all our problems: an ultra-modern villa built only two years earlier for a wealthy French author of popular novels, on the sand-strip seperating the sea from the western extremity of the Ebrié lagoon, between Anda and Toukouzou, some eighty miles West of the capital. The owner, who was homosexual, had found it expedient to leave the country after a scandal involving an accusation of drug peddling, which was probably unfounded but might have been difficult to disprove.

The villa really was a dream-come-true and perfectly suited to our requirements. Road transport conditions contributed to its isolation, as there was no bridge across from the mainland, motor traffic having to use the ferry from Sogno to Ndyéni about twenty miles West of the capital, whereafter fifty miles of dirt track, that could only be negotiated with four wheel drive transport in the rainy season, ran along the sand strip just behind the beach as far as Toukouzou, the nearest village, where it came to a dead end.

This was ideal, as the villa's isolation meant we would be able to do more or less what we liked without the staff being able to tell the neighbors, as the nearest house was ten miles away. In our Range Cruiser station wagon, or even in the Safari Range Cruiser we used for the really rough stuff, Abidjan was three and a half hours drive in normal weather conditions, but — and this was one of the site's main attractions for Etienne — there was an even faster and more comfortable way to the capital: by water in less than two hours.

We did not have to look further for the right boat than the end of our noses, as the villa's owner suggested we buy his 42 foot, air-conditioned Livorno, whose powerful diesels whisked us in absolute luxury into Abidjan by way of the lagoon, from the private jetty behind the villa. We even 'bought' the skipper-cum-mechanic at the same time as the boat, the trustworthy Joseph, a miniscular four foot six inch member of the Gagou pygmy tribe from the nearby Bandama river, as he literally went with the boat and was the answer to the launch owner's prayer. Later, I was to discover he had other ways and means of being of service to female passengers.

The villa itself was situated on the crest of the sand bank seperating the lagoon from the Gulf of Guinea, a strip of land which, at that point, is less than a mile wide. Standing in a man-made gap in the curtain of giant palms which cover both slopes, it had direct views out to sea towards the South, with an awe-inspiring spectacle of uninterrupted breakers, and northwards over the calm waters of the lagoon. The site was particularly well chosen, not just for the Eden-like perfection of the setting, but also for the inexhaustible supply of fresh water from its artesian well, making it possible to satisfy all the considerable requirements of the villa and its occupants, as well as those of the small colony of servants, a certain number of whom had very specific functions, as I will shortly explain.

The architectural style was a marvellously Italianate version of an expanded West African chieftain's dwelling, surrounded, at a somewhat lower level, by a semi-circle of satellite huts in which the servants were housed. The staff was made up of a male cook, a housekeeper, an imposing major-domo, three maid servants from the local Adjoukrou tribe and two Senoufo gardener-bodyguards. Etienne had only taken on the staff provisionally until the end of the year, as there seemed to be an inordinate number of over-highly paid domestics to look after a main house having only three guest bedrooms in addition to the master and reception suites. We rapidly discovered that the Senoufos, who were magnificent specimens, had been the owner's hired lovers, being compensated for this unsavory task — as they were anything but homosexual — by the stunning Adioukrou girls and substantial salaries.

However, to return to our arrival at the airport, we cleared customs and security without anyone asking to look under my mantle, and the briefest of chauffeur-driven rides took us to the edge of the lagoon near Port Bouet airport, where the undersize and grinning Joseph was waiting in his outsize launch to whisk us off to the West and the earthly paradise that was to be the scene of every conceivable permutation and combination of the components of the original sin.

In the meantime I set about repairing the damage occasioned by the night flight, and after stripping off in the master bedroom passed through into the impeccably equipped shower, where a great deal of soap, shampoo and water were needed to remove the traces of our aerial orgy, particularly from my knee-long main of hair which was clogged with a congealed and unmistakable substance. Yasmina, responding to my call for assistance, came down from the rear deck and, seeing what was required, disrobed rapidly and joined me in the cubicle, helping me to deep soap all the interesting places and unravel my four foot long tresses before shampooing them thoroughly.

While she was rinsing my hair, I reciprocated by soaping her all over, expressing astonishment at the number of patches of coagulated come I had to wash off her body. She sheepishly confessed she had spent most of the night in one of the toilets, with a queue of eager travellers — most of whom were manual laborers from inland tribes returning home under a French-sponsored repatriation scheme — waiting their turn outside and paying fifty francs each to Houari for the right to spend five minutes with his sister. When I feigned to be shocked by such petty prostitution, she said she had done it for the pleasure, and that Houari had kept the money, an explanation which left me feeling vaguely jealous at the thought she had been screwed by upwards of forty black ramrods while I was only having two, even if one of mine was first class.

I gradually forgot my irritation as she coaxed the lather into my remotest nooks and crannies, and our ablutions soon degenerated into an unrestrained suck and fondle,-finishing on the bed with the two of us scissor-fucking with all our might, our wrists interlocked in the mountaineer's security grip, enabling us to grind our crotches together by pulling hard against each other's forearms. Clit against clit, panting and sweating like a pair of all-in-wrestlers locked in some unheard-of hold, we both finally came, our bodies shaking with the shock-waves of climax and our slits seathing with the secretions of love.

After a few minutes of breathless detumescence, we oiled each others' bodies all over — a process that had us caressing and fondling again, until I put my foot down and insisted on going out onto the sun deck to give my hair a chance to dry a little before we arrived. The expression on Joseph's face was positively comic when he saw the two of us emerging stark naked from the catwalk alongside the main cabin, to install ourselves on the foredeck sun bed, with Yasmina holding my shining mane clear of my oily back as if it were a bridal train.

During the whole of the rest of the trip I could feel his eyes boring holes in my body, which I turned this way and that, partly to benefit evenly from the already powerful morning sun, and partly to keep Joseph amused. Yasmina plugged in a hair dryer and went to work on my locks, diverting the nozzle from time to time to shoot down my sex at short range, reverting to the more normal function when my overheated clitty stood up and begged for mercy.

To remove the oil I took another quick shower before we arrived, and slipped into a simple, mid-thigh length, V fronted, sleeveless smock dress in natural linen, with a matching pair of espadrilles, before disembarking in the presence of the assembled staff. I could feel every eye, male and female, focus on my tall, athletic figure with its full breasts and exuberant main of hair falling tumultuously over the shoulders, spreading out to hide my back right down to the knees. No one present could ever have seen anything like it before, and my loins moistened in excited expectation.

I slept for most of the day and then, after a galvanizing interlude of expert marital sex, fell asleep again for the rest of the night. Our adulterous escapades did not prevent us making love together, although other people were going to be so busy with my body there would not always be much room for my husband, who in any case really preferred watching me perform while masturbating as a tribute to the sacrifice of my virtue. Even when his self-abuse took the form of relations with another human being, cerebrally it remained masturbation and proof of his absolute mental fidelity to the young wife he both revered and feared since her Pandora's box of debauchery had been thrown wide open.

I was woken the following morning, long after Etienne's departure for Abidjan, by the major-domo hovering round the bed with a breakfast tray in his hands. This would have been fairly normal had it not been for the fact that the bed clothes were thrown back and I was lying there in all the splendor of my nudity.

Akba, as he was called, who was the undisputed head of the servant universe, was also a Senoufo from the North. He was an impressive rather than a fine figure of a man, standing over six feet tall, in his late fifties, and somewhat overweight as a result of his age, lack of exercise and the perquisites of his position. His wirey hair was almost white and stood out from his head like a halo. He invariably wore a wide sleeved, safran colored caftan that fell almost to his ankles.

How he happened to be in my bedroom ogling my nakedness was another matter, and I suspected the connivance of Yasmina, as she herself or one of the other maids should have brought in my breakfast, as the master suite was no place for male servants at that time of the morning, unless they were exercising some other function.

Akba finally placed the tray on the bedside table and stood facing me only inches from the side of the bed, as if mesmerized by the sight of so much Nordic nudity. Despite the bulge of his stomach, which pushed the caftan well clear of his lower limbs, there was a distinct protrusion of material further down, which could only have been a tribute to the aphrodisiac effect of my charms, that he was anxious to bring to my attention.

As I had to start my inter-racial rutting somewhere, and as there is no time like the present, I looked at him perversely through half closed eyelids and sat up, sliding my bottom up the bed. Using the truncated French which is the local means of communication with the uneducated, I whispered hoarsely: "Put behind back", pointing to the pillows on Etienne's side of the bed. This was asking for trouble, as to get to the pillows he either had to walk round the bed, in which case he would avoid accute proximity, or he could lean across, bringing the protrusion to within inches of my face.

He of-course chose the latter method, lifting the caftan so he could place one knee on the edge of the bed without pinning it down, a method he would not have adopted unless he was hoping I would have a look under the garment to see what was happening. As he slid the pillows into position, allowing his hands to touch my skin in a manner that was quite superfluous, but made me shudder with excitment, I surprised him by making a move he could not possibly have anticipated.

Stretching over to the breakfast tray, I scooped a spoonful of marmalade from the cut glass dish and smeared it over my right nipple. I then lifted the breast upwards and outwards, arching my back as I did so, murmuring slyly, so the major-domo should left in no doubt as to the course of duty: "Bon appétit Akba!"

After a moment's incredulous hesitation, during which his eyes rolled comically, he took the proffered titty from me respectfully and, once he had licked it clean, his thick lips closed around the erect and sticky nipple, which he started to suck with the intensity and dedication only black men seem to be able to muster, making it harden even further before yielding up a trickle of milk, which produced the usual astonished reaction, but encouraged him to return to the task with even greater application.

I then made the move he had been expecting in the first place, sliding my hand under the caftan to find out what the bulge was all about. My reconnaissance revealed the presence of a great big thick black cock, as stiff as a poker and pulsating with pent up energy. What struck me first was its incredible width, but I soon realized that something about its feel was peculiar, as the skin of the sheath, instead of being silky and smooth, was rough and abrasive, the penis itself seeming to be gnarled and twisted. This was unusual, as the skin of blacks is normally softer and more velvety than that of whites, and when I lifted the hem, I had visual confirmation of the tactile impression of my fingers, the penis being disfigured by injuries sustained, as I was to learn later, during an initiation rite of a genital worshipping sect in an upcountry backwood.

The mutilated member, which seemed to have lost not only its foreskin but most of its sheath, nevertheless posessed a strangely compelling beauty, and in any case its thickness and rigidity commanded absolute respect, as did the blissful sensation it produced when scratching and scraping around feminine innards.

Deferentially I took it in my hand, discovering that its calloused surface provided a perfect non-slip grip for busily masturbating fingers, and leaned across to take the disfigured glans between lips eager to practice a new type of fellation in which roughness and asperity would replace the smooth and silky.

My excitement at the strangeness of the experience was

fuelled by the battle I had to wage with Akba to shake him clear of my boobies, as after having managed to get almost half my right breast into his mouth, he was repeating the exercise with the other, while kneading its twin with a hand that slid down it lengthwise, progressively increasing the pressure until a jet of milk was expelled which would carry several feet before splashing onto the marble floor.

When I could feel he was on the verge of something wet and sticky, he disengaged his member and applied his thick lips to mine, leavering them apart with his tongue to exchange a mouthful of unswallowed milk, allowing it to swill round a little before we each disposed of our own fair share. Maintaining the hem of his caftan round his hips, he clambered up onto the bed, lay down between my thighs and plunged his gnarled old tree into my sex without checking whether I was ready to receive it, knowing instinctively that a woman who could behave as I had just behaved was ready for anything. He was one hundred per cent right as I had secreted so much love juice I had wet the bed: there was no question of whether I was ready or not — I was dying for it!

The problem was would he be able to get it in without splitting me asunder? Again the answer was yes, as not only did I want him inside but my sex wanted him as well, as if it had been an independent person with its own likes and dislikes. We both agreed, my sex and I, that it had to go the whole way in, and one lunge was enough for Akba — who was still giving my mouth a regular Frenching — to drive it all the way home.

What made Akba's lovemaking so effective was its earthiness. There was no attempt at finesse or sensuality, only a single-minded determination to accomplish the inevitable without haste or consideration for the female partner, who was no more than an object at the service of his massive sexual appetite. What really turned me on was the sensation of being a worthless utensil whose only function was that of a vessel needed by the all-dominating male to achieve orgasm.

I adored every minute of a personal insignificance intensified by the lacerated stump's remorseless occupation of my distended orifice, an occupation that went on for ages and during half of which I was in a delirious state of continual come, with my lips imprisoned and a tireless tongue rotating incessantly around my mouth.

Our morning session, whose routine never varied, became a regular fixture to which I was virtually addicted, to such an extent that when I had to pass a night in Abidjan and there was no Akba the following morning, I used to wander round like a junky who had lost her fix. Despite, or possibly because of my physical superiority to most women, not to mention men, I missed my moment of inferiority. On one occasion I could stand the craving no longer and went out into the street to trap a male, dragging back an incredulous street sweeper whom I raped in the the building's trash bin room.

With Akba I would occasionally try and assert myself by thrusting back with my loins, but he would just continue to grind away imperturbably until he had forced me back down onto the bed, where I would soon forget the tattered shreds of my self respect as the orgasms logjammed in my libido, and the groans of my fulfilment echoed round the room. When I finally burst into hysterical tears he would open the sluice gates of sperm, making me rear convulsively, grasping his massive biceps for support.

Between our morning fixtures we would treat each other with distant disdain, as he had no administrative function which would have necessitated any other contact with me as mistress of the house. Occasionally he would find me fornicating with another member of the staff or a visitor, elsewhere than in the master suite, and would take no notice whatsoever, other than to brush me aside contemptuously if I happened to be in his way. I always tried to be, as I loved it when he pushed me roughly to one side as if I were a beggar on a private sidewalk.

Try as I might, I could never tempt him with my ass, as he must have felt such dirty habits were beneath his dignity. I just longed to feel his rasping corkscrew in my rectum, but he would have none of it, and when I tried to trap him by expelling his member and raising my hips sufficiently to line him up with my alternative, he would always correct the trajectory, leaving me swearing silently at the reticence which deprived me of a blissful bumfuck.

Chapter 9

My remedy for sexual satiety is sleep — an hour's sleep recharges my batteries and I am ready again for everything the next brigade of lovers may have to offer.

After Akba's first onslaught, I slept until midday, when I was woken by Myriam. At seventeen she was the oldest of the Adioukrou girls, all of whom had been chosen for their beauty by Akba, who had been the owner's procurer and no doubt received a commission on the substantial indemnities paid to the younger girls' parents. Myriam herself had been married but childless, and it was her husband who received the idemnity for her repudiation. She was almost my height with a broad and superbly muscled frame which in no way detracted from her essential femininity, as her ankle and wrist joints were slender and perfectly formed.

As I stood naked beside the bed, my hair cascading over my

shoulders and down thighs still streaked with the seminal evidence of Akba's incursion, Myriam, who had slipped off the white mini smock which was the maids' standard dress, took me gently in her arms and kissed me as naturally as if we had been lesbian lovers for years, darting a lecherous tongue between my lips, to which I responded in kind, digging inquisitively into the corners of her mouth.

My heavy breasts hung lower than her's, but because of the difference in height our nipples were almost at the same level when we stood face to face, and all we had to do to benefit from this anatomical coincidence was wriggle our torsos to give the four red points a heavenly rubbing. I made it even more fun by using some of Akba's ejaculation as a lubricant, helping them slide slipperily over each other to start with and then more and more stickily, increasing the effectiveness of the caress.

After we had practiced a little Myriam led me into my bathroom, where the Italian bubble bath was gurgling with delicately scented, luke-warm water. I wallowed happily, turning this way and that to line up my holes with the master jet, which had obviously been designed for such a purpose, as the high pressure column of water forced its way into my intimacy like an infinitely adaptable penis. I then stood up to allow Myriam to soap me all over, devoting particular attention to those awkward corners which were still partly full of virile effusion.

It was from Myriam I discovered the truth about the goings-on in the villa when the owner was in residence. The two young Senoufo warriors — as that is what these magnificent specimens would have been in a more noble age — were his hired lovers, who had been chosen not only for their physique, but also for the size and beauty of their genitals, which even in repose would dangle down to mid thigh level. The owner liked to caress and suck them before being sodomized, even requiring they be permanently naked so that whenever he encountered them, in or around the villa, he could admire and fondle their members and testacles without having to wait for them to undress.

As I have already explained, the Adioukrou girls were the Senoufo's outlet for their natural inclinations. Girls of their beauty and self indulgence would under normal circumstances have tended to drift into the Abidjan night club circuit, and live a sleazy existence based on part-time prostitution. In the Villa Laguna, for such was its appropriate name, what they were doing was morally not much better, but had the considerable advantage of being just as well paid — as Etienne had discovered to his pained surprise — and infinitely more agreeable, as it was no sacrifice for them to be made love to by a pair of handsome young studs, whom they in any case adored. The only unpleasantness was the special service, which consisted of catering to the owner's fetichistic and masochistic cravings, involving them in a certain amount of fancy dress and meting out of punishment.

Myriam sheepishly confessed that she rather enjoyed her role of whipper-in-chief, dressed up in white leather boots, bra and panties, and listening to her description of their sessions was really quite exciting. A typical performance would consist of tying the owner face inwards to a sort of St Andrew's cross, whereafter Myriam would apply vaseline to his anus, before lashing him until he thrust out his rump, which was the sign for her to force the handle of the whip up his rectum, as if it had been a diljo, only reverting to the whipping when he withdrew his bottom and rounded his back. While she was doing this the other two girls would be tormenting his genitals and nipples with a variety of ferocious gadgets.

Once the owner felt ready for the Senoufos, Myriam would stand aside to let them fulfil their part of the contract, which consisted of sodomizing their employer, one after the other, both of them having to discharge inside him, while the two younger girls continued their frontal ministrations. The other objectionable feature was that when the owner was finally ready to come, one of the girls would have to swallow his sperm, but it was a small price to pay for such an easy life, as after one of these happenings, the owner would take a week to ten days to recover, during which they all did more or less as they liked.

I was so stirred by Myriam's account, that I asked her to put on her sado-maso outfit, which really was delicious, as the white leather enhanced the lustre of her jet black skin. The bra was in fact only a lifter, as all the bosom was visible, and the panties were little more than a string, the boots being hand made, mid-thigh models which must have cost a small fortune.

Using as many gestures as words in a strange, erotic pantomime, I explained to the girl that although I was not a masochist, I liked having my bottom smacked with a cupped hand, providing a lot of noise and just enough pain to make it interesting. We returned to the bedroom, where I knelt on the bed with my backside high in the air and my head down on the pillow, and Myriam went to work on my buttocks, slapping first one then the other, making a noise like a pistol shot once she had learnt how to adjust the cup of her palm to the contour of my cheeks.

It hurt more than I expected, but I soon adapted to the pain and began to enjoy it, whimpering with pleasure after each report. She was sensually very gifted, as she would use the finger tips of her free hand to caress and stroke the insides of my thighs with great delicacy, sucking and lick-kissing my holes between slaps. She soon discovered which of them was my favorite, and gave it a momentous tonguing before gently pushing a finger past the sphincter on a mission of exploration. Feeling I was on the verge of an orgasm, I gasped hoarsely: "Quick the whip! stick the handle up my ass!" It was no sooner said than done, and I bucked as she pushed it in a long way, pressing down the end where it joined the thong to stop interference with the corporal punishment.

My eyes were moist with tears of pleasure, and I bucked again as a first orgasm shouldered its way through my loins. "Now stick it up my cunt!" I sighed dreamily, and was rewarded by a truly wicked lunge that took me quite by surprise, releasing a resounding climax which made me rear up so sharply that Myriam was unable to hold the handle in position. She compensated for its ejection by grasping me firmly by the buttocks, pulling them well apart and eating everything within range, licking and sucking and chewing like a famine victim at a banquet. I reclimaxed so thoroughly I fell off the bed, followed by the girl, who continued to hold me tightly in her arms, kissing me passionately on and in the mouth until my shuddering subsided and I came back in to land.

Myriam must have left me on the bed, as I woke some time later to find her standing there holding a tray with a light luncheon snack. Although the sleep had restored my energy, I really did not feel ready for more sex, but as I was equally unattracted by the idea of visiting the villa and gardens with the housekeeper to discuss administrative problems, I decided to watch somebody else take the center of the stage, reasoning that as I had all those love-puppets at my disposal at prohibitive cost, I might just as well pull a few strings to see how they jiggled.

I therefore told the girl to fetch Banda, the handsomest of the Senoufos, and a minute later she returned with the young man, who was only wearing the scantiest of loin cloths, which I at once told Myriam to remove. I had glimpsed him when disembarking the previous evening, but the true extent of his beauty and bodily perfection came as a breathtaking surprise. He stood all of six foot three with the physique of a perfect athlete, as if the Greek sculptor Lysippus had translated his canons of the ideal male into a black marble statue, which had been miraculously brought to life in Africa more than two thousand years later.

However, Lysippus would never have sculpted such genitals, as he would have considered them to be completely out of proportion, which they were in purely artistic terms, but not in those of the subjugation of the human female, being impeccably shaped and probably three times as large as the classical Greek model. As with all perfect works of art there was a minor flaw: the foreskin was too long, as it fell down at least an inch below the end of the glans, but in the presence of such an overall masterpiece I was in no mood to cavil over a detail which I personally considered to be an advantage, as it meant more popgun to play with. I caught my breath in amazement, and feeling I had to do something to mark my respect for such a thing of beauty, I dropped to my knees at his feet and, without using my hands took his overhang between my lips and nibbled it gently.

The reaction was of course immediate, as the glans thrust its way along the enclosing passage and into my mouth, surging forward to slide down my well trained throat, where it discharged immediately with a force that would have pushed it back out again had Banda's hands not been holding my head. As if nothing had happened, the young warrior began to fuck my face with long, virile strokes, withdrawing almost completely before plunging the superb column of black flesh back in again until his fuzzy pubic hair compressed my nose. Lying on her back on the floor behind me, Myriam slid her mouth between my feet and under my crotch, lapping greedily while I used my hands to caress my breasts, pinching and pulling the nipples.

When I felt Banda's member start to jerk in my mouth prior to a second ejaculation, I removed my lips and pointed it at my breasts in preparation for his splash down, which covered them with a layer of thick white cream I massaged into the skin of the taut globes while dribbling happily into Myriam's eagerly receptive mouth.

Banda and I both realized instinctively something special had happened, without being able to explain its significance. All we knew was that a bond had been created between us, as if the exceptional beauty of our bodies somehow predestined our union in a manner which had not as yet been made clear, but required that we hold ourselves ready.

I rose slowly to my feet and we merged in a kiss which turned us into a single mouth. I felt that in Banda I had met my ideal male and we would never part, but if we did it would only be after something momentous had happened, in which we would both be involved together. It was not love at first sight, as there were none of the romantic symptoms of falling in love. What had happened was purely sensual, as its instrument was our bodies, our bodies and genitals that had recognized their exceptional affinity, independently of our minds and emotions.

I felt no immediate need for further sex with him, and when our lips finally seperated the spell had been broken, and I was back in my world of lucid lechery. Turning away towards Myriam, I made her kneel on the edge of the bed, and reaching out I took hold of Banda's glorious sceptre, which rose again to its full length at the mere touch of my fingers, as if recognizing its mistress. The Senoufo understood what was required, and lined himself up behind the girl, whose vagina had been tantalized into a state of oozing impatience.

I myself threaded the splendid phallus into the gaping sex, before kneeling down behind Banda and respectfully seperating his sculptural buttocks as a prelude to my act of supreme adoration. Apart from Myriam's gasping, the silence was only broken by the lapping sound made by my tongue as I did homage to the tight little orifice, approaching my nostrils from time to time to savor the pungent odor.

As I had not turned on the air conditioning, Banda's servicing of the groaning Myriam, who must have been at her third or fourth coming, produced a stream of sweat which ran down his back into the cleft of his buttocks. Withdrawing my tongue and nose, I allowed the little rivulet to continue on down over his asshole and scrotum, where my mouth collected the acrid drops reverently, one by one. After a while I stood up to rub my breasts across his dripping back, my nipples tracing patterns in the shining sweat.

"Come on my breasts Banda", I whispered in his ear, "Spout on my titties again, they are still stiff with desire for your come!" He must have understood, as he turned to face me, and taking his black bludgeon in my hand I whisked the sheath to and fro, squatting down to receive my anointment. Feeling the member jerk I passed my other arm under my breasts, lifting them towards the glans which I pointed into their cleft. Another flick and his seminal fluid flew through the air, splashing into the deep divide and running on down to my navel, whence I scooped it back onto my nipples, rubbing them sensuously. Banda joined in by chastizing my bosom with his formidable weapon, wielding it with one hand as if it were a truncheon. The tension that had been building up in my loins was released as I came in a convulsion of quaking limbs while bitter sweetness trickled down my thighs.

Chapter 10

After the first few days I gave up wearing clothes almost entirely when Etienne was away in Abidjan or on one of his other trips. Cultivating my 'golden girl' image, which was becoming quite a fad, I would receive my dark-skinned lovers dressed only in jewellry fashioned from the precious metal, which, added to my sun-tan, gold make-up and nail varnish, created the effect of a Hollywoodian pagan goddess invested for penis worship, which is what I practiced. Admittedly I spent most of the time in our suite, whose huge bedroom had an integral sitting room with all the necessary amenities in the way of hi-fi, video and a keep-fit corner. The suite gave directly onto the terrace, which in turn overlooked the pool built at a slightly lower level.

I rarely ventured down to the ocean, as the size of the breakers precluded normal water sports, although during calm periods it was a surfers' paradise, and on such occasions the two young Senoufos, Myriam — who was a natural athlete — and I, might be seen riding the crests of the waves on our boards with the salt spray lashing our naked bodies. Two or three runs would be enough for even Banda, and after our exploits we would lie fucking in the sand, the rigid black columns of flesh sliding voluminously in and out of our distended cavities until, drunk with sun and love, we would stagger back up to the villa, surprising the occupants of the occasional vehicle using the track between Anda and Toukouzou.

On the other side of the villa the lagoon was normally as calm as a mirror, whose gleaming surface was only occasionally ruffled by warm breezes from the interior. From time to time a brisker blow would provide ideal wind-surfing conditions. We had two rubber dinghies, one of which was the tender to the Livorno, while the other, which was a larger model with a 90 hp outboard, was used for water skiing and local excursions, a small, sporting catamaran completing our flotilla.

The logistics of such a sophisticated dwelling, dozens of miles from the nearest town, were impressive, most of the supplies being brought in across the lagoon on the Livorno, which picked them up at either Dabou or Abidjan, being equipped with a special cold storage compartment for the transport of foodstuffs. The diesel which was our life blood, driving the generators that supplied the power for all our requirements, including air-conditioning, was delivered by tanker barge to a sea line, enabling the filling operation to take place three hundred yards off shore. Water was supplied by a prolific artesian well, everything surplus to our needs being injected back into the water bed.

On that first memorable day, having already accounted sexually for two of the male staff and one of the female, I had yet another shower and then walked out onto the terrace and down to the pool, where I decided to brush up my tan, which was in need of refurbishing after a European autumn, despite the use of the helio center I had installed at my keep-fit club in France. Although the sun was far past its zenith, it was still powerful by any standards, and every ten minutes or so I had to plunge into the pool to remove the latest layer of sweat and cool off.

I must have been out there for three quarters of an hour when I saw the second of the younger Senoufos — a certain Wakaba — ostensibly tinkering with the floating vacuum cleaner, without there being any apparent need for him to do so, his real interest being clearly centered on my sweat-soaked nudity. The good news about my promiscuity had obviously already reached him, and he was no doubt wondering when it was going to be his turn.

He was wearing the same symbolic loin cloth as Banda, and it was standing out from his body at right angles, born aloft by a rampant mainmast hidden from view by the folds of the material in which it was draped. This was not however the case with his testacles, as the lifting effect of the erection unveiled them in all their stallion splendor, hanging low at the bottom of a big black sack that swung pendulously with the movements of the crotch from which it was suspended.

Unlike Banda, whose powerful body was a poem of willowy elegance, Wakaba, who was short and stocky, had the massive physique of a weight-lifter with gnarled and knotted muscles in permanent movement, as if animated by a life of their own. Making love with him — as I was shortly to discover — produced the strange sensation of having a seperate affair with muscles that writhed and twitched as if intent on taking part in the event on their own account, independently of the main frame of which they were a part.

I was lying on my front when I sensed his presence behind me on the other side of the pool, and had to prop myself up on my elbows to rotate my head sufficiently to see what he was doing. When he realized I was looking his way, he turned sideways-on so I should not fail to notice the readiness of his condition, although out of respect for my position as the wife of his employer he remained hesitant, and it was clearly for me to make the first move.

The assault of the sun on my wide-splayed sex, and the sight of that black muscle machine had by now aroused my baser instincts, which in any case never required much encouragement. As we were clearly in complete agreement as to objectives, I decided to forego any of the conventional signs of willingness, which might have needed a certain amount of decoding. Sliding the upper part of my torso down the mattress without moving my knees, I forced my rump up into the air and, supporting the weight of my body on the side of my face, reached back to pull my ass-cheeks apart, giving the African an unimpeded view of the hairy nests which were his for the roosting.

As I had turned my body to bring my genitals directly into his line of vision, I could not hope see his reaction, but first of all I heard it, when the noise of a human body diving into water reached my ears, as he applied the principle that the shortest distance between two points is a straight line. Then I felt it as two giant hands replaced mine on my buttocks and my legs were framed by the Senoufo's, pressing my thighs tightly together. Finally I adored it as a formidable black phallus drove straight between the constricting lips of my sex and into the depths of my tunnel, without any of the usual preliminary niceties. This assault typified the difference between my two in-house studs, who were the heads and tails of the coin of virility, Banda's approach to physical love being all finesse and sensuality, whereas Wakaba's had no more subtlety than a charge of heavy cavalry.

Although I was psychologically prepared for what had happened, my ever-active love glands were taken by surprise, as they had only just started to respond to growing excitement, with the result that I was not quite ready for such an inconsiderate onslaught. My loins were transpierced by a searing sensation which made me cry out so loudly that Yasmina put her head round the sliding windows of the main suite to see whether I needed assistance. I signalled to her irritably that this was not the case and she reluctantly withdrew, leaving the two of us locked in single combat.

The shock of unoiled penetration had made my torso snap up into a vertical position, with my back against Wakaba's chest, underlining the fact I was perhaps an inch taller, which I somehow found exciting, as his body must have been half as broad again as mine, and the concentration of all that sinew and muscle into a smaller longtitudinal frame gave a different dimension to the points of contact between our bodies. Imprisoning my breasts from below with the palms of his hands, he milked them in time with his coming and going, his balls bouncing off my upper thighs while his teeth gnawed the back of my neck playfully, like an excited stallion.

I still had not actually seen his manhood, and could not therefore compare its appearance with Banda's, but I was certainly feeling its effects, which, if anything, were more brutally exciting than those of his fellow Senoufo, to whom I was bound by an almost mystic link. My only bond with Wakaba was the ten inches of rigid gristle that was reaming my vulva, as well as those rippling and quivering muscles I could feel under the skin of his buttocks and every other part of his body that was in contact with mine.

I came at least twice, gasping with breathless pleasure and recoiling before the thrust of his pelvis, while milk seeped from my nipples around the curved underside of my breasts, forming drops which pearled off onto the mattress. He finally relinquished his grasp, transferring his hands back to my buttocks, where he placed them with the tips of both thumbs exercising an outward pressure on the rim of the sphincter. Pressing harder and harder against the circular muscle, with an occasional visit to the neighboring hole for a shot of lubricant, he continued the obscene massage for what seemed to be an age, but there were no complaints, as it was a deliciously dirty sensation in exactly the right place.

When he could feel that my asshole was in a fully receptive condition, he withdrew his penis from my sated sex and at the same time pressed in hard with both thumbs while pulling my buttocks apart. I felt the skin of my rear cleft stretch to what must almost have been tearing point, followed by the extraordinary sensation of his organ entering my widespread anus between thumbnails which remained locked in place like a pair of clamps, keeping me so wide open that the big black member gave the impression of having enough room to rattle round inside. He withdrew his thumbs suddenly, allowing the rubbery collar to encircle the glistening stem as it shuttled to and fro, passing his hands around my hips and between my loins, where one of them was transformed into a two fingered stopcock which set about my front entrance, while the thumb and forefinger of the other hand became a pair of pincers that went to work on my clitty, pinching it into one of the most aggressive erections of its overmolested career, before jerking it off as if it had been a spare prick.

As all this left my hands idle I used them on my milkers, lifting a breast so I could take the nipple in my mouth, while raising the other one even higher, tempting my marauder to leave off nibbling my neck and lean over my shoulder to take the teat between his teeth and give it a lusty chewing.

My orgasm was by now a quivering continuity, and only the presence of the nipple in my mouth stopped me advertising the intensity of my enjoyment. The speed of our movements crescendoed as we neared a joint climax which swept both of us away like a tornado, uprooting everything in its path as cocks and fingers and nipples were torn out of their temporary housings. I was so devastated by the violence of our coming that my self control collapsed, and I could do nothing to stop myself peeing profusely down my thighs onto the already saturated towel, before noisily parting company with most of my anal injection.

His reaction to such unladylike behavior was to roar with laughter and aim a series of well directed slaps at my buttocks, making them glow happily through the sheen of sweat and sperm. My pleasure was greatly increased by the realization that the rest of the sexually involved staff, with the exception of Akba, had gathered in the bedroom and were watching the spectacle through the windows giving onto the terrace. Turning to face my benefactor I lent forwards, still on my knees, to take his dribbling limpness in my mouth and gulp down the last few drops, feeling the wrinkled black tube harden under the sucking and sliding until it regained its commanding stature.

Using his jutting member to pull him to his feet, I slid my tongue between his thick, protruding lips for a wet one, encouraging him to pinch my angry nipples before leading him into the pool by the steps at the shallow end. Once the cool artesian water had refreshed our bodies Wakaba took me in his arms, standing behind me at a point where the depth allowed my breasts to float like the marker buoys of an aquatic orgy. Then, pressing his body against mine, he pushed his rampancy through the underwater opening at the top of my thighs, running it to and fro to protrude in front and slide lewdly over the base of my slit.

During our cooling off neither of us had noticed the skimmer which Wakaba had left on the water when he had joined me on the mattress. Ever since it had been criss-crossing the surface and had finally meandered near to where we were standing.

The mechanical sucking noise gave me one of my bright ideas, and disengaging from yet another tongue fight I said: "Leda want in! You hear? Right in! Frontside, backside!"

For a moment he did not appear to have understood, so I picked the suction-head off the surface and made a gesture with its extremity in the direction of the parts of my body I had in mind. His mouth opened in a knowing grin resembling a lecherous leer, and gesturing to me to stand with my thighs against the rim of one of the sides near the shallow end, where my buttocks were just clear of the water, he removed the circular, floating attachment from the nozzle, which then made even ruder noises as if in excited anticipation. Wakaba demonstrated the strength of the suction by placing the palm of his hand over the intake and showing the effort needed to remove it.

I bent over the rim, my dangling breasts coming to rest on the burning marble surface of the pool surround, but I was more worried by the effect the suction might have on my insides. Yet I had to have it, whatever the consequences, even becoming impatient, as my hands had been holding my buttocks apart for what seemed like an eternity, while Wakaba just fingered my fanny without apparently getting any nearer to implementing my plan.

At last one of the Adioukrou girls arrived from the direction of the villa holding a small jar of vaseline, as the reason for the delay was the concern of the Senoufo over the problem of getting the nozzle into me rather than getting it out if anything went wrong. He was however right about the need for an artificial lubricant, as the inner diameter of the pipe must have been two inches, to which had to be added the thickness of the plastic material itself as well as that of the screw thread which was particularly prominent.

Applying a generous quantity of the viscid grease to both my holes, he worked it well in and spread it around before pressing the nozzle against the lips of my sex. This produced a series of stifled snorts from the mouth of the pipe as its intake choked, as well as my first sigh of gratitude as the device sucked all the air out of my reproductive parts, creating a vacuum which tugged at the remoter reaches of my inner-woman to herald the start of the experimental suck-fuck.

However, it soon became clear we had another problem, as the screw thread acted as a brake on the pipe's progress into my sex, and to have forced it might have caused laceration. It was Myriam who found the answer, which, like all the best solutions was simplicity itself, as what better way could there be of using a screw to screw someone than by screwing it in? This is exactly what Wakaba did, turning the end around and around until the first ten inches had disappeared out of sight between my thighs, scraping blissfully against the sensitive but well greased vaginal walls. When the end of the nozzle reached the mouth of my uterus I thought the decompression would make my insides implode. I must have been in at least an eighth or ninth heaven, particularly on the return journey, as a straight pull on the way out took most of my lining with it, and having started to orgasm as soon as the tube entered my sex, I had not stopped since, nor was there any sign I was likely to do so in the near future.

Then I felt something new happening behind, as once the pipe was sucking me to everyone's satisfaction and particularly mine, Wakaba had straddled the protruding extremity and, inching his way along it, had used the upper side of the nozzle as a launching ramp from which to slide his hard-on directly into my ass.

"Sod it you buttfucker", I yelled, "Be careful can't you? Watch it you ass-jerk! There's not that much room; you'll rip me to pieces! Ah! Ah! That's better now! That's better! Ooh Yes! Yes! That's it! Slide them both in together! Aah! Aah! What a gutsuck! Now, Sock it to me! Ooh Yes! Harder! Faster! Harder! Faster! Ooh! Drub me that doublefuck!"

I did not see him make a signal to Banda, who may have had the idea all by himself, but I became conscious that the vacuum pressure was being varied from maximum down to minimum, then back up to maximum again, before the pump was reversed and a blast of warm air blown up my cavity, followed by a switch back to suction.

That was a lot more than I could take. As the comewaves crashed over me I bucked like a bronco that had just been stung by a swarm of hornets, lifting Wakaba off the floor of the pool, as he was holding the outer end of the nozzle between his thighs. My writhing pushed the tube even further in, at the same time as driving him in deeper as well so that when I reared he was born aloft on his improbable seat. Finally he could hold on no longer, and after ejaculating prematurely in my alimentary canal, deserted the sinking ship. This is precisely what happened, as with the nozzle still firmly embedded I keeled over backwards to disappear from view, leaving him to lifesave me, unscrew the ecstatic appliance and then carry me up the stairs at the shallow end, coughing and spluttering out the aftermath of my first submarine sodomy.

Chapter 11

When Etienne returned from Abidjan on the Livorno it was already late. As a dutiful wife, I gave him a full account of the day's events, sparing no detail likely to tickle his perverted fancy, punctuating my description with a pensive mouthing of his glans while he distractedly fingered my fork, using a hand that had taken the long way round between buttocks. Even he was surprised at the amount of inter-racial intercourse I had packed into a few brief hours, and was disappointed at having been unable to witness any of the debauchery. He was so obsessed by what he might be missing as a voyeur that he decided to take on a living-in photographer to film the wifely fornication, and although the idea appealed to my exhibitionist streak I could not help wondering how he would be able to find anyone prepared to take on such an assigmnment without wanting to join in.

In the middle of my narrative I suggested we order a couple of our special planter's punches, made from best Barbados rum with extra ingredients noted for their aphrodisiac effect. I expected Yasmina to bring in the drinks, but it was in fact the youngest of the Adioukrou girls, the adorable Dagouba who opened the door, her spikey plats sticking out from her head like some rigidly stylized depiction of a sunrise.

She put down the tray on the side of the bed and, when she saw what I was doing to Etienne, quite casually unbuttoned her smock, allowing it to fall to the floor. Then, with a dazzling, white-toothed smile, she jumped skittishly onto the bed, taking the rigid stem of my husband's penis between her beautifully tapering fingers to slide the glans into her mouth as if it were an outsize lollipop.

We were both so fascinated by the spectacle of this lovely adolescent practicing fellation with a skill that would have done credit to a middle aged harlot, we refrained from making any movement, being quite happy to drink in the intensely erotic spectacle with our eyes. Every now and then, with a broad grin, she would rub the end of the glans over her nascent breasts, inserting her small but rigid nipples in the hole at the top. After a few minutes of teasing the bulging pink object, she would whisk the sheath up and down the stem without interrupting her mouthing of the extremity, using her free hand to play with the testacles as if they were an exciting new toy, occasionally giving the scrotum a brisk lick before really pumping the glans, her cheeks hollowing with the effort of suction.

The inevitable outcome was not long in the making, as my husband's breathing became more and more irregular while his balls heaved in forewarning, and although Dagouba remained glued to the glans like a blood-starved leach, it was evident that transfusion had taken place. I expected her to make a swallowing movement, but nothing happened, and I was intrigued to know why she should have retained the sperm in her mouth.

I was soon to find out as, straightening up into a kneeling position, she smiled at us enignmatically before allowing her mouthful to trickle slowly out of the corners of her lips and down onto her mini-breasts, where she spread it around with an infinite suggestiveness, using only the tips of her shapely fingers. For sheer naughtiness it was hard to beat, particularly as she then straddled Etienne's legs, with her nipples at the level of his mouth and said "Mister lick!" with a great peal of laughter.

My husband of course obeyed, affectionately licking the viscid mixture of sperm and saliva from the boyish breasts. But that was not all, as the stimulus of the girl's lewdness was such that his penis had reared up again, causing her to slide her legs around his hips with a suppleness that even I would have been hard put to imitate, clasping her hands behind his neck to lift her body briefly off his thighs. She then sat down again as naturally as on a stool at school — which is probably where she should have been — with the difference that all eight inches of Etienne's rampant shaft and heavyweight glans had disappeared as if conjured out of sight!

We were both so surprised by her expertise that we left the organization of our amorous get together in her hands, as she was obviously brimful of ideas and quite capable of stage-managing the next phase of the action. She continued by crossing her ankles behind my husband's back to obtain enough leverage to lift her body sufficiently to produce the required length of penis travel. After a few experimental runs, punctuated by further gusts of laughter, she looked me in the eyes with her mysterious and intensely erotic little grin and said: "Leda go backside!"

It was a clear-cut order, so I edged in behind Etienne, kneeling with my thighs spread as far as they would go, whereupon Dagouba unclasped her hands and used them to pull my breasts over my husband's shoulders on either side of his neck and take one of the nipples in her mouth. She then stretched her arms round both our bodies and really began to fuck in earnest, lifting herself until the glans was on the point of breaking free, then flopping down again with all her inconsiderable weight, which was however enough to drive the rigid member home to the innermost limit of her immature sex. Upon completion of each stroke she would change from one of my nipples to the other, giving them alternating sucks whose vigor was remarkable for such a small mouth and physique, as I could feel the milk flowing regularly with each pull.

And even that was not all, as she adjusted the height of her feet behind Etienne's back to the same level as my loins, and by pressing their tiny soles one against the other and bunching her toes together as tightly as possible, she created a wicked little wedge of flesh and bone which she worked into my sex, with of course my willing cooperation, as I wriggled and pushed until her instep impeded deeper progress.

In any case the number of inches was unimportant; what mattered was that her combined assault on my breasts and sex should be so unusual and so perversely exciting. With my husband being fucked by her at the same time, and both of us being virtually reduced to the role of sexual stage props, I just had to come, annointing her feet with my trickle and not stopping until Etienne ejaculated.

In the meantime she must have had at least five or six spasms amid further peals of golden laughter, which, it must be admitted, became somewhat strained at the precise moment of orgasm, but was a much more musical sound than Etienne's snorting and my grunting and gasping. As there was little I could do with my hands, I used them to pinch her burgeoning nipples, and was punished by a series of retaliatory bites that cut off my milk supply for the rest of our orgy, much to Dagouba's annoyance.

Rising and falling with surprising ease, like a boat in a gentle swell, with movements which were as sensually feline as they were graceful, our infant prodigy once again got the better of

Etienne's legendary self control. The tightness of her semi-virginal cunt combined with a supple rotation of the hips proved irresistible, and he emptied himself deeply inside her at the same time as her own well synchronized climax. This made her release my nipples and throw her arms round her lover's neck, thrusting her tongue into the back of his mouth as she shuddered her way through an orgasmic implosion that would have done credit to a woman three times her age.

After the needle on her Richter scale had returned to a normal reading, she allowed her body to fall back onto the bed, where she lay with her legs and arms asprawl. Finding the spectacle of her outspread nudity more than I could resist, I slid my head between her open thighs, whose terminal triangle glistened with overflow, parting the lips of the little conch and licking my fill, savoring Etienne's familiar flavor laced with the more acrid taste of her own effusions.

Chapter 12

For some obscure reason, quite possibly related to the memory of my mother as the white ham in a black sandwich, I had always shied away from double penetration, although the prospect excited me like mad, and I knew it had to happen sooner or later. All sorts of objects had already been in an out of one of my holes while a male organ was in the other, but I could not somehow make up my mind to take the final plunge, and had always stopped any second man, who happened to be taking part in a sex situation in which I was involved, from occupying my spare opening. It may have been the same reflex as that of a child saving till last what tastes the best!

The inevitable loss of my double virginity happened one morning when Akba had left for several days up country on family business, and Etienne had spent the night in the apartment in

Abidjan. Deprived of the night-time recreation supplied my husband, and my morning session with the major domo, the pressure was starting to build up in my boiler, and I encouraged Yasmina, who had brought in my breakfast tray, to caress my breasts and fondle around further down, but as I was used to something more substantial at that time of day, for once I found her expert mouthing and fingering a trifle irritating, even if the familiar warm sensation did pervade my loins.

Feeling instinctively that something worth recording would happen, without having any idea what it might be, I rang the bell three times, which was the agreed signal for the camera operator to standby to film. I never knew where Etienne had unearthed her (as it was a she), but he had found the ideal solution: a sixty year old Senegalese who had worked on French porno movies as an assistant cameraman. But that was only half the battle, as there was also the question of sexual neutrality, and from this point of view she was perfect as well, as any risk of her wanting to take part was obviated by the horrible fact of having undergone clitoridectomy in childhood; a barbarous form of traditional mutilation which permanently eliminates enjoyment of sex. Etienne paid her handsomely by result, ensuring that she zoomed in on us from every conceivable angle, almost standing on her head to take the most incredible close-ups, producing shots and sequences which would have won every Oscar in the porn trade. Between reading my diary and editing these films my husband's voyeurism had good value for a lot of money.

While Yasmina's graceful hands stroked and coaxed my sexual awareness out of the lethargy of sleep, she chattered on, between kisses, about her love life during the past twenty four hours, astounding me, as always, with its incredible density. For the lovely Algerian girl life was one long unbroken fuck, all of her bodily orifices seeming to be permanently and even simultaneously occupied. I knew her lurid accounts were not exaggerated, as you could not take a few steps in the villa or its grounds without stumbling over a copulating Yasmina, were it standing up, sitting, kneeling or lying down, with either man, woman or object, not to mention the suspicions we entertained on the nature of her relations with the Korhogo guard dogs.

Usually Yasmina's hands and mouth were effective part-time penis substitutes, soothing my copulative frenzy for hours on end, but on that day she was only exciting me without being able to finish me off, as my pending orgasm obstinately refused to respond to lesbian loving, requiring a male member in fighting trim, so taking her head between my hands I kissed her juicily and told her I had to have either Banda or Wakaba as a matter of urgency.

Pouting angrily she left the room, and barely a minute later Banda's perfect silhouette was framed in the window. He had always been my favorite, as quite apart from his physical beauty, his skin was absolutely jet black without a trace of a mark or scar, and had that uncanny, velvety softness characteristic of the black races. Sometimes, after we had finished making love, I would take a Banda bath by rubbing myself all over him in every conceivable position, kissing and caressing all the recesses and protrusions of his sculptural body.

His lips were thick and of the consistency of tender rubber, which he could twist into all shapes to apply pressure anywhere and anyhow. When kissing he would trap my lips between his and munch them gently, while using his long and muscular tongue to spring-clean the corners of my mouth. A prolonged kiss from Banda would be enough to make most women come; but there was all the rest as well!

Taking his semi-erect member in my mouth, to complete the stiffening process and cover it with a sheen of lubricating spittle, I felt it jerk to attention between my lips, and as my need for impaling had reached the stage where my limbs were trembling with desire, I pulled the Senoufo down onto the bed, installed him on his back, straddled his body and sank down onto at least ten inches of unconditional bliss.

Kneeling astride his thighs, with his column of ebony filling my loins to way up beyond my navel, I could just manage to raise my sex far enough to allow the massive, black staff to slide slowly out of my vagina until my gaping slit was poised over the shapely glans. Then, equally slowly, I would sink down again until I was sitting on the African's thighs and the pulsating shaft had been driven back in to the limit of painless penetration. To enhance the sensation Banda would rotate his hips almost imperceptibly, adding a further measure of erotic pressure to the waves of pleasure that were already eroding the sandbanks of my self control.

While this was going on, he would support his torso on his elbows to bring those intimidating lips within range of my nipples, which met him half way through my forward-leaning position. The big rubbery flanges would close over one dark red teat and then the other, pulling them out to full stretch with the assistance of a lowering of his head and a straightening of my back, until the traction was such that the lips could no longer retain the nipple, and the whole breast would spring back into its normal position.

I was just starting to come nicely, dribbling a rivulet of fore-juice over my lover's bulging scrotum and trembling with lust, when I felt the mattress yield under the weight of a new arrival, and turning my head saw Wakaba climbing onto the bed behind me, with a cock so rampant that it stood up and out diagonally from his crotch. I remember thinking hazily through the orgasmic mists: "But I told Yasmina either Banda or Wakaba", as it was an unwritten but inflexible rule of villa life that no one should enter our suite without having been invited to do so, other than for domestic service.

It was only afterwards that I discovered the reason for this departure from established routine. Yasmina had found Wakaba almost immediately, as he was in the Adioukrou girls' hut, pounding away at the second of the native servant girls, the lovely and sensuous Dala, who, apart from her prodigious appetite for regular sex, had a quite unquenchable thirst for come, that she would gulp down in whatever quantities were available, complaining bitterly if a partner came in her loins instead of ejaculating in her mouth. Such was her oral longing for seminal fluid she would accost perfect strangers to propose her body in return for the right to swallow the contents of their balls.

Yasmina had been so excited by the spectacle, she had fallen to her knees to service the Senoufo's anal furrow, encountering endless difficulty in maintaining contact, as he was screwing the Adioukrou with such long and rapid strokes that it was no mean feat to keep a tongue in his rectum. After ten minutes of acrobatics, just when Dala was quaking with climax, Yasmina suddenly remembered why she was there, and hauled Wakaba off his partner — who almost had hysterics — to propel him in the direction of our suite, where he found me already fucking frontally with Banda.

Not realizing Banda's presence was accidental, he obviously thought I had decided to take the plunge, and started to straddle my calves, nevertheless hesitating for a moment to see whether I would have the usual negative reaction. I did in fact murmur: "No Wakaba, not that!" but my tone must have lacked conviction, and as he was in no mood for prevarication after the untimely coitus interruptus, he continued to position himself astride my legs, inevitably prodding my cleft with his cock, as it was sticking out so far he would have had to turn his body sideways to avoid contact.

I was suddenly creeping with gooseflesh from head to foot, and the adrenalin began to flow as I realized I was about to engage the fateful process, but I did nothing to help Wakaba or make him aware that I had decided to go on with the experiment. In fact, he needed no encouragement as, without knowing it, my readiness for a two-way ride was visible yards away for anyone standing behind me, as my asshole was yawning cavernously, without even having been touched by anything or anyone, as if trying to to say: "Come and get it!". All he had to do was ladle off some of the drippings from the adjoining hole to anoint the rim of my gaping sphincter, press his cock down to a suitable angle, and slide it in right up to the pubics, which is precisely what he did, choosing the moment when Banda was at the end of an out-stroke, leaving the vaginal channel unoccupied with plenty of room next door.

I nonetheless cried out, more from principle than pain, as the sensation was of such intensity I started to climax, just retaining enough mastery over my reflexes to continue on the basis of 'one in and one out', while Banda, giving up his mouthing of my breasts, clamped his lips over mine to silence my normal verbal reaction to any form of buggery. Wakaba took over my titties where the other had left off, seizing the nipples between finger and thumb to pinch and rotate them in time with the basic rhythm.

When I had loosened up sufficiently to change to the 'both in at the same time' method, Banda had precious little to do, playing for him the unusually supine role of the stake on which the willing victim impaled herself. Even Wakaba's contribution was essentially passive, as the 45° inclination of both my torso and of his erection meant that by raising my body off Banda's thighs at the same angle, and sinking down again without changing planes, I myself ran both of the black battering rams up and down the adjacent channels. They felt as if they had to burst, as each phallus must have been one and a half inches thick, and better than ten inches long, on a day when my cavities felt particularly short and narrow owing to their simultaneous occupation. Shake my head as I might I could not free my mouth from the grip of Banda's lips, and it was in terms of stifled moans and groans that I expressed my ecstasy.

It was all so hermetically tight we had to take it easy at the start to keep the pain within agreeable limits, but as we progressed, and my suffering gradually diminished, I was able to step up the speed until the sky became the limit, and the two black pistons flailed in and out of my privates as I rose and fell back again, rose and fell, rose and fell. We were so used to making love together that after a prolonged crescendo, during which the intensity of our collective pleasure became more and more difficult to contain, with the men voicing their increasing erotic tension in bursts of gutteral dialect, while my liberated lips contributed their usual cascade of obscenity, we all achieved a precisely synchronized climax, with both members burried deeply inside at the moment of effusion.

The feeling of those two thoroughbred stallions hosing my innards simultaneously with cataracts of come was as unforgettable as it was hysterical, and it needed the combined strength of the two of them to hold me down until I came back to land on the same planet. But there was also the realization I had gone and done it again, as with Akba I was never sodomized first thing in the morning, and had not therefore thought of going to the little room to be a clean girl before allowing a big black man to fill my beautiful bottom with nature's most powerful enema.

It was self-evident that if I allowed Wakaba to withdraw, my sphincter, after the basting it had received, would not close rapidly enough to avert disaster, and I therefore had to keep Wakaba where he was until he could remove the stopper without involving us all in a ghastly accident.

Passing my arms behind me and around his back, I said beggingly: "Wakaba stay Leda asshole! Leda big tummy shit!" Fortunately he understood the position immediately, helped by ominous rumbling noises from the lower part of my abdomen.

Passing his hands underneath my thighs, I felt those steely biceps flex as he lifted me clear of the soiled sheet, prior to sliding back over the edge of the bed and onto his feet, without relaxing the pressure of the all-important bung that remained firmly wedged in my butt. Still holding me under the thighs, with my back against his body and my legs dangling from the knees, he strode easily out of the bedroom and into my bathroom, positioning himself in front of the john. We then executed the difficult movement of rotating my body around the pivot of his penis so I was in a head down position.

It was then easy for me as a gymnast, by opening my thighs as we held on to each other's forearms, to do an upside down splits followed by a pull up of the torso to resume a sitting position the other way round, facing him, with of course the bung still tightly in place. All he then had to do was flex his knees to lower my buttocks until they were on a level with the seat, pull out his prick, deposit me rapidly and leave the room hastily like a perfect gentleman, closing the door quietly as he went.

It had been as near a miss as on the occasion of my anal defloration on my sixteenth birthday, and I swore out loud I would never again allow myself to be caught unprepared for my favorite pastime!

As for the film produced by the Senegalese operator, it was so unbelievably lurid that just looking at it made me come, let alone Etienne!

Chapter 13

The days and the weeks passed by in a blissful convergence of sex and sun — in that order — and if I were to describe all my love making I would spend so much time writing about rutting there would be none left for lechery. As it is, I have difficulty finding the odd minute to scribble the few lines of reminiscence I manage to commit to paper almost every day, with the result that this account is limited to the events which, through their novelty or originality, seem to me to be worth placing on record.

Why I should wish to describe my sexual self-indulgence in writing is yet further material for the psychiatric couch, deserving analysis at the same time as my exhibitionism, of which it is probably no more than a projection. Even if I wanted to give up keeping these note books, as they are diaries only in name, Etienne would not hear of it, as ever since he discovered their existence at the start of our marriage, when their contents were less outrageously explicit, he has read them avidly.

In fact, ever since I launched into maritally condoned adultery on a spectacular scale, Etienne has been so excited by my descriptive gifts he has made me do most of the reading on my knees, with the diary in front of me on the bed, while his hands or mouth or penis, or all three do conjugal things to my relevant parts.

I passed every day at the Villa Laguna indulging in some form or other of amorous activity, going the rounds of my five male and four female regulars, not to mention occasional visitors of both sexes, who were usually chosen for the degree of innovation they could be expected to introduce into our world of libido. Finally there were the chance encounters, as well as those Etienne would lay on when I accompanied him to Abidjan, where he rented a two-bedroom service apartment in a fashionable block, as he frequently had to spend the night in town.

From time to time he would use my body to further his business interests, and I rather enjoyed the feeling of being prostituted, just so long as the beneficiary was black and as horny as all hell. More and more frequently Etienne preferred to watch me performing with others, either masturbating while I was being inseminated by one or more strapping African athletes, or himself making love simultaneously with a partner or partners of either sex.

On these occasions he often placed himself in a position from which there was no risk of missing the smallest detail of my fornication. One of his favorite configurations was to lie on his back and make me stand over him with my feet on either side of his head, bending over to touch the floor beside his chest with the palms of my hands. My lover would then penetrate me anally, giving my husband a perfect view of the action taking place just over his face, while he masturbated with one hand and fondled my crotch or smacked my swinging breasts with the other.

Sometimes, when Banda or Wakaba were doing the ass-fucking, he would make them withdraw so as to be able to suck and lick their glistening members, visibly savoring the acrid taste of my insides. He even filmed me from this angle, but the take was not a success as the lens kept becoming clouded with easily foreseeable smears. Come to think of it Etienne is the biggest sexual freak I know — and I have met some prize specimens in my time — but I love every perverted moment of his depravity, seizing on his most revolting ideas with lecherous abandon to improvise even more vicious variants of my own, hoping he will then find some way of making them worse!

My sexual automatisms include an unusual preliminary phase due to the exceptional activity of my lubricant glands. This is triggered by either foreplay or just plain anticipatory excitement, and is different from the normal female moistening process in the amount genital fluid produced, which is so plentiful that it drips or even dribbles, wetting my thighs, my skirt and even the floor when I am standing (as I never wear panties) creating all sorts of embarassingly fertile situations. This is followed, in the event of sexual intercourse or intense masturbation, by a double-decker climax, consisting of a clitoral phase starting as a series of peaks and troughs on the graph of my sensory perception, from which the lows gradually disappear.

It is characterized by bodily writhing and squirming accompanied by gasping, sighing and a rush of blood to the cheeks, lips, nipples and clitoris. This leads to a vaginal climax or 'Big Bang' as I call it, which is marked, to a greater degree, by the same symptoms, but can also involve a partial loss of control of certain bodily functions. When the climax is anally induced and the ejaculation prolific it is not uncommon — as we have already seen — for the sperm which has just been pumped into my rear to be blown back onto the donor's thighs!

The main and possibly only victim of my passion for Africa

and the African male was my marvellous knee-length hair — my pride and glory — which proved to be incompatible with love in a hot climate. When it was loose it was like copulating under a thick blanket in an ambient temperature of 100°F, whereas platting, pinning up, shampooing and drying not only took longer than in temperate climates, but consumed time I could no longer spare, being busy using it to make love from morning to night!

Amid the lamentations of my dusky lovers, for whom it was the most exotic symbol of my whiteness, I had it cut off just over the shoulder, and cried as I had never cried for the other virginity I had never seemed to lose. Once it had gone I enjoyed a sensation of liberation which seemed to last for weeks, and was due as much to my release from the main vestige of revolt against maternal authority, as to freedom from the bondage of a four foot hawser of hair that seemed to get in the way of almost every amorous initiative. My head had lost its ball and chain, and the dancing, wavey buoyancy of my new pageboy style soon became everyone's favorite and a combing range for hosts of eager black fingers.

I had fulfilled my unconscious ambition of becoming the African's ultimate white phantasm, and would have given myself to the whole male population of the Ivory Coast had it been physically possible, which was why it was indispensible to shut me up in the villa, where my hired stallions could satisfy my inordinate sexual appetite without everyone knowing. If I was left on my own in Abidjan anything could happen — and sometimes did — as without a massive injection of sex every morning, I could become hysterical with desire and do anything to procure the black manhood without which I went off my butt.

To start with, Etienne did not guage the risk he was running in leaving me alone and unfucked in the apartment, as he had not measured the extent of my new greed for sex. I have already mentioned the incident with the street sweeper, but it took what I call the 'trash bin scandal' to make him realize I could not be left alone without more than enough penis to contain my craving for come.

One morning in Abidjan I had a bad case of the coital shakes, and nothing I could do to and by myself did anything to alleviate my chronic yearning for negroid virility. In the entrance to the apartment a pair of smallish elephant tusks were mounted on stands, and such was my desire I straddled one of them, forcing the point far up into my loins until the sheer width of the ivory way down from the tip stopped it sinking in further and causing serious injury. I stood there half crouching, squeezing the gleaming object between my thighs and moaning with frustration.

Then, despite total nudity, I strode out onto the bedroom balcony, which overlooked a service courtyard behind the building, hoping to discover some means of calming my seething sex, just as the trash disposal vehicle drew up downstairs and two burly blacks entered the bin compartment to start emptying the contents of the cans into the shredder. Suddenly, without really knowing what I was doing, I found myself hurtling down the service staircase three at a time to arrive in front of the door of the compartment just as one of the men was about to emerge.

He dropped what he was carrying in amazement, giving me an opening to fall on my knees in front of him, jerk down his shorts and gobble his gift to womankind, which even when limp must have been six inches long and promptly doubled in size as a result of my oral adoration. Pulling him down onto the floor I straddled his thighs to impale my still distended sex on his upright pylon, and then bent forward from the hips, as a new but zealous convert to double-fuck, to arch my back and make my anus gape cavernously at his colleague, who was not slow to take the hint and stab it with his spear.

Shouting encouragement and obscenities at my partners I lunged forward until my frontal lover could penetrate me no further, and then thrust back with my buttocks to force my sodomiser in as far as he could go. After a few minutes of delirious duality I was coming ecstatically, just as the driver entered the compartment in search of his team. I received him in my butt, pulling his predecessor round front where I could take him in my mouth and taste my netherness before gulping down his discharge, resurrecting his virility with a spate of sucking while the underman guzzled my breasts.

At that moment the janitor arrived, having been disturbed by the amount of noise I was making, and was accommodated, in my regular hole, by the expulsion of the original trashman, who almost took my boobies with him. Rolling my new sodomiser onto his back, without interrupting penetration, I presented my widely spread thighs to the newcomer, whose member was rapidly mouthed into an adequate state of stiffness before being jammed into the vacated slit. I entertained the two who were waiting for a hole by mouthing their members, one after the other, while they kneaded my breasts, occasionally withdrawing their sexes from between my lips to bend down for an oozing of milk.

Having come more than my fill I felt enough remorse to want to return upstairs to relative respectability, but my gang of bangers still had unfinished scores to settle with my sex, as having sowed the wind of desire I was about to reap the whirlwind of virtual rape. Thrusting me down on my back onto a floor littered with random refuse, they took it in turns to posess me contemptuously as if I was less than the cheapest of harlots, goading each other on in my strangely listless loins with bawdy comment and helping hand. At least between the four of them they extinguished the fire in my furnace, and having immobilized a trash disposal unit for at least an hour, I staggered back upstairs to the shower, where, as soon as I directed the water onto my sex I was shaken by a delayed-action, depth-charge of a climax and had to hold on to the taps for support.

I showered every inch of my befouled back, but the stain of moral degradation was indelible, whatever the degree of physical cleanliness achieved, even if in secret I jubilated at the almost morbid intensity of a sensation I had never felt before, even in the throes of the most flagrant perversion.

It cost Etienne a fortune to put a lid on that one. He finally managed to buy silence with hard cash and promises his wife would be waiting for them next time she was in Abidjan, which was at least one way of keeping me out of all sorts of public mischief, as the next time I had a seizure I might have run naked down the main street in search of sex.

At last I had exorcized the demon of my mother's example by doing the same thing myself, but on a larger and obscener scale. In addition, I now had an alternative to Akba for my mornings in Abidjan, which were afterwards staged with an identical cast, but in the discreeter and more comfortable setting of the apartment. It was all so easy; whenever I wanted to wile away the time I only had to ring the janitor and ask for room service!

Parts of the lagoon were a scuba diver's paradise, and I was like a fish in its native element, having made the semi-finals of the state junior free-style championships when I was fourteen. I would spend hours out on the water in our rubber dinghy with Banda, who was also a powerful swimmer. He would drive the dinghy to a point on the sand dune some two miles East of the villa, opposite Deblay Island, where a small hut had been erected between the palms to house bulky equipment such as our wind surf boards and air bottles. I would usually ski out to our base behind him wearing only a mono ski and a wedding ring, sometimes doing without the mono and skiing on the soles of my feet.

With the help of Wakaba, who did not ski but could drive the outboard, Banda and I managed to perfect love making on twin skis, even being pulled out of the water in a state of interpenetration. Before take off he would place his feet on the skis behind mine, spread his knees wide apart to get close enough to enter me, and it was in this posture that we were hopefully pulled out of the water, with the outboard revving madly to overcome the resistance of our bodies. It was of course an act requiring almost uncanny equilibrium, as our pelvises had to keep up the copulatory movement, and there were quite a few splash-downs amid shrieks of laughter, but once we were underway, and lechery replaced mirth, we rang a surprising number of changes on the basic position imposed by the placing of our feet and the need to maintain balance. When I took the rope Banda would encircle my body, doing everything he could to excite me, the converse applying when he took the tow, leaving my hands free to do the feeling. The game consisted of trying to get the other skier to come and lose his or her balance, as an orgasm on water skis at thirty miles and hour almost always resulted in a crash landing.

On the way to our base we would occasionally pass native fishermen in their primitive outriggers made from hollowed-out tree trunks, giving them as wide a birth as possible, not out of any modesty on my part — as I simply loved exposing my naked body to the lustful gaze of onlookers — but to avoid troubling them with our wake.

One sharp-eyed and grey-haired old fisherman, who must have been well into his sixties, spotted me just as we were drawing into the beach, and paddled over to have a closer look at the golden Venus in all the glory of her nudity. He must have been as tall as Banda, with an emaciated body which was all bone and sinew and a loin cloth that was thrust aside by the erection of a gnarled and wrinkled old cock, seemingly as long and thin as the rest. It pointed at me ominously as if indicating a personal choice.

There was something about the cragginess and scragginess of his aged carcass, with its carpet of wirey, grey hair, that made me want to rub my velvety smoothness against all that abrasiveness. As I was for once ashamed to let Banda into my secret, I told him to ask the old man of the sea to take me fishing in his boat, although it was quite obvious what would happen, as there was not enough room in his unstable craft for the three of us, including his rigid member, without a certain interaction. As Banda was no fool, he looked at me with open hostility and said: "Leda no get fish; Leda get bad cock!"

As the obscene side of my nature was starting to freak at the idea of being banged on the bottom of a dirty old dinghy, in the sediment, scales, sea water and smell of fish, I stared back at him with a certain irritation and snapped impatiently: "Banda tell man Leda want fish!"

After an angry exchange, in which I suspected Banda of trying to queer the deal, the fisherman gestured to me to climb into the bark, helping me up with a calloused hand that scratched deliciously over my thigh. Pushing off, he jumped in with a litheness surprising for a man of his age, his Long John Silver of a stump asserting itself more and more rigidly as the time for its consecration approached.

Standing astride the stern, he propelled the craft forward with the long, easy strokes of an ornately carved paddle, staring at me with incredulous lust as I sat facing him in the hollowed out bottom of the trunk, with two inches of sand and sea water swilling around the lips of my sex. He was no doubt wondering how such a miracle of naked white beauty could possibly even exist, let alone have found its way into his impoverished universe.

To make it clear I was interested in a rod that had nothing to do with fishing, whatever Banda may have said, I hooked my legs over the sides of the boat and lifted my back off the inside of the trunk, raising my genitals so they emerged from the water to become fully visible at the apex of my thighs. As this did not produce an immediate result, other than a further increase in the angle of upstand of the fisherman's phallus, I took hold of my breasts in both hands and teased the nipples into their most persuasive state of stiffness, pulling the orbs back towards my mouth to lick and nibble the rubbery points while staring the navigator meaningfully in the eye.

All this was finally too much for my oarsman, who dropped the paddle and fell to his knees in the bottom of the boat with such precipitation that we almost capsized. As he knelt between my legs, after removing his loin cloth, I had my first full view of his member, which was still just as spindly as when I had glimpsed it on shore. I could not however have foreseen how much its length would increase as a result of visual stimulus, as it must have measured at least thirteen inches, or on average two or three more than my well hung team at the villa, and I was concerned that I might not be able to host it all that easily.

At least I could make certain that my working parts were well oiled, as after their submergence in sand and salt water they were ready for a little fingering. As soon as the resultant secretion had prepared my slipway for his launching, I freed a hand for the sinister looking spindle and, after running the rough-skinned sheath up and down the stem, slid the bullet-shaped glans into my mouth and down my throat.

The fisherman's only immediate response was to hold my nipples between finger and thumb, twisting them first one way and then the other, increasing the pressure until it was difficult to distinguish between his selfish grunts of pleasure and my grateful groans of pain. Having achieved a preliminary orgasm through my own efforts, I withdrew my remaining hand from an impatient slit which gaped up invitingly at the rubbery relic I had just removed from my mouth. Pulling down the tip until it was opposite my entrance, I slid it well in, leaving a hand around the base of the shaft as a buffer in case he should forget the length of the weapon he was wielding.

As it was the glans banged painfully into my longstop on the first lunge, but there was no way I could tell him to take it easy, as, quite apart from the language problem, he was beyond the limit of lust at which unrestrainable desire outruns any form of consideration. I clamped my other hand round his stem as a secondary shock absorber, while his hirsute body scraped over mine, the horse-hair of his chest maintaining my breasts in a state of rubbery rigidity. As the weight of his body forced me back against the crudely hewn wood of the hull he pushed his tongue repeatedly into my mouth.

It was the mixture of the primitive and the painful which finally made me flip, fuelling my enjoyment of a situation that up to then had brought only chronic discomfort. I began to kiss back aggressively at his molesting lips, suddenly discovering I wanted a lot more of that interminable cock in a place where there was room to spare.

He was well on the way to winning the battle of tongues, having forced his leathery thong half way down my gullet, leaving me with no choice but to strike back in another area. Using all my vaginal strength, I forced his phallus out of my slit at the end of a withdrawal stroke, quickly raised my buttocks clear of the bilge, aligned the straining penis with the center of my sphincter, and let go just as the down stroke got under way. I felt a searing flash as I was gate-crashed by the helmet, followed by the sensation of being cauterized by a soldering iron, before a resounding thump announced the collision of thighs and the limit of incursion.

Although I enjoy a little civilized pain from time to time, things had got out of hand and I started to snivel. Far from showing pity, the fisherman put his hands on what would have been the gunwales of a less rudimentary vessel, and by placing his feet on the seat in the stern was able to get his thirteen inches the whole way in and the whole way out by doing good, old fashioned press-ups, using the entire length of his arms. I do not know what happened to the pain — it quite probably continued — but instead of being quite unbearable it had become perfectly delicious, and I wimpered with delight as he stabbed me into a state of blissful submission, thrusting back at him longingly with all the strength of my pelvic girdle.

Only two perfectly adapted muscular systems could have sustained sodomy for twenty minutes in such a physically extenuating position. I eased the strain a little by placing my ankles on his shoulders, supporting the weight of my body with my elbows on the gunwhales, allowing it to swing to and fro like a pendulum under the effect of the blows meted out by his thighs.

Howling anal obscenities across the unruffled waters to the screen of palms that echoed them back over the lagoon, I slammed my swinging torso onto the incoming harpoon, whose formidable length was now fully uncovered at the end of each stroke. We were both streaming, as the violent exercise under the midday sun had activated our glands to the point where he dripped sweat onto my stomach and breasts like a shut-off shower with a leaky washer.

I was really building up to something big when his voice mingled with mine to herald an ejaculation which seemed to go on for ever, as he filled me to anal overflow with what must have been a three month backlog, but before I could reach my own climax his member collapsed irretrievably, leaving my libido standing up on end.

As nothing could be done with the defunct organ I struggled out from under his body, grabbed the paddle and jammed in the handle as far as it would go, rowing a private boat race to try and catch up with a climax that was becoming more and more elusive, but try as I might it remained exasperatingly out of reach. As there was nothing else I could do unaided to attain the coveted goal, my only hope was Banda, and I threw myself over the side to cover the three hundred yards to shore in my best time ever, emerging like an outraged sea nymph shouting: "Banda! Banda! Help me Banda! Leda want come!"

But there was no Banda anywhere to be seen, and I fell to my knees sobbing with anger and frustration. I had never known such a feeling of pent-up sexual energy seeking an outlet it could not find, and however relentlessly I clawed at my clit and slid absurdly inadequate fingers in and out, the prospect of achieving the hoped-for heaven receded further and further.

Sobbing and sniffing on my knees, I searched the ground for something I could use to ease the intolerable yearning that was gnawing away at my loins. After an interlude of undignified crawling and crying, I came across a small conger eel that must have escaped from the basket the fisherman had removed from his boat to make room for me. It was now lashing around with its tail in an effort to propel itself back down the beach to the lagoon and survival.

The spectacle took my mind off my own misery for a moment, as although the conger could not have been more than a foot long, the strength of its tail was nothing short of remarkable. I continued gazing vacuously at the stranded apode when, out of the blue, I had a providential inspiration I hastened to put into practice. Approaching it with considerable care, as the young eel already had formidable jaws, I grabbed its head tightly in my right hand and, lying on my back, parted my thighs to position the terrible tail at the entrance to my slit, which I hastily fingered into a state slippery acquiescence.

Suddenly I was very excited, and my nipples and clitty stood up stiffly in instant recognition of erotic potential, as if they knew something quite out of the ordinary was about to happen. With my shoulders raised off the ground I watched and waited for the moment when the conger would stop flailing for an instant, having to be patient all of three or four minutes. When the moment came I made no mistake, thrusting the rubbery object deep into my yearning cavity. For a moment I thought I was going to lose my grip not just because the eel went mad and almost forced its way out of my grasp, but also because the flailing of the tail in my sex made me come so hard and so quickly I went faint with pleasure.

I was noisily proclaiming my temporary relief when the Senoufo returned. Reluctantly, as it really was the most sensational outside aid to self abuse I had ever encountered, I withdrew the writhing eel from my intimacy and stumbled down to the water's edge, throwing it back into the sea as a sign of gratitude for the consolation it had unwittingly provided.

But I was still yearning for my full rectal climax, and standing knee-deep in the water touched my toes with my feet together and my back towards the young African. In this position I whispered through my legs: "Banda bugger Leda; Banda butt-fuck!" Thanks to the fisherman's fertilization I was so slippery he penetrated me fully with his first thrust, despite the tightness of my stance, catching my torso in his arms as it snapped upright under the shock of his entry, grasping my breasts to knead them with untypical roughness as he flag-staffed my innards, resucitating the still-born orgasm and raising it to heavenly heights of fulfilment.

Standing upright in the superb Senoufo's arms, I remained sufficiently lucid to realize he had not ejaculated, and when I had recovered enough breath I turned to ask what was wrong, allowing his still erect organ to slide out of my anus. As soon as I was facing him he slapped me so hard the blow spun me round and precipitated me into the water, where I lay sobbing, more from mortification than physical pain, being too astounded to react in any other manner.

Then I felt Banda's hand grab my hair to wrench me up into a kneeling position, in which he penetrated my regular hole with a brutality that was quite uncharacteristic, as was the pistoning violence of his assault, which induced an almost immediate climax. When he ejaculated it was with a savage thrust that again knocked me flat in the water, and an imprecation shouted across the lagoon with all the power of his lungs.

I only discovered the reason for such extraordinary behavior later, in a moment of quiet confidence, as at the time he refused to talk to me at all, driving the dinghy back to the villa in tight-lipped silence. It turned out that the cause of his anger had been my defilement by the fisherman, as for the Wasagu tribe, by whom Banda had been brought up, copulation with anything that had been in contact with dead fish and not ritually cleansed was a form of sacrilege for which I had to be punished, although he had been unable to resist the magnetic field of temptation which drew our bodies together.

Thinking things over during our speechless return, I realized I had rarely experienced such a dream of a climax. On subsequent occasions I tried to find other means of defilement that would make Banda rape me again, but the most revolting perversions I could devise failed to produce the desired reaction; not even a repetition of the fish trick, as in the meantime he had exasperatingly arranged for a spell to be cast which gave me immunity from ritual contamination.

Chapter 14

Some time later Etienne told me he had an important client in Abidjan to whom he would like to show the film of my first double-fuck. He asked me pointedly if I would not mind being present at the viewing, and although he tried to give the impression that my role would only consist of a limited amount of what might be called 'advanced friendliness', it needed little imagination on my part to see what was likely to happen with a man who had just seen me go through the hoops with the two strapping Senoufos.

So the important client should have plenty to look at off screen as well as on, I decided to wear a white camisole top in silk crepe with a plunging U decolleté and very bare midriff, accentuated by a slim, above the knee skirt in light grey linen hanging low on the hips. The outfit was completed by a matching kimono style top which provided the necessary degree of above-the-belt modesty until the time came for its removal.

To add a Bohemian touch I went barefoot, underlining this boldly erotic initiative with gold chains around my ankles, wrists, neck and waist and my special golden girl make-up that I had decided to wear on occasions when my body was due for intensive collective use. I became quite excited at the prospect of dressing up, as at the villa I would sometimes go for days, when Etienne was not there, without even slipping into a pair of shoes, and the idea of putting on all those expensive clothes just to take them off in the presence of a complete stranger seemed deliciously sinful.

Yasmina hung them up in the master cabin, and I boarded the Livorno behind Etienne, democratically wearing one of the white mini-smocks that were standard uniform for female staff. The pygmy boatman Joseph feasted his eyes on the visible parts of my body, no doubt wondering why he was the only male member of the staff not to have been inside his employer's wife. The reason of course resided in his stunted physique, as such an insignificant creature could hardly hope for the favors of a blond Juno surrounded by black Hercules — at least in theory.

As soon as we disappeared into the stateroom, the V8 diesels gave a throaty roar, the prow lifted out of the water and we were on our way. After a few minutes Etienne looked at me slyly and said: "Why don't you go up onto the fly bridge? You will have a much better view of the lagoon from up there". As my husband had just put a new film in his camera, I needed no further explanation of the reason behind such an apparently innocent suggestion, as out in the middle of the lagoon there was strictly nothing to see but water, and Etienne knew I liked to spend the trip on the forward sun deck, as there was no better place for improving my tan. I had somehow never thought of Joseph as a potential lover, as he really was much too small and ugly, but now my husband was more or less ordering me to give myself to the

Gagou pygmy, so he could gloat over my abasement while recording it for more or less private projection, the wanton grotesqueness of the situation appealed to the slutty side of my nature. I was in fact so fascinated by the idea of fornicating with a fully grown adult of four foot six that I began to moisten.

Etienne made the purpose of his invitation even clearer by undoing the top two buttons of my smock and folding the lapels back under to create a dazzling decolleté, which was so deeply becoming that he slid an inquisitive hand into the divide to fondle his property, while we exchanged a very unhygienic kiss of complicity, a kiss that had become standard procedure when he was on the point of giving me to another man, as if saliva sealed our compact of infidelity. He then confirmed my adulterous assignment by reaching down between my loins to run a finger into my seeping slit before raising it to his nose and saying: "I think you're going to have yourself a ball up there, if not two; don't forget to give me a lens-friendly field of vision!"

Blushing despite my ingrained immodesty, I walked out onto the rear deck and lithely scaled the ladder to the flying bridge, where the unsuspecting Joseph, who did not know his luck, was sitting on a special cushion on the pilot's seat that enabled him to see over the bulwark. I greeted him almosy casually and sat down on the neighboring chair. After a few minutes silence, during which he spent more time thinking about my long legs and bulging breasts than navigation, I swivelled to face him and placed one of my feet on the edge of his seat. Making certain the hem of my minismock rode well up the thighs, I proceeded to coax my nipples out of their inadequate refuge and pinch and twist them into a state of livid protruberance.

He was staring so fixedly at my improvised peep-show that the boat veered violently off course, and he had to spend the next few seconds wrestling with the wheel to get it back on an even keel and going in the right direction. Before he could recover a little composure I took my foot off the rim of his seat, unbuttoned my smock, and sliding it slowly off my shoulders liberated breasts which were each twice the size of the pygmy's head. "Now Joseph", I said winningly, seeing no point in beating about our bushes, "Leda and Joseph make big fuck! Joseph take off shorts!"

He obeyed incredulously, with the jerky, wooden movements of an automat. Once the pathetically small garment was lying crumpled on the deck, I could survey his manhood, which made up in stiffness what it lacked in size, straining back against the base of his stomach in a manner worthy of the rampant Houari! Out of the corner of my eye I caught sight of Etienne sitting on the stern with his lens aimed in my direction, reminding me that I had to organize our fornication in such a way as to compensate for the disadvantageous angle.

After one or two revealing set piece poses, which told the inquisitive zoom all it ever needed to know about my fork, followed by a panoramic display of holes, both of which were well smeared to provide the camera with flattering reflections, Joseph was made to stand facing outwards beside the starboard seat, which was the nearest to Etienne. After having checked the course, reduced speed and set the radar to sound warning of floating objects within a range of 500 yards in a 20° segment in front of the boat, he was told to switch on the automatic pilot.

No other precautions were necessary, as at that rate it would take us more than an hour to reach Dabou, and on our chosen course the lagoon was free of any fixed obstacles such as rocks, wrecks or sand banks. Still stunned by his good fortune he obeyed, apparently uninhibited by my husband's presence, and I sank to my knees to provide a two-thirds frontal view of my body, turning Joseph slightly to his right towards the camera. Taking hold of his upright mini-penis, I flicked the sheath to and fro several times with my right hand — to leave the photographic field unobstructed — and then, bending it down to a realistic angle, I lowered my head to compensate for his lack of height and licked and sucked the tiny glans before sliding the rest of the diminutive stem into my mouth.

A few strokes were all that Joseph could take before coming, as he was living the thing of a lifetime, and when I felt him jerk in my mouth, I gave my husband a clear shot of the pygmy ejaculating between my widely parted lips, as well as of the last drops running down my chin and onto my breasts. Taking him back in my mouth, I allowed two white rivulets to escape from the corners of my lips, before removing the shining black beetle to smile a mouthful of bubbling come at the camera, only swallowing it with an ostensible gulp when my movie magnate gave me the go-ahead.

Planting a very viscous kiss on his tiny mouth, prior to removing the surplus sperm from my chin with my fingers to spread it over my nipples, I gestured to Joseph to help himself. Suddenly freed from the embarrassment and even fear that had paralyzed him up to then, he lunged at my breasts, trying to cup them in his minute hands while licking their coating of semen, sweat and milk, finishing inevitably with an oozing nipple deep in his mouth. We were both so excited I forgot the existence of the camera, and was rudely called to order by an irritated Etienne, who had been deprived of a licentious take. One of the biggest kicks I get out of adulterating in my husband's presence and under his supervision, is the humiliation of being ordered insultingly to do the most abject things as if I was the lowest whore on earth.

Something about the pygmy made me feel maternal, but in a perverted way, as if he were my mother-fucking baby. This was of course a patent absurdity, as he was a lot older and racially so different that no such bond of relationship was conceivable. Nevertheless, when he started to suck my titties, I cradled his little head and crooned: "That's it! Suck your mummy you little black bastard! Fill your mouth with her milk!" With a shudder of guilty delight I began squeezing my breasts, which suddenly felt much too full, helping his toiling lips to take their toll of my ample resources.

After a few minutes of the suckling routine Etienne began to find our improvisation boring, despite the secondary spectacle of a dusky finger and thumb overhauling holes at the photogenic apex of my widely splayed thighs, and shouted at me to get on with the action. Reluctantly, as I was starting to feel nice and slutty, I tried to remove my nipple from the eagerly sucking Joseph, but there was no way he would let go, a refusal which at least provided the camera with shots of my left breast being pulled right out of shape as the pygmy held on with his teeth.

Finally he unclamped, enabling me to stand up and force him down onto the seat, which I swivelled to face the camera, but when I sat down on his lap facing Etienne, there was no way he could focus on our centers of erotic gravity, as the whole area was cut off, from where he was standing, by the edge of the seat. He therefore decided to drop the slender pretence of a scene filmed without the participants' knowledge, and climbed up onto the flying bridge, where he could insert his zoom in my anus, like a medical probe, if he felt it was the best way of getting a good shot.

It all seemed a trifle unreal, with the boat roaring across the mirror-calm surface of the lagoon, under a cloudless blue sky occupied only by the flaming fullness of midday sun. Yet there could be no doubt about the tangibility of Joseph's rigidity, which was pressing into the divide of my buttocks as I straddled his lap in what appeared to be a reversal of the normal order of things, due to the difference in our sizes, as even from his new vantage point my husband was having difficulty in finding the male partner behind the screening body of the full-scale female.

I reached behind me to take hold of the rampant midget, that could not have been more than three inches in length, which was very small beer indeed for a woman who regularly accommodated many of the finest cocks on the Ivory Coast. And yet he continued to turn me on, despite the unimpressive statistics, and I affectionately slid the insignificant object into the farthest hole from the camera.

For some time I sat there barely moving, just feeling it prod my sphincter, before the realization dawned that its incredible stiffness could in fact be put to good account, as even if little joy was to be obtained from standard copulative gymnastics with such a small penis, its monolithic rigidity — as it really was like an iron peg set in a block of concrete — lent itself perfectly to a circular movement of the pelvis. The result would be to stretch the rim or sides of whichever hole was being used as far as elasticity would permit — the bigger the radius of the circle of rotation of the hips, the harder the pressure against the rim of the orifice, as, unlike normally tumescent organs, whose effectiveness is often in direct proportion to their length and breadth, the advantage of Joseph's tiny prick was that it was totally unyielding in any direction.

I had the same feeling of momentous discovery as Archimedes in his bath, and holding on to the back of the chair, to take the strain of the weight of my body, I began to rotate my buttocks around the little linchpin, stretching the rim of my butthole as I did so. The anus is of course the perfect orifice for such an exercise, as the tension of its elasticity makes the stretching process easier to control than with the looser vagina.

As the concrete cock reamed my rotating butt I gasped and groaned, much to Etienne's surprise, as he could neither see nor film what was going on, as my buttocks hardly cleared the pygmy's thighs. When I told him about my invention, he ordered me to place my feet on the seat on either side of Joseph's legs and squat down on my haunches. This made it easier for me to lift my buttocks clear of my partner's thighs and show the camera what was happening when I increased the speed of rotation and the radius of the circle.

Now that he had something worthwhile to put in the box,

Etienne ran down to the cabin and returned with a formidable diljo that must have measured all of twelve inches, zooming in for a macro close-up as I gaspingly worked it up my tunnel of love, until only the handle protruded from the inner lips. We were ready for the main take, and after making certain there was no more than an inch of penis in my ass, giving the camera a clear field between our two bodies, I carefully initiated the rotary movement, gradually increasing the radius of the circle until I reached the point where my butt-hole could stretch no further without coming off the rails. To begin with I had to use my arms to steady myself, but once my balance was secure I was able to do a 'look no hands', freeing them for the upping and downing of that mother and father of all diljos.

Once the basic routine was fully operational I could concentrate on coming, which I did uninterruptedly, shouting my usual ass-talk into the lagunar winds and the perch mike Etienne had suspended over my head, just out of the camera's field. Joseph manifested his presence, other than as the inert owner of that crazy little cock, by taking a breast in each of his infantile hands and kneading them gently with a back to front motion that soon had the nipples glistening with milk.

Finally, when I could take no more coming, only just managing to keep my balance, I was shaken by a Stromboli of a climax that flattened my body against Joseph's, pinning him to the back of the seat. The same eruption expelled the diljo clatteringly onto the main deck, as well as releasing an unprogrammed fountain of scintillating pee, which flew outwards and upwards, dissolving into a fine spray that trailed off in the wind to defile the flag of convenience which fluttered proudly from the stern.

Before signing off, I can remember receiving another prolific discharge in my anal tract and wondering dreamily where he could possibly get it all, as for a second service from a pair of balls no larger than cherry stones it made no sort of sense.

Chapter 15

Etienne's small but luxurious apartment in the downtown Plateau district of Abidjan comprised an open plan office, a reception and living area, two bedrooms with their bathrooms and the other usual amenities.

Joseph would drop off his passengers at a jetty on the Bay of Cocody, just South of the new aquarium and swimming pool, which the apartment overlooked, as well as having a panoramic view to the East across the harbor and the district of Cocody on the far side. Carrying my finery over my arm, I slipped my smock back on to walk the two hundred yards to the block, adding a pair of long white pants at my husband's insistence, as otherwise my bare legs tended to attract a crowd of fascinated he-men, even over such a short distance.

When we arrived, Etienne explained that his mysterious client was the headman of a group of villages on the Abi lagoon, sixty miles to the East of the capital, where he was hoping to construct a holiday complex for a German tourist consortium. The headman in question, who was almost eighty, had seen a monokini photo of me on the desk, that I suspected Etienne of displaying as a sort of catalogue item for any influential visitor who might be interested in a little quid pro quo. At a difficult stage in their discussions, the chief had implied that further progress in the negotiations would be linked to a cooperative attitude on my part. As the stakes were enormous, and the lecherous old headman the key to success, Etienne had been quite undeterred by the prospect of prostituting his lovely young wife.

The headman and certain other influential elders had been invited to a buffet lunch at the apartment to examine a model of the proposed village. The bit about the other influential elders was new, and when I questioned him on what they would be doing while I was busy showing the headman my film and a lot else besides, Etienne replied there would be no problem, as he would arrange for the two of us to slip away into one of the bedrooms. In any case I was only expected to submit to a little heavy petting while watching the film, as he was completely impotent, not even the young girls of his tribe, over whose adolescent bodies he exercised positively feudal rights, being able to arouse his defunct vitality.

It all sounded a trifle specious, and there was something evasive in my husband's attitude which made me feel I might well find myself in a different situation from the one he described. However, it was a big deal, and I owed him a considerable debt of gratitude for all that heavenly inter-racial fucking at the villa, not to mention the even more shameful set up in Abidjan following the 'trash bin scandal'! A little whoring was not too much to ask of a loving wife in return for such perverse and expensive connivance, quite apart from the fact that my libido might well find food for lechery in resurrecting the venerable tyrant's extinct virility.

I cold showered to remove the usual pellicle of sweat and dried sperm from my skin — a reason that seemed to motivate most of my ablutions in Africa — and put on my outfit, which really was very naughty indeed. I slid on the gold chains and — following a sudden inspiration — pushed a gold sovereign I carried round in a jewel case into my belly button, wedging it there like a monocle. I then stood in front of the full-length mirror in the bathroom, admiring the electifying effect of the naked midriff with its golden chain and bull's eye, and the skirt which hung so low on the hips that the merest slip of the waist-band revealed a flurry of high-growing pubic hair. What I saw in the looking-glass was good enough to eat, and while waiting for the headman I decided to help myself to a plateful.

Inching my close-fitting skirt up my legs until I could see the other end of my hairy growth, I squatted down on my haunches in front of the wardrobe mirror and opened my thighs, obtaining a revealing view of the target area. Starting by nonchalantly pinching and pulling my clitty into a state of slippery stiffness, I amplified the movements as it grew in size and became easier to catch. Bunching the finger tips of the other hand, I pushed them into the mouth of my slot, which was already dribbling with satisfaction, rotating my wrist as far as it would turn in both directions. Savoring the truth of the French saying that you are never better frigged than by yourself, I was starting to sigh and gasp and utter little come-come cries when I heard the bell ring in the hall, and orgasmed with a piercing squeal of delight as the sound of my husband's welcoming remarks filtered through the enjoyment of self-abuse.

I wondered whether I should wash the clean but acrid smell of come off my fingers, before leaving the bedroom to greet our rather special guest, who had arrived in advance of his colleagues.

Deciding instinctively against it, I slipped on the kimono top and opened the door into the reception area to discover Etienne in the company of a big, bald African dressed in a ceremonial kaftan, whose eyes lit up with undisguised sexual glee at the sight of the original of the photograph.

Like many of the older inhabitants of the Ivory Coast who had passed most of their lives under French colonial administration, the headman had acquired a veneer of Gallic manners, and, instead of shaking my proffered hand, raised it to his lips for the baise-main that had previously singled him out as a member of the ruling classes. However, when my hand reached the level of his chin, his sensitive nose detected the unmistakable smell of orgasm, and instead of brushing it lightly with his lips, his widely dilated nostrils hovered over the tips of my fingers, inhaling their pungent odor before he unexpectedly darted out his tongue to lick them avidly.

Etienne was amazed by such a promising start, but quickly collected his wits and said: "Leda darling, Chief Zakareko was kind enough to say he would be interested in the little film we made the other day; be a dear and show it to him before the others arrive; I will bring you drinks in the second bedroom where I have fixed up the screen and projector.

When we reached the bedroom I removed my kimono top, attracting a lot of attention from the African dignitary, but did not have time to switch on the projector before Etienne arrived with a couple of large koutoukos in colorful ceramic beakers, and we toasted each other's good health.

Downing my glass I glanced slyly at the headman and said: "Cul sec", the French equivalent of 'Bottoms Up', meaning literally 'dry bottom'; referring of course to the empty glass, but the play on words was not lost on the headman who replied smilingly: "I hope not!"

The powerful drink — whose intoxicating properties where a

local byword — soon dissolved what was left of our inhibitions as if they were no more than an instant coffee mix, particularly as my husband had added a little powdered Annamese ginger noted for its aphrodisiac effects!

The more I thought of it the less I felt Zakareko's impotence was likely to survive our encounter, as he was already flushed and breathing heavily, and could not make up his mind whether he wanted to stare at my legs, which I had crossed way up high when sitting down on the edge of the low bed, or ogle the other exposed parts of my body, as I had slightly rounded my back and advanced my shoulders to emphasize cleavage.

The ginger was starting to play havoc with my respect for the basic decencies, and I was just dying to roll up the Kaftan and get to lips with his problem. I hardly heard Etienne switch on the projector and leave the room, as I was busy pulling the headman down onto the edge of the bed beside me. The film had been advanced to the point where the rampant Wakaba was climbing onto the bed behind me, as straddling Banda's body, I rose and fell, impaling myself on his sacrificial stake.

I do not know what Zakareko was expecting — may be a few shots of nude sunbathing — but when the full realization of what was happening on the screen penetrated his mind, he gave vent to a sort of snarl. Without letting his eyes stray from the spectacle, he reached out roughly with his left hand to grab my hair and drag me round to face him, with my back to the screen, pulling the hem of his kaftan as far up as he could with his free hand, before thrusting my face down between his thighs.

Having shown me what was expected, he let go of my hair and devoted all his attention to the film, gasping incredulously at what must have been the moment when Wakaba entered me from behind, as he forced a hand down the back of my skirt, bursting it at the seams, to stuff the end of a stubby forefinger into my anus, as if to ascertain whether there was in fact room for such a maneuver. I squirmed my bottom in grateful approval to indicate there was, and that my asshole was his to do with as he pleased, provided of course he could achieve the necessary degree of stiffness.

This was now my problem, and I concentrated on the mass of inert man-meat that hung limply between his legs, framed by a forest of tightly curled and greying pubic hair. The trouble with men who have big ones is they require a much larger and more powerful injection of blood to achieve rigidity, a situation that becomes more and more problematic with advancing age, and it seemed that a great deal of stimulus would be needed to enable Zakareko to become operational.

We were however some way down the road to success, as the initial excitement of his discovery of my real-life body, added to the erotic impact of my movie double-fuck had broken the ice, as the huge tube had already lengthened appreciably and was beginning to rear up clear of the low-dangling scrotum.

Supporting the member sensuously in one hand, I gently scraped the finger nails of the other along the underside of the sheath, and was rewarded with a series of starts which must have increased the angle of erection by at least twenty degrees. Inspecting the half-rigid column more closely, I realized its tip was tightly enveloped in an overtight foreskin which would no doubt have been removed during childhood in a more medically advanced age, as the glans was impeded by the restraining effect of the constricting hood of skin.

After playing at kissy-kissy with the voluminous black sack and its bulging contents — a treatment that added another five degrees to the critical angle — I concentrated on the tight little aperture, sucking and licking busily while easing the rim with a firm but gentle jerking movement, the object being to get as much lubricating saliva as possible under the retentive turban of skin, while easing its resistance with oral and manual massage.

Finally my experience and imagination succeeded where the efforts of other partners had presumably failed, as the glans suddenly surged out of its retaining mantle in a manner that was somehow reminiscent of the uncoiling of a snake, and immediately rose to the occasion with an unimpaired vigor which totally dispelled any suggestion of impotency.

Zakereko did not know whether he should pay more attention to his deliverance from a frustrating and humiliating impediment, or to my 16mm saga that had now reached the 'both inside together' stage. I solved the dilemma by standing up, slipping off my skirt and turning my back to him, placing my buttocks just in front of his nose, with my legs wedging his thighs apart. I then bent down supplely from the waist, and passing my head between my knees took his resurrected penis in my mouth and gave it the gobbling it deserved.

My unusual stance was by no means disinterested, as apart from taking the headman's attention off what was happening on the screen, by interposing a wall of buttock and thigh, it focused it on my own genital area, which I brought into contact with his thick lips by simply inclining my thighs a few degrees to the rear. At the same time his nose came to rest against my anus, and I heard him sniff deeply to sample its distinctive bouquet, as his tongue went to work probingly on the neighboring crevasse.

We were soon both in dire need of bodily junction, which I brought about with the utmost simplicity by unmouthing his phallus, which was now of fittingly regal proportions, and sitting down on it with an undignified bump, as my aim was not quite as good as the rest of my performance to date. The glans bounced off the no man's land between my two orifices to totter on the brink of cunt, before changing its mind to sink abrasively into asshole, making me cry out with a mixture of pain and lecherous elation.

Clasping my hands behind Zakereko's bull-neck to obtain the purchase I needed to raise my body, I let go when my sphincter felt the glans nestle against its puckered rim, allowing my weight to drive it back in to the bottom of my bowels. The headman helped me ring the changes from time to time by grasping my hips and pulling my buttocks back against his paunch when the glans reached the exit position, ensuring that when I sat down again his ebony pile would be driven into my regular hole, repeating the maneuver the other way round when he wanted to return to my butt.

We had almost perfected the 'one in the one and then in the other' routine, with Zakareko playing his part like a well-oiled machine, never missing out on the 'lift hips then backwards and let go — lift hips then forwards and let go', and I was far gone in continuous come, with the usual atrocious verbal accompaniment, when the door bell rang and I heard Etienne welcome the elders who had arrived on time.

However, instead of showing them the holiday complex model as agreed, while I finished off the headman and he finished me, he threw open the bedroom door and said: "There you are gentlemen, my wife will be only too happy to look after you once she has satisfied your chief. As you can see from the screen there is plenty of room for two, and the longer you are the more she will like it. In fact those of you who are waiting your turn can try her mouth and breasts to pass the time until she can offer you one of her major inlets!"

"You lousy shit!" I said to myself; "You had it planned this way the whole time!" But even as these thoughts raced through my mind I knew I was grateful to him for laying on yet another lay of a lifetime. Even if he had added that he had also commandeered the Pretorian Guard from Messalina, I would have screwed them the whole way to the Forum and back in time for a switch to the Foreign Legion, as my libido was careering around quite out of control!

As the first of the elders approached in incredulous

astonishment, I reached under his kaftan to discover a shrivelled old weed, which I nevertheless lent forward to take between my lips, while tightening my sphincter round the headman's cock for long enough to bring it to the boil and drain off the contents of his incredibly prolific danglers.

Under the vacuum effect of fellation the unpromising shoot of the first elder had become a serviceable plant, and while holding on to the members of his second and third colleagues, that I was coaxing into a state of preliminary readiness before giving them some oral uplift, I gestured to him to lie on his back on the floor, and when he was in position straddled his hips to impale myself frontally.

The second elder's member took up its appointed place in my mouth while I groped for the fourth elder's organ under his kaftan, freeing my lips for long enough to shout: "Take off your kaftans! all of you! otherwise we'll get tied in knots!" and to Etienne, who was staring wide-eyed at the incipient wifely gang-bang: "Unbutton this bloody camisole top so they can guzzle my tits!" As he did so I gave him a long and juicy kiss before returning orally to the member of the the third elder, having already pulled the second one round behind to stuff him up my ass, whereas the fifth was now receiving a thorough jerking before moving up in the batting order. The sixth was allocated my left breast, which he gobbled greedily when he realized it was full of erotic nourishment, and the headman got back into the ball game with the right one to make seven who were sexually involved with my body in one way or another.

Once the cycle was complete, and I was coming in sporadic bursts that jostled the mountain of elderly black manhood under which I was half-interred, there was more than enough of me to go round, as I used my formidable control of vaginal and anal muscle to hasten ejaculation at the end of each elder's major hole entitlement. During our forty to fifty minutes of fucking several went to the back of the queue more than once, after coming in one or other of my basic holes, so as to have a shot at the other one, with some even coming in my mouth. Finally one breast became free and then another, permitting those who were still engaged elsewhere to fondle and knead them. Then the time came when I even had a free hand, until the last of the Mohicans squeezed out his few remaining drops before withdrawing from the only hole that remained in service.

It was then and only then that Etienne, who had been raptly masturbating while surveying the scene with an intense and unhealthy interest, slapped my face brutally before coming all over it. He then voraciously licked me clean from the end of my anal cleft to the top of my pubic triangle, turning my body this way and that to run his tongue in and out of everything. While he was eating I squeezed my breasts to extract the last few drops the elders had left untapped, lifting the nipples to my lips, but as they closed round the jutting points I was shaken by a final convulsion that left me quaking on the floor.

As a pay off Etienne received an even larger contract than he expected, and afterwards, when I was in Abidjan and short on sex in the afternoons, I was always welcome in the headman's apartment, where his glans — which had been entirely liberated by a minor circumscision — would treat me to a 'one in the front then another behind', but only after two of his athletic young tribesmen had thoroughly aroused his libido by lengthily double-fucking me into a state of quivering acquiescence, having themselves already been treated to one of my double-sucks to drain off the main cause of early ejaculation.

Chapter 16

I had not seen Vicky for years.

After our unforgettable days together at school, we had continued to meet regularly when she went on to a rather lowly-rated upstate college to major in psychology and sports administration, but after my departure for France our contacts had been limited to the occasional greetings card on birthdays and at Christmas.

Just before we left for Africa she had written to say she was making a trip to Paris with her husband and would like to see me again. Unfortunately their visit to France was due to take place a fortnight after our arrival on the Ivory Coast, and I had to reply we would no longer be available, adding almost jokingly that if they cared to come and see us on the Dark Continent they would be more than welcome.

gave the matter no further thought until a few months later, a letter arrived from New Jersey saying she and her husband would simply love to spend their annual vacation with us if our invitation still held good. I was of course delighted, as the idea of seeing the woman with whom I had been passionately in love during my adolescence intrigued me no end, and we agreed on a date some two months later in an exchange of correspondence whose undertones were alive with ambiguous anticipation, particularly as I hinted broadly at our unusual way of life.

Our meeting at the airport, after ten years of seperation, was pregnant with uneasiness. This was amplified by the surge of sexual interest shown by almost every man present in the arrival lounge, as we were just the sort of phantasm with whom the African male dreams of making endless macho love: the blond, blue-eyed, Viking and the red-haired, freckle-skinned, green-eyed Celt. At thirty-one Vicky, the mother of two children who had been left behind with relatives, was at the zenith of her physical beauty.

For a moment we stood in embarrassed silence, then suddenly the ice melted and we fell into each other's arms with a display of fondling emotion that had all males within range eying us with undisguised lust, a hush falling over the airport hall as we kissed uninhibitedly with an ardor that was quite out of place in a normal friendly greeting.

We had always been of the same height and build, to such a degree that when we stood facing each other, with our bodies barely touching, our nipples would meet head on, as was also the case with Myriam. We had used this particularity when very young to make nipple love in public, without anyone else really knowing what we were up to, as we appeared to be simply standing close together, facing each other. However, as we were both had hypersensitive breasts, when our four burgeoning buds made contact, even through a bodice or T shirt, with barely perceptible movements, compounded by the excitement of public misdemeanor, we could drive ourselves out of our minds, dribbling love-juice down our inner thighs until one or the other could take it no longer and flee in blushing confusion.

This was what was starting to happen in the main hall of Port-Bouet Airport, as in the midst of all our kissing and sobbing we instinctively lined up our bodies so our nipples would touch. We were of course both 'braless', I with a cotton debardeur and Vicky with a light silk corsage, and although the form of our breasts had matured in the intervening period, it must have done so in exactly the same proportions, as our teats still met perfectly head-on, offering, through the flimsy materials, the vision of four provocatively upstanding silhouettes.

Etienne was the first to realize what we were doing and snapped: "Cut that out or we'll have a bloody riot on our hands!" Vicky obediently hid her protrusions under a cardigan she was carrying over her arm, and I achieved the same result by placing my left forearm at an angle across my breasts, and we hastened over to the doorway where a limousine was waiting to convey us to the launch.

Vicky had introduced her husband in the usual off-hand manner, but it was only on the way down to the boat that I had a chance to study the features of the male who had transformed one of the most dedicated lesbians on the East Coast into a heterosexual housewife — or so I thought. I found myself looking at a man in his late thirties who was totally bald, making up for this lack of conventional hair with a thick and perfectly groomed walrus moustache. He had a sallow complexion, pronounced Mongolian features and the physique of a weight-lifter on a frame of no more than five feet eight. His handshake was of the sensually sinister variety which transmits an unmistakable message to any woman who cares to receive it.

When we boarded the Livorno, Etienne and Kardar — for such was the husband's name — stayed on deck and Vicky and I disappeared on down into the master cabin for what we hypocritically described as a 'good chat'.

No sooner were we installed on the edge of the bed than our hands and mouths started a grope of rediscovery, and we were soon lying enlaced together as naked as Eve. During a first, glutinous, mouth-probing kiss that was seemingly endless, we used our fingers to tease each other's nipples back into a state of rubbery response. Surprised by the feeling of a sticky fluid, Vicky released my lips to examine the substance and then sought the origins of the cream-colored liquid, crying out in delighted surprise when her suspicions were confirmed by the sight of a nipple that had quite obviously just been oozing.

"Oh my God!" she exclaimed, "It's not true! how perfectly divine! However do you manage to do it? You clever little thing! And it's just in time for tea!"

So saying she took the source of the trickle gently between her lips and settled down to a sensual suckle, while sliding a hand between my thighs to relieve the longing that throbbed almost painfully in the pit of my loins, which her skilful fingers knew how to exorcise from long experience. I just let myself go, allowing her to drink her fill while I welcomed the other fluttering, probing caress with all my libido, arching my back and sighing her name repeatedly through half-closed lips.

I could have gone on like that indefinitely, but sooner or later Vicky was going to want something in return, as an exploratory finger told me when I slipped it into her slit to find the whole furrow brimming with juice. The gasp with which she greeted my intrusion made it evident I could not go on hogging all the fun, so I lent over to a bedside cupboard where I kept a toy I allowed Yasmina to play with when she was a good girl. The plaything in question was a double diljo I called my Janus, as it faced both ways and was a hand made marvel from a collection of antique Chinese erotica that Etienne had picked up on a visit to Hong Kong.

It consisted of two mock penises which were so real that, at first sight, they appeared to have been amputated from the bodies of victims of some hideous oriental tragedy, as the glans had the texture of human flesh. This sinister first impression was partly dissipated by the fact that the sheaths — which were masterpieces of the leatherworker's art — were made from the skin of newly-born crocodiles to provide a divinely chafing effect, but nevertheless the grisly feeling of doubt persisted. They were mounted back to back on a spring-loaded mechanism which forced them apart when their users, who had to be in the fork to fork position, pressed their crotches together, winding up the spring.

Each organ was about eight inches long, the spring device adding a further six inches to the overall length, meaning that when the mechanism operated, as a certain amount of pressure was necessary to rewind it and trigger the release catch, the diljos were completely embedded in their hostesses, and unless they timed their withdrawal movement with considerable accuracy they could receive a painful punch in the backdrop. The instrument, which was housed in its own exquisite lizzard skin case, was part of a set which included what I called — for lack of better terms — two clitty and four nipple clips, all of which were needless to say hand-made as well and were items of jewellry in their own right in the form of finely worked flowers in silver-gilt and enamel.

At the sight of the set Vicky almost jumped for joy, as when she was younger she had always been an ingenious inventor and keen collector of lesbian gadgetry and, as a connoisseur, was genuinely appreciative, quite apart from her excitement at the idea we were about to give the equipment a full test run. Neither of us really needed any further preparation, as our clitties and nipples were already swollen with excitement and lust, but it still took a certain amount of time to prepare ourselves for the event, and amid a lot of obscene giggling we set about fitting the flower-clips to our secondary sexuals.

The stems of the flowers were in fact composed of small, hollow, cylindrical plaques of silver, whose ends overlapped, making it possible, with an integral, screw-operated clamp, to tighten the cylinder around whatever it contained, that is to say either a nipple or a clit. This stopped the device falling off and, above all, gave a degree of masochistic pleasure which could be tailored by tightening to suit individual tastes. When Etienne brought the set back from Hong Kong, the adjustable stem-clamps were tiny, being obviously intended for the miniature privates of decadent, Chinese ladies of the middle Ch'ing dynasty, and not the king-sized protrusions of twentieth century, American athletes. This necessitated the intervention of a specialized jeweller to adapt them to my personal specifications. Wearing only the three flower-clips I had danced for my husband on many an occasion prior to nights of uninhibited love, with Etienne in my back-passage and the diljo up front, giving him a good return on his investment!

Each clip had to be screwed on individually, and as I had personal experience of their use, I showed Vicky how to fix a set to her pink protruberances. Although she was already so stimulated I could have foregone any further titillation, I had up to then been on the receiving end with no opportunity to revisit the lovely anatomy that had charmed my adolescence. So I took my time, starting with the nipples, which were even larger than those I could recall, having no doubt been developed by maternity as well as by all the greedy mouths that had worked on them over the years. Sucking, nibbling and tonguing, I managed to get them to swell even further, intensifying their stiffness and making her sigh with contentment as she kissed the top of my head. When they were as hard as vulcanized rubber I ceased caressing and adjusted the diameter of the clamp to the dimensions of the aggressively prominent teats, sliding on the first one and tightening the screw until my poor Vicky winced with pain.

The centers of the enamel flowers were hollow to allow the ends of the nipples to protrude out of their cylinders, swelling abnormally because of the constricting pressure round their bases, and I licked the bloated extremity tenderly, extracting another long drawn-out sigh from my darling. The other nipple clip produced the same reactions, but the clitty clamp took ages to fix, as every time I sucked her love-button into a state of upstanding stiffness, the wretched little beast would shrink back into its pouch when I started to to tighten the device — which was little more than a tiny wire lasso. Finally, after a lot of exasperated micro-fiddling, I managed to trap the little beggar, which then swelled up perversely to a splendid size with its tip sticking out cheekily through the flower. My own three clips were on in a jiffy, and we kissed moistly and lengthily, with much slithering of mucous membrane, before turning head to tail for a quick lick at the swollen ends of our imprisoned clitties, prior to lining ourselves up for the main event.

Owing to our vaginal secretions the insides of our thighs were completely awash, and in the crotch-to-crotch position the two heads of Janus slid abrasively into our viscid pits of love. Further pressure was then needed to wind up the spring mechanism to the point of its automatic release — a point that could only be foreseen after a lengthy experience which I alone posessed.

Vicky and I grasped each others' wrists, as for the classic lesbian fork-fuck, and pulled our sexes gingerly together, compressing the spring, but the dice were loaded in my favor, as I alone knew when. At the precise moment dictated by knowledge, I pushed myself away with my legs, which were locked around her body, allowing the spring to direct its unpent energy straight into my sweetheart, pile-driving the eight inches of diljo already embedded in her love-nest against the mouth of her uterus. This elicited a howl of pain followed by a stream of invective, as she cursed the miserable bitch who had failed to let her know what was going to happen!

"You just wait!" she snarled, "I'll get you — you treacherous harlot! Seconds out for the next round!"

We both laughed, but were too excited for any lasting mirth, as our nipples and clitties were throbbing with a mixture of pain and desire. We settled back into position for a second try, but after her initial misfortune Vicky shied off too quickly, causing both of us to lose the benefit of the thrust of the spring. Practice finally made perfect, and within next to no time, as Vicky was a gifted pupil, we were synchronizing to perfection, drawing back fractionally less on each occasion to let the eerie glanses thud more and more firmly into our internal buffers. Scraping their scaley sheaths along our vaginal walls they propelled us towards a joint climax, proclaimed at the top of our voices, while our bodies were shaken convulsively by the shock-waves of come.

The door to the cabin was suddenly thrown open and Etienne's voice trumpeted: "Would you two bloody dykes mind making a little less noise with your rutting, as we are about to birth at Dabou to pick up supplies, and I don't want the police to think we're castrating a hostage!"

The door slammed, and we would have blushed had we not already been flushed with erotic excitement and far beyond the pale of shame. As it was we fell silent other than for heavy, irregular breathing. Vicky withdrew the Janus completely and we unscrewed the flower-clips and lay there side by side allowing ourselves a few minutes to decompress, as it had been a big one. After recovering we turned to face each other on the bed, our sore nipples touching as if by magnetism, despite the gravitational slant of our breasts, and Vicky gave me a quick rundown on the last decade of her life.

Her studies in the field of sports administration had brought her into contact with her future husband, who was a successful importer of foreign sports equipment, with a business based in New Jersey. Vicky had met him on the occasion of an internship in his offices, organized by her college. Having seen her walking around in a mini skirt, he called her into his office, and within three minutes our inveterate lesbian was writhing in ecstasy with her back on the executive desk and her feet on the presidential shoulders.

Initially she was fascinated by his endless macho virility, and just wanted to live a one-off experience without any intention of becoming a full-time hetero, but she got hooked on his massively muscular and abnormally hairy body, as well as on his thing. This was decidedly freakish, as of respectable proportions when normally erect, it would swell inside the female sex, remaining jammed until discharge, procuring the most heavenly wrenching feeling when he tugged against the resistance. In addition, his stamina and self-control were phenomenal, enabling him to continue for literally hours until his partner was reduced to the state of a gibbering human jelly.

"It's not as if I even like him, let alone love him", Vicky exclaimed, "But I'm the same as a junky in need of a fix, I've just got to have him in me — he's my needle!"

She had finally accepted one of his innumerable proposals of marriage, simply to be sure of getting her daily jab of pure-bread Mongolian penis, and had become Mrs Kardar Tsakir and her husband's toy, not to say sex-slave. He had decidedly oriental ideas on the status of women, distributing her body to friends and above all clients as if it were some form of transmissible property, being however careful to recover his chattel after use. She therefore found herself in the beds of endorsing athletes, retailers, wholesalers and foreign manufacturers of sports equipment, several times a week if not a day, as no one had ever been known to refuse such a sensational incentive.

This was all very well when they were strapping young

champions, but not so good when a fat, old, beer-swilling, German, skate manufacturer was programmed, as she had not as yet acquired my taste for the perverse. In addition, every night her husband would reduce her to the state of a quivering plankton, fortunately leaving her alone in the mornings, otherwise she would not have had enough energy to crawl out of bed to perform the functions of a high-class commercial whore, as well as her considerable duties in the running of the business.

On one occasion, during the negotiation of a contract to supply football gear to a large mid-western university, her husband had promised to lend her as a mascot for the opening match of the season. This was all very well where the cheer-leading and wearing the diminutive outfit were concerned but, after the match's triumphal conclusion, the team carried her shoulder-high into the changing room, stripped her naked and bundled her into the shower area where, on the tiled floor of the open central alley, in a slippery deluge of sweat, sperm, soap and water, all eleven players and three reserves posessed her collectively, with never less than three brawny athletes using the available holes at one and the same time.

She recalled that at one moment she was servicing no fewer than nine footballers: two in her basic holes, one in either side of her mouth, one under each armpit, one with each hand and a loner who somehow managed to get under the scrimmage and make love to the channel between her breasts, which were in any case being gobbled by two other players. In fact she loved every delirious moment and orgasmed continuously, but as she could never come with out telling everybody, she kept repeating: "I'm coming! I'm coming!" whereupon fourteen male voices would respond with the college cheer routine!

Vicky almost suspected Kardar of having suggested they have children to satisfy the craving of an Italian manufacturer, who only enjoyed intercourse with women in an advanced state of pregnancy. As soon as she was seven months gone, he would fly over to New York weekly, and Vicky would visit with him everyday in his suite in a well known Fifth Avenue hotel. He would take her contemptuously, greedily sucking her swollen breasts and withdrawing at the moment of orgasm to ejaculate over her distended stomach.

At this point her narrative was interrupted by the noise of our arrival at the jetty, and we hastily threw our clothes back on to disembark under the eyes of the staff, who drank in the splendid red head with an even more vibrant lechery than had been the case with my own arrival, for with Vicky there were no secrets, as I had told Banda and Yasmina all about our adolescence together, and they knew they could rely on me to lay on the Celtic fire-ball as soon as possible.

Chapter 17

Vicky's only experience of dusky virility had been after the famous football match, as three of the burliest players were black, although among the fourteen male organs which gave her the biggest workout of her life, she was unable to remember which one was doing precisely what or when or where, even if she knew why and how. All she could recollect was that they were all in there rooting.

After dinner on the Tsakirs' first evening at the villa, our husbands left us alone in the master suite, as Etienne, who seemed to get on surprisingly well with Kardar, wanted to show him the Adioukrou girls at closer quarters, leaving us to our own devices.

Already when getting off the boat, Vicky's observant eyes had sized up Banda's magnificent physique, and her hands trembled with excitement when I remarked laughingly that as hostess I felt bound to make up for my husband's discourteous absence by asking Banda to stand in for him and join us for coffee.

The superb Senoufo arrived in his most symbolic loin cloth, and sat down incongruously on the other side of the low table. Vicky and I were dressed as for a gala night at the Opera, Etienne having insisted that on our guests' first evening we make an effort to attire ourselves other than for instant sex, with the result I was wearing a long, white, shoulderless evening gown with a lot of jewellry and flesh-colored stockings, and Vicky a halter-top, knee-length, backless dress in a green shantung which had been chosen to match the devastating color of her eyes.

I continued talking in English about social niceties, as if in the presence of a conventional guest in a dinner jacket, revelling in the perversity of the situation, while Banda shuffled his feet uneasily and a feverishly excited Vicky tried to pretend she was not going down on him with her eyes.

After five minutes or so I started to become excited myself, as Vicky and Banda had not only given up all pretence of not blatantly ogling each other, but the red head had helped her skirt ride well up over her knees so that the lowness of her chair, and the fact she was not wearing any panties, presented the Senoufou with an unimpeded view of her bright pink gash and its halo of flaming pubic hair.

Banda responded by parting his ebony thighs to give Vicky an equally revealing view of his voluminous scrotum, as his organ was still partly hidden by the loin cloth that it had lifted clear of his legs, announcing his readiness for the next move. Standing up, I crossed over to his side of the table and, raising him to his feet, bent down to slip off the superfluous piece of cloth, uncovering his superlative stem in a state of stiffness which spoke highly of the red head's powers of visual stimulation.

I was just about to give it a quick lick myself when I heard Vicky groan behind me: "Come on you sadistic sow! Stop torturing me!" and looking round saw that lying back in her chair with her thighs widely spread, she had pulled her skirt right up to her waist and was busy running three tightly bunched fingers in an out of her wellhead, which was obviously in chronic and immediate need of the largest possible virile insertion.

"Alright! Alright!" I replied, "But I'm going to put it in; don't be so damned impatient!" Taking hold of Banda's formidable protrusion I led him round the edge of the table to position him between the red head's gaping thighs. I had to tell Vicky, whose mouth was set in an ugly rictus of lust, to stop screwing herself so I could collect some of her juice for transfer to the tip of Banda's rigid member, which felt so good and rapesome it was as much as I could do to resist the temptation to bend over and slide it into my own underworld.

Sensing how near I was to betrayal, she finally removed her hand and let me help myself to her streaming, which was so abundant there was enough to coat the whole of the African's glans and sheath. I then made him kneel to bring his organ down to the right level, placing my left hand under the small of her back to take the weight of her body and ease it forward onto the gleaming black pylon I was holding in the other hand, which I removed as it glided in. She was soon sobbing: "Oh my God! It's paradise! It's heaven! It's.....! But no one will ever know what her third metaphor for the celestial penis would have been, as at that moment their tongues met in deep-delving encounter and did not seperate until they climaxed some fifteen minutes later.

Rare are those whose sexual affinity is so intense they can simply look at each other from a distance and come. Vicky and Banda were of that ilk, as proximity alone made them almost hysterical with desire, and when they were actually plugged in, the sensation they experienced was so all-consuming that the usual gymnastics of sex became superfluous. All they had to do was lie virtually still and wait for it to well up all by itself and submerge their senses. Once inside her, barely moving, just an inch or so either way and very slowly, he undid the halter neck of her dress and, pulling down the corsage to bare her breasts, took hold of the nipples almost respectfully to pinch and twist them with a strange tenderness.

I was right out of the picture and yet I desperately wanted in, but they were locked together in a bodily communion in which I had no place, only Banda's backside and scrotum forming a visual link between me and their hermetic intimacy. Without ever having actually been in love with Banda, as our relationship was much more of a concentrated apotheosis of sex than a sentimental link, I nonetheless felt an accute pang of jealousy at not being the uncontested object of his desire. For Vicky it was clearly a case of love at first sight — Vicky who had loved many a woman, but never a man, was now experiencing hetero love for the first time, and was living it with a black Adonis. And when I say love I do not just mean sexual desire but the real old fashioned June-Moon-Croon variety.

I sat there listening to them groaning ecstatically as they came in slow motion, lost to everything but the sensual consummation of their new-found affection. Staring dejectedly at Banda's almost motionless buttocks I started to feel bored, as there is nothing more tedious than having to watch people who are in love actually making love, as all the wanton wickedness of lechery is missing, apart from the odds on being able to get into such an act being discouragingly long.

Deciding that Banda's bottom was my only chance of storming their citadel of romance, I fell to my knees and, parting the statuesque hemispheres, pushed a forefinger into his anus, provoking a contraction and a reflex of withdrawal. Leaving the finger buried up to the second joint I waited patiently, and after what could have been no more than thirty seconds, but seemed like an eternity, the magnificent buttocks began to move back in my direction, driving the finger the whole way in, with the African easing his knees apart to make my task easier and provide proof that he at least had not forgotten Leda.

Feeling elated at having been allowed back into his magic circle, and to give him tangible proof of my gratitude — as his mouth was still stuck to Vicky's and his sex deep down inside her — I withdrew my finger from his rectum to slip it into my own. I then applied my lips to his tight little opening with my nose wedged in the top of the shapely cleft, and started to suck and kiss the tightly puckered sphincter, fondling the splendid testacles with my other hand, until I felt the circular muscle relax. Pulling his buttocks apart, I was able to slide my tongue into his rectal cavity, scraping the outside of the rubbery ring with my teeth while inhaling the heady odor of his great divide.

Whether by coincidence, or because of my tonguing and teething, the testacles heaved and Banda ejaculated, making Vicky croon with delight as she responded with a vaginal eruption. Realizing that unless I did something about it I would be left out of the orgasmic picture, I roughly pushed a handful of fingers into my sex, working away until the familiar feeling of rising tension and release enveloped the pit of my loins, freeing me to sit back on humid haunches and smile.

Vicky, with a crumpled, shantung dress covering little more than her navel, had lent forward as soon as Banda withdrew to swallow his final spurting directly from the jerking glans, leaving nothing for me, as from my position behind I had no chance of getting there first, and pump as I might there was no way I could squeeze even the smallest drop out of his still impressively rigid penis when I finally arrived on the scene, as the greedy ginger bitch had guzzled the lot.

Despite her resentment of my reappearance, Vicky had lain back on her chair after swallowing her lover's effusion, dreamily caressing her breasts, with her thighs asplay, the oozing of overflow from the vivid gash between her legs making a pretty picture. One of Banda's most endearing qualities was the sheer quantity of come his balls produced, even after the shortest recovery period, and he had really topped up his latest conquest to the short and curlies.

"Well", I whispered to the Senoufo, "If I can't have it directly from the supplier I must go down on the go between". So saying I knelt in front of Vicky's yawning almond to lap its greater lips, before applying my mouth to the inner ones on which I could get a better labial grip. Breathing through my nose, I began to suck deeply and was rewarded almost immediately with a few drops which soon became a trickle. To start with the red head lay back savoring the new source of pleasure, until she realized what I was stealing. Sitting up with a jolt she exclaimed: "You horrid little thief! Give that back! It's mine! I earned it!" So saying she darted an agile tongue between my lips in an attempt to recover her lost treasure, engaging me in a mock battle of mouths that soon degenerated into a girly kiss as we briefly reverted to Lesbian type, with Vicky sinking back again onto the cushions.

However, what was about to happen at the other end of my body was as far removed from the world of dykes as vice from virtue, as Banda, who had been left with an unimpaired stiffer, had followed my sperm-recovery operation as an amused spectator for a minute or so, leisurely masturbating to keep his beautiful erection in fighting trim, but when my exchange with Vicky gave signs of lasting, his patience ran out and he turned to the nearest means of satisfying his rekindled desire, which happened to be my backside.

There was still however an obstacle between his black ramrod and one or other of the holes which would give him the relief he sought, and that was the long evening gown I was wearing. I felt him feel around the bottom of the skirt in the hope of being able to raise it high enough to allow penetration, but as I was kneeling on it, there was no way I could raise both knees simultaneously to free the hem without letting Vicky know what was happening. Like all my other clothes, and in keeping with my husband's wishes, the dress had been made to allow instant removal, by the simple expedient of a zipper which ran the whole way down the back, but as the gown was beautifully made, the zip was discreetly hidden under an overlap of material that gave the impression of being an integral part of the cut of the dress.

It took Banda some time to work this one out, and I could feel his hands groping around for a solution, which in itself excited me no end, in addition to the suspense of wondering whether Vicky would find out and try to spoil our fun. In fact I managed to divert her attention with our girly games, and Banda finally discovered the zip, which he pulled as discreetly as possible, allowing the dress to fall open and reveal my complete nudity other than for the self-supporting stockings.

Once again I managed to put Vicky off the scent by clutching the front of the dress to my breasts with a natural caressing gesture which did not awake her suspicions, and even stifled a gasp of pain when Banda, having moistened his glans with no more than a meager application of spittle, perversely ran his member into my unlubricated asshole rather than into the neighboring cunt, which was aching drippingly for his intrusion.

Unfortunately all good things must come to an end, and Vicky ultimately realized something lewd was happening, not from any movement of my body, as the Senoufou was careful to slide in and out of my tail without any tell-tale percussion, but from the ecstatic glazing of my eyes.

When the truth dawned she sat up again with another jolt, saw what Banda was doing, and gave a shriek of anger before exclaiming: "You miserable pair of cheats! You promised me it was my turn this evening! Oh and he's giving it to you in the butt! Just what I was dreaming of!"

In a flurry of frustration she began to pinch and pull at her clitty, but Banda and I were beyond the point of no return on the other side of the mirror of lust. Nothing anyone could do, short of physical violence, could stop our runaway rut. Now that I had nothing to hide I arched my back, raising my buttocks higher to give Banda a more effective angle of slide, whispering to him hoarsely: "Banda put knees outside Leda's: tighter bumfuck!"

The Senoufo willingly complied, loving it when I felt in the mood for what we called a 'tighty', as it gave him a more intense orgasm. Because there were relatively few assholes which would accept his mammouth member in this gut-grazing position, he always jumped at the opportunity whenever I made the suggestion, whose frequency depended on my sphincter's state of soreness following other moments of maltreatment.

Nobody could teach me and Banda anything about buggery; we were in a class of our own. Our timing, technique and sensual inspiration are of an order that enables us to use every inch of the African's vibrant phallus, which he withdraws with nerve-racking slowness to expose the whole of the glans, before plunging it back until arrested by my buttocks, which I thrust back to enhance the shock of impact. Then, to attain the very quintessence of sodomy, we add a rotating movement of my backside to the contra-rotation of his pelvis.

I often increase excitement by using my gymnastic training to adopt inventive positions well beyond the muscular possibilities of the normal female, athletically exploiting the natural or unnatural features of a random setting, which might be anywhere from a telephone booth to a suburban cemetery, depending on the whims of desire and geography.

On that particular day, as soon as we began our 'tighty', I started to come, oozing secretion down my thighs in such quantities that it stained the modern carpet which was one of the owner's most prized posessions. As usual I started to eruct my standard stream of verbal filth, but Vicky — whose attitude had progressively evolved, while masturbating introspectively, from one of petty jealousy to fascination at the rigorous perfection of our performance — remembering from way back one of the best ways to silence me — slid her slit to the front of the cushion, canted her loins upwards, put a hand behind my neck and pulled my mouth down onto her sex.

The smell and taste of her freshly irrigated vulva pulled out my big bass stop, while Banda's equivalent of the thirty foot pipe did the rest, raising both of us to a fortissimo climax, his powerful hands gripping my hips and pulling me back fitfully against his thighs, as if he were trying to follow his ejaculation through into my ass.

I had never known Banda like it before, as for ages after ejaculating he held roughly onto my hips with both hands, pressing my rump against his pelvis as if trying to force his member further and further into my butt, which was patently absurd, as there was no way he could hope to go deeper, as my buttocks were compressed to the maximum and there was nothing else that could possibly give. For all I cared he could stay in there as long as he liked, as he was still as stiff as a lamp post and lovely to have on board, even if there was no chance of his making further progress. He must have known it, but it was as if he wanted to stake an indefinite claim to my asshole.

It was finally Vicky who broke it up, disengaging herself from my mouth to move round behind Banda and start fondling his cleft, as with his knees pressing mine together she could not get his buttocks far enough apart to give him a 'feuille de rose', and had to be content with second best. While dandling his balls she felt him come, and was surprised that he should continue to thump my buttocks, at the same rate, as if nothing had happened. Deciding to find out what it was all about, she forced a hand between our sweating bodies, somehow managing to grasp Banda's member and pull it out of my cavity. She discovered, to her surprise — proving her lack of experience of the Senoufo's stamina — that he was none the worse for wear, even after two major shake downs at such short notice. Far from it, he was still as stiff as a crowbar and ready to go the distance of a third round, hence my selfish attempt to keep it all for myself!

Vicky and I were now one all in our contest for the Senoufo's semen, and neither intended to stand by while the other won the best of three by default. But we were confronted with the problem of the eternal triangle the wrong way round, having two cunts and only one cock, and although one into two may be good arithmetic it only results in deficient fucking. We were on the point of starting a war of posession when I remembered a technique I had seen used in a porn film, consisting of one of the women lying on her back with the other stretched out on top of her, on her front, their sexes being lined up face to face at the edge of the bed and their widespread legs supported at the same height as the mattress by a pair of chairs. After lubricating the two superimposed slits, the kneeling male slid his member to and fro between them, rubbing it against both of the clitties in the process, and continuing until everyone took off.

That at least was the theory, but as none of us had any practical experience of the method we were going to have to play it by ear. In fact it could not have been easier, as I volunteered to be the spreadeagled underbitch with Vicky lying on top of me, our bodies touching the whole way from our outstretched arms to our outstretched legs, with our breasts squashed bulgily together. All Banda had to do, after applying vaseline to our vulvas, which were pressing tightly against each other, was kneel against the side of the bed between our thighs, adjust the height of his intact erection, and force it between our slits until the tip ran to and fro over our clitties, flattening them divinely on each round trip.

Far from resenting having to share Banda's black banana we were both delirious, as our nipples were teasing each other and our mouths housed a regular tongue fight, while our clitties were rubbed apart at least twenty times a minute by the Senoufo's two-way ticket. It did not take long at that rate for all of us to hit the highlights and, despite the emptiness of our holes, have resounding climaxes at the moment of Banda's blow-out, which injected his discharge into the compressed area between our sandwiched bodies like a grease-gun lubricating the zones of contact between moving parts.

Chapter 18

Even Banda needed a rest after his third inning, as we had made no allowance for the calls Yasmina and the Adioukrou girls might have made on his seemingly infinite manhood earlier in the day, and his heavenly member was allowed to resume its handsome off-duty proportions. At one stage I thought Vicky might try and turn our evening's entertainment into a Marathon, as she was simply dying to discover how the Senoufo felt the other way round, but fatigue got the better of lechery and Banda returned to his quarters, leaving the two of us to sleep the sleep of the wicked in each other's arms.

I shudder to think how our men folk must have spent the night, or for that matter the following morning, which we passed alone together in the master suite, rutting and reminiscing. Etienne finally appeared at four in the afternoon to announce a very special 'exhibition'.

The reason was that when he and Kardar had gone looking for Yasmina the previous evening, with the intention of including her in their festivities with the Adioukrous, they had caught her red-handed in her hut — which she shared with her brother Houari — in the act of being sired by the larger of the two Korhogo guard dogs. These formidable creatures are a local variant of the Bull Mastiff and appropriately as black as charcoal. Etienne felt that the spectacle of my lady's maid being posessed by such an animal was an edifying experience we should not be allowed to miss, hence, for the first time on any stage, the appearance of the adorable Yasmina and her furry friend.

From the time of our arrival the dog, who was passively hostile towards the other inhabitants of the villa, apart from his handler Akba, had been visibly interested in Yasmina, as even when she obeyed my orders on the subject of below-the-belt hygiene, she smelt sexually stronger than the rest of us; a peculiarity I personally found exciting just so long as she kept things under control with plentiful applications of soap and water.

The dog would often nose around the lower reaches of her body, and as she never wore more than the standard mini-smock, when not actually naked, there was no barrier between the animal's muzzle and her private parts. I had noticed that it frequently managed to get in a lick or two before being pushed away half-heartedly, giving the impression that had I not been on the scene she would have allowed it to take matters a stage further.

One day I had confirmation of this when entering the master suite unexpectedly to discover a rear-view of Yasmina, whose smock was obviously undone, with one foot on a chair and her leg at a wide enough angle to expose her genitals for the dog, which was almost entirely hidden from my sight by her body. I could nevertheless see, from the position of its front paws on the floor in relation to her feet, that it must have been licking her sex, an impression corroborated by an unmistakable lapping sound, to which the girl responded with salacious little sighs and gasps. The animal was just as excited as its human partner, as could be seen from a long and slimey stem which had slid the whole way out of its sheath. From the position of her arms and neck it was evident that Yasmina was fondling and kissing her breasts, and was in any case so absorbed by the excitement of her dirty little pastime that she failed to notice my presence.

The rhythm of her breathing increased progressively, punctuated by the occasional strangled sob, until a shudder followed by a long groan denoted a clitoral orgasm, which must have been accompanied by a secretion of love-juice, as the animal redoubled its efforts, increasing her obscene enjoyment by repeatedly pushing its muzzle into the exposed angle of her thighs.

She had just dropped to her knees with the obvious intention of letting the dog go even further, when I decided things had in fact already gone far enough, at least for the time being, and coughed loudly, making her jump with surprise.

"You filthy little slut!" I exclaimed, "Are there no depths to which you would not be prepared to sink? Get that bloody animal out of my bedroom and then come back immediately!"

The animal did not appreciate my tone of voice, as it bared its teeth and snarled threateningly in my direction, but Yasmina whispered some endearment in Arabic and it followed her meekly to the door. When she returned smiling insolently, with her smock still wide open in front, I told her to kneel down over the bed, holding the skirt well clear of her buttocks, as I was going to punish her for such bestial behavior.

Her grin became even broader and more impertinent, but she obeyed my orders to the letter, arching her back to make her bottom stand out invitingly. Cupping the palm of my hand to fit the beautifully rounded contour, I started with the left buttock, gradually improving my aim and the profile of the hollow of my hand to produce pistol-like reports which became clearer and louder with each successive smack.

I changed regularly from one buttock to the other, making her sigh and squeal and even snort, dosing the strength and frequency of the blows to keep her suffering within delectable limits, as only the sensually insensitive and unimaginative need to inflict or suffer excessive injury or mutilation to achieve orgasm through pain, often at the inadmissible price of permanently damaging erotic potential. In fact the slogan for acceptable sado-maso should be: 'All done by kindness!'

However, to return to Yasmina, although I could see and feel she was perfectly clean, the more excited she became the stronger she smelt, possibly as a result of the dog's fore play. What is certain is that she was making me feel increasingly rutty, and I slapped more and more distractedly, occasionally sliding my hands lovingly over and between the perfectly rounded orbs, which were now a deep and angry red, allowing my fingers to wander feelingly around her hole of stickiness.

Finally, her emanations became so obsessive I abandoned my punishment of her misdeeds to concentrate my faculties of taste and smell on the source of the exhilirating odors, gently prying her buttocks apart to apply my lips to the clean-shaven gash of her sex, the tip of my nose coming to rest in the contrasting entanglement of anal hair, while my tongue went questing for the wellhead of acrid outflow.

The more I licked the more excited we both became, until I could contain myself no longer. Lifting her bodily onto the bed, I clasped her divide in the scissors of my thighs so we could grind our crotches together in a contrarotating fork-fuck which made both of us come breathlessly. It took me a little time to notice there was something abnormal about the warmth and volume of the girl's effusion, as my powers of observation were temporarily dimmed by the intensity of our intercourse, and it was only after a few seconds of the wierd but enthralling sensation that I realized she was peeing into my sex.

There was a time when I would have been scandalized, but I was now an old and enthusiastic hand at the use of urination to further the cause of sex, even if it was the first time with a woman. Instead of showing anger and indignation I responded in kind, pissing straight back with all the force of my bladder, clutching her buttocks to keep our gushers pressed tightly together until the last drops had drained off our thighs, while our bodies writhed their way through the contortions of a dual vaginal climax that left both of us quaking on sodden sheets.

I thanked the gods of foresight for having taken the precaution of inserting a plastic sheet between the under-blanket and the mattress, as it enabled us to destroy the evidence of our delicious incontinence. Having discovered yet another exhilirating variant to the standard catalogue of perversion, I was pleased with myself, although I was really sorry the dog did not love me in the same way as Yasmina!

The purpose of this long digression was simply to show that the Algerian girl was already suspected of bestiality, but I was carried away by my eloquence and my interest in my favorite subject. What I was going to say was that when Etienne and Kardar walked into her hut, she was in fact in the middle of taking matters a stage further, as the dog was actually up her.

She was of course naked and kneeling at the right height to allow the animal to mount her with its front paws jammed under her armpits on either side, but it was clearly having a problem staying put in her hole, as its long, unsheathed member kept coming out, to the girl's unconcealed annoyance, as every time she started to build up her sexual tension the doggy prick would pop out of her kennel and she would have to reach back to reinsert it. Her task was not made any easier by the fact that her mouth was full of fraternal phallus, making it impossible for her to devote as much attention as she would have liked to her canine lover.

All Yasmina did, when she became aware of their presence — as she knew no such thing as sexual shame — was to turn her neck after having released her brother from between her lips, while continuing to jerk him off, and smile at them invitingly as if to say: "If you wait your turn there will be plenty of room for both of you"! She hardly had time to turn back to Houari before he ejaculated all over her face, freeing her to devote her entire attention to the guard dog without even bothering to wipe the come off her features.

This time, when she threaded the dog's penis into her pussy, using the same technique of reaching between her thighs, she passed both arms behind her back to grasp the animal by the folds of skin on the sides of its rib cage, with which she held it in position. As is usual with dogs, once inserted it ejaculated quickly, after a few sharp thrusts, which looked as if they hurt, as Yasmina winced at the end of each jab, but she then settled down to enjoy the interesting part as the animal's member swelled inside her, making it impossible for it to withdraw before detumescence.

This was where Houari showed his gratitude for his sister's expert fellation, by baiting the dog to make it struggle to withdraw, wrenching at its swollen penis and almost pulling the lining of the girl's vagina inside out, making her come like the end of creation. My husband was so impressed with her performance, and by her caterwauling when her vaginal walls were submitted to violent traction, that he told her he would like to stage her little act in public.

After dinner Etienne installed everyone, with the exception of the actors, on the far side of the pool, looking back towards the terrace, which was to be used as an impromptu stage and was floodlit for the occasion. We were all told to undress and kneel facing the house, the women in front and the men behind, excluding of course Akba, who would never have demeaned himself in such a way. As an artistic touch the two white female bottoms were placed between the three black ones.

When everything was ready, the all-nude cast walked on stage amidst embarrassed applause, Houari holding the guard dog tightly on a choker leash to stop it assaulting Yasmina before the moment came, as it was in a state of excitement that bordered on the dangerous, no doubt induced by a certain amount of foreplay as it was prominently tumescent.

Yasmina, who acknowledged our applause by pulling her tongue at us in a particularly suggestive manner, was obviously just as excited as the animal, as well as relishing being the center of so much lascivious interest; indeed there were times when I wondered whether she was not an even greater exhibitionist than I.

As Houari was clearly having difficulty holding the animal, which had tried to round on him more than once, his sister hastened to lie down on the edge of the improvised scenery, consisting of a large mattress and sheet, and the dog was freed. It literally threw itself at the girl's open thighs, snarling horribly, thrusting its muzzle repeatedly into the gap, and the audience fell tensely silent wondering whether we were not on the verge of an ugly incident. In fact, it was only the animal's way of asserting its male superiority over Houari, and once satisfied it had established ascendancy — glancing furtively in the direction of the audience to make certain we did not constitute a challenge — it stopped growling and began licking the girl's scarlet gash with a relish and a length of tongue that soon had her shuddering with breathless delight.

Judging his female sufficiently prepared, the dog placed its front paws clumsily on her breasts, crushing them out of shape, but could not penetrate properly. despite her help in guiding the glistening object, as the angle of attack was quite wrong. By arching her back and raising her buttocks off the mattress, she managed a few hesitant half-strokes before the animal's member failed to re-enter, and it soon became obvious she would have to abandon the classic human position for one better adapted to canine anatomy.

The frustration of its attempt had not only made the dog angry, as it was again growling and snarling, but had produced a negative effect on its virility, as of the formidable phallus of ten minutes earlier only a small pink extremity remained. Lying on her side and sliding her head under its stomach, Yasmina was able, by raising her neck, to take the unsavory object in her mouth, easing the sheath back with her fingers to suck the lewd stem lovingly until it had recovered its menacing proportions.

With the canine penis back at full stretch, Yasmina knelt with her buttocks at what frequent experience told her was the right height, and the animal once again started to lick her genitals, spending however a lot of time on her ass, which seemed to fascinate it, quite probably for reasons on which I would prefer not to dwell. Finally it clambered up with its paws under her armpits and its sex prodding away clumsily at her cleft.

Feeling good and ready, the girl reached back between her thighs to take hold of the slithery member, placing its tip at the entrance to her sex in a position that would ensure penetration when the dog lunged forward. The animal seemed to hesitate, and Yasmina reached back again to caress its scrotum, hoping to trigger a reaction, which was precisely what she did, but not with the result she anticipated, as the dog, lurching clumsily, drove its penis into her ass, which, unlike her sex, whose lubricant glands had been thoroughly activated by the canine tongue, had on the contrary been licked bone dry.

Two things happened simultaneously: the dog, feeling itself

at long last embedded in something suitable, ejaculated instantaneously and remained jammed in Yasmina's asshole as its organ swelled up to a distended, post-coital size, whereas the girl cried out in pain at having been unexpectedly raped in what unusual circumstances had made the wrong hole.

Generally speaking Yasmina's asshole was a happy hunting ground for anyone or anything with a stand on, and although it was not what she had intended, she would normally have welcomed the change, provided her alternative hole was in a sufficiently slippery state to receive the intrusion. But it was not, hence the howls of protest.

They really were genuine screams of unsimulated pain, and for a moment we all seriously considered going to her assistance. Houari, who was shamelessly standing on the terrace, jerking himself off at the spectacle of his sister's bestial buggery, made a half-hearted move, only to freeze into immobility when the dog bared its fangs and lunged in his direction as if to bite off his dick. However, as was usually the case with our womenfolk, what was initially made to sound like unbearable suffering turned out, a few minutes later, to be heavenly bliss. This proved to be the case with the saga of Yasmina's anus and the guard dog, as within a matter of seconds the cries of agony had subsided, to be replaced initially by grunts of concentration, themselves superceded a minute or so later by gasps of satisfaction, followed shortly by squeals of unmitigated glee.

Yasmina, who was reputed for her smiling silence when in the throws of sex, even went as far as to murmur: "C'est ça! Encule-moi mon amour!" (That's it! Bugger me my beloved!), expressing herself in the French that was our common language of communication.

Houari hesitated before baiting the dog into premature withdrawal, as pulling the lining out of an asshole is not the same thing as pulling one out of a cunt, but his sister spat out something in Arabic, making it clear she wanted her rectum to have a good ripping. He therefore began teasing the dog, which promptly tried to tear itself free, making Yasmina weep and almost faint with erotic joy, as the animal tugged at her sphincter while she contributed to her happiness with an energetic pinching and twisting of a remarkably rigid clitty.

While all this was going on the spectators had not remained idle. Etienne had set the rules of the game in advance: the male onlookers were not entitled to start screwing until he gave the signal, or the women to move from their pre-allotted kneeling positions, meaning the four men could only take the five girls from behind — one way or the other!

To pass the time of day pending the starting signal, Etienne had invented a divine distraction for the ladies. Among the many gadgets the owner of the villa had left behind was a portable, high pressure, electric pump, which was mainly used for washing the cars and launch. This device could project a thin jet of water with great accuracy at very high pressure, and my lecherous angel of a husband was quick to appreciate the erotic potential of such an implement in a warm climate. Having lined up the five adorable behinds of his bevy of beauty, all he had to, once the pump was connected, was to to aim the nozzle at one or other of the exposed targets, choose the precise point of impact of the high pressure jet, and press the trigger.

To start with, from twelve feet, he used a fairly wide jet at less than maximum pressure, which struck our vulvas and anuses simultaneously, producing a deliciously erotic sensation and plenty of giggling, each bottom receiving a blast of about fifteen seconds, which was nothing like enough and we all cried out for more. Etienne then increased the pressure and reduced the diameter of the jet, making it possible for him to target the vulva independently of the anus. This time the were fewer giggles, more excited gasps and a general feeling that fifteen seconds a hole was a fair share.

Finally my husband adjusted the nozzle to produce a pencil thin jet at very high pressure, explaining that no one would be able to stand more than five or six seconds directed seperately at each of the three erogenous zones: the ass, the clitty and the cunt. When Etienne called our names we were to say which of our zones was to receive the first blast, and cry out when we had had enough, indicating whether we wanted him to continue with another of our targets.

Vicky, as our guest, was entitled to the place of honor, and chose to receive her first blast on the clit. Etienne aimed carefully and scored a direct hit on her already prominent and clearly visible appendage, the powerful jet making a noise on impact like a cataract hurling itself over a precipice. Within what could hardly have been three seconds the sexually unstoppable Vicky was crying out for mercy, trying to protect her battered button with a hand which was swept aside by the almost solid jet.

She knelt there gasping heavily, as if having difficulty recovering her breath after an exceptional physical effort, and all she could do, when Etienne asked her whether she wanted to continue with another zone, was shake her head wearily. Because of her kneeling position, two places down the line, I had difficulty catching the expression on her face, but when she finally turned in my direction, I could see she was smiling in bewilderment, but with an expression of ecstasy that spoke highly of the effects of the jet, once the moment of immediate and almost traumatic shock had passed.

Without breaking the rules by leaving my kneeling position, I allowed my torso to fall backwards until my head was touching the ground, and then turned it to discover what the effects of the blast had been on her clitty, and was astounded to see it protruding from her vulva like the last two joints of a little finger. Vicky's clit had always been very big when rigid, but this was crazy, as it must have been twice its normal maximum size, and realizing I was on the verge of a unique experience, the adrenalin started to flow. I would have liked to join her, to be the first to make love to her wonderful new plaything, but when I started making the move that would have taken me in her direction Etienne cried out to remind me I had to stay where I was.

As hostess I was next in the batting order before the staff and, bracing myself in the bent over kneeling position, I told Etienne bluntly that I wanted it straight in the ass. It was no sooner said than done, and the solid cable of water crashed into my sphincter, forcing it open and flushing its way up my rectum to produce an instant orgasm, but I managed to hold on, gritting my teeth, for seven or eight seconds before screaming for relief. Gasping for breath, as if winded by a punch in the solar plexis, I was nevertheless determined to outdo Vicky, and when my husband asked me whether I wanted a second blast I said I did, choosing my womanhood to receive the renewed Niagara.

Biting a thumb to try and retain some self control was of no avail, as when I felt the jet brush aside my lesser lips and surge straight up my slot into the uterus and God knows where else, I was paralyzed by a vaginal climax which knocked me sideways, making it impossible for Etienne to continue the torture as the target was hidden from view. Like Vicky I was stunned for the best part of a minute and then, as the water started to leak out of my loins, I had first one delayed action orgasm, then another, and then a whole chain of them, each sensation provoking a bodily convulsion that made me writhe fitfully like an epileptic, twitching around on the tiled surface.

One after the other the three Adioukrous received the same treatment. Dala was so fascinated by the size of Vicky's clit she chose the same zone, and must have stood up to the treatment for five seconds. She then had such a fit of hysterics it took three men to hold her down. Finally the shock waves were replaced by the same feeling of sensual fulfilment that Vicky and I were enjoying, happily stroking our sexes and drooling with delight. Myrian chose the cunt and was power hosed into a vaginal heaven, whereas little Dagouba preferred the ass, and although I suspected Etienne of reducing the pressure for his favorite, she also had what looked and sounded like a fit, before returning to the land of the living with a blissful smile on her face and a middle finger buried deeply in her butt.

No one asked for more except me. I wanted a clitty like Vicky's and I wanted it badly, whatever the pain. In any case, it would not have been entirely true to say it hurt abominably, as it was like a blinding flash in the sex, almost what the atom must feel when being split. I came out of it crying like a baby, but with an even bigger clitty than Vicky, although it was so sensitive I could not touch it for at least twenty minutes without sobbing and coming, whereafter the pain subsided and only the responsiveness to pleasure remained.

During these antics we were supposed to be watching Yasmina on the stage. She did attract a certain amount of attention, but not as much as she deserved, particularly when the dog finally made it into her ass, as it was then that Etienne put away his new toy and gave the signal for the gentlemen to join the ladies, making a sign to Houari, who could not approach his sister on the stage because of the violently posessive dog, to make up the party on our side of the pool when he had finished inciting the animal to withdraw.

I did not know how the women had been allocated in advance, but I drew a rampant Wakaba, whom I had never known so stiff or inconsiderate. He knew perfectly well that my ass would be as dry as a desert, having had a high pressure wash out only twenty minutes earlier. Despite this, while chewing the back of my neck, he grabbed my hips with his two manual clamps to stop me moving, thrust my legs apart roughly with his knees and rammed his cast iron cock the whole way up my rear entrance, scorching my sphincter with the friction of his entry. I moaned pitifully, and for a moment it looked as if Etienne, who was stuck into Dala on my right, might tell the Senoufo to take it easy, until he saw that my bottom had started to rotate and was pushing back contentedly against the accelerating thrusts.

Everyone seemed to be coming in every direction, starting with me. I had an excellent excuse, as after Wakaba had emptied his prolific balls into my burning butt, I felt another pair of hands take hold of my hips and, looking round, saw Kardar about to penetrate my slit with a penis that was already of substantial size. Remembering it would swell up even further when inside, I braced myself for the big stretch, and sure enough once he was up me his phallus grew considerably, and Yasmina was no longer the only one to be stuck to her lover, even if her's did have four legs.

Once he felt his organ had reached its apogee, Kardar made as if to withdraw, but as there was no way he could extract the grossly swollen weapon, the fact of pulling backwards exercised traction on the walls of my cunt, which were partly dragged out into the open, although there was a point beyond which they could not stretch any further, and when this was reached he would come back in again, bringing my lining with him.

While this was happening and keeping me in a state of uninterrupted come, as the effect of Kardar's inside-outing was sensually devastating, the women, who just could not get over the size of my clitty, crawled underneath my body to touch and stroke it, adding a further dimension to my already hysterical pleasure by superimposing a second layer of orgasm on top of those initiated by the Mongol, as the merest contact of my hypersensitive female penis with anything else automatically triggered a full climax, and I was reaching the point where I could not take much more pleasure without becoming completely delirious.

The women must have understood my problem, as despite the fascination exercised by my giant clitty-prick they disappeared, leaving me alone with the prodigious Kardar, who continued to belabor my loins for another two hours, holding me against his thighs, as otherwise I would have slumped down onto the tiled surface. This is what happened when he finally came, contemptuously discarding my body and cursing and swearing in Mongolian as if I had stolen his birthright, rather than having been the instrument of sublime sexual pleasure.

When Vicky appeared I was lying there in a state of ecstatic torpor, wondering where I would find the strength to crawl back to the bedroom. I knew immediately what I had to do, slipping naturally into the sixty-nine position that brought her clitty-cock opposite my lips and mine opposite hers. We sucked them like homosexual boys enjoying a feast of adolescent fellation, coming continuously with an intensity which was well nigh unbearable, sobbing out a mixture of pain and pleasure that ended in a searing climax during which we held tightly onto each other's bodies to avoid being torn apart by our convulsions.

Chapter 19

The parting of Banda and Vicky at the end of the Tsakirs' stay was heartrending, as they were completely infatuated with each other and could not bear the idea of seperation.

Kardar had not realized what was brewing between his wife and the Senoufo, as he himself spent all his time with the Adioukrous, particularly Dagouba, with whom he must have made love two or three times a day. As it took him at least two hours to come, it is hardly surprising he was too busy to see what Vicky was up to, and when he finally understood he was pathologically furious, not out of jealousy — as just so long as his wife was present when he needed her to assuage his sexual appetite, or when he required her services to satisfy a client, he did not mind what she did — but from an outraged sense of property, as Vicky was his thing, and not entitled to give as opposed to lend a part of herself to another man without his consent, above all her love, which was something he had never shared.

He must have given her one hell of a beating, as she appeared in the morning with a black eye the size of a grapefruit, infuriating me as much as Banda, and Etienne had to intervene to seperate the two men. As a result of this incident Vicky and her husband left two days early, with the redhead in tears, and it was as much as I could do to prevent Banda going to dangerous extremes, as he was out of his mind.

Life at the villa gradually resumed its normal rhythm, with Akba posessing me regularly every morning, and Wakaba and a disconsolate Banda helping themselves to me whenever they or I felt so inclined, that is to say at least once a day each, either seperately or together. Etienne and Houari were also entitled to frequent incursions into my intimacy, although the Algerian boy's rabbitting did not send me in the same way as the three mightily hung Africans, above all when there were two of them in me at the same time.

I suppose I must have averaged about six full fucks a day under normal conditions, in addition to a fair amount of lesbian loving, but on special occasions I could manage several times this figure, accurate accounting being made difficult by the problem of deciding where one fuck ended and when the next began. For instance, was it right to give the same score to a double-fuck as to two seperate screwings, or should it only have been counted as one? As a matter of personal pride I adopted the latter method, but if I had wanted to show off I could have used a more flattering basis for my computations.

Had it not been for my insatiable sexual curiosity, I would have gone on fucking away happily like that for years, as even for an appetite the size of mine, which was inexorably increasing, there was still more than enough cock to go round, above all when the gang-bangs in Abidjan were taken into consideration.

However, one day when I was unexpectedly taking my siesta alone, Myriam came in to clean the master suite, and having started talking to me from the middle of the room, finished on the bed eating me as messily as if I had been some over-ripe tropical fruit, making enough noise to be overheard on the terrace. She would therefore have had difficulty replying intelligibly when I asked her about the secret sex sects, even if she had known anything of interest, which was not the case, but the little she knew did at least whet my appetite for further information.

It would have been impossible to live in contact with the inhabitants of that part of Africa without hearing something about these sects sooner or later, and as my contacts were essentially sexual, it was normal I should become aware of their existence quite rapidly. It was finally from Banda that I obtained my first few shreds of enlightenment, but when I tried to make him give more than a general picture he shut up like a obstinate oyster, and there was nothing I could do to make him reveal details. He was known to have been a participant in the rites of one of the sects, and excused his reticence on the grounds of having been sworn to secrecy.

The few scraps of knowledge I was able to garner from him, and from other local sources, suggested that the ceremonies associated with the main rites took place once a year at the summer solstice — which incidentally coincided with my birthday — in a nebulous northern border district between the Ivory Coast and Burkina Faso, where the Wasagu sect was known to survive, despite having been banned by the French colonial authorities more than forty years previously.

What these rites consisted of was another matter, and only the haziest indications were available, but were singularly intriguing for someone with my obsessive interest in outlandish sex. It appeared that the sect practiced a form of virility cult whose supreme being was an 'Ape-God'. A certain number of the most beautiful married women in the Wasagu Territory were chosen to become candidate-brides for the legendary creature, and either lent by their complaisant husbands, whose justification was supposed to reside in the honor involved, or simply abducted in the event of marital opposition. Having reached this point my sources dried up, and it was clear that a more methodical approach would be necessary if fuller information was to be obtained.

I therefore had to resort to the Anthropological Section of the Beauvoir Library in Abidjan, where I was confronted with a reference system designed for specialists rather than uninformed amateurs, making the assistance of a librarian indispensable. The one who happened to be on duty was an unattractive specimen of indeterminate age, ungroomed beard and disproportionate height in relation to his skinny frame. In addition, he made it perfectly clear — to the point of downright rudeness — that he had no time to waste on non-professional or non-academic enquiries, particularly from white women of a certain social standing.

Seething with suppressed anger I withdrew to the apartment to rethink my plan of campaign in the light of this unexpected obstacle, and did not have to rack my mind to discover the best means of turning a hostile masculine librarian into a malleable informant. On the occasion of my first visit, not imagining I would encounter a male-relationship problem, I had given no thought to my appearance, throwing on a very concealing trouser-suit, hiding my hair — which needed washing — under a scarf and my eyes behind dark glasses. It was therefore hardly surprising I should have obtained such an unfavorable result by comparison with my usual success story. For my next visit to the library I was going to do a great deal better!

Despite my impatience — as I was now genuinely excited by what I sensed about the Wasagu rites — I decided to wait until my next stay in the capital before returning to the library, hopefully allowing the bad impression I had created to be at least partially effaced by time. For my second attempt I was simply but revealingly dressed in a white, U necked, sleeveless, cotton bodice, which moulded my breasts as if it was being used to take a cast, a white, pleated, mid-thigh length skirt in the same material, and white leather ballerinas that set off the shapely muscles of my long golden legs to perfection. My sun-bleached hair was freshly shampood and fluffy, and I was good enough to knock down and eat, my main problem being how to reach the library, which was some three blocks away, without that actually happening. I solved it by slipping on a long, lightweight linen cape, which I removed upon reaching the floor of the Tribal Customs Department.

My luck was in, as the thin man of African anthropology was all alone in his section of the library and stared at me as if I were an apparition from another more beautiful world. I sensed a flicker of recognition in his eye, and there was a moment when the issue hung in doubt, but not for long, as leaning over the counter to allow my U neck to billow becomingly, I appropriately told a big black lie: "Please forgive me for my rudeness the other day; I don't know what must have come over me as you are just the type of African intellectual I admire!"

He really wanted to believe that one, not just for the bit about his intellectual distinction, but even more so for what he could see bulging out of the U neck, as well as for the two arrogant nipples silhouetted against the thin material, having been sharply tweaked and pulled into their present state of prominence on the way upstairs. As his eyes remained glued to my neckline, I decided to exploit my tactical advantage and added: "I need your learned assistance for a little reserch into sexual practices", flashing him a knowing smile and running a very pink tongue around sensuously parted lips.

Having initially been unable to believe his eyes, he was

now unable to believe his ears and gasped in a stifled, little voice: "What do you mean by sexual practices?"

It was obvious from his attitude, quite apart from his visual violation of the contents of my corsage, that he would have traded all the information in the world on sexual practices in return for being able to play at Mummies and Daddies with just one of my bouncing boobies. Standing up I seated myself familiarly on the edge of the counter, giving him a fine view of thigh by allowing my skirt to ride up to the point where the ends of my pubic fringe were just visible.

I said: "I want to know about the Wasagu rites and whether there is any chance of my being able to take part in them".

I though he was going to choke, as the shock of hearing this half-undressed, blond goddess declare she wanted to participate in what he knew were wantonly bestial ceremonies, was more than he could take.

"But the Wasagu rites have been banned for years!" he spluttered, "In any case, no white woman has ever taken part; it's dangerous you know, the god is not a human being but a large ape; women have been killed — that's why the French banned them!" It was a sweltering tropical day, and even at that early hour the heat was producing unsightly stains under the armpits of his cheap white shirt, which was not as clean as it might have been.

"Could you at least show me the material you have?" I replied, turning my torso even further in his direction and leaning forward again to let him enjoy the full benefit of my vertiginous cleavage: "I am making a detailed study of African sex practices, and there is no better way of finding out about things than by doing them yourself; don't you agree?"

He was leaning so far forward to stare at my breasts that for a moment I thought he might fall into my decolleté, but he managed to recover his balance and gasped: "Stay where you are; I will see what we have". He started by consulting a dog-eared card index in a rusty metal box, grunting when he found the appropriate entry, removing the card and exclaiming: "You will have to wait here; it may take some time". With a farewell, visual dive into my divide, he tore himself away from the phantasm of a lifetime to disappear into a labrynth of giant wooden filing racks; no doubt a heritage from the colonial era, as they were massively made from a hardwood of currently prohibitive cost.

It was clear that the librarian was so chronically timid I could probably have obtained everything I wanted without giving anything in return, not even a nipple. But that old black magic had me in its spell, and I already knew that out of sheer vice I just had to get myself laid by the insignificant employee, back there somewhere in the middle of all the books, racks, dust and dead flies. I could not bear to have to leave the whole stuffy set up until I was stained with sweat and sperm and dust, until my neat little outfit was soiled and crumpled, so that when I wore it walking the few blocks back to the apartment everyone would know I had just been giving away my ass on the floor in a dingy corner, simply because I could not stop myself rutting like a bitch on perennial heat.

Almost mechanically, like a robot programmed to carry out a specific function which could hear only a metallic voice repeating: "Fuck the librarian! Fuck the librarian!" I walked round the counter into the no-man's land of anthropological science, where I could hear my victim shuffling around between two rows of racks a few feet away. I went up to him slowly, rolling my hips invitingly.

"What are you doing here?" he cried agitatedly, "What are you doing? Visitors are not allowed in this part of the library! Go away! Go away immediately!"

"Oh there you are!" I replied, as if surprised by my good fortune, "I just thought I might be able to help; Ah! Look! May be it's up there!" Pointing irrelevantly to a shelf from which a mobile ladder was hanging, I slipped past him, turning to rub my still erect nipples across his chest, and was several rungs up the ladder before he had time to react. I stopped climbing when his angle of vision was at its most revealing and hitched up my skirt, giving him a panoramic view of the barest and most beautiful white bottom he had ever seen, sliding my feet to the opposite ends of the rung and holding on to the ladder higher up, so I could push my ass out and give him a close up of everything that makes life livable.

As nothing happened I turned to see what was delaying his reaction, being already very excited myself, as the librarian would have seen had he taken the trouble to look closely at my slit, which was glistening with love-juice. But the silly goon was standing there like a statue with his nose only a few inches from my privates, seemingly incapable of making the move which would transport both of us into a sordid heaven of sweaty sex.

His breath was coming in staccato gasps, but something was grounding his take-off. To make the visual effect of my backside even more impelling, I reached back between my thighs, and after ostensibly dipping a middle finger into the source of the secretions, I slid it away from the exquisitely shaped lozenge to push it firmly into my asshole.

That must have been the 'Open Sesame', for suddenly everything hit the fan, as two clammy hands seized my hips and a bristly mouth crashed landed on my vulva, giving me hardly enough time to pull my finger ploppily out of my butt. Never had my meat been eaten with such ravenous abandon, hanging there on the ladder with the African chewing away at my loins like a half-starved cannibal, his incisors scraping over my clitty with a sensual finesse that belied his apparent inexperience.

When he reached the point of drawing his lips back between his teeth to give me a bloodless vaginal munching, I started to flip; but it was only the beginning, as once he had prepared the terrain,

I felt a very boney finger slide into my slot, followed progressively by its four companions, including the thumb. I had never known fingers like them, not just because they were abnormally long and seemed to reach up into places where no fingers were ever intended to go, but they were virtually skeletal, having hardly any flesh or sinew. Feeling as if I was being violated by the hand of death, I thrilled to the morbid sensation as he pushed his bunch of elongated bones in and out of my sex, rotating them as far as his wrist would turn, and jumped when I felt his over-length tongue, which was in proportion to the rest, slide snakily into my other orifice.

But it was above all those scrawny fingers that were driving me crazy, scraping away at my vaginal walls until I was on the verge of a psychotic fit. When suddenly he pushed in the whole of his hand, right up to the wrist, I thought I was going to faint, as I opened up as if in childbirth, enabling his fingernails to reach the downtown end of my womb. "Further!" I groaned, "Further you bastard!" and, removing one of my hands from the upright I was grasping to support my weight, I jerked up the front of my bodice to liberate my nipples, which were as stiff as starch, so I could rub them against the rough jute bindings of the volumes on the nearest shelf.

He must have fingered me to the extent of at least three orgasms up there on the ladder, before unplugging his handfull of abrasive knuckles and passing an arm round my waist to lift me down for a gum-running kiss, prior to pushing me onto a concrete floor which could not have been swept let alone washed for months if not years. While he was unzipping his fly I discarded my clothes and sat there primly, dressed only in ballerinas, pinching and twisting my nipples to keep them sprightly pending the unveiling of the librarian's penis, which seemed to be giving some trouble owing to the tightness of his jeans and the rigidity of his erection. Finally the jeans slid down his legs with a jerk, and his manhood, which was also as thin and long as the rest, sprang vigorously into view.

I was not so much impressed by its length of around ten inches, which although respectable was rapidly becoming commonplace in my stud-starred universe, but by the abnormal thinness of its stem in relation to the swollen grossness of the deep purple glans, which was similar to my husband's, and I was almost sorry he was not there to see someone else fucking me with his prick. Reaching out excitedly I forced it down to an angle that enabled me to thrust it between my lips, and then jammed the bloated toadstool down my throat, only stopping when my nose collided with his abdomen.

It was now my turn to do the eating, and I was very greedy indeed, sweating in the humid heat of the South-facing room while shuttling his fossil voraciously in and out of my mouth at a speed which had him off in less time than it takes to say sodomy. Releasing the glans to direct the sperm-splash onto my boobies, which hardened all over when I rubbed in the viscid effusion, I gave him no time to recover his breath, immediately remouthing his member to discourage any tendency to go limp. When the response was a heart-warming reassertion of rigidity, I pulled him down by his emaciated manhood and threaded it gratefully into my sex.

Lusting there in the dust and the dirt, with the bodies of generations of dead insects etching itchy patterns in the skin of my back, soaking with sweat and smeared with sperm, I said to myself that if this was not the crummiest fuck of a lifetime there must be something pretty horrendous still to come! But did it turn me on! The idea of defiling my impeccably clean and perfumed body with the accumulated grime of the Tribal Department's filthy floor was so ecstatically humiliating that my loins dribbled anew at the mere thought of the abasement, and I writhed around on my back to cover as much of my anatomy as possible with all that heavenly muck.

Goatee was grinding away with utter dedication, socking it to me as thoroughly as I had sucked him earlier on, withdrawing completely before stabbing my slit with his distorted dagger, while grabbing my breasts as if they were essential to his balance, his boney fingers leaving angry weals on the otherwise unblemished skin. Wrapping my calves around his emaciated buttocks to increase the impetus, I came and went and then came back in again, but even more volcanically, sobbing with erotic elation. My God was it good while it lasted, but he could not hope to keep it up at that rate for long, and I was shortly flooded by a second spouting, way down inside, that felt almost as plenteous as the first, most of which was now spread stickily over the off-white shirt.

We lay there panting like long distance runners after an uphill stretch, bathed in sweat and as stained and dirty as a pair of ragamuffins who had spent the morning in a city gutter. Before offering me so much information on the Wasagu rites that I could have written a thesis, goatee spent at least five minutes tenderly mouthing my breasts as we sat there recovering on the fouled-up floor. He was out of luck as I was in the middle of a dry spell, but as he had no means of knowing anything about my milky ways he never knew what he missed.

Finally, I threw my skirt and bodice away behind a pile of packing cases, promising to send someone to collect my prize of information. Returning to the apartment clad only in the cloak, my predatory instincts thoroughly aroused, I ran into a burly black leaving the building by the service entrance, which I had used in the hope of just such a chance encounter. Without either permission or preamble I slid my hand into the front of his shorts, grabbed his huge appendage and towed him into the trash bin room which had already been the scene of some of my more spectacular misdemeanors.

In a trice we were naked and in another he was rampant,

undeterred by my general state of dirt, his massiveness sliding deeply into my mouth as if such a transition and my misconduct were the most natural things in the world. I just had time to scoop a little of Goatee into the neigboring tunnel, while rising, turning and bending, before he arrived at the speed of an express, crashing clumsily into my secondary siding, which is were he was programmed, as I had canted my hips at an angle that made sodomy a certainty.

Gasping and sobbing with unholy joy, I orgasmed immediately and continued to do so until his piston-like penetration ended in a surging that filled me with ineffable fullness.

Afterwards it was easy to run up the stairs to the nearest bidet and soap myself back to cleanliness in a bubbling bath.

Chapter 20

Reducing my love-making to the minimum necessary for psycho-sexual survival, and taking a lot of it kneeling, from behind, so as not to interrupt my reading except during orgasms, I spent the next three days at the villa totally immersed in the profuse documentation lent by Goatee in violation of his library's most cherished rules and regulations.

In fact I need only have read two works: 'Bestial Wasagu Practices', a Ph D thesis written in 1961 by Henry M.Kirchner, an American anthropological student who had spent several years in what was then the Upper Volta on a research grant, and 'Les Rites Sexuels Bestiaux des Wasagu de la Haute Volta' by the French ethnologist Charles Leroy-Vallon, written in 1932 before the the ban drove the sect underground, a work which therefore had the merit of having been compiled at a time when its life was not distorted by a need for secrecy.

Although neither of the authors had of course been present at any of the ceremonies, they had both questioned numerous participants and eye-witnesses and painstakingly cross-checked their information before drawing conclusions. The ban remained in force, as it had been confirmed by the two newly independent nations, but was in fact more respected in the breach than in the observance. In practice the authorities tended to turn a blind eye to what was going on, provided there was no scandalous publicity, as the cult operated in a poorly defined frontier area, and to do anything effective would have required energetic joint action on the part of both states. This was not forthcoming as they had more important problems on their hands.

As with many African oral traditions its origins are lost in the proverbial mists of time, and in any case I was more interested — for obvious personal reasons — in the details of the rites insofar as the female participants were concerned, above all the woman chosen for the final honor which, in bygone days, had sometimes ended in tragedy.

To cut a long story short, the paramount deity of the Wasagu was a virility god believed to be incarnated in an extremely rare species of large ape, known to science as the 'Schlieberg Ape' after the name of the German zoologist who had identified the strain. The three specimens which had found their way into western zoos before the last world war had failed to survive captivity by more than a few months, and since 1945 the open hostility of the Wasagu, intent on protecting their sacred animal from extinction, had precluded any further captures and even resulted in the death of one well known trapper.

Standing up to five feet eight, the origins of the animal are still a matter for learned speculation, Schlieberg's original conjecture being that the species had developed from crossings between female gorillas and male chimpanzees. No plausible explanation could be found for such an exceptional zoological deviation, other than the chance encounter of isolated groups of female gorillas and male chimpanzees, after the accidental destruction of their normal partners, coinciding with the absence of any other groups of the same types of animal in the region. The Schlieberg Ape is only found in small numbers in the Wasagu area.

The rites can only take place in years when a suitable male specimen has been trapped — on average about two out of three. They start with an initial phase devoted to the selection of the best candidate from among fifteen women, themselves chosen in the manner already described. I should perhaps emphasize that cases of marital opposition are extremely rare, as husbands genuinely perceive the choice of their wife as a great honor. The successful candidate takes part in a ceremony whose purpose is to secure the ritual mating of woman and animal.

The first phase of the selection process could not be simpler. It involves the fifteen candidates being made love to by all the fully-fledged warriors of the tribe, that is to say seventy-five males in their prime. This collective love-making takes place in a jealously guarded and purpose-built compound enclosing four large huts, three of which are disposed around its perimeter at points corresponding to the positions in the heavens of certain ritually significant stars at the time of the summer solstice. The fourth hut, in the middle of the compound, contains a caged area which is only used for the mating ceremony. All these installations are entirely razed when the rite has been completed, as the venue is changed every year for security reasons, and only chosen ten days before the start of the first phase by a chapter of co-opted elders, who also decide which women are acceptable candidates.

During the love-making each woman is served by a handmaiden who carefully washes her mistress after every act, as the female participants are called on to make love fifteen times a day.

At the end of this phase, which lasts eight days, the warriors meet in conclave for two days with the elders in the central hut, to recommend the best candidates. This debate is lengthy, detailed and surprisingly solemn, no facetiousness being tolerated. The qualities of each woman are examined individually and commented on by the warriors, after which the elders withdraw to make their choice in secret.

The chosen candidate is then subjected to a ritual preparation and cleansing lasting for a further two days, during which she is fed — or more accurately feeds herself — exclusively on warrior sperm, having to swallow the semen of all the male participants who are made to ejaculate in her mouth.

When these preparatory rites have been completed, the ape-god's bride is led into the central hut, where her would-be lover is waiting for her in the cage, and in the presence of the elders and the warriors she offers herself to the formidable animal. Failure to achieve coitus involves disgrace and casting out from the tribe, and there is always the risk of a nasty accident, as in theory, under no circumstances would the audience intervene (although they do in fact), because for all those present the Schlieberg ape is the inviolable incarnation of their God of Virility, whose every act is sacred, and closely studied by the tribal soothsayers for augurs, the best of course being a successful copulation and the worst a brutal assault on the bride.

The risks are not however anything like as bad as they used to be, as since the ban, and the relatively tolerant attitude of the authorities following independence, the sect uses various means to reduce the risk of accidents that might result in unwanted publicity, the most effective being the sedation of the ape with a local laudanum brew. A nice balance has to be struck between over-sedation, which would result in a somnolent fiasco, and the under-sedation which could bring with it the risk of the dreaded accident. As for the bride, she is given a powerful aphrodisiac to enable her to overcome any old-fashioned aversions. In fact, the chosen woman is finally in such a state of psychological and sexual elation she requires little encouragement, particularly in view of the consequences of failure.

In the event of a successful outcome, the woman becomes High Priestess of Love and officiates at the sect's virility ceremonies during her year of office. At the end of this period she hands over to a successor, whose assistant she becomes, but in the event of her not being replaced, for one or other of the reasons already mentioned, she continues in office with reduced prerogatives until a successor materializes. For the Wasagu such provisional tenures are deemed to be bad omens, and additional ceremonies have to be held to try and propitiate the evil spirits responsible for the interregnum.

I could go on to describe the ritual aspects of the ceremonies in detail, but this is not a treatise on West-African folklore.

What I had learnt had made me highly excited, as to be chosen to become the bride of the Ape-God and a sort of high priestess of sex, would be the apotheosis of my adoration of the African male. In his work on the subject, Charles Leroy-Vallon mentioned the fact that an eighteen year-old French girl, the sister of the school teacher at Gaoua, had been a voluntary candidate in the 1920's and had completed the first phase, thereby giving the lie to Goatee's assertion that no white women had ever taken part.

With this precedent on the books it never entered my mind I might be unable to enter the strange competition, as that was now my unshakable and even frantic ambition. If chosen for the supreme honor I felt calmly confident of my ability to seduce and master the monster; otherwise what a wonderful way to die — being raped by the divine descendant of a gorilla!

But I had a problem: the summer solstice that year fell on June 21st, my birthday, and allowing for the eleven days of preliminary rites, there was little time left. It was already June 2nd and I had to convince Etienne — or more precisely tell him of my decision, as there could be no question of a refusal — drive 350 miles over frequently rutted tracks to reach the area, find out where the rites were to take place and get into the act.

Etienne had been following my research activities with an amused condescension, but when I told him of my project he hardly surprisingly refused outright. The reason was typical: he was not concerned by the idea his wife might be laid by seventy-five black studs and a gorilla and be mangled in the process, but by the fact he could not get away to make the trip with me and watch, as he had a series of important meetings in June that could not be postponed.

After the biggest quarrel of our married life, I told him that even if he did not agree I would go in any case, as by then I was financially independent, having inherited a substantial sum under my father's will two years earlier. It was a choice between the break-up of a marriage, or rather a perversion pact with an remarkably beautiful woman, who shared and humored his depraved tastes to an exceptional degree, or allowing her to take an initiative fraught with considerable danger to satisfy her obsessive sexual curiosity and appetite, which he would have surely approved had he been able to be present as a voyeur.

Finally he gave in, as he could see I was absolutely determined, and even had it been possible for him to accompany me he would have seen almost nothing, as all outsiders could hope to glimpse were the comings and goings in the compound, as copulation took place indoors out of sight of bystanders.

It was agreed I would take the two Senoufos as body-guards and the Range Cruiser, which was a heavy duty safari model, and the following morning we left the villa with thirteen days to spare until my birthday.

My pilgrimage to the supreme shrine of black sex was on the road.

Chapter 21

We travelled light, there being no call to do otherwise. As I needed only the simplest not to say the scantiest of clothes, our luggage consisted mainly of such utilitarian items as sleeping bags, a tent, a first aid kit, a chain-saw, two rifles, currency, a purse of gold coins and boxes of hygienic inserts. I may have been leaving the world of the bidet but had no intention of abandoning my notions of personal cleanliness, although I would soon learn to copy the irreproachably clean Wasagu who did it all by hand! We also took a crate of Scotch as a well known way to make friends and influence people!

There were no road problems for the first 350 miles, as after the ferry over the lagoon we followed the major highway running North from Dabou through Toumodi, where we spent our first night. At my insistance the three of us slept in a room containing only one double bed.

It was the first time I had actually slept as opposed to gone to bed with an African, even if there was little emphasis on sleep! Being a lucky girl, I had not just one ardent black bedfellow but two, who had both been rationed for the past few days and were intent on catching up on their Leda-loving in the space of a single night. I have no clear recollection of how we fitted into the bed or how Banda and Wakaba fitted into me, other than very well, very stiffly and very often. Everything seemed to merge into a half-waking and half-sleeping amalgamation of perspiring bodies, joined together by columns of rigid black flesh in an obscurity relieved only by a guttering night candle, lit by Wakaba to provide a more congenial setting for love than the hotel's neon tube.

In a half world of flickering twilight reflected off sweaty skin, my golden sheen stood out in sharp contrast to the Senoufos' black lacquer. There was permanently at least one rampant ebony organ to contain, as with the possible exception of Vicky, I was the most powerful aphrodisiac either of them was ever likely to take, with the result that during the time needed to bring one of them to orgasm, the other had recovered any momentarily impaired virility and was ready for further insertion.

There was no oral sex as it would have been superfluous. The two Senoufos relayed each other in my body without any time or need for stimulation, other than that provided by the guttering illumination of my glistening nudity. We did not even kiss, except when I imploded under the pressure of come, causing the lover who happened to be on that side to take my lips in his mouth to prevent me waking the whole hotel with one of my bouts of erotic hysteria.

The room resounded to my heavy breathing, interspersed with gasps and sighs, to which the Africans responded with grunts and growls of pleasure when they came. My night was a long drawn-out climax made up of troughs and peaks which paraded in uninterrupted succession down my highways of love, producing secretions which merged with the acrid sweat of my loins to form a strong-smelling deposit on my inner thighs, whose bitter fragrance filled our nostrils with the odor of human bitch on heat.

Most of the time my active lover would take me from behind, stretched out on his side, leaving room for his resting colleague to lie facing me, either half asleep or fondling and sucking my throbbing breasts. They had rarely been so prolific as on that night, seeping unaided to add a further flow of stickiness to the moisture in which our bodies were already bathed. From time to time the bitter bouquet of my thighs made my waiting lover impatient, and I would ease the member of his laboring partner out of my sex, turn him gently onto his back and sit down on his stake, impaling my rectum and freeing my regular hole for a frontal approach. However, if the rigidity of my lower lover's erection was not equal to the tightness of my anal tunnel, I would turn and kneel over him, receiving his jack in my vaginal box while presenting my acquiescent asshole to his accomplice in sex.

Occasionally, if one of my partners looked like flagging when it was his turn, I would raise my thighs to offer him a lick of my elixir of love. As its virilizing effect was immediate, the momentarily interrupted round of rutting would resume, with the resurrected member storming my citadels of sex. It must have been when the candle finally guttered itself into extinction that we fell asleep — none too early for the hard day's travel ahead.

The following morning we continued on through Bouaké and Ferkessédougou, whereafter the road was unsurfaced, crossing the Burkina Faso frontier to reach Banfora, whence the track to

Gaoua and the Wasagu Territory branched off to the right. We passed the night near Banfora, lying on top of our sleeping bags — one of which was double — as the humid heat made them quite unsuitable inside other than for a lecherous Turkish bath!

We pitched our camp on a beach on the left bank of the Komoé River. To obtain some relief from the broiling humidity, which was as bad as I had ever known, I would kneel naked in the tepid water, bending forward from the waist, my buoyant breasts floating on the surface from which my buttocks emerged, enabling a Senoufou to kneel behind me and use or abuse whichever of my holes tempted him most, while splashing cooling water over our shuttling bodies.

At one stage Wakaba's thighs were busily slapping the back of mine as he remorselessly plumbed my rectal privacy, causing his cannon balls to swing wildly in their supple sack and thump my clitty divinely at the end of each pendular cycle. I was on the point of coming, and concentrating on making the the most of it, when I had a feeling we were being watched. Looking up the river bank I saw an adolescent standing some twenty yards away, drinking in the spectacle we were providing and masturbating quite openly.

"Get him for me!" I cried out to the watching Banda, who only needed ten seconds to catch up with the fleeing boy and bring him down to the edge of the water. The young African was rolling his eyes and struggling feebly in the Senoufo's arms, as if in fear for his life, although my plans for him were far from ill-intentioned, as I was about to help him enter the sublime universe of adult sex, rather than waste time and sperm on self abuse. Banda held him in front of me, knee deep in the river, and with Wakaba still basting my butt as if nothing else mattered, I reached out for the now flaccid sex — whose former arrogance had disappeared during the scuffle — and started by running a finger nail round the inside of its surprisingly long foreskin.

He liked that, and his confidence started to return at the same time as his erection, which revealed a surprisingly well developed member for such a youthful subject. Pausing for a moment to ride the wave of an anal orgasm brought on by Wakaba's skilful sodomy, my face screwed up in a grimace of lust, I advanced my lips towards the adolescent glans, provoking a further bout of struggling on the part of the boy, who must have thought I was a cock-eating cannibal, which I was in a certain manner of speaking, although no one ever got hurt!

Of course, when I slid him the whole way in he liked it even better, particularly when I held the sheath nibblewise between my lips to run them back and forwards over the stem. But I could already feel from the heaving of his testacles, which I was cradling in the palm of a hand, that he would not keep us waiting, and sure enough, a few seconds later I received confirmation as his ejaculation bounced off the roof of my mouth.

Up to then I had paid little attention to the taste of sperm, having gratefully swallowed everything I received orally without asking any soul-searching questions. Why I should have started to think about it at that precise moment, when the boy's effusion was still bubbling around the back of my throat, I will never know, but it suddenly struck me that the substance I had always taken for granted had a subtle flavor which varied from one pair of balls to another. This was also true of its density, which went from thin and diluted to thick and creamy, the latter requiring more of a conscious swallowing effort.

May be it was the knowledge I might have to live off sperm for two whole days, if I was chosen to be the Ape-God's bride, that made me conscious of the fact I not only liked the taste of come, but that my considerable experience had sensitized my palate and made me something of a connoisseur. There were the nutty ones, the milky ones, the salty ones and the sweet ones, to mention only a few of the main gastronomic groups of semen. No sooner had I realized I liked its taste than I felt a craving for large quantities, as if suddenly hooked on sperm, and greedily swallowed the sample which was already available, before starting to suck the boy's penis again with redoubled energy, as I wanted everything his immature sack could give, right down to the last drop.

After two or three minutes of devoted fellation, he laboriously managed a second coming, trickling a few drips of an anaemic liquid which confirmed my suspicion there was nothing more to be obtained from that source, as he had probably ejaculated two or three times when watching my Wakaba ass-fuck. However, as he was still as rigid as a metal girder, I pushed him round behind, telling my reluctant servant to withdraw and let the boy take his place. Once installed he proceeded to rabbit-fuck my rectum — whose gaping distension made it an obvious first choice — at a Houari-like speed, reaching under my body to pinch and pull my nipples with a surprising brutality, until a third and arid orgasm put a breathless end to his initiation.

Thrusting him out of the way I turned to face the still unsatisfied Wakaba and, sitting with my buttocks planted firmly in the mud of the river-bed, I finished him off by hand and mouth, swallowing the whole of his member, flicking the sheath several times on the way out, before sliding it back in again right up to the hilt. When I felt him holding on and trying to fight it, I speeded up the action until he could no longer stand the pressure and came prolifically in my mouth. "That's more like it!" I thought, reasoning more in terms of quantity than of quality, as the taste was a trifle bitter and difficult to classify.

Banda, who was still standing in the water, must have wondered what had got into me (apart from a lot of cock), as he was my next victim, albeit a willing one, laughing happily like some playful black Apollo when I spun round to face him and, taking hold of his hips, caught the end of his god-like member between my lips. It was already half erect from the spectacle I had provided, and slid easily down my well-trained throat, but to make him discharge was quite another matter. Unlike Wakaba — who was still kneeling disconsolately in the water, looking as if he had been conned out of a proper coming — Banda refused to comply, and try as I might he simply got stiffer and stiffer but did not ejaculate, not out of any desire to frustrate, but because he was used to hosing me further down.

I realized I was going to have to do some explaining if I were to enlist their support for my training campaign, and said to both of them: "Leda eat come for Wasagu". It worked like magic, although Banda had to utter a few words to Wakaba by way of translation, as the latter's understanding of my pidgin French was unreliable. He then pushed his penis back between my lips, with the obvious intention of cooperating, as after no more than a minute of mouth-fuck, which I amplified by sucking steadily and tonguing the underside of his glans as it slid to and fro, he blew his balls, which were at least as full as Wakaba's. Unlike the sperm of the burlier Senoufo it tasted like nectar, and to avoid waste I was careful, when finishing him off, to jerk the terminal spurts directly onto my tongue, before greedily licking the residual drops off my hands and fingers.

The next day we struck East along the track towards Gaoua, as the Wasagu area we had to reach was some fifty miles from Banfora, near the headwaters of the Kéléworo, a tributary of the majestic Komoé, one of the great rivers of Africa. For the first few miles the going was tolerable, but we were at the end of the rainy season, which had been severe, and the track soon degenerated into a series of quagmires which had to be negotiated with the winch, attaching the hawser to one tree after another to pull the car through seas of mud that could be hundreds of yards long. I remained at the wheel while the two Senoufos attached and detached the tackle.

At one point the track passed through an expanse of forest where it disappeared entirely under a layer of mud more than a foot deep at its shallowest, with hidden pot holes of up to three or four feet in depth. It was in one of the latter that the Range Cruiser came to grief, the winch proving useless as the vehicle had tilted over forwards into the depression.

Fortunately a gang of lumberjacks were working nearby, and Banda — who could speak the local dialect, as he came from a branch of the Senoufo who had their roots on the border of the Wasagu Territory, where he had lived for many years — sought and obtained their assistance with a powerful winch used for hauling tree trunks out of the undergrowth after felling. They succeeded in pulling the car out backwards, and it is certain we would have been helpless without the aid of their specialized equipment.

I was wearing only rubber boots and a mid-thigh length débardeur, which was already far from immaculate, as although my place was behind the wheel, I inevitably got down from time to time, and my legs were spattered with mud. The débardeur, owing to a heavy shower, clung to my body in a most revealing manner, particularly for my nipples, which were not only visible through the thin material, but prominently outlined as well.

Once our vehicle had been salvaged, we returned with the lumberjacks to their adjacent camp to down the customary drink, producing one of the bottles of whisky we had brought along for bartering purposes, as in those parts a quart of Scotch or Bourbon could be worth its weight in gold. The effect of the alchohol was to arouse the lumberjacks' interest in the beautiful blonde — as the beautiful blonde's interest in the lumberjacks could be taken for granted — and I was the object of ribald comment I could not understand, but whose general sense was perfectly clear and exciting, as they really were rippling mountains of primitive, black muscle, whose girths would have made the average Sumo wrestler look like short rations on a long diet.

I smiled engagingly at the foreman, a colossus of upwards of three hundred pounds, with a huge stomach and biceps which were as big as my waist. I had already singled him out as a must for my collection of do-it-yourself phantasms, and dreamed happily of wrapping my golden thighs around his mighty carcass, always assuming they would stretch that far! Banda and Wakaba looked at me nervously, as the atmosphere was becoming more and more feverish. They suggested we pay the lumberjacks for their services and leave, as they were afraid the situation might degenerate, which is precisely what I wanted and I was not to be deflected from my purpose.

"Tell chief I show what pay" I said to Banda, who dutifully translated, imagining I was going to ask him to produce a bank note or even a gold coin so we could settle and clear out. The colossus nodded and stared at me, his expression becoming more and more incredulous, as the blond goddess peeled off her sodden débardeur to reveal a torso that would have made Praxitiles want to scrap the Cnidian Venus. He was so astounded, I also had time to step out of my rubber boots before he reacted by sweeping me up in his arms and running out of the clearing to find a suitable place to collect my down payment.

However, I had my own ideas on that subject, as watching the giant wading around in the mire earlier on had reminded me of a female mud wrestling match in New York to which Etienne had taken me two years previously. My husband had disappeared with a friend a minute or so before my desire suddenly got out of control — an unusual event at the time — leaving me with no other outlet than the men's toilet. Chosing the mightiest specimen from the array at the urinals, I cock-towed him into the nearest cubicle, blithely oblivious of the spraying the backs of my legs were receiving in the process. Bending low over the john for what I intended to be a lightning if frenzied fuck, after having wrenched my mini-skirt up over my hips, I reckoned without my improvised lover's ideas on duration, as he gave both my holes such a blissful and lengthy amount of punishment that the soreness took several days to subside. Therefore, when the lumberjack put me down to take me leaning against a tree, I skipped agiley passed him and ran like a hare for the scene of our debacle with the car, as nearby the mud was just the right depth and of an almost creamy consistency.

Floundering into the quagmire with just enough lead to avoid being hauled out, I turned at bay when the morass came up to my knees, scooping up handfuls of the oozy substance to smear it lovingly over my breasts, depositing particularly generous daubs on the nipples, before reaching down to run a mud-coated finger repeatedly in and out of my slit. After a moment's hesitation on terra firma, my increasingly incredulous Goliath, bellowing like a wounded bull, ripped off his shorts to dive in after me, and as he waded laboriously towards his goal I had my first sighting of his massive member, trained sights-down on my sex like the barrel of a naval gun being used to shoot a minor target out of the sea. Gulping with trepidation, I wondered whether my highly extensible but human-sized aperture would really be able to accommodate all that manhood.

But it was too late to turn back, as there was no way I could stop the oncoming Juggernaut. The only course was to throw myself under it like an oriental devotee, hoping the crushing process would leave some of my sexual organs intact for the future. Crouching down on my haunches, I felt my buttocks sink into the mud and, splaying out my arms behind me as supports, I arched my body upwards, spreading my thighs to receive the inevitable.

To my surprise, as I was expecting a direct onslaught, the

lumberjack fell to his knees in front of my proffered sex and, pressing his mouth gently against my muddy vulva, started to eat it with lips and a tongue whose suppleness and strength soon had me on the verge of hysterics. He had a way of sealing his upper lips hermetically against my lower ones and then blowing me up like a balloon before sucking the air back down into his lungs, driving me out of my mind at the same time as softening up my vaginal cavity. Once he could feel I was ready for his excessive overcrowding, he dipped his monument in the creamy morass and pressed its end against my gaping inlet to effect an unexpectedly painless entry, the huge mudlark sliding slowly into my private depths, incredibly sinking the whole way in without splitting me assunder.

On the contrary, I enjoyed a feeling of erotic bliss which racked my body with instant come, although I somehow managed to avoid collapsing into the mud, despite a momentary faintness following another orgasmic earthquake. My partner placed his hands on either side of my shoulders to support his body over mine, obtaining the necessary impulsion by flexing both arms and ankles, while I responded by thrusting my pelvis upwards to meet his incoming tree trunk, falling back as he withdrew until my buttocks hit the mire. At the third or fourth coming I could take it no longer, and collapsed in the ooze, whereupon the giant picked me up as if I had been a feather, spun me round, plopped me down on my knees, and penetrated me from behind as easily as an outsize piston sliding into its cylinder.

I kept on climaxing, losing all count of the number of orgasms, which merged together indistinguishably, my breasts swinging at each impact with their nipples trailing in the mud. I somehow sensed he would be a one-come client but that it would be one hell of a discharge, and before he signed off I badly wanted to feel his Eiffel Tower in my alternative. The mud was so fine it acted as a painkilling lubricant, but suffering or no suffering I still had to have it, and reached back between my thighs to remove the massive bludgeon from my regular slot and line it up with my butt.

It was not as easy as with the front door, and I cried out in passing pain as his massiveness sundered my sphincter. Little by little the clouds of suffering dispersed, and I signalled to the lumberjack to continue, as he had considerately stopped his inward movement when he sensed that my distress was genuine. After a few slow motion strokes he was able to speed up progressively until I started to come again, even more intensely than before, while broadcasting my usual anal filth:

"That's it you butt-bugger, mud-fuck my bung! Do you hear? You black bastard! I want to die of dirt! Rip me open and fill me fully! Ram the rest into my butt you randy shit! There's still some outside. Further! Do you hear me! Oh My God! My God! Now! Now! Bang harder! Come now you lousy shit-holer! Aah!"

He came in no uncertain manner, hitting me with such a final thrust that I went headlong as he collapsed, pressing me heavily into the ooze while filling my bowels to bursting with a flood of molten, mud-stained cream.

When he rolled off my flattened carcass I lay there half-immersed for several minutes, fighting for the recovery of both breath and mind. I then struggled out of the morass and made it to shore, only to find the three other lumberjacks waiting in ambush, after having followed the spectacle I had just provided with palpably erective interest. No one then setting eyes on me for the first time could have imagined there was a strikingly beautiful woman under the layers of filth that covered me from head to foot. But the lumberjacks knew, and grasping me by the ankles and wrists they transported me bodily to another clearing, where various machines and vehicles were parked, dumping me unceremoniously on the ground to start up a motor. This I was shortly to discover belonged to a pump, as two of them lifted me by my hands and feet, while the third hosed me with a powerful jet of water, changing me back into a human being in a matter of seconds.

No sooner had my hair been rinsed than I was set on by all of them together. One lay on his back while I did the splits to straddle his elephantine loins, my widely distended sex avidly swallowing his already erect penis, the second ponderously transpierced my other, well oiled orifice, as I crouched astride his colleague, and the third worked his organ laboriouslyly in and out of my mouth. Of course, they were not individually as phenomenally hung as their foreman, but were nonetheless mightily equipped, and there was so much of them in me at the same time they took up a heavenly amount of space. While coming, I muttered a passing prayer of gratitude to the genie of genes who had endowed my inlets with such an infinitely extensible elasticity.

From time to time they changed positions with my willing assistance, and as the ground was little more than a marsh, at every switch I was hosed down again. Of course I came like crazy, for once without vociferating, as my mouth was full, and it was to become even fuller, as I asked Banda — who was nervously watching our happening, wondering if and when he should intervene — to explain that I was a potential ape-bride candidate, and was practicing my swallow. All three of them readily and bawdily agreed to come in my mouth, and as they had been isolated in the forest for the best part of a week, three of the biggest sack-fulls of sperm in West Africa went gurgling down my throat.

When it was all over Banda whisked me muddy and naked into the Range Cruiser, before any of them decided to come back for further helpings, starting off down an alternative track the lumberjacks had cleared when the permanent way become unpracticable, and not stopping for another two miles. Although I was almost out for the cunt, I have a recollection of my breasts aching as they have rarely ached, and of pleading with Wakaba, on whose lap I was sitting, to suck them for me. The pain may have been due to low atmospheric pressure, but when Banda stopped I made him take over one of the throbbing boobies, and it took my two big black babies, whose heads I kissed and cradled lovingly, almost twenty minutes to suckle off enough milk to cure the pulsating discomfort.

After the end of this digression, we soon reached the junction with the secondary forest track that led to Dapchi, which had suffered less damage from rain and traffic. We made good progress by jungle standards, emerging on the edge of a wide plateau some two hours and twenty miles after leaving the lumberjacks, including the time needed to look after my dairy problem.

The atmosphere had become less oppressive since we had started to climb steadily, weaving our way through a universe of scrub and wilderness with virtually no sign of human activity other than the track, which was no more than a rough path widened by a bulldozer. The rutted surface and the heavy duty springs made the life of the rear passenger, on the seat over the wheel arch, a living hell of vertical knocks and shocks, as the suspension faithfully telephoned every irregularity.

I do not know what had got into me on that particular day — maybe it was the excitement of knowing I had arrived in Wasaguland — but I was still as whoresome as all havoc, despite the epic hammering received from the lumberjacks. The sight of poor Wakaba banging up and down in the back and being projected three or four inches into the air when the Range Cruiser hit a bump, gave me a lecherous idea that even Vicky would not have been ashamed to call her own. Telling Banda to stop to let me climb up behind, I helped a perplexed Wakaba remove his shorts, and stiffened him up nicely with a bout of greedy mouthing.

The débardeur and boots I had been wearing before disrobing, to pay off the lumberjacks, had been abandoned in the forest, and I had replaced them, after our stop to relieve my breasts, with a long T shirt, which was all I was now wearing, other than for a lot of dry mud. Once Wakaba was erect it was easy for me to sit down and impale myself on him by simply rolling the shirt up over my hips.

Telling Banda to drive on to Dapchi as fast as he could, I used the grab bar on the inside of the roof to raise my buttocks just clear of the Senoufo's thighs, allowing the road to do my fucking for me, as every few yards there was a jolt that projected Wakaba into the air, that is to say into me. As we could not anticipate where the bumps would come, and Banda, once he got the hang of the game selected the worst ruts to give us plenty of action, there were occasions when Wakaba's cock was rammed into me so hard, before I could compensate by raising my body, that the repeated impact of his steely thighs on my velvety buttocks left weals which took time to disappear. The same was true of my breasts, as they were the only things Wakaba could grasp to keep his balance, a squeezing that also left tell-tale milk stains on the shirt.

By the time we reached the outskirts of Dapchi I had come twice, although it needed a lot of concentration not to be put off by the lurching and bumping of the vehicle. We stopped again briefly to allow me to go down on Wakaba, as I wanted him to come in my mouth, being rewarded with yet another bumper scrotum of sperm — my fourth of the day.

As I was taking my training seriously, there was no reason why I should not achieve the highest Wasagu standards in time for the trials!

Chapter 22

Once we had made ourselves presentable, involving me in a thorough wash and a further change of T shirt, we forded a shallow, fast-running stream to enter the village of Dapchi where Banda had lived out most of his adolescence. As the altitude was nearly two thousand feet, the buildings, which radiated from the headman's dwelling in the central clearing, were mainly rectangular adobe huts, as reed walls of the lowland regions were not the best protection against the chilly nights of winter. On the day of our arrival the weather was that of a perfect late afternoon in June, with a temperature of 90°F and no trace of the mugginess we had left behind in the forest.

The appearance of a Range Cruiser and a white woman was a local event, drawing a crowd of idlers, among whom Banda's foster father, who could hardly believe his good fortune when he saw the splendid young man standing by the vehicle in the central square. After they had embraced and launched into a lengthy exchange accompanied by much gesticulation, Banda introduced me, and despite the purpose of our voyage, which was hardly respectable by Judo-Christian standards, I was interested to note that he treated me with the utmost deference.

Later Banda explained that everything relating to the rites was sacred, particularly the persons of the candidate brides, and any manifestation of derision or disrespect would not just be out of place, but certain to destroy any hope of my candidature being accepted. This was fine by me, as sex was about the only thing I took very seriously, and as the Wasagu rites had become the mainspring of my existence, there was no likelyhood of my being anything but spontaneously enthusiastic.

Banda's most important discovery was that the rites were about to be celebrated for the first time in two years, as after more than six weeks of unsuccessful stalking, a fine young Schlieberg ape had been trapped three weeks earlier. My heart bounded when I heard the news; we might not yet be in business, but at least we knew there was a market for our product if only we could sell it!

A hut was put at my disposal, consisting of a single room with rush matting on a compacted earth floor. The Senoufos installed my meager posessions before we followed Banda down to the washing place, which consisted of a dam across the stream where those wishing to take a bath did so in public with other like-minded people. There were already several bathers of both sexes and all ages and as there was nothing else for it, I slipped off my ridiculously elegant Parisian bath robe and stood there on the bank in the nude, savoring the sudden silence that descended on the milling crowd as they all — man, woman and child — stared at my exposed body. The women did so in envious fascination and the men with undisguised lechery, as few if any of them could ever have seen a naked white woman before, or for that matter such a desirable female of any color.

A group of young boys waded across from the other bank and clustered around me, unabashedly visiting my parts with their busy little fingers until their attentions became so pressing Wakaba had to chase them off. But the feeling of their eager fondling remained, particularly the one who had thumb-nailed my weeping pussy from behind, as in the state of overwrought excitement which had been building up ever since the beginning of the Wasagu expedition, any sexual contact was enough to make my nipples and clitoris erect and start me secreting with desire.

Standing knee deep in the water, protected by my bodyguards as much against myself as against the greatly increased number of bathers — above all men — who had suddenly taken to the water and were trying to get as near as my guardian angels would allow, I occasionally felt an exploratory hand, that had managed to avoid their surveillance, furtively caress a breast or buttock or try to insinuate itself between my thighs before a Cerberus drove it off. Nothing would have pleased me more than to have given myself to everyone who touched me or even just wanted to, as the fleeting contacts made me feel giddy with lust, and I remember hazily saying to myself: "If you're like this now, what on earth will you be like when they've given you the aphrodisiac?"

I washed myself all over, crouching down on my haunches to deal with the corners that were in chronic need of soap and water, an initiative that really tested my protectors' effectiveness, as every man within touching distance seemed to be trying to help me, and quite a few did. As soon as I was hauled out from under the scrimmage — where I felt one very stiff member slide into me from behind, but only once, or maybe twice, and it really was exquisitely rigid — I waded out into deeper water to shampoo my hair, before turning to emerge from the foam like my Botticelli original.

As I did so, I saw a group of older men, among whom I

recognized Banda's foster father, standing on the bank and scrutinizing my body as if it were an objet d'art undergoing appraisal. The intervening bathers had disappeared, as if by magic, and I heard Banda's voice telling me to remain where I was and turn round slowly, making a sign to me when I had completed one revolution to turn back again the other way.

After they had finished studying my anatomy from all angles they actually applauded, before approaching and starting to touch and feel me without any of the consideration due to a masterpiece, kneading and prodding my flesh in the same way as a butcher assessing the worth of an animal in a livestock market. I of course understood this was part of the initial selection process, and even enjoyed their dispassionate fingering, which was quite different from the earlier bathing romp. They finally pushed me down on my knees to allow several pairs of hands to explore my vulva, pulling my inner lips wide open and generally probing around, making such a thorough job of it that despite the clinical approach I became even more excited and doubled my dribble.

One of them, who appeared to be their leader, was then passed a smooth truncheon-like object, which must have been all of three feet long and two inches in diameter, with knotches down one side. He proceeded to push into my vagina, only stopping when he could force it in no further, and although I regretted its sudden withdrawal, I was proud to note the expression of admiration on his face when he saw the number of notches I had been able to contain. Expecting a repeat performance with my anus, I arched my back in pleasurable anticipation, knowing the position would make for a seductive gape and offer easy access. I was so sure that an ass-test would take place, and of their unstinted approval when they saw how far their yardstick had gone in that way round, I was frantically disappointed when Banda told me to get to my feet as the inspection was over.

Petulantly refusing to move, I stayed there pouting like a

spoilt child and spat out: "Leda want ass rod!" at the bewildered Senoufo. His reaction was admirable, as after the barest moment of hesitation he had exactly the right reflex, which consisted of taking his hand back to shoulder height and giving me the biggest slap on the fanny I have ever received. I yelped in pained surprise and the crowd of by now entirely male onlookers, many of whom were unashamedly masturbating, burst out laughing, which did not stop two anonymous donors from directing splashes of sperm onto the middle of my back. Returning to my hut in the nude, I twisted myself this way and that to scoop them off, licking my fingers with the uninhibited enthusiasm of a street urchin savoring an unhoped for ice-cream.

No sooner had I cleaned myself up than Banda turned on me furiously, berating me in his basic French for running the risk of upsetting the whole apple cart by behaving like a randy white slut. When I laughed unheedingly he pulled me across his knees and gave me a marvellous hiding, the noise of his palm striking my willingly proffered buttocks echoing round the walls and filling me with a frenzied excitement he did nothing to relieve. When I tried to seize his member under the loin cloth, he pushed me roughly against the wall and strode out of the hut, leaving me in a state of chronic erotic anguish, with only my own fingers to calm my craving. For the time being, in Wasagu territory, Banda was the lord and master and I the humble servant! But all that might change.

Squatting down in one of the corners, I opened my thighs until my legs were at right angles, pressing them back against the walls, and started to make the best of a bad job, stroking my clitty into an upright posture before pinching it rythmically in time with a lingering caress of the sensitive inner surface of my vaginal lips. But it was not the same thing as Banda's gorgeous banger, and I had to work much harder to obtain a less conclusive result.

I was finally on the point of being rewarded with an orgasm

when, above the sounds of my own gasps and groans, I heard a rustle of feverish whispering outside the hut, followed by the appearance around the door of a boyish face. It belonged to the ring leader of the group that had tried to molest me in the bathing pool, and to say he was dumbfounded by my pose would be an understatement. His eyes protruded from their sockets as they focused on fingers which flickered in and out of the gaping, almond-shaped gash at the point of my furry triangle, while his loin cloth was contemptuously brushed aside by the force of an instant erection.

Overcoming a surge of disappointment, as I had hoped the noises off signified the arrival of my bodyguards intent on doing a lot more to my body than guarding it, I beckoned to the boy, who entered the room followed by no fewer than six other adolescents. This raised my hopes, as I felt it ought to be possible to get as much milage out of seven smaller members as out of two big ones, provided they were handled with care and imagination. In any case I was simply spoiling for a fuck, as my orgasm was still waiting impatiently for an opportunity to happen, and as nothing more promising was likely to materialize, I decided to take the plunge.

Wasting no time, I fell to my knees and reached out for the ring leader's hardness, which was much bigger than I had anticipated, as seven solid inches is a lot of cock for a boy of his age, although I was to learn later that big male organs are a well known Wasagu characteristic, being one of the facets of their veneration of virility.

Giving the gleaming helmet a quick coating of spittle, I pulled him round behind me, using his member as a tow-bar, as my vaginal tension was unbearable and I was grateful to feel him sink to his knees and jam himself clumsily into my seeping socket, making us both come instantaneously, as I could hold on no longer. His premature ejaculation was due to the intensity of the stimulus of an unprecedented situation, as he was actually and incredibly sticking his black banger into a golden goddess, whereas I was already so worked up that all he had to do was push the plunger down once for me to blow my bottom, shuddering and clenching my fists until the knuckles went white.

The next boy tried to rush round behind me to stop my gap as soon as the first withdrew, but tripped over my arm in his headlong haste, and I hauled him back round front to pop his skinny six-incher between my lips, where it was literally child's play to provoke a discharge which filled my mouth with a thin but nutty brew that I gulped down avidly. Only after I had emptied the last driblet from his hose-pipe was he allowed to return to my rear and spear me with unabated stiffness. While he was sawing away methodically at my slot, for what must have been his first, unsimulated fuck, I started to mouth number three, who was short and thick, forcing me to part my lips to a surprising degree for someone of his age.

When I realized the extent of their adolescent impetuosity, I delayed their orally-induced ejaculations by squeezing the necks of their scrotums to stop the semen escaping until the duty fucker out back had hosed me with his second coming, whereupon I would release the stranglehold and empty the boy I was fellating with a few deft sucks, after which he would pass round behind me for his turn in my passage. It went on like that until all seven had done the grand tour, the five who were queuing up killing time by playing with my danglers or rubbing their admirably erect organs over my sweaty back.

I changed to a crouching position at the end of round one and pressed my asshole into service. Using an eloquently obscene sign-language to convey my wishes, I soon got the message across that they should wriggle feet-first between my widely parted knees and under my raised buttocks when it was their turn in front, while one of their comrades went backside to enjoy a much more accessible bumfuck. But this was not all, as taking a leaf out of

Vicky's football saga, apart from the obvious one in the mouth and two on the sides chewing my nipples while I jacked them off, I also managed to fit the remaining pair of pricks into the hairiness of my armpits, although my other commitments made it difficult for me to keep them sufficiently tight, and they kept slipping out.

During the organization of all this team work I had not been consciously able to spare a moment for my own pleasure, but when the boys were finally sorted out into neat little sucking and fucking units I let myself go, screwing and guzzling and frigging away frantically under the writhing blanket of tender, ebony flesh, until my self control disappeared in a July the 4th of a climax, to which those of my young lovers who still had something left in their little black sacks contributed according to their means. It was the end of a perfect orgy, and all seven of them picked themselves up wearily but contentedly and made for the door, giving me juicey thankyou kisses and titty-fondles on the way out.

Chapter 23

After a further round of tumultuous public bathing the following morning, with Banda and Wakaba fending off one attack after another as the local lady killers made the most of my still unofficial status, Banda returned to the hut with me to confirm I had passed the purely physical selection procedure with flying colors, and that a further examination would take place during which my capacity for making love would be put to the test.

Smiling in lecherous anticipation, I reached tentatively under his loin cloth to see if he had forgiven me for my unseemly behavior the previous evening. His hardness said he had, but he regretfully told me I was no longer entitled to make love, other than as directed by the elders. If I passed the forthcoming test — and it was evident I would romp through it unless they produced a rhinoceros — I would have to abstain from sexual intercourse until the start of the ceremonies, when I would of course give myself to the warriors. My case was special, as I was white, foreign and unmarried, involving ritual complications I could not hope to understand. The purpose of Banda's tutorial was to explain the Wasagu rites, but after a certain amount of hesitation on his part, and a lot of specious argumentation on mine — as I maintained that the love ban he had just announced did not extend to a little fondling — he agreed to being caressed during his narrative.

Watching my blond head bob up and down over his member, as I crouched between his outspread thighs, Banda explained the Wasagu set up, adding little to what I already knew other than for one or two details. He told me, for example, that he had been the youngest participant ever, when granted special temporary warrior status at the age of nineteen to enable him to take part alongside his fully-fledged seniors. Certain women whose beauty and reputation for passionate love-making were local by-words were automatic candidates, whether they were willing or unwilling, the only admissable grounds for refusal being illness or pregnancy.

Selection was signified by the village elders, who were also responsible for examining voluntary candidatures such as my own, which were in fact extremely rare, only three others ever having been entertained. A woman who had already taken part could not be drafted a second time unless both she and her husband were willing. Widows were not eligible as deemed to be unlucky.

So ended the lesson, which was probably a good thing, as his breathing was becoming more and more labored. My head bobbed up and down faster and faster as, open throated, I slid his pulsating member in and out and out and in until I felt his balls, which I was caressing almost reverently, tremble in their velvety sack. Bracing myself for an ejaculation that completely filled my mouth, I lifted it up to his face as soon as I had swallowed the fragrant sperm, for a deeply delving kiss, as although I was not truly in love with

Banda in the normally accepted sense of the word, during our actual love-making I adored him so intensely that it came to the same thing.

"Banda fuck Leda before others come", I whispered, running my tongue round the inside of his ear. I do not know how he reconciled his reaction with what he had just said on the subject of my present status, but, sacrilege or no sacrilege, he spun me round onto my knees, cradled my breasts in his hands and homed his sex directly into mine without any guidance. He had developed an almost supernatural ability to penetrate me in any position without either of us touching his member, which was drawn into one or other of my holes as if by some form of magnetism. In the villa, when we met casually, all I had to do was put a foot up on a chair or bend over a little for Banda to enter me without any preparation or manipulation, as if our genitals were permanently seeking each other, only requiring a sufficient degree of proximity to be drawn inexorably together.

I responded passionately, as we had both suddenly realized we were about to forgo this uncanny compatibility for at least two weeks, and possibly even longer if I became high priestess. With other men I might come until I could hardly talk let alone walk, but with Banda it was just as intense without even trying, the mere fact of his presence turning me on immediately, doing away with the preparation cycle as he erected and I humected instantly and spontaneously as soon as we looked at each other.

In our last weeks at the Villa Laguna, without even trying, we would often be sexually linked more than thirty times a day, wherever we happened to meet, for a few strokes at a time, or even just to remain genitally joined for a second or so before passing on. Unless our union developed into a full scale act of love, these moments of fleeting penetration replaced the smile or nod of recognition we would probably have exchanged under normal circumstances. There were times when I would sit for ages impaled on his lap while he fondled my breasts and nibelled my neck, talking quite naturally to him or other people about everyday topics, as if it was no more than a brotherly arm around a sisterly shoulder, even if I did make rude noises and pull impolite faces every now and then when I came. After having experienced such phenomenal harmony as part of one anothers' bodies, we were shocked by the size of the void their seperation would leave. Because of this our farewell love-making in the hut had a quality of slowness and reverence which recognized the exceptional nature of the moment. We came as one, our mouths sealed together in clinging suction.

We had barely unplugged when a formidable matron entered the hut carrying a saffron-colored bodice and full-length skirt. She signified to Banda that the time had come for him to leave, eying both of us suspiciously. When he had gone she used sign language to indicate I should put on the clothes, whose modesty came as a surprise after the revealing nature of my own wardrobe, although their concealing function was to be short-lived. Once she was satisfied I was properly dressed, she told me to sit down in the middle of the end wall, and when I had done so went out. A few seconds later the elders of the village filed into the hut and squatted down against the other three walls, with the headman facing me at the opposite end of the room.

The matron then returned and helped me disrobe, making me squat down again on my haunches in the same place, pushing my legs as far apart as possible and showing surprise when the outsides of my thighs touched the wall on either side of me, as she obviously could not have known how supple I was. Despite the fact the elders had already not only seen but manhandled my body, they fell strangely silent when it was exposed in such a revealing posture, as they could see deeply into the dark recess of my sex, whose humid inlet yawned back at them invitingly.

The matron again disappeared, and from outside I heard a

rattling sound which I could not identify, and a rhythmic pounding of feet followed by the precipitate arrival of a personage who must just have escaped from the cast of a down-market remake of 'King Solomon's Mines'. There could be no mistaking the witch doctor of childhood adventure stories, although this version was dressed in a manner which would have given the Hays Office second thoughts about suitability for a general release as with the exception of a monkey-head mask, he was stark naked. This might have been acceptable on the grounds of authenticity were it not for the fact that his penis and scrotum, of a goodly size even in repose, were painted bright pink, as was the divide of his buttocks. He was brandishing a scourge of knotted leather thongs mounted on a thick cylindrical handle which ended in a minute monkey skull.

In spite of a state of wild elation he stopped dead in his tracks when he saw the vision of exposed white beauty against the wall, and I was proud to note the stimulative effect of my charms was such that the frightening pink object between his legs jerked convulsively and began to stiffen. It would have seemed this was not in the script, as he tried to hide the tumescence with his free hand, breaking into what must have been a spell-casting dance to the accompaniment of a single tom-tom, jumping around in time with the drum beats and thrusting the handle of the scourge repeatedly in the direction of my vulva while barking a series of blood-curdling imprecations. There was however nothing he could do to curtail his erection, which just got harder and harder until it was sticking out at better than right angles. Finally he had to give up pretending it did not exist, and seemed surprised when the elders' reaction indicated they thought it was a good omen, even if it was not in the plot.

This restored his confidence, and he started to scourge my breasts with a symbolic gentleness. When he saw I liked it, as I cupped them in my hands and held them out for more, he increased the dose, without ever going beyond the point of no return, as if I were to be the village's candidate — and it was an honor for a community to present a candidate, let alone a winner — I must on no account be disfigured in any way. This suited me fine, as I was all for a little painful stimulation just so long as it stopped short of the stupidly excessive.

When the witch-doctor had started his antics it was all I could do to remember Banda's advice about keeping a straight face, but the scourge was quite another matter, as it really turned me on. My nipples were so hard I thought they were going to burst, and when he began handing out the same treatment to my widely exposed loins, using a little backhand flick, I really flipped, running the whole gamut of erotic sound effects while the thongs of the scourge grew moist with the secretions of sex.

Finally, when my ecstasy became insurmountable, I lunged forward onto my knees to catch his hips in my hands, swallowing the whole of his pinkness in an effortless movement which was the result of years of practice. He was so surprised he tried to shake me off but I held on with all the strength of my lips, and no doubt fearing damage to his sheath if he tried too hard he abandoned his attempts to dislodge me. The elders must have told him to stop resisting, considering what I was doing to be interesting proof of my love making abilities, as I suddenly felt his opposition cease, leaving me free to display my mastery of fellation.

It took me no more than twenty seconds, combining hand and mouth irresistibly, to obtain ejaculation, which I made visible to the elders by holding the glans three inches away from my mouth when I felt his baubles tighten, allowing the jet to fly across the intervening gap before surging down my throat. Alternatively jerking and sucking I finished him off to the last drop, noting with relief that none of the pink paint seemed to have come off at the same time as the sorcerer.

To a man the elders gasped in admiration, but I had much more to show. Arching my body over backwards with my feet apart, until the palms of my hands touched the ground behind me, I again offered my wide open sex to the witch-doctor for what I had rightly guessed would be the crowning feature of his act. Sure enough, he reversed his grip on the handle of the scourge and placed the monkey skull against my inner lips, which were still brimming with Banda.

Very gently he rotated the abrasive object, pressing slowly inwards to the accompaniment of my groans of pleasure, and was surprised when my sex sucked in at least ten inches of the formidable instrument without any further effort on his part. As there was none of the resistance he had expected, he increased the speed of the in and out movement, shuttling the handle rapidly to and fro in my loins, which I stimulated even further by rotating my hips. The tension due to my position, and the vaginal friction of the fast moving cylinder, soon boiled over into an orgasm I proclaimed out loud for all to hear, flailing my thighs together against the hand which held the protruding exremity, before allowing my streaming body to slump down breathlessly onto the rush matting.

The chastened witch doctor left the hut feeling I had stolen his thunder, and still realing from the effects of the most diabolical blow-job of his bedevilled career. After a long drawn out murmur of approval the elders became quiet again, but this was a more ominous silence than before, and I wondered apprehensively what could possibly be in store for me. I resumed my 'back to the wall, squatting on the haunches with the thighs wide open' position and waited, pinching my nipples to keep them sprightly.

I did not have long to wait, as a curious shadow fell across the doorway, announcing the arrival of the most extraordinary creature — I suppose he or it was human — I had ever seen outside a museum, as the mammal which was now standing framed in the doorway was a perfect specimen of the cave-dwelling pithecanthropos — the missing link between monkey and man.

He stood no more than five feet two, with a sharply receding forehead, cavernous eye sockets, a flat nose with widely flared nostrils, a barrel chest and long arms falling almost to the ankles of his short, bandy legs. His body was entirely covered with bushy brown hair, the only indisputably human feature being hands and feet which looked strangely out of place on a frame that was animal in every other respect. He was naked — if the term can be applied in such a context — and, half hidden in the jungle of coarser, pubic hair that overgrew his loins, I was conscious of the shadow of a large and menacing presence.

The headman made some gutteral noises, and the creature, whose eyes had been rivetted on my vulva, looked at him and replied with a deep, rumbling grunt. Glancing at me in a way that made my flesh crawl, he or it reached down for the shadowy object, which was already starting to protrude, and began to fondle it with one of those grotesquely human hands, while a sinsister parody of a smile revealed long yellow teeth that could never have belonged in the mouth of any mortal man.

At that particular moment I came as near as I had ever been to running away, and suddenly found myself wanting, of all people, my mother — a woman I had hardly known, let alone loved. I wanted to cry on her lap and ask why I always had to make love with people whose oversized things hurt her poor little baby, hoping to hear her reply that the nightmare was over and I could go back to my own warm little bed in the room with the pink curtains. The crisis only lasted ten seconds, but I very nearly made a break for it before returning to the realm of rutting reality and the feeling of fascination which was normally the first stage in my progress to sexual delirium.

Later Banda told me that the creature, who was clearly about to posess me, had been born some fifteen years previously to a woman who had been the ape-god's bride nine months earlier, and given birth to him during her tenure of the office of high priestess, dying in the process, as her changeling weighed more than fourteen pounds. Although the idea the Ape-God should have fathered this thing is biologically untenable, those are the facts.

The Wasagu did not herald this offspring as the true reincarnation of the god, as the omens at his birth could not have been worse, but as there could be no question of openly repudiating what might have been a divine manifestation, he was brought up and provided for at the community's expense, being shown every sign of respect. From time to time he was used for ritual sexual acts such as the one he was about to perform, and lived with a half-crazy woman who had the physique of a weight-lifter and was capable of standing up to the strain of his sexual appetites. No western specialists had ever been allowed to examine this strange specimen, who was fiercely protected by the Wasagu, with the result that the blood test which might have revealed a genetic miracle was never carried out. Test or no test, it was clear to me that the first step up the ladder which might lead me to the Ape-God, was going to be an ape-man!

The fondling of the once indistinct object, which had developed into a slow masturbating movement, had produced a threatening erection whose pale pink helmet — which owed nothing to the artifices of paints or dyes — pointed at me like an instrument of capital punishment.

"Take it easy Leda!" I said to myself, "Take it easy, it's going to be OK, you're going to love every inch of it as you always do when people stick things into you! Relax!"

I took a hold on myself, as success in this ordeal would be my meal-ticket for the big banquet later on. To show good will I pouted provocatively in the thing's direction, looking it straight in the eye, and, running my finger invitingly up and down my gash, noticed with mild surprise that even allowing for Banda's contribution I was very moist indeed, my assertive vulva having taken over the decision-making process from a hesitant mind. Muttering a prayer to heaven knows what deity — maybe the Ape-God — I slid down onto the floor and lay there on my back with my thighs wide open, offering my overflowing loins to the biological freak.

His eyes lit up lewdly, and lumbering ponderously towards me he fell to his knees prior to slumping down between my legs, supporting his weight on his hands, which he placed on the ground on either side of my shoulders. In this position, his bushy hairs divinely scratching my inner thighs, he made an unsuccessful but relatively gentle attempt to penetrate, his glans missing the hole and riding up over my clitty, which jumped excitedly at the clammy contact.

Stretching down to where his organ was lining up for a second attempt, I took hold of the inhuman object, which had the unpleasant feel of raw meat, rubbing it lengthily over my clitoris, whose response was to become as hard as hell and send lascivious signals all over a body that was now erotically alive to the potential of monkey business. Lowering the glans I threaded it carefully between my inner lips where, once engaged in the channel, it slid easily the whole way in, the ape-man then allowing his body to sink down onto mine to give my vulva a prehistoric pummelling.

For me this was when the balloon went up, as the feeling of a savage, hairy body in contact with my skin, and the pungent smell of aroused animal, suddenly had all my sensory glands working overtime. Raising my thighs so I could cross my legs behind his back and pull his torso further in, I slid my breasts from side to side to scrape my nipples over his barrel of coconut matting, reaching round behind his thighs to grasp a pair of formidably bristly buttocks and press them into me for even better measure.

Although his mouth was within inches of mine, to start with I could not bring myself to kiss it, the feeling of revulsion being too strong, even when the scraping of his pubic bristles set my clitty on fire. But after a few minutes, when the effect of his coming and going was beginning to take its toll and I was shaping up for my first major climax, I myself planted my lips against the dark brown folds and forced my tongue into the unlovely chasm.

I am sure he had never been kissed like that, even assuming he had ever been kissed at all, as to start with his lips remained motionless. Then, little by little, he got the idea, reciprocating with his abrasive tongue to give me a high ride on the big dipper of sex, as it was so unnaturally long and strong he could push it right down my throat and tickle my tonsils. Pulling at his buttocks more and more frantically I speeded up the action, gasping for breath as one orgasm collided with the other until I felt him flood me with my first skinful of Neolithic sperm.

Spinning round unexpectedly into a sixty-nine position he started to guzzle away at my gash, emptying it of both his own and Banda's effusions, while at the other end, his unabatedly erect member fucked my mouth excitedly until he came again, filling my throat with the bitter taste of his viscid semen. In a flash he was back in my sex, but this time lying on the floor so I could straddle his hips, offering swinging breasts which he squeezed and teased, extracting their milk immediately. After the usual astonishment of discovery, he nibbled away almost apologetically at the nipples with those formidable yellow teeth.

We finally had to be seperated by the elders, as neither of us wanted to stop; he having no desire to return to his weight-lifter of a wife after making love to a white woman of exceptional beauty and erotic devotion, whereas I would have loved to go on fucking the only authentic cave man left over from the dark ages. It goes without saying that after such an exceptional performance the elders approved my candidature without even withdrawing to deliberate, and as they filed out of the hut there was not a dry foreskin between them.

Chapter 24

Most of the following day was devoted to the leisurely choice of the handmaiden who would attend me during the candidature phase, continuing to do so during my year of office as high priestess should I become the Ape-God's bride and survive my wedding night.

I was escorted to a nearby hut, where the prettiest girls in the village had been assembled, and sat down on what must have been a headman's stool — as I had become a V.I.P — while the adolescents were presented one after the other. Each of them was stripped naked and made to turn round slowly, before executing a series of movements whose purpose was to exhibit the most intimate parts of their bodies. In the event of my becoming high priestess my hand maiden would be one of two female assistants, and as such have to take part in ceremonies which, by their nature, called for physical beauty and an insatiable craving for sex, being of course exonerated from the obligation to remain a virgin until marriage. There was much squealing and girlish giggling, except from the lovely teenager I chose without hesitation, as she appealed to me not only for her beauty, but for a feline sensuousness suggestive of a lesbian streak.

We returned to the house together between two ranks of idlers to pass our last night at Dapchi before journeying to the site chosen for the rites, which was kept secret until the very end, only the headman being aware of our destination. Katiola, as my young companion was called, had the formidable task of transforming my curly blond hair into something resembling the ceremonial style required of all female participants, which consisted of screwing it up into a series of 'sun-ray' plats across the top of the head from ear to ear.

As soon as we reached the hut I drew the rush curtain across the doorway, and removing the distinctive skirt and bodice supplied by the matron, squatted down on my haunches in the typical African position I was now starting to enjoy, as when in the nude the revealing angle of the thighs appealed to my exhibitionism. Gesturing to Katiola to undress and stand in front of me, I examined her even more closely than when making my choice earlier in the day. There could be no doubt she was a very lovely creature indeed, with boyish breasts whose contrastingly pronounced nipples were an invitation to inquisitive lips and fingers.

When she turned her back to me I was struck by the perfection of her legs, which were not only exquisitely shaped and muscled, with slender ankles and swelling calves, but the all-important fold at the back of the knee, which frequently lets down otherwise beautiful legs, was as flawless as mine. Without being asked, she placed her feet apart and bent down until her head was between her knees, revealing an uncommon degree of suppleness and the absence of inhibition I had sensed when I first saw her. Her skin was much lighter in color than the almost charcoal black of the pure bred Wasagu, and I was to learn this was due to her being a grand daughter of the French girl who had taken part in the rites in the twenties.

With the intention of testing her love-making ability, as their could be no doubt about her beauty, I beckoned to her to squat down on the floor facing me, as close as possible. She did so with the grace of a trained dancer, having been groomed to take part in certain Wasagu ceremonies involving a high degree of professionalism in this field, and as such was exempted from the normal chores of village existence, which accounted for the fineness of the skin of her hands, knees and elbows.

She was obviously thrilled by and grateful for my choice, and her devotion was soon to develop into a passionate affection she did her best to conceal from others, while leaving me in no doubt as to the nature of her feelings. Far from being displeased, I was delighted with this alternative source of lesbian pleasure, which I found restful after tumultuous heterosexual love, particularly as Katiola was an excellent masseuse, who skilfully mingled surprisingly advanced physiotherapy with the most devastating caresses.

Wanting to see what her reaction would be, I squatted there smiling, doing nothing myself. She smiled back at me enigmatically for a while, before making another move which was so graceful I only really noticed it when I felt her body touch mine, as she had edged up to me until her left instep slid under my sex with her knee pressing into the divide of my breasts. To make this possible she had passed her right foot under her left buttock to support her weight, enabling her to maintain her left leg at the correct angle, as in this way she could flex her ankle at will, using her instep to caress the inner lips of my sex. When I was thoroughly wet with secretion, she continued to fondle me with an incredibly versatile big toe, running it around the edge of the vaginal lips, prior to flicking my clitty in a way that had me begging for both more and mercy.

After declining all the possibilities of this unique position, she used her few words of French to tell to move slightly out from the wall, kissing me with a rare erotic fervor, her tongue fluttering round my mouth like a captive butterfly. She then slipped out of my arms, and lying on her back with her head between my thighs, lifted my vulva so she could slide her mouth under my crotch and start eating me behind. At the same time she stretched up with her legs to push my shoulders over backwards with her feet, so as to be able to take a nipple between each of her big and second toes, squeezing and pulling them with a dexterity that thrilled me to the sensual core. While she was doing all this, and a lot more besides — as her fingers refused to leave my genitals in peace — I admired the symmetrical perfection of her vulva, reaching out to touch the immaculate ellipse and run a pensive finger round the faultless almond of her greater lips.

She finished her delicious demonstration by massaging me to sleep, as she would on many a future occasion, whatever the number or sex of my bedfellows, relaxing my body with expert movements and pressures prior to stimulating it with artful caresses, the tips of her fingers transforming the most pedestrian parts of the body into centers of lascivious delight. My last memory before sleep was of an infinitely gentle orgasm that could have been either a waking dream or a dormant reality.

Next day I was awoken by Katiola in the same way she had used to lull me to sleep. I dreamt I was making love to a beautiful black swan, which was holding me in its wings and thrusting something wonderful between my thighs. The feeling was sublime, and as I came the swan pressed its beak between my lips, which was when I awoke to find Katiola's tongue saying good morning, my inner thighs being covered with the secretions of an orgasm that had dovetailed into my dream. We kissed lengthily and lovingly before walking down to the bathing area, where Katiola washed me intimately and openly before a strangely deferential public, not allowing me to do anything for myself.

Returning to the hut for the last time, my handmaiden dressed me in a white cotton toga that left the right shoulder bare, slipping on a garment which was identical except for its reddish color. She then arranged my hair in the ritual style, which was no mean accomplishment, as it had never been allowed to grow to the required length. After a struggle that retarded our departure, she obtained what all considered a satisfactory result, although I refused to look at myself in the mirror for fear of bursting out laughing. The headman then arrived and blindfolded both of us, after which we were lifted onto mules with primitive side-saddles, and set out for the site chosen for the celebration of the Wasagu rites: my ultimate phantasm was about to become a reality!

At what I judged to be midday we were allowed to dismount, retaining our blindfolds, and after food and drink resumed our journey. The afternoon ordeal seemed to be even longer, but I had no means of knowing what time it was when we arrived at our destination, as my watch, together with all my other western paraphernalia, had been confiscated. The journey seemed interminable, as we left an hour or so after dawn and only arrived when the sun was starting to set, having covered a distance of maybe thirty miles at little more than walking pace.

Our blindfolds were not removed until we had been led into a rush hut which must have been forty feet long by almost twenty feet wide. It gave every appearance of having just been completed, as the air was full of the distinctive smell of freshly sawn wood. Down either side there were series of rush mattresses in pairs, one slightly higher than the other and obviously destined to serve as beds for the candidates and their handmaidens. Against an end wall was an oblong platform with a wide bed whose head was set against the wall. Between it and the edge of the dais, facing the main body of the room, was a rectangular block of ebony with rounded-off corners which proved to be an altar. There were three doors, one in the other end wall, and two in the side walls alongside the podium.

It seemed I was one of the last candidates to arrive, as the room was abuzz with the chatter of women dressed in white or red togas, but when I entered a hush fell over all present about which I could do nothing, being unable to express myself. Katiola came to the rescue and said a few words in her seductive, low-pitched voice, which I assumed were an introduction, as I heard my ritual name, Akala, but there was virtually no reaction, the silence continuing unbroken. Deciding to do something myself I walked towards a group of women who were clustered together near the altar, but they seperated and turned their backs as I approached, and any attempt to reduce the tension was neutralized by their refusal of any form of contact. It was clear that there was something about me they found deeply disturbing.

Apart from their hostility, I noticed that all the candidates were beautiful, as it would have been an affront to the deity to offer him a plain or ugly bride, the same being true of their handmaidens, although Katiola still stood out like an exotic flower among untended weeds. My progress through this unfriendly gathering had taken me as far as the altar and the large bed, which I had no difficulty in recognizing as the one which would be used by the incumbent high priestess, who ruled over the candidates during the eight day period of love-making with the warriors.

Drawing on the experience accumulated in the two years that had passed since she had taken office, she would advise us on ways and means of becoming more sought-after and, above all, endeavor to detect and eliminate any attempts to discourage selection by being intentionally unattractive and frigid. When, after the first few days, it became evident who were the front-runners, she would try to prepare them psychologically and sexually for the ordeal, going as far as to take them into her big bed for personal tuition should she deem it necessary.

I knew all this thanks to my reading of Leroy-Vallon and Kirchner, as I was of course deprived of the benefit of any advice, having been incapable of communicating with anyone since leaving Banda, Katiola's few words of French not being equal to even the most elementary conversation. And yet, within a matter of days, the closest of links would be forged with Yamala, the high priestess, as although we had no language in common, from the moment of our first encounter we became intimate, as we both felt the same impulses at the same times in the same places.

In those few days we developed an improvised sign language which enabled us to exchange simple messages, but it was not until I recovered Banda that I was able to communicate with her in any depth. Physically she was the living image of the Rice-Burroughs jungle goddess I had imagined in the role of the Ape-God's bride, surviving the ordeal through a mixture of strength and energy, swinging from tree to tree on liana tendrils and running barefoot through the hostile jungle. She was perfectly built in an entirely different, much more robust mould than Katiola, her splendid musculature looking like an ad for a body-building method.

One of the two most extraordinary aspects of her appearance was her body-profile, as she had a rump which protruded way out on one side, and breasts that did the same thing on the other, making any form of movement in the nude a very voluptuous business. Her other exceptional feature was eyes which, instead of being the customary dark brown or black, were tawny gold with outsize pupils. Under her scrutiny you had the impression of being appraised as potential nourishment by a man-eating lioness, a comparison reinforced by the supple, undulating strength of a gait that recalled the Queen of Beasts stalking her prey.

While I was standing in front of the altar wondering how to

overcome the barrier which seperated me from the other female participants, the high priestess made her entrance, wearing a white, ground-length mantle with a silver hem which hid her body completely, as well as ritual headgear consisting of a wide and finely chased silver diadem surmounted, above the forehead, by a silver monkey mask the size of a human hand. She was flanked by two female acolytes, dressed in what looked like red, mid-thigh length gym slips, one of whom was the previous high priestess, who ordered us to stand at the foot of our beds, while the three doors were sealed from outside.

Upright, behind the altar, Yamala made a short speech in a low, vibrant voice, and then addressed a remark to her assistants, who promptly knelt down at either end of the block of ebony, where two leather-bound caskets had been placed, opening them to extract a series of liturgical objects which they laid out on the altar in an order and positions obviously governed by ritual considerations. The last articles to be removed from the caskets were two mummified sexual organs with scrota attached, that I recognized from their appearance, as well as from Leroy-Vallon's description, which referred to them as authentic, naturalized penises of Schlieberg apes.

When the acolytes resumed their places on either side of the high priestess, they lit the contents of two incensories, which gave off a dense blue smoke with a heady smell that rapidly pervaded the entire hut, obscuring the already ineffectual light dispensed by four oil lamps placed on low tables at intervals between the beds. Yamala began to intone a litany in her contralto voice, and I sensed, without any knowledge of the meaning of the actual words, that its subject had to be the exaltation of protracted physical love as an ideal prelude to bestial intercourse.

My deduction was soon to be confirmed, at least in part, when one of the acolytes went behind Yamala and, unclasping the silver fibula which held the mantle together at her throat, slid it off her shoulders to reveal the body I have just described, which was naked except for silver anklets and amulets carved with monkey themes. The spectacle of the nude priestess brought a murmur of awe from the lips of almost all the women present, a reaction which was only due in part to the sight of her spectacular physique, the other reason for this collective reflex being the psychological impact of a human body that had actually copulated with the Ape-God.

This was the signal for a general disrobing, and the example of the other fourteen candidates sliding out of their togas was all the explanation I required to imitate their gesture. Picking up a mace-like object from the altar, that proved to be similar to the scourge handle with which I had been consentingly violated at Dapchi, the high priestess, accompanied by one of her assistants, started off down the line of beds opposite mine. Stopping in front of each candidate, she would utter a few words before the acolyte pushed the woman down onto her bed, seperated her thighs and applied a viscid, white unguent to the inner lips of her sex. Yamala, reciting a further liturgical formula, would then place the monkey skull end of the mace in the proffered opening and press until it sank in as far as it would go, a limit she would only acknowledge when the candidate cried out in pain.

When my turn came, it was Yamala herself, looking me in the eyes the whole time, who took the unguent jar, leaning over me to apply the lubricant to the lips of my sex while allowing her huge breasts to dangle down onto my slightly raised thighs. I took this to be an invitation, and caught hold of their nipples, which protruded from deep purple halos the size of small saucers, stiffening them while she slid the monkey-wrench slowly into my vagina, stopping of her own volition at a certain point, no doubt out of fear of damage to my insides. Still staring into her eyes I grasped her wrist with both of mine and forced the object in even further, until the tears welled up and I had to stop with a strangled sob. When she withdrew and looked down to see how far it had penetrated, I was proud of her expression of incredulity, as I knew from the pain that I must have taken all of fourteen inches.

The next sequence in the preparatory ritual involved the use of the altar, each of the candidates being spreadeagled over it with their arms and legs hanging down over the corners. They were then penetrated by one of the ape-diljos — which were decidedly sinister in their state of perpetual rigor mortis — wielded by an acolyte in time with a tom-tom played by the other, starting slowly and then speeding up until the woman on the altar cried out. While this was happening, Yamala stood behind the altar facing down the hut, hand-fucking herself with the other diljo, really playing for keeps, as it was clear from the groans, speed and depth of penetration that she was not putting on an act.

As usual, I made a better showing than the others, arching my back to accentuate the penetration and thrusting my hips forward to meet the oncoming fossil. The high priestess was so near the altar I could touch her, and did so, deflecting the hand that was driving the diljo into her sex to make her understand I wanted to take over, supporting the weight of my arched body on my shoulders to free my left arm. She soon understood what I wanted, and staring at me intently with those astonishing eyes, which smiled without letting her facial expression betray any trace of humor, she handed me the diljo, probably thinking my awkward position would prevent me using the instrument effectively. That was to reckon without my muscular control, which enabled me not only to keep up the momentum but to increase the speed, reducing her to a state of trembling ecstasy in which I joined, as the acolyte had also intensified her pummeling of my loins.

Afterwards we went to bed, and I had fallen asleep following a Katiola orgasmic massage when one of the acolytes shook me awake, taking hold of my hand to lead me back to the dais and the double bed, on which the naked Yamala was waiting impatiently.

I needed no encouragement to wrap my body round that extraordinary physique, chewing her thick, negroid lips, fondling endless expanses of breast topped with rigid protrusions and fighting my way through impenetrable undergrowth to reach the promised land of loins.

Yamala, or Yamy as I was to call her, resembled me in one unusual respect, that of her hairiness, as the bodies of black women are normally devoid of hair, even the pubic variety being sparse. This was not however the case with the Wasagu, who cultivate their pubic hair with great care, snipping it off from early adolescence to make it bush out luxuriantly. In common with her fellow women, Yamy had the most riotous tangle of jet black, crinkly hair between her thighs and under her armpits, but in addition her legs and forearms were also covered with a sheen of hair, that continued over the bottom of her stomach and on her buttocks, but was so fine as to be almost invisible.

Our love making that night was like a fight for supremacy, as we instinctively realized we were destined to spend a lot of time together, and our desire for each others' bodies was mingled with the will to mark out our territories and not surrender the initiative. The result was a lesbian copulation of a rare intensity, during which we held back our orgasms for as long as possible, each climax being looked upon as a sort of delicious defeat, ending with our crotches interlocked around the monkey-mace, whose twenty-five inches of overall length were completely submerged in our struggling sexes.

As the high priestess took part in the final selection process along with the elders, being the only woman present, I could not help thinking, as I returned wearily down the hut to my bed, that I had not hurt my prospects!

Chapter 25

The giant gong which rang out at sunrise stood on the edge of the compound looking like a survival from a pre-war movie credit; at that time of the morning it signified we had one hour in which to bathe and eat before entering the arena.

Katiola made no attempt to disguise her jealousy of Yamy following my elopement to the high priestess's bed the night before. She knew what had happened as she had come and knelt in the nude beside the bed on the dais, hoping someone would invite her to join in the fun, but I was too absorbed by the tactics of my amorous assault on the high priestess and in defending myself against her counter-attacks to pay any attention to poor Katiola, who nevertheless stayed there quietly until we had gasped our last gasp of lecherous pleasure, and then guided me back to bed before massaging me to sleep and a last orgasm.

Far from tiring me or reducing my sexual stamina and appetite, these 'last thing at night' and 'first thing in the morning' comings stimulated both these qualities. I had never felt on such fine erotic form or had such a hunger for intercourse, the latter having increased in such proportions that there seemed to be no limit to my capacity for sex, to the point where I sometimes wondered whether I was not after all becoming a clinically certifiable nympho. And yet my partners almost invariably satisfied me, whereas in theory the true nympho remains permanently frustrated, hence her craving for more and more sex to achieve the perpetually elusive orgasm. The number of orgasms that eluded me could be counted on the fingers of one hand out of a total of maybe a hundred a week, and even they had a job getting away with it!

The compound had been built near a stream which supplied the bathing room of the dormitory hut with running water, where the handmaidens, after having filled jugs from a reservoir would pour their contents over their candidate's bodies before washing them carefully and intimately with palm oil soap. Being deep-washed by Katiola was as good as making love, as her supple fingers discovered recesses I never knew existed and conjured voluptuous sensations out of every pore of the body. When she concentrated on the sexual organ, caressing lather up and down my slit before diving in at the deep end I would come violently, clutching at her for support and sensual contact.

After drying ourselves we would pass back into the main hut for a breakfast consisting of meal cake and fruit, set out on trestle tables between the two rows of beds. We were still naked, only being issued with clean togas after leaving table.

At the second sounding of the gong we would file out into the enclosure, where fifteen warriors would be waiting to take their pick. The warriors were a co-opted body of seventy-five members aged from twenty to forty-five, being a survival from the tribal era when, as the personal bodyguard of the Chief of the Wasagu, they went into battle with him in the van. The selection criteria were now rather vague, unimpaired virility being of course a prerequisite, and although nepotism was inevitable, they were a fine body of men the mere thought of which made me tremble in lascivious anticipation and reach for my sexual attributes. Banda was in every way the model of the perfect warrior, but the fact of having left the territory disqualified him from re-election.

The fifteen Wasagu who were already strutting round the compound were veterans aged between forty and forty-five, and would be succeeded by the next fifteen in order of seniority, and so on until the fifth and final relay composed of the youngest and most recently co-opted. In the event of a warrior being taken ill or being impeded from exercising his functions for any other reason, he was immediately replaced by a reserve — the same procedure applying to the candidate-brides. After each bout of love-making the women would return individually to their quarters to be washed and then the routine would start again with another fifteen warriors.

The senior warrior in each group was entitled to make his choice known as soon as the last of the women, who entered the compound in any order, had left the hut, but tradition required that the candidates, dressed in their togas, parade to and fro like so many models in a fashion show whose purpose was to sell the mannequin and not the merchandise. After five minutes or more of this sauntering spectacle, the senior warrior would indicate his preference, who would then remove her toga and stand naked in front of him, turning round slowly to show off her body from all angles.

This routine was a survival from bygone days, when the warriors could and did exercise a right of refusal if the body revealed by the disrobing process did not live up to their expectations. Although this right continued to exist in theory, it had disappeared in practice, as all the bodies were well nigh perfect, and the striptease in question had become the occasion for the other warriors to compare bodies for future reference, as well as for the more determined candidates to reveal their persons as excitingly as possible to improve their chances. When this charming ceremony was over, the chosen candidate would follow her temporary master across the compound to the love hut, which was unfurnished other than for a thick carpet of fresh, sweet-smelling rushes, which was all that was proposed in the way of bedding.

The other women walked nervously around the enclosure in twos or threes and were visibly apprehensive. They still spurned me, no doubt resenting the presence of a foreigner who gave every impression of being able to win the nomination, and I found myself completely isolated. The warriors were now standing round in small groups, all of them staring overtly in my direction, as apart from my beauty and elegance of carriage, the participation of a white woman was a unique occurrence. The last warrior to have taken part when the French girl was a candidate in the 1920's had died two years earlier, and these different factors made me the automatic cynosure of male attention. I paraded past and around each of the groups, pirouetting to show off a body whose forms were emphasized by the thin and clinging cotton of the toga, as I had deliberately chosen one that was too small so that my contours would be more revealed than hidden by its folds.

When the five minute period had elapsed, the senior warrior — a strikingly handsome man with greying hair whose beautifully muscled body gave the impression of being half its real age — chose me without a second's hesitation. Turning to face him from a distance of only a few feet, I undid the primitive clasp which held the folds of the garment together, allowing it to slide off my shoulder and fall to the ground. After a moment of silence, the other warriors expressed their admiration as one in an outburst of excitement, all fourteen sending me soaring to the top of their pops, while the senior who had chosen me gave every impression of being unable to believe his good fortune.

Playing the game by the rules, but with much more erotic imagination than most, I stood naked in front of my future lover, looking him steadily in the eye, and slowly raised my hands to my breasts, lightly stroking the nipples before dropping a finger down to my loins to repeat the caress. I then turned slowly to the right, in the midst of one of those strained silences of which I had the secret, my hands still toying lazily with the sensitive buttons. When I was facing away from my senior, I seperated my feet to bend over forwards and provide him with an unimpeded view of everything, pouting back at him from between my knees.

He did not even give me time to complete the turn, sweeping me into his arms and running effortlessly across the compound to the love-hut, our lips joined in a deep-down kiss while my hand fondled his irreproachably rigid member, which had refused to continue in hiding under the loin cloth. Laying me gently on the rushes, he was inside me at the same instant, as my caress had lubricated my loins and prepared them for his arrival.

God it felt good! It was the first living member to have been up me for three whole days at a time when my craving for cock was increasing exponentially, and not even the artifices of Yamy and Katiola could hope to compensate for the absence of the real thing. And this one was incontrovertibly real, as it came and went in my channel, withdrawing completely at the end of each stroke to provide the thrill of re-entry at the start of the inward surge. It was too concentrated to last, something having to give way when our orgasms met head-on like express trains in a tunnel on a one- way track, with a resounding crash whose silence shook us to the genital core, as our mouths were still joined together in tongue-twisting conflict, stopping us giving audible vent to our climax.

When our lips finally left each other alone we lay side by side gasping for breath, as if we had just narrowly escaped drowning, gulping air into our heaving lungs while an overflow of sperm trickled stickily over my sphincter. I remember thinking dreamily that it was almost worth suffering three days of penis privation in return for such an orgasmic Hiroshima. But it was only the start, as although he might not have recovered his breath, he had never lost his erection, which was jutting skywards for all to see and waiting for the next countdown.

Rolling over onto my knees I straddled his hips, impaling myself expertly on the vertical stake. It was my turn to raise my loins slowly to a height that liberated the tip of his glans, before allowing my body to subside, driving the rigid bludgeon between my inner lips and back into the moist midnight of my sex. Raising himself on his elbows, he took first one of my jutting nipples in his mouth, and then the other, drawing his lips back between his teeth to be able to munch them without drawing blood. During his attendance on a breast I would pinch and roll the other nipple with one hand while doing the same thing to my clitty with the other, until I began to come, tightening my vaginal muscles to intensify our pleasure.

Rising and falling repeatedly I plunged his black sword of sex into my reproductive depths, imploring Priapus, the God of Penes, to accept them as a sacrificial offering and transfix me for ever in his Kingdom of Come. His only reply — if he ever even heard my prayer — was another geyser of sperm which gushed upwards at the top of an out-stroke, when the glans was momentarily released from my gaping tunnel, splashing my mucous membranes before creaming back down my thighs. I delayed lowering my body to savor the suspense, prior to collapsing onto the rearing column for the last time, just as my genitals were devastated by a force nine convulsion which made me writhe and cry out so loudly everyone else in the room stopped making love to see who was suffering such exquisite torture.

At the entrance to the hut two women looked after a strange little oblong table. When a couple began making love they would light a small candle and place it in a position corresponding to the situation of the lovers on the floor. The candles would gutter and go out after twenty minutes or so, and if a couple had not finished when this happened, one of the attendants would tap the man on the shoulder to signify that time was up.

After the senior's second orgasm I had rolled over on my back, as there were only two or three minutes left, which my partner spent investigating my breasts, having just discovered their secret. But I was going through a virtually dry phase, which was probably just as well, as it avoided what might have been a pointless distraction at a critical stage of my campaign.

Between each love-period and the time spent promenading and walking to and from the huts, each phase lasted half and hour plus twenty minutes washing and resting for the women. As there were five teams of fifteen warriors, just over four hours were necessary to complete a cycle. There were three full cycles every day meaning that each woman had to make love fifteen times, anyone who was unable to execute her contract being automatically and definitely replaced by one of the reserves, who took over her bed in the hut as well as her handmaiden. When the turn of a team of fifteen warriors came round again in a subsequent cycle, the warrior who had had first choice the last time went to the back of the queue, ensuring that everyone had at least one first choice during the eight days of love-making.

I should perhaps point out that although fifteen times a day may not sound impressive when compared with the scores of many prostitutes, it has to be remembered that all the women were supposedly participating whole-heartedly, with an average of maybe three or more orgasms a lover, putting an entirely different complexion on any such statistical comparisons.

Katiola was of course waiting for me proudly when I returned to the hut for washing, as it was a great honor that her mistress should have been the first choice on the first day, and she seemed to have forgiven me for deceiving her with Yamy the previous night. She cleansed me deeper than soap and water had ever been before, standing behind me when she washed my front, dropping progressively to a kneeling position to kiss my back from top to bottom. She would then stand in front of me when washing my back to be able to repeat the performance the other way round, her fingers playing havoc with my erogenous zones. I would remain upright with my eyes shut and head thrown back, my gasps of excitement annoying the other candidates, whose initial disapproval was now tinged with jealousy, although the fact of having been given a good screwing seemed to have made them less nervous.

As soon as the last arrival had been washed, Yamala herded us out into the compound again, and after the five minute parade I was once more the immediate first choice of a burly, thickset man in his early forties, whose eyes devoured me with blatantly animal desire. When he gestured to me to approach I obeyed with becoming meekness, pouting invitingly with half-veiled eyes as I slid out of the toga. Cupping my breasts to lift them clear of my body, I started to rotate, smiling equivocally at the groups of warriors. But this time I did not even reach half way, as I suddenly felt a stubby middle finger slide roughly into my sex while the hand to which it belonged lifted me bodily off the ground, helped by the other arm which he passed under my thighs. I in turn raised my arms to clasp my hands behind me around my future lover's neck, and in this position was transported to the love hut.

Mr 2's attitude was as different from his predecessor's as his physique, which was square and stocky with bulging knots of muscle. His regard was callously lewd as it surveyed my body, which he had thrown down on the rushes as if it were no more than a sack of potatos. Brushing off an attempt on my part to take his rigid member in my hand, he thrust a pair of horny fingers into my sex, treating it with as much respect and delicacy as a farmer checking out the genitals of a cow. Rubbing his glans roughly up and down my slit — not out of consideration for my pleasure, or to reduce the pain of entry, but uniquely to lubricate his penis for his personal comfort, he grasped my knees to force them as far apart as they would go and rammed his warhead straight into my trench.

The ease with which I accommodated the entire length of his ten-incher surprised my new lover, as he was probably hoping to inflict pain. Yet he did not allow his astonishment to distract him from the main purpose, and was soon devoting his entire attention to a pitiless pummeling of my loins. However, what my macho-man did not know was that not only did I revel in rape, but that I gave as good as I got. Arching my back to raise my buttocks off the rushes, I began counter-thrusting energetically, crying out elatedly every time our pubic buffers collided with a muted thud. He tried to force me down onto the ground by using the whole weight of his body, but I locked my shapely and formidably efficient leg, arm and abdominal muscles into a fully supporting position, making it impossible for him to overcome my resistance. We continued like that until he abandoned his terrorist tactics, realizing he had met his match, and we settled down to a formidable fuck for which I lay back on the ground, wrapping my legs around his buttocks to provide added impulsion for bigger and better banging.

We even became friendly to the extent that for the last five minutes, while waiting for the terminal tap on the shoulder, our mouths joined in lingual discovery. Until then I had held back my climax, but when the time finally came I released it at the same time as my lover, my body so convulsed with the outsurge of energy that I would have bucked him off had my arms not been tightly entwined round his neck to keep our lips together.

After the intensity of the sensation, my second greatest reward was the crooked grin with which he actually gratified me when we parted, as it must have been the first time he had smiled at any woman other than his mother, and even she was probably rationed to a small smirk on birthdays!

I finished by establishing an outright record by being everyone's automatic first choice throughout the whole of the eight-day period, making 120 times in all that I was preferred to the other candidates. As there were 75 warriors but only 120 copulations, the system meant that many of the younger bucks, including my adored Zala — of whom much more later — had to be satisfied with only one turn. I could easily have taken them two at a time, had it not been strictly forbidden, as only frontal relations were permitted. This was my only cause for complaint, as I badly missed buggery, to the point of having Yamy work me over rectally every night with her monkey mace, after Katiola had prepared me with one of her inimitable 'feuilles de rose'.

I will not even try to describe my other 73 lovers or the other 118 fucks, as an encyclopaedia would be necessary, and even then I could not hope to remember all the details, as during the period of the rites I of course had no diary, and for this account I have had to rely entirely on memory. I recall that I never once failed to come with each of my partners, often managing several orgasms, which in no way diminished my appetite for more and more sex, and I would throw myself into the arms of each new warrior with unabated, man-eating zeal.

However, I will tell the tale of Zala, a young stud of twenty who was last in the batting order, meaning we only made love once, on the fifth day.

I do not think he could be described as more beautiful that Banda, but he was certainly just as handsome in a different way. Banda was probably more graceful, but not quite as tall, Zala being a giant of six foot five whose muscular developement was more pronounced than the Senoufo's, although his hips and waist were deliciously slender and his buttocks prominent spheres of steely muscle. He also had the darkest of coal-black skins and his genitals were mountains of virile perfection, the massive penis, with its long drooping foreskin, hanging down to just above the knees in front of ram-sized balls which swung lowly and loosely in their silky scrotum.

The strength of his erection made his member describe a perfect upward curve, which brought the gleaming glans to within inches of a point midway between his nipples: an overall length of more than fourteen inches. Because of the natural upward thrust of such a shape, the pressure it exercised against the roof of the vaginal passage was nothing short of heavenly, and love with Zala, after the first few minutes, became an almost uninterrupted climax. Every now and then he would pump an incredible quantity of sperm deep into my downstairs and continue with unabated virility, as if nothing had happened, frequently repeating the dose.

The first and only time I fucked him during the rites I fell head over heals in love with his cock, taking it out of me at regular intervals to kiss it tenderly and tell it I loved it. The fourteen inches I had proved I could take at Dapchi were almost a case of predestination, as I did not have to waste a single inch, but when he laid me on the reeds in the love-hut, I nevertheless had to make a quick decision on how to deal with the sheer size of the problem, concluding it would be best to make him sit down with his legs outstretched.

As his member was too long for the kneeling position — there being no way I could raise my sex high enough to clear the glans — I had to crouch facing him over his upper thighs, with my feet on either side of his hips and my knees apart. In this manner the whole length of my legs was available to elevate my loins to a point higher than the end of his penis, whereafter all I had to do was pull it out from his chest, line it up with my happiness and sink down ecstatically, feeling it slide slowly and inexorably into what must have been the depths of my womb.

Then, using my thigh and calf muscles, with the Wasagu's hands guiding my buttocks, I would raise my hips by the fourteen or so inches required to expose the base of the glans (I dared not release it completely as the back pressure of the erection would have torn it free). Afterwards I would start the long descent until I was again sitting on his thighs with his main mast feeling as if it were a second spinal column driven up the middle of my body. My breasts were by no means neglected, as on the way up and down they passed in front of Zala's vast, thick-lipped mouth, which gleefully engulfed the halos and most of the surrounding flesh, holding onto the nipples when the rest of the orbs had slid out, stretching the breasts themselves to the limit of their elasticity.

Impaled on such a formidable implement, my orgasms followed one another in giddy succession, like bursts of machine-gun fire. I made so much noise that people came running from the other huts to see what such strident sounds in a strange foreign tongue could possibly signify, standing round us in a circle to admire the seering intensity of our junction.

Why one climax should have been stronger than the others I really do not know, but it was, winding me up and throwing me backwards over Zala's knees, my head touching the floor as I gasped almost painfully for breath, while the huge, half-hidden hose pipe continued to fill me with its geysers of sperm. There was enough come inside me to conceive a hundred million twins, which was much too much for the space available, forcing it to ooze back out past the gleaming, black bung and trickle over its maker's ebony thighs.

Zala and I were destined to see a lot more of each other, but for the time being we seperated with a feeling of bitter privation, and when I saw him in the compound during the choosing sessions it was as much as I could do to not to drop to my knees and take him forcibly in my mouth.

Chapter 26

At the end of the ninth day, when all was over, the elders, the warriors and the high priestess withdrew to the central hut to deliberate on the choice of the Ape-God's bride.

In the candidates' hut we settled down to a vigil which could in theory have lasted up to two days, in the event, as was usually the case, of the elders and the high priestess being unable to agree on a unanymous choice. One by one, starting with the oldest, the warriors would give the names of their three favorites in order of preference, whereafter a discussion took place during which the elders cross-examined the warriors on the reasons for their preference, after which they would confirm or change their lists. The electors then sat in conclave and designated the successful candidate, unanymously if possible, otherwise by a simple majority vote.

The atmosphere in the hut was tense, the relatively relaxed and cheerful attitude of the previous week having given way to to a feeling of apprehension and even fear. It was evident that almost all of my companions would have been only too happy to call it a day and return there and then to their hearths and husbands, forgoing the honor of being selected for what was objectively a dangerous and terrifying experience.

Eight days of being screwed by the most virile men in the tribe was paradisiac, but enough was enough! According to Yamy there were possibly two other women who would not have been averse to being chosen, but were not entirely convinced. On the contrary, I was completely dedicated to my bridal vocation, as well as being composed and confident, feeling not only no fear, but a definite elation at what I considered the certainty of being selected. I had always been the equal if not the superior of my sexual partners, subjugating them with the intensity of the desire I aroused and then satisfied through my identification with their most intimate phantasms. I was certain of my ability to control the situation and turn it to my advantage and enjoyment. In other words I was simply rearing for that monkey-fuck; it was just that easy!

We had hardly been waiting for more than an hour on that first morning, when the two acolytes entered the room and ordered us to stand at the end of our beds. I did so imagining some new purification rite was about to be performed, an impression reinforced by the arrival of Yamala in full regalia.

She took up her position behind the altar, and made a declaration which drew a collective gasp of nervousness from the other candidates. Her assistants then undid the fibula, and her mantle slid off her shoulders revealing her usual, aggressive nudity, only relieved by the regalia and a silver object over the mons veneris which was too far away to identify, but turned out to be a monkey-skull mask attached to an ebony diljo, which was pushed well home into her sex.

Stretching out both arms, she picked up the other two diljos from the altar, where they had been placed by the acolytes, and holding them out sideways at arms' length, uttered three or four words, one of which was 'Akala', the Wasagu name I had been given for the duration of the rites. Thirty-two heads turned as one in my direction, and gasps of relief were heard all round as the faint-hearted realized that for them the terrible ordeal was no longer even a remote eventuality.

I remained outwardly calm and unflinching, never having doubted I would be chosen, but was nevertheless filled with a feeling of elation, accompanied by a sense of psychological shock at the imminence of bestial copulation. Yamala gestured to me to approach the altar, and when I reached it the acolytes helped me remove my toga and lie down on the ebony slab in the same spreadeagled position we had all adopted for the earlier ceremony. Three silver, monkey-head incensories were placed on either side of my hips and between my thighs, prior to the high priestess starting what was for me a meaningless incantation that lasted several minutes, and in which my ritual name was repeated frequently.

At the end of her litany Yamala handed the two diljos to her assistants, and then, spreading her thighs as far as her standing position would allow, grasped the silver monkey head and laboriously withdrew it from her loins, revealing an ebony shaft which was almost as long as Zala's penis. Its removal was clearly a delicate business, as rear-facing notches ensured that it remained embedded in the loins unless forcibly withdrawn. Yamala then walked round to the end of the altar opposite my wide-open thighs, briefly fingering my slit to check that it was in a sufficiently lubricated condition to receive the implement, which was still moist from her own secretions. Having satisfied herself on this point, she inserted the extremity between my inner lips and pushed until the back of the monkey head — which was connected to the ebony phallus by a curved, swan-neck attachment whose purpose was to achieve the necessary alignment — came to rest against my thighs.

The high priestess, smiling a fleeting smile of approval, returned to her place behind the altar and began to intone another litany, accompanied by a repeated kissing of my breasts. When this was over she helped me to my feet, indicating I should push the diljo back in if the movements of my body tended to expel it, as for the next two days, during which I would feed only on warrior sperm, it would serve as a symbolic hymen as well as a highly effective chastity bung whose purpose was to preserve my new-found, ritual virginity for the Ape-God. This was deemed a necessary precaution against any tendency on my part, or on that of my seventy-five suppliers of semen, to carry our sexual relations to their logical conclusion. Until it was ceremonially removed when I entered the nuptial cage, I was only allowed to withdraw it to urinate and to wash in the presence of the ex high priestess, who now became my principal acolyte, or more accurately mentor, with Katiola as her assistant. I must say it felt perfectly at home in its temporary lodging, and very nice to have inside in a randy sort of a way.

Yamala then removed the silver band from her temples and pressed it down over my head, sliding the amulets and anklets over my hands and feet. She witheld the mantle of office, as this would only be passed around my shoulders in the event of a successful mating with the Schlieberg ape, which would be my official consecration.

Leading me round to the altar front she turned me to face the unsuccessful candidates, whose hostility had disappeared, not only through the respect they now owed the high priestess elect, but from relief that they themselves had escaped the intimidating ordeal. I had in fact broken every record, as to my previous achievements during the love-making period I had added the final prowess of being the warriors' unanymous first choice, an unprecedented honor, as never, in the annals of the Wasagu rites, had a bride been designated before the morning of the second day of deliberation. When allowance was made for the time devoted to formalities, my selection had in reality only taken a matter of minutes. In my mind there had never been any doubt I would be chosen — a conviction shared by everyone else after the first two days of love-making — but it was astounding that I, a white foreigner, should have won such a landslide victory in the face of family ties and local preference.

One further rite remained to be accomplished before the fateful day of my marriage: the two-day ceremony of purification, during which the only nourishment to which I would be entitled was warrior sperm, having to swallow the semen of all seventy-five supermen.

Because of my lightning election, the start of the two day Feast of Sperm had been advanced to the following morning, and after the departure of the other candidates and their handmaidens, the three of us piled into the big bed, which I still thought of as Yamy's, and passed the time of day using the ebony and silver diljo for one of the purposes for which it had been devised, which was enlarging the new high priestess's sex for pentration by her hairy bridegroom. After its removal had been ritually condoned by Yamy, the slot-stopper, whose notches considerably reduced the pace at which it could be withdrawn, was run slowly in and out of my loins, and then rotated at an angle of some 25 from its axis, to stretch the vaginal walls in every direction.

As my sex had long since achieved the necessary length and degree of elasticity, these exercises were strictly for fun, with Yamy and Katiola seeing how often they could make me come, while I retaliated by eating and fingering their breasts and genitals with the same intention. They of course won, but I did not do badly, particularly with Katiola, whose lesbian leanings made her an exceptionally responsive partner.

Yamy also had a taste for womanly love, but required a more assertive approach if she were to give of her best. She had one of the most erotic anal rose-buds I had ever encountered, which opened gapingly after a little imaginative tongueing and fingering. As it would have been lèse-majesté (or monkey) to use my silver stoppered ebony gadget, which had been returned to its official lodging, I told Katiola to take one of the ape diljos out of the casket, despite a show of reticence on the part of the ex high priestess — who was worried about the ritual propriety of such a move — and slide it the whole way into Yamy's nether opening while licking her clitty, which, when really rampant, would stand out almost as far as mine.

We also spent an hour or so teaching Katy the basic rules of fellation, using a ritual diljo instead of the real thing, as she was going to have to help us process all those gorgeous warriors. Apart from that we mouthed and munched, and fingered and fondled, and sucked and stuffed in the empty hut, hardly stopping to touch the food which was passed to us through a hatch in the wall, so feverish was our excitement, until we fell into a sleep of sexual exhaustion, our bodies still intermingled in the attitudes of love.

Next morning, after a lascivious three-way wash, the second gong announced the start of the Marathon sperm-swallow. Naked apart from the high-priestess's silver regalia, I squatted on what looked like a low, milking stool on the edge of the dais in front of the altar, flanked on my right by the nude and kneeling Yamy and Kati, an arrangement that placed our mouths at just the right height to fellate the men filing past at floor level.

Yamy, who had already dealt with the problem of sucking off seventy-five warriors in two days, proposed this disposition as being the most effective for combatting the fact that the warriors did not have to cooperate by having a rapid orgasm, being fully entitled to make the pleasure last as long as possible, which was quite naturally what most of them did. This was not the only problem, as there would be those who came too soon, in the mouths of my assistants or over their bodies or mine, that is to say elsewhere than in my mouth, as in such cases the warrior would return to the end of the queue and be entitled to a second sucking.

The 'three in line' array meant that Kati, who had no experience at all in such matters other than our practice together the day before, received the warriors one at a time as they arrived through the door in the wall to the right of the altar. Her job was to warm them up, only turning them over to Yamy when they were totally rigid and starting to breathe heavily. Yamy, with her unrivalled experience, cradling the scrotum in one hand and shuttling the sheath backwards and forwards with the other, while running the whole member in and out of mouth and throat, would bring them up to fever pitch, leaving me the theoretically easy task of finishing them off and swallowing their discharge.

Yami knew from first-hand that the best obtainable average would be ten minutes a man, as two or three minutes rest every quarter of an hour was indispensable, plus a certain amount of time off for longer breaks, as apart from occasional bouts of cramp, the jaw and throat muscles just had to have a protracted rest every now and then. This boiled down to an overall twelve and a half hours once a margin for misfortunes had been posted, so there could be no question of taking it easy. On our side was the fact that the younger studs, whose turn would come on the second day, would have such a sack-full of sperm waiting for an outlet, it should be possible to deal with them quite quickly, my main problem being swallowing thirty times their backlog of semen without choking.

All these niceties and by-laws gave rise to a lot of good-natured bluffing, maneuvering, giggling and even screams of mirth, as warriors who gave the impression of being almost frigid suddenly came all over Kati's face, while I had to scramble for others who were on the point of ejaculating in Yamy's mouth, without losing control of the one I was sucking myself. During the first three hours there were so many miscarriages we must have seen at least ten heros return to the back of the queue for a second turn, but gradually we became very good at calling our opponents' bluffs, and finally settled down to the average we had fixed as a reasonable goal.

We perfected an uncounterable gambit I called the 'SS' or 'scrotum-squeeze', which enabled the other two girls to stage a delaying action until I could intervene, making it possible for me to freeze the situation I was dealing with at any given moment, and take over from one or other of my acolytes, who would hand me a warrior on the point of ejaculation. All I had to do was take him in my mouth and swallow when my assistant let go of the neck of his sack, while I continued to choke-off the warrior I had been fellating myself to prevent him from playing any tricks while I was occupied elsewhere!

Even allowing for the fact that I must be one of the most avid come-guzzlers in the cosmos, and had emptied an inordinate number of testicles in the past weeks since formulating my plan to take part in the rites, this ball game was national league standard. Every ten minutes I had a real skinful, and although I enjoyed every drop, by the end of the first afternoon, when the younger men started to fire off their seemingly endless salvos, I was so full I thought I could hear the stuff swilling around my windpipe. Fortunately the substance seemed to have a diuretic effect, and the call of nature came frequently to my rescue in the form of a liquid of an unhealthy grey color and strangely viscous consistency, whose laborious evacuation made room for the next intake.

I obviously inherited a few master-bluffers who had genuinely appeared to be on the point of ejaculation with Yamy, but proved to be unamenable when I took over. In such instances the only solution was hard work, combining ultra high speed sheath-flicking with deep-throating, glans kissing, tongue jabbing and whatever. Those who could stand up to more than three minutes of such an assault, after all that my attendants had done to them, were few and far between, and received my special 'depth charge' therapy consisting of a sudden finger-up-the-ass, which destabilized their self control and usually did the trick!

I of course gave my favorites preferential treatment, particularly Zala, whose turn was not until half way through the second morning. I made him come everywhere except in my mouth: in my hair, on my breasts, in my eyes, in my ears and on my navel, to name only some of the random targets, as this allowed him, quite legitimately, to return to the back of the queue eight times, until he was there all by himself and we had to work on him collectively to squeeze a few drops into my mouth as the regulations required.

I finished my contract about two hours before sundown on the second day with Zala's nineth effusion, and the paramount chief of the Wasagu in person came into the hut to acknowledge my 'purification' officially. I shudder to think what he must have thought of our appearance, as we sat and knelt on the edge of the dais in a state of total exhaustion, like survivors from some epic defeat, our bodies coated in patches of congealed come which glistened wierdly in the lamplight. I remember trying to reply quite pointlessly in French to a question he had put in Wasagu, which I did not in any case understand, only managing to produce a resounding belch whose cause was the undigested sea of semen surging noisily around my stomach.

As the selection procedure had been so rapid, there was still a full day to go to the summer solstice: my twenty-ninth birthday and second wedding. I smiled at the thought I might be laying myself open to a charge of bigamy, and could imagine my defence in court: "Your honor, the charges should be set aside as my second husband is only a gorilla and therefore not legally capable of committing the alleged offence!"

I had slept uninterruptedly following the chief's departure until three or four hours after sunrise the following morning. As the entrances to the hut were sealed and guarded to prevent any sort of communication with anyone other than my two official acolytes, we had a whole day of doing nothing apart from each other. This was a good thing, as I had not completely recovered from ten days of an erotic mayhem that would have sent most women to the hospital, the asylum or the cemetery, if not all three.

During the 'Feast of Sperm' both Yamy and I had been surprised by Katiola's sudden and unforseeable conversion to cock, as for a dedicated lesbian she had seen the heterosexual light with an astounding rapidity, revelling in a type of relationship only the initiated are supposed to enjoy. Far from being reticent, she had become a go-downer of the most extraordinary versatility, running the whole gamut from the crudest of gobbling to the most delicate of lick-kissing.

For the time being we were unable to offer her the supreme consolation of the real thing, but Yamy and I spent our day treating her to the two ape-diljos, and by evening she was able to take both of them simultaneously without any side effects other than her own untrammelled delight. She really had one of the most perfect bottoms I have ever seen, which I spent hours sucking and kissing, while working my fingers in and out of the tight little sphincter to prepare it for the monkey diljo, Yamy having an easier task with the other orifice.

All this hard work on someone else's pleasure was exactly what the shrink would have ordered for my own psychic and sexual balance, which were given a full day's rest from male interference for only the second time since my arrival in Africa — as the Feast of Sperm could hardly qualify as abstinence from cock — allowing me to freshen up for the bridal ordeal.

Chapter 27

When the first gong rang out on the morning of my twenty-ninth birthday — the summer solstice of June 21st 1976 — I was sleeping the sleep of the innocent, unlike my two attendants who had been awake and anxious for more than an hour, but had not dared to move for fear of disturbing the bride-to-be, who lay there slumbering peacefully as if her greatest concern was how to make the most of a morning in bed.

I opened my eyes, smiled at them, and then propped myself up on one elbow to kiss Yamy's opulent breasts good morning, and then on the other to repeat the greeting with Kati, stretching luxuriously while they returned the compliment, coaxing my nipples into their first erection of the day. When they suggested we go through to the wash room I refused, feeling instinctively that my animal lover would prefer the acrid odor of the juices I had secreted during our girlie games of the previous evening to the alien smell of soap.

However, the condemned woman ate a hearty breakfast, as I was still ravenous after my two day stint on sperm, whose nutritive value is distinctly inferior to its psychological impact on the libido. Under the astonished eyes of my companions I waded into yams, pineapple, maze biscuits and the host of other local delicacies that made up my special bridal menu, including a cup of sweet-tasting liquid which was undoubtedly the aphrodisiac, as I felt an immediate flush of sexual excitement.

When I had finished, the acolytes dressed me symbolically in the high priestess's silver regalia, leaving the rest of my body naked apart from a white hood with eye holes, which they slipped over my head, as on that wedding morning no other male was entitled to see my face before I unveiled it for the Ape-God. When the gong sounded for the second time I was ready to pass through the end door, facing the central hut, and walk between the two lines of warriors who made up my guard of honor, as well as being a disincentive to any last minute change of mind — an eventuality which was as far from my thoughts, after all the trouble I had been to to get that far, as becoming a Carmellite nun!

At the entrance to the central hut I was met by the chief holding a monkey skull talisman, which he passed over my head several times while grunting a series of incantations in what sounded like an imitation of a gorilla call. When this formality was over, he beckoned me into the building.

The interior was lit only by rays of sunlight filtering hazily through the loosely woven rushes of the circular walls, and my eyes took some time to accustom themselves to the semi-obscurity. In the center stood a large cage that must have been all of twenty foot square, made from massive bamboo canes. Apart from this structure, the inside of the hut was furnished with four benches facing inwards, on which the elders were already installed, with the warriors standing behind them. In one of the angles Yamala was sitting on a stool, dressed in the high priestess's ceremonial toga.

My own attention was rapidly drawn to a large form huddled against the bars in one of the corners, and no introductions were necessary for me to recongnize the Ape-God in person, squatting somewhat dreamily, no doubt a trifle overcome by the precautionary laudanum he had absorbed in his feed. Understandably, as he was an awe-inspiring giant, I felt the skeletal hand of fear clutch at my consciousness for the briefest of moments as the adrenalin hollowed out my loins, and the vestiges of a conventional upbringing cried out that this whole thing was crazily unthinkable.

Objectively, it really was a superb specimen, resembling a gorilla in many more bodily respects than a chimpanzee, weighing everything of 550 pounds for a height of about five feet six. Its facial appearance was however more akin to that of the chimp, whose friendly curiosity the animal seemed to have inherited — although this could easily have been a dangerous illusion. Its coat was of an unusually deep auburn tint. I felt my cheeks flush with excitement at the sheer proximity of the unbelievable, the blood rushing to my lips while my nipples and clitoris stiffened of their own accord and my sex began to secrete.

The chief led me to a circular wooden plaque on the floor, half of which was outside the bars of the cage and the other half within. Making me stand on the external part facing outwards, he withdrew the virginal diljo from my sex and applied an unguent to its lips to facilitate the monstrous entry, although I was already so awash with my own licqueur of love he need not have bothered. This did not deter him, as he clearly found the task agreeable — as did I — and some time passed before he resigned himself to abandoning my genitals to their fate. His last gesture was to rotate the plaque on which I was standing, transferring me to the interior of the cage, where I found myself face to face with my husband, whose nut-brown eyes seemed to reflect a gleam of interest.

The silence in the hut became almost painful as I removed my hood and slid it behind me through the bars, revealing my face to a male for the first time since the end of the Feast of Sperm. The fortunate recipient of the honor did not seem at all impressed — having no notion of the elevated place I occupied in the scale of human beauty — being visibly more concerned with the presence of a foreign body in one of its widely-flared nostrils, which it teased and scratched busily with the jagged nail of a formidable forefinger.

Dominating my desire, which had been dangerously fuelled by the totally unnecessary aphrodisiac — as it was indispensable that my first contact with the animal be positive and securizing — I moved slowly across the cage to within three or four feet of the ape, who greeted my intitiative with a series of deep and vibrantly sonorous grunts, which did not however seem to contain any message of hostility.

Squatting down facing it with my knees apart I began to caress my sex in an attempt to attract its attention, while making a crooning noise which I somehow thought would be appropriate. I do not know whether it was the mixture of the unguent and the juices secreted by my unwashed loins, but I could not help noticing I smelt very pungent indeed. Whatever it may have been, there could be no doubt that my stirring of the pot was producing a definite effect on my bride-groom, as little by little it abandoned its lethargic attitude and started to bounce up and down on its haunches, accompanying the movement with a further more excited series of grunts, forgetting the nostril to devote its entire attention to the strange but apparently friendly creature that had invaded its territory.

Still squatting, I moved my weight forwards so I could take two or three waddling steps towards the animal, as in a sudden triumphant flash of intuition I had realized that the show of intrerest was being generated by my intimate odors, there being no other means whereby, from a distance, I could hope to attract the desire of an animal whose perception of sex is based almost entirely on the sense of smell.

Controlling a violent impulse to grab its long pink organ, which was starting to jerk convulsively in what I hoped was a preliminary manifestation of desire, I swore to myself at the stupidity, under such perilous circumstances, of administering an aphrodisiac to a woman of my torrid temperament, and began to run my fingers up and down my slit to cover them with what I sensed was my main asset in my attempt to engage the ape's sexual interest.

When my fingers were running with the stuff I advanced my hand gingerly in the direction of the animal's nose, starting with apprehension when I felt a vice like grip close over my wrist. I need not have worried, as the only reason for this move was to convey my fingers to a position under its nostrils, where it could concentrate its nasal attention on an aroma which was obviously awaking some form of longing.

It was in fact the type of desire I had been hoping to kindle, as the giant ape started to gibber excitedly and, after turning my hand first one way and then the other, to sniff the fingers from every possible angle, it began to lick them greedily, punctuating this pastime with a volley of staccato grunts. There could be no doubt about it: I had discovered the Open Sesame, a glance between the monkey's shaggy thighs revealing the presence of a stiffening organ which could not have been far from its maximum development, as it was already bigger than the ebony diljo.

I simply had to find a way of directing the ape's attention to my sex, where the smell was strongest, as rapidly as possible, as I could not afford to allow its interest to either wax into frustration — in which case an accident could easily happen — or wane into boredom. The laudanum, which was in a certain sense my ally, could easily become an enemy if its effects were allowed to overcame the present display of interest, as I might then find it impossible to reactivate the animal's desire.

My most delicate problem was how to withdraw my hand without triggering a violent reaction. For the time being it was the Ape-God's only link with the source of the intoxicating smell, but I needed that arm, along with the other, to support my weight. My intention was to bring my vulva to within inches of the monkey's nose, by arching my body with my back well clear of the ground and my thighs widely splayed, hoping its sense of smell would guide it to the source of the odors, and that instinct and my ability to adapt would do the rest.

Having succeeded in recovering my hand without setting off any fireworks, I started to raise my loins, with thigh, calf, arm and abdominal muscles tensing under the strain of the most provocative and vulnerable of female postures. When I had achieved the intended position, with my upcurved body resembling a fully drawn bow, I shuffled forward like a crab until my shins came to rest against the insides of the squatting animal's outspread legs.

I need not have been concerned about the ability of the ape to find the source of the fun. Suddenly I felt those two terrifying hands encircle my upper-thighs from below and lift me bodily off the ground as if I had been no more than a feather, enabling the animal to inspect the strange-looking, almond-shaped gash that smelt so delicious. Grunting delightedly, it stood up and started to smell my sex, appraising the state of my readiness with a repetitive sniffing which was so obscenely suggestive I came, twitching helplessly in mid air.

I will never know whether the erruption of my orgasm was visible to the monkey, whose eyes were only inches away from my slit, or whether it released some particularly motivating odor. One way or the other the Ape-God had obviously got the message, as, holding me aloft with my head and torso lolling over backwards, it pressed its bristly mouth against my vulva and started to eat me as I had never been eaten in the whole of my life, or could ever possibly be eaten again.

Gasping and sobbing deliriously, I came as if I never intended to stop. This must have been exactly what the monkey liked, as he ate me harder, faster and deeper, making me come bigger and better in a giddy spiral of lust, squeeling like a sacrificial pig, with that bristly mouth and chin busily rasping around where they could do the most good. So much blood had flowed into my lips they felt like horizontal stays supporting the mask of my face, and my clitty and nipples were stiff to the point of being positively painful. From time to time the brute's bristles would scrape over my clit, making me start so violently that even my monument of animal muscle had to make a small effort to stop me convulsing my way out of its grasp.

Looking down and round under my back, I could see its member was completely tumescent and much larger than anticipated. With a final shudder of delighted dread I realized it would soon be doing something about it and with it, which is precisely what happened, as I was suddenly deposited on the floor, to a background of frenzied grunting and gibbering, and realized I was going to have to move very quickly into a feasible position if I wanted to reap the benefit of all my hard work. But what indeed was a feasible position? Every naughty girl, who has been able to escape parental supervision when visiting the monkey-house in the local zoo, knows that the male takes the female from behind, which would not have involved any alignment problem had it not been for the difference in our heights, which meant that my target area was too high when I stood up, and too low when I knelt down.

I therefore had to settle for a precarious, half-crouching position, reversing inch by inch until I felt the bright pink glans bump into the cleft of my buttocks, providing me with guidance as to height. I raised my rump a little, as despite my taste for sodomy this was no time for a stupid mistake. Feeling the gland collide with the lips of my sex, I reached back ever so gently between my thighs, as I had not as yet touched its organ, and did not want to trigger a panic reaction through any ill-conceived move.

Barely fingering the clammy stem, I managed to line it up with my slit without any adverse side-effects, the ape even appearing to enjoy the subtle contact, to judge from the contented-sounding grunts from behind. Mentally crossing my fingers, I made the momentous move and pushed back in a dead straight line, hoping against hope the animal would not shy away. My concern proved unfounded, as far from recoiling, the Ape-God moved forward at exactly the same time, and I suddenly found myself massively impaled, with what felt like a pubic scrubbing brush scraping across the lower surfaces of the cheeks of my bottom.

I again lived a moment of fear as the two huge, abrasive hands closed round my slender waist, but there was no problem, and all I had to do was relax and enjoy the ride. The Ape-God was in charge, thrusting forward to meet my buttocks, which he himself pulled back in the opposite direction, resulting in a dull thudding sound and bone-shaking impact as my ass-cheeks took most of the shock.

With a sex fuller of penis than at any other time in my copulative experience, for an unforgettable moment in time I lived the quintessence of erotic ecstasy. But it was relatively short-lived, as apes have no time for such niceties as the avoidance of premature ejaculation, particularly as I must have been by far the tightest screw in its anthropoid existence. In any case, petty considerations of duration do not apply to thirty seconds of celestial bestial that could only be judged by different time and value scales, being sufficiently concentrated to last most women a dozen normal lifetimes.

I can only vaguely recall the irrelevant image of my grotesquely swinging breasts and then, much more clearly, as we both came simultaneously, the explosion of an orgasmic ammunition dump that corkscrewed my writhing body, and would have knocked me off my feet had it not been for the animal's retaining grasp.

No human being had ever made me come like that. My frame twitched with an almost epileptic frenzy as it was racked by a series of erotic shock waves whose intensity was partly due to the psychological effect of defilement. Afterwards came the great flood, as my insides were inundated with enough monkey come to restock all the jungles of Africa. For an instant, in the middle of a chain reaction of climaxes, I found myself hoping obscenely that somehow I would be fertilized and give birth to a bonny Schlieberg ape, which I would suckle contendedly, crooning some native lullaby, while Zala and Banda and Wakaba and every other mightily hung African stud within ass-fucking distance took it in turns to service my butt.

Far away in the infinity of distance I heard myself intoning: "I Leda Akala Schlieberg formerly Swanhurst, a well brought-up product of the middle classes of western consumer civilization, hereby solemnly declare that I rejoice in having copulated with the half brother of the gorilla, and in having adored every impure moment of my ultimate abasement". My reverie was rudely interrupted by an authentic extract from a jungle movie, as my mate, still deeply imbedded in my weeping loins, expanded his barrel chest and pummeled it mightily with his fists, releasing a blood-curdling shriek that almost shattered my ear drums.

And then it was all over. With glazed eyes, clutching my breasts in ecstasy, I was kneeling gasping and alone in the center of the cage. My dream lover had returned to the delicate problem of the upkeep of its left nostril, a task that clearly enjoyed priority over the servicing of a female on heat, even and perhaps above all a female belonging to the human species.

Somehow I managed to drag my trembling body over to the plaque and pull myself up against the bars to enable the device to function, like some primitive mechanical deity, expelling me from an earthly paradise and the scene of a singularly original sin.

Chapter 28

I can recall being carried more than helped back to the hut by a group of cheering warriors, and being inspected by Yamy for genital damage. She failed to realize that my semi-fainting condition was due to the devastating effect of a series of particularly violent climaxes, and had nothing to do with any form of maltreatment or injury, despite the outrageous size of the intrusion. My only battle scars were a sore patch at the rise of the buttocks in the vicinity of my sex, due to the scraping received from my ape-mate's pubic coconut-matting, and a few scratches around my waist caused my his nails. Apart from that all I needed was a good sleep, as not even I could stage an instant recovery following a comparable draining of energy.

After such a copy-book mating the omens read like rave-notices. I subsequently discovered — when Banda could discuss matters with Yamy — that mating was a very elastic concept, any semblance of penetration with or without ejaculation being good enough to qualify, the elders having a vested interest in success without problems, as repeated failure, or an insistance on complete consummation that might lead to injury or worse, could have meant the end of the road.

Yamy herself had been half penetrated once by a somnolent animal, whereafter the elders had decided honor was safe, and called in the warriors whose job it was to immobilize the ape with long staves, which they slid through the bars of the cage, giving the bride time to escape. In my case their intervention was not required, as, apart from the nose-picking, my Schlieberg lover had behaved like a perfect gent, and not even the most venerable of the elders could remember a mating where, kissing apart, the partners had made love like human beings, including a long moment of oral foreplay.

I woke in the middle of the afternoon to find Yamy and Kati sitting on the bed gazing at me in admiration. They lead me through to the wash room for long overdue ablutions, before applying balm to my scratches and soreness. I could not help noticing that their attitude, although still tender and loving, was tinged with a respect which was entirely new, as in their eyes the Ape-God, in honoring me with a complete mating without violence, had not only confirmed my status as his ritual wife and high priestess, but, at the same time, had conferred on me a god-like aura that commanded reverence and obedience from all members of the sect. In a matter of minutes I, a white woman, had become one of the most important personages in the whole of the Wasagu territory: this really was African adventure fiction at its best!

One final ceremony was to take place to celebrate my full investiture as high priestess, whose main feature had originated as a war dance, but evolved over the years into an event with a blatantly sexual connotation in keeping with the main object of the sect: the glorification of virility.

Just after sundown the paramount chief entered the hut accompanied by the two senior warriors and Yamala, who had disappeared after preparing the altar and helping me put on my silver regalia, including the headband, retrieved from the floor of the cage where it had fallen when the ape had picked me up by the thighs. They took up positions behind the altar with the chief in the center, lit the incensories and told me to lie down on my back on the block of ebony.

The chief reeled off a long incantation, frequently passing the monkey-head talisman over my body, and then helped me down, turning to Yamala who handed him the ceremonial mantle of high priestess, which he draped around my shoulders. Leaving me standing in the center, behind the altar, flanked by my acolytes, the three men descended from the dais and prostrated themselves in my direction prior to leaving the hut.

After an interval of a few minutes the gong sounded, and Yamy led me out through the end door, where I found myself facing a central building whose walls had been removed. In the place of the cage there was a tribune with an important looking stool in its center, and on either side were the benches on which the elders were sitting, the warriors being drawn up in a square formation facing the stool at a distance of about twenty feet. The compound was lit by a series of bonfires around the boundary fence and torches fixed to the supporting poles of the roof of the central hut. With Yamy holding up my right hand and Kati holding up my left, I crossed the intervening space, using my best 'one foot in front of the other' mannequin walk, stepped up onto the tribune and sat down graciously on the stool, modestly gathering the mantle together over my knees.

As soon as I was seated, the warriors, who were in full battle regalia, which consisted of precious little dress but a great deal of paint, shouted my Wasagu name three times and then prostrated themselves on the ground. From the edge of the compound resounded the slow beat of a deep base drum, which was the sign for the warriors to get to their feet and move off with a shuffling step, one line after another, in time with the drum beats, until they formed a complete circle around the central hut.

After a brief pause the base drum started up again, but this time the rhythm was a more animated quick-quick-slow tattoo, and the chain of warriors began to move clockwise around the spectators, stamping their feet on the ground as if to echo the drum beats. They completed one whole circle in this manner, but as they entered the second tour, the leader, who was my favorite senior, introduced a body movement consisting of quarter pivots to the right and left for each measure, continuing on round the hut on this basis. Thereafter, each successive tour was made more elaborate by an additional movement — some of which necessitated extra drum beats — such as a forward thrust of the pelvis, a rythmic brandishing of fists above the head and a rolling of shoulders, until the dance was of such a complexity, and required so much physical effort, the sweat streamed off the warriors' bodies and many of the seniors were hard put to stay the pace.

The last movement to be added was a lolling rotation of the head which proved to be the undoing of the older dancers, who dropped out one after the other, falling exhausted beside the fence to leave the field to their juniors. The speed of the drum beats increased, the base drum being joined by a tom-tom which embroidered the warp of the larger instrument with a tracery of high notes. It was soon the turn of the younger warriors to fall out, until there was only a small group left which rapidly diminished in size, leaving only five, then four, and so on until one warrior danced alone in the flickering fire light, one warrior who had to be; who could only possibly have been the magnificent Zala!

Stepping down from my rostrum I ran lightly across the

compound to where he was still dancing, my mantle, which was only held together at the neck by the silver monkey fibula, billowing open. As I reached the giant Wasagu I signalled to the drummers to stop — which they did immediately, as my gesture could have been understood in any language — and threw my arms around his neck, pressing my exposed breasts against his streaming torso and exploring his mouth with a deeply probing kiss, before avidly licking the salty sweat from the unpainted areas of his chest and shoulders. I felt his manhood stir spectacularly under the loin cloth and surge through the gap between my upper thighs, pressing hard against the base of my slit, but I knew the right moment had not come and there would be time for all that later.

I returned to my ceremonial stool with a body whose breasts and inner arms were smeared with a Van Gogh palette of war paint from the Wasagu's sweltering skin, all of which was hidden, for the time being, by a mantle that remained immaculately white on the outside. After an interlude to allow the warriors to recover, they reformed their circle, with the exception of maybe fifteen or so of the oldest, who were not equal to another bout of such gruelling exercise.

This time it was clearly going to be much more fun, as the participating warriors had all removed their wide, ceremonial loin cloths to appear virtually naked with the exception of their head gear, shin and forearm guards, which were all the protection they wore, the Wasagu in battle having relied more on agility to avoid injury than on armor.

The second dance started in a similar way to the first, with the base drum pounding out the quick-quick-slow rhythm. It was mouth-watering to see such a forest of black genitals bouncing up and down, particularly Zala'a huge member which I watched for as long as it remained in my field of vision, feeling the renewal of the familiar sticky sensation between my thighs. At the end of the first tour the pattern started to change, as the pivotal movement was replaced by a pelvic thrust, and there was no more brandishing of fists above heads, as hands were going to be needed for other purposes.

The first three rounds brought nothing else in the way of innovation, but I was quite entranced by the spectacle of fire light reflecting off incandescent skin, and the lurid exposure of dozens of dancing organs. When the leader appeared opposite me again at the start of the fourth turn, he took hold of his half-rigid member, and pointing the glans directly at me gave the sheath a down-up-down flick, in time with a new quick-slow-quick drumbeat, each of the succeeding dancers imitating his example when they reached the same point.

The obvious result of these manipulations, apart from advancing the process of tumescence, was to expose the glans when the foreskin was pulled back, which would have been unremarkable had it not been for the fact that the first bulging helmet to emerge had been painted bright yellow. As the dancers passed before me one by one and unveiled the extremities of their virility (as for the Wasagu circumscision was only allowed for medical reasons and involved disqualification from participation in such events), I was confronted, to my delighted astonishment, with glans decorated with all the colors of the rainbow. I learnt later that this singular art-form was rendered possible by the use of non-irritant vegetable pigments, which were not however water-resistant, with the result that all these masterpieces — as certain must have taken devoted wives ages to execute — were rapidly effaced by sweat, not to mention their worst enemy: fellation, which was encouraged by the sugary taste of the product!

The sticky area around my loins was starting to get out of hand, and I allowed the folds of my mantle to fall apart so I could finger my nipples and clitty, which were standing stiffly to attention in anticipation of early employment and responded eagerly to the caress. When the warriors had completed their tour, instead of starting on a fifth giration, the leading dancer continued straight on to the edge of the compound to allow the others to form a long line across the enclosure facing the central hut. When this maneuver had been completed, each warrior took his organ in both hands and turned in my direction. The drums then fell silent and the warriors stopped dancing, their only movement being a to and fro of the sheaths of their members, as they pointed their ornamental objects at the new high priestess in mute and rigid supplication.

It was obvious from the context that I was expected to do something, but as I had no idea what custom required, I could only improvise. Standing up, I undid the fibula clasp, allowing my mantle to fall to the ground, and took off the silver head band, as I knew from recent experience that it would not stay on under the circumstances likely to prevail. Wearing only the amulets and anklets, I stepped down from the tribune and advanced, with breasts and blond hair bobbing (as I had insisted on a return to my normal style) to within ten feet of the line of warriors.

I must have been doing the right thing, as the base drum started up again with a leisurely slow-slow-quick-quick-slow-slow beat, and I began to dance as I had never danced before. I was performing for the sixty multi-colored tips which were pointing their virile preference in my direction, and my body responded to their sexual solicitation with a rhythmic display of exhibitionism that whipped everyone's desire into a frenzy. To start with I just rotated my hips voluptuously in time with the drums, cupping my breasts to control their bouncing and point them defiantly back at the warriors, before caressing the rest of my body with a feline suggestiveness that induced even more pronounced tumescence among all concerned.

I then pirouetted off down the line, first one way and then the other, stopping every five yards or so to threaten my viz-à-viz with a pair of jutting nipples, which I licked lewdly and rhythmically before moving on, interspersing these tableaux with views of the other side of my medal. Turning my back to the line and bending down with my feet apart, I would spread my buttocks revealingly, integrating this feature into a full programme of rhythmic gymnastics without ever missing a drumbeat, but adding such a wealth of obscene gesture and erotic detail that any normal panel of judges would have called in the Vice Squad as a matter of urgency. When I had worked my way up and down the line and returned to the center, the leading dancer started off again round the hut, followed by the rest of the warriors, joining up with the last in line to complete the circle.

The problem was what to do next, as it was clearly up to me to make the running, otherwise the ring of warriors would simply continue to turn round the hut, and I would never come to terms with those sixty gleaming members, all of which were superbly stiff. Deciding that the only thing to do was to take the bulls by their horns, I dropped to my knees, within inches of the moving wall of human flesh, to grasp a passing phallus and, while still undulating in time with the drums, slip it in and out of my mouth before releasing it to grasp the next one, repeating the gesture with each successive warrior.

This of course played havoc with the rhythm of the first dancers to arrive, as they were thrown off beat. As luck would have it one of them, who had seen what I was trying to achieve, realized that all he had to do was synchronize two thrusts between my lips with the last slow-slow measure, to restore order to the general impulsion and make it possible, without interrupting the circular progress, for each warrior to penetrate my mouth twice before moving on to allow his successor to do likewise.

My initiative was such a success it continued for three whole rounds, during which I recognized quite a few organs from the qualification ceremonies and the Feast of Sperm, particularly the big balled ones that had given me a real mouthful. Having already seen what I could do, it never occurred to any of them they might not be able to get the whole of their members into my mouth under the changed circumstances, and as there were quite a few ten inchers and better, the sides of my throat were given severe punishment as a result of inconsiderate jabbing.

By the time the fourth round started and the decorative effects of the glans were starting to blur, I decided there was no reason why I should not use the same method at the other end of my body, as it would not even be necessary to change the rhythm. I managed the transition without missing a beat, as all I had to do, when a penis withdrew from my mouth, was use the next four beats to spin round, rise to my feet and bend over forwards. Fortunately the dancer who arrived at that precise moment, seeing a moist and gaping cleft instead of widely parted lips, understood what was required of him, and drove in his plunger right up to the pubics, almost knocking me over with his second thrust.

As with my mouth, I had to make allowance for the difference in height between a giant like Zala, taken on tip-toe, and the shorter warriors for whom I sometimes had to bend my knees, having only a second or two between dancers to turn my head and guess the correct hole-level for the next fucker. It was a heavenly feeling, as I was penetrated by a new prick every six beats, and revelled lecherously in a gamut ranging from fat to thin, rough to smooth, pointed to blunt and crooked to straight, all of them however sharing the common Wasagu characteristic of length.

To obtain maximum pleasure from mini-fucking I would thrust back to meet the incoming joy-sticks, and had it not been for the sound of the drums, the slapping noise as buttock met thigh would have been audible all over the compound. After the first full tour, considering no doubt I would not last long under such pressure, quite a few of the warriors had been jacking themselves so that when their turn came again they would be ready to ejaculate, and as I was coming continuously myself that made a lot of stickiness, either oozing out of my gash, or spattering my thighs and buttocks for those who had problems with their timing.

Halfway through the second lap I made a pantomime signal to the drummers to speed things up, as at the sedate rate at which we were going the fuck-dance could last all night. The acceleration produced the hoped-for result, as one by one the dancers fell out. I do not know how I managed to stay the pace myself, as every twenty warriors or thereabouts, I would be racked by a major spasm, which, added to the fatigue of my position, and the effort needed to remain upright after certain of the better hung had rammed me with all their might, seriously taxed my endurance. There were also those who, to my vociferous delight, stuck it in the wrong hole, as they were both gaping so invitingly that many warriors chose one orifice first time round and the other the next, collectively putting an end to my asshole's unwanted continence.

The drummers were both consummate artists, the base drum representing the male organ and the tom-tom personifying female pleasure. The low, slow beats, coinciding with the penetration strokes, were varied according to the physique of the dancer and the size of his member, whereas the tom-tom would chatter and prattle every time I came, identifying itself uncannily with what was happening in the pit of my stomach.

The last survivors, after six full circles, had to rush round the central hut in a strange parody of musical chairs to get back into the queue in time to avoid missing their turn, until finally the pace became too exhausting, and the number of participants rapidly diminished. One of the finalists, in the precipitation and confusion of the last moments, lost control of his functions, as instead of coming in my bum, which was the hole of his preference that time round, he failed to ejaculate after the normal two stroke allowance and re-entered me for a third attempt. Suddenly realizing he was breaking the rhythmic rules, he withdrew in a panic, tried to come before it was too late, got his lines crossed and peed at high pressure between my thighs and over my dangling breasts, presenting me with an unscheduled climax as the turgid depths of my libido stirred perversely under the effect of defilement.

The victorious warrior who emerged from the other side of the hut, for the last time, was of course Zala the Invincible. When he appeared behind me to claim his prize, I deliberately canted my hips to direct his weapon unerringly into my ass, where it disappeared right up to our crinkly tufts of hair. Reaching behind my head I ran my arms round his neck, raising my breasts, whose undersides he cupped in his hands, kneading them as our tongues intermingled greedily. We stood there in the middle of the compound, watched by all the elders and warriors, while Zala ass-fucked me with long, deep strokes whose length of recoil eliminated any waste of penis.

We came prodigiously, holding on to each other as his member jerked convulsively in and out of my anus, filling my entrails with a swirling sea of sperm, while his huge hands crushed breasts which unexpectedly spurted milk onto the dusty ground as I suddenly came back on stream after days of drought. We stood there heaving and panting, my body smeared with sweat and war paint, until detumescence and the natural expulsive thrust of my rectum rejected his manhood, which even in repose was larger than life. Then, gently releasing my lower lips from between his teeth, he walked slowly over to the side of the compound. Returning to the tribune I picked up my mantle and diadem, bowed incongruously to the chief and elders, and strode as majestically back to my hut as circumstances would allow.

It was all over and yet had only just begun, as my year of office as high priestess was about to start. The following day I was allowed to retrieve my personal belongings, enabling me to write up my diary for the first time since Banfora. I also recovered Banda, whose basic French was taxed to the limits of endurance by my flood of questions.

I told him that with Zala, he was to become one of my male attendants, accompanying me on my travels through Wasagu territory as the High Priestess of Love. I was jubilant at the prospect of serving the God of Virility in the backwoods of Africa, where an untold number of black stallions of all ages and sizes were waiting to make inroads into my vulva as a religious duty.

Somewhere in those same backwoods my bristly lover of the bamboo cage had returned to his normal habitat and the company of the females of the group, who were now the only recipients of the long, pink penis that had transported me into a world of an inhuman orgasmic intensity. My journeying may one day bring us together again; only time will tell.

KATE PERCIVAL

Volume One

CHAPTER ONE

CHILDHOOD

I am about to do a bold thing. I am about to give to the world the particulars of a life fraught with incident and adventure. I am about to lift the veil from the most voluptuous scenes about which I shall disguise nothing, conceal nothing, but shall relate everything that has happened to me just as it occurred. I am what is called a woman of pleasure, and have drained its cup to the very dregs. I have the most extraordinary scenes to depict, but although I shall place everything before the reader in the most explicit language, I shall be careful not to wound his or her sense of decency by the use of coarse words, feeling satisfied there is more charm in a story decently told than in the bold unblushing use of terms which ought never to sully a woman's lips.

I was born in a small village in the state of Pennsylvania, situated on the banks of the Delaware, and about thirty miles from Philadelphia. My father's house was most romantically situated within a few yards of the river.

It was supported as it were, at the back by a high hill, which, in summer, was covered with green trees and bushes. On each side of the dwelling was a wood so dense and thick that a stranger unacquainted with the paths through it could not enter. In front of the house, the river on sunshiny days gleamed and glistened in the rays of the sun, and the white sails passing and repassing formed quite a picturesque scene. At night, however, especially in the wintertime, the scene was different. Then the wind would howl and moan through the leafless trees and the river would beat against the rocks in a most mournful cadence. To this day, I can remember the effect it had on my youthful mind, and whenever I hear the wind whistling at night, it always recalls to my memory my birth place.

My father was a stern, austere man, usually very silent and reserved. I only remembered seeing him excited once or twice. My mother had died in my infancy (I was but fifteen months at the time) and my father's sister became his housekeeper. I had but one brother, a year older than myself. How well I remember him, a fine noble-hearted boy full of love and affection. We were neglected by our father and aunt, and left to get through our childhood days as best we could. We would wander together hand in hand by the riverside or in the woods, and often cry ourselves to sleep in each other's arms at our father's want of affection for us. We enjoyed none of the gaieties, none of the sports of youth. The chill of our home appeared to follow us wherever we went, and no matter how brightly the sun shone, it could not dissipate the chill around our hearts. I never remember seeing my father even smile. A continual gloom hung over him, and he usually kept himself locked in his room except at mealtimes.

This life continued until I was ten years of age, when one day my father informed me that the next day I was to go to Philadelphia to a boarding school. At first I was glad to hear it, for any change from the dull monotony of that solitary house must be an agreeable one to me. I ran to the garden to tell my brother, but the moment I mentioned it, Harry threw himself sobbing in my arms.

"Will you leave me, Kate!" he exclaimed. "What will I do when you are gone, I shall be so lonely—so very lonely without you."

"But Harry, darling," I returned, "I shall be back again in a few months, and then I shall have so much to tell you, and we shall have such nice walks together."

I succeeded in calming him, especially as our father informed him before the day was over that he too was to go to a boarding school in the city of Baltimore. That evening we took our last ramble together before we left home. It was the month of June, and all nature was decked in her gayest apparel. It was a beautiful moonlit night, and the air was fragrant with the odor of June roses, of which there were a large number in the garden. We wandered by the side of the river and watched the moon rays playing on the surface of the water, while a gentle breeze murmured softly through the pine trees. On that evening we settled our future life. It was arranged between us that when Harry grew up to be a man I should go and keep his house. We dwelt a long time on the pleasures of such life. At last it was time for us to return to the house, we embraced each other tenderly and separated.

The next morning I left very early, and in a few hours reached my destination and was enrolled among the pupils of B—— Seminary; I shall not dwell long on my school days, although I might devote much space to them. I was not a popular girl in the school— I was too cold, too reserved, and some of the girls said, too proud. I took no pleasure in girlish sports, but my chief amusement was reading. I would retire to a corner of the schoolroom and while the other girls were at play, I would be plunged in the mysteries of Mrs. Radcliff's novels, or some other work of the same character. Frequently the principal insisted on my shutting up my book and going out to play, but I would creep back when she had left the schoolroom, and resume my favorite occupation. I remained at school seven years, and during that time I never once visited home, for my father made a special agreement that I was to spend my vacation at school.

It is strange that, considering the prominent part I had played in the Court of Venus, that up to the age of seventeen, not a single thought concerning the relation of the sexes ever entered my head. I had up to that age never experienced the slightest longing or desire and looked on all men with the utmost indifference. And yet I knew that I was called beautiful and was the envy of all my school fellows.

I have not yet given a description of myself to the reader and it is nothing but right that I should do so. At the age of seventeen my charms were well developed, and although they had not attained the ripe fullness which a few years later was the admiration and delight of all my adorers, still I possessed all the insignia of womanhood. In stature I was above the medium height, my hair was a dark auburn and hung in massive bands on a white neck. My eyes were a deep blue and possessed a languishing voluptuous expression; they were fringed with long silky eyelashes and arched with brows so finely pencilled that I have often been accused of using art to give them their graceful appearance. My features were classically regular, my skin of dazzling whiteness, my shoulders were gracefully rounded and my bust faultless in its contours. My more secret charms I shall describe at some future time when I shall have to expose them to the reader's gaze.

I have said that up to the age of seventeen I had never experienced the slightest sexual desire. The spark of voluptuousness which has ever since burnt so fiercely in my breast was destined to be lighted up by one of my own sex. Yes, dear Laura, it was you who first taught me the delights and joys of love; it was you who first kindled that flame of desire that has caused me to experience twelve years of delirious bliss; it was to your gentle teaching, sweet friend, that I owe my initiation in all the mysteries of the Court of Venus; it was your soft hand that pointed out to me that path of pleasure — and all the delight shown on the wayside. The incident happened in this manner:

About three months before I left school we were told one morning that a new music and French teacher would take her abode in B—— Seminary the next day. We were all extremely anxious to see her, and at the expected hour she made her appearance. Her name was Laura Castleton, and her father lived in St. Mary's County, Maryland. She was a brunette, about twenty years of age, and one of the most beautiful girls I ever saw. She was nearly as tall as myself, but considerably stouter, and her body was molded in a most exquisite manner. Although her eyes were very black and her hair like the raven's plume, her skin was as white as alabaster. Her teeth were as regular as if they had been cut of a solid piece of ivory, and her hands and feet were fairylike in their proportions. I was the eldest girl in the school and Laura immediately made me her companion. She was exceedingly intelligent, well educated, and well read. I was soon attracted to her and we became inseparable. We would pass all our spare time reading to each other or in conversation on literary subjects. I agreed to love her with my whole heart, and was never happy outside of her company.

"Laura," I said to her one day when we were walking on the playground with our arms around each other's waist, "why can't we sleep together?"

"Would you like it, Kate?" she asked,

bending her black eyes upon my face with a peculiar gloom in them which sent the blood rushing to my cheeks—but why and wherefore I did not know.

"Indeed I would, Laura. It would be so nice to lie in your arms all night."

"Well, darling, I will ask Mrs. B——. I have no doubt that she will give her consent."

The lovely girl drew me towards her and gave me a warmer kiss than she had ever before bestowed upon me. The contact of her easy lips to mine sent an indefinable thrill through my body which I had never experienced before. In the evening she informed me that she had spoken to Mrs. B——and that the latter had consented that we should sleep together. I was overjoyed at this news and longed for night to come so that I might recline in my darling's arms.

At last the hour of bedtime arrived and I followed Laura to her chamber. She put the lamp on the dressing table and, kissing me affectionately, bade me undress myself quickly. We began our toilette for the night. I was undressed first, and having put on my nightgown, I sat down on the side of the bed and watched Laura disrobing herself. After she had removed her dress and her petticoats, I could not help being struck with her resplendent charms. Her chemise had fallen off her shoulder, beautifully rounded, and two globes of alabaster reposing on a field of snow. She appeared to be entirely unaware that I was watching her, for she sat down on a chair exactly in front of me, and crossing one leg over the other, she began to remove her garters and stockings. This attitude raised her chemise in front, and allowed me to have a full view of her magnificently formed limbs. I even caught sight of her voluptuous thighs. Laura caught my eye.

"What are you gazing at so earnestly?" she asked.

"I am gazing at your beauties, Laura."

"One would think that you were my lover," returned Laura laughingly.

"So I am, dear—for you know I love you."

"You little witch you, you know well enough what I mean. But if you want to admire beauty, why not look in the glass, for I am not nearly as beautiful as you are, dear Kate."

"What nonsense, Laura," I replied, "but come, let us get into bed."

So saying, I jumped between the sheets and was followed almost immediately by Laura, who first, however, placed the lamp on a chair by the bedside. She clasped me in her arms and pressed me to her breast, while she kissed my lips, cheek and eyes passionately. The warmth of her embraces and her glowing limbs entwined in mine caused a strange sensation to steal through me. My cheeks burned and I returned her kisses with an ardor that equalled her own.

"How delightful it is to be in your arms, dear Laura," I exclaimed.

"Do you really like it?" she replied, pressing me still closer to her. At the same time our nightdresses became disarranged, and I felt her naked thighs pressing against mine.

Laura kissed me again with even greater warmth than before, and while she was thus engaged she slipped one of her soft hands in the opening of my night-chemise, and I felt it descend on one of my breasts. When I felt this, a trembling seized my limbs and I pressed her convulsively to my heart.

"What a voluptuous girl you are, Kate," she said, molding my breasts and titillating my nipples. "You set me on fire."

"I never felt so happy in my life, Laura. I could live and die in your arms."

I now carried my hand to her globes of alabaster and pressed and molded them, imitating her in all her actions. Nay, more, I turned down the bedclothes and, unbuttoning her nightdress in front, I exposed those charming, snowy hillocks to my delighted gaze. The light of the lamp shone directly upon them, and I was never tired of admiring the whiteness, firmness and splendid development of those glowing semiglobes. I buried my face between them and pressed a thousand kisses on the soft velvet surface.

"Why Kate, you are a perfect volcano," said Laura, trembling under my embraces, "and I have been laboring under the delusion that you were an icicle."

"I was an icicle, darling, but now I have been melted by your charms."

"What a happy man your husband will be," said Laura.

"Happy—why?"

"To enfold such a glorious creature as you in his embrace. If you take so much delight with one of your own sex, what will you do when clasped in a man's arms?"

"You are jesting, Laura. Do you suppose for

a moment that I will ever allow a man to kiss and embrace me as you do?"

"Certainly, my love—he will do a great deal more than I do."

"More? What can you mean?"

"Is it possible, Kate, that you do not know?"

"I really do not know. Do tell me, there's a dear girl."

"I can scarcely believe it possible that you are seventeen years of age—a perfectly developed woman, and that you know nothing of the mysteries of love. Are you not aware, darling, that you possess a jewel about you that a man would give half his lifetime to ravish?"

"You speak in riddles, Laura. Where is this jewel?"

"Lie perfectly quiet, and I will show you where it is."

My cheeks burned and I was all aglow, for I had pretended to be more ignorant than I really was. Laura fastened her lips on my breast and placed her hand on one of my thighs. She then slowly carried it up the marble column and at last invaded the very sanctuary of love itself. When I felt her fingers roaming in the mossy covering of that hallowed spot, every moment growing more bold and enterprising, I could not help uttering a faint scream—it was the last cry of expiring modesty, and I grew as hardy and lascivious as my beautiful companion. I stretched my thighs open to their widest extent, the better to second the examination Laura was making of my person. The lovely girl appeared to be strangely affected while she was manipulating my secret charms. Her eyes shot fire, her bosom heaved, and she began to wiggle her bottom. For some time she played with the hair which thickly covered my mount of Venus—twisting it around her fingers, she then gently divided the folding lips and endeavored to penetrate the interior of the mystical grotto—but she could not effect an entrance but was obliged to satisfy herself with titillating the inside of the lips. Suddenly flows of pleasure shot through my entire body—for her finger had come in contact with the peeping sentinel that guarded the abode of bliss, an article whch until that moment I did not know I possessed. She rubbed it gently, giving me the most exquisite pleasure. If the last remnant of prudery had not taken flight before, this last act would have routed it completely. With a single jerk I threw off the bedclothes, and thus we both lay naked from the waist down.

"How magnificently you are formed, dear Kate," said Laura, examining all my hidden charms with the aid of the lamp. "What glorious thighs, what a delicious bijou, what a thick forest of hair, and what a splendidly developed clitoris. Now, sweet girl, I will make you taste the most delicious sensation you have ever experienced in your life. Let me do with you as I will."

"Do what you like with me, darling. I resign myself entirely in your hands."

Laura now commenced to gently rub my clitoris with her finger, while she kissed my breasts and lips passionately. I soon began again to experience the delicious sensation I have spoken of before; rivers of pleasure permeated through my system. My breasts bounded up and down—my buttocks were set in motion from the effect of her caressing finger, my thighs were stretched widely apart, and my whole body was under the exquisite influence of her scientific manipulations. At last the acme came, a convulsive shivering seized me, I gave two or three convulsive heaves with my buttocks, and in an agony of delight I poured down my first tribute to the god of love.

For a quarter of an hour I lay in a complete state of annihilation, and was only recalled from it by the kisses of Laura.

"Darling Kate," she exclaimed, "you must give me relief or I shall die—the sight of your enjoyment has lighted up such a fire within me that I shall burn up if you do not quench it."

"I will do my best, dear Laura, to assuage your desires. You have made me experience such unheard-of delight that I should indeed be wanting in gratitude if I were not to attempt to make you some return."

I rose up and, kneeling across her, began to examine at my ease her lovely Mons Veneris.

It was a glorious object, covered over with a mass of black silky hair, through the midst of which I could discern the plump lips folding close together. I placed my finger between them and felt her clitoris swelling beneath it until it actually peeped its little red head from its soft place of concealment. I now advanced one finger and found that it entered her coral sheath with the utmost ease; at the same time it was tightly grasped by the sensitive folds of her vagina. I began to move it in and out, while I kissed her white belly and thighs.

"Stop, darling," said Laura, rising up and going to a drawer, "I will contrive something better to bring on the dissolving period. You are rather a novice as yet in the art of procuring enjoyment."

She took from the drawer a dildo, which she fastened securely around my waist, and making me lie on my back, she leaned over me and guided it into her sensitive quiver. She then commenced to move herself rapidly upon it. It was a delicious sight to me; I could see the instrument entering in and out of her luscious grotto while her features expressed the most entrancing enjoyment and her broad white bottom and breasts shivered with pleasure. Her motions did not continue long, however. In a few minutes she succumbed and the elixir of love poured down her white thighs. The voluptuous sight before me and the rubbing of the dildo on my clitoris caused me to emit again at the same moment that she did, and we both sank exhausted on the bed. I shall not detain the reader with all the exquisite enjoyments I experienced for the next three months in my lessons with the beautiful Laura; suffice it to say that we exhausted every method that two young girls of ardent imagination could propose. At last the time approached for us to separate, and with tears and embraces we bade each other adieu.

I returned home and it was several years before I saw the sweet companion of my school days again.

CHAPTER TWO

THE MYSTERIES OF A CONVENT

When I returned home I found my father as gloomy and austere as ever. He welcomed me with a cold kiss and asked me a few questions as to the progress I had made in my studies. My replies did not appear to satisfy him and I had not been home a week before he declared his intention to send me to school again. I was by no means sorry to hear of this resolve, for my brother was finishing his education in New York, and the house was insufferably dull. I was at once dispatched to Mount de Sales, a convent near Baltimore. The inmates of the convent consisted of pupils and nuns — the latter acting as instructresses to the former, assisted by two or three priests.

I had been in the convent a year when we received a new pupil named Margaret Maitland, the daughter of a distinguished lawyer, residing in Baltimore. Margaret was a beautiful girl about my own age. She was rather tall, her eyes and hair were black, while her skin was of a whiteness ravishing to behold.

She was exceedingly religious and spent a great portion of her time in prayer, fasting and vigils. I noticed that she confessed to a Father Clark very frequently and always appeared very happy and contented when she left the confessional. I felt satisfied that there was something going on which partook more of the flesh than the spirit, and I determined to watch.

Father Clark's apartment was situated at the eastern extremity of the convent. It contained a large closet, and one day I concealed myself in it at the time I knew his penitent would visit him. I had been there but a few minutes before the priest entered. He was about forty years of age, stoutly built and rather handsome. He did not wait long before Margaret made her appearance. She looked positively beautiful. Her eyes sparkled, her cheeks were flushed, and her bosom rose and fell, showing that she was laboring under some excitement. To my extreme surprise, the moment she entered the room she ran up to Father Clark, and throwing her white arms round his neck kissed him passionately on the lips. He returned her embraces and drew her on his knee. This sight was entirely novel to me, and my cheeks burned while my eyes almost started from their sockets watching what would be their next proceeding. I had not long to wait, for I saw the priest's officious fingers unbutton Margaret's dress in front and deliberately pull it off her ivory shoulders, thus exposing two globes of snow, round, firm, exquisitely formed, and surmounted by two strawberry nipples, which stood out stiff. He pressed and kissed her breasts, absolutely burying his manly face between the soft cushions. He was, however, soon not satisfied with this, but canting her slightly up in his lap, he put his hand up her clothes, and invaded the most secret recesses of her body. This action raised her petticoats in such a manner that it exposed, to my gaze, one of her ivory thighs, which was large, well developed and beautifully rounded. I could see that he was moving his hand rapidly while Margaret seemed on the point of dying with delight. After amusing himself a short time in this manner, he suddenly desisted and, slipping her off his lap, placed her on her hands and knees on the floor. He then went to a cupboard and took from it a bunch of rods. Margaret remained in the position which he had placed her without making the slightest movement. Father Clark now walked up to her and, raising her petticoats, threw them over her head, thus exposing, in a moment, all her hidden charms to my excited eyes. It was a delicious sight, sufficient to have seduced the most rigid anchorite. I could see Margaret's white buttocks, admirably formed, her two beautiful thighs, and exquisitely formed legs; all was naked from her waist down. Situated at the lower portion of her white bottom, between her lovely thighs, I could discern the pouting lips of her bijou, with a line of coral marking the spot where they met.

Father Clark raised the rod and brought it down gently on her broad, white buttocks—their hue was immediately changed to a blushing red, while Margaret twisted and turned under the flagellation, every movement revealing more of her exquisite Mon Veneris. While the priest plied the rod, he appeared to be experiencing the most delicious sensations. Margaret's bottom was soon as red as a cherry, but she did not appear to mind the flogging which she was receiving the least bit.

When the priest had continued this excerise a few minutes, he threw down the rod, and kneeling on the ground behind her, he unbuttoned his pantaloons, and out leaped his staff of love, stiff, firm and with its ruby head uncovered. He nestled it for a moment between her buttocks, and then gently driving the vermilion lips of her coral sheath with his fingers, he brought his instrument to bear on the luscious opening, and seizing her by the hips, in another moment he was plunged to the very hilt in her beautiful body. When Margaret felt that the conjunction was complete she uttered a faint exclamation of joy and wiggled her buttocks from side to side as if to prevent her prisoner from escaping her. The priest now began to move himself in and out of her — and as he did so, I could distinctly see his staff appear and disappear in its warm nest. Every time he withdrew, her vagina clasped his intrument so tightly that he drew out the interior lips, and each time that he plunged it into her palpitating body, they were carried in with it. You can imagine my sensations, dear reader, when I saw all this. I instinctively raised my clothes and carried my hand to my own moss-covered retreat, and forcing a finger between the lips, I found it tightly grasped by my vagina, and I imitated all their motions, thrusting it in and out, my eyes being all the time fixed on the amorous couple. The priest was evidently in the seventh heaven of enjoyment, his hands wandered from one beauty to another as if at a loss to know which to take possession of. At one moment it would be her snowy globes which still remained uncovered; at another it would be her white belly, and then again it was the top of her Mount of Venus. Suddenly his motions grew quicker, his staff entered in and out of the coral retreat so rapidly that I could no longer detect the motion. The crisis came, and with a smothered exclamation of joy they both discharged. At the same moment the exciting scene I had witnessed drew from me my tribute to the god of sexual desire.

I cultivated Margaret's friendship after this, and when I was intimate enough with her I told her all I had seen. She blushed at first, but when she saw that I could be discreet, she confessed the whole truth to me. I found her an able instructress, and was soon even more perfectly *au fait* in all the mysteries of love, except the actual experience of sexual intercourse with the other sex. She made me a witness of many scenes between herself and Father Clark, and I soon found they were both perfectly adept in the art of procuring sexual enjoyment.

One day I discovered further evidence of the great morality pervading in Mount de Sales. The Lady Abbess was a handsome, fine-looking woman of about forty years of age. She was very strict with all the boarders of the convent, except with two sisters named Emily and Fannie Dawson. These two girls were her pets and were always with her. They were both beautiful girls, with flashing dark eyes and beautiful complexions. On the day I refer to, Margaret Maitland came to me and whispered in my ear that if I would come with her she would show me a pretty sight. I followed and she led me to the Lady Abbess's room and told me to peep through the keyhole. I did so and saw a very strange scene which I will endeavor to describe to you.

Seated on a low chair near a large sofa was Father Price. His pantaloons were down and the lower portion of his body all uncovered; his instrument of love stood stiff and erect. Seated sideways towards him on the sofa I have just referred to, was the Lady Abbess. Her dress was off her shoulders, revealing her well-developed bust. The lower portion of her body was entirely naked; one of her feet rested on an ottoman, the other on the ground; by this means one of her thighs was elevated. Father Price had one finger in her lustful slit, while she had grasped his staff in her hand. He was slowly pushing his finger in and out of her warm nest, and every now and then kissing her broad white buttocks which were entirely at his command. But this was not all; Emily and Fannie Dawson were also there, acting their parts. Emily stood on the sofa with her petticoats raised above her naval, thus revealing her delicious thighs, her white belly and the moss-covered domain of Venus. She was exquisitely made. The Lady Abbess was titillating her clitoris with her unoccupied hand, while Emily's excited face, the tip of her tongue slightly protruding from her coral lips and the heaves of her alabaster buttocks rising to meet the Abbess's deflowering finger, sufficiently showed the intense delights she was enjoying. Fannie was at the other end of the sofa. She had her back turned towards Father Price; she knelt on the sofa with one knee, while the other leg rested on the ground; her skirts were thrown over her head, and her head was buried in the sofa, thus elevating her white bottom in the air. Between her ivory thighs we could see the panting lips of her luscious bijou. She was rubbing the top of her slit with one finger, and by the quivering of her buttocks, I guessed she was enjoying herself to her heart's content.

Margaret and I watched all their proceedings. Their motion soon grew fast and furious, and we were both so excited by what we saw that we instinctively raised each other's petticoats and imitated their actions on each other. I forced a finger in Margaret's lovely grotto, and at the same time felt her finger caressing my clitoris. I opened my thighs to the widest possible extent to admit her manipulation more readily and she did the same. It was a delicious sensation, feeling her delicate finger force its way into my warm vagina. We kept time with the actors in the next room, and at the very moment that I saw the sperm go from Father Price's instrument to the broad, white buttocks of the Abbess, both Margaret and myself emitted, and the Abbess and the two sisters were not a moment behind. We then ran to our dormitories for fear of being discovered.

A few weeks after this occurrence my father took me away from the convent and I returned home. Here my time passed monotonously enough, and I wished myself back to Mount de Sales a hundred times. But an event happened which more than reconciled me to my change of life. This was nothing less than a visit from Harry Duval, a cousin who resided in Baltimore.

Harry was a fine, handsome young fellow, about twenty-two years of age. The moment I saw him, I felt irresistibly attracted towards him. But I disguised my admiration with all the hypocrisy common to young girls.

One day we were out walking together in the beautiful grounds surrounding my father's house. The weather was deliciously warm and the birds filled the air with their melodies. I was clad very lightly, wearing a low-necked dress with a light scarf thrown over my shoulders. We wandered for some distance, conversing on everyday topics, when my cousin proposed that we should rest ourselves on the grass under the shade of a fine, large elm tree; I consented and we sat down. Harry took my hand in his and kissed it. I blushed at this familiarity but did not withdraw it from his grasp. By degrees he grew more enterprising, and drawing me towards him, imprinted a kiss on my lips. I now made an effort to withdraw myself from his grasp but he held me tightly.

"Dear Kate," said he, "I love you with all my heart and soul."

"Oh Harry," I replied, "you have said that to hundreds of others."

"Pray, darling—it is you alone that possesses my heart. I swear I love none but you."

So saying, he imprinted fresh kisses on my lips in spite of the resistance I made. To tell the truth, my resistance was getting weaker and weaker, for I felt a delicious feeling run through my body such as I had never experienced before. He grew bolder and almost devoured me with kisses. In our struggle the light scarf which I wore on my shoulders became displaced and my neck and the upper portion of my bust were bare. The sight of my white shoulders appeared to electrify Harry, for he immediately brought his lips to bear upon them, and caressed and patted them with his hand. He did not stop here, however. My dress was rather loose in front and he had the audacity to invade the secrets of my bosom. The pressure he made caused some of the buttons to give away behind and my frock fell completely off my shoulders, revealing to his gaze my two "orbs of snow," as he called them. He immediately took possession of them and molded and pressed them with his hands, at the same time gently titillating the strawberry nipples which, under his lascivious touches, stood out stiff. I was now completely on fire and no longer opposed him. To tell the truth, I was as anxious as he to experience the acme of love. Harry kissed and caressed my bubbies for some minutes, and while thus engaged, one of his hands was furtively raising my petticoats. At last I felt one of his hands on my naked thigh—a shiver of desire ran through my frame. He cautiously ascended the snowy columns, and in a moment or two I felt an impudent finger in the outskirts of the domain of Venus. I instinctively lifted up my thighs in order to facilitate his curious researches, and soon experienced the most delicious sensations, for his finger had already divided the lips which formed the entrance of my moss-covered retreat. He gently pushed it forward until it was clasped tightly by the warm sides of my vagina. While he was acting in this manner he kissed me repeatedly on the lips and breast, only pausing to suck the rosy nipples which surmounted the two semiglobes. Although he addressed every term of endearment to me, I was too much excited to make any reply. For in a few moments he continued his delicious play, titillating the interior of my Mons Veneris, while he caressed my clitoris with his thumb, sending a lava of delight through my frame. In spite of all my endeavors not to appear too lascivious, I could not help moving my buttocks in response to his soul inspiring touches —I felt the crisis approaching. At that moment I saw him tear open the front of his pantaloons and out jumped his member, as stiff as an iron bar. With his unoccupied hand he seized mine and bore it down on the menacing object. I seized it in my grasp and began to imitate his motions. This was more than Harry could bear, for I had scarcely made half a dozen movements when my cousin, frantically seizing me around the waist, stretched my length on the green sward. In one moment he was between my thighs, which I am willing to confess were opened wide enough to receive him, and in another moment his instrument had penetrated the lips of my most secret charms, and was imbedded to the very hilt in my body. Oh God! the ecstasy I felt when the conjunction was complete I can never describe. He reposed for a moment or two in this condition and then began to gently heave his buttocks. I responded with a corresponding motion and no tongue can tell the delights I enjoyed as his delicious staff rushed in and out of the sheath destined by nature to receive it.

"Oh, Harry," I exclaimed, "this is too much —I am suffocating with pleasure—darling, dar —dar—"

The crisis came; a flood of rapture escaped from me while I felt his copious discharge lubricate the very mouth of my womb. I absolutely fainted with pleasure.

When I recovered my senses I found that Harry was drying me with his pocket handkerchief. This done, he stooped and imprinted a kiss on the sheath of his joys, and then assisted me to rise. We then returned to the house fully satisfied with our delightful experiences.

"Darling Kate," said he, as we reached the door, "leave the door of your bed chamber open tonight."

I pressed his hand as a sign of affirmation and we separated. You can easily imagine, dear reader, how anxiously I waited for night. My bedroom was far removed from any other occupied part of the house, and I had no fear that we should be interrupted. At last the hour for retiring came, and I took up my candle and went to my chamber. I did not undress myself, but sat on the beside anxiously awaiting my cousin's coming. I had been there about a quarter of an hour when I heard his footsteps, and in another moment he was by my side. He rushed to me, kissed my lips and then, with trembling fingers, bared my breasts, which he covered with kisses. He then absolutely tore off my clothes, not even sparing my chemise, and I stood before him as naked as I was born. In a few seconds he was in the same situation and I saw for the second time in my life his splendid member, so stiff and firm that its ruby head nearly reached his navel. All my modesty disappeared as if by magic, and I removed my hands which I had instinctively placed over my center of attraction and, rushing towards him, seized his burning rod in my grasp. I capped and uncapped the fiery head and played with the purse containing the two witnesses to virility. My cousin's eyes shot fire and he began to move his buttocks in reply to my touches. He placed his hands on my bottom and pressed me close to him, and I could feel his staff of love pressing against my white belly. In another moment he had thrown me on my back on the bed, and then set about examining the charms of my person at his ease. His first proceeding was to open my thighs to the widest extent, thus exposing to his gaze and touches the whole of love's domain. He played with the hair covering the hillock of Venus; he divided the lips with his finger and, seeking my clitoris, almost sent me crazy with pleasure by gently rubbing it. He then turned me over on my belly and patted the cheeks of my buttocks, which he swore were whiter than driven snow. He titillated both my clitoris and bottom at the same time, but noticing by my convulsive movements that I was on the eve of spending, he suddenly desisted. Restoring me to my former position on my back, and throwing himself on top of me, he inserted his staff of love into the pouting lips of my moss-covered slit. No sooner had I felt the delicious morsel pierce me to the quick than I passed one of my arms round his neck and pressed him convulsively to my bosom. I then clasped his loins with my thighs and legs and strained myself so closely to him that the very hair of our genitals intermingled. A large mirror hung beside the bed and I could see our forms reflected in it. I could see his instrument imbedded to the very hilt in my Mons Veneris, the tips of which clasped it tightly. He now commenced to work his plump buttocks up and down. I replied by a corresponding motion and we kept time admirably together. The thrilling rapture, the delicious sensations of that ecstatic period is out of my power to describe. When I felt his hot pego rushing in and out of my sensitive vagina, I squirmed and wriggled under his fierce thrusts, and I thought my breath would leave my body. At last the dissolving period approached. I could tell it was coming on by his more rapid thrusts, by his half-drawn sighs, by his interrupted breathing, and more especially, by a peculiar suction which my vagina exercised on his rod. I spurred his bottom with my heels, I pressed him to me, I bit him in the agony of my delight, and just as I was discharging, I passed my hand underneath his thigh and tickled his testicles.

"I am coming, darling Kate," he exclaimed. "Oh God, I come, I co—!"

"I too, Harry," I exclaimed, "there, there! there!"

He made two more vigorous thrusts to which I responded with such vigor that it made his testicles butt against my bottom, and the next moment we were both dissolved in bliss.

He then withdrew from me and lay down by my side. A delightful conversation followed in which he told me how much he loved me and how faithful he would always be to me. While we were thus conversing I had hold of his instrument while he was playing with my center of love. In a short time I felt his staff swelling beneath my grasp, and it was soon in a state of princely erection again. We again resumed the rites of Venus.

This time he stretched himself all his length on his back and drew me on top of him. He clasped me around the waist, while I myself guided his dart into my bower, which was burning to receive it. He then insisted that I should pump up his spermatic treasures myself while he would remain perfectly passive. I was quite agreeable, and began an up-and-down motion. My vagina fitted his pego like a glove, and I had not played horsewoman a dozen times before I felt his boiling sperm inundate my womb, while I also poured down my share of love's elixer in such profusion that it wetted both thighs and belly.

I shall not detain the reader by detailing how many times we sacrificed ourselves to the shrine of Venus that night, nor shall I depict all the postures and modes we persued, as I have many similiar scenes to depict; suffice it to say that when we got up the next morning we were both thoroughly exhausted, and pale and feeble from our unwonted exertions.

For six weeks I enjoyed sexual delights in every possible form—not a day passing without at least one experience of my cousin's capabilities. At the end of that time he was compelled to return home. He left me with the most ardent protestations of love and devotion, and took an oath that he would marry none but me. I had such a confidence in him that I firmly believed his word.

CHAPTER THREE

A NEW SCENE

After Harry's departure, my father's house grew more and more distasteful to me, and I resolved to make an effort to leave it. One day I went to him and expressed a wish to take a situation as governess—he made but slight objections, and at last gave his consent. I immediately sent an advertisement to the Philadelphia papers and received several answers; amongst them was one from a Mr. Herbert Clarence who lived in the village of Chester. He offered me such advantageous terms that I at once accepted them, and the next day started for my new home.

Riverside Lodge, as Mr. Clarence's residence was called, was situated on the banks of the Schuylkill, and was fitted up with all the elegance wealth could command. The grounds were handsomely laid out, the gardens cultivated to the extreme of art, and in short, it bore more resemblance to the residences we meet on the other side of the water which are occupied by the proud aristocracy of England than the mansion of a simple American gentleman.

Nature too had done an immense deal to enhance the beauties of the dwelling. The scenery around was pastoral and beautiful—what it wanted in grandeur it more than made up with the picturesque view to be seen from all sides of the house. The lodge was situated on a rising hillock and fronted the river, from which it was not more than a hundred yards distant. To the north of the house was a thick wood, containing trees of many years growth. In this sylvan retreat Mr. Clarence had fitted up rustic chairs and seats, and in the heat of the summer it afforded a delightful shelter from the sun's rays. On both the other sides of the dwelling was a handsome sloping lawn, also covered with fine trees.

I was met at the door of the house by the owner, a fine handsome man of about thirty-five years of age. He introduced me to his wife, a confined invalid who never left her chamber. I then saw my pupils, two little girls, the eldest not more than six years of age. I found Mr. Clarence to be a perfect gentleman, courteous, polite and agreeable. I soon felt quite at home with him. Mrs. Clarence never interfered with me, and days passed without my even seeing her. I pitied poor Mr. Clarence having such a sick wife, for it was easy to be seen that he was a man of a very amorous temperament, and it was also certain that his wife could afford him no satisfaction in this respect.

I was naturally thrown much into Mr. Clarence's society and noticed that he daily grew more tender to me. When shaking hands with me he would press my hand and retain it in his, and when I wore a low-necked dress I observed that his eyes were fixed on my white shoulders, and that when he caught a glimpse of my bosom his face would flush and a decided protuberance would manifest itself in his pantaloons.

Things went on in this way for two months. Then one day Mr. Clarence asked me if I would like to go out riding with him. I had always been fond of equestrian exercises and consented very willingly. The horses were brought round to the door and I mounted a handsome bay pony, while my companion rode a large gray horse which appeared but half broken. Mr. Clarence assisted me to mount and in doing so I exposed a considerable portion of my limbs, my petticoats getting entangled in the saddle. When he saw my leg above the knee, for I wore no drawers, a crimson flush suffused his face—but it was not one of shame but desire. He recovered himself, however, almost immediately, and off we started.

We had ridden about six or seven miles when Mr. Clarence's horse suddenly took fright and galloped off with him. At the turn of the road, from some cause or other, the rider was thrown off and deposited on the green sward. Fortunately he was not injured—his horse, however, galloped away towards Riverside Lodge.

"A pretty situation, Miss Percival," said Clarence as he rose to his feet. "Here am I, six miles from home, and nothing left for me but to tramp it on foot."

"Nay, Mr. Clarence, that must not be. If you do not mind, you can ride behind me. The pony can bear us both very well, and we can proceed slowly."

"I am afraid to discommode you, Miss Percival."

"Not at all—our ancestors, you know, used to ride pillion."

"I accept your kind offer," he returned, and springing on the pony's back took his place behind me.

He passed one arm around my waist for the purpose of holding himself securely in his position. We then slowly started in the direction of the lodge. We had not advanced a mile, however, before I felt something pressing stiffly against my bottom. My previous experience made me know what it was and you may easily believe, dear reader, that I began to feel a strange sensation running through me. Whether my companion detected my sensations or not, I cannot say, but certain it is that the arm that encircled my waist was raised until his hand rested on my bosom, outside my riding habit; however, I made no attempt to remove it, and encouraged, doubtless, by my seeming tacit consent to his enterprises, he furtively inserted two of his fingers in the opening in front of my dress and I felt them on my naked breast. The contact of my bubbies appeared to electrify him, for I felt his staff of love beating against my buttocks, still more plainly than before.

"Mr. Clarence," said I, "this is wrong—remember you have a wife."

"My darling girl," he replied, "I cannot help it. I am deeply enamored with you. My wife is sick and unable to receive my embraces. Dearest Kate, be kind to me. I swear I will not injure you."

What could an amorous, love-sick girl reply? I was too fond of sexual pleasures to refuse them when time and opportunity offered. I made no reply whatever. My silence evidently encouraged him, for he now unbuttoned the front of my habit and placed his hand on my naked breasts, molding them and titillating the strawberry nipples. With his other hand he managed to raise my petticoats from behind, and I felt myself sitting bare-bottomed on his lap. This was not all, for between my fleshy thighs was his instrument, which he had managed to disengage from his pantaloons. He now raised me up slightly and in another moment his hand invaded my mossy crevice. No sooner did his fingers come in contact with the hair surrounding the domain of Venus than all reserve left him and, inclining me slightly forward, he directed his instrument and in a moment forced it into my moist and burning passage, and drove it home with a sudden plunge.

"Oh God! Mr. Clarence! how delicious!" I exclaimed when I felt the hair surmounting his pubes tickling my bottom, and I wiggled myself from side to side on his splendid staff. The pony now began to canter and the motion he made was sufficient to cause his lance to move in and out of me. During this exciting proceeding, Clarence was titillating my clitoris in front, and turning my head around he kissed my lips in the most passionate manner. The pony really seemed to have some idea of what was being transacted on his back, for he set off in a gallop which soon brought a climax to our pleasure, for we both discharged simultaneously.

He then withdrew his weapon and we proceeded quietly home, indulging, however, in most delicious conversation on the way. When we reached Riverside Lodge we dismounted and entered the drawing room. It was unoccupied.

"Darling girl," said Herbert, "I must enjoy you once more—we shall not be interrupted."

"I am yours, dear Herbert, do with me as you please," I replied.

He led me to a sofa and laid me on my back, and then threw my clothes up above my navel. He paused awhile to gaze on my hidden charm, and ran his hands over the various objects that met his gaze.

"What magnificent limbs! What splendid thighs!" he exclaimed, "and what a graceful, rounded and polished belly, and then what a delicious Mons Veneris! What a profusion of curly hair adorns this lovely spot!"

He was not content with the unveiled charms of the lower portion of my body, but he must needs release my large and plump breasts—and these afforded him a new theme on which to expatiate. He did not moralize long, but unbuttoning his pantaloons he released his stiff lance and, bringing it to bear between my widely stretched thighs, I soon felt it forcing its way into my sensitive vagina. I raised my buttocks to meet his thrusts and experienced the most delicious sensation. His motions grew quicker and the end approached. I wiggled my bottom from side to side. I gave utterance to my rapture in words, sighs and exclamations of pleasure and received his whole discharge at the same moment that I myself emitted. When he had finished he leaned over and kissed my breasts and assisted me to rise. We heard steps approaching the room and I hastily retired to my chamber.

My time after the adventure with Mr. Clarence passed very agreeably. My amorous desires were fully satisfied and I enjoyed a repetition of the scenes I had passed through with my cousin. I found Herbert very ardent and very ingenious in his mode of performing the sexual act—I shall have to refer to some of his experiments by and by.

One day I was informed that Mr. Clarence's sister-in-law was coming to spend a few weeks at Riverside Lodge. Herbert gave me the information with manifest pleasure painted on his face and I felt sure her coming pleased him; for my own part, I cannot say that I was especially delighted, for I was afraid her presence would interfere with our enjoyments.

On the appointed day, a carriage drove up to the entrance and Amy Denmead, Mrs. Clarence's sister, alighted. The moment I saw her, truth compels me to state that she was one of the most beautiful women I had ever beheld. She was about twenty years of age, above the medium height and her form was molded in the most exquisite manner. Her face was really lovely, her features faultless, her complexion fair as Parian marble and yet the hue of health was on her cheeks—the white and red contrasting in admirable manner. Her hair was a dark glossy brown and hung in natural ringlets on her snowy neck and shoulders. Her bosom was full, voluptuous and beautifully rounded. Her hands and feet were small, almost to a fault, her carriage was full of grace and when she smiled she allowed to be seen a row of pearly teeth which, if they had been cut out of a solid piece of ivory, could not have been more regular.

When I was introduced to her she received me with a good deal of warmth in her manner and observed that she was certain we would be good friends. During the evening she asked me if I had any objections to her sleeping with me, as she was too timid to sleep alone. I replied that I should be very happy for her to share my bed. We retired early as she was tired from her journey. She undressed very quickly and was soon between the sheets. I quickly followed her example. The moment I lay by her side she clasped me in her arms and pressed a warm kiss on my lips. I returned it, for I began to feel attracted by this delicious creature, and the warm contact of her beautiful semiglobes to mine sent a thrill through me. But we made no further progress that night, confining ourselves to conversation only. She asked me a great many questions concerning Herbert Clarence, as to "how I liked him," "how he behaved towards me," and a hundred other interrogatories. At last we went to sleep.

When I awoke the next morning I found Miss

Denmead already risen. I got up, dressed myself and went down to seek her. I searched the house and found she was not there, and then came to the conclusion that she must have gone into the garden for a stroll. I followed and directed my steps to a summerhouse situated at the bottom of the lawn. The pathway that led to it was of grass so that the sound of footsteps could not be heard. When I approached the arbor I heard the rustling of a dress inside, and instead of opening the door I peeped through the keyhole. Great God! I saw a sight which sent the blood boiling through my veins. Herbert Clarence was reclining on his back on a divan which he had drawn into the middle of the floor. His pantaloons were slipped down to his heels, leaving the whole of the lower portion of his body uncovered. Straddling him, with one foot resting on the ground and with the other on the divan was the beautiful Amy. Her dress was open in front, leaving her splendid breasts entirely bare. Her petticoats were elevated above her navel and thrown behind her white belly, her voluptuous thighs, her magnificent limbs, and above all that masterpiece of nature, her lovely Mons Veneris entirely exposed to my gaze, for she stood directly facing me. His instrument had penetrated the luscious lips of her slit. While I was watching he gave one tremendous heave upwards with his buttocks and sent it into her body clear up to his testicles. She was evidently gorged with delight and enraptured, for her lovely face expressed the most intense enjoyment, and by the quivering of her eyelids I felt assured the crisis would soon come. They now commenced to move together, he directing his thrusts upwards while she worked her bottom in reply to his motions. While this delicious play was going on, I could distinctly see his staff entering in and out of her coral sheath, the lips of which embraced it so tightly that they seemed to be afraid it should escape from them. It was the most voluptuous sight I had ever seen. As the acme approached, Amy leaned over and kissed Herbert—their tongues sought each other's mouths and they imitated the sexual act. So intense was their feeling of pleasure that they actually bit each other. The working of his lance in her sensitive vagina caused a suction sound delightful to hear.

"Dear Herbert, I am coming," suddenly exclaimed the lovely girl.

These words seemed to increase Clarence's ardor, for he commenced to work his bottom with lightning rapidity, and suddenly giving a tremendous push upwards which she replied to by a corresponding motion downwards, they both remained motionless, his staff so deeply engulfed in her that the hair of their genitals was intermingled. Convulsive movement then seized her whole frame and she fell on his belly. He was still imbedded in her.

They remained motionless for ten minutes when she opened her eyes and kissed Herbert repeatedly on the lips. The warmth of her caresses appeared to reanimate him and he returned her embraces.

"I must now go, darling," said she. "Someone may come."

"I must once more taste the delights of

heaven," he returned. "We shall have no opportunity until tomorrow, dear Amy, and I am not half satisfied yet."

He withdrew himself from her and wiping the throne of love gently with his pocket handkerchief, he stooped down and kissed her Mons Veneris. He then drew her on his knee and began gently to titillate her clitoris with his finger, she performing her part by covering and uncovering the ruby head of his lance. They continued this play for some little time—every motion evidently bringing them nearer the consummation.

"Herbert, I shall spend if you continue your titillations much longer," said Amy, beginning to wriggle her buttocks.

"Come then, darling," replied Herbert. "I too am ready."

And so saying he reclined her on the divan, and taking her thighs in his arms, he drove his lance to the hilt into her body. They seemed no longer to know what they were about. Joined as they were together, they seemed to experience the utmost voluptuousness. Amy especially appeared to be enjoying the delights of heaven. Her rapid movements, her exclamation of supreme pleasure, the trembling of her eyelids, and the convulsive manner in which she pressed Herbert's bottom was sufficient proof of her intense pleasure. A few reciprocal motions and they again discharged.

They now rose, adjusted their clothing and I thought it better to retire, which I immediately did. A few minutes afterwards Amy entered, apparently as fresh as ever, and greeting me with a kiss, stating that she had been taking a long walk. I did not say a word, determined to take my own time to tell what I had seen. That night when we retired to bed, Amy addressed a few words to me and then fell asleep. When I woke up in the morning she was still sleeping. I turned down the bedclothes and found that the lower portion of her body was entirely naked. Her nightdress, too, was open in the front, leaving her delicious breasts exposed. They were firm, round and white as the driven snow, and surmounted by delicate pink nipples. Her beautiful hair covered the pillow like a veil. Her ruby lips were slightly separated, revealing her pearly teeth, and her lovely cheeks were tinged with a slight color which made her appear most lovely. Her belly was the smoothest and whitest I had ever seen. Her magnificently molded thighs were stretched widely apart, and at the lower part of her belly was her glorious domain of Venus. It was indeed a pretty bijou. Imagine to yourself, dear reader, a hillock surmounted with curly brown hair, between which could be seen the pouting lips to the entrance of bliss, folded so closely together that a line of coral only showed where they joined. It was a sight that would have tempted an anchorite. I do not know what possessed me but I leaned over her and imprinted a kiss on that fountain of delight. I then gently divided the lips with my finger and sought for her clitoris, which I soon had swelling under my touches.

In a few moments it grew quite stiff. A shiver of delight ran through the lovely girl, but she did not awake. With a finger of my other hand I penetrated into the coral passage and began to move it rapidly in and out, while with my other finger I titillated her vagina. Amy, still asleep, replied to my titillations by working her bottom up and down.

"Oh Herbert," she exclaimed, "it is too delightful! Faster darling, faster."

I moved my finger with such extreme rapidity I could feel her vagina beginning to contract on my finger; she wiggled herself to and fro.

"I am coming, darling, dear Herbert, I am com—com—"

She could utter no more, but pushing her bushy mount close up to my hand I felt my fingers endowed with the love potion I had distilled from her. At the moment of discharging she awoke, and opening her eyes gazed with astonishment on me.

"Is it you, dear Kate?" she exclaimed as soon as she could recover her breath. "I really thought it was—" she seemed suddenly to remember and hesitated to finish her sentence.

"You thought it was Herbert Clarence," I remarked.

The lovely girl blushed, but made no reply.

"I saw your proceedings with him yesterday in the arbor," I continued, "but do not be alarmed, dear Amy, for I am willing to confess he has done exactly the same thing to me."

"If that be the case, there need be no reserve between us," replied Amy, and raising from her reclining posture she seized me by the waist and throwing me on the bed she divested me of my chemise almost before I knew what she was about. When she saw my naked body she uttered an exclamation of pleasure and ran her hands rapidly over my charms. She first of all kissed and molded my bubbies, sucking the very nipples—from this she descended to my belly, smoothing it down with her soft hand—at last she attacked me in the very center of pleasure, running her fingers on the hair surmounting my Mons Veneris, opening the lips and gazing curiously in the ruby cavity. Then she seized on my clitoris, exciting it with her lascivious touches, and at last, as if unable to control herself longer, she forced a finger into the deepest recesses of my vagina and commenced to move it rapidly in and out.

"Amy, Amy!" I exclaimed, "you are killing me with pleasure."

"Have you not given me the most intense enjoyment this morning, and shall I not be equally kind to you? But stay, darling," she continued, "I have something that will give you even greater delight."

She suddenly desisted from her manipulations, and running through her trunk took from it an India-rubber dildo, shaped exactly like a man's instrument.

"This is what I amuse myself with when alone," said she, "and now I am going to give you a taste of it. Place yourself on your knees dear Kate, and recline your head on the pillow."

I placed myself in the position she indicated,

by which means my buttocks were elevated high in the air.

"How glorious you look in this position, Kate," said Amy, pressing her hands over my bottom. "What a pretty object is your bijou between your swelling thighs, how closely the plump lips come together and how delicately they are shaded by the curling hair growing on that precious buttock! I must—I must kiss it."

So saying she stooped down and imprinted a long kiss on the object presented to her regard—nay, she did more, for I actually felt her tongue divide the mysterious portals of Venus and penetrate into the most secret recesses of my covered way of love, rendering me almost crazy with the delicious titillation. She was one of the most lascivious girls I ever met with, and evidently enjoyed one of her own sex almost as much as she did one of the male kind. She moved her tongue rapidly for a few moments and I verily believe, had she continued five seconds longer, I should have spent in her mouth. But she suddenly ceased.

"Now, darling, for something more substantial," she exclaimed.

And bringing the point of the dildo to the entrance of my vagina, she suddenly plunged it to the very hilt into my glowing sheath. She now commenced to move it in and out of me somewhat slowly, as if for the purpose of prolonging my exquisite feelings. Soon, however, she saw by the motion of my buttocks that I was on the eve of discharging, and placing her hand scientifically between my thighs, she titillated my clitoris and bottom at the same moment, while with the other hand she drove the dildo with lightning rapidity into my lustful cavity. I could hold out no longer.

"I must come, dearest Amy," I gasped. "There—there—th—"

And with a half murmured ejaculation of pleasure I poured down a flood of love's tide and sank motionless on my belly in the bed.

In a few minutes I recovered and we both lay side by side. Again and again we tasted bliss in each other's arms, I sought to repay her for the delights she had afforded me, and I may say, I succeeded. At last we were unable to do anything more and fell asleep in each other's arms. We were awakened by a tap at the door. Amy rose up and ran to open it and who should be there but Mr. Clarence. A few hurried whispers ensued between them, then Herbert stepped into the room.

"Dear Kate," said he, coming to me as I lay in bed. "Amy has informed me that you have come to a good understanding together, and I need not tell you how much gratified I am to hear it. God forbid that two such beautiful girls should be rivals. I love you both and I believe I can satisfy you both. My wife, tomorrow, goes to Philadelphia to spend a few days—there is no reason we should not enjoy pleasure all together. I propose that tomorrow evening shall be our initiation—we shall have the house entirely to ourselves. Do you consent, Kate?"

"Willingly," I replied. Jumping up from my

bed, regardless of the exposure of my person, and throwing my arms around his neck, I kissed him on the lips.

"What do you say, Amy, do you consent?"

"I shall like it most of all things," replied his sister-in-law, following my example. As we both hung about his neck he pressed us to him, and the sight of our naked charms evidently affected him, and I thought he would there and then give us proof of his prowess, but he controlled himself and advised us to husband our strength for the following night as he intended to do. He then kissed us both and retired from the chamber.

CHAPTER FOUR

AN ORGY

The next day at two o'clock Mrs. Clarence and her two children started for Philadelphia, leaving Amy, Mr. Herbert and myself the sole occupants of Riverside Lodge. We passed a delightful afternoon together, wandering about the grounds, reading amorous books, and filling up intervals with tender conversation. I found Amy to be a very intelligent girl who conversed on almost every subject. We stayed out in the open air until it began to grow dark, then we all reentered the house. We then sat down to a delicious repast followed by a bottle or two of champagne. The wine caused our eyes to sparkle and unloosened our tongues.

"Come, girls," said Herbert, rising from his chair after we had finished dessert, "follow me, and I will conduct you to the room destined to be the theater of our joys."

We obeyed and he led us to a part of the house I had never visited before. At the end of a passage he unlocked a door and ushered us into a magnificently furnished chamber, in fact it was furnished with a luxury which I had never before imagined. The apartment was of octagon shape and was lighted by a chandelier which hung from the ceiling, suspended therefrom by silver chains. The ceiling itself was beautifully frescoed and was painted with scenes from heathen mythology. Placed here and there throughout the chamber were statuettes made of Parian marble which almost seemed to breathe in the soft artificial light. The floor was covered with a gorgeous medallion carpet and around the walls were placed easy chairs and sofas of the most costly description. A peculiar intoxicating perfume was shed through the room, which had the effect of inducing a soft languor. There were eight panels formed by the octagon shape of the room. The upper portion of each panel was filled by a beautifully executed oil painting, the lower portion by a mirror or plate glass descending to the floor.

Each painting was numbered from one to eight, and they were such exciting subjects and so beautifully executed that I cannot refrain from giving a description of them to the reader. Number one represented a beautiful girl reclining on a sofa, her petticoats raised to reveal the lower portion of her body. Her head was thrown back, her breasts were bare, and her thighs were elevated in the air. In front of her was a young man with the insignia of his sex proudly elevated, menacing the domain of Venus with his formidable weapon. Another girl seated on the sofa behind him was endeavoring to pull him away from her more fortunate companion—her clothes too were raised above her navel, revealing all the secrets of her person. The artist had painted her charms so perfectly that it was difficult to believe they were not real. The lips of her slit and the hair surmounting the hillock of Venus was done to the very life. This picture was labeled *The Dispute.*

Number two, labeled *A Water Party*, represented a boat gliding down a silver stream. On the edge of the boat sat a man entirely naked with a girl in the same condition in his arms. Her arms encircled his neck while he grasped her around the body. Her thighs were wrapped tightly around his loins while his instrument was buried to the very hilt in her salacious slit. In the water, a girl was resting on her hands, her plump bubbies just kissing the stream, while behind her stood a man with her legs in his grasp, his staff of love deeply imbedded in her sensitive vagina. The lips of her bijou were beautifully depicted at the lower part of her white bottom. Another nymph was getting into the boat with her back turned to the spectator, thus showing the glorious slope of her back and her voluminous white buttocks and thighs.

Number three, labeled *A Complete Seat*, represented a man sitting on the edge of a low wall, a lovely girl completely in a state of nature in his lap. She sat sideways. One of her thighs rested on his arm, the other hung down. The elevation of her thigh enabled the spectator to see his pego hovering between the lips of the warm nest destined by nature to receive it.

Number four, entitled *Rural Felicity*, depicted a beautiful girl seated on a rock beside a stream of water. She was naked, as also was her companion, a stalwart man who kneeled over her belly in such a manner that he had placed his staff between her bubbies, which she squeezed together for the purpose of holding it tightly in position; below his buttocks could be seen the whole of her domain of love, his bottom resting on the hairy mount.

Number five, entitled *Mutual Enjoyment*, represented a man and a woman lying on a couch together, but in reversed position. The man's tongue had penetrated into her lustful cavity, while she had his engine in her mouth, at the same time tickling his testicles with her fingers.

Number six, labeled *Garden Studies*, represented a beautiful flower garden in the midst of which was a man seated on a rustic bench. A girl was standing over him with her clothes raised up, and his rod was just entering her sheath at the same time that he was titillating her clitoris with his finger.

Number seven, labeled *A Scene In The Rocky Mountains*, represented a naked nymph seated on a rock, while in front of her stood her lover with her thigh resting on his arms. She had seized his weapon and was just forcing it into her lascivious cavity. A short distance off was another girl, also seated, amusing herself with a dildo, which she had imbedded into her sheath.

Number eight, entitled *A Kitchen Scene*, represented a naked man embracing a girl from behind. Her head rested on an ottoman placed on a bench, her thighs rested on his shoulders, and he was kissing her bottom, molding her breasts and driving into her vagina all at the same time.

The reader can imagine how the sight of these lascivious pictures acted upon two such excitable girls as we were. I forgot to mention that in the center of the apartment was a long divan, evidently made purposely for the sexual act. It was perfectly certain from our sparkling eyes, from our heightened color, and from our trembling limbs that we were almost crazy with desire and that we were ready to do anything to appease our passions. Still, there was for a moment or two a kind of restraint as to who should begin. Amy was the first to break.

"We have come here to enjoy ourselves," she exclaimed. "Let us lose no time. I propose the first thing we do is to strip ourselves entirely naked."

"Agreed," I returned, commencing to unfasten my frock, and in a few moments we had divested ourselves of every particle of clothing.

When we all three stood naked, we saw our forms reflected over and over again in the mirrors. Herbert came up to us and clasped us both in his arms. He kissed us all over: now it was our bubbies, now it was our whole bellies, now it was the center of love itself until we were all so excited that the consummation could no longer be delayed. Amy, indeed, was beyond herself, for she threw herself on her back on the divan and, opening her white thighs to the widest extent, begged for someone to come and give her relief.

"If someone does not come and quench the fire burning in me, I shall die," said she.

"My slit is on fire—come Clarence, drive your delicious pego into my vitals—see, I open the door for you—come, darling, come."

And the voluptuous girl, with her finger and thumb, opened the lips of her coral sheath and showed up the pink interior. Who could resist such an appeal as this? Certainly not Herbert, for he rushed to the suffering girl and in a moment his pego was knocking at the mouth of her womb, imbedded to the very hair in her salacious cavity. Great God, what a delicious sight it was! Amy was crazy with delight; she folded her legs and thighs around his loins and jutted up her Mons Veneris to meet his thrusts. They had already commenced to move together when Amy suddenly called to me.

"Come here, Kate," said she, "you must have your share too—just turn your bottom towards me and straddle across my face."

I did as she requested, and my position was such that my notch came directly over her mouth.

"Now, Herbert," said Amy, "I will titillate her clitoris with my tongue while you imitate the sexual act with your tongue."

I threw my arms around Herbert's neck, he brought his face to mine, and his tongue penetrated my lips. In the meantime, I could feel Amy's tongue seek out my clitoris, which she no sooner found than she began to titillate it in the most entrancing manner. I was gorged with love and so was Amy, for I could feel her whole body shiver with her delicious sensations. Herbert began to drive most furiously into her body. Amy kept time with her tongue in my slit. We were much too excited to be able to prolong this scene. The crisis soon arrived: Amy's burning womb received Herbert's boiling sperm while she responded in such profusion that it actually ran down her white thighs; nor was I behind, for Amy's tongue brought down from me a copious shower of the elixir of love. This exciting scene over, we all took a bath, which was conveniently situated in an adjoining chamber, and partaking of a few glasses of champagne, we rested ten minutes.

"Come, dear Kate," said Clarence, "it is your turn now," and throwing himself on his back on the divan, he drew me on top of him. In another moment his engine of love had penetrated my slit and I felt it rubbing one side of my sensitive vagina. Amy stationed herself behind us and watched with flushing eyes and heightened color the in-and-out motion of his pego into my body. At last unable to control herself any longer she passed one hand between our bellies and titillated my clitoris while with her other hand she tickled alternately my bottom and his testicles. Soon, however, she changed her tactics and applied some vigorous slaps on my broad buttocks, turning the white cheeks into a rosy hue; each time she struck me it seemed to impale me on his fiery staff, causing it to enter a prodigious way into my mount.

I insisted that Clarence should remain perfectly passive while I did all the work, and I can assure the reader that I moved my buttocks in fine style. The mirrors around us reflected our actions, and not only was I feeling gratified but, owing to their agency, I could see his weapon entering in and out of my coral crevice. It was a delicious sight and enhanced our pleasures tenfold—I was, however, so full of love's juices that I could hold back no longer.

"I am coming, dear Herbert," I exclaimed, "come at the same time that I do, darling—come—co—co—"

I could perceive that Herbert was responding to my invocation, for he suddenly heaved up his buttocks and placing his two hands on my bottom he pressed me so closely to him that the hair surrounding our private parts was mingled in one mass together and I could feel his hot semen rush into me, meeting my own discharge which I emitted most copiously. Amy expressed herself as much gratified at witnessing our entrancing enjoyments as if she herself had been the recipient.

After half an hour's enjoyment of more wine, Herbert's erect weapon, which we had never ceased handling, showed us that he was again ready for combat. This time he devised a new mode for satisfying his desires. He had been playing with my bubbies, admiring their whiteness, firmness, and volume. He pressed them closely together and remarked that the narrow channel thus made would just fit his instrument. He placed me half sitting on an ottoman and made me recline on my back on the divan. He then made Amy straddle my chest, her bottom just resting on the top of my breasts, her face turned towards me, thus presenting her delicious buttocks to his gaze. He now stood between my thighs, his right knee coming in contact with my hairy mount. He then placed his instrument between my breasts, and at the same time entered Amy's slit from behind. I squeezed my bubbies together and held his staff tight. It was a curious position but it gave us all infinite enjoyment—for while he was satisfying Amy's greedy crevice with his pego, he was rubbing my clitoris with his knee—we all discharged together.

All these experiences in the field of Venus were not sufficient to quench our desires, so excited were we with the voluptuous surroundings. After a few minutes' rest, Amy proposed the next tableau. She lay down lengthwise on the divan and made me lie on the top of her with my head between her thighs, by which position my mouth came in contact with her notch, while hers did the same with mine. As I supported myself on my knees my bottom was raised. She then directed Herbert to enter me from behind. No sooner was his staff embedded in my vagina than she commenced to titillate my clitoris with her tongue, while I performed the same office for her. I shall not attempt to describe my feelings during this delicious combat. Not only did I feel his soul-inspiring thrusts, but the titillations of her tongue almost sent me crazy with delight, to say nothing of the pleasure I experienced from biting and sucking her voluptuous clitoris. We all discharged sooner this time than we had done before.

We were now somewhat exhausted and sat down to a splendid collation and drank some delicious wines. After this was over we all reclined on the divan together.

"Herbert," said Amy, "while we are resting,

tell us your love adventures—they must be very racy."

"Willingly, my love, but it is a long story and I am afraid of shocking your modesty for I shall be obliged to use plain language."

"I tell you what to do, Herbert," said I — "use French terms, that will be an excellent way of getting over the difficulty."

"A good idea, Kate — and I will follow it. When I want to speak of the throne of Venus I will use the word 'Con.' When I refer to man's organ I will say 'Vit'—the buttocks I will call the 'Fesses' and 'Cul' indiscriminately. I warn you beforehand, some phrases I shall express entirely in French as they cannot be translated without offending American ears. Besides which I love to speak of matters of which I believe you are ignorant; for I am free to confess there is no greater rake than myself."

We placed ourselves in listening posture, he with a hand placed over each of our mounts, he then commenced his history in the terms which will be found in the next chapter.

CHAPTER FIVE

HERBERT CLARENCE'S HISTORY

"I was born at Temperanceville, a village in the interior of the state of New York. My father was a rich man, and the house in which we lived was a fine mansion, beautifully situated in the midst of a grove of trees. Up to the age of sixteen, nothing occurred worthy of note. Since the time I was eight years of age my father had employed a private tutor to instruct me—but he was a very easy man and allowed me to slight my lessons with impunity; the consequence was that at sixteen I was, comparatively speaking, ignorant. One day my father asked me to write a note for him, and when I handed it to him he was shocked at the numerous mistakes in orthography and composition, and forthwith decided that I must be sent to school. My tutor was dismissed and the very next week I was sent to a large boarding-school in Brooklyn, kept by a Mr. Ames.

"I soon felt at home in my new position and liked the change very much, making rapid progress in my studies. I was one of the biggest boys in the school, and having, in more than one instance, proved my courage, I was spared much annoyance from the other boys, who although they might surpass me in learning were not my masters in fisticuffs.

"A year passed in this manner, and during that period I almost recovered the time lost in my early education. I was a favorite, both with the boys and the principal of the school, and the days passed very pleasantly until an event occurred which changed the entire tenor of my existence.

"I had often heard Mr. Ames speak of his daughter Cordelia, who was in France finishing her education. During my second year at school she returned home and the following day I saw her for the first time in the garden attached to the house. At the moment I first beheld her, she was stooping down gathering flowers. This posture elevated her clothes behind and I saw a considerable portion of her beautiful legs, the sight of which for the first time inspired me with sexual desire. I anxiously waited for her to turn around that I might see her face. In a few moments she did so and I was immediately struck with her beauty. She was a brunette with dark glossy hair, intensely black eyes, regular features, luscious red lips, white teeth, a laughing expression on her countenance, ivory shoulders, rather short stature, broad hips, and a glorious figure. She detected my earnest gaze, but instead of being abashed at it, she merely smiled at me and passed. I judged her to be about twenty years of age.

"I could not forget Cordelia's smile all that

day. It haunted me wherever I went. I was too young to understand its real significance, but it was sufficient to cause an indefinable feeling to take possession of me. When I retired to bed that night (my father had insisted that I should have a room to myself), I noticed that the chamber adjoining mine, which had been shut up ever since I had been at school was now open and fitted up with new furniture. In answer to my inquiry I was told that the room was destined for Miss Cordelia; I felt pleased to think that I should have her for such a close neighbor, and I began to think we might become more intimately acquainted.

"About three nights after this, I retired to bed quite late—in fact, the whole house had already retired. When I came to Miss Cordelia's room, I was surprised to find the door half open and a brilliant light streaming from it. My curiosity was so much aroused that I peeped into the chamber. Great God! a sight met my eyes which took away my breath and riveted me to the floor.

"The beautiful Cornelia with nothing on but her chemise, was lying on a sofa; but this was not all. Her back was towards me and her sole garment was raised above her hips, revealing to me her lovely bottom, the back portion of a pair of the whitest thighs in the world, and the whole of her magnificently formed legs. In lying down she had a curious position which jutted out her buttocks and allowed me to see between her fleshy thighs the luscious lips of her bijou shaded with black hair.

"I stood confounded for a moment but soon

recovered myself, as the lovely creature appeared to be asleep. I determined to venture into the chamber that I might obtain a closer view of her concealed beauties; I cautiously glided into the chamber and found that she did not wake. I advanced close to her and, kneeling down behind her, examined at leisure the beautiful objects before my eyes. I can find no words to express her exquisite *con*. The two fleshy lips met close together, showing only a line of coral which curved from her bottom and was lost in a mass of black curly hair. Of course I was perfectly excited at this sight. And in spite of all prudent considerations, I could not resist bending my head down and imprinting a kiss on the object offered to my regard. She evidently felt the embrace, for a shiver ran through her body, but she did not open her eyes. I now grew more bold, and dividing the lips of her bijou with my tongue I sought the interior of her grotto and met at the entrance her stiffened clitoris, which I had no sooner touched than as if by instinct she pressed her bushy mount close to my face. I now moved my tongue slowly in and out of the luscious opening and she responded by heaves of her buttocks, and in a few moments she poured down a flood of love's elixir. I rose to my feet and was about to withdraw when Cordelia opened her eyes and gazed on me, full in the face. I blushed all over with shame and was about to make a precipitate retreat, when the dear girl smiled on me and, seizing my hand, conveyed it to her splendid bubbies. I already read my pardon on her face, and clasping my arms around her, I pressed her frantically to my heart. I kissed her deliriously, gluing my lips to her, at the same time forcing my tongue into her mouth. She returned all my caresses.

"After toying in this manner a little while, I slipped her chemise off her shoulders and exposed her two semiglobes to my greedy gaze. What lovely objects! I kissed them, sucked the nipples, buried my face between them, stroked her belly and played with her hairy mount. She, too, was not unoccupied, for she had unbuttoned my trousers and was caressing my staff with her hand, capping and uncapping its red head and with the other hand she tickled my testicles. In a broken voice she confessed to me that she had only pretended to be asleep during my manipulations of her charms; that she desired to enjoy me as much as I did her, and she begged me at once to satisfy her longings. I was all primed and loaded for the combat, and kneeling on the floor I drew her towards me; she stooped down and with her own hand guided my instrument into her salacious notch. I felt it tearing up her vagina, and in a moment our conjunction was complete.

"She now commenced to move her bottom rapidly on my staff, while I, with my arms clasped round her handsome body, pressed her towards me in such a manner that her snowy breasts beat against my face. I took one of her rosy nipples in my mouth, and while she was pumping up my spermatic treasures, I sucked and titillated the cunning little strawberry top of her alabaster globes. Nor was this all, for I lowered one of my hands and tickled her bottom—sometimes gently slapping her fleshy cushions, at others forcing a finger in *le trou de son cul*. When she felt this last operation she could no longer withhold her emission, but throwing her arms round my neck she discharged profusely at the same moment that I anointed her vagina and thighs with my love juices.

"I enjoyed her three times before leaving her. We came to a very good understanding together, and it was decided that I should visit her again the next evening when everybody had retired to bed. I slept soundly that night and rose the next morning extremely happy, for I was cheered up by the thoughts of the joys I was about to experience.

"I stole into her chamber at the time agreed upon and found her already in bed. I undressed myself as quickly as possible and placed the lighted candle at the foot of the bed. I then laid down by her side. During this proceeding, Cordelia pretended to be asleep. I placed my hand on her delicious bubbies, and throwing down the sheet, kissed them; she then opened her eyes and smiled sweetly upon me. I placed my hand over her night dress and raised it gently until I reached her pretty *con*. I played with the hair of her mount and inserted a finger into her warm vagina. While I was doing this I kissed her lips and my tongue met hers. I then felt her bottom and thighs, roving from one to the other. All these touchings excited us both to the highest pitch. I suddenly threw off all the covering of the bed and by the aid of the candle examined all her charms. Cordelia made no resistance whatever, but grasping my stiff rod in her hand, commenced to move the foreskin backwards and forwards. I kissed her on the eyes and mouth, and addressed the most endearing epithets to her. She was almost crazy with delirious delight.

" 'Come, darling,' she exclaimed, 'put it into me or I shall die.'

"I immediately rolled on top of her and in a moment I had pierced her to the very quick. A few rapid motions and I had inundated the mouth of her womb with a flood of boiling sperm.

"It would take me too long to relate all the different ways in which I enjoyed the beautiful Cordelia. Sometimes I lay on top of her—at others she lay on top of me. Sometimes I did it sideways—sometimes I did it kneeling, sometimes before and sometimes behind. Sometimes when I was in a hurry and met her in a retired place, I would place her on a trunk, a chair, a mattress, and achieve the results in the most extraordinary position. More than once I made her stoop forward with her head and hands resting on a trunk, and throwing her pettticoats over her head from behind, I would regale myself by the sight of her delicious white *cul*, with her delicate *con* peeping between her white thighs, and releasing my member from its ordinary place of concealment, I would force it to the very hilt into her body, her beautiful bottom just fitting the hollow of my thighs.

"One night I stripped her entirely naked as well as myself. I then strewed a large quantity of roses on the floor and made her pick them up naked as she was, all the time watching her by the light of the lamp; the different postures she assumed were delicious to contemplate. I then rubbed some essence of jasmine on her polished skin and applied some on my own body. We threw ourselves on the bed and assumed a hundred different positions. At last I caused her to kneel before me, and handled at will her belly, her thighs, her bubbies, and at last, though not the least delicious, her *con,* pressing the two lips together, playing with the hair on her mount, titillating her clitoris and exploring the innermost recesses of her vagina. She appeared to enjoy all these follies as much as myself. I then made her incline forward on her hands and knees and mounted on her back. I maintained this position some little time, then I brought my member down between her two fleshy buttocks, and knocked at the *trou de son cul.* I did not, however, enter there, but opening the lips of the legitimate passage with my two fingers I inserted my dart into her ruby sheath, and a few in and out motions soon brought down a shower of bliss.

"We now rose up, and naked as we were, sat down near the fire. I produced a bottle of cordial with which I had provided myself, and the fire of desire soon burned in our eyes again. We kissed each other over and over; at last I took her by the arm and drew her from her seat in a standing posture and tried to enter her while in this position, but I could not accomplish it. She was so excited that she seized my member in her hand and, dragging me to the bed, fell on her back, pulled me on top of her and guided my instrument into her salacious slit. The bed creaked with our motions, but I paid no attention to it and drove into her delicious body with all my might—she returning heave for heave. We both soon discharged copiously.

"We rested an hour, and then I inclined her with her belly on the bed. By this means her beautiful *cul* was completely exposed to my attack. In the first place, I put my instrument between her buttocks and moved it backwards and forwards in this position. I do not know how it was, but the head of my engine struck against *le trou de son cul*. The contact evidently titillated her, for she wiggled her bottom and begged me '*l' enculer*.' Without any further ceremony I moistened the head of my instrument and, separating the two cheeks of her *fesses*, I forced my *vit* into the narrow passage. She aided me by every means in her power, raising her buttocks to meet my attack. In a moment I was plunged *au fond de son cul*.

"How delicious it was. How tightly was my engine grasped by the narrow sheath. I passed my hand around her belly, and put one of my fingers into her *con*, titillating the lips of this seat of happiness. Cordelia was beyond herself; she lay palpitating on her belly and her whole body was in agitation; every thrust that I gave from behind caused my fingers to be buried deeply into her sensitive quiver, and the cheeks of her bottom trembled with the shock. Her sensitive vagina contracted and she discharged before me, but when I felt my fingers moistened, I withdrew them from their warm nest and, seizing her by her hips, pushed my member for the last time into the narrow path, and she drew from me the liquor of love in such great profusion that when I withdrew my lance from its asylum the white cushions of her buttocks were inundated with my mettle.

"When all was over, I assisted her to rise and we were satisfied for the time, for our scene had been a prolonged one. I left her after assuring her of my devotion.

"At last the time came for me to leave school and I lost sight of the beautiful Cordelia. When I returned home I was quite a young man and my experience with my preceptor's daughter had lighted such a fire in me that I was soon looking about for a means to gratify my passion. I determined that Margaret Murdock should be the next to receive my embraces and I began immediately to lay my plans for the purpose of effecting that object.

"Margaret was the daughter of a widow lady who resided in the village. She was a gloriously beautiful girl, about eighteen years of age. Her hair was a sunny auburn and hung in natural curls around a snow-white neck. She was voluptuously made and extremely graceful. I managed to get introduced to her, and visited the house quite frequently. I had frequent opportunities to see her alone, and you may rely upon it, I did not let the grass grow under my feet. In a few days I had advanced so far as to put my arms around her waist and kiss her. Although at first she somewhat resisted those embraces, she eventually submitted to them and even returned my kisses.

"One warm day in the spring of the year,

I called at her mother's house as usual and was informed by the servant that Mrs. Murdock was not home and would not return before evening; but that Miss Margaret was in the drawing room. I ran upstairs and found her seated on a rocking chair engaged in sewing. I ran up to her and shook her by the hand, asking tenderly after her health. She answered me with civility and I took a seat close by her side and gazed fixedly on her beautiful face. We conversed on different subjects a little while, then I passed my arm round her waist and kissed her. She made no resistance but a deep blush suffused her face and neck.

" 'Kiss me darling,' I whispered in her ear.

"The charming creature advanced her face toward mine and brought her lips in contact with my own; before she was aware of it, I gently inserted my tongue into her mouth. This species of kissing appeared to please her, for a shiver ran through her body and I met with hers in reply. I now glided my hand down the front of her dress and felt her plump, firm white bubbies, first molding and pressing them, then forcing my hand as far as possible toward her smooth belly. She murmured a few words of objection to these enterprises on my part, so I withdrew my hand and drew her on my knees. I now commenced to kiss her eagerly, during which time I was cautiously raising her petticoats with my fingers; at last my hand came in contact with her naked thighs. When I felt her deliciously formed limbs I could scarcely restrain myself, but pressed her frantically to my heart. Margaret appeared to be as much excited as I was and I saw her direct her eyes to the front of my trousers, which I assure you stuck out in a very unseemly manner.

" 'Someone might come,' said the charming girl, her cheek dyed with the deepest crimson. And she suddenly jumped from my lap and, running to the door, shut and bolted it. She then returned to me and I drew her between my legs.

" 'I love you darling,' I exclaimed, and while speaking, I raised her petticoats from behind with one hand until it rested on her magnificently formed buttocks—how firm and smooth were those white cushions and what pleasure I took in manipulating them at will! With my unoccupied hand I seized one of hers and brought it down on my rampant member, which was so stiff and unruly that it was ready to burst the bonds which confined it. Finding that she made no resistance to my proceedings, I unbuttoned the front of my trousers, and my staff nestled itself in her grasp. She was evidently astonished at the size and condition of my member.

" 'You must be aware, darling,' I exclaimed, 'that this ought to be hidden from sight, and you have a place proper to receive it.'

"So saying, I carried her in my arms to a sofa, and placing her on it on her back, I threw her skirts over her head, disclosing to my gaze her body, naked from her belly to her feet. Ye gods, how I feasted my eyes on the glorious sight! I passed my hands over all her hidden charms, now it was her smooth white belly, now it was her voluminous thighs, now it was her delicious bottom and at last it was her lovely *con*, embowered in a mass of auburn hair. I pressed the two lips of this abode of bliss together; I turned my fingers in the curly thicket adorning her mount, and even advanced one into the narrow opening of her vagina. I was now determined on action, and seating myself on the sofa I drew her onto my lap with her face towards me and my knees between her thighs. I let down my trousers, raised my shirt and directed my lance towards her rubicond opening. I soon felt it come in contact with her hairy slit. I then opened the two lips of her *con* with my fingers and thumb, and jutting my buttocks forwards I felt myself penetrate a little way into her warm vagina. I hurt her, however, a good deal, and she begged of me to desist—but I only altered my position slightly, and making her open her thighs to the widest extent, I again pushed forward, but she again compelled me to stop, complaining that I hurt her dreadfully. I explained to her that the pain would be but momentary, and that when I had once forced a passage, the most delicious pleasures would follow. But seeing she still resisted, I determined to try another mode.

"I again placed her lengthwise on the sofa and threw myself on top of her—but it was of no use, I could not enter. I withdrew from her and began to curse my ill-luck. I kissed her, felt her *con* and advanced a finger into her vagina to see what progress I had done—I found it was very little indeed. To my great joy I saw on the chimney piece a pot of pomade. I immediately appropriated it and anointed my staff. I now placed the dear girl on her hands and knees on the floor and, throwing up her clothes, I entered her from behind. It was now comparatively easy work and in a second, her magnificent bottom was in contact with my belly, my instrument having entered her vagina to the very hilt. I paused a moment to observe the beauties before me, and then commenced slowly the in-and-out movement. Margaret was already in the seventh heaven of enjoyment—her white buttocks shivered with the shocks of my thrusts—I passed my hand in front and handled her bubbies, her belly and the upper part of her slit, titillating her clitoris. At last the die-a-way moment approached and I seized her by her buttocks and drove furiously into her—her thirsty vagina sucked from me the essence of life which mingled with her own discharge, and she sank exhausted on her belly.

"When she had recovered, I took her to her chamber, which was the very next room, and we both threw ourselves on the bed, having both stripped naked. The contact of our warm bodies soon restored our powers and we indulged in a thousand follies. In a state of nature she appeared perfectly lovely, and I was never tired of admiring her smooth, satin skin, her voluptuous bosom, her swelling thighs, her whole belly and her delicious Mons Veneris. She too gratified her curiosity by falling all over my body. She half threw herself on top of me, and gluing her lips to mine she at the same time amused herself titillating my testicles. While thus engaged, her snowy bubbies beat against my chest, while her moss-covered slit rubbed against my thigh.

"These touchings and titillations worked me up to such a pitch that I could endure it no longer. I drew her to the edge of the bed, first placing a pillow under her bottom, and raising one of her thighs in the air, I rested it on my arm. By this means her lovely slit was completely exposed to my attack. She opened the luscious lips herself with her finger and thumb so that I could see the coral interior. I brought my staff to bear on the inviting entrance, and with a single heave of my buttocks I completely gorged her vagina. I rode, however, easily in the harbor, and the dear girl experienced all the joys of a perfect conjunction without any pain. At first my motions were slow, but as our delirium increased they grew faster. She met my thrust by responsive heaves of her bottom until we could both hold out no longer, but both discharged simultaneously.

"I shall not tell you, dear girls, how many times I enjoyed the beautiful Margaret before I left her, for fear that you should think that I exaggerate. I only know that when I quitted her apartment I was completely exhausted, and that it took several days for me to recover my wonted energy.

"I found Margaret adept in the science of love. She soon learned every mode and posture for performing the sexual act and we had many, many happy hours together.

"One day we were together in the summer house attached to the house. She began the play of love by kissing me, and forcing her tongue into my mouth, she imitated with that organ the conjugal act. By this mode of procedure she illumined a fire in my body and I pressed her to my heart in delirium. She then unbuttoned my trousers, and seizing my instrument, rubbed it between her hands. I drew her on my knees and raised up her petticoats at the same time. I let down my pantaloons, and felt her naked bottom resting against my belly. How delicious was the sensation of her warm buttocks! My staff forced an entrance between her two thighs, and she leaned forward and kissed it a thousand times, occasionally rubbing it against her lovely *con*. She even lodged it between the two lips, and by moving her buttocks, titillated it in this position. Supreme pleasure began to run through my veins, and I was on the eve of discharging when, slightly raising her *cul*, she guided the stiffened dart of love to the entrance of her vagina, and in another moment, I was *au fond de son cul*. She leaned forward in such a manner that I could see my staff enter in and out of her coral sheath. She moved her buttocks, and after a few violent thrusts I felt her parts contract on my piercer and she pumped the sperm from my testicles at the same moment that she herself discharged profusely.

"My acquaintance with Margaret lasted four months, during which time we took our surfeit of love's enjoyments. At the end of that time I left to pay a visit to an uncle who lived in the village of B——, in the state of Pennsylvania, a few miles from where I now reside. My uncle was a bachelor, possessed of large wealth, and it was generally understood that I was to be his heir. The village I have just referred to was a very quiet place consisting only of about two hundred inhabitants. It contained however, a church and a clergyman who was a widower with an only daughter. I first saw Helen Roberts at chapel the Sunday following my arrival. I was immediately struck with her beauty. Her features were perfectly regular and classical. Her eyes were large, lustrous and dreamy. Her bust was faultless, and her whole form was as if it had been molded by the god of love himself. I was soon destined to know her more intimately.

"One afternoon, after I had been at my uncle's about two weeks, I happened to stroll into the church and the first sight that met my eyes was Helen Roberts herself lying fast asleep in one of the pews. The day was very warm and she had doubtless entered the holy edifice for the purpose of resting herself and, feeling tired, sleep had overcome her. Her dress was slightly discomposed at her feet, revealing a considerable portion of her magnificently formed limbs. I advanced cautiously to her side and saw that she slept soundly. I could not resist the temptation offered me, but gently raised her petticoats. She wore no drawers and all the secrets of her charming person were entirely exposed to my gaze. The sight of her lovely white belly, her naked thighs and her pretty hairy bijou inflamed me in the highest degree, and in a moment my lance was as stiff as a poker. I passed my hand over her belly, and although a shiver ran through her at the contact, she did not awake. I then gently divided her thighs and handled at pleasure all the charms of the domain of

Venus. I played with the hair surmounting that lovely spot, I inserted a finger in the passage and titillated her clitoris, which I found finely developed. My touches became more and more exciting until I believe she was on the point of discharging when she suddenly awoke and found herself in my arms. My instrument was rubbing against her thighs, but I had not effected an entrance. The charming girl, when she found the condition of affairs, took it in good part; she kissed me. However, we were so excited that we both discharged before the act of coition was effected.

"I now led her into the vestry-room near the pulpit, and seating myself on a chair, pulled her on my knees. I unfastened her dress and, exposing her two breasts, repeatedly kissed and handled them. I made her put one of her feet on the table while her other leg hung between mine, by this means leaving her thighs streched widely apart. I forced a finger into her slit while she seized my instrument. I commenced moving my finger, she did the same with her hand, and in a few moments we again discharged, experiencing the most delicious sensations.

"After a little repose we recommenced. She longed for something more satisfying and endeavored to excite me. She seized my staff, covering and uncovering the ruby head. She even took the whole of my rod into her mouth, palating it with her tongue, while at the same moment she tickled my testicles and bottom. Nor was I idle, for I pressed and kissed her bubbies, sucking the strawberry nipples, stroking down her belly and titillating her anus. I then kneeled down, and making her open her thighs widely apart, I inserted my tongue into her slit, titillating the sides of her vagina and sucking her clitoris. Helen was almost mad with the intensity of her desires, and was ready to spend again, when she had the satisfaction of seeing my instrument attain such an enormous size that when she again took it in her mouth it filled it completely. Giving it a last kiss she threw herself on a hassock and pulling up all her clothes above her navel, thus leaving her body entirely naked from there downward, spreading her legs open and slightly bending her knees, she exclaimed:

" 'Come love, embrace me well—bury your staff into the deepest and most secret recesses of my body. Do not spare me.'

"I did not have to be told twice, for I was on her in a moment. I gently introduced the head of my instrument between the lips of her slit, but it would not enter.

"It was in vain, I pushed, I could make no headway, but only gave her a great deal of pain. After a little trying of this nature, she was getting exhausted and told me for God's sake to finish my work. I then withdrew my instrument, and, wetting the end of it with spittle, again brought it to bear on the entrance of the abode of bliss. As soon as I got the head well between the lips I began to shove. She was determined, however, to be aggressive with me, and with a tremendous heave of her bottom impaled herself to the hilt on my rod, so much so that the hair surrounding our genitals intermingled. She could not avoid shrieking out, but the pain soon began to pass off and after a few more shoves she evidently began to experience the most delicious sensations. Every thrust I gave sent a liquid fire of delirium through her veins. When she felt my instrument rubbing the sensitive sides of her vagina she appeared as if she would die with pleasure. Her breasts rose and fell and her buttocks actually quivered with the delights of her sensations. My motion grew faster, my testicles tingled with delight at every shove against her bottom. She threw her legs about in confusion and met every thrust more than halfway. She wiggled herself from side to side on my staff. The finale came.

" 'Herbert, I am coming—O God! what pleasure! Dear Herbert—closer—clo—ser—clo—' she pantingly exclaimed, and a profuse discharge from the innermost recesses of her body met my own.

"We got up and adjusted our clothing and I promised her I would visit her the next night in her own room, the access to which was very easy, and I returned home to reflect on all the pleasures I had experienced."

"Stop, Herbert," said Amy, interrupting her brother-in-law in his recital. "Before you continue your history, you must give me relief. Your descriptions are so voluptuous and lascivious that my slit is on fire—come, darling, you are in fine condition."

I seconded Amy's request, being no less excited myself. Herbert was indeed in splendid condition for performing the rites of Venus. We all rose from the couch.

"Stand up, Amy," said Herbert. "Put one of your feet on this chair and let the other rest on the ground. There, that's it; now your plump thighs are widely separated and I can manipulate your pretty little *con*."

"Oh, do, darling," returned the delighted girl.

"Now I am going to titillate your clitoris with my tongue," said Herbert.

Amy placed herself in the position required. Herbert seated himself on the ground between her thighs and brought his mouth in contact with her slit. He divided the lips of her bijou with his tongue and forced it in and out of the rosy cavity.

"Amy," said Herbert, when he had indulged in this play a few moments, "you have got the prettiest little *con* in the world. What soft down adorns this hallowed spot! What delicious folding lips, and what a sweet morsel is your clitoris! How glorious it is to enjoy you to one's heart's content. Just fancy this the first time you had ever come in contact with a man. Let me rehearse the scene: he would first of all play with your bubbies, he would press and kiss them as I do now, he would suck these rosy nipples until he had excited you to the last degree. He would then grow bolder, but you must lie down for me to perform the scene properly."

Amy threw her entire length on the divan while I watched with delighted eyes this delicious scene, enjoying it as much as if I were the recipient instead of his beautiful sister-in-law.

"When he saw your delicious white belly," continued Herbert, "he would shiver with delight and fasten his lips to it, thus and thus. He would then pass his hand backwards and forwards on this smooth white plain and endeavor to peer into the mysteries seated below. In another moment his hand would invade your delicious little *con*—just as mine does now—his finger separates the lips and he gently rubs your clitoris—you are mad with delight, you open your thighs and wriggle your bottom under his touches. He pushes one of his fingers into your *con* and moves it in and out as I do now."

"Oh, darling, it is too much; I cannot bear it," cried the delighted girl, writhing and wriggling her body about in the most delicious manner possible, at the same time seizing Herbert's staff and rubbing it up and down.

"Having toyed with each other some time," continued Herbert, "he suddenly fixes his lips on your delicate slit, and pushes his tongue between the lips, and while thus employed he tickles your bottom. You are just ready to spend and beg him for heaven's sake to finish with you. He divides your thighs as I do now and mounts you in this manner."

Herbert suited the action to the word and threw himself on Amy's belly. She herself guided his instrument into her coral sheath, and they both commenced the work of thrust and heave.

"Delicious, splendid!" exclaimed Amy. "I can feel your lovely instrument in my vagina. Go on! go on!"

"He moves his bottom as I do mine—and soon discharges—as I do now. My darling girl, your lovely slit has extracted the last drop from me."

"I too," gasped Amy, "there—th—"

I was so excited at witnessing this voluptuous scene that I was obliged to give myself relief by rubbing my clitoris. I emitted at the same moment they did.

"What delight I have enjoyed," said Amy when she had somewhat recovered. "But continue your history, dear Herbert."

Herbert recommenced in the terms to be found in the next chapter.

END VOLUME ONE

KATE PERCIVAL

Volume Two

CHAPTER ONE

HERBERT CLARENCE'S HISTORY CONTINUED

"I was punctual to the moment with my engagement with the beautiful Helen, and the moment I saw her I rushed into her arms. I then proceeded to strip her of her clothes and she did the same office for me. I made her sit naked as she was on my knee, and began kissing her body all over, caressing her breasts and sucking the rosy tips surmounting them. I descended to her belly, smoothing it with my hand, and then I attacked the very center of pleasure, first putting in one finger and then another, and twisting the hair surrounding her mount. I then made her stand with her legs wide apart, and I kneeled before her, and put my tongue into the coral passage, giving her intense pleasure. I seized her clitoris between my lips, at the same time titillating the inside of her *con* with my finger. I thought she would expire with delight. I stroked down her thighs with my hands. I then made her stoop forward, by which means she exposed her handsome buttocks completely to my gaze. I slapped them with my hand until they were as red as a cherry. This was too much for me, for making her lean with her head on the bed, I had a fine opportunity to enter her from the rear. I was on her in a moment. I felt her warm buttocks rubbing against my belly while my instrument entered a prodigious way into her body and I commenced my movements. At every push I made I could feel my testicles strike against her bottom. My hands at the same time were passed round her body; with one hand I handled her breasts—with the other I rubbed the top of her slit. The pleasure was so great that it could not last—and we both actually swooned away when the crisis came, I falling all my length on her back and she falling on her belly on the bed.

"A few minutes' repose served to renew our energies. I now placed a large cushion on the bed, and taking her in my arms I made her recline against it in such a way that I could easily enter her body while in a standing posture. She passed one arm around my neck, the other around my body and her two breasts beat against my chest. My instrument was soon buried in her glowing sheath. I pushed vigorously, and her breasts rebounded, quivered with the shock—even our very hair intermingled. She was beyond herself and could continue her passion no longer, but opening her thighs to the utmost extent she discharged, and I did the same, her pleasures being a hundred times increased as she felt the warm liquor rushing into her womb.

"We soon recovered ourselves. This time I seated myself on the bed and drew her, naked as she was onto my knees. How delicious was the sensation of her warm bottom to my thighs! She impaled herself on the object of her divinity—she now moved herself rapidly up and down, but I did not let her finish in this manner, but turning her around with her face towards me, I carried her to a sofa and lay panting and heaving on her bosom. She began to wiggle her bottom again and in a few moments we again dissolved in bliss.

"The time had now arrived for us to separate, and hurriedly dressing ourselves we bade an affectionate farewell to each other. I never saw Helen after this—for my uncle died suddenly, leaving me his heir, and Helen was married shortly after and went south to live.

"Soon after coming into my uncle's estate I moved to New York, and took up my residence at the St. Nicholas Hotel, determined to see a little life before settling down as a steady man. I had been at the hotel but a few days when I made the acquaintance of a gentleman about my own age. His name was George Darville and he was a first-rate fellow. In the course of conversation we struck on subjects of an amorous character and I soon discovered that my friend was no novice in the field of Venus. That same evening we went together to Niblo's Garden and took our places in the parquet. Just before the curtain rose I stood up from my seat to gaze around the house. My eyes were immediately arrested by a beautiful girl stationed in one of the private boxes. She was the most perfect blonde I had ever seen. Her hair was a glossy auburn, and shaded a face that might have served for the model of Titian's Venus. Her features were regular, her eyes a deep blue, shaded by long eyelashes which gave a dreamy expression to her lovely countenance. Her lips were full and sensuous; a lovely carnation hue, evidently nature's own coloring, adorned her soft velvet cheek. Her neck and shoulders, for she wore a low-necked dress, were as white as Parian marble and her bust was full and voluptuous. I immediately turned to George and asked him if he knew her.

" 'Why that's Harriet Wells,' said he—'the most lascivious woman in all New York. She does nothing in the common way, not even the act of sexual intercourse. She is a young girl of immense fortune and puts no restraint on her passions. But come with me and I will introduce you to her. I am in favor with her just now and perhaps we may get an invitation to supper—if we do I can tell you we will see a scene that you will remember to the longest day of your life.'

"We immediately proceeded to the box where the beautiful girl was seated. She received us with a charming smile and I was soon on terms of the closest intimacy with her. After we had conversed for about a quarter of an hour, she whispered something to George to which he made the reply 'all right!' She then turned to me and asked me to sup with her that evening after the play was over. To this invitation I gave a willing assent.

"The first act of the play was over and the curtain rose for the second.

" 'What a dull piece!' said Harriet. 'Let us retire to the rear of the box, where we shall not be seen by the audience—we can then converse with more freedom. I dare say, you don't care about seeing the play, Mr. Clarence?'

" 'Not at all,' I replied, 'I would a thousand times rather converse with you than see the finest play in the world.'

" 'That's a very pretty compliment,' said she, rising from her chair and taking up her position at the back of the box, where I followed her.

"George now excused himself and said that he would return when the piece was ended, leaving me alone with Harriet. In the position we had taken no one could see us, neither from the stage nor from the theater. When we were alone I put my arms round the lovely girl's waist and drawing her towards me imprinted a moist kiss on her soft dewy lips and then begged her pardon for my boldness.

" 'There is no apology necessary,' said Harriet. 'I like it as much as you do yourself, and I like men to be bold.'

"She then kissed me of her own accord and I could even feel her tongue penetrate my lips while a deep flush of desire suffused her face.

"Thus encouraged, I grew more bold and placed my hand on her white shoulders; I gently let it slide down inside the front of her dress and it came in contact with her glorious bubbies. Of all the breasts I had ever felt there were none could be compared with hers— so voluptuous, so white and so firm. I handled them at will, pressing them and pulling down her dress, exposing them to my ardent gaze.

Harriet placed one of her feet on a chair and placed her other leg across my lap. This movement raised her petticoats in such a manner that it showed me a considerable portion of her gloriously formed limbs. In a moment my hand was under her clothes, handling at will her lovely *con*. She stretched her thighs widely to assist me in my researches —nay, more, she raised her petticoats with her own hand and exposed to my delighted gaze the lovely domain of Venus.

I frantically seized the beautiful girl and stretching her length onto a settee, I strode over her and, forcing my head between her thighs, I kissed her mount over and over, while she nestled my rod between her breasts. I sought out her clitoris, which I easily found, for it was extremely largely developed, and began to titillate it with my tongue.

" 'Stop,' cried Harriet—a convulsive shudder running through her system, 'you must reserve yourself for tonight.'

"I now desisted and we contented ourselves with feeling and touching only until the piece was ended. Just before the conclusion of the play, Harriet sent a note to the green room, and informed me that she had invited two well-known actresses to sup with us. They were both beautiful girls—but more of them by and by. As we were leaving the theater, George and the two actresses who had been invited found us and we all proceeded to Harriet's house in her carriage.

"Miss Wells resided in a magnificent mansion on Fifth Avenue. When we entered I was struck with the elegance seen everywhere. The drawing room especially claimed my attention. A delicious perfume was distilled in the atmosphere and the brilliant gas burners shed an effusion of light throughout the apartment. The most elegant furniture was spread through the chamber, consisting of canopies, sofas and chairs of the most costly description. On the floor was spread a carpet so soft that the sound of footsteps was inaudible. The walls were a mass of mirrors extending from the ceiling to the floor, relieved here and there by magnificent paintings, representing woman's form in every attitude and every variety of costume. In fact the most beautiful women could be seen, from those most simply clad to those without a particle of clothing to cover their nakedness. I was transported with the scene. I felt my blood boil in my veins with undefined desires.

"We all five sat down to a magnificent supper and partook plentifully of champagne. The three girls looked beautiful in the evening costumes. They were all very lightly clad, revealing a considerable portion of their womanly charms. Their dresses were cut very low in the neck revealing almost the whole of their lovely breasts; their dresses too were of the thinnest description and allowed their voluptuous limbs to be distinctly traced through them. One of the actresses was named Ernestine, a beautiful girl of about twenty; the other was named Isabelle, and was a year or two younger.

"After supper we entered a delicious boudoir evidently fitted up purposely for performing the rites of Venus. We had no sooner entered the chamber than Harriet exclaimed:

"'Come ladies and gentlemen, you all know what we have come here for—let's have no reserve.'

So saying she deliberately pulled up her skirts above her navel, and seating herself on the ground, stretched her thighs open to the widest extent, giving us a full view of her hidden charms. She then pulled me to her, and unbuttoning my trousers, released my staff and began to kiss and embrace it, titillating the head of it with her tongue. Nor was this all; Ernestine also raised up her skirts and showed us her magnificently formed thighs and Mons Veneris, and putting her arms round my neck kissed me passionately. Isabelle sat down before George, and shaking her dress from off her shoulders, she nestled his staff between her lovely bubbies. Her petticoats too were elevated so that we could see all the lower portion of her naked body. I glanced in the mirrors around the room and beheld a glorious scene. First of all there was the beautiful Harriet with her milk-white thighs, stretched widely apart and her pouting bijou, covered with its downy moss, staring me right in the face. Then there was the charming Ernestine with her luscious *con* rubbing against my thigh. While Isabelle showed me her white buttocks wih the lips of her slit peeping between the posterior portion of her splendid thighs. Of course the sight of these beauties fired my blood in such a manner that I was completely beside myself—and if Harriet had continued her titillations with her tongue a minute more I must have emitted in her mouth. But she suddenly stopped.

" 'Let us all strip,' she exclaimed, 'our clothes are only in our way.'

"We all seconded her motion, and in a few moments we were all as naked as we were born. Ye gods! what a glorious sight it was for me—just imagine, three beautiful women entirely naked before my eyes. Thighs, breasts, bellies, bottoms, *cons*, all merited my admiration and deserved my embraces. I paid my *devoirs* to all three without any distinction—now it was Harriet's beautiful bubbies, now Ernestine's lovely bottom, and now Isabelle's glorious slit. I kissed them all over, not even omitting their lovely mounts of Venus—indeed I can say with truth that before three minutes elapsed I had explored all three of their vaginas with my tongue. Nor had they been passive spectators the while for they paid back with interest on my person all that I did to them. They sucked my pego—they titillated my testicles, they forced their fingers into the *trou de mon cul*. Ernestine breathed on my belly while Isabelle slapped my buttocks. George went through exactly the same thing; the consequence was we were all inflamed to the highest degree.

"When Harriet thought we were all sufficiently excited, she raised her finger as a token for us to cease and exclaimed:

" 'I proclaim myself the priestess of this assembly, and shall take upon myself the ordering of all tableaux. First of all I give as your motto — Voluptuousness, Lasciviousness, and Sexual enjoyment—there must be no modesty, no shamefacedness and everybody must obey the slightest of my commands—let them be ever so *outre*. I shall make use of the common words when referring to the organs of generation and shall expect everyone else to do the same.' I shall still continue to use the French words, but you must understand that whenever I do so the English common words were used by Harriet and her companions.

"'And now to begin,' continued Harriet. 'Fond as I am of being embraced by a man—I like almost equally well to receive the embraces of my own sex, and still more to see others performing the desired act of copulation.' She now sat down on a low sofa and stretched her thighs widely apart. 'My first order is that Ernestine shall kneel before me and *fete my con* with her delicious tongue and that while she is thus engaged, Mr.—— shall embrace her from behind while George shall satisfy Isabelle's pouting slit with his magnificent staff so close to me that I can feel them both when in the act!'

"We immediately began to work in the manner prescribed to us. Ernestine knelt down and fastened her head between Harriet's lovely thighs, and separating the lips of the latter's *con* with her finger and thumb, she plunged her tongue into the coral cavity. The position Ernestine assumed caused her splendid bottom to be elevated in the air, and between the cheeks of her buttocks I could plainly discern the luscious lips of her *con*. In a moment I was behind, and pointing my staff, it was quickly imbedded in her warm vagina, the lips of her sheath clasping it like a glove.

George took Isabelle and placed her sitting on the sofa beside Harriet. The lovely girl raised her thighs in the air. George rushed between them and his instrument pierced her to the quick. Harriet clapped her hand as a signal that we were to commence, and we all began to push for the very life. Harriet, by means of the mirror, had the whole voluptuous scene before her eyes. While she felt Ernestine's tongue in her salacious slit, she could see my instrument enter in and out of the latter's *con* and saw also George's rod appear and disappear in Isabelle's beautiful body. Now more, while the two latter were thus enaged our priestess stretched out her hand, placed it underneath Isabelle's thighs and titillated their sexual organs while in the act of coition—sometimes it would be the lovely girl's clitoris, another time it would be her bottom, and another George's pendants which she gently squeezed. These touches had the effect of causing those two to go before we did. I suddenly saw Isabelle's eyelids tremble — she raised her white thighs high in the air, while a convulsive shudder of delight ran through her whole body. George's strokes now became faster and more furious—his buttocks quivered and he fell palpitating on his companion's belly, while a low cry from her announced that he had sent his fiery mettle up to her very womb, meeting her own emission on the way. About a minute afterwards I felt Ernestine's vagina embrace my penis tightly, a convulsive trembling seized her bottom and she wiggled herself from side to side on my staff. In another moment I had inundated her with my sperm while she discharged so copiously that it trickled down the inside of her beautiful thighs.

" 'I too come,' said Harriet, seeing that we were all *hors de combat*, and she elevated her buttocks and pressing her mount tightly to Ernestine's face, found relief in a shower of love's dew, and then sank back exhausted on the sofa.

"In a minute or two we all rose, washed ourselves and were ready for another bout.

" 'Seat yourself on the sofa, Mr. Clarence,' said Harriet.

"I obeyed. She came and sat on my lap and guided my stiff dart into the innermost recesses of her *con*. She then leaned forward and making George sit on the other end of the sofa, she took his staff between her magnificent breasts and squeezing them close together, held it a tight prisoner there. She now made Isabelle take her place by my side, and Ernestine sat next to George—she then ordered us to put our hands on each of their *cons*. We obeyed. Harriet had one of the most delicious bijous in the world—it was so tight and warm that it embraced my pego very closely. I forced the middle finger of my right hand into Isabelle's coral passage while I titillated her clitoris with my thumb. With my other hand I tickled Harriet's bottom. George did the same for Ernestine and we all moved together. I noticed that while George's staff was moving between her two bubbies she frequently bent forward and titillated the ruby head of his rod with her tongue. All at once

I saw the white semen gush from his engine all over her white breasts, at the same moment that I shot my charge into Harriet's vagina and received Isabelle's emission on my hand. Ernestine too, almost at the same moment, bedewed George's fingers.

"This last engagement seemed rather to increase our sexual desires rather than to quench them. Acting according to the orders of our priestess, I sat myself on a chair before a large mirror. Isabelle came and straddled my thighs and Ernestine guided my engine into Isabell's lovely grotto. I cast my eyes in the glass and had a splendid front view of my companion's thighs, notch, etc. I could see my staff imbedded in her vagina and had a distinct view of the luscious lips embracing it. The lovely girl was delighted to be so thoroughly gorged. Ernestine laid on her back exactly in front of us and Harriet knelt down before her, and with her tongue titillated her clitoris, while George entered Harriet from behind. It was a magnificent sight to us, and we all soon emitted.

"We now partook of some spiced wine, which had the effect of entirely restoring our energies, and our rampant instruments proved that we were quite ready for another engagement in the courts of Venus.

"Harriet now ordered me to lie on my back on the floor and pushed Ernestine on the top of me. My pego entered her *con*. Harriet began to tickle our genitals when we were thus joined while George entered her *en cul* at the same time passing his hand in front of her and titillating her clitoris with his finger. With her unoccupied hand, Harriet took possession of Isabelle's *con* and forced two fingers in it—and in this manner we all again succumbed. I should tire you if I were to enumerate all the manners and modes in which we accomplished the sexual act—suffice it to say that we kept it up until five o'clock the next morning and only ceased from sheer inability to proceed further. During that time I had embraced three girls in every part of their bodies—*en con, en cul*, between the bubbies, the buttocks, and in short every portion of their bodies.

"I took a week's rest after this night's experience. My history is already too long, but I have one more adventure to describe and then I have done.

"About a month after my adventure with Harriet Wells, I received a note from an aunt of mine who kept a ladies' seminary in Westchester County, New York, asking me to come and spend a month with her. Having no particular business to attend to I determined to accept this invitation, thinking perhaps I might meet with some adventures among so many young girls—besides which I knew that my aunt had a very pretty daughter, and I thought perhaps she and I might become better acquainted. In a few hours I was at my aunt's door, and was received with the utmost cordiality by my aunt. I had scarcely entered the drawing room before my cousin Emmeline made her appearance. The moment I cast my eyes upon her I was almost struck dumb with surprise, for she was so much more beautiful than I had expected to find her. It was at least ten years since I had seen her; she was at that time twelve years old and promised to be very pretty, but I never expected to see such an embodiment of female loveliness as now appeared.

"My cousin Emmeline was twenty-two years of age. She was tall, stately and voluptuously formed. Her face was perfectly oval and her features were regular almost to a fault. Her hair, which was very abundant, was a dark glossy brown and fell in massive bands on a neck as white and pure as alabaster. Her eyes were dark and flashing and shrouded with long eye-lashes while her figure was perfect. She was dressed *en neglige* but through her morning wrapper I could trace the round form of her voluptuous bust.

"She received me with the utmost frankness and made no objection to the kiss that I imprinted on her ruby lips with a cousin's liberty. During her temporary absence from the room, her mother informed me that she was to be married in three weeks to a very rich gentleman who was a good deal older than herself and for whom she did not profess any deep attachment. In the afternoon I was ushered into the schoolroom and found myself surrounded by thirty or forty beautiful girls of all ages and styles of loveliness. Some of them were excessively beautiful and all cast on me curious glances as if they wondered what my business could be there.

"In the evening, my aunt, cousin and myself met in the drawing room, and the evening was passed with music, singing and conversation. If Emmeline looked beautiful in a morning costume, she was perfectly lovely in evening dress. She wore her frock cut so low in the neck that the contours of her lovely bust could be plainly seen. In fact, while she was performing on the piano I bent over her for the purpose of turning the leaves of her music, and as she bent forward I had a most distinct view of the two white semiglobes of her bosom. They were separated by a white valley which led to other hidden charms. The sight of her delicious bubbies so excited me that I was compelled to hold my pocket handkerchief in front of me to hide the protuberance produced by her charms.

"Several days passed, during which time I attempted to take several liberties with my cousin—but she always stopped me at a certain point, no doubt actuated by the fact of her approaching marriage. I was in despair for I saw no way of accomplishing my designs. The thought struck me, however, that if I could only succeed in exciting her passions I might move her to my will—I determined to make my attempt. I had in my stock amorous books, one in French, entitled: *L'Académie des Dames*, an exceedingly lascivious work, interspersed with the most magnificent engravings. It was something like Aretino's famous *Putante Errante* — but much more full and complete. It purported to be a dialogue between two young girls and gave the fullest information in all sexual matters, interspersed with vivid and glowing descriptions of the sexual act. This book I stealthily lay in my cousin's way, as if I had left it there by accident. I rejoiced to find half an hour afterwards, on returning to the place where I had put it, that it was gone, and I had no doubt but that it had fallen into Emmeline's hands.

"The house in which my aunt resided was an old-fashioned building, containing very large rooms, all communicating with each other. The bedroom allotted to me was situated next to Emmeline's chamber, and there was a communication between the two apartments by means of a closet which served for both rooms. This closet was only divided by a green curtain. I retired to bed very early that night—and the first thing I did was to cut a hole in the curtain and leave my side of the closet door open. I then put out my light and waited for events. I had not to wait long, for I soon heard Emmeline's light step ascending the stairs. I had only just taken my position in the closet when she entered the chamber. As luck would have it she did not close her closet door, but immediately began to undress. Great God! What beauties she revealed to me as she removed her garments one by one. First it was her beautiful shoulders, next her voluptuous limbs, and lastly her resplendent bosom, for when she stood in her chemise I had a full view of her naked bubbies. No words that I can utter can give the faintest idea of the glories of their form and beauty. They were beyond comparison. She now went to her trunk and took from it a book, which I discovered in a moment to be *L'Académie des Dames* and then she threw herself, lightly clad as she was, upon the bed.

"Her couch was placed exactly opposite my hiding place, so that I had a most perfect view of her as she reclined there. One of her milk-white breasts was entirely bare and her chemise was raised sufficiently high for me to see a portion of her lovely thighs. She began to read and soon I saw a strange change take place in her. Her face grew flushed, her bosom heaved and she began to twist her legs and thighs about in a curious manner. Suddenly, without any previous intimation of her intention, she seized the lower end of her chemise and slowly raised it above her navel. By this action all her hidden charms were entirely exposed to me. Heavens! I glanced on the picture. Imagination cannot paint the delicious sight that met my eyes, her 'con' was one of the loveliest I had ever beheld. I could distinctly trace the two pouting lips through a forest of umbrageous covering—while her white belly, her delicious thighs and voluptuous breast formed the adjuncts to a picture which I feel it is in vain for me to attempt to describe. The lovely Emmeline still continued reading, little suspecting that prying eyes were eagerly devouring her most secret charms. She held the book in her left hand, her right fell carelessly by her side, her fingers coming in contact with the hair surrounding her Mons Veneris. A shiver ran through her system when she felt the place on which her hand had fallen, and she instinctively raised up her thighs to admit more easily her researches into her own beauties. The book had evidently grown now quite interesting, for I saw the middle finger of her hand slowly separate the pouting lips of her bijou to find a refuge in her warm vagina. She now began to move it in and out, slowly at first. It appeared to fit very tightly, for every onward motion brought out the myphae, and they disappeared again when the deflowering finger advanced inwards. These titillations were more than the lovely girl could bear, for she threw away the book and set earnestly about giving herself relief. Her finger now moved with lightning rapidity in and out of her vagina, while with her thumb she titillated her clitoris. By Heavens! she is about to come—I can read it in the voluptuous motions of her charming body. I can read it in the trembling of her buttocks and the heaving of her bubbies. I can read it in the frantic motion of her finger and in the twitching of her eyelids. There—dear girl—now it flows—there—there. The acme was reached and she fainted away.

"I was so excited by what I had seen that, regardless of consequences, I rushed into my cousin's bed chamber. She did not hear me for she had not yet recovered her consciousness. I pulled out my pocket handkerchief and wiped her lovely bijou perfectly dry. I then knelt down by the side of the bed and tenderly kissed the theater of her pleasures. The warmth of my embrace doubtless recalled her to herself, for she opened her eyes and gazed on me. The moment she saw me she uttered a faint scream.

" 'Hush, dear Emmeline,' I exclaimed. 'It is I, your cousin Herbert. After what I have seen, all further reserve would be folly. I love you, my dear cousin, and must enjoy your beautiful body. No one need know anything about it.'

" 'Promise to conceal what you have seen

this night, and you may do anything you please with me,' she replied.

" 'I swear it,' I answered.

"The beautiful girl no sooner heard me utter these words than she threw her arms round my neck and kissed me passionately. I twined her beautiful limbs in mine and rolled over her on the bed. I now laid on my back and, turning her magnificent buttocks towards my face, she herself guided my lance into her ruby cavity. A slight upward motion on my part caused it to enter completely, and I had the gratification of seeing my instrument enter in and out of her coral crevice during the act of coition. Emmeline, when she felt my proud engine pierce her vitals, was almost delirious with joy. She knelt with my thighs between hers, and in the delirium of pleasure convulsively grasped the bedclothes. I felt that I was about to emit, and finding that she was not quite ready to come, I passed a hand round her hips and titillated her clitoris with my finger. This had the effect of immediately bringing down her emission. We both discharged together.

"I have already, my dear girls, made my history too long, or I could detain you for hours yet with an account of the various modes in which I enjoyed my cousin. I could also tell you how I overcame the virtue of five of my aunt's eldest scholars, and how one night we all enjoyed an orgy in my cousin Emmeline's chamber. But in such a relation I should necessarly have to repeat scenes I have already depicted so I forbear.

"My cousin Emmeline was married on the

day appointed. I returned home, became acquainted with my present wife and was married. Some little time after my marriage I managed to get Amy to accept my embraces. I shall leave the details for her to tell."

Amy blushed and would fain have been excused—but we both insisted.

Amy was not obdurate, and could not withstand our entreaties. She commenced her history in the terms which will be found in the next chapter.

CHAPTER TWO

AMY DENMEAD'S HISTORY

"I was born in Philadelphia. My father was a large and successful merchant, doing business there. We lived in a large house in the upper part of Chestnut Street, and my father's wealth procured me every luxury that the heart could wish for. I never knew my mother, for she died when I was quite young. My sister was married to you, Herbert, when I was seventeen years of age. My ideas up to that time were very vague regarding the sexes, but I was soon destined to be fully enlightened.

"I felt very dull after my sister had gone away, and my father proposed that I should write and ask my old school fellow, Florence Maltby, to come and stay on a visit with us. I cordially agreed to this proposition, for I loved Florence and had not seen her for several years, although we kept up a constant correspondence.

"Florence accepted my invitation, and on the day agreed upon she took up her abode with us.

"Miss Maltby was a beautiful girl about twenty years of age, her hair and eyes were black—in fact she was a decided brunette. She was fiery, impulsive and amorous. We had a thousand things to converse about, and in a few hours all our old friendship was reknit, and we became more intimate than ever. Of course, we slept together.

"For two or three nights nothing occurred of special moment. I noticed, however, that Florence would kiss me with a great deal of warmth and press me tenderly in her arms when we were in bed together, but I thought nothing of it.

"One night, about a week after she had been an inmate of our house, when we retired to our chamber, instead of undressing as usual, Florence seated herself on the side of the bed and watched me in the process of disrobing. I had unhooked the front of my dress, and it had fallen on my shoulders, and my chemise, being open in front, allowed my two breasts to be seen; nay, even a portion of the white plain below was visible. Florence no sooner saw this than her eyes brightened and she ran up to me and began to mold my bubbies. Although this action somewhat surprised me, I made no resistance, and to tell the truth the contact of her soft hands on my breasts was very agreeable.

"'What delicious breasts you have,' said Florence. 'How well formed they are, and yet how large! See how stiff the rosy nipples stand out from this field of snow! Oh, how I would love to kiss and press them!' And she buried her head between the two semiglobes. 'And then your belly, how soft and white it is,' she continued, passing her hand over it, 'how happy will the man be who presses that belly to his own.'

"'Oh, fie, Florence, you should not talk in that manner,' I replied, my face flushing with the fire kindled in me by her lascivious touchings. 'But you exaggerate my beauties. It is true my breasts are a little larger than yours—but they are not one bit more handsome, more firm, nor more elastic. Come dear, let us compare them, for I do not see why I should not be gratified as well as yourself.'

"I now unhooked Florence's dress and pulled it down to her waist. Her two semiglobes were completely exposed. They were beautifully formed, firm, elastic and standing boldly out from her chest. I pressed and caressed them, sucking the rosy nipples which stood out stiff with desire.

"'You naughty girl,' said Florence, 'you will devour me. Your kisses send a fire through my veins—and these delicious globes too—'

"'Could it be possible to see prettier bubbies than these,' I interrupted. 'Just see how stiff the nipples are, and then you talk of my belly —look at yours. How deliciously smooth! How beautifully white.'

"'Come, darling,' said Florence, 'let us rub breasts together—I am sure it will give us mutual delight.'

"'I will do anything you wish, Florence, for I feel a strange fire burning in me—come, love—come.'

"We pulled down our clothes as low as possible so as to leave us a clear field. We then brought our chests together in such a way that our breasts rubbed against each other. To show how amorous we were, I need only say that this strange action gave us great delight.

" 'Is it not exquisite?' said Florence. 'The sensations of your breast against mine fires my whole blood.'

" 'I experience the same feelings,' I returned. 'Oh, it is charming.'

" 'Amy,' said Florence, after a few minutes repose, 'do you know what I would like to do?'

" 'No, what?'

" I should like to explore your more secret beauties.'

" 'With all my heart,' I replied, 'if you will allow me the same privilege.'

" 'Willingly—I should love it,' returned Florence.

" 'Come then, darling,' I exclaimed, 'I am ready—do with me as you like.

" 'Dear girl, how good you are!' returned Florence. Lie down with your belly on the bed that I may admire and manipulate your beauties; that's right, darling.'

"I threw myself on my face on the bed. Florence came behind me and, lifting up my petticoats, exposed my bottom to her gaze. Of course she saw also the pouting lips of my bijou at the bottom of the fleshy cushions, faintly overshadowed with hair. She moved my thighs slightly apart, by which movements the lips of my sheath were slightly separated, revealing a line of coral between them. Florence absolutely threw herself on my bottom and devoured it with the most lascivious and ardent kisses.

" 'Does that position suit you, dear Florence?' said I, with my face buried in the bed.

" 'It is charming—delicious,' said Florence, molding and pressing my buttocks. 'Great

Heavens! Amy, how the sight of your beauties fires me! What magnificent buttocks, how white and firm, how well developed,' and again she bent down and smothered them with kisses. 'I should never be tired kissing your lovely bottom,' she continued, 'and the edges of that dear little cleft I see between your thighs—how inviting it looks! How beautiful it is, shaded with silky down. Oh! I must—I must!' And she put her finger between the lips of my sheath and titillated my vagina. 'How charming, how delicious,' she repeated. 'Amy, I am in a blaze—my slit is on fire. How deliciously tight your vagina clasps my finger and what a delightful warmth is there. There! Now I have your clitoris! How stiff it is!'

" 'Dearest Florence,' I exclaimed, wiggling my buttocks, for the in-and-out motion of her finger was more than I could bear—'your touchings and titillations are bringing on a crisis. Stay the motion of your finger or I shall come—there—there—there it is! Oh! I die! I die——'

"During this last speech of mine I moved my buttocks up and down, imitating the conjugal act—Florence all the time continuing her manipulations until the crisis came and I fell motionless on my belly.

" 'Come, Amy,' said Florence, withdrawing her dripping finger from my sheath, 'for heaven's sake give me relief or I die.'

"I rose from my recumbent posture and, seizing Florence by the waist, pushed her on the bed. She fell on her back. I threw her petticoats over her head. This action revealed all the lower portion of Florence's body—and a beautiful sight it was. Two magnificently developed thighs led up to a charming grotto covered with black hair, between the pouting lips of which could be seen her clitoris, stiff with intense desire. I admired for a moment Florence's beauties, and then commenced my manipulations. First of all I stroked her belly, implanting kiss after kiss upon it. I then played with the hair covering her Mons Veneris, twisting my finger in and out of it. I then divided the lips of her sheath and titillated her highly excited clitoris.

" 'Great Heavens, Florence,' I exclaimed, 'what a beautiful bijou yours is! What delicious pouting lips! What a forest of black hair and then your clitoris—how finely developed! Let me kiss it! Let me suck it.'

"I now stooped down and inserted my tongue between the lips of Florence's ruby passage, and titillated her clitoris with the tip of it.

" 'Great God! how delicious,' I exclaimed, 'I feel ready to come again—I do indeed darling.'

" 'Amy, darling, keep on—keep on—' said Florence, almost crazy with delight, 'pass one hand behind and press my buttocks.'

"I did as she desired and advanced one finger in the narrow canal adjacent to the legitimate road and kept time with my tongue and finger.

" 'There — that's it!' she continued, 'I am coming. Oh! now—now! there! there! th—'

"She opened her thighs to the widest extent and lifted her legs high in the air. A convulsive shudder ran through her frame and she discharged profusely, appearing to be perfectly annihilated by the deliciousness of her sensations. I threw myself by her side on the bed. After a long pause we both rose and kissed each other tenderly.

"Such was my first initiation in the sports of Venus. Florence remained with us some months and scarcely a day passed that we did not enjoy the pleasures of the gods. When she left us I was for a time disconsolate—but soon after I received an invitation to visit Herbert and my sister. He has left it to me, dear Kate, to give the history of my first amour with him. I shall do so, freely speaking, as if he were not present.

"I was received with the utmost kindness by my brother-in-law, and truth compels me to state, rogue that he is, that he has always treated me with the most unvarying affection. At the time of my visit my sister was very sick, and I really pitied poor Herbert, that he was debarred from those sexual enjoyments of which I felt assured he was so fond. But the thought of taking her place never for a moment entered my mind.

"Herbert was very polite to me, and time passed very agreeably. One day I stumbled in an obscure corner of the library on some amorous books. I secured them and conveyed them to my chamber. I then examined them and found that they contained pictures of a very lascivious character. In fact men and women, as naked as they were born, were performing the sexual act. I read them with avidity and they soon made me adept in sexual knowledge. One evening when Herbert had gone to Philadelphia, and my sister was confined to her chamber by sickness, I entered the drawing room with one of those prizes in my hand, determined to enjoy it all myself. I was in a state of delicious languor and, throwing myself carelessly on the sofa, began to read my book. I wore a low-necked dress and the weather being warm I had unfastened two or three of the top loops—thus leaving a considerable portion of my breasts exposed. My dress too was disarranged at my feet—revealing a considerable portion of my limbs. As I read, my cheeks became flushed, my bosom heaved, and I was altogether in a state propitious for an attack. I was suddenly startled by the sound of a voice at my elbow.

" 'What is the name of that book which seems to engross so much of your attention?' said the voice.

"I raised my eyes, and who should I see but Herbert himself gazing on me with heightened color and burning eyes.

" 'It is too bad, Herbert,' I replied, raising from my seat, revealing by this movement a considerable portion of my legs; nay, I believe he even caught a glimpse of my thighs, 'you ought not to come so stealthily into the room.'

" 'My dear girl, you are wrong,' replied Herbert, 'I did not come here stealthily, but it was your preoccupation which prevented you from hearing me enter. But you have not replied to my question—what book are you reading?'

" 'Oh, it is a stupid work I found in the library, I have only just glanced at it and do not find it worth reading.'

" 'Will you allow me to judge for myself, my

charming sister-in-law,' he replied, taking a seat by my side.

" 'No, Herbert, I will not allow it,' I returned, pressing the book to my bosom.

" 'I insist,' he cried, endeavoring to snatch the work from my hands. In the struggle his hand came in contact with my bosom and he even touched the strawberry nipples surmounting the semiglobes. At last he conquered and obtained possession of the book. I looked imploringly at him, but he opened it deliberately and read the title. It was *The Memoirs of a Woman of Pleasure*.

" 'So, so, Amy,' said he. 'This is the subject of your studies, is it?'

" 'I assure you I have not read a page of it—it appeared to me foolish and uninteresting, and I was just about to return it to the library when you entered.'

"He knew that I did not tell the truth, for I blushed and cast my eyes down on the ground. He no longer hesitated, but throwing his arms around me, pressed his lips to mine and kissed me ardently. I was astonished and confounded and endeavored to escape him, but he held me tight and pressed his breast to mine.

" 'Herbert, Herbert, this is wrong, let me go, I beg of you.'

"He replied by pressing another kiss on my lips. It was in vain I struggled; he appeared to be endowed with the strength of Hercules.

" 'Do have done!' I murmured between each embrace, 'someone might come.'

" 'My love, there is no cause for fear, there is no one in the house but you and I. Your sister is confined to her chamber by sickness and I have given positive orders that I am not at home to anyone. We are absolutely alone.'

"I could not disguise the pleasure that this news gave me, for my whole body became agitated with the warmth of his embraces, and my bosom palpitated against his. I even dared to return his caresses, and reimbursed with interest the kisses he gave me.

"'Amy, I love and adore you,' said he.

"'Herbert, I love you! I love you,' was the only reply that I could make.

"Again he pressed his lips to mine and sucked in my breath. He even inserted the end of his tongue in my mouth, and he met mine, which was as ardent as his own. I believe I should have died if nature had not given me relief at that moment. I believe the same thing happened to him, for he threw himself upon me, and two or three convulsive shudders ran through his system; he then became calmer and reclined negligently in my arms.

"'My beloved, this is true happiness,' said he, 'oh, that we could remain thus forever, and that we might never part again.'

"After a few moments repose he rose up, and leaning over me, seized one of my hands and felt my bubbies with his unoccupied hand. The contact renewed the fire in his body and his eyes reassumed their brilliance. When I felt his hand descend on my breast, I shivered and made a pretense of snatching it away, but it was in vain. He cautiously unhooked my dress; I no longer restrained him. My frock fell off my shoulders and my naked bust was entirely exposed to his view. He passed from one to the other of my ivory globes, as he called them, and molded them with his hands, playing with the nipples and applying his lips to them so that he almost sucked my life away. But he was not yet satisfied. He knelt down before me and, placing his head between my bubbies, began to play with my feet. I made but little resistance and he began to raise my petticoats. He touched my legs, he reached my knees, and at last his hand came in contact with my fleshy thighs. He rested here a moment and excited me by kisses. I trembled in his grasp like a leaf — my desires overcame me and I was completely in his power. He then became more bold and his agitated hand ascended the marble columns which would lead us to the center of love. At last he reached my bijou and ran his fingers in the down covering that mossy spot—he even forced one more bold than the rest between the lips, and gently rubbed my clitoris. It was too much for me, I opened my thighs to the widest capacity and absolutely cried with pleasure. He then raised his head from my palpitating bosom, and applied his lips where he had just put his hand. He kissed my Mons Veneris a thousand times, and inserted his tongue between the folding lips; he again sought out my clitoris and played with it at will. But this could not continue long. I was absolutely drunk with delirious joy.

" 'Oh, what pleasure!' I cried, 'do what you will with me, my dear Herbert.'

"His only reply was to divest himself of his clothes; he then performed the same office for me, and we were both naked as we were born. He turned me round and round—he patted my buttocks and caressed my body all over. My hands too were not idle. I seized his magnificent instrument and gently rubbed it and tickled his purse. We were both almost crazy. He then reclined me on my back on the sofa and threw himself on the top of me. I eagerly opened my thighs to receive him and guided his fiery dart to the entrance of my 'con.' He entered the lips and met a little resistance, but was not to be conquered, for raising my buttocks I gave a sudden heave upwards, and his instrument was suddenly imbedded in the sheath destined by nature to receive it. Then commenced the delicious movements. The motion was delightful. I looked around me and saw our naked bodies reflected in the mirrors. I could see his instrument entering in and out of my coral sheath. At last the consummation came.

"'Oh, Herbert,' I cried—'I die! I die!—closer!—closer—clo——'

"Thus muttering, I closed my eyes. My eyelids trembled and with a convulsive movement I threw my legs around his loins and pressed him so tightly that I almost took away his breath. All was over, for I felt the essence of love rush into my thirsty womb, while I at the same moment poured down my share of Venus' libations. My hold relaxed and we both fell all our lengths on the couch.

"After remaining without motion a few minutes, he kissed me again, for he was not yet satisfied. He soon rekindled my desires.

"He rose from the couch, and raising me up, placed me on its edge and again commenced his labor of love. With one hand he raised one of my arms in the air in such a manner as to leave my bosom entirely at his discretion. He took one of the nipples in his mouth and pressed me to him with his other hand. My thighs were widely separated and he had no difficulty in entering my vagina. He slightly bent his knees and was soon buried in my grotto. How delicious was the sensation of his lovely engine rubbing against the sides of my vagina. I assisted him by every means in my power, and in a short time we were again inundated with our mutual emission.

"Such, my dear Kate, was the manner in which I first became carnally acquainted with Herbert. How many times we have enjoyed each other since, I need not tell you. But this I do assure you, no other man has enjoyed me but Herbert, and as long as he is kind to me no other shall. My history is ended."

We thanked the charming girl for her confession. It was now getting daylight and almost time for us to separate. During Amy's recital we had partaken freely of spiced wine, and all of us felt almost as vigorous as ever; we decided we would not separate until we could enter the lists of love no more. Herbert brought a new auxiliary to our pleasures into the field, for going to a cupboard, he took from it an India-rubber dildo, which he strapped round Amy's waist.

And placing me on my side on the couch he made Amy insert the dildo into my vagina, while she put her finger on my clitoris and began to rub it, at the same time moving her buttocks as if she were a man. He then went behind me and entered me *en cul*. Amy acted her part splendidly. Herbert passed his hand over her bottom and inserted his finger in her sheath. Both Herbert and Amy moved together, and I had the delicious pleasure of enjoying a double embrace. Herbert's finger too, was active, and we all discharged simultaneously.

After we had recovered we danced naked about the room. Herbert kissed our breasts, bottoms and mounts. He placed his staff between our bubbies, he tickled our clitorises, and committed a thousand other follies. At last he lay down on the couch and pulled Amy on the top of him. She guided his instrument into her coral sheath, and moved herself rapidly up and down, while I clapped her broad white bottom with my hand until they were cherry red, and while I was thus engaged, Herbert's toe entered my slit, and in this manner we all again discharged.

It would tire the reader to tell all the ways we adopted to arrive at the same result. Herbert embraced us *en con, en cul*, between the bubbies, between the buttocks—in fact in every possible mode and we did not separate until we were thoroughly exhausted and until the morning sun was several hours in the heavens.

CHAPTER THREE

A CHANGE OF FORTUNE

The very next day following our orgy, I received a letter from my father's lawyer informing me of the death of my only surviving parent, at the same time informing me that he had left all his property to be divided equally between my brother and myself. His wealth was large, for his habits had been penurious, and I found myself the possessor of at least $10,000 a year. This of course entirely altered my prospects in life and it was natural that I should immediately throw up my engagement as governess and return home for the purpose of assisting the settlement of my father's affairs.

I bade an affectionate farewell to Herbert and Amy, and even shed tears at parting with them. In due time I reached home. How still and quiet the place seemed! My brother was abroad, so that everything connected with the property was left to me. I worked energetically and soon produced something like order. I had been home about a week when I received another letter from my father's lawyer, who resided in New York, stating that my presence was absolutely required in that city to sign certain documents relative to my father's property, and advising me to come at once. I did not hesitate to obey his wishes, and that same evening entered the cars for New York.

It was about six o'clock when we started, and I took a seat in the rear end of the car. For some miles I was alone, but a young gentleman of about eighteen got into the car from a way station and sat down by my side. I could see by the dim light that he was very polite and we had quite an agreeable conversation together.

By and by it grew quite dark, for the lamp stationed in the middle of the car threw very little light where we sat. Our conversation grew more confidential, I may even say affectionate. The young gentleman grew somewhat bold, and taking my hand, pressed it in his. The novelty of the situation and the fact that for ten days I had tasted no sexual pleasure rendered me oblivious to all resemblance of modesty and I allowed him to do as he pleased. Nay, I even encouraged him, for I allowed my hand to fall as if by accident on a certain protuberance in front of his pantaloons. I had no sooner touched this sensitive spot than a shiver ran through him and he immediately retained my hand there as a prisoner.

All reserve now left him. He had spread a shawl over our knees so that our actions could not be seen by the other passengers. I suddenly felt the rogue dragging up my skirts and petticoats, and in a few moments his hand was on my naked thigh; he glided over it and his fingers came in contact with the hair covering my Mons Veneris. He had already divided the lips of my coral cavity with his digits and was advancing one in the very center of my vagina when the train entered Philadelphia. Of course this put a stop to his progress, and we were compelled to assume a decent position.

He was very attentive to me on the boat when we crossed the Delaware, but he had no opportunity to renew his enterprises. At last we were safely seated in one of the Camden and Amboy Railroad cars. As luck would have it the car was very empty, there not being more than two other persons in it besides ourselves. We took our places as far from them as we could. The young gentleman turned the seats so that he now sat opposite to me.

The train had not left the station a hundred yards before he commenced operations by making me rest my two feet in his seat, one on each side of him, so that he sat between my thighs. He now raised my petticoats and amused himself by feeling my thighs, bottom and slit. He played with me for some minutes, titillating the interior of my vagina with his finger, pressing my thighs and tickling my bottom. In the meantime I had released his instrument from its place of confinement, and grasping it in my hand, I covered and uncovered its red head, and at the same time tickled his testicles. After a little time he drew me to the very edge of the seat and, pointing his rod, entered my salacious slit. After a few pushes which sent a thrill of delight through me, he turned up all my clothes and regaled himself with the sight of his engine entering in and out of my coral sheath. I responsively moved my buttocks in answer to his thrusts and in a few minutes we both discharged profusely.

Four times did he thus embrace me during our journey from Philadelphia to New York, and four times did I pour down my libation of love's dew. We parted the best of friends, and from that day to this I have never seen him but the pleasure I enjoyed with him will never be effaced from my mind.

Late the next day I called on Mr. Ralph Pitman, my father's lawyer. I found him to be a fine looking man of about thirty-six years of age. He was nearly six feet high, and stout in proportion. He appeared to be very strong and evidently enjoyed the most robust health. He received me very warmly and I saw his fine eyes sparkle when he gazed on my womanly charms. My business with him was soon concluded and it was decided that he should visit my late father's residence the ensuing week for the purpose of finally settling up his affairs.

I made up my mind that I would return home the next day, as the city with all its noise and confusion was not agreeable to my taste. The next morning I walked out on Broadway for the purpose of making a few purchases, when who should be the first person I met but Laura Castleton, my old teacher at B . . . Seminary—and the first who initiated me in the delights of love.

Laura was dressed in the height of fashion and was as beautiful as ever. She recognized me immediately and kissed me affectionately. We immediately adjourned to Taylor's, where we could converse in private. I told her everything that had occurred to me since I had seen her, disguising nothing. Her eyes sparkled and her bottom heaved when I depicted all the love scenes I had gone through.

"And now, dear Laura," said I, when I had finished, "tell me what you are doing now."

"I am the mistress of the head *maison de joie* in New York."

"What!" I returned, "do you mean to tell me that you keep a house of that kind?"

"I do indeed, and a delightful time I have of it."

"How I should love to know its mysteries."

"That you can easily do—come and spend tonight with us. You shall see everything without being seen yourself. I have twenty-four magnificent girls living with me and every one of them will be gloriously embraced tonight, you may depend upon it. The rooms are so arranged that we can see everything that transpires in them. Say you will come."

"My dear, I should love to—only tell me where it is, and at what hour I should come."

"I live at No.——Mercer street, and come at seven o'clock."

"I will be there, you may depend on it."

Soon after this we separated. I made my purchases, put off my departure until the next day, and at the appointed hour I was at Laura's door.

My old friend met me at the entrance.

"You have just come in time," said she, "for Horace Greenwood has just taken Olivia, one of the handsomest of my boarders, upstairs. She is from New Orleans and one of the most lascivious girls I ever saw; I have no doubt we shall see some fun."

So saying she led me upstairs and ushered me into a closet which communicated with the adjoining room. Olivia and her friend were already there. I was struck with the beauty of the couple. The girl had intensely black hair and eyes, the latter of which were lighted up with desire and passion. Her bust, which her low-necked dress allowed to be seen, was really magnificent. Her companion was a fine handsome young fellow of twenty-two or twenty-three.

"Well, darling," said Horace, pressing her voluptuous bosom close to him, "I have come to see you again. The thoughts of once more tasting the delights of your lovely person has kept me in a continued state of excitement all day. My staff is in a state of the fiercest erection."

"Let me have oracular demonstrations of the fact," said Olivia, opening his pantaloons in front; out jumped his member, stiff and erect as a poker.

"Oh you bad boy," she continued, taking it in her hand and rubbing it up and down— "how gloriously stiff you are. I must kiss you then, you bad child."

So saying, she took his member in her mouth and rolled her tongue over it, at the same time tickling his testicles.

"Great God!" he cried, "this is too much —I shall spend, dear girl, if you do not cease. All my blood is in a flame."

"It is so delicious, I hate to give it up," she returned, giving it a last kiss. But I am excited as much as yourself. Slip your hand underneath my petticoats and feel how stiff my clitoris is."

He lifted up her skirts and took possession of Olivia's luscious *con* with his hand and evidently found the little sentinel as stiff and firm as his own lance, for I saw by his motions that he was rubbing it between his fingers.

"How delightful," said Olivia, a shudder of delight running through her frame. "It is too much! Stay! let me open my thighs a little wider—there, that is much better, now you can manipulate my slit a great deal easier. What intense pleasure! Rub my clitoris harder and titillate the interior of my mount with your other finger."

"Yes, darling, I will, but, your petticoats are in the way," replied Horace. "I want to see my finger enter in and out of your luscious grotto."

"I will soon remedy that," she replied, lifting her petticoats above her navel, thus exposing her magnificent thighs, a portion of her white belly, and above all, her delicious *con*.

"How beautifully you are made, dear Olivia," said Horace, devouring with his eyes the luscious sight before him. "What a luscious belly, and then this masterpiece of nature—this splendid bushy mount . . . what words can I find to express its beauties—what fine silky down surrounds this luscious little *con!* How deliciously the lips pout, inviting a visitor. Let me examine the interior of this abode of happiness."

So saying, Horace seated himself on the ground between Olivia's thighs. With the fingers of one hand he opened the lips of her slit and peered curiously into the ruby cavity. He passed the other hand behind her, molding and pressing her buttocks, even advancing one finger into the narrow passage adjacent to the haven of love. After continuing this play for a minute or two, he inserted his tongue between the lips of her bijou, titillated the interior of her grotto, sucking her clitoris. Olivia was almost mad with pleasure, and showed it by opening her thighs to the widest extent. When she felt his tongue come in contact with her clitoris she experienced the acme of delight.

"Stop, dear Horace," said Olivia, throwing her arms around his neck, "or I shall spend —I shall indeed—Oh darling, darling—for heaven's sake, stop."

"It is a hard matter to leave the interior of your luscious grotto," said Horace withdrawing his tongue from her slit and looking into her face. "The sensitive folds of your vagina embraced my tongue so deliciously, and your clitoris is so beautiful that I hate to give it up. But, darling, let me see your beautiful bubbies."

"How fond you are of molding and pressing a woman's breasts," returned Olivia, unhooking her dress and shaking it off her shoulders, thus exposing her magnificently developed semiglobes. "Then here they are. Do what you like with them. See how stiff and firm the nipples stand out."

Horace then began to toy with her breasts,

molding and pressing them and then sucking their rosy nipples. While he was thus engaged, Olivia took possession of his staff of love—capping and uncapping its large ruby head.

"This is too beautiful," said Horace, burying his head between her breasts. "I can contain myself no longer. Come dearest, let us perform the last act of love—I must embrace you. You see how eager my member is to enter your delicious *con*."

"I assure you my slit is not less eager to receive it. Dear Horace, I burn for you—come, my dear angel—come! Embrace me. Bury this delicious instrument into the deepest recesses of my vagina. Do not spare me—push it in to the very hilt, make your testicles knock against my bottom. Come, darling, into me quick. See —I open the portals for you—there—now you have a fair mark—come darling—come!"

While she was thus speaking, she half reclined herself on the sofa and opened her thighs to the widest extent. He then divided the lips of her salacious *con* with a finger of each hand and revealed the interior of that ruby grotto. Horace rushed between her thighs, and passing one arm around her neck, brought his instrument to the entrance of her slit. Olivia placed one of her feet on a table, standing close by the sofa, thus stretching her thighs as widely apart as possible. In another moment he was plunged to the very hilt in her body.

"There, dear girl, you have it now," said Horace—when his instrument was clasped by the lips of her coral sheath. "Oh, how deliciously warm your vagina is! Oh, how tightly your lovely *con* clasps my penis, and your delicious belly, how soft it is! Your charming bubbies too, how delightfully they beat against my chest! Stay, I must suck the nectar from those rosy lips once more." He continued bending forward and took one of the strawberry nipples in his mouth, at the same time continuing his energetic thrusts. "There, how heavenly! how delicious! how exquisite!"

"It is too much, darling!" returned Olivia, throwing her legs around his loins. "Closer—closer still. Look in the mirror and see how deliciously your penis fills my vagina. Stay, let me raise my thighs a little, you will see it better then. There, now you see it. How lusciously it enters in and out of the coral cavity —now—I can see its ruby head—now it is lost in the hair covering my mount," (his strokes quickened) "Oh! Oh! I can stand no more," she continued, wiggling her buttocks. "Dear love, I spend—I come—I come!—Oh! Oh——."

"I too am coming—there, dear Olivia—come! come!"

During this scene their motions had increased rapidly. Horace giving violent thrusts and Olivia meeting him with corresponding motions of her buttocks. As the climax approached they seemed crazy with excitement and at the moment of emission their legs and thighs mingled together in confusion.

You may be sure that I was no passive inspector of this scene; during its continuance, Laura had taken possession of my Mons Veneris, and with her finger sought to give my excited feeling relief. At the moment of their discharge, I too succumbed, and was so much overcome that I was compelled to sit down to catch my breath for a few minutes.

When I had somewhat recovered I again took my station at the post to enjoy commanding a view of the chamber.

Horace was now stretched lengthwise on the sofa; he was perfectlly naked and Olivia was lying on the top of him, also stark naked. His arm was passed around her loins and he pressed her tightly against his belly. His left hand rested on her shoulder. Her mouth was fixed to his, and her breasts rested on his chest. Her thighs were stretched widely apart and Horace's staff was so deeply imbedded in Olivia's slit that the very hair of their genitals intermingled. They evidently experienced intense pleasure. Olivia's buttocks were elevated high in the air and she moved them energetically. Every time she raised her bottom I I could see Horace's lance entering in and out of the lips of her bushy mount, and sometimes I could even see the rosy head of his dart as he plunged it again and again into her coral slit. This motion became more rapid, and soon the lips of Olivia's glorious *con* seemed to contract and embrace Horace's staff closely. She then gave two or three convulsive struggles and ended by falling without motion on Horace's belly, at the same moment I saw the sperm trickle down her thighs.

"They have done for the night," whispered Laura to me. "Come with me and I will show you something else. For I am very much mistaken if Rose has not a visitor by this time."

So saying we left our place of concealment and entered a similar apartment at the other end of the corridor. We entered a closet in this room and peeped through some cracks in the boarding into the next apartment.

I saw a very pretty little plump girl entirely naked on her hands and knees on the bed, presenting her delicious white buttocks with her lovely slit, shaded with brown hair between them. Behind her was a tall, fine looking man, about forty years of age, also naked. In his hand was a birch—with which he was gently tickling the lovely girl's bottom.

"What does this mean?" I asked of Laura.

"That girl you see there is Rose Monson," she replied. "Nothing gives her so much pleasure as to be soundly whipped on the bottom by her lover. They always begin in this way. Her companion is George Coulson, a very rich gentlemen—but watch them and you will see something amusing."

I peeped again and saw that George was using the rod a little more freely than when I had first looked, already the cheeks of her buttocks were turned a rosy hue. His instrument was so stiff that it stood boldy up against his belly.

"Harder, George," murmured Rose, her face buried in the pillow. "I scarcely feel it, harder my dear boy, flog me harder."

George obeyed her wishes and let fall a shower of cuts on her plump backside. He continued this for a minute or two, when suddenly throwing down the rod he rushed to her, and to my surprise instead of entering her by the legitimate road, he entered her *en cul* —and passing his hand in front of her, buried two of his fingers in her hairy mount. Every thrust of his buttocks sent his fingers deeper into her vagina, giving her intense delight. Suddenly I saw her put her hand between her own lily-white thighs and tickle his testicles; it immediately brought on an emission from both of them and they sank exhausted on the bed.

Laura now led me to another apartment and again we took up our position. Here I saw a strong man standing in the middle of the room, holding in his arms a naked girl. Her arms were clasped around his neck and her thighs around his hips. His instrument was buried to the very depth in her vagina; he had one hand clasped round her body and the other supported her bottom. He moved her rapidly up and down. Every time he did so his staff entered in and out of her cavity and in a few moments they both discharged.

In the next chamber I saw a somewhat different scene. A beautiful girl, entirely naked, was seated on a low ottoman with her lovely thighs stretched widely apart. Her lover was kneeling on the floor before her and was caressing her lovely *con* with his tongue. I was so placed that I could see his organ of speech enter in and out her ruby sheath—the lips of which appeared to caress it lovingly. This act alone was sufficient to make him discharge copiously at the same moment that his tongue made her dissolve in bliss.

In another chamber a couple appeared to relish giving themselves manual pleasure instead of the act itself. For a lovely girl reclined on the bed with nothing but her chemise on, but still having her breasts and the lower portion of her body bare. Her companion lay by her side—he had his fingers imbedded in her slit, while she had hold of his instrument. They moved their hands together while he had hold of her bubbies and tickled her bottom with his other hand. A few rapid motions caused the sperm to fly from his staff, and he drew his finger dripping from her vagina at the same moment.

Another couple had chosen a strange way to satisfy their desires. The girl lay with her head on a pillow near the edge of the bed. The man was behind her and had passed her thighs around the upper part of his chest—supporting her belly with his hand. They were closely joined together—he appearing to be able to enter a prodigious way into her by this mode—her bottom almost touching his face. While he embraced her, he bent his head forward and kissed her buttocks. They both soon emitted.

I saw a great many other couples, but as they were for the most part a repetition of what I have already described, I shall omit referring to them. I thought I had seen all when I suddenly heard a ring at the bell, and almost immediately afterwards I heard a gentleman's voice say something in French in the hall.

"It is Alphonse de la Tour," said Laura. "Now I shall have to show you something really worth seeing. He is the particular friend of Eudoxie, the most beautiful girl in my whole establishment and more amorous and lascivious than all of them put together. She is lately from France, and does not speak a word of

English. She is perfectly crazy when enjoying the sexual act and acts in the most preposterous manner. Her naked body is worth going a hundred miles to see, she is so gloriously beautiful. But come, let us get to her room first for it is best not to miss the slightest preliminary of their love meeting."

I was very curious to see this paragon and followed Laura to her chamber which joined that of the French girl. We were soon installed in a convenient place of observation. We had been there but a few moments when Eudoxie, followed by her lover Alphonse, made her appearance. At the first glance I cast on the girl I was struck perfectly dumb at her surpassing loveliness. She was about nineteen years of age. Her face was perfectly oval and her features as regular as if they belonged to a Grecian statue. Her complexion was a rich brown. Her hair was intensely black and hung in a thousand little ringlets on her magnificently formed neck and shoulders. Her eyes were shaded with long black eyelashes—her teeth were beautifully white and regular, her arms might have formed a model for a sculptor, while her bust, which her low-necked dress allowed to be seen, was the most beautiful I had ever beheld. Imagine two lovely globes of snow which were so beautifully developed that they seemed to struggle to get free from the slight bonds that confined them. Every breath she drew caused those magnificent orbs to heave in sight. Her hips were fine, her figure magnificent, and her hands and feet excessively small.

Her companion was a fine, handsome young

man of about thirty. He was well made, evidently of a very amorous disposition. The moment they entered the chamber she ran up to her lover and throwing herself in his arms, imprinted some hot kisses on his lips. I could even see her velvet organ of speech enter his mouth in search of his, and they remained for a moment glued together. Suddenly the amorous girl released one of her divine breasts from its bonds of confinement and pushed it forward for him to kiss.

"*Baisez mon teton, mon cher Alphonse, je meurs pour vous!*" (Kiss my breast, my dear Alphonse. I die for you) said she.

And she herself slipped the rosy nipple in his mouth. While he was thus engaged she kissed his hair, his ears and forehead.

"*O foutez-moi—foutez-moi—mon cher,—Mon con est en feu!*" (O fuck me, fuck me, my cunt is on fire) she exclaimed.

And with that she began to tear off his clothes, and in a few moments he was quite naked. She then, with trembling fingers, began to disrobe herself, and every garment she took off only revealed new beauties. At last she stood with nothing on but her chemise.

"*Olez ma chemise. Je suis si excitee, que je ne le puis pas.*" (Take off my chemise I am so excited that I cannot do it.)

Alphonse slipped her sole remaining garment over her head and she stood in all her naked beauty before us. I had seen many naked women, but none to compare to Eudoxie; she was grace, beauty and voluptuousness combined. Her skin was dazzling white, her limbs models of beauty—her tapering legs, her plump thighs, her white belly, her magnificent buttocks and her mount of Venus, were the most magnificent objects I had ever beheld.

The moment she was naked, she knelt down before the object of her adoration (the position she assumed slightly opening the lips of her slit, and giving me a glimpse of the coral interior) and, taking his instrument in her hands, she nestled it between her breasts, and bending her head forward, kissed it again and again. She then rose to her feet again and making him lie with his back on the bed, she kissed his whole body, now it was his staff, now it was his testicles—now she even caressed his buttocks. She placed one of his feet against her mount and, dividing the lips with her fingers, forced his toe into her coral sheath and moved herself rapidly up and down on it. This curious proceeding was very exciting to behold and her lascivious caresses caused Alphonse's instrument to assume a prodigious state of erection. Now she got on the top of him and, turning her bottom to his face, impaled herself on his staff. I saw its bulbous head distinctly separate the luscious lips of her slit, and then beheld it slowly dissappear in her sensitive vagina. But she only kept it there for a minute, for jumping up again she placed it between the fleshy cushions of her buttocks, and holding it there with her hand, moved her bottom up and down. Then she suddenly turned around and rubbed her white belly against it—now she put it between her swelling thighs—now her armpit. In fact, there was no part of her body to which she did not conduct it. These manipulations were more than the young Frenchman could bear. He suddenly rose up and pressing her palpitating body in his arm, he laid her on her back on the bed. She opened her lovely thighs to the widest extent and revealed to him all the delights of the domain of Venus. How can I describe the spectacle that we saw from our hiding place! An eminence shaded with a mass of hair as black as jet, the beauties of which the most delicate pencil could not trace. In a moment he was between her magnificent thighs. Eudoxie seized his member and guided it into the delicious interior of her rosy *con*. It grasped his penis like a glove. Eudoxie was almost wild with excitement, she breathed short, and her bubbies rose and fell in the most delicious confusion. Their images were reflected in the mirrors surrounding the apartment. It was a glorious sight. There lay Eudoxie extended on the bed, her head reposing on the pillow, and her long hair streaming by the side of the bed. One of her legs rested on the ground while the other was a little elevated, by this means extending her thighs to the widest capacity. Alphonse was between them, his staff buried in her *con*, with one of his hands molding a globe of snow while the other was passed round her body. How delicious the contact appeared to be.

He suddenly leaned forward and imprinted a thousand kisses on her lips; he then withdrew himself slowly from her, only, however, to plunge more deeply into the innermost recesses of her *con*. So delicious, so transporting, so celestial was the pleasure that they both felt, that Eudoxie threw her legs around his loins and pressed him closely to her and they twisted and writhed in each other's arms. Eudoxie suddenly exclaimed:

"*O ciel! quel transport! O, O, O!*" (O heavens! what transport.)

And finishing with a prolonged sigh, she poured down her tribute to the god of love, and then with a few convulsive heaves of her divine bottom, she let go her hold and fainted away. He also emitted copiously and fell annihilated by her side. In a few moments they had both recovered. Eudoxie wiped Alphonse perfectly dry and her lover performed the same office for her. Neither of them appeared to be satisfied, for I could see that the Frenchman's instrument was still in a state of fierce erection and Eudoxie, by her touches and manipulations, proved that she was as amorous as ever. They now performed a strange action which only shows how foolish young people can be when they sincerely love each other.

Eudoxie went to a cupboard and took from it a bottle of champagne. She now placed herself on the edge of the bed in a half reclined position. Alphonse sat on the floor with his head underneath her thighs so that his mouth came in contact with her hairy mount. Eudoxie now uncorked the champagne and, drinking a glass herself, she poured another glass on her belly in such a manner that it ran down to her slit, and from there into Alphonse's mouth. He swallowed it with the greatest gusto and the operation was continued until the bottle was emptied. This sight, strange as it was, inflamed me wonderfully. The parties were so beautiful and every portion of their bodies so scrupulously clean that all disgust was removed. The bottle was no sooner empty than they again proceeded to satisfy their amorous desires. Alphonse lay on the ground, resting his head on a low stool. She straddled his face so that her Mons Veneris came in contact with his mouth. As she stood exactly opposite our place of concealment, we could see his tongue enter in and out of her luscious sheath; while he was feting her *con*, he advanced a finger into the narrow passage adjacent to the legitimate road and kept time with his tongue and finger. Every time his tongue came in contact with her clitoris, a convulsive shudder ran through her and her bottom moved responsively to his titillations. At last they both succumbed—he from the force of imagination and she from the actual contact of his organ of speech on her excited clitoris.

It was now quite late, and after Alphonse had departed, the house closed for the night. I bade my friend an affectionate farewell and returned to my hotel. The next day I started for home.

CHAPTER FOUR

MY FATHER'S LAWYER

When I arrived home I busied myself putting my father's papers in order, and was so absorbed by the occupation that not even an amorous thought entered my head. This took me a whole week and I had only just finished when Mr. Ralph Pitman was announced. I received him very cordially and treated him so freely that he soon felt quite at home. He had been there but two days when we so far understood each other that he ventured to kiss me. I made no resistance. From his manner of kissing I saw that he was of an excessively amorous temperament, and the fact that I had been ten days without indulgence in sexual pleasure made me very desirous of tasting his capabilities in the school of Venus.

The next day I entered the library rather suddenly and found my friend deeply engaged in a book. When he saw me he hastily endeavored to conceal the volume.

"What are you reading, Mr. Pitman?" I asked.

"Something that I cannot show you, Miss Percival," he replied.

"Nonsense," I returned. "You need not be afraid, I can look at anything."

"You will not be angry or offended if I show you this book?" he exclaimed.

"Certainly not—I wish to see it, and rest assured that whatever it may contain will neither offend me nor shock me."

"Then take it and judge for yourself," he answered after a moment's pause, at the same time giving me a burning kiss which sent a thrill through me.

I opened the book and found it to be one of a most lascivious character, filled with amorous pictures. I gloated over these engravings and felt my blood all on fire. The engravings were from steel plates and represented the famous thirty-two positions of Aretino. As they were extremely curious I will give a short description of them to the reader. Their titles were in French and consisted of as follows: first, *La Patte Debout* represented a man and woman standing face to face with his instrument plunged deeply in her coral cavity; second, *La Grue*—the same position, but with one of the legs raised in the air; third, *La Porte de Devant* represented a woman seated with a man standing between her thighs, her lustful crevice completely filled by his instrument, while her legs closely embraced his ribs; fourth, *Le Cheval Fondu* represented a girl on her hands and knees, while a man was embracing her from behind, her head being reclined forward and her bottom elevated; fifth, *L'allemande* the same position with the addition that the man has his hands on her *con*; sixth, *La Brebis*—the same position with the woman resting her hands on the ground; seventh, *Faire des Chandelles de Suif* —the girl seated across the thighs of the man; eight, *A L'arbre*—the same position but with the girls legs raised, and with her feet placed against the man's buttocks; ninth, *L'enfant Qui Dort*—the girl leaning against the man's stomach, her shoulders against his right arm, and her two legs resting on his right thigh; tenth, *L'etendue*—the girl lying down on her back and the man standing between her thighs, embrace her in front, in which position he can see his instrument working in her *con*, eleventh, *Au dos Presse*—a girl seated on a man's thighs with her legs wrapped around his loins; twelfth, *Cornuse*—the same position, where a man rests one of the girl's thighs on his arm and presses the other down against his buttock; thirteenth, *Se Seoir Au Col*—the same position when he raises one leg in the air; fourteenth, *Chaussebotte*, a man taking the two lips of the girl's *con*, and drawing them on his penis; fifteenth, *Courir La Bague*—a man running towards a girl with thighs extended to receive him, and in this manner inserting his instrument into her *con;* sixteenth, *A la Plaine* —the woman extended all her length on her back, with the man lying between her extended thighs; seventeenth, *A la Grenouille*—the same position with the woman resting her feet on his heels; eighteenth, *La Jannette*—the man lying all his length on the top of a woman; nineteenth, *A L'ondrenette*—when the girl stoops forward and the man embraces her in a standing posture from behind; twentieth, *Au Profil* —a girl and her companion lying on their sides;

twenty-first, *A la Botte Badine*—the man with one of his legs resting on the woman's flank; twenty-second, *Derriere en Con*—a woman lying with her back to a man, with one of her legs raised in the air; twenty-third, *Riche en Fleuve*—the man lying across a woman, belly to belly; twenty-fourth, *Chevaucher l'Asne*—the woman lying on the top of a man with his instrument in her *con;* twenty-fifth, *A la Galère*—the same position with her side turned to the man; twenty-sixth, *Chevaucher en Bast*—the woman lying across him; twenty-seventh, *A la Mauresque*—the man seated on the bed with his legs open, the woman seated in the same position, but with her thighs resting on his; twenty-eighth, *Au Clystere*—the girl with her bottom brought to the edge of the bed, separating her buttocks with her hands, and the man standing behind, imbedded in the *lrou de son cul;* twenty-ninth, *Sonner du Cul*—the woman seated on the edge of the bed with her feet resting against the wall, and during the act of coition she keeps raising one leg and lowering the other; thirtieth, *Les Jambes au col a la Revêche*—the woman lying on her face with her legs resting on the man's shoulders; thirty-first, *La Cloche* represented a man reclining on the ground, resting on his hands and feet—his belly uppermost, while the woman is seated in a basket without a bottom, so that her *con* comes through the open space, to which was affixed a pulley, so that every time the rope was pulled it brought the woman's notch in contact with the man's penis, and the amorous combat is finished by continual pulling on the rope; thirty-second, *Bran-*

ler la Pique represented a man with his finger in a girl's *con*, and by his touches making her discharge—while she was doing the same thing for him. In this manner they enjoyed pleasure without conjunction, either standing, sitting or lying.

When I cast my eyes on the magnificent plates, the color mounted to my face, and I involuntarily pressed my thighs closely together.

"Ah! Kate," said Ralph, again kissing me and forcing his tongue into my mouth. "I perceive you are as fond of amorous sports as I am. I am delighted to make the discovery. I can foresee some delicious pleasures together," and he pressed my palpitating bosom to his, kissing me in the same manner as before.

"Dear Ralph," I replied, returning his caresses by imitating his actions, and advancing my tongue to meet his, "I have already been initiated in the mysteries of love, and have determined henceforth to devote my whole life to its enjoyments."

"Bravely spoken, Kate" returned Ralph. "But come, darling, take me into your bed chamber, and we will talk the matter over."

I led the way into my own private room. I had caused it to be neatly furnished, and it was replete with every luxury. A carpet soft as velvet was spread on the floor; capacious sofas, soft and springy, just fitted for the performance of the conjugal act, were placed around the apartment. Immense mirrors adorned the walls, relieved by beautiful pictures. No light of day was permitted to enter this nest, but it was illuminated by means of brilliant gas burners, and to crown all, a perfume of the most intoxicating description was distilled through the atmosphere.

When we entered this apartment a delicious languor stole over me, and my amorous feelings were excited to an intense degree. I threw myself into Ralph's arms, squeezing, kissing, nay even biting him. He returned my embraces with as much ardor as my own. I placed my hand outside his trousers and felt his stiff instrument.

"Stop, darling," said he, "these invidious clothes are in the way—I should love to feel your hand on my naked staff."

So saying he began to undress, and in a few moments he was entirely naked. It was glorious to see his manly form in a state of nature. I rushed to him, I kissed his naked body all over. He shivered in my arms, and I really believe he would have discharged had he not torn himself from my embrace. As for myself I was on fire. The contact of his firm flesh sent a thrill of joy through my system, and I had to exert the greatest control to prevent myself from pouring down the elixir of love.

"Now, Kate," said Ralph, "it is nothing but fair that you should let me see you naked."

"Dearest Ralph, do with me as you will; my whole body is yours."

"Bless you, darling, I only hope I may be able to satisfy you to your heart's content."

So saying he actually tore off my clothes and reduced me to a perfect state of nudity. He then led me to a sofa and reclined me upon it.

I never saw a man so amorous and lascivious as he was. Sexual enjoyment appeared to be a perfect passion with him. When he had placed me on the sofa he stood a few feet off that he might better observe my naked beauties.

"Great God," he exclaimed, "what glorious beauty! How magnificently formed your body is, dear Kate. What a delicious bust, what glorious semiglobes, how firm and hard, and then your belly, how white and smooth! What well developed thighs, what straight legs, and above all that masterpiece of nature—your delicious *con*. Open your thighs a little, dear Kate, that I may get a better view of it. There, that's it, now I can see it perfectly. How inviting the lips look amidst that mass of black hair! How closely they fold together showing a line of coral between them! Oh, how I long to taste the sweets of that delicious grotto. Now, dear Kate, turn on your belly, and elevate your buttocks a little—there, that's it exactly. Great heavens, the back of the picture is even more glorious than the front! What a delicious bottom! How closely the cheeks come together."

He now began to kiss what he had admired. He embraced my bubbies, my belly, my bottom and the mount of Venus. I could stand no more, but jumping up from the sofa, I rushed into his arms and exclaimed:

"Dearest Ralph, give me relief or I shall die."

He pressed me to him—my bubbies came in contact with his chest—our bellies met. The contact of the warm flesh almost drove us mad—we squirmed and wiggled in each other's arms—we hugged, kissed and bit each other—we rolled on the floor, interlacing our thighs, his staff touched my *con*, the hair of our genitals intermingled—we rubbed our bubbies together. I rolled myself on the top of him and moved myself backwards and forwards—he placed a hand on each cheek of my bottom, and pressed my hairy slit to his testicles.

"Great heavens!" I exclaimed, "it is coming—Ralph—Ralph—I must spend—I must—I must—"

"Dearest Kate, I too—there—now it flows—now—now—now—"

A convulsive shudder ran through both our frames; we closed our eyes in the ecstasy of our sensations, and both discharged profusely, the divine liquor running from one to the other. All this had been effected without any actual conjunction.

A few minutes' repose followed and we recovered our energies.

"Kate, my darling," said Ralph, "lie down on the sofa again, I want to manipulate your charms a little more at my ease. We were so carried away by our feelings that we discharged before we had sufficiently prolonged our pleasures—let us be more prudent this time."

Acting upon this wish, I threw myself on the sofa, and Ralph seated himself on an ottoman by my side, and commenced to excite me by his caresses. Fastening himself on the first instance on my breasts, he sucked my nipples, patted and molded my bubbies and tickled me under my arms. He was not satisfied with his tribute of admiration to my bust, but he straddled my chest and brought his instrument and testicles directly over my two ivory globes. He then lowered his bottom and rubbed his staff and pendants against soft cushions, nay more, he pressed my breasts closely together and nestled his engine between them. Great heavens, how these delicious touchings excited me; nor was he less moved, for his buttocks actually quivered with delight.

"Kate," said he, "how delicious your breasts feel to my pego; I could almost fancy it was its own proper nest," and he commenced to move his buttocks backwards and forwards.

"For heaven's sake stop, Ralph, or I shall spend, I shall indeed," I exclaimed, "I can feel the crisis approaching."

"So do I, darling, but it must not be yet."

He then dismounted and took a seat by my side on the sofa and began to play with my belly. He stroked it, rubbed it backwards and forwards with his hand and tickled my navel. He then descended to my slit. There he made a full stop, and a convulsive thrill ran through his body when his hand came in contact with the bushy forest of dark auburn hair surrounding my Mons Veneris. He twined it in his fingers, gently pulling it, just to cause me the most pleasing titillation without giving me the slightest pain. He then invaded the sanctuary of love itself, and gently dividing the lips of my bijou, cautiously advanced one finger into my vagina. After allowing it to rest there a few moments, he pushed it further in until it was wholly engulfed in my glowing passage.

"Oh, Kate," he exclaimed, moving his finger gently in and out of my slit, "what a charming *con* you have, how tight it is! And only to think that I am to bury my staff in this lovely cavity."

"Darling," I replied, "your lascivious touches almost take away my senses."

He withdrew his finger from my vagina and carried it to the top of my slit, and tickled my clitoris.

"There now, I have the little sentinel between my fingers. Heavens, how soft it is," he said, rubbing it gently.

During these manipulations on his part, I was not idle, but paid him back in his own coin. I stroked down his belly and rubbed his staff in my hand, making him squirm and wriggle again.

Had anyone peeped in the door at that moment they would have seen a delicious spectacle. Such an observer would see a naked girl and man seated together on a sofa. Our faces were close together. Ralph had one arm round my neck, his hand resting on my left shoulder; the other arm was pressed underneath my right thigh, which was elevated in the air, and the finger and thumb of that hand were buried in my *con*, the lips of which clasped them tightly. His left leg rested on the ground while the other was placed on the sofa, thus stretching his thighs widely apart. I was engaged in rubbing his stiff member up and down with my left hand, and intense pleasure was painted on our faces.

"It would be impossible to find such a pretty little slit as yours," said he; "it is a veritable bijou—there now, my finger is wholly inserted." He continued forcing his finger to the very hilt into my vagina, so much so that it actually touched the neck of my womb. "How deliciously warm it feels, and it is so tight that when I withdraw I take with it the inner lips. Now just fancy my finger a man's pego—now it's in, now it's out—now it's in—now it's out —now——."

"For Heaven's sake stop! I don't want to spend just yet. It is too delicious," I exclaimed.

He then made me get up from my recumbent posture, and placing me in a standing position, put one of my feet on a chair, while the other foot rested on the ground. By this attitude my thighs were stretched widely apart, and my *con* was fully exposed to view. He then seated himself again on the ottoman between my legs. His face by this means just reached my mount. He commenced to bury his visage in the hair surrounding my slit.

"Darling Kate," he said, "I must now taste the delights of your delicious *con*. I have felt it, played with it, but I have not yet performed the act which is the most delicious of all to me."

"Do with me as you will," I replied. "I experience nothing but delight from your touchings."

"Push your belly a little forward—there, that's right, now I have it exactly."

So saying he deliberately separated the lips of my slit with his tongue, and worked it into the innermost recesses of my *con*. God, how delicious it felt! He then moved his tongue in and out, at the same time by scientific movement caressing my clitoris with his lips—giving me the most intense pleasure. I stood directly before a large mirror, and by looking into it, saw a most delectable sight. There I stood in my nudity, my naked body borrowing roseate hues from the artificial light, and seated between my thighs, his face also turned towards the mirror was the naked form of the handsome Ralph. I could see his tongue enter in and out of my coral sheath, while my breast rose and fell with the delights of my sensations. I could tell when his lips came in contact with my clitoris, not only by my sensations but by the tremor and writhings of his thighs. His legs were widely open, and I could see reflected in the glass his glorious engine in a state of princely erection. The motion of his tongue increased.

"Darling Ralph, I am going to spend—harder—come—O—co——."

I could hold out no longer, but with a convulsive heaving of my whole body, I emitted a profusion of the elixir vitae.

"Kate, dear Kate!" exclaimed Ralph in an excited tone—"I must have relief; I am in flames."

I clasped him in my arms, and pushed him to the sofa. I made him place himself on his hands and knees, by which position his buttocks were elevated high in the air. Great God, how magnificent he looked thus! His splendid buttocks shone in the gaslight. Between his thighs I could see his magnificent pego all surrounded with hair, and the two well-developed pendants. I patted his buttocks, I separated the cheeks, and titillated the division between them. My fingers came in contact with *le trou de son cul*. I cautiously penetrated it and tickled the narrow canal, and kissed his bottom over and over again. When I had wrought him up to the highest pitch of desire, I proceeded with further operations.

"Open your thighs a little wider, dearest Ralph, so that I may get my head between them—you have given me the most ecstatic pleasure, and I am determined to do the same for you."

"Will that do?" he answered, opening them to the widest extent.

"Beautifully," I returned, fixing my head in such a manner that the insides of each of his thighs rested against my cheeks. I laid on my back and was so placed that my mouth came in direct contact with his splendid staff. In a moment I had taken his engine entirely in my mouth. I titillated the end of it with my tongue and forced the foreskin backwards with my lips. It was too delicious—I was ready to spend again.

"Oh, how heavenly!" exclaimed Ralph. "How beautiful, dear Kate, titillate my anus."

I passed my hand behind him, and forced one of my fingers into the narrow way, moving it in and out, and keeping time with both my mouth and finger. I soon had the satisfaction of seeing the climax approach. He pressed his buttocks together, his muscles stiffened.

"Now I am coming! now—Oh! Oh! Oh!" he exclaimed.

And with a cry of pleasure he emitted profusely.

When we had rested some little time, I went to a recess and took from it a delicious cordial—of which we both partook freely. It had the effect of completely restoring our energies.

We commenced our touchings and titillations and were soon in a glorious state of desire again.

"Kate," said Ralph, "I am going to give you a glorious embracing, and if I don't make you spend as you have never spent before, I shall be very much deceived. I intend to treat your delicious little *con* to a delicate morsel. Now, Kate, on your back—open your thighs, and let me engulf my staff in your salacious slit."

I laughed heartily and threw myself on my back—he was on the top of me in a moment, and in another second his pego was imbedded in my *con*. It touched me to the quick and I experienced intense pleasure. Ralph, while he was working his instrument in me, sucked my breasts and played with my belly, and just when I was about to spend he placed his hand on the top of my slit and rubbed my clitoris. This finished the business, and with a cry of joy I again discharged—he at the same time pouring down his share of the nectar of Venus.

This last bout appeared to arouse my amorous desires instead of quenching them, and I exclaimed in a frenzy:

"Ralph will you do a favor for me—you know that flagellation increases amorous pleasures. I want you to birch me on my bottom, while I make myself come with a dildo."

"Get me a rod, dear Kate, I should like nothing better than to birch your naked buttocks."

I went to a cupboard and procured from it a birch and a dildo—the former I handed to him. I then placed myself on my hands and knees on the sofa, thus elevating my bottom in the air. I then brought the dildo to bear on my coral sheath, it entered the lips and in another moment it was plunged to the very hilt into my vagina. He placed himself behind me and began to lay the birch gently on my bottom. The skin turned a rosy hue and I twisted and wriggled under this delectable excitement. I moved the dildo gently in and out of my *con*.

"Harder, flog my bottom harder," I exclaimed. He obeyed by letting fall a shower of stripes on my buttocks. The motion of the dildo in and out of my coral slit grew faster. I wriggled my buttocks—I am coming—my bubbies trembled—I was now working for my very life—the instrument moved in and out of my lustful sheath so quickly that its motion was no longer perceptible. "Ralph, I spend, I die glorious—delicious—del—del—"

A convulsive shudder ran through my frame—the motion of my hand suddenly stopped, leaving the dildo still imbedded in my *con*, and I fell flat on my belly without any sign of life. I was recalled to life again by the energetic thrusts of Ralph's instrument—for seeing my delirium, he could not restrain himself any longer but felt that he must share it.

Before we separated we enjoyed each other several times more. The next day he returned to New York and I saw him no more.

I was now left entirely alone, but I was very busy, for the house was full of workmen embellishing the house and grounds.

I have but a few more words to add. In due time all the improvements to the house were finished and I began to feel very lonely.

One winter's evening just as I was about to retire to bed I was startled by the ringing of the front door bell—and almost immediately afterwards I was clasped in my cousin Harry Duval's arms. He had just returned from abroad.

I shall draw a veil over the pleasures of that night sufficient to say that Harry had become more dear to me than ever, and I paled before him in the art of giving sexual delight.

The next week we were married, and since that time we have settled down into a quiet life. Neither Harry nor myself desire any change—and our existence has been fraught with every blessing. The confidence between us is so great, that I have not hesitated to tell him my history. He has reposed the same confidence in me by telling me his, and some day I may perhaps give it to the reader.

And now, dear reader, my task is done. I bid you an affectionate farewell.

THE END

ANGELICA

THERESE

Are you serious, my dear count? Do you really want me to write down my story? Do you truly desire that I recount the mystical happenings between Miss Eradice and the Most Reverend Father Dirrag? That I tell you all about the affair between Madame Catherine and the abbot? And you request from a girl who has never written anything in all her life that she give a detailed description with all the systematic arrangements. Milord, you are insisting upon a lascivious painting which shows everything I have told you about; and of which we, ourselves, have been a part. And at the same time you want me to recount the metaphysical contemplations, telling you about the tremendous impact they made upon me. Truly, my dear count, this is a task way too heavy for my feeble powers. Besides, Eradice was my best friend, Father Dirrag was my confessor, and I have nothing but gratitude for dear Madame Catherine and the abbot. Am I to betray the trust of those people toward whom I feel the greatest admiration? Because the deeds of the one and the good advice of the others have slowly opened my eyes against the prejudice of youth. But then, you say, if their advice and example have made you happy, why shouldn't you make others happy and contribute to their pursuits with the wisdom you have learned? What is that fear which prevents you from writing down the truth which can be of such tremendous value to the society of man?

All right, my dear benefactor, I shall no longer resist your reasoning. I will write everything down. Well-read people will have to excuse my lack of style which may occur from time to time for the sake of clarity, and I don't give a hoot about those self-styled faultfinders. No, your sweet and loving Therese will never deny you any of your wishes. I will show you every little fold of her tender heart, from early childhood, and you will get to know every nook and cranny of her trusting soul. I will give you an exact description of every little adventure which has slowly but surely carried her, so to speak, without her doing anything for it, step by step to the highest peaks of lasciviousness and delight.

Foolish people! You, who believe you have it within your power to kill the passions which Nature has given you! No, they are God's work! And you want to destroy those passions, guide them into narrow paths. Idiots! You pretend to be new creators, more powerful and wise than the Old One? Will you never realize that He saw that everything was good, and that everything is exactly as it was meant to be? That everything belongs to God and not to you? That it is as difficult to create a thought as it is to make an arm, or an eye, or a leg?

My career is undeniable proof of these eternal truths. Since early childhood I had been told that I should harbor love for virtue and disgust for vice. I had been told: "You will only find happiness in proportion to living these Christian and moral virtues. All that causes you to swerve from that path is vile and unnatural, it is vice! And vice causes depravity and wickedness and their natural results are shame and guilt!" Convinced of the excellence of these teachings, I have severely tried to live up to them till I had reached the age of twenty-five years. I will show you how far I have been successful.

* * *

I was born in the province of Vencerop. My father was a good, solid citizen, a merchant, in a nice little town where everyone was happy and the atmosphere free of troubles. The amorous life seemed to be the only thing in which the people were interested. They began to love as soon as they started to think, and their only reason for thinking was to dream up different ways and means to increase the pleasures of making love. In my mother the vivaciousness of the women from her homeland was admirably blended with the sensibility of those in her new country. My parents lived modestly from their small income and from the money which was brought in by father's business ventures. Their labors neither increased nor diminished their income noticeably because father paid a young widow who had a shop down the street. Mother, however, had her own income from a rich nobleman who was kind enough to honor my father with his friendship. Everything was marvelously well-organized and both parties knew exactly where they stood. Never had any marriage created a better impression of unity than theirs.

The years passed in laudable harmony, and then, after ten years, my mother became pregnant and brought me into the world. My birth caused her to suffer enormously and brought her a fate worse than death. Due to a sudden movement during the birth pangs, a big tear developed. This made her swear off forever the joys which had been responsible for my birth.

The changes in my parental home were enormous. My mother became pious. The frequent visits of the ardent marquess ceased, because my mother had told him to stop seeing her. In his place she received Father Guardian, a Capuchine monk. My mother's need for loving tenderness changed. Out of necessity she started giving to God what she had been giving to the marquess out of inclination and temperament.

Father died when I was still a babe in the cradle. For some reason, unknown to me, mother moved to the famous harbor town of Volno. The most amorous woman had turned into the most chaste, and possibly also the most virtuous creature that had ever lived.

I was barely seven years old when my sweet and dear mother, who was constantly worried about my health and well-being, noticed that I rapidly lost weight. A famous doctor was called into consultation about my mysterious illness. I was ravenously hungry all the time, yet I had no fever and felt no pain. Nevertheless, I lost my vivaciousness and my poor legs were barely capable of carrying my skinny frame. Mother feared for my life; she never left me out of her sight and she made me sleep with her in the big bed. Who can describe her enormous surprise when, one night, she discovered that I was rubbing in my sleep that part of my body which makes me differ from a boy? It seemed to her that the rhythmic rubbing gave me joys which one would expect in a fifteen-year-old girl but which are generally not expected from a little one of seven years. Mother could not believe her own eyes. She quietly lifted the blanket and the sheet, fetched a light and, being a woman of experience and wisdom, awaited further developments. It happened exactly as she expected. I started to move and rotate my lower body, sighs escaped my tender little lips, my body quivered and finally shook with little convulsions and . . . the delight I had experienced woke me up.

Mother was so excited herself that she scolded me thoroughly. She asked me who had taught me the horrors she had just witnessed. I started to cry and answered her that I did not know what I had done to upset her so much, and that I had no idea what she meant with all those expressions that rolled from her lips. All those words—fingering, coming, indecency and mortal sin—meant absolutely nothing to me. The naiveté of my answers convinced mother of my innocence. I fell asleep. The tickling started again. And . . . mother scolded me again. After she had observed me closely for several nights there was no longer any doubt in her mind. The strength of my passions caused me to do in my sleep what so many poor nuns do in their waking and praying hours. Mother decided to tie my hands close together behind my back so that it would become impossible for me to continue my nightly exercises.

Soon I had regained my health and former

strength. I discontinued the vile habit but, unfortunately, my secret passion grew. When I was about nine or ten I noticed a curious unrest and I felt desires well up in me whose goal I did not know. I often played with other little girls and boys of my age in the attic or some quiet little room. We had our little games: one of us was elected to be the teacher; the smallest offense was punished with the rod. The boys lowered their little pants and the girls lifted their skirts and petticoats. We viewed each other with great curiosity. Five or six little behinds were the object of intense concentration; we admired them, petted them and whipped them. The wee-wees of the boys —that's how we called them—were little playthings for the girls. A hundred times we would take them between our fingers, caress them, kiss them; we took them between our fingers and made little dolls out of those instruments, having no idea of their use and value. Then our little behinds got their turn. They were kissed and caressed, too. Only our centers of joy were completely ignored. Nobody bothered about them. Why this terrible disregard? I don't know. But, those were our games; simple Nature guided them, and I tell things as they actually happened.

After I had abandoned myself for about two years to these harmless escapades, mother placed me in a convent. I must have been about eleven years old. The main interest of the old nun was to prepare me for my first confession. I was without fear for this first judgment, because I had no qualms whatsoever. I told old Father Guardian, the Capuchine monk who also advised my mother's conscience, all the stupid little sins a girl of my age was supposed to commit. After I had told him every single little mistake I believed I had made, the good father said to me, "One of these days you will become a saint, if you follow all the good advice your dear mother has given you. Especially, let me warn you, never, never listen to the devil of the flesh. I am your mother's confessor, and she has told me of your lack of chastity, this foulest of all evils. I have been seriously concerned about you. But, I am happy to discover that she has made a mistake. The illness from which you suffered four years ago must have given her that idea. Without her infinite care, my dearest child, you would have been doomed; body and soul. Yes, I am sure that those certain movements she noticed must have been involuntary and I am convinced that the conclusion she drew in regard to your salvation was absolutely wrong."

The strange language of my father confessor upset me terribly and I asked him what on earth I had done to give my mother such horrible ideas about the state of my immortal soul. He told me without further ado exactly what had happened, in clear, plain language. He also said that the immediate steps my mother had taken to correct my terrible mistake could have saved me from the most horrible consequences. He also added that he hoped I would never have to find out those evils on my own person.

His words reminded me suddenly about those games in the attic about which I have told you. My cheeks were covered with a deep red blush and my eyes dropped to the floor. I remained mute and silent. For the first time I had an inkling that our harmless little games could have been sinful. The priest asked me why I suddenly became so quiet and sad. I told him everything. Then he wanted to know more and started to press for details. The innocence of my expressions, my unembarrassed description of our positions and the simple, yet open statements about our pleasures, convinced him even more of my innocence. He reproached me about those games but he did it wisely and carefully and with a tact which is highly unusual for a servant of the church. But the expressions he used proved without a doubt that he had guessed my temperament correctly. He ordered me to fast, pray and think. To this arsenal he added yet another weapon. I had to wear a penitent's hair shirt. This, he said, would aid me in the fight against my passions.

"Never," he told me, "never ever touch with your hand that filthy part of your body. Don't even cast a glance upon it. It is the very apple which tempted Adam and which caused the fall of the race of Man and the expulsion from Paradise. In it lives the devil who brought us to our doom. It is his home, his throne. Don't allow yourself to be captured by this enemy of God and Man. Soon, Nature will cover this filthy part of your belly with ugly hairs, like those of the wild beasts in the forest. It is our punishment to remind you that you have to be ashamed of it, and from then on it will be hidden in darkness, and, God grant you, forgetfulness. But, my child, be even more careful with that piece of flesh the little boys have. You may have thought it fun up there in the attic, but, my daughter, that piece of flesh is the snake who tempted the Mother of all of us, Eve. Don't allow yourself to become dishonored by touching this piece of meat, or even by looking upon it. It is intent upon biting you, poisoning you, and, if it can, gorging itself upon you."

"But how, Reverend Father," I answered, extremely excited, "is that possible? Could it really be a snake, and is it truly as dangerous as you say it is? I thought that it was a rather soft and harmless little animal. And it never bit me or any of my girl friends. I tell you it has a very tiny mouth and absolutely no teeth at all. I have looked it over very carefully . . ."

"Go, my dearest child," interrupted my father confessor. "Believe me when I tell you that the snakes you have held so boldly in your innocent little fingers were too young and too small to cause all the dangers which I just described to you. But, I assure you, they will grow; they will become heavier, longer, and firmer. They will throw themselves upon you, pump their unholy venom into you. You will have to learn right now to fear the results of their ruthless onslaught. They are scheming and plotting monstrosities, eager to squirt their poison, intent upon destroying your body and your eternal soul."

After this and several other lessons, the good father let me go, leaving me in a state of terrible confusion and inner turmoil.

I returned to my room and stayed there for several days, fasting and praying. The words he had spoken to me had made a great impression upon my young imagination, but nevertheless, the thoughts about those pretty little snakes did not leave me. They seemed more charming than ever, despite the terrible sermon which the well-meaning priest had given about them. The desire to touch and hold one was stronger than the fear to leave them alone. Nevertheless, I kept my promise. I resisted the temptations of my vile temperament. I prayed, I fasted and did penitence, and soon I had become a veritable example of virtue.

Oh, the struggles I have fought, my dear count! Finally my mother took me out of that goddamned convent! I had barely turned sixteen when my feverish thoughts had weakened my body. It was obvious that two different passions ruled my body and soul. I was unable to make the one reach accord with the other. On the one hand I felt a true love for God: I wanted to serve Him with all my heart in the exact way they had told me. He wished to be served. On the other hand I noticed fierce desires without being able to guess their purpose. The picture of the pretty snake had burned itself indelibly into my soul. It was perennially before my mind's eye, in my waking as well as in my sleep hours. Sometimes I became so excited that I believed to hold the snake in my hands; I caressed its head, I admired its noble, proud posture, its firm erectness, even though I had no idea of the purpose of this beautiful animal. My heart would pound with unusual speed; at the peak of my excitement, or in the middle of my dreams, a voluptuous quiver would run through my body. It nearly drove me out of my mind. The apple attracted my hand as if it were a powerful magnet, my finger would take the place of the snake.

Excited by the many possibilities of delight, I was incapable of any other thoughts, and even if the earth had opened up before me and the tortures of hell had yawned at me, I would have been incapable of stopping. Oh, the useless pangs of conscience! I would wallow in lasciviousness. But the restlessness afterward! Fasting, flagellation, prayer and penitence were my only recourse. I practically drowned in my own tears of remorse. Gradually these practices destroyed my passions. But, they not only wrecked my sensuality, they ruined my health as well. I had ultimately reached a state of weakness which had carried me to the brink of the grave. Finally my mother decided to take me away from the convent . . .

Answer me, treacherous or ignorant priests, who credit us with nonexistent crimes: Who has implanted both passions in my soul? Those two desires which I have been unable to reconcile: my love for God, and my desire for carnal knowledge? Was it Nature or the devil? Make up your minds! Or do you really dare to insist that either the devil or Nature are more powerful than God who created both of them? Because if they are less powerful than God, then it must be Him, Who has given me both passions; then it must have been His handiwork.

But, you will undoubtedly answer me, God has given you the intelligence to make up your own mind.

Sure. But not to decide about my will. My intelligence has made it possible to discern the two different passions which struggled for the possession of my body and mind. Through them I have been made to understand that both are gifts of God, just like everything else is a gift of God. But even though my intelligence has made this clear to me, I still did not have the willpower.

But God has given you the power over your own free will, you will say. You are free to decide the path of good or the path of evil.

That is the purest form of nonsense, a mere play of words. The strength of this will, and the momentary freedom to decide, are directly proportional to the strength of the passions and desires that drive us along the path of life. For instance, I am theoretically free to kill myself, to throw myself out of the window. Not at all true! As soon as my love for life is stronger than the desire to kill myself, I'll never commit suicide.

But, you will say, you are absolutely free to give alms to the poor, or to hand a hundred gold francs to your father confessor, if you happen to have that amount in your pocket.

That, too, is not true. If the desire to keep your money is stronger than to throw it away on a useless forgiveness of imaginary sins, then it is rather obvious to me that one does not wish to throw his money away. In one word, everyone can, with a simple test, convince himself that intelligence is only a means to show how strong a certain desire really is and whether giving in to that particular desire will cause pleasure or remorse. And the result of this intelligent realization is our so-called free will. But this will depends as much upon our passions and desires as the movement of a scale which will sink toward the level of a four-pound weight if we counterblance it with only three pounds on the other end.

But, you will ask, is it then not my own free will to order a bottle of Burgundy or a bottle of champagne with my meal? Am I not master of my own destiny and choose to stroll in the Tuileries or sit at a sidewalk café on a boulevard?

I admit that in all cases where the decision is rather irrelevant, where our desires and wishes keep each other more or less in balance, our lack of freedom is not immediately apparent. From a distance we don't notice the single objects any longer. But as soon as we come close to those objects we notice very clearly that our lives are influenced heavily by the mechanical laws of checks and balances. We realize that Nature operates consistently by this one law. Set yourself down to dinner. You are served oysters. Obviously you will select champagne.

But, you will answer, I could have selected Burgundy. I was perfectly free to do so.

I say: No! Obviously, some other reason, a different desire which would have been stronger than the first, natural impulse, could have caused you to drink Burgundy. But in that case it would have been this strong, and rather odd desire which would have influenced your so-called free will.

Let's assume you are strolling in the Tuileries and at the terrace of the Feuillants you see a charming woman of your acquaintance, and you decide to walk over and talk to her. Meanwhile, for some other reason, you suddenly decide to continue your stroll, or follow some other pleasure or business, and you are not going to talk to her. Whatever you decide to do, it is always some desire which is stronger than the other that causes your ultimate decision, quite independent from your will.

To admit that Man is a free agent, one must assume that his decisions are entirely free from outside influences. And as soon as his decisions are caused by two or more struggling inner desires, implanted in him by Nature, he is no longer free. The strengh of one desire or the other will influence his actions as surely as a four-pound weight causes the three-pound weight to go up.

And I also ask you: What prevents you to think about these questions the same way I do, and why can't I bring myself to have the same opinion as you? Undoubtedly your answer will be that your thoughts, your opinions and your feelings force you to believe the way you do. This consideration must convince you therefore that it is not agreeable to you to think as I do, and consequently that it does not depend upon me to think as you do. And out of all this it follows crystal clear that we cannot believe as we please. And since we seemingly are not free to think as we please, how on earth can we act with total freedom? Our thinking is the cause and our actions are merely the result of our thinking. And would it be possible that out of a cause which is not free, a free action could result. Such reasoning would hold an absolute contradiction.

I will show you the truth of this reasoning

with the following true story. Gregory, Damon and Phillip are three brothers. They have been educated by the same teachers till they are twenty-five years old. They have never been separated from one another, they have received exactly the same upbringing, and they have had precisely the same lessons in morals and religion. Nevertheless, Gregory loves to drink wine. Damon loves to wench, and Phillip is extremely devout. What was the cause of this triple diversity in the will of these three brothers? It cannot be their knowledge between morally good and evil, because the same teachers have given them the same lessons. Every one of them must have had different principles and different passions carried within him since birth, and despite the similarity in upbringing and education they must have had a different will. But, I'll go one step further. Gregory, who loves the wine, is an honorable man, a charming host and the best friend a person might wish to have, as long as he is sober. The moment he has tasted the magic drink he changes and becomes, to name a few, vicious, lazy and quarrelsome. He would have cut the throat of his best friend with pleasure. Was Gregory master over the changes that came over him? No, not in the least, because when he was sober he abhorred the things he did when he was drunk from the wine. Of course, a lot of stupid idiots admired the abstinence of Gregory who did not like women, the sobriety of Damon who could not stand wine, and the piousness of Phillip who hated both wine and women, but who got the same pleasure out of his devotions which the others derived from either their wine or their wenches. That is how most people lie to themselves with their provincial ideas about the human vices and virtues.

I would draw the following conclusions: The organs of the body, the nervous system, the presence of certain juices; their presence and their strength or weakness influence our will during important decisions we have to make in our lifetime. Therefore, there are passionate people, wise people, and crazy people. The crazy ones are neither more nor less free than all the others, because they are what they are according to the same principles. Nature never varies. So, if we assume that Man is free to act as he wants and can plot his own path through life, we make him equal to God . . .

But, let's go back to my story!

As I said, I was almost dead when my mother decided to take me out of the convent. My entire body was exhausted; with my yellowish skin and my thin lips I looked like a living skeleton. My piousness had turned me into a suicidal maniac and I surely would have died if I had not returned in time to my mother's home. The very good doctor whom she had sent to me in the convent had immediately recognized the source of my illness. That divine juice which is capable of giving us physical delight, the only delight whose enjoyment does not leave one filled with bitterness, that juice whose outflow is just as necessary as the intake of good food, that juice had left the vessels for which it was intended and had penetrated other vessels in my body. That was the reason that my entire body was sick. My mother was advised to look posthaste for a husband for me; this was the only way to save my life. Mother talked very kindly to me about the prospect, but I was so caught in my own prejudices that I harshly told her I would rather die than displease God by contracting a marriage which would be a despicable affair at best and which He only tolerated in His infinite goodness. All the reasons she gave me were of no interest to me; my weakened constitution left me without any desire for this world and the only happiness I counted on was that of the next world about which I had heard so much from the nuns.

I continued my pious exercises with undiminished fervor. I had been told about the famous Father Dirrag; I looked him up and he became the advisor of my soul. His most fervent visitor, Miss Eradice, soon became my best friend.

You know, my dear Count, the history of these two famous people. I have no intention to repeat everything that public opinion knows about them and has told about those two. But I have been witness to a rather strange occurrance and maybe you would delight in listening to my side of this story. If it is only to convince you that, even though Eradice ultimately knew what she was doing, she allowed the old lecher to embrace her because she was betrayed by her own voluptuous piousness.

Miss Eradice had become my dearest girl friend; she confided her deepest secrets to me. We did the same religious exercises, we thought about the same godly things and we were in complete agreement about the salvation of our eternal souls. Possibly we also had the same temperament. Anyhow, we were inseparable. We were both extremely virtuous and our one overriding passion was the desire to be considered very pious. Secretly we hoped to achieve the sanctity which would enable us to perform miracles. This passion ruled my friend so powerfully that she would gladly have borne all the tortures of the early Christian martyrs if she had been told that it would enable her to raise a second Lazarus from the dead. And, Father Dirrag had developed his gift to make her believe whatever he wanted to perfection.

Rather vainly, Eradice had told me on several occasions that Father Dirrag had assured her in secrecy that she only needed a few more steps to achieve complete sanctity. She had, so she told me, visited him frequently in his home, where he had held various confidential sessions with her. God had told him in a dream that she would soon be capable of performing great miracles if she would allow him, Father Dirrag, to help her practice virtue and mortification of the flesh.

Jealousy and envy are two normal human vices, but pious virgins are most prone to them.

Eradice must have noticed that I was envious, begrudged her her happiness and, worst of all, did not seem to believe her! I must admit that I was very surprised about her tales of his confidential talks with her at his home, especially since the good father had always carefully avoided talking to me, one of his most ardent penitents, about anything else but mortification of the flesh. And I knew another penitent, also a good friend of mine, who, like Eradice, also carried the stigmata of our Lord. He had never been as confidential to her as he had been to Eradice, and this girl friend, too, had all the requirements of becoming a saint. No doubt, my sad face, my yellowish complexion, my utter lack of any sign of stigmata were enough reasons for the venerable Father Dirrag not to have any confidential talks with me at his home. The possibility existed that he saw no reason to take on the extra burden of spiritual works in my behalf. But to me it was a bone of contention. I became very sad and I pretended not to believe any of Eradice's stories.

This irritated Eradice no end. She offered to let me become an eyewitness to her happiness that next morning. "You will see for yourself," she contended heatedly, "how strong my spiritual exercises are, how the good father guides me from one degree of mortification to the next with the purpose of making a saint out of me. You will be a witness to the delight and ecstasy which are a direct result of these exercises and you will never doubt again how marvelous these exercises are. Oh, how I wish, my dearest Therese, that my example would work its first miracle upon you. That you might be spiritually strengthened to totally deny the flesh and follow the only path which will lead you to God!"

We agreed that I would visit her the next morning at five o'clock. I found her in prayer, a book in her hand. She said to me, "The holy man will arrive soon, and God shall be with him. Hide yourself in that little alcove, and from there you can see and hear for yourself the miracles of Divine Love wrought upon me by the venerable father confessor. Even to such a lowly creature as I."

Somebody knocked quietly on the door. I fled into the alcove; Eradice turned the key and put it in her skirt pocket. There was, fortunately, a hole in the alcove door, covered with a piece of tapestry. This made it possible for me to see the entire room, without, however, running the risk of being seen myself.

The good father entered the room and said to Eradice, "Good morning, my dearest sister in the Lord, may the Holy Spirit of Saint Francis protect you forever."

She wanted to throw herself at his feet, but he lifted her off the floor and ordered her to sit down next to him upon the sofa. Then the holy man said, "I cannot repeat too often the principles which are going to become the guidelines for your future way of life, my dear child. But, before I start my instructions, tell me, dear child, are the stigmata, those miraculous signs of God's everlasting favor, still with you? Have they changed any? Show them to me."

Eradice immediately bared her left breast, under which she bore the stigma.

"Oh, oh, please, dear sister! Cover your bosom with this handkerchief! (He handed her one.) These things were not created for a member of our society; it is enough for me to view the wound with which the holy Saint Francis has made you, with God's infinite mercy, His favorite. Ah! it is still there. Thank the Lord, I am satisfied. Saint Francis still loves you; the wound is rosy and clean. This time I have with me a part of our dear

Saint's sacred rope; we shall need it for our mortification exercises. I have told you already, my dear sister, that I love you above all my other penitents, your girl friends, because God has so clearly marked you as one of the beloved sheep in His flock. You stand out like the sun and the moon among the other planets and stars. Therefore I have not spared any trouble to instruct you in the deepest secrets of our Holy Mother Church. I have repeatedly told you, dearest sister, 'Forget yourself, and let it happen.' God desires from Mankind only spirit and heart. Only if you can succeed in forgetting the existence of your body will you be able to experience Him and achieve sainthood. And only as a saint will you ever be able to work miracles. I cannot help, my little angel, but to scold you, since I noticed during our last exercises that your spirit is still enslaved by your body. How can that be? Couldn't you at least be a little bit like our saintly martyrs? They were pinched with red-hot irons, their nails were torn off their feet and fingers, they were roasted over slow fires and yet . . . they did not experience pain. And why not? Because their mind was filled with pure thoughts of God's infinite glory! The most minute particle of their spirit and mind was occupied with thoughts of His immense glory. Our senses, my dear daughter, are mere tools. But, they are tools that do not lie. Only through them can we feel, only through them can we understand the evil and the good. They influence our bodies as well as our souls. They enable us to perceive what is morally right and what is morally wrong. As soon as we touch something, or feel, or hear, minute particles of our spirit flow through the tiny holes in our nerves. They report the sensations back to our soul. However, when they are filled completely with the love they owe their God and Creator, when YOU are so full of love and devotion that none of these minute particles can do anything else but concentrate on the Divine Providence, when the entire spirit is given to the contemplation of our Lord, then, and only then is it impossible for any particle to tell our spirit that the body is being punished. You will no longer feel it. Look at the hunter. His entire being is filled with only one thought: his prey! He does not feel the thorns that rip at him when he stalks through the forest, nor does he notice cold or heat. True, these elements are considerably weaker than the mighty hunter, but . . . the object of his thoughts! Ah, that is a thousand times stronger than all his other feelings put together. Would you feel the feeble blows of the whip when your soul is full of the thoughts of happiness that is about to be yours? You must be able to pass this all-important test. We must know for sure, if we want to be able to work miracles, whether we can reach this degree of perfection, whether we can wholly immerse ourselves in God!

"And we shall win, dear daughter. Do your duty, and be assured that thanks to the rope of the holy Saint Francis, and thanks to your pious contemplations, this holy exercise will end for you with a shower of unspeakable delight. Down on your knees, my child! Reveal that part of your body which raises the fury of our Lord; the pain you will feel shall bring your soul in close contact with God. I must repeat again: 'Forget yourself, and let it happen!'"

Miss Eradice obeyed immediately without uttering a single word. Holding a book in her hands, she kneeled down in front of a little prayer stool. Then she lifted her skirts about the waist, showing her snow-white, perfectly rounded bums that tapered into two gorgeous alabaster, firm-fleshed thighs.

"Lift your skirts a little higher, my dear child," he said to her, "it does not look proper yet. Fine, fine . . . that's a lot better. Put the prayer book down, fold your hands and lift up your soul to God. Fill your mind with thoughts about the eternal happiness which has been promised you!"

The priest pulled up his footstool and kneeled next to her, bending slightly backward. He lifted his cowl and tied it to the rope around his waist. Then he took a large birch rod and held it in front of my penitent friend who kissed it devoutly.

Piously shuddering I followed the whole procedure with full attention. I felt a sort of horror which is very difficult to describe. Eradice did not say a word. The priest gazed upon her thighs with a fixed stare, his eyes sparkling. He did not let his gaze wander for a single moment. And I heard him whisper softly, full of admiration, "Oh, God, what a marvelous bosom. My Lord, those gorgeous tits!"

Now he bent over and then he straightened up again, murmuring biblical language. Nothing escaped his vile curiosity. After a few minutes he asked the penitent if her soul was prepared.

"Oh yes, venerable Father! I can feel my soul separate itself from my unworthy flesh. I pray you, begin your holy work!"

"It is enough. Your soul will be happy!"

He said a few prayers and the ceremony started with three fairly light blows of the rod, straight across her firm buttocks. This was followed by a recitation from The Bible. Thereupon another three blows, slightly stronger than the first ones.

After he had recited five or six verses, and interrupted each of them the same way as before, I suddenly noticed to my utter surprise that the venerable Father Dirrag opened his fly. A throbbing arrow shot out of his trousers which looked exactly like that fateful snake about which my former father confessor had warned me so vehemently.

The monster was as long and as thick and as heavy as the one about which the Capuchine monk had made all those dire predictions. I shuddered with delightful horror. The red head of this snake seemed to threaten Eradice's behind which had taken on a deep pink coloration because of the blows it had received during the Bible recitation. The face of Father Dirrag perspired and was flushed a deep red.

"And now," he said, "you have to transport yourself into total meditation. You must separate your soul from the senses. And if my dear daughter has not disappointed my pious hopes, she shall neither feel, nor hear, nor see anything."

And at that very moment this horrible man loosened a hail of blows, letting them whistle down upon Eradice's naked buttocks. However, she did not say a word; it seemed as if she were totally insensitive to this horrendous whipping. I noticed only an occasional twitching of her bums, a sort of spasming and relaxing at the rhythm of the priest's blows.

"I am very satisfied with you," he told her, after he had punished her for about fifteen minutes in this terrible manner. "The time has come when you are going to reap the fruits of your holy labors. Don't question me, my dear daughter, but be guided by God's will which is working through me. Throw yourself, face down, upon the floor; I will now expel the last traces of impurity with a sacred relic. It is a part of the venerable rope which girded the waist of the holy Saint Francis himself."

The good priest put Eradice in a position which was rather uncomfortable for her, but extremely fitting for what he had in mind. I had never seen my girl friend in such a beautiful position. Her buttocks were half-opened and the double path to satisfaction was wide-open.

After the old lecher had admired her for a while, he moistened his so-called rope of Saint Francis with spittle, murmured some of the priestly mumbo-jumbo which these gentlemen generally use to exorcise the devil, and proceeded to shove the rope into my friend.

I could watch the entire operation from my little hideout. The windows of the room were opposite the door of the alcove in which Eradice had locked me up. She was kneeling on the floor, her arms were crossed over the footstool and her head rested upon her folded arms. Her skirts, which had been carefully folded almost up to her shoulders, revealed her marvelous buttocks and the beautiful curve of her back. This exciting view did not escape the attention of the venerable Father Dirrag. His gaze feasted upon the view for quite some time. He had clamped the legs of his penitent between his own legs, he had dropped his trousers, and his hands held the monstrous rope. Sitting in this position he murmured some words which I could not understand.

He lingered for some time in this devotional position and inspected the altar with glowing eyes. He seemed to be undecided how to effect his sacrifice, since there were two inviting openings. His eyes devoured both and it seemed as if he were unable to make up his mind. The top one was a well-known delight for a priest, but, after all, he had also promised a taste of Heaven to his penitent. What was he to do? Several times he knocked with the tip of his tool at the gate he desired most, but finally he was smart enough to let wisdom triumph over desire. I must do him justice: I clearly saw his monstrous prick disappear the natural way, after his priestly fingers had carefully parted the rosy lips of Eradice's lovepit.

The labor started with three forceful shoves which made him enter about halfway. And suddenly the seeming calmness of the priest changed into some sort of fury. My God, what a change! Imagine, my dear count, a satyr. Mouth half-open, lips foam-flecked, teeth gnashing and snorting like a bull who is about to attack a cud-chewing cow. His hands were only half an inch away from Eradice's full behind. I could see that he did not dare to lean upon them. His spread fingers were spasming; they looked like the feet of a fried capon. His head was bowed and his eyes stared at the so-called relic. He measured his shoving very carefully, seeing to it that he never left her lovepit and also that his belly never touched her arse. He did not want his penitent to find out to whom the holy relic of Saint Francis was connected! What an incredible presence of mind!

I could clearly see that about an inch of the holy tool constantly remained on the outside and never took part in the festivities. I could see that with every backward movement of the priest the red lips of Miss Eradice's lovenest opened and I remember clearly that the vivid pink color was a most charming sight. However, whenever the good priest shoved forward, the lips closed and I could only see the finely curled hairs which covered them. They clamped around the priestly tool so firmly that it seemed as if they had devoured the holy arrow. It looked for all the world like both of them were connected to Saint Francis' relic and it was hard to guess which one of the two persons was the true possessor of this holy tool.

What a sight, my dear Count, especially for a young girl who knew nothing about these secrets. The most amazing thoughts ran through my head, but they all were rather vague and I could not find proper words for them. I only remember that I wanted to throw myself at least twenty times at the feet of this famous father confessor and beg him to exorcise me the same way he was blessing my dear friend. Was this piety? Or carnal desire? Even today I could not tell you for sure.

But, let's go back to our devout couple! The

movements of the priest quickened; he was barely able to keep his balance. His body formed an "S" from head to toe whose frontal bulge moved rapidly back and forth in a horizontal line.

"Is your spirit receiving any satisfaction, my dear little saint?" he asked with a deep sigh. "I, myself, can see Heaven open up. God's infinite mercy is about to remove me from this vale of tears, I . . ."

"Oh, venerable Father," exclaimed Eradice, "I cannot describe the delights that are flowing through me! Oh, yes, yes, I experience Heavenly bliss. I can feel how my spirit is being liberated from all earthly desires. Please, please, dearest Father, exorcise every last impurity remaining upon my tainted soul. I can see . . . the angels of God . . . push stronger . . . ooh . . . shove the holy relic deeper . . . deeper. Please, dearest Father, shove it as hard as you can . . . Oooh! . . . ooh!!! dearest holy Saint Francis . . . Ooh, good saint . . . please, don't leave me in the hour of my greatest need . . . I feel your relic . . . it is sooo good . . . your . . . holy . . . relic . . . I can't hold it any longer . . . I am . . . dying!"

The priest also felt his climax approach. He shoved, slammed, snorted and groaned. Eradice's last remark was for him the signal to stop and pull out. I saw the proud snake. It had become very meek and small. It crawled out of its hole, foam-covered, with hanging head.

Everything disappeared back into the trousers; the priest dropped his cowl over it all and wavered back to his prayer stool. He kneeled down, pretended to be in deep communication with his Lord, and ordered his penitent to stand up, cover herself and sit down next to him to thank God for His infinite mercy which she had just received from Him.

What else shall I tell you, my dear count? Dirrag left, Eradice opened the door to the alcove and embraced me, crying out, "Oh, my dearest Therese. Partake of my joy and delight. Yes, yes, today I have seen paradise. I have shared the delights of the angels. The incredible joy, my dearest friend, the incomparable price for but one moment of pain! Thanks to the holy rope of Saint Francis my soul almost left its earthly vessel. You have seen how my good father confessor introduced the relic into me. I swear that I could feel it touch my heart. Just a little bit deeper and I would have joined the saints in paradise!"

Eradice told me a thousand other things, and her tone of voice, her enthusiasm about the incredible delights she had enjoyed left no doubt in my mind about their reality. I was so excited that I was barely able to answer her. I did not congratulate her, because I was unable to talk. My heart pounded in wild excitement. I embraced her, and left.

So many thoughts are racing through my mind right now that I hardly know where to begin. It is terrifying to realize how the most honorable convictions of our society are being misused. How positively fiendish was the way in which this cowl-bearer perverted the piety of his penitent to his own lecherous desires. He needled her imagination, artfully using her desire to become a saint; he convinced her that she would be able to succeed, if she separated her mind from her body. This, however, could only be achieved by means of flagellation. Most likely it was the hypocrite himself who needed this stimulation to repair the weakened elasticity of his flagging member. And then he tells her, "If your devotion is perfect, you shall not be able to feel, hear, or see anything!"

That way he made sure that she would not turn around and see his shameless desire. The blows of the rod upon her buttocks not only increased the feeling in that part which he intended to attack, but they also served to make him more horny than he already was. And the relic of Saint Francis which he shoved into the body of his innocent penitent to chase away impurities which were still clinging to her soul, enabled him to enjoy his desires without any danger to himself. His newly-initiated penitent mistook her most voluptuous outburst of carnal climax for a divinely inspired, purely spiritual ecstasy.

All Europe has heard the history of Father Dirrag and Miss Eradice; the whole world has talked about it, but only a very few know about the true circumstances which led to the quarrel between the Jansenists and the Molinists. I won't repeat everything that has been said about this whole affair. You know the entire sordid story. You have read the pamphlets that have been distributed by both factions and you know the results of the whole process and the fights that ensued. Whatever little I know from my own experience, I shall tell you now.

Miss Eradice is about my age. She was born in the city of Volno and she is the daughter of a merchant. My mother moved in with him when we came to live in that town after my dear father passed away. Eradice has a beautiful figure, her skin is extraordinarily beautiful and has a snowy complexion. Her hair is black as ebony and her beautiful eyes make her look like the Madonna. We were playmates when we were children, but I lost contact with her when mother put me in the convent. Her main interest was to be better than her friends and excel in everything she undertook. This peculiar passion made her select piety, since this is the easiest way to reach a goal. She loved God as if He were her lover. When I met her again she had become Father Dirrag's penitent and all she could talk about were pious thoughts, retreats and fiery prayers. This was, at that time, quite a fad with this particular mystical sect in the provinces. Her virtuous demeanor had already given her quite a reputation of saintliness. Eradice had a good mind but she used it only to satisfy her unbound desire to become capable of performing miracles. Everything which claimed to make this possible became for her unquestionable truth. That's the weakness of us poor, ignorant people. Our ruling passion—and everyone of us has one—absorbs all the others. We act only upon whatever satisfies that one passion, and everything that contradicts it is instantly dismissed from our minds. Thus we are never bothered by little facts which could so easily destroy our little, comfortable illusion.

Father Dirrag came from the village of Lode. At that time he must have been about thirty-three years old. He had a face like our painters use when they want to portray a lustful satyr, but despite the incredible ugliness, his features conveyed a powerful, irresistible spirit. His eyes were lustful and shameless. But his actions only indicated his concern for the souls of his flock, and his devotion to the greater glory of God. He was an extremely talented preacher, his speeches were friendly and unctuous. He possessed the gift of persuasion. And he spent his entire inborn shrewdness to achieve the reputation of God's favorite Evangelist. And indeed, an incredible number of women and girls from the best of society have done penitence under his skillful direction.

As you can see, my friend, the good father and Miss Eradice had a lot in common. Their characters and their goals were so basically similar that it was almost impossible for them *not* to get together. As soon as Father Dirrag arrived in the city of Volno, where his reputation had preceded him, Eradice veritably threw herself into his arms. And they had barely gotten to know each other when one recognized in the other the perfect instrument to achieve the great goal: perfection and fame I am quite sure that Eradice initially acted in good faith, but Dirrag knew exactly what he had bagged. The beautiful face of his new penitent had captivated him and he knew that he could easily lead her astray. He knew that he would have no trouble at all to swindle this softhearted, prejudiced, basically innocent girl who had a mind which willingly and with full conviction soaked up his ridiculous mystical insinuations and admonitions. That was the framework of his plan whose execution I have just described to you. This plan promised him a whole series of voluptuous entertainments long before he had reached his goal, especially the act of flagellation. The good priest had used those exercises already upon several others of his penitents, but his lecherous actions had never gone further. But the firm flesh, the beautiful figure and the immense white buttocks of Eradice had heated his imagination so much that he decided to take this last, important step.

Great men can overcome great obstacles. This priest invented the intromission of a piece of robe which had girded the waist of the holy Saint Francis. This relic was supposed to expel all the impurities of the soul and the last carnal thoughts which were still plaguing the members of his flock. It was also supposed to cause divine ecstasy. At the same time he also invented the stigmata with which the holy Saint Francis had been afflicted. In deep secret he invited one of his former penitents to come to Volno. This woman possessed his full confidence, especially since she had played the role voluntarily and knowingly which he now intended to play with Eradice. But he had found her too young and too full of enthusiasm about the possibilities of performing miracles. He did not dare make her his confidante and decided to play a trick upon her rather than reveal his secrets.

The old penitent arrived and soon this bigoted woman became well-acquainted with Eradice as her fellow-devotee. It was the old girl friend of Father Dirrag who managed to fill Eradice's mind with the special devotion to the holy Saint Francis. The priest had given her a liquid to create a phony stigma. The old bigoted penitent washed Eradice's feet that next Maundy Thursday and used the occasion to apply some of the fluid, which immediately did its job.

A few days later Eradice took the old woman into her confidence and told her that she had a wound on each foot.

"Oh, what happiness! The miracle of it! And the fame for you!" exclaimed the old hypocrite. "Saint Francis has imparted his most holy stigmata to you, his handmaiden! God surely intends to make a great saint out of you. Let's find out if you don't have the stigma on the side, like the one of all great and venerable saints."

And her hand touched Eradice under the left breast, quickly applying some of the acid liquid. And sure enough, the next day there it was . . . a brand new stigma.

Obviously Eradice talked to her father confessor about the miracle, but he wanted to avoid unnecessary publicity and advised the girl to be humble about it and keep the entire affair a deep secret. To no avail; the main passion of our poor girl was her incredible vanity and her desire to become a great saint. She was totally incapable of keeping the signs of her belonging to the chosen few from her friends and she began to make all sorts of confessions. Her stigmata caused a considerable consternation and soon all the penitents of Father Dirrag wanted to have a stigma of their very own.

Dirrag understood the necessity to keep his fame and to divert the attention of his flock from Miss Eradice. A few penitents received the same stigmata and everything went along fine again.

Meanwhile, Eradice devoted her entire being to the holy Saint Francis and her father confessor assured her that he had the utmost confidence in the miraculous powers of that particular saint. He himself had performed many a miracle through a section of the rope of this holy man. A priest from his order had brought it with him from the Holy Father in Rome. With the help of this relic he had exorcised many a devil from some poor possessed soul, either by sticking it into the mouth of the victim or by penetrating another body opening. Finally he showed her the so-called rope. In reality this was nothing but a ten-inch long piece of hemp which had been soaked in tar to make it smooth and slick. He displayed it to her in a case, covered with purple velvet. Eradice, who was too innocent to know this, begged the priest for permission to kiss the instrument. He had told her that she would have to reach a state of utter humblenesss, because any touching by profane hands would be a great and mortal sin in the eyes of the Lord.

This is how, my dear count, Father Dirrag succeeded in allowing his young penitent to endure for many months his lecherous embraces. And all that time she firmly believed she was enjoying the purely spiritual ecstasies of Heavenly grace.

She told me everything after the sentencing at that notorious trial. She confided to me that a certain monk—one who had played a great role in this whole unpalatable affair—had finally opened her eyes to reality. He was young, very handsome, strong, and passionately in love with her. He was also a friend of the family and therefore dined frequently with her. She became confidential, and the monk exposed the brazen Dirrag. From what she told me, it was rather obvious that she had no doubt whatsoever what happened during the embraces of her friendly monk. She gave herself to him out of her own free will. It seems that his behavior did not do any harm to the reputation of his order but that may have been because he was young, strong and handsome. He doubled the exercises to twice weekly and his new convert felt so richly rewarded that she began to neglect the weekly devotional sessions with the old druid.

After Eradice had began to enjoy the wonderful effects of the natural member of the young monk and she realized that she had been cheated with this so-called rope, she felt grossly disappointed. Not only that, but her vanity had been hurt and she decided to revenge herself. She started the entire proceeding which is well-known to you and she was assisted by the passionate young monk, who was not solely interested in his party, but furious at the old Dirrag who had received so many favors from his beloved Eradice by playing tricks upon her innocence. After all, in the opinion of the young, strong and handsome monk, Eradice was created only for his pleasure. The priest had clearly committed theft and he had to be punished spectacularly. His rival had to be burned! Only this could satisfy his injured feelings.

As I already told you, I went straight home as soon as Father Dirrag had left my girl friend's house. I had barely reached my little room when I threw myself down upon my knees, begging God for the grace to be treated like Miss Eradice. My mind was in a turmoil which had reached the proportions of near-insanity. An inner fire consumed me. I sat down, then I stood up, again I threw myself upon my knees, but I went nearly out of my mind, regardless of the position I was in. I threw myself upon my bed; the deep penetration of that red snake into the private parts of my girl friend had burned itself in my mind's eyes. It did not occur to me to think of carnal pleasures. I did not connect what I had witnessed in any way with voluptuous pleasure, any more than I realized the criminality of what I had just witnessed. Finally I trailed away in a deep slumber and I dreamed that the member of Father Dirrag had left his body and was now in the process of penetrating me.

Half asleep I took the same position which I had observed from Eradice and, still half asleep, I backed up, crawling on my belly till the bedpost was in between my legs and touched that part of me which itched, driving me out of my mind. The contact with the bedpost caused a sharp pain which woke me out of my reverie without diminishing that infernal itch. To free myself from the position into which I had gotten, I had to lift my behind. Rubbing against the bedpost was unavoidable and it caused a rather peculiar tickling. I moved once more, then again, and again. The effect was amazing. Suddenly I was caught in a frenzy. Without really having any particular thought in mind I began to pump my behind against the bedpost. Finally I rubbed my private parts with incredible speed against the beneficent bedpost. And soon a delightful feeling came over me; I lost consciousness and sank into a deep, relaxing sleep.

A few hours later I woke up, clamping my beloved bedpost between my thighs. I was on my belly, and my behind was naked. I was quite surprised about this peculiar position because I had forgotten what had happened. In a similar way a dream disappears at the moment of awakening. I had quieted down considerably; the release of those divine juices had freed my mind of its obsession. I began to think about what I had seen at Eradice's home, and I tried to remember exactly what I had done. However, I failed to realize any connection. I could make no sense out of what had happened to me. The part which I had rubbed against the bedpost hurt awfully, and the insides of my thighs were sore. Despite the firm warnings of my former father confessor from the convent, I gathered all my courage and dared to look at that part of my body which was giving me so much pain. I could not bring myself to touch it, the terrifying threats of hellfire and brimstone were too firmly implanted in my mind.

Just when I had finished my inspection, our maid entered my room and announced that Madame Catherine and the abbot had arrived to take dinner with us and mother had ordered me to come downstairs and keep them company. I went downstairs.

It had been quite some time since I had seen Madame Catherine. Though she was befriended with my mother, who had done her a few great favors, and though she was considered to be a very devout woman, I had not visited her for a long time, because I did not want to incur the displeasure of my father confessor. She made no bones about the fact she abhorred the principles and the mystical exhortations of Father Dirrag. And this venerable priest in turn was very firm about his opponents: he did not allow any member of his flock to associate with the penitents of other father confessors, his competitors. Without doubt he feared confidential exchanges and therefore enlightenment. Anyhow, it was an absolute condition which the venerable Dirrag extracted from all his penitents and one which they carefully kept.

We sat down to dinner. The meal was very pleasant and I felt a lot better than usual. My usual dullness had made place for a certain vivaciousness; the pains in my back had disappeared, and I felt as if I had been reborn. None of our neighbors was slandered during the dinner conversation, although this is usually the case when priests and pious women dine together. The abbot, who is a very bright man and who has traveled a lot, told us many an amusing story without harming anyone's reputation, at least not anyone we knew personally. We were all in a very good mood.

After we drank our champagne and had taken our coffee, my mother took me aside and berated me about not having visited Madame Catherine for such a long time.

"She is a darling lady," said my mother, "and one of my best friends. It is because of her that I enjoy such a good reputation in this town. Her virtue and her enlightened knowledge are proverbial, and she is revered by all who know her. We need her assistance and it is therefore my wish, nay, my express order, Therese, that you do everything in your power to acquire her friendship."

I answered mother that she did not have to be afraid and that I would do everything I could to make Madame Catherine like me. Oh, the poor woman. She had no idea about the lessons I was to receive from this woman who had such a splendid reputation in our small home town.

Mother and I returned to our company. A few moments later I told Madame Catherine that I was terribly sorry about having neglected her for so long. I asked her to forgive me and to allow me one of these days to explain to her why I had been so thoughtless. I would be more than happy to tell her in detail what had kept me from visiting such a good friend. But Madame Catherine did not let me finish and said with a sweet smile, "I know everything you want to tell me, my dear. This is neither the time nor the place to talk about it. Every person is convinced he has his own good reasons and it is quite possible that they are right. One thing is for sure: it would be a pleasure to have you visit me and to prove this to you." She continued, raising her voice slightly, "I invite you right here and now to have late supper with me at my home. Is that all right with you?" she asked my mother. "Obviously I expect you and the reverend abbot, too. Both of you have things to talk over, so Miss Therese and I are going out for a stroll; you know when and where we shall meet."

Mother was delighted. Neither the principles nor the behavior of Father Dirrag met with her approval and she hoped that the good advice of Madame Catherine would help me to swear off my inclination to mortification of the flesh, for which she held my father confessor directly responsible.

The possibility exists that Madame Catherine and my mother had made some secret agreement. If that was true, my mother's wishes were fulfilled very soon and far beyond her wildest expectations.

Madame Catherine and I left the house, but I had barely walked a hundred steps when a terrible pain tore through my body. I was incapable of standing up straight and Madame Catherine asked, "But my dearest Therese, what on earth is the matter? Don't you feel well?"

Though I told her that it was nothing, she asked me a thousand questions. Women are curious by nature and her questioning was very embarrassing to me. This, obviously, did not escape her attention.

"Don't tell me," she said, "that you, too, belong to the stigmatized females of this town. You are not even able to stand up straight. You are beside yourself! Come into my garden, dear child, and recuperate yourself. Let us sit down and wait till you have come to rest."

The gardens of Madame Catherine were in the neighborhood. We walked over there slowly and sat down in a delightful little summerhouse close to the lakefront.

After some idle talk about common generalities, Madame Catherine asked me again if I really had stigmata, and how I felt under the spiritual direction of Father Dirrag. "I am very sorry, my dear," she said, "but I cannot deny that this particular kind of miracle surprises me terribly, and I am dying to see some of these miraculous wounds with my own eyes. I have a fervent desire to convince myself of their existence. Oh, please, my dear child, don't refuse me my wish. Tell me where and how and when these wounds appeared. You can be very sure that I shall not misuse your confidence and I believe that you know me well enough to be convinced that I speak the truth."

Not only are women curious, they also love to talk. I myself suffered from this little fault of my sex, and moreover, several glasses of champagne had loosened my tongue. I was in pain and needed no prodding to talk at length. I decided to tell her everything. Of course, I had to admit to her immediately that I was not fortunate enough to belong to the select group of brides of God, but that I had witnessed the sacred wounds of Miss Eradice that very morning and that the venerable Father Dirrag had inspected them himself when I was there. A little more artful prodding from Madame Catherine caused me to tell her slowly, bit by bit, everything I had seen and heard that morning. Not only what I had witnessed at Eradice's home, but also what had happened in my own room. I told her that I suspected that the pain I suffered was a direct result of my rubbing the bedpost.

During this remarkable confession, Madame Catherine was smart enough not to show the slightest surprise. She nodded her agreement with everything I said and caused me therefore to tell her every single little detail. Whenever I became confused because I did not know the proper words to describe what I had seen or felt, she asked me to describe the situations graphically. Undoubtedly, the lechery and voluptuousness of the situations, coming from a girl as young and innocent as I, must have been very funny to this world-wise woman. Never before have such vile and obscene situations been described so seriously.

When I had finished my story, Madame Catherine seemed to be far away with her thoughts. I asked her several questions, but her answers were very vague and short. Finally she pulled herself together, and told me that the things she had just heard were very remarkable indeed and they deserved her full attention. She would tell me later what she thought about it, and what I should do. But first things first, and I had to get rid of that pain. She advised me to bathe the spot with warm wine, especially in between my thighs which had been chafed by the bedpost. "Be very careful, my dearest child," she said to me. "Don't tell anything of what you have told me to someone else. Not even to your own mother, but especially not to Father Dirrag. You have done something good and you have seen something evil. Come and see me tomorrow morning around nine o'clock, and I will be able to give you some better advice. You can count upon my friendship. Your noble character is quite obvious. Well, I see your mother. Let's go and meet her, and talk about something else."

About fifteen minutes later the abbot arrived also. Late supper, as they call it in the provinces, actually is rather early. It was barely seven-thirty when food was served and we sat down to supper.

In between courses Madame Catherine could not help herself, and she made some rather satirical remarks about the good Father Dirrag. The abbot seemed to be quite surprised and he scolded her gently. "Why," said he, "shouldn't everyone behave himself exactly as he deems proper and correct, as long as it does not violate the concepts of proper society? And so far we have not seen Father Dirrag breech propriety. I therefore beg you, Madame, to allow me to disagree with your remarks, till the opinion you have about my confrere is substantiated by facts."

To prevent a direct answer. Madame Catherine artfully guided the conversation in another direction. Around ten o'clock we got up from the table; Madame Catherine whispered something into the abbot's ear, he nodded, and escorted mother and me to our home.

You should know, my dear count, to understand my story, who Madame Catherine and the abbot were. I will therefore interrupt my story and give you some idea of their backgrounds.

Madame Catherine is a member of a noble family. Her parents had married her off to an old naval Officer of about sixty when she was only fifteen years old. The man died five years after the wedding, leaving his young widow pregnant with a boy. The birth of this child almost killed the mother and three months later the baby died. Through her son's death, Madame Catherine inherited a substantial fortune. The beautiful widow, barely twenty years old, was besieged by matrimonial offers from bachelors all over the country. But she was now her own boss and made no bones about it that she liked it, and that she had no intention to ever again run the risk of dying in childbed. It was only a miracle, she said, that she had remained alive; she intended to keep it that way, and she was so firm about it that soon even her most ardent admirers lost courage and left her alone.

Madame Catherine had a marvelous mind; she was very firm with her opinions, but she did not form them unless she had subjected them to many tests. She read a lot, and enjoyed conversation, especially about philosophical and abstract matters. Her behavior was beyond approach. She was a true friend and she would offer assistance whenever she found an opportunity. My mother, for one, knew this out of her own experience. The time I am talking about, Madame Catherine must have been close to twenty-seven years old. I will have more than sufficient opportunity to describe her physical charms later.

The abbot, who was a very dear and special friend and at the same time spiritual advisor of Madame Catherine, was a truly deserving gentleman. He was around forty-five years old, small but well-built, and had an open, very intelligent face. He carefully observed the demands required by his station in life and the high society whose advisor he was, loved him and lavished its attention upon him. He was very intelligent and his knowledge was remarkable. These qualities made him excellent for the high position he held in Volno and though I am very sorry, I am not at liberty to reveal its nature without giving away the abbot's true identity. He was the father confessor and true friend of many respectable and noble people, in the same way that Father Dirrag was father confessor to every bigoted, hysterical old maid, the professional devout female and an assorted bunch of fanatical bitches.

That next morning I returned to Madame Catherine's home at the appointed hour.

"Well, my dearest Therese," she called out at the front door, "how is my sore little friend? Did you sleep well?"

"I feel a lot better, my dear Madame," I answered truthfully. "I have done exactly what you told me. I have thoroughly bathed the sore parts in warm wine and it has relieved me tremendously. I only pray that the Lord will have mercy upon me and not doom me to the deep pit of fire in hell."

Madame Catherine smiled; she poured me a small cup of coffee and said, "What you told me last night is far more important than you could possibly believe. I have become convinced that it is imperative to talk with the abbot about it. He is waiting for you at this very moment in his confessional. I want you to visit him and to repeat to him, word for word, everything you told me last night. He is a man of honor, and I am sure that he will give you proper advice. You need that very badly. I also believe that he will give you a few new rules to follow, and if you are as smart as I think you are, you would do well to follow them! It is imperative not only for the well-being of your immortal soul, but also for your own good health. Your dear mother would die of misery if she ever found out what you have seen at the home of your girl friend Eradice. If she every found out what I know, she would have a stroke. I cannot hide from you the fact that what you have witnessed at Eradice's was horrible. Now, go with God, my dearest Therese. Take the abbot into your confidence. I assure you that you will be very glad if you do."

I burst out in tears and left her home, trembling all over. I arrived at the abbot's mansion and, as soon as he saw me, he went into the confessional.

I did not leave out the tiniest detail. He listened patiently and with full attention till I had finished my entire story. He only interrupted here and there to ask for an explanation about a few things that did not seem quite clear to him.

When I had finished he said, "You have made quite remarkable observations. Father Dirrag is a swindler, an unhappy soul who allows himself to be torn down by the strength of his passions. He is inviting his own doom and, worse, he will take Eradice along in his fall. And you, Miss Therese, are more to be pitied than to be scolded. We do not always have the strength to resist temptations. The happiness and unhappiness of our lives are quite frequently decided by chance, or, if you prefer, by good or bad opportunities. I advise you to avoid the bad opportunities. Stop all contact with Father Dirrag and his penitents but do not speak evil about them; God in his infinite love for His children, would not like that. I also advise you to visit Madame Catherine quite frequently. She means very well and she will be able to give you lots of good, solid advice. It would indeed be a lot better for you if you tried to follow her example.

"And now, my child, we shall have to talk about that unendurable itching which you often notice in those parts of your body which you have been rubbing against the bedpost. That itching indicates certain needs of your temperament which are as important as eating and drinking. It is not directly necessary to goad on these certain needs but it would be foolish to deny their existence. If they are bothering you too much, there is absolutely nothing wrong in the eyes of God our Father when you bring relief to that certain part of your body by rubbing it vigorously with a finger. I absolutely forbid you to stick your finger into the small hole you will find there. All you need to know now is that the husband, whom I am sure you will find one of these days, might get the wrong impression. But otherwise, I cannot repeat this too often, it is a feeling which Nature has implanted in us, and it is necessary to release the tensions which it creates at times. And Mother Nature also gave us a hand with fingers to satisfy the needs of our body.

"And, since we are nowadays convinced that the laws of Nature are also created by God, we cannot insult our Creator by not using the things He has given us to satisfy the needs whose impulses were His gift to us. Especially since by doing so, the prurient interests of society are not disturbed if we only remain discreet about it. It is something entirely different, my dear daughter, between the hypocritical priest Dirrag and his penitent Miss Eradice. He has swindled her, endangered her by possibly making her the mother of his bastard, because the so-called relic of the holy Saint Francis was nothing else but the male member which is used to impregnate women. Therefore he is sinning against the law of Nature which commands us to love our neighbor like ourselves. And I ask you, is it Christian charity when a priest puts a girl like your friend Eradice in a position to lose her good reputation, and to dishonor her for the rest of her natural life?

"You have seen, my dear child, how the priest rammed his tool into your girl friend and how he moved it back and forth. The connection of these two body parts, which are created for procreation, is only permissible when a woman is married. To do it with an unmarried girl can cause misery for an entire family. It is against the rules of society and therefore reprehensible. As long as you are not bound by the sacrament of marriage, don't allow any man to do this to you, regardless of the position you take. The simple means I have just advised you will suffice to keep the desire in check and to dampen the fire which may be caused by the wish. This simple cure will soon heal your failing health and I assure you that your body will bloom forth in beauty. I do not doubt that then your beautiful face will call forth suitors by the dozens who will try to lead you astray. Beware of them, and be very careful in your selection of a final partner. Never forget the lesson I gave you today. That will be all. I expect to see you next week at the same time and do not forget that the secret of the confessional is as sacred to the penitent as it is to the confessor. I must warn you that it is a mortal sin in the eyes of God, if only the smallest detail is talked about to outsiders."

I must admit that the prescriptions of my new father confessor delighted my soul. I recognized instinctively a truth and Christian charity and I also realized the ridiculous sham of Father Dirrag's unctuous lectures which I had held, alas, so sacred for so long.

After I had contemplated the advice all day. I sat down on the edge of my bed before I went to sleep. I wanted to wash the chafed, sore parts again with warm wine. I spread my thighs as wide as I possiby could and began to inspect those parts very carefully and intensely. I shoved the lips of my cunny to the side and started to look for the little hole in which I had seen Father Dirrag shove his enormous prick at Eradice's home. I finally discovered the little orifice but I could not believe that it was the same. It seemed so tight and tiny! I tried to stick my finger into it when I suddenly remembered the abbot's warning. Quickly I pulled my finger back and traced the little slit. Suddenly I touched a little protuberance. A little quiver ran through my body. I touched it again, and the shudder became voluptuous delight. I started to rub this little knob and soon I had reached the peak of delight. What a happy discovery for a girl who possesses such a richly flowing spring of life juices!

For almost six months I swam in a sea of sensual delights, carried by waves of orgasms and whirlpools of lasciviousness. My health had become perfect, my conscience was unruffled thanks to my new father confessor who gave sensible advice which was adjusted to human passions. I saw him regularly every Monday in the confessional and almost every day at the home of Madame Catherine. I spent a lot of time with this lovely lady. The darkness which had for so long engulfed my spirit had disappeared; it had become a habit to think rationally and to judge calmly. Father Dirrag and Miss Eradice had almost disappeared from my memories.

How perfect can mind and spirit be molded by example and regulations! If it is true that they do not give us anything, and that we carry the seeds of everything within ourselves, then it is at least sure that examples and regulations serve to develop these seeds. They are able to make us realize thoughts and feelings of which we are capable and which would have remained hidden from our consciousness, in their bolster, if we had been without example or without rules and regulations.

Meanwhile, mother had carried on with my late father's wholesale business. The results were disastrous, she had more enormous debts, and she had extended too much credit to a merchant in Paris who was now threatened with bankruptcy. This would ruin my mother, too. After she had consulted with her friends, she decided to undertake a voyage to our marvelous capital city. My sweet, lovely mother loved me too much to leave me back home. The trip might be prolonged for quite some time, and she could not stand the idea that we should be separated for an indeterminate period. She decided therefore that I would accompany her to Paris. Ah! the poor woman had no inkling that she would find a miserable end in Paris and that I would find the wellspring of my happiness in the arms of my count!

The decision was made and we were to undertake our voyage in a month's time. It was agreed that I would spend the remaining time of our stay in Volno at the little country home of Madame Catherine which was about a mile away from town. The abbot visited us regularly and slept quite frequently in the guest room whenever his duties in town allowed him to do so. Both he and Madame Catherine showered me with attentions; they no longer feared to make remarks in my presence which were rather revolutionary and to talk about subjects of morality, religion and metaphysics which were in flagrant contradiction to what I had been taught previously. I had already noticed that Madame Catherine liked the way I thought and reasoned about certain subjects, and that she was delighted whenever she succeeded in changing my opinion about a certain subject. She always forced me to come up with undeniable proof whenever I maintained an opinion about something. It annoyed me occasionally to notice that the abbot sometimes shook his head as if to warn her not to go too far on certain subjects. This discovery hurt my pride. I decided to try everything in my power to find out what they were trying to hide from me. It had at the time not occurred to me that these two people could have more than intellectual ties which bound them together. But soon, I was fully enlightened. I will tell you about that in a moment.

You are now about to learn, my dear count, the source from which I have acquired my moral and metaphysical principles which you have so carefully developed. These principles have enlightened me about what we are in this world and what we have to fear in the next. I thank them for the peace of mind and a way of life whose entire delight is made up by you.

It was a beautiful summer. Madame Catherine had the habit of getting up at five in the morning to take a stroll in the little forest near the end of her property. I had also noticed that the abbot, whenever he stayed overnight with us, had the same habit. After about two hours they would return home, go to Madame's bedroom and come downstairs around ten o'clock for a second breakfast.

I decided one day to hide in the bushes in such a way that I could overhear their conversation. Since I had no idea that they were lovers, I also did not think that I would lose anything if I were not able to see them.

I looked the place over very carefully and decided to hide in a place which seemed perfect for what I had in mind.

During supper the conversation drifted toward the workings and products of Nature.

"But what is Nature?" asked Madame Catherine. "Is it a particular creature? Isn't everything created by God? Could it be possible that Nature is a subservient deity?"

"It is really not very intelligent of you to

talk in such a manner," exclaimed the abbot, his eyes twinkling. "I promise you that I will explain what we are supposed to think about the Mother of the race of Men when we make our early stroll tomorrow morning in the gardens. It is too late now to talk about such a heavy subject. Can't you see that Miss Therese is dead tired? A discussion like this would bore her to death. I advise you, my dearest ladies, to go to bed. I shall recite my prayers and then follow your example."

We took the abbot's advice and retired to our rooms.

The next morning, before sunup, I hid myself in the bushes I had selected. They were behind some trees which were connected by trellises along which roses climbed, thus forming a charming natural summerhouse, decorated by a few benches and little statues. After I had impatiently waited for a full hour, my two heroes finally showed up and sat down upon that bench behind which I had hidden myself.

"Yes," the abbot said when they walked into the little clearing, "she becomes lovelier every day. Her breasts have developed so well that they would completely fill the hands of some honorable priest. And her eyes have a sparkle to them which betrays her vivaciousness and her passionate temperament. Because she is very passionate, our little Therese. Imagine, I have given her permission to relieve herself with her finger and would you believe that by now she uses this form of satisfaction at least twice a day? You must admit that I am almost as good a doctor as a father confessor. Not only have I cured her spirit and mind,

I have also healed her body and brought it to bloom."

"Oh, come on now, my darling," exclaimed Madame Catherine, "have you finally finished with your dear Therese! Did we come here to talk about her beautiful eyes and fiery temperament? I really believe, Mister Joker, that you are tempted to tell her to save the trouble and you will help her relieve her tensions. You know darned well that I am not a jealous mistress, and I would instantly give you permission if I did not fear that it could land you in a lot of trouble. Therese is a very smart and intelligent young girl, but she is too innocent and does not know enough about the ways of the world. You simply cannot afford to take her into your confidence. I have noticed that she is very curious. It is very well possible that she can be of great use to us, but we must be very careful and willing to wait. She suffers from a few great faults. I just enumerated them to you. If she did not have those, I would not hesitate for a single second, and I would personally invite her to share our delights. Beecause it is really ridiculous to be jealous at our best friends and to deny them their happiness, especially since it would not in the least diminish ours."

"You are absolutely right," said the abbot. "Jealousy and envy are two passions which can do a lot of useless harm to people who cannot think intelligently. But there is a difference between envy and jealousy. Envy is a passion which is born into Mankind and it belongs to his nature. Little children in the cradle are already envious at other children when they see what they get. Through education we may be able to weaken the results of this passion with which Nature has endowed us. But it is a different story altogether with jealousy. Jealousy is related to the joys of love. It is a result of our vanity and our prejudices. After all, we know of entire populations where the men offer the guests the enjoyment of their wives, in a manner very similar to where we offer our honored guests the best stock of our wine cellars. A native caresses the lover who is enjoying his wife, and all his acquaintances are envious of such a friendship. They laud him, and they congratulate him. A Frenchman, in a similar predicament, would make a long face, his acquaintances would point him out and laugh at him. A Persian would stab both his wife and her lover, and all his friends would honor him for it.

"Consequently I do not believe that jealousy is one of the passions which Nature has implanted in us. It is fostered by education and by whatever the prejudice might be of the society in which its victim is brought up. A woman in Paris reads about, and is told as a young girl, that infidelity of her lover is an insult to the woman; a young man is assured that a mistress or a wife who cheats a little bit on him, dishonors the lover or the husband. They imbibe these ridiculous principles, in a manner of speaking, with their mother's milk. Out of it grows jealousy, the green monster which tortures mankind with unspeakable suffering which in reality is not worth bothering about.

"Nevertheless, we must make a distinction between fickleness and infidelity. I am in love with the woman who loves me; her character is sympathetic to me; her beauty and her passion make me happy. She leaves me. In this case the resulting pain is no longer caused by some prejudice. It is justified. I lose something which was really good and beautiful, I lose a delight to which I had become accustomed and of which I am not sure whether I will be able to find it back with all the joys and happiness to which I had become used. But what is the meaning of a fickle sidestep? This can be caused by a temporary mood, a sudden passionate feeling, or sometimes gratefulness. A sensitive soul which is easily attuned to the pain or joy of another one, and which gives in a little too easily, maybe. One really shows little intelligence to worry about something like that, a tempest in a teapot which has no meaning at all, neither good nor evil."

"Aha!" Madame Catherine interrupted the abbot with a smile. "Now I understand what you are leading up to. You are trying to tell me that you are not unwilling, out of the goodness of your heart, or to give her a little pleasure, to give our little Therese a small lesson in voluptuous pleasures, to give her a little love enema which, as far as I am concerned, is neither good nor bad. Well, my dear abbot. That's all right with me. It's a pleasure, because I love both of you. The two of you will gain something, and I stand nothing to lose. Why did you expect any resistance from me? If I would get excited you might rightfully conclude that I am only in love with myself, that I am merely interested in my personal satisfaction, and that I want to increase that at the expense of something which you could find somewhere else any time you wanted it. But that is far from the truth. The happiness which I have acquired has nothing to do with throwing your satisfaction away. You don't have to be afraid, my dearest friend, to come close to me without being able to nibble to your heart's content at the little pussy of our dear Therese. Personally I think that it would do the poor girl a lot of good. But I warn you, my dear friend, be very careful!"

"That is a lot of nonsense. I did not even think about the little Therese. I only wanted to explain to you the mechanism which Nature . . ."

"Oh, please, let's stop talking about that!" answered Madame Catherine. "But now that you mention Nature, you remind me of something. You forgot to tell me, if I remember your promise correctly, exactly who and what this so-called Mother Nature of yours really is. Let me hear how good your explanation succeeds, because you always insist that you can explain everything rationally."

"I will fulfill your wish," answered the abbot, "but, my dearest love, you know what I need first. I've got to do it now. My imagination is terribly excited. I am absolutely useless. I can't think of anything else. My thoughts are confused and everything is absorbed by this one single thought. I have told you what I used to do when I studied in Paris, and my thoughts were primarily absorbed with reading and exact sciences. The moment I noticed the first carnal desires I would instantly procure a girl. The same way one gets himself a pot to piss in when the bladder gets irritated. I would make her once or twice in a manner which you unfortunately won't allow me to do. My mind would be cleared, my spirit would be calm, and I could go back to my studies. I maintain that every student, and every statesman with an ounce of passion in him, should use this kind of a cure. It is as necessary for the health of the body as it is for the sanity of the mind. I will even go further. I maintain that every honorable man who knows his duties toward society, should use this method to make sure that he does not forget his duties because of undue excitement, or tempts the wife and daughters of his best friend."

"Now, you may ask me what the women and girls should do. They have, as you say, the same needs men have, because they are created out of the same flesh. But, alas, we cannot use the same methods. A false sense of modesty, or fear of slander and gossip, a blunderer or a childmaker . . . No, my friend, all these possibilities don't allow us to use the same means as men. And besides, where would we be able to find men who are instantly ready and willing, like your little girls in Paris, to service us?"

"Listen, my darling. Women and girls are allowed to do what you do and what Therese is doing twice a day. And if this game does not really satisfy you (and I know that there are lots of women who don't really like it), then you always have the choice to use that fantastic invention which they call a dildo and which is a rather correct copy of the real thing. And moreover, your imagination will help you with the rest. No, I still maintain that men and women are only allowed to find those satisfactions which do not disturb the order of society. But when women start to enjoy just about any delight that strikes their fancy, then they have to voluntarily bear the yoke which society puts on their shoulders. You may call this injustice, but it is an injustice which is for the greater good of society."

"Aha, my poor abbot. Now you have really talked yourself into a fine mess. You are trying to tell me that a woman or a girl can enjoy a man whereas a man of honor cannot enjoy a woman. It would destroy the very fabric of your precious society if he were to try and lead an honorable female into temptation. But you, yourself, you little hypocrite, have tried on hundreds of different occasions to lead me astray and you would have succeeded a long time ago if I had not been so deadly afraid of pregnancy. So, you have acted against the welfare of society to satisfy your own little desires."

"Well, we are back on our old theme again," said the Abbot. "It's always the same song, my little love. Haven't I told you a hundred times that there are certain precautions which make such an accident impossible? Haven't you, yourself, admitted that women should only be afraid of three things: the devil, the loss of reputation, and pregnancy? As far as the first is concerned, I'm quite sure that you are not worried. I also don't believe that you have to be afraid about point number two as far as I am concerned. Only a mistake from you could damage your good name. And thirdly, a woman can only become a mother through the stupidity of her lover. I have told you a thousand times that because of its very construction nothing is easier to avoid as far as a man's prick is concerned. And though I have told you so often, I will gladly repeat it once more:

"A lover can only get into the mood for screwing by two things: his own imagination, or the sight of his loved one. The flow of blood makes his prick thick and stiff. Since they both want to do it, they get into the proper position. The prick of the lover is shoved into the cunt of his mistress, and through mutual rubbing and pumping the juices are being prepared to flow out of the respective parts. The moment the jism is about to be expelled the wise lover who knows how to control his passions will pull the bird out of the nest and with his own hand, or the hand of his loved one, only a slight jerking is necessary to shoot the divine load. And there is absolutely no worry about being knocked up.

"A lover who does not use his brains, or one who shoves it in too deeply and who cannot pull out of the cunt in time, he is the one who squirts his seed deep into the womb, and that is the spot where the child develops.

"That is the precise mechanical way of the enjoyment of love. You know me well enough. Could you truly believe that I belong to those I mentioned lastly? The ones that do not use their God-given intelligence? No, my dove. I can speak out of experience when I tell you that I have proof of the opposite a hundred times over. I implore you. Let me prove it to you now. Today. Look at the triumphant state of my little boy; you are holding it in your hand. Oh, please, squeeze a little bit harder. You see, he is begging for your mercy, and I . . ."

"No! Please, no! No, my dearest abbot!" exclaimed Madame Catherine. "I beg of you, don't do it! No matter what you say, I cannot get over this horrible fear. I would give you an enjoyment of which it would be absolutely impossible for me to partake. And that would be terribly unfair. Allow me to bring sense to this fresh little one . . . Well," she continued after several moments of silence, "are you satisfied with my breasts and my thighs? Have you kissed and caressed them to your complete satisfaction? And why are you trying to shove my sleeves above my elbows? The gentleman undoubtedly enjoys the sight of a moving, naked arm. Am I doing all right? You don't say a word. Oh, you rascal! Look at the way he is enjoying himself!"

For a moment everything was quiet. Suddenly I heard the abbot exclaim, "Oh, my dearest little one, I can't stand it. Please, hurry! Quick, quick . . . come, come . . . with your darling little tongue, aaah . . . it's . . . squirting!"

Imagine, dear count, the situation in which I found myself. I tried to get up at least twenty times to find some little opening in the bushes which would allow me to see what was going on. However, the rustling of the leaves prevented me from doing so. I sat upright and tried to stretch my neck as far as I could. A fire consumed me and I used my normal way to contain it. Extinguishing had become quite impossible.

After a moment, during which he undoubtedly put his clothes in order, the abbot began to speak again. "Really, my dearest. Come to think of it, I am afraid that you were right again. I am glad that you denied me the enjoyment I wanted because I am afraid that I would have lost my mind completely and I would never have pulled out in time. I felt such an enormous delight, and such a great ecstasy that I would have come right smack into your belly."

"Yes! I know, we are truly weak creatures and not very capable of controlling our desires. I know all that, my dearest abbot. You are not telling me anything new. But tell me, are we really not going against the interests of society by giving in to the enjoyments we just experienced? And those so-called intelligent lovers who are so careful in pulling the bird out of the nest, and who allow the juices of life to dribble away on the outside. Don't they commit a similar crime? Don't they rob society of a possible member who could have become very useful?"

"That sounds reasonable," retorted the abbot, "but you will see, my love, that your reasoning is rather superficial. There is neither a human, nor a divine law, which invites us, let alone forces us, to work on the multiplication of the human race. All the laws we have force an immense amount of bachelors and maidens, as well as droves of filthy monks and useless nuns, to observe continence. They allow a married man to fuck his pregnant wife and you could hardly call that useful. He merely spends his jism in a place that needs it the least. As a matter of fact, being a virgin is considered more desirable than being a married woman.

"Don't you agree that those people who cheat a little while fucking, or those who enjoy licking a pussy, don't do anything more or less than all those monks and nuns, and all the other ones who remain unmarried. They keep their seed in balls that are basically as useless as those who come outside of a cunt. As far as society is concerned, they are in exactly the same position. Neither one of these groups contribute any new members to society. But our common sense tells us that it is a lot better to waste the seed and enjoy doing it, especially since it does not do anyone a bit of harm, than to keep it and save it at the expense of our health and sanity. So you see, Madame the philosopher, that our enjoyment does no more harm to our precious society than the accepted celibacy of monks, nuns and the whole rest that prefer to remain unmarried, and so we shall be able to continue our enjoyment like we have always done."

The following exclamations left no doubt in my mind that the abbot was of the opinion that he had to offer certain services to Madame Catherine, because I heard her exclaim, "Oh, please, don't do that, you naughty abbot! Get away with that finger. I am really not up to it today, I am still worn out from yesterday's playing around. So please, don't do it till tomorrow. And besides, you know very well that I like to do it in comfort. I prefer my soft bed over this hard, uncomfortable bench any time. Quick, stop it. All I want from you now is your explanation of Mother

Nature. Well, big philosopher. I helped to clear your thoughts, didn't I? Now talk . . . I am listening."

"You want to know about Mother Nature? That is simple. Soon you will know as much about her as I do. She is a creature who only exists in our imagination. She is nothing but the useless sounds of words. The first founders of religions and the first leaders of nations were at a complete loss to explain to their people the concepts of moral right and moral wrong. And therefore they invented a creature who stands between God and us. And then they made this creature the founder of our passions, the originator of our illnesses, the reason for our crimes. How else could they possibly have explained the infinite love and goodness of God? How could they have given a reasonable explanation for such human vices as murder, theft, treason and rape, just to name a few. Why are there so many illnesses and so much physical suffering? What has the poor cripple who is doomed to crawl in misery all his life done to incur God's wrath?

"A theologian gave us the simple answer to all those questions: It is the work of Nature. But, what and who is this Nature? Is it another God we don't know? Does it act all by itself, independently from the will of God? Oh no, the theologian will answer smugly. Since God is incapable of doing evil because of His infinite love, it follows that evil can only exist through Nature. —What incredible nonsense! Am I supposed to complain about the whip that is hitting me, or about the person who is wielding it? Because isn't he the one who causes the pain I feel?

"So why don't we simply want to admit that Nature is an empty word, a concept which has been created by our weak human intelligence? Why can't we admit that God is everything! That a physical suffering which may be harmless to one, can be beneficial for another. In other words, as far as God is concerned, there is no evil in the world. The things we call good or evil are only so in relation to their effects upon our society, not in relation to God through Whose will we operate in the first place, following precisely the laws and principles which He has laid down at the time of creation. A person steals something. If he is successful, it is good as far as he is concerned, bad as far as his victim is concerned. If the victim is of value to society, the thief is very bad. But, I maintain, that from God's point of view, the thief is neither good, nor bad. He has been created a thief and fulfills his function. I must admit that the man may have to be punished, even though he has acted under compulsion, and I am convinced that he was not free to commit his crime or not commit it. But he has to be punished, because punishment of a person who has disturbed the mechanism of an orderly society is deemed necessary to prevent other criminals from doing the same thing. The punishment which the unfortunate law breaker has to suffer is supposed to be for the common good of society which, in this case, must take precedence over the well-being of the individual.

"Actually, my dearest love, I presume that you now have an inkling of what I mean when I used the term, 'Mother Nature.' It is a meaningless invention, because we cannot stand the mere idea that God could not care less about the little doings of a handful of mere mortals. We have invented a system of morals where the Creator of the universe has been degraded to a village shopkeeper who is the confidant of all the gossipy housewives. For certain acts He is supposed to shake His head, for others to nod agreement and for a few He should arise indignantly. We have perverted our religion into a snooping system of bed manners, we have made our body into a temple of filth and the pleasures of the body into a sin. Finally we have decided that it cannot be the shopkeeper's fault, and we have invented Mother Nature who can take the blame, because only lowly peasants and total morons are still willing to believe in the devil. But that is another subject which I intend to discuss with you tomorrow morning. I will tell you precisely what I think of religion in general. It is a very important subject, especially since it concerns our happiness. But for today I have talked enough. I would love to sip a cup of hot chocolate."

"That is fine with me," said Madame Catherine, straightening her dress. "My dear gentleman philosopher undoubtedly needs the physical strength of this heartening drink, especially since I have taken away a considerable amount of your procreative powers. You have been on your very best behavior and told me some marvelous things. Your remarks about Nature were absolutely fantastic, but I am afraid that you won't be able to enlighten me in a similar manner on the subject of religion. Besides, how could you expect to convince me with proof about a subject which is largely based on belief?"

"We'll talk about that tomorrow," answered the abbot.

"Fine, but don't think that I will let you get away with mere words. Tomorrow, with your permission, we shall retire early to my room, because I will need my comfortable bed and your caressing fingers . . ."

A moment later they walked back to the house. I followed them from a distance, slipped through the back door, and raced up to my room to change dresses. Then I walked downstairs to say good morning to Madame Catherine and the abbot who were already drinking their chocolate. I was afraid to stay too long in my own room, because the possibility existed that the abbot would start his conversation about religion anyway, and I did not want to miss a single word of it. His discourse about Nature had made a tremendous impression upon me. I saw now clearly that God and Nature were one and the same thing, or at least that it is Nature which carries out the will of God. I drew my own conclusions from that momentous discovery and I began to think, perhaps for the first time in my life.

I trembled when I walked into Madame Catherine's room. I felt as if she knew that I had spied upon her and the abbot, and I was incapable of hiding my excitement. The abbot looked at me carefully. I pretended not to notice it. But I heard him whisper to Madame Catherine, "Look at our little Therese. Isn't she pretty! Her complexion is charming, her eyes sparkle and her face is twice as intelligent as it was yesterday."

I don't know what Madame Catherine answered him, but they both smiled. I pretended as if I had heard nothing, and stayed with them all day like a devoted watchdog.

That night, when I had retired to my room, I developed my war plan for the next morning. I was so afraid that I would oversleep that I decided to stay awake all night. Around five in the morning I saw Madame Catherine hurry toward the little clearing where I knew that the abbot was awaiting her. After what I had heard the previous day I also knew that they would return soon to Madame Catherine's room with the enormous, comfortable bed. Without further ado I went into her room and hid behind the curtains at the head of the bed, leaning against the wall and making sure that I could shove the curtain slightly aside without making noise. I did not want to miss anything! They could not whisper the slightest word without me being able to pick it up. I waited for a long time and I began to become impatient. I was afraid that they had changed their minds and that my plans would fail. But finally the two heroes of the comedy, which I shall describe now, entered the room.

"Do it good to me, my dear friend," said Madame Catherine, leaning back on her bed. "Your story about the evil painter of Chartreux has made my blood boil. His portraits are beautifuul and very true to Nature; if they had not been so dirty the book would be a true classic of art. Stick it into me, my dearest abbot. Today I have decided to let you do it. I implore you! I am dying with wild desire and I am ready to bear the consequences!"

"I don't dream about it," said the abbot.

"And I have two good reasons for it. In the first place, I love you and I am too decent to gamble with your good reputation. Besides, I am sure that afterward you would accuse me of carelessness. And in the second place, as you know, the doctor is not always capable of performing his duties. Now, I am not a peasant . . ."

"All right, all right! That's enough!" Madame Catherine exclaimed impatiently. "Your first reason was good enough and took too long to explain. I can't hold it much longer. But please, sit down here," she continued with a voluptuously purring voice, stretching languidly out on the bed, "and let's bring a little sacrifice, as you call it."

"Ah! I would love nothing better, my dearest angel!" said the abbot. He stood up and carefully uncovered her breasts. Then he lifted her skirt and chemise to well above her navel, spread her thighs and lifted her knees a little, pushing her heels together.

In this position the abbot kissed every single part of the body of his loved one. Madame Catherine remained motionless, her eyes were closed, she groaned softly and it seemed as if she was dreaming about unspeakable delights yet to come. The tip of her tongue moved rapidly across her lips, her eyelids opened slowly and her eyes were glazed. Her rosy lips began to quiver and the muscles of her face began to twitch. She had reached a state of voluptuous excitement. "Hurry up with your kisses," she exclaimed. "Can't you see that you are killing me. Stop it or start it . . . I can't stand this any longer!"

The agreeable father confessor did not have

to be invited for a second time. He lowered himself on the bed, put his left hand under Madame Catherine's head and his lips touched hers. His tongue slid slowly into her mouth and slipped out again, sliding back and forth, licking her lips, her teeth, filling her mouth and sucking her tongue. Meanwhile his other hand turned to the main business. He caressed her with true artistry. Madame Catherine's cunt was richly covered with black curls and it was here that the abbot's finger lingered and played his virtuoso game. I was in a marvelous position to see the entire procedure. The rich fleece of Madame Catherine was exactly in my field of vision. Under it I could see a large part of her behind which she was moving in a slow undulating motion, a sure sign of her inner turmoil. Her thighs, the most beautiful, firm, whitest, well-rounded thighs one can imagine, and her knees, were also in motion. They weaved slowly back and forth from left to right and vice versa. It seemed to contribute to her delight and the finger of the abbot, which had entirely disappeared in the black curls, followed every one of her moves.

It would be a rather fruitless attempt, my dear count, to try and tell you what I was thinking at that particular moment. I mechanically imitated everything I saw. My hand did the same to me that the abbot's deft fingers were performing on the lower belly of Madame Catherine; I even imitated every single movement my dear friend was making.

"Aah! I'm dying!" she exclaimed suddenly. "Put it in, my dearest abbot . . . shove it as deep as you can. Please, deeper . . . yes, I implore you, shove it up as hard as you can

... shove it, push it, deeper, harder! Oooh, that feels good ... the darling little one is doing his job well! Ooh, what delight ... I am coming ... I am coming ... it's flowing ... I ... I ..."

I imitated everything I saw, and without thinking for a single moment about the warning of my father confessor, I pushed my finger up as high as I could. The stabbing pain did not prevent me. I pushed as deep and as hard as I could, and soon I reached my climax.

The excitement had subdued and I almost fell asleep, despite the uncomfortable position in which I found myself. When I heard Madame Catherine approach the spot where I was hiding, I almost died of fear. But fortunately I remained undiscovered. She pulled the bell cord and sat down at the little table in the other corner of the room. Her servant brought two cups of chocolate, and while they slurped it quietly, they talked about the joys which they had just experienced.

"But why aren't you absolutely innocent?" asked Madame Catherine. "You can tell me as often as you want that you do not encroach upon the rights of society, that we are driven by a need which for certain persons has to be treated like the satisfaction of thirst and hunger. You have proved to me beyond a shadow of a doubt that all our actions depend upon God's will, and that the concept of Nature is merely an empty word. But what is your honest opinion of religion? The only thing I know is that religion prohibits the extramarital delights of the flesh. Does that make religion an empty word, too? What? Have you already forgotten that we are not free to act? That all our actions are predestined? If we are not free, how can we possibly commit sins?"

"You seem to be bound and determined to talk about religion. I have studied for years and years about the subject and God knows that I have tried to unravel the many mysteries connected with it. I have come to the following conclusion: God is good. His goodness is for me a guarantee that He shall not want me to make a mistake if I am truly and whole-heartedly devoted to the search for truth. But I have to know if God really wants me to follow any particular cult. It is obvious that if God is just, I must be able to recognize the true cult. Otherwise God would be unjust because He has given me the intelligence with which to make correct deductions and decisions.

"When a true Christian is unwilling to search for proof that his religion is the correct one, rather than to accept this blindly on faith, why would that same Christian, for example, demand that a Mohammedan, who is equally convinced that he has the proper religion, come up with convincing proof? They both believe that God has revealed their religion to them. The one by Jesus Christ, and the other by Mohammed.

"Our belief exists only because certain people have told us that God has revealed certain truths. But other people have told other members of different religions exactly the same thing. So, who are we to believe? To find the truth, we have to devise certain tests. Because everything which has been thought out by people must be subservient to our intelligence.

"All the founders of religions, wherever they may be found on Earth, have claimed that God has revealed His eternal truth to them. Which one are we allowed to believe? We could, of course, start to investigate which one of those religions is the true one. However, we have been prejudiced in favor of the one into which we have been brought up. The first thing we have to force ourselves to do is to sacrifice all our prejudices to God, and then take the light of our intelligence and inspect every question that arises in our mind.

"I would like to mention that from the entire civilized world, at the most one-twentieth embraces the Roman Catholic religion. The inhabitants of the other parts of the world maintain that we idolize a human being, that we pray to a slice of bread; they insist that we commit idolatry, pray to humans, and they also maintain that the Church fathers contradict each other in their writings. To them, this is absolute proof that our holy books are not inspired by God.

"All the changes in religion which have occurred since the time of Adam, and which have been brought about by Abraham, Moses, King Solomon, Jesus Christ, and later the Church fathers, are proof of the fact that religion is a human undertaking. God himself has never changed, because He is unchangeable.

"God is everywhere. Nevertheless the Scriptures tell us that God looked for Adam in Paradise and asked, 'Adam, where art thou?' They also tell us that God walked in the Garden of Eden and talked with the devil about Job. My reason tells me that God cannot be passionate, because he would have to be subject to something stronger than Himself. Nevertheless, the sixth chapter of Genesis tells us that God was sorry to have created mankind, and his revenge is not idle. In our Christian religion God is so weak that he is unable to make Man do his bidding. He punishes him with water, then with fire, and Man remains invariably the same. He inspires the prophets. Man does not change. He has only one Son. He sends Him down to earth, and sacrifices Him because He loves the world so much! And still, Man does not change. What a ridiculous weakling has the Christian religion made out of its God!

"Everyone admits that God knows everything that will happen in eternity. Out of this follows that the God who allowed us to be born, knew beforehand that we were totally doomed, and that we were born to be unhappy throughout our lives.

"Nevertheless, the Scriptures tell us that God sent the prophets to warn us and to admonish us to change our ways. But, the all-knowing God must have known that Man would not change. It follows that the Scriptures themselves assume God to be a cheat. Does that make any sense to you? Is that in accord with your belief in God's infinite goodness?

"The all-powerful God has an opponent. The devil. Against God's will, the devil manages constantly to acquire about three-fourths of the souls of Mankind, the Mankind which God allegedly loved so much that he sacrificed His only begotten son! However, it seems to me that God couldn't care less about the fate of the majority of Mankind. Now, how stupid am

I supposed to be to believe all this idiotic nonsense?

"According to the Christian faith we only commit sins because we are led into temptation. The tempter, we are told, is the devil. All God has to do is to destroy the devil. Since he obviously has not done that it follows that either He is too weak, or unwilling. If He is unwilling He is unjust, if He is too weak He cannot be God.

"A fairly large amount of the servants of the Roman Catholic Church maintain that God gives us orders. However, we are incapable of following those orders, unless we are graced by God's infinite mercy which He only bestows upon those who have found favor in His eyes. Nevertheless, God punishes those who are incapable of following His orders. Don't you see the contradiction? The monstrous perversity of it all?

"Can you think of anything more miserable than the thought that God is vengeful, jealous, full of wrath? Can you imagine any more pitiful sight than a bunch of Roman Catholics, down upon their knees, praying to a bunch of saints? As if those saints, like God, were omnipresent? And what if those saints could read the hearts of these people and hear their voices?

"The ridiculous double-talk that we do everything to the greater glory of God. Do you truly believe that God's infinite glory could be increased one iota by the thoughts and deeds of little mortals? Could they increase anything on Him? Isn't God complete onto Himself?

"How could people possibly start an idiotic

belief which tells them that God is more happy and satisfied when they eat a herring instead of a chicken, onion soup instead of beef bouillon, filet of sole instead of a steak? And especially that this God would throw them in hell for all eternity if they happen to prefer a simple slice of bacon on a specific day rather than an expensive filleted fish?

"Oh, the stupid people who believe that they are capable of offending God. Even a prince and a king, if they use their brains, are above being insulted. Your religion teaches you that God is an avenging God, but at the same time you are being told that vengeance is sinful. The contradiction. On one hand we are assured that forgiveness of an insult is a virtue, while on the other hand our entire concept of original sin, the eternal threat of hell, is God's revenge for an unintentional insult.

"We are being told that, if there is a God, we do need a cult. But nobody can deny that God existed before the world, and at that time a cult was obviously not needed. And since the creation of the world, this earth has crawled with all sorts of animals who are obviously not in need of a cult. Without people, there would still be a world, there would still be animals, there would still be a God, but there would be no cult. People suffer from the sickly delusion that God cannot do His work without their meager help! They judge the acts of God according to their own little deeds.

"The Christian religion gives us an entirely false picture of God. According to its teachings, our human justice is based on the justice of God. But, if we apply the rules of our human justice, we would have to condemn God for his vile actions, especially those against His own son, against Adam, against the multitude of populations who have never had a chance to learn about His existence, and—most important of all—against all those little innocent children who died before they were given the chance of being baptized.

"According to the teachings of Christianity, we have to strive for perfection. In the opinion of the saints and the fathers of the Church, virginity is more perfect than the married state. It follows therefore, clearly, that the Christian concept of perfection equals the total destruction of the human race in the shortest time possible, because if we were to follow the exhortations of our priest literally, it would not take more than sixty or eighty years and the human race would have vanished from the face of the earth. Could a religion like that, such an abominable perversion, truly be inspired by God?

"And, since I am mentioning it, can you imagine anything more stupid than the idea that priests, monks and nuns, total strangers, have to do our praying for us. A communication with God through others? Their concept of God is as if He was a king on a throne who has to be pacified by lackeys.

"What an unbelievable nonsense is the idea that God caused us to be born so that we would do nothing else but everything that is against our nature, and that we are doomed to be as miserable as we possibly can be! We are required to give up everything which can satisfy the passions and desires that God has planted into our being. No tyrant could be worse. In all mankind the fiend has not yet been born who follows us with such sickening vengeance from the moment that we are born till the day we die, with the added possibility of eternal torture in hell.

"To be a perfect Christian, one has to be ignorant, capable of blind faith, disdain all pleasures, give up joy, honor, riches, leave friends and family, and maintain virginity. In short, one is supposed to do everything which is against so-called Nature, while this same Nature has been ordained by God, and surely is part of His unalterable will. These unbelievable contradictions are supposed to belong to a Being which is all-knowing, all-just and all-good!

"In my opinion, since God is the creator and master of all things, we are obliged to use our facilities for the purposes for which they have been created. We can try and find out those purposes with the intelligence and the feelings with which God has endowed us. It is our duty to find out His goal and purpose, and to bring that in accord with the goals and purposes of human society. Obviously Man has not been created to do nothing. He is supposed to do something which serves his own purposes and which does not damage society. God has not created a multitude of people just for the benefit of a few; He does not want the happiness of a single person, He wants the happiness of all. Therefore we are obliged to be of service to each other, provided that this does not damage one branch or the other of human society. If we keep this in mind, we will all do our duty towards God. The whole rest of the religious structure can then be summarily dismissed as pretentiousness and prejudice.

"All religions, without exception, are the work of men. There is not a single one that does not have its martyrs and saints who have allegedly performed miracles. What do the miracles of the Christian religion prove to me, if other religions claim the same miracles?

"In the first place, all religions are based on fear. Thunderstorms, snow and hail, and unbearable heat destroyed the fruits of early Man's labors. They were at an absolute loss to defend themselves against those forces of Nature, they were at their mercy, and consequently they assumed that there had to be a force stronger and more powerful than themselves. They assumed that these forces would be appeased by prayer and sacrifices, and that these 'gods' found a special delight in torturing defenseless people. In the course of the centuries, and in various countries, many people decided to organize those beliefs and form religions. They invented the most fantastic and incredible gods. They organized themselves into orders and societies whose members had to be subdued and kept in fear. They became their leaders, political as well as religious. They realized that they could only remain in business if they kept fear among their followers and ordered them to keep their passions in check. They also realized that mere exhortation was not enough, that they had to hold out rich rewards and horrible punishments. Only then can people be brought to obedience.

"These politicians invented our religions. Every single one of them promises rewards, and threatens with punishments. This way they have induced the majority of Mankind to act against the natural impulses, passions and desires. Some of those passions, I must admit, are reprehensible. They include the desire to possess the neighbor's wife, or to rape his daughter. Among them are the impulse to wreak vengeance in a terrible manner, or to soil another's good reputation to make one's own questionable deeds seem less reprehensible by comparison. Some religions have even invented the concept of honor. There is nothing wrong with that in itself, because in general this is to the greater good of society and can, at times, be useful for the individual.

"I don't doubt the fact that there is a God Who has created everything and Who has set this universe in motion according to His own laws. Everything is therefore necessary and interlocking. There is no chance. The three dice which a player throws upon the table, will show necessarily a certain amount of eyes. The number of eyes depends upon the manner which the dice were shaken and the strength with which they were thrown. All the actions of our life can be compared with a game of dice. All our actions are a direct result of previous actions, which in turn, are a result of their previous actions. We can go back and forth into eternity.

"Therefore, when I am told that a person wants something because he desires it, I consider that a meaningless statement. Throughout our life we are forced to do something as it is dictated by the combination of our intellect, our passions and our own previous deeds. Life, indeed, is a game of dice.

"Let me assure you, my dearest friend, that I do believe that we should love God. Not because He desires us to do so, but because He is good. We should obey the human laws because those laws have been designed to protect the best interests of society. Since we are a part of that society, they are also in our own best interest.

"I have only told you this, because I consider you my best friend. This slight discourse is the result of twenty years of study, and thinking, and long, arduous, sleepless nights. I have tried to the best of my knowledge to separate wisdom from superstition, truth from lies. Let us therefore conclude, my dearest, that the joys we are giving each other are pure and innocent, they cannot insult God, and they do not insult society because we keep them secret. For all appearances we stick to the rules of propriety and the laws of men. If we were not to fulfill both conditions, I admit that we would excite the prurient interests. Our example could lead young and innocent people astray."

"But," protested Madame Catherine, "if our pleasures are as innocent as you say, and I am inclined to believe you, why don't we go out and teach the world how to enjoy their pleasures? Why don't we tell our friends and acquaintances about the results of your metaphysical research and let them share our peace of mind and our happiness? Haven't you told me a hundred times that your greatest joy would be to make people happy?"

"Yes, I did. And I did not lie," answered the abbot. "But beware of telling the ignorant masses about self-evident truths. They don't feel it in their bones, and they would only misinterpret their meanings. Only those who know how to think intelligently, who understand the art of keeping their passions in balance, and who will not be brought down to their knees by others, are worthy of knowing the truth as I have come to understand it. But men and women of that caliber are a rarity. Among a hundred thousand of them, not twenty are capable of thinking, and of those twenty there may not be more than one capable of some original thought. Most of us will be swayed by our ruling passion. That is the main reason why we have to be exceedingly careful about voicing thoughts like the one we have been talking about this morning.

"Very few people understand the necessity of caring about the happiness of their fellow men as the only way to secure happiness for themselves. That is why it is dangerous to point out the inherent weakness of religions, because it is the only thing that forces them to care about others. The rules and regulations, no matter how silly and stupid the reasoning behind them, makes them work for the greater good of society, and therefore for themselves. Religions are a mere veil, the real incitements are the promises of eternal happiness and the threats of eternal damnation. These fears and hopes are the guiding forces for the weak, and their number is huge. Honor, justice and concern for the common good guides those who can think. Alas, their number is so small as to be almost negligible."

The abbot fell silent. Madame Catherine thanked him in terms that left no doubt of her happiness. "You are the most darling friend any woman could wish for," she exclaimed, embracing the abbot with ardent fire. "How lucky am I to be in love with a man who can think as clearly as you do. Be assured that I will never misuse your confidence in me, and I promise to follow your intelligent principles for the rest of my life."

They exchanged kisses, lingering passionately in each other's arms. I was bored silly, especially since I was sitting in a very uncomfortable position. But finally my pious father confessor and his learned pupil went downstairs, and I ran to my room where I locked myself securely in. Only a few moments later the maid called that Madame Catherine would enjoy the pleasure of my company. I told her that I begged Madame to be excused for a few more hours, since I had slept very badly that night. I spent the time writing down everything I had heard.

The days passed in pastoral tranquility. We became the best of friends. Suddenly, one day, my mother arrived, informing me that we had to depart the next day to Paris. We had dinner with Madame Catherine for the last time, and I said my farewells, crying hot tears. The darling woman caressed me, and gave me many a good advice without making me feel inferior. Unfortunately the abbot had gone to a nearby town, where his duties would keep him for at least a week. I did not see him. Mother and I returned to Volno where we spent the night. That next morning we took the coach to Lyons and from there we transferred to Paris.

* * *

As I already told you, my mother had decided to make this trip, because a merchant in Paris owed her a considerable amount of money. Mother's entire fortune depended on his payment. She, too, had enormous debts, and business was bad. Before she left Volno, she had given power of attorney to one of her distant relatives. This man ruined us completely. One day, mother learned that all our possessions, including the house in Volno had been sold to satisfy her distant cousin's gambling debts and that same day she found out that the Parisian merchant had gone bankrupt. This was too much for her. Within a week she died of a brain fever.

There I was. Alone in the big city; no friends, no family, no one to take care of me but myself. I was, as I had been frequently told, very pretty, I possessed considerable knowledge but I had no practical experience.

Before her death, mother had handed me a purse with four hundred gold pieces in it. Since I had plenty of linen and clothes, I considered myself rich. Nevertheless, my first thought was to enter a convent and become a nun. Fortunately I gave up the idea when I remembered in a flash all my previous misery and suffering with the nuns in Volno. Besides, the woman who lived next door to me and with whom I had a fleeting acquaintance, gave me very good advice.

This woman, a certain Mrs. Bois-Laurier, lived in a furnished apartment adjoining mine in the same hotel. She was so kind to take care of me in the first weeks after mother had died, and she did not leave me out of her sight for one single moment. I was eternally grateful to her for that and felt very much obliged to her.

As you know yourself, Mrs. Bois-Laurier was one of those unfortunate women who had been forced since early childhood to serve the bestial desires of the public. And, like so many others, she had assumed a different name when she could afford to live as a respectable woman. She had bought herself a pension with the earnings of her previous profession.

The mourning which consumed me those first few weeks made way for some serious thinking. I began to get worried about my future. I confided in my new friend and told her about the bad financial state I was in, expressing my fears about my terrible predicament. But she had a healthy intelligence which had been strengthened by experience.

"Oh, you are so dumb," she told me one morning. "Never fear about the future. The future is as unpredictable for the rich as it is for the poor. And you, my dear child, have no reason to worry at all. At least far less than others. With your nice figure, your pretty face and clear complexion, with your intelligence and sparkling wit, a girl should never have to be afraid about the future. Especially not if she knows how to be smart. No, my dear, you don't have to be afraid. Leave everything to me, and I will find you what you need. I think you need a good husband, since you seem to be intent on doing it with the blessings of the sacrament. Oh, my dear child, you have no idea how dangerous such a wish can be. But, let me take care of it. A woman of forty with the experience of one of sixty knows precisely what a girl like you needs. I will take the place of your mother and I will introduce you to the possibilities of the great world. I shall introduce you tonight to my uncle, who is a rich man, a very decent man, and I am sure that he will find someone for you who deserves you."

I threw my arms around Mrs. Bois-Laurier's neck and thanked her profusely. I must admit that the soothing words had wiped away my fears, and I was convinced that from now on my future would be rosy.

How stupid can a girl be when she has a lot of confidence and absolutely no experience. The lessons of the good abbot had opened my eyes and I knew that we had to obey the laws of God and Man and I also knew that at times we could break the laws of Man when they were in contradiction with the laws of God. Not to be caught was the main concern. But, alas, I had no idea of the depths of human passion.

Everything I saw and heard seemed as justified as the ideas of Madame Catherine and the abbot. I thought that the only villain in the world was that infamous priest, Father Dirrag. Oh, poor innocent girl! What an incredible mistake! The rich Mr. Bois arrived that evening around five o'clock at the home of his niece. The first few hours of his visit were spent on something else than talking about my plight. The niece was, as she herself admitted, too clever to show me immediately to her uncle, because she did not want, as she put it, to upset him with the immediate view of my considerable charms. She wanted to talk to him alone and it was past seven o'clock when she called for me. I greeted him as demurely as I possibly could, but he seemingly did not deem it necessary to get up. He invited me to sit down upon the chair that was put beside his huge easy chair upon which he was half-sitting, half-reclining. His enormous belly was covered only by a shirt and his manner was like that of most financiers. Nevertheless, I thought he was a very nice man. He paid me many a compliment, including one about the firmness of my thighs. Suddenly he stretched out his pudgy hand and squeezed me so strongly that I cried out with pain.

"My niece has told me about you," he said gruffly, without bothering about the pain he had caused me. "Goddamn, what beautiful eyes. Marvelous teeth, and the firmest flesh I have felt in a long time. Oh, I promise you, we'll make something out of you. Tomorrow I will make an appointment for you with a colleague of mine. You shall meet him at dinnertime. The man veritably swims in gold, and if I know him as well as I think I do, I assure you that he'll instantly fall in love with you. Just be nice to him. He is a man of honor, and he will satisfy you completely. Well, children, it's getting late," he added, buttoning his vest and hoisting himself out of the chair. "Good night, my children, give me a kiss, and treat me like you would your own father. And you, dear niece," he continued, "see to it that she is on time in my pleasure home, and that there is enough to eat and drink for all."

When the rich uncle had left, Mrs. Bois-Laurier said to me, "You can congratulate yourself, Therese. My uncle liked you very, very much. Sometimes his manners leave something to be desired, but he has a heart of pure gold. He is a true friend. You know how much I like you and therefore you must let me take care of all the little details. Just follow my advice to the letter, and I assure you that soon you will not have a worry in the world. One thing I must impress upon you: For God's sake, don't be a prude. That could ruin everything we are trying to do for you. With prissiness nobody has ever managed to make a fortune."

I had dinner with my newfound protectress and she managed to find out all about my life, my thoughts and ideas with a very clever line of questioning.

She was very open and honest, and this caused me, too, to make many confessions. I talked much more than I really wanted, and it seemed that she was rather shocked to find out that I had never had a lover. However, she was quickly put at ease when I confessed to her that certain ways of love were not unknown to me and that I had already tasted a considerable amount of sexual satisfaction. She embraced me, kissed me and tried to do everything in her power to talk me into spending that night with her. However, I declined politely, went to my room, filled with joyful thoughts about my promising future.

The women of Paris are vivacious and helpful. That next morning, Mrs. Bois-Laurier entered my room, woke me up and asked me if she could help me dress. She offered me to curl my hair, but, since I was still in mourning for my dear mother, I declined and kept my little bonnet on my head. Bois-Laurier was very curious and exceedingly prankish that day. She inspected with her eyes and her hands all my charms before she reached me my chemise. She insisted on helping me put it on. Suddenly it seemed that a thought hit her, and she exclaimed, "Wait a minute, you little rascal! You are putting on your chemise without having brushed your pussy! Where is your bidet?"

"I really don't know what you mean. What is a bidet?"

"What? No bidet? Don't let any of your suitor's hear that you don't have a girl's most important piece of furniture. My God, child, it's almost more important than a clean chemise. For today you can use mine, but tomorrow, it's got to be the first thing you will have to buy for yourself."

Mrs. Bois-Laurier's bidet was brought into my room; she made me sit down upon it and despite my violent protests she insisted on brushing my pussy. She used a lot of lavender water and I could not figure out why she washed my private parts so thoroughly. But then, I did not have the vaguest idea of the big party she had intended for my pussy . . .

That afternoon we drove to the pleasure home of the uncle, which was situated outside the city. Uncle Bernard was already there when we arrived, together with his friend and colleague, a man of about thirty-eight to forty years old. He was reasonably handsome. His clothes were very expensive and he wore many rings, flashing the diamonds with seeming delight. His snuff box of pure gold, his gold watch on a heavy gold chain, and several other pieces of golden jewelry seemed to play an important part in his life. But he nevertheless deigned to walk toward me, take my hand in his and look me over very carefully. "Goddammit, she is pretty!" he exclaimed. "Upon my word, she is charming; I swear, I'll make her my little wife."

"Oh, dear sir," I stammered, "you honor me greatly, and as soon as I no longer . . ."

"No, no," he interrupted, "don't you worry your pretty little head. I will take care of everything and I will see to it that you are totally satisfied."

The servant announced that dinner was served. We sat down and I was pleased to know that Mrs. Bois-Laurier knew what form of conversation was acceptable and usual in the better circles of Paris. She was simply brilliant, her wit sparkling, and she set a marvelous example for me to follow. However, I did not really feel at ease. I did not say much, and the few things I said seemed to make the wrong impression. The two gentlemen looked at each other with lifted eyebrows and my future fiancé became rather quiet. He looked at me with big eyes and it was obvious that his mind was racing. It seemed to me that he regretted his enthusiastic outburst when he first saw me. However, a few glasses of champagne must have enlivened his imagination because soon he did not seem to care about my rather sober replies and he laughed at everything I said. He became more insistent, and I became a little bit more pliable. His good looks impressed me and it was obvious that he was a man of means and standing in Paris society. His hands took all sorts of liberties and I did not dare to push them away because I assumed that it was a form of good manners and I hated to act against the rules of good Paris society. I had to think about the splendid advice of the good abbot which proved to me that violation of the rules of society was much against God's intentions. I also believed that I should let things go as they were, because Uncle Bernard and his niece were sitting on the sofa in the other room and the liberties uncle and niece were taking with each other exceeded everything I had ever witnessed in Volno. Anyhow, I resisted the bold advances of Uncle Bernard's colleague so slightly that he assumed he would have no trouble whatsoever with becoming a little bit more serious. He invited me to sit down upon the bed opposite the sofa upon which we were seated. "Oh, I would be delighted, dear sir," I answered innocently. "I am quite sure we will be far more comfortable because I am afraid that your present position on my lap must be terribly tiresome for you."

You see, he had sat himself squarely upon my lap. Without further ado he lifted me off the sofa and carried me toward the bed. I saw that Mrs. Bois-Laurier and her uncle got up and left the room. I, too, wanted to get up and follow them, but the passionate gentleman with whom I had been left alone seemed to have different ideas. He told me in no uncertain terms that he was deeply in love with me, that I drove him out of his mind, and that he intended to make me happy right on the spot. At the same time he had grabbed my skirts and lifted them high above my waist. He held me with one hand and with the other he took his long and rock-hard member out of his trousers. He pushed his knee between my thighs; by pressing and squeezing he managed to part them. He patted my pussy and covered my face with slobbering kisses. He tried to wiggle his tongue between my lips and when I chanced to look down I saw the monstrous size of his prick. It reminded me of the holy water sprinkler which Father Dirrag used to chase the evil spirits out of the bodies of his penitents. It was huge and the red knob was throbbing.

Almost simultaneously I remembered what the abbot had said about the results of those actions. My innocent cooperation suddenly changed into a burning fury. I grabbed the bold rascal by his necktie and held him at arm's length so that he was incapable of fulfilling his attack. Without taking my eyes off the enemy, because I was afraid he would penetrate me with one mighty shove, I hollered as loud as I could for Mrs. Bois-Laurier's assistance. Whether she had been in league with my so-called fiancé or not, she could hardly do anything else but come to my aid and scold the bold knave about his clumsy attack upon my honor.

Furious about the insult, I wanted to scratch the gentleman's eyes out. I told him in no uncertain terms what I thought about his miserable attitude and Uncle Bernard and his niece had the greast trouble to restrain me and prevent me from counterattacking the man who had tried to make me pregnant. We struggled silently. Finally, this silence was interrupted by the loudest laughter. The monster who had not ten minutes ago tried to attack me, was splitting his sides in one outburst of laughter after another. He had to sit down and wipe

585

the tears from his face with a silken handkerchief. He put his tool, which now hung limply down, back in his trousers and said, "I'll be damned. That little provincial bitch. Well, you must admit that I scared you, didn't I? Oh, oh, I can't believe it. They still make them that way in the villages. Such a silly goose. She doesn't have the slightest inkling what we were supposed to do here! Just imagine, my dear Bernard," he continued, "I put the young lady down upon the bed, I lift up her skirts, I show her my prick and what do you think happens? That stupid little goose thinks there is something wrong with that! She makes a noise as if she is going to be murdered, succeeds in getting the two of you out here and then goes into some kind of hideous spasm which would make you believe I did God-knows-what to her. I thought I would die laughing!" And he started to laugh again. But suddenly he turned serious and said, "But listen, Bois-Laurier, don't procure any of these idiots for me in the future. I am not a school teacher, and I have no desire to go through the trouble of telling every silly little goose from the provinces how to behave in my presence. You would do the little girl a favor if you taught her how she is supposed to act in a big city. Especially if she intends to meet other people of the rank and standing of Bois and me!"

I must admit that listening to this strange conversation made my head spin. I was totally flabbergasted, and I did not say another word. Bernard Bois and the gentleman disappeared without bothering to say good-bye and I lay half-conscious in the arms of Mrs. Bois-

Laurier who murmured something between her teeth to the extent that I, myself, was not entirely free of blame. We got into the coach that was waiting outside and drove back to our hotel.

The excitement had been too much for me. As soon as I was back in my room I broke down and burst out in tears. My chaste friend was very nervous and wanted to know exactly how I felt about the whole affair. She took extremely good care of me and did not leave my side for a moment. She tried to convince me that all men are curious and invent numerous ways to find out how far the girl they intend to marry is willing to go before they have exchanged the vows. It also gives them an excellent opportunity to discover how much the girl already knows about the joys of love. She closed her beautiful speech with the assurance that I had handled it correctly, though she hated to say that my vivaciousness might well have killed the goose that laid the golden eggs.

I answered furiously that I was no longer a little child, that I was very well aware what that miserable bastard would have done to me if I had given him the chance and, I added rather rudely, not any amount of money in the world was large enough to pay for having my body used that way. And in my excitement I told her what I had seen between Miss Eradice and Father Dirrag, and about the lessons which Madame Catherine and the abbot had given me.

To make a long story short, the clever Bois-Laurier managed to get the entire story out of me, and once she knew everything, her attitude toward me changed magically. She had noticed that I was rather unfamiliar with the customs and morals of the world and she was therefore very surprised about my knowledge of moral philosophy, religion and metaphysics.

Mrs. Bois-Laurier was a very good-natured soul. She embraced me, full of love, and exclaimed, "Oh, how happy I am to get to know a girl like you. You have just taken away the veil from my mind, and in a flash I realize the mystery which was the cause of my unhappy life. I cannot help but constantly think about my former profession and I know that I will never be able to rest. Who, more than I, is afraid of the punishments of hell with which we are constantly threatened? And you, my dearest angel, have proven to me beyond a shadow of a doubt that my so-called crimes were involuntary. The beginning of my life was an incredible mixture of cruelties, and though it takes me all the courage I can muster, I will repay confidence with confidence and your wisdom with my experience.

"Therefore, dear Therese, I shall tell you the story of my life. It will teach you about the moods and tricks of men, and it is time for you to learn about them. They will contribute to your conviction that vice and virtue depend entirely upon temperament and education."

And she began to tell me the story of her life.

* * *

THE STORY OF MRS. BOIS-LAURIER

You see before you, my dear Therese, a strange creature. I am neither a man nor a woman, neither a girl nor a widow, nor a wife. I have been a professional prostitute and yet, I am still a virgin. I am sure that you will think I am crazy, but please, be patient, and I will give you a full explanation. Capricious Nature has the path of delight which makes blooming women out of shy virgins blocked with an obstacle that cannot be overcome. The entrance is closed by a piece of skin that even the thinnest arrow Capid carries with him cannot penetrate. And you will be even more surprised to find out that nobody has ever succeeded in talking me into undergoing the simple operation which could cure my affliction. I am fully capable of enjoying the delights of love, and many girls who were born with a similar thick piece of skin in front of their pussy's entrance have shown me their operated parts and I have witnessed their pleasures with men. Ever since I was a little girl I knew that one day I was going to be a whore. And the mistake Nature had made seemed destined to ruin any profitable career. But, odd as it may sound, it has contributed greatly to my happiness.

I have already told you that my story will teach you a lot about the strange ways of men. I could talk to you about the many positions they have invented to penetrate a woman and to increase their carnal pleasures. But all these voluptuous positions have been described so completely by the famous Pietro Aretino, who lived in the sixteenth century, that there is not much left to say. What I am going to talk to you about is those flights of fancy, those curious services which many men desire from us, giving them the greatest delight and ecstasy, either because they have a preference for it or because they suffer from a physical defect. I'll come directly to the point.

I have never known my father or my mother. A woman, named Lefort, who lived in Paris, and who was reasonably well-to-do, had raised me as her daughter. One day she took me aside, very secretively, and said, "Dearest, you are not my daughter, and it is about time that I set the record straight and explained a few things to you. You were about four years old, and you must have lost your way to your home when I found you wandering in the streets. I took you into my home and till today, out of love and Christian charity, I have clothed and fed you. I have tried to find out who your parents were, but despite all my efforts I have never been able to discover them.

"You have obviously noticed that I am not very rich or important, but nevertheless I have spared neither money nor trouble to give you a good education. But now you have to secure your own happiness. And, to be able to do this, I will make the following deal with you. You are very well-built, pretty and better developed than many a girl of your tender age. The president of the bank, my benefactor and neighbor, is in love with you. He has decided to keep you, provided you are willing to do his bidding. Well, Manon, he expects an answer today. What do you want me to tell him? I shall be honest with you. If you refuse his proposal, I shall be forced to throw you out of my house, today. You have to accept his offer and do whatever he desires from you, because if you don't, I'll no longer be able to feed and clothe you."

This devastating news, together with the harsh conditions, filled me with a terrible fear. It was as if an icy hand had gripped my heart and tried to squeeze it out of my bosom. I burst out in tears, but my mother knew no mercy. I had to make an immediate decision. After I had been told what I might expect, and after I had been informed about the ways a man may know a woman, I promised to do whatever was desired from me. Mrs. Lefort assured me that she would still care for me and love me as her own daughter, and she allowed me to keep calling her mother.

The next morning she gave me full instructions about my new profession, told me about my duties as a whore, and pressed upon me the importance of doing exactly what the president might desire of me. Then she made me take off all my clothes till I was completely naked; she bathed me from top to toe, curled my hairs, brushed my pussy and washed it lavishly with lavender water. Then she handed me clothes which were prettier and cleaner than anything I had ever worn.

At four o'clock that afternoon we arrived at the home of the president. He was a tall, gray-haired, skinny man, whose tallow skin made his wrinkly face look yellow. His face almost disappeared behind a ridiculously high, white-powdered wig, which made his neck look scrawnier than it already was. This honorable personality invited mother and me to sit down, and he said in a very serious tone of voice to my mother, "Well, well, well. So this is the little creature. She is very pretty. I have always told you that she had all the possibilities to become well-built and beautiful. The money that she has cost me was spent well, I see. But are you sure that she is still a virgin? We'll have to check that at once, Mrs. Lefort."

My mother made me lie down backwards upon a couch in the room, she lifted my skirts and petticoats, and was about to spread my legs when the president barked at her, "Come now, come now. These damned females have a positive mania of always showing the front! Now, let's turn her around!"

"Oh, I beg you a thousand pardons, my dear sir!" exclaimed my mother, cowardly wringing her hands. "I understood that you wanted to see if she . . . hurry, Manon, get up! Put one knee on this chair and bend your body forward as far as you can!"

As a victim I did everything I was ordered to do. I was terribly humiliated, but I did not dare to refuse the woman who had treated me as her daughter, and I was terribly impressed by the importance of the president. My dear mother lifted my skirts again, the president came closer, bending over to look, while my mother spread the lips of my cunt apart. The honorable gentleman stuck one finger in and tried, without success, to penetrate. He said to my mother, "Beautiful, beautiful. I am absolutely satisfied. There is no doubt in my mind, she is still a virgin. Now, I want her to stay in that position and I want you to give her beautiful buttocks some light slaps with your bare hands."

The command was fulfilled, and a deep silence followed. My mother held my skirts with her left hand, and with the right hand she slapped my buttocks rhythmically, but lightly. I was very curious what the president would be doing and I turned my head slightly so that I could have a better look. There he was, sitting about two feet behind my buttocks, peering up my ass with a little looking glass, and his hand was busy shaking something dark and limp which was hanging between his legs. He never succeeded in getting it up, though he was trying very hard. His hand flew up and down, but the thing remained limp and ugly as ever. My position was not too uncomfortable, and my mother's slapping had brought me a rather pleasant glow. Nevertheless I was glad when, after about twenty minutes, the honorable gentleman got up off the floor, dragged himself on his spindly old legs toward his comfortable big leather chair. He handed my mother a purse and told her that it contained the one hundred gold pieces he had promised her. He honored me with a kiss upon my cheek and he told me that he would personally see to it that I would have everything my little heart desired, provided that I always stayed as nice to him as I had been today, and he would let me know when he needed my services again.

When mother and I had returned home I thought seriously about everything I had seen and heard during those past twenty-four hours. My thoughts were like the ones you had, after you had witnessed the treatment Father Dirrag gave Miss Eradice. I started to remember a lot of the things that had been said and done since my childhood in the home of Mrs. Lefort. And while I was still trying to make any sense out of the multitude of thoughts that stormed through my brain, my mother entered my room and rudely interrupted my daydreams.

"I now have nothing to hide from you my dearest Manon," she said, embracing me, "because you are now my accomplice in a profession which I have profitably conducted for over twenty years. Listen therefore carefully to what I have to tell you. Follow my advice and you will be able to get full compensation for what you have to suffer from the president. Ten years ago I took you into my home upon his express orders. During that time he has given me a modest yearly income which I have spent entirely for your education. Yes, I have even added some of my own money to his. He has promised me that he would give each of us a hundred gold pieces as soon as you are old enough for him to deflower you. He wanted to be the one to take your virginity. But the lecher has forgotten one thing. When you were old enough, he was too old. It is not our fault that he could not get that limp and wrinkled prick of his stiff enough to shove it up your cunt and take your maidenhead away. Since he could not do it, he has only given me one hundred gold pieces, because you are still a virgin and have not earned your share. It is too bad for you, but look at it this way: You can still sell it. Therefore, my dear daughter, I don't want you to worry. I will find you someone else, and you will earn more than the measly hundred gold pieces the old piker had promised for your defloration. You are young, you are pretty and, most important, you are not well-known, yet. It will be a pleasure to spend the entire hundred gold pieces that were my share on a new and beautiful wardrobe for you. Let yourself be guided by me, and I assure you that together we will make more money than I used to make in former years when I had ten or twelve girls working for me."

She had a lot more to tell me, but one thing was terribly clear to me, and that was that my dear mama had kept one hundred gold pieces all to herself. We made a pact. She would spend the hundred gold pieces on a new wardrobe, and I would repay her out of my first earnings with a modest twenty percent interest. After I had paid her off, we would share my earnings on a fifty-fifty basis, for which she would guide my career and continue to take care of me as if I were really her beloved daughter.

Mrs. Lefort had an inexhaustible supply of good friends in Paris. In less than four weeks I was introduced to at least twenty of them and one after the other tried in vain to rob me of my virginity. Mrs. Lefort was a very careful woman and she made it a habit to be paid in advance. She was, by now, convinced that nobody would ever succeed in tasting the joy of taking my maidenhead.

These twenty athletes were followed by more than six hundred others in the course of the following five years. Priests, officers, civil servants, lawyers and financiers made me take the most ridiculous positions, they contorted my body and theirs in the fruitless attempts of shoving their pricks into my minute little orifice. Needless to say, none of them ever succeeded. Either the sacrifice was brought at the entrance of my temple, squirting the jism into my pubic hairs, or the tool was bent and my virginity remained unharmed. Finally the story of my impenetrable cunt became too well-known and the police got interested in it. The commissioner decided to put a stop to all the fruitless attacks upon my innocence. Fortunately we were forewarned and Mrs. Lefort decided that the time had come to put a little distance between us and the city of Paris in the interest of our safety. We moved away about thirty miles into the province.

Three months later the heat had cooled down, because a distant relative of Mrs. Lefort, who happened to work in one of the police departments, had taken it upon himself to quiet down the upset feelings of his colleagues. We paid him thirteen gold pieces for his troubles, and returned to Paris, brimming with ideas for a new project.

My mother, who had for a long time insisted that I would undergo an operation, had realized that my affliction was a true gold mine. I did not need medical inspection, there was absolutely no fear of pregnancy, and I did not have to go to confession because the mortal sin of loosing my virginity without the holy sacrament of marriage had never been committed. Unfortunately I, myself, found absolutely no enjoyment in my profession and I was forced to use the same means with which you, too, relieved yourself.

As I told you, we had come up with a few new plans, and as soon as our voluntary banishment was over we went back to Paris and moved into another home, without, for one thing, bothering to notify the bank president of our return. We took a home in the Faubourg St. Germain.

The first acquaintance I made was with a certain baroness who had served the joys of famous men of the world together with her sister, a countess. She now graced the household of a rich English bachelor with her title and the sparse remnants of her former charm. He paid for them way out of proportion, but he was rich and happy with the mere idea of possessing a member of the nobility. Another Englishman, his friend, saw me and fell in love. We made an agreement. I confided in him and my confession delighted him instead of being repulsive to him. His first experience with a woman had been rather sickening to him, and he had sworn that he would never touch another one. Ever since, his hand had been his sole lover. However, he needed some additional excitement. His pleasure could only be served when I would stand in front of him with lifted skirts, while he jacked away furiously at his tool. But a maid, hired for the express purpose, had to cut little curls of pubic hair from my belly. Without this peculiar preparation the man was totally incapable of getting a hard-on and ten pairs of hands would not have been enough to get his prick stiff, let alone squeeze a single drop of jism out of his balls.

Minette, the third sister of the baroness, had a friend with a similar peculiarity. Minette was tall and rather skinny. Her face was ugly, her skin sallow and her temper was not always the most pleasant. But she had beautiful eyes, and her voice was fabulous. She tried to show off her passion and her intelligence but she actually possessed neither one. But her voice could charm the dead. And it was this beautiful singing organ which had slowly given her a bevy of admirers. The one she had at the time I knew her was only capable of getting his tool stiff when he heard the sound of her marvelous melodious voice. Only when she was singing was he able to shoot off his load.

One day the three of us had a big party. We sang and danced, made a lot of jokes and talked about all sorts of experiences, and also about the peculiarity of my cunt. We showed each other our charms, and mine was unanimously elected to be the most interesting. Minette's lover became excited, he pulled her toward the edge of the bed, shoved up her dress and stuck his prick up her pussy. He then ordered her to sing. After a few introductory warbles, Minette began a song in waltz tempo; her lover tore into her, shoved it up and pulled it back, the muscles of his face began to twitch as if indicating the rhythm and his buttocks pumped up and down to set the speed. I was lying on the same bed, looking at this ridiculous performance, laughing till the tears ran down my face. Everything went fine till Minette started to reach her climax, before her lover had reached his. She suddenly hit a sour note and fell out of rhythm. Then she shuddered and emitted a shrill shriek.

The effect upon her lover was devastating!

"Oh, you goddamned broad, you!" exclaimed the music lover. "That horrible note went through bone and marrow. And look what you did!" He was furious and pulled out his tool. The member which had been so proudly erect, which had been used like a conductor's stick, had, at the sound of the flat note, turned into a limp rag.

My girl friend was desperate and she tried everything in her power to bring her hero back to life. But the most tender kisses and the softest caresses were unable to bring about an erection. His tool remained limp and useless. "Oh, my dearest friend," Minette cried, exasperated, "don't leave me. Only my love for you, and my fiery passion, caused my voice to break; please, don't leave me at this moment of my happiness. Manon, dearest Manon, help me! Show him your pussy! That will bring his powers back. It will surely make him regain his strength and save my life. I would die if he could not bring it to a finish. Please, Bibi," she said to her lover, "put her down upon the bed and make her take the same position as my sister, the countess. Manon's friendship for me guarantees that she will do it for you."

During this entire ridiculous exchange I had been laughing. And really, has anyone ever seen somebody get fucked while she is singing? And then, can you imagine a man who fucks like a bull suddenly turning into a zero because the woman he screws hits a sour note? Of course, I realized that the baroness' sister was not as deeply in love as she pretended to be, but I could understand her exasperation because she was being paid very handsomely for her odd services. But I still did not know the role of the countess whose place I was supposed to take. I was not left in the dark very long. I had to turn over on my belly, and they put about three or four pillows under me. My arse stuck high up into the air. Then they bunched my skirts, petticoat and chemise under me so that I was absolutely naked from the navel on down. Minette lay down upon her back and her head rested between my thighs. The hairs around my cunt framed her face like a wig: Bibi undressed his darling Minette and laid himself down on top of her, resting upon his hands. In this position her face, my cunt and my arse were all right in front of his nose. He licked and slurped without distinction. Now his tongue was between Minette's lips, then between my thighs, up my arsehole, into my pussy, and back between Minette's lips again. He even started to lick my buttocks. And meanwhile his member started to grow again and he began to pump away. Minette's hand guided his member back into her cunny and she began to swear and move her behind rapidly. I had turned my head around to get a good look and laughed till I ran out of breath. After they had labored for what seemed like an hour, the two lovers finally reached their climax.

Not long after that I met a bishop who had the rather dangerous habit of roaring during the act of copulation like a maddened bull. Aside from the fact that it compromised some of his female visitors, it also endangered their eardrums. Whether it was to increase his satisfaction, or because of some organic disorder, as soon as His Eminence felt the tingling of his climax approach, he started to scream and roar, "Aaah—eeek; aah—eeek!" The eeks and aahs were in direct proportion to the strength of his orgasm; the louder his roaring, the greater his ecstasy and satisfaction. The force of the fat prelate's ejaculation could always be measured by the loudness of his roaring shrieks. Were it not for the fact that His Eminence's manservant had been smart enough to cover the doors and walls of the bishop's mansion with thick, sound dampening mattresses, the souls in Heaven would have been disturbed every time that holy man came.

I can go on almost indefinitely with descriptions of the strange things men do while they are in the act of coitus. With some it is the preliminaries, with others it is the additional little things they desire. Most of them wish a woman to be in a most peculiar position while they fuck them.

One day I was brought to the rear entrance of the home of one of this country's richest and most famous men. Every morning for the past fifty years he had received the visit of a girl he had never seen before. That particular morning it was my turn, and I had been fully instructed as to what to expect and how I was supposed to behave. The great, gray-haired lecher could only come in one particular way. He opened the back door personally, and, according to my instructions, I instantly dropped the clothes I was wearing and stood before him mother-naked. He sat down upon a big easy chair and with a serious face I turned around and offered him my backside for a good-morning kiss.

He planted a smacking kiss upon each one of my buttocks and cried out, "Run, little girl, run!" fumbling in his trousers for his limp old tool. He shook it furiously at me and in the other hand he held a birch rod with which he threatened to beat my behind. I began to run and he followed me. We ran five or six times around the room, all the while he was jacking himself off and screaming at me, "Run faster, you goddamned bitch, faster, I tell you!" Finally he sank exhausted and deeply satisfied into his easy chair; I dressed, he threw a few gold pieces at me, and I left.

Another man put me mother-naked on top of a chair in the corner of his living room. I had to rub my pussy with a dildo while he was watching me from the other corner of the room. I liked that one, because it was one of my few clients who wanted me to come first. When he noticed that I started to pant his trousers would bulge, when I started to groan he would whip out his enormous dong with its big ruby-red knob, and at the moment I reached my climax, enormous squirts of jism would flow into his hand.

A third one—and this one was a doctor!—would be incapable of giving any sign of life unless a girl friend of mine and I had given him a hundred sharp blows with a whip. Then my friend would kneel in front of him, bare her breasts and he would start sucking her nipples. I would switch from the whip to a cane and hit him some more. Then my friend would begin to manipulate his balls and together we would jack off his slowly ripening tool. Finally we would be able to squeeze a little drop of jism out of it. This doctor maintained that flagellation would cure the worst forms of impotence and, moreover, that it would cure infertility. He had beaten several barren women, he claimed, and within the year they all had given birth to healthy boys.

The fourth one was a voluptuous courtier whose senses had been blunted by his youthful excesses. He, too, always invited me and my girl friend to his home. His bedroom walls and the ceiling were covered with mirrors. From his huge, red-velvet-covered bed—which stood in the middle of the room—one could see everything that was going on. "You two darling girls are the most adorable little ladies I know," he used to say, "and I am terribly sorry that today I am not able to fuck you myself. Instead, if it is all right with you, I have instructed one of my manservants to have you. He is a very handsome and strong young man, and I am sure that he is willing to make both of you come. Yes, what do you expect, my beautiful little girls? One has to take his friends with all their little faults. One of my little faults happens to be that I'd rather do in my imagination what I see others do in reality. And besides, what could be more vulgar than a common fucking bout with a couple of ordinary peasants? It's too, too common. What would the world come to, if one of our standing would lay an ordinary, plump whore?"

After this honey-voiced introduction one of his servants would enter the room. All he would wear was an extremely short, flesh-colored kilt. My girl friend was told to lie down upon the bed and the servant started to take off her clothes. Meanwhile I would take off my blouse and bare my breasts and shoulders. He only wanted to see my upper body naked. Everything had to be done with care and precision, and most of our movements were timed. The courtier would sit in a chair, watching the proceedings in the various mirrors from different angles. I would then walk over to him, open his fly and take his limp tool out of his trousers. Then he would wave me away with his hand, indicating that I had to sit down at the foot of the bed. Meanwhile my friend was supine and naked on the bed, the servant leaning over her, his marvelous prick stiff and proud as a rod. The happy man would look with expectant eyes toward his master, who would finally give the sign that the servant could proceed. The boy would pounce his weapon into my friend's body and remain motionless, waiting for further orders. His taut behind would be quivering.

"My dear little girl," the cavalier would say to me, "give yourself the trouble and walk over to the other side of the bed. And now, please, tickle those enormous balls of my trusted servant. Don't you see them, you stupid little female, those big things dangling between his thighs. Go on, tickle them!"

When I had followed his orders, the lordly gentleman would tell his servant to go at it. The boy would start to pump away at tremendous speed, and I would hold his balls, squeezing them lightly. The courtier looked in every mirror, his hot eyes soaking in every detail of the love game all around him. Finally he would succeed in getting his limp prick stiff and he would start jerking it like a maniac. When he knew that he was about to come, he'd shout at his servant, "You can come now, my dear boy. Hurry up, squirt it into her!"

The servant would double his jolts and shove away with increased strength. Finally master and servant would simultaneously achieve ecstasy and squirt their juices in enormous spurts.

The things I just told you remind me of a rather funny adventure I had. It happened that same day and I tell it to you, because it should give you a good idea how firm the Capuchine monks cling to their chastity vows.

I had left the mansion of the cavalier and said good-bye to my girl friend. I walked around the corner and was just about to call for a coach, when an old friend and competitor of my mother stopped me on the street. Actually she was not so much a competitor as a colleague. Mrs. Dupuis was also a procuress; but whereas my mother catered mainly to the well-to-do and off-beat circles of Parisian society, Mrs. Dupuis' specialty was catering to the Roman Catholic clergy.

She exclaimed, "Ah, my dear Mizzi. What a delight to see you. As you know, I am honored by serving the clergy of Paris, and today it seems as if those dogs have made an agreement. They are all rutting at the same time. It's driving me crazy. I have been running all over town trying to find girls enough to satisfy their animal lusts. Now I am looking for one who can help me serve three Capuchine monks who are waiting in the front room of my own home.

"Please, dearest Mizzi, help me out of my predicament. My feet are sore from running around and those men are getting hornier by the minute. Pretty soon they will run out of my home and rape the first woman they see. Please, Mizzi, come home with me, they are nice devils, and you will enjoy it."

My protestations did not help. I told Dupuis that I was not a monk's chicken, that I knew the clergy well enough to know that they were not satisfied with using their imagination, that they did not enjoy a hand or a blow job, but that they demanded girls whose gates were wide-open.

"Goddammit, are you crazy!" answered Dupuis. "Do you care about their satisfaction? That is the craziest answer I have ever heard from a professional whore. Listen, all they pay me for is to procure them a girl. What they want to do with her is their business. Here, look, they gave me six gold pieces. Three of them are for you if you will come along with me."

Well, anyhow, she talked me into it. I did come along more out of curiosity than because of the money. We got into a cab and drove to the home of Mrs. Dupuis in the neighborhood of Montmartre.

Immediately three Capuchine monks entered the room. It seemed that they were not used to seeing an appetizing young morsel like me, because they threw themselves upon me like three hungry dogs. I had just put one foot up on a chair to loosen my stocking. One, who had a huge red beard and a foul smelling mouth, pressed his mouth upon mine and tried to stick his tongue between my lips. The second one was grabbing at my tits with his plump, hot fingers. And the third had lifted my skirts and was pressing his nose against my buttocks, trying to worm his tongue inside my little opening.

Something prickly—I thought it was made out of horsehair—chafed between my legs. I grabbed it and pulled. What do you think I held in my hands? The beard of Father Hilarius. When he noticed that I had no intention of letting him go, the foul bastard bit me in the groin. I let go of his beard and screamed loudly. Fortunately this scream scared the horny monks for a second and they let go of me. I rushed to the other corner of the room and sat down upon the bed. But I barely had the chance to recuperate from my scare, when I found myself cornered by three huge, throbbing pricks. I called out, "Please, venerable Fathers, wait a moment. What we have in mind should be conducted with some dignity. I realize that I have not been hired for the role of the Holy Virgin, but, for God's sake, let's find out which one of the three I am supposed to take on first . . ."

"Me, me, me!" all three exclaimed simultaneously without giving me a chance to finish.

"Hold it, you milquetoasts," said one of the three in a scornful voice. "You dare to go ahead of your superior? What is happening to subordination?"

"Jesus Christ!" one of the two others exclaimed indignantly. "What do you mean, subordination? There is no such thing in the whorehouse of Dupuis. Father Anselm has the same value here as Father Angelo."

"You liar," retorted the second of the two, hitting the venerable Father Anselm squarely between the eyes with his fist. This one, not a cripple either, jumped up and attacked Father Angelo. The two rolled across the floor, working each other over with fists and teeth. Their cowls were wrapped around their faces and necks, and their lower bodies were naked, the once enormous pricks flopping limply around. Dupuis tried to separate the two fighters but she succeeded only after she had emptied a bucket of cold water over their bellies.

During the fight, Father Hilarius thought it better not to pay too much attention to unimportant details. I had to laugh so much that I was half-conscious, reclining upon the bed. The good father made all the preparations to taste the oyster over which his two comrades were fighting on the floor. He was surprised by the resistance. He stopped and inspected my pussy closely. He opened the lips with his fingers and found to his surprise that the entrance was blocked. What now? He tried to penetrate again, but to no avail. He tried and tried and worked himself into such a state that he suddenly came and squirted his juices over the oyster which he could not swallow.

Suddenly everyone was very quiet. Father Hilarius had told the two fighting cocks about my physical disability and informed them that it was absolutely impossible to get a prick into that tiny little hole. They heaped scorn and abuse upon old Dupuis who defended herself laughingly. She was a very experienced woman and she knew how to rescue herself out of such a situation. She fetched several bottles of Burgundy which were soon emptied.

Meanwhile the tools of our venerable priests had resumed their firmness again and the sacrifices to Bacchus were interrupted to bring sacrifices to Priapus. Even though I did not measure up to the qualifications of the clergy, they seemed to be very satisfied, because my breasts, my armpits, my thighs and my behind at one time or another were the altars of their sacrifices.

It did not take long ere a true mood of festivity had taken hold of all of us. Our guests took off their clothes and dressed up Mrs. Dupuis and me in their cowls. They thought that I looked positively charming in this outfit. Dupuis, who was quite drunk, exclaimed loudly, "Don't you people think that Mizzi is the most charming little monk you have ever seen in your life? Doesn't she have a pretty face?"

"Who gives a good goddamn about her face!" roared Father Angelo. "Did you think that I paid my good money to see a pretty face! I came to your stinking whorehouse to fuck a cunt, not to see a pretty face. Why do you think I am holding my dong in my hand? To stick it in a cunt, that's why! And I swear before God Almighty that I won't go home till I have fucked somebody, even if it were the devil himself!"

"If it were the devil himself," repeated Dupuis, drunkenly staggering through the room till she stood in front of the venerable father. She bunched her skirts together, hoisted them up above her navel and exclaimed, "Look at it, you miserable bastard! Do you see this venerable cunt? It is as good as two others. I am a perfect devil, so why don't you fuck me if you dare and I swear that you will have double your money's worth."

And she grabbed Father Angelo by his beard,

pulling him across her belly. The good father was not in the least shocked by the outburst of the old Dupuis. He was ready for a good battle and he put his lance in her before she had finished babbling. He shoved it into her with all his might and started to pump away. Dupuis, who was sixty years old, had not found anybody in the past twenty-five years with enough guts to fuck her. All her pent-up emotions released themselves before the good father had had a chance to pump away more than six times. She started to trample and thrash wildly on the bed where Father Angelo had pinned her down firmly. Her voice changed and she exclaimed, "Oh, dear little Father, please fuck me good. I am only a tiny fifteen-year-old virgin as you can see, and I need it so badly. Can you feel how good I try to help you? Oh, oh, oh, I am so happy. Pump away, my dearest little cherub, you are giving me back my life. God will reward you, because you are doing a true labor of love."

In between those terms of endearment, Mrs. Dupuis kissed the monk wherever she could reach him and with her few remaining teeth stumps she tried to give him little love bites. The good father, who was loaded with wine, fumbled away as if he were a rank beginner. Finally the wine started to work upon Father Angelo, and Father Anselmus and Father Hilarius who, with me, were interested onlookers in this battle of the century, noticed that the good Father Angelo rapidly started losing ground. His movements were no longer regular and the force behind his shoves diminished rapidly.

"You goddamned bastard," screamed the

frustrated Dupuis. "I believe you're not even in! You miserable squirt, if you have the gall to . . ."

I will never know what Dupuis wanted to tell the brave Father Angelo because at that moment he came slightly to his senses, his stomach turned and he vomited all over Dupuis; part of it flowed into her screaming mouth. When the old lady was covered by the stinking mass, her stomach turned over also, and she answered Father Angelo in a similar way, spewing all over him. The two of them swam around in their own filth. Father Angelo collapsed and fell heavily on top of Dupuis who tried with all her strength to free herself from his weight. Finally she succeeded in crawling out from under him. Dupuis suddenly turned vicious. She stomped and trampled upon Father Angelo, who did not even notice it, because he was peacefully snoring away. The two monks and I were laughing so hard that we did not have the strength to stop her. Finally we succeeded in calming her down and waking Father Angelo.

We washed them, dressed ourselves and at nightfall we all went our own way.

I do not wish to talk to you about those unnatural monsters who only find enjoyment with their own sex, whether they are active or passive. France, today, produces more of those monsters than Greece and Italy ever did. Of course you know about the story of one of those afflicted who could only climax during his wedding night by summoning his manservant and ordering that wretch to do to him in the asshole what he, himself, was trying to do in his wife's cunt.

These faggots may make fun about our scorn for them, yes, they even defend their evil tastes by saying that they don't act any different than their opponents, namely by following the dictates of their own natural feelings. These fiends say namely we are only looking for pleasure in the way we consider natural, and our opponents are trying to do exactly the same. So what is the difference, if our partners are willing? What business is it of you people who claim to be interested in women, and what business if any, is it of the women who scorn us anyway? You must admit with us that we are not the masters of our own destinations and we cannot help having different tastes than you. We are being accused of following a taste which is punishable by law. How ridiculous to outlaw a preference which has been given us by God. Why shouldn't we follow our desires since it is only a satisfaction of partners who both want the same thing? What business is it of yours? Whom are we doing any harm? There is no such a thing as a punishable delight. And your argument that it is against Nature makes no sense at all, because it is Nature who gave us this particular taste to begin with. We are being accused that we cannot procreate the human race. What utter nonsense! Is there one person alive who gives in to his passions for the express purpose of creating a child?

In short these pederasts give thousands of reasons why they should be neither pitied nor scorned But no matter what they say, I think they are monsters.

I have to tell you about a trick which I played upon one of them. My mother had made arrangements for one of those enemies of our sex to visit me. Even though I break wind often by Nature, I had prepared myself for his visit by eating enormous quantities of beans. I allowed the man to see me only because I did not want to disappoint my mother. Every time he visited us he spent two hours bending over my buttocks, sticking his finger up my hole and squeezing my bums, opening and closing them, and I knew he would have loved to stick something else up my arsehole. But, I had told him my opinion about him, which means, I abhorred him.

At nine o'clock that night he arrived. I had to lie down flat on my belly. He lifted my skirts and as usual he held a candle so that he could inspect me closely and gaze upon the object of his adoration. I had been waiting for this moment. He kneeled down and brought the candle and his face very close to my bumhole. His nose was almost in it. At that very moment I farted with all my strength, breaking a wind that I had been keeping back for almost three hours. It escaped its prison with a horrifying roar and blew out the candle. The curious pederast jumped back and the only thing I regret to this day is that I was not able to see his face in the darkness. He fumbled around for the candle which had slipped out of his hand, and by the time he had managed to light it, I had slipped out of the room and locked myself in my own little room upstairs. Neither begging nor threats could induce me to unlock my door, and finally the man who had received the biggest fart I ever let, left our home forever.

* * *

I thought that this was the most hilarious story I had ever heard and had to laugh so long that Bois-Laurier had to stop her storytelling. Two gentlemen of her acquaintance were announced and she told me that she was terribly sorry that I had only heard the seamy side of her life's story. She hoped that she would soon be able to tell me the good part so that I might learn how she had succeeded in escaping the sordid life into which the reprehensible Mrs. Lefort had introduced her.

I must do Bois-Laurier the justice she deserves. Throughout my acquaintance with her she has never done anything to bring my good name in disrepute, except for that one time with her Uncle Bernard's colleague, even though she denied any knowledge of that man's intentions up to the very last moment we were together. Four or six friends formed her entire circle of acquaintances, and I was the only woman she ever saw, because she said that she hated females. Whenever we were in company, our conversations were quite respectable but whenever we were together, just the two of us, we could have made a soldier blush. We had absolutely no secrets from one another and exchanged every little confidence we could think of. The gentlemen who visited her were all, without exception, respectable gentlemen of means. We usually played cards for very small amounts of money. The only man who was permitted to see her alone and in private was her so-called Uncle Bernard.

As I just mentioned, two gentlemen were announced. They entered, we sat and talked, played our game of cards and had supper together. Bois-Laurier was in an excellent and most charming mood; it is possible that she did not want to give me any opportunity to think about what had happened that morning, because she insisted that I would spend the night with her, after the gentlemen had taken their leave.

We said and did all sorts of things, but about that I may tell you some other time.

* * *

The day after that particular night, I met you, my dear count. It was to be my happiest day! Without you, without your advice, without your friendship and without the attraction we felt for each other the moment we saw one another, my life would have ended miserably, because I would have walked into my doom with open eyes.

It was a Friday, I remember it well. You were sitting in the amphitheatre close to the box in which Bois-Laurier and I had our seats at the Opera.

Our eyes met quite accidentally but we both seemed to come under a strange spell, and we kept staring at each other. One of your friends who was supposed to take late supper with us after the Opera came to visit us in our box, and shortly after that you were talking to him. I was kidded about my strange opinions on morals and theology, and you expressed curiosity. You seemed to be interested in finding out a little bit more about me and you seemed pleased when you were successful. The fact that you agreed with many of my opinions attracted my attention. So far, most people have raised their eyebrows in amused tolerance. I listened to you and I liked to look at you, finding a pleasure in these two simple acts which I had heretofore never experienced. The pleasure was so strong that it gave me new inspiration, vivaciousness, and it developed feelings in me of whose existence I had been totally unaware.

This is the way sympathy between two souls works. It is as if one thinks with the organs of the other. The moment I intended to ask Bois-Laurier to invite you to our supper, you made the same suggestion to your friend. We reached an agreement and when the Opera was over the four of us got into your cab and we drove away to your little palace. We played a game of cards in which you and I were partners, and we were so engrossed in each other that we had to pay dearly for the many mistakes we made. Then we had our late supper and Bois-Laurier and I had to leave. It was terribly difficult for me to say good-bye to you, and I was awfully glad when you asked my permission to continue our acquaintanceship and if it was possible to meet me again soon. Your tone of voice convinced me that this was not mere idle talk and that you meant what you said.

When we drove away, Bois-Laurier was bursting with curiosity and she tried to find out, pretending to be totally disinterested, what we had been whispering during supper. I told her very simply that you had wanted to know what on earth brought me to Paris and, most of all, what kept me here.

I told her that your behavior had been impeccable, that I trusted you, and that I had told you honestly what had happened to me. I furthermore told her that you seemed interested in me and had offered me your help and assistance. I repeated to her that you said that I had released certain feelings in you which you hoped to realize one day and prove by action that your passions were not mere words.

"You don't know men as well as I do," answered Bois-Laurier curtly. "Most of them are liars and are only looking for an opportunity to get a girl in trouble, after they have used her innocence. It is not that I believe the count to be such a person, on the contrary, he seems to be a man of honor."

Bois-Laurier told me a lot of things, especially how to get to know the characters of the various types of men on the prowl. We went to bed together and again we played with one another till we had reached several climaxes in each other's arms.

The next morning, when we woke up, Bois-Laurier said to me, "Yesterday I told you the miserable part of my life; you have seen the bad side of it. But now I would like you to listen to me and hear the other side of the coin.

"For a long time I began to dislike the seamy life I had to lead, but I had absolutely no idea how to escape it. The money I earned always seemed to disappear somehow and the continual poverty kept me in bondage to the only profession I knew. Moreover, Mrs. Lefort, who handled my affairs, also was the only woman who ever gave me advice, and since she had brought me up from when I was a four-year-old waif, she exerted an enormous influence upon me.

"Fortunately she became ill and died very soon thereafter. May God grant me forgiveness for the thought. Since no one doubted that I was her daughter, I inherited everything from her. Part of it turned out to be cash money, there was a considerable amount of silverware and jewelry, plus, of course, the house, the furniture and sundry other articles that make up a well-stocked household. I kept whatever was necessary for a decent household and sold the remainder. It took me about a month to put my affairs in order and I bought a pension which gives me thirty-four hundred francs a year. I gave a thousand francs to the poor and departed for the city of Dyon where I intended to spend the rest of my days in a quiet atmosphere where nobody knew me.

"On the way to Dyon, near the village of Auxerre, I attracted a case of the pox. My face changed so much that nobody recognized me. This fact, plus the fact that the treatment and care in the province was horrible, induced me to return to Paris. I figured that if I stayed away from the areas where I had lived before my illness with Mrs. Léfort and where I had plied my trade, I could easily live in a neighborhood where nobody would recognize me.

"I have been here since last year and only Mister Bernard Bois knows about my past. He allows me to call myself his niece since I am now considered to be a lady of noble descent. You, Therese, are the only woman with whom

I have ever exchanged any confidences and with whom I have ever been intimate.

"I am firmly convinced that your principles make it impossible for you to misuse the confidence of a friend, a confidence which you have won because of your outstanding character and your sense of justice."

*　*　*

Mrs. Bois-Laurier had finished her story. I assured her that she could count on my silence and I thanked her profusely for her confidence in me. She had proven to be a great friend, because it must have been difficult for her to overcome her natural reluctance to bare her sordid past. Yet, she had done it to me as a favor, so that I might draw a lesson from the mistakes she had made.

Meanwhile, it had become afternoon. Mrs. Bois-Laurier and I were still paying one another those meaningless compliments which are demanded by polite society, when the maid entered and announced that you wanted to see me. My heart jumped for joy; I got up and ran toward you. We had very early dinner together and spent the rest of the day in each other's company.

Three weeks raced by, so to speak, and we did not leave each other's side. I did not notice at all that you used that time to convince yourself that I was worthy of you. My soul was engulfed in happinesss and I could not think of anything but your nearness to me. I simply had no room for any other feeling than my passion for you, and though my greatest wish was to possess you for the rest of my life, it never occurred to me to devise a plan and assure me of so much future happiness.

Meanwhile, I can now admit this, I was constantly worried about an apparent lack of enthusiasm whenever you talked to me, and a certain coolness which I could not properly define whenever we were intimately together. If he really loves me, I told myself, he will hotly pursue me, just like all the others who keep assuring me that they feel nothing but the hottest passion for me.

Yes, I was very worried. I did not know then that intelligent people are also intelligent in their love life and that the fly-by-nights are flighty in everything they undertake.

Finally, my dear count, after a whole month had passed, you told me rather coolly that the situation in which you had found me the first time we met, had rather upset you. My face, my character and my absolute trust in you had caused you to think of a way to keep me out of the mire in which, you were convinced, I would sink shortly. "Without a doubt," you said, "I must appear rather cold to you, my dear Miss Therese. Especially since I am a man who says that he loves you. I do not doubt that I love you, but stronger than my love for you and my desire to possess you, is my desire to make you happy."

I wanted to interrupt you and thank you, but you did not let me, and continued, "There is no time for that, dear girl. Please, be so kind and let me finish what I started to say. My yearly income is twelve thousand francs. Without making too much of a financial sacrifice, I am able to assure you of two thousand yearly for the rest of your life. I am a confirmed bachelor and determined never to marry. I have decided to leave the city because I am getting sick of the hypocrisy and idiocy that stares me in the face wherever I go. I have a nice and comfortable retreat about forty miles outside of Paris. I intend to live there from now on, and I depart in four days. Would you accompany me as a friend? Possibly you might decide to live together with me as my mistress. It entirely depends on whether you will find pleasure in such a relationship. You can be sure that such a decision can only have good 'results if you feel for yourself that it will contribute to your happiness merely by wishing it. It is proven that a person cannot feel the way he wants. To become truly happy, a person must be able to secure those delights which conform with his nature and his passions. He must, however, calculate the advantages and disadvantages these delights will bring him, not only to his own person, but also to those around him. It has been amply demonstrated that a person, because of his numerous needs and desires, can never achieve happiness without the help of a lot of other people. And he must take care, therefore, not to do anything which might harm the quest for happiness of those others. Whoever deviates from this rule will find that the happiness he chases keeps eluding him. This is my firm conviction, and the logical consequence is that true happiness is only possible for honest people. Men or women who cannot act with integrity will never be able to achieve happiness. The severity of the laws, their own pangs of conscience, their guilt feelings, the hatred and scorn of their fellow men, will be their constant companions.

"Take your time, my dear young lady, to think over what I have just told you. Find out for yourself, if you can become happy by making me happy. I will leave you now and come back tomorrow to hear your answer."

Your words shook me deeply. I wanted nothing else but to make a man who thought like you the happiest man in the world. But at the same time I, too, saw the danger of making a grave mistake and I realized that your generosity would be able to prevent me from making that mistake. I loved you. But prejudices are extremely powerful and difficult to destroy. I was afraid to be known for all the world as a kept mistress, because it had not escaped my attention that a certain aura of disdain was drawn around those who were known as such. Moreover, I was terribly afraid to get with child, because both Madame Catherine and my dear mother had almost died in childbirth. Besides, I was used to providing my own climaxes, and I had been assured by everyone that they were as ecstatic as the embraces of a man. Therefore, I was unaware of the heat of my passions. I had never any carnal desire, because the mere thought of it was usually followed by immediate self-satisfaction. There were two reasons left for a decision. First, the possibility of a miserable end in the gutters of Paris and, second, the desire to make you happy and to achieve my own happiness by doing so. The first reason did not really disturb me, because its possibility seemed so remote. It was the second reason that caused me to make up my mind.

Oh, the impatience with which I awaited

your return that next morning as soon as I had made up my mind! The next morning you arrived and I threw myself into your arms. "Yes, oh, yes!" I cried out. "I want to be yours and yours alone. Please, be considerate with the feelings of a young and innocent girl who adores you! Your feelings toward me assure me that you will never force me. You know my fears, my weaknesses and my habits. Allow time and your good advice to do their work. You know the human heart. You know the power that feeling has over the will. Please, I beg of you, use the opportunity to develop in me those properties which in your opinion are the best to contribute to your own happiness. Already I am your best friend . . ."

I remember that you interrupted me when I poured out my anguished heart. You promised never to go against my desires, and you also said that you would not force me to change my taste or to belittle my inclinations. Everything was taken care of and the next day I informed Mrs. Bois-Laurier of my happiness.

She cried when we said our farewells and finally we departed to your estate upon the date you had decided to leave Paris forever.

Once arrived at that pleasant place, I had absolutely no time to think about the sudden change in my situation because my mind was constantly occupied with only one question: How to make you happy and give you satisfaction? Two months passed and you did not once insist upon my giving you certain pleasures, though you tried to awaken in me the desire to give it to you out of my own free will. I fulfilled all your wishes happily and voluntarily, only that one I was unable to give you, the one which you praised as the most ecstatic experience a couple could undergo. I could not possibly conceive that anything could be more pleasant than the delights I gave myself and which I offered to share with you. On the contrary, I shuddered at the mere sight of the monstrous arrow you showed me and was horrified at the thought that you would penetrate me with it. How on earth is it possible, I thought, that such a long, thick and stiff thing, with a head as knobby and big as that one, could get into a little opening into which I could barely stick my little finger? Besides, I was convinced I would die if I were to become a mother.

I begged you often to avoid this one dangerous cliff. "Please, my dearest friend," I would say, "let me do it for you!"

I caressed, kissed, licked and rubbed your little Peter, as you called him. I moved him up and down and sideways, took the knob between my fingers and the shaft in a firm grip of my hand. My other hand would play with the bullocks hanging under your Peter and, whether you wanted or not, you would reach your climax and spill your divine seeds in my hand or upon my lips. The voluptuous delight would overwhelm you and you would quiet down again.

As soon as the carnal desires had disappeared, you would use my love for metaphysical theorizing and my habit of discussing moral problems to sway my opinion through the power of your word. One day you told me:

"Love for oneself determines all the actions of one's life. And with love for oneself I mean all those satisfactions we feel when we do something that gives us pleasure. I love you, to give an example, because I derive pleasure from loving you. What I have done for you is probably very pleasant and useful for you, but you don't owe me any gratitude. It is self-love which made me do the things for you I have done, because it gives me pleasure and satisfaction to do them. I am happy when I can contribute to your happiness. Therefore you can only make me completely happy when I know that your self-love is totally satisfied by doing so. Somebody gives alms to the poor. He may even go so far as to suffer certain inconveniences just to be able to give money to the poor. His actions are very useful, for the poor, as well as for society at large, because he is alleviating a certain burden of the community. Therefore his actions are considered very laudable. However, the almsgiver deserves no particular praise. He has given alms because his pity for the poor has caused him unpleasant feelings. And it was less unpleasant for him to give away his money than to look upon the plight of those who are poverty-stricken. It is possible that a certain amount of vanity contributed to his actions, because he liked to be seen by his fellow men as a philanthropist. But even in that case he was striving for a fulfillment of a certain desire. That fulfillment gave him satisfaction and the desire to attain that satisfaction is a form of self-love. All the actions in our life are caused by only two principles: To acquire more or less satisfaction, or to avoid more or less pain."

At other times you would elaborate upon the lessons which I had received from my former father confessor, the abbot, proving to me the inanity of my prejudices. And finally you began to get tired of my eternal refusal. Then you had a brilliant idea. You ordered from Paris a collection of erotic paintings and books. Since I liked the books, and found as much enjoyment in viewing the pictures, you came up with two suggestions. You were finally on your way to success. "Ah, you are reading, Miss Therese," you said jokingly. "Erotic books and pictures! Well, well, well! I am very glad to see that you are interested. I will secure for you the best available works in this field. But, with your permission, let's enter into an agreement. I will lend you for two weeks my entire collection of erotica. But you must promise me solemnly not to touch with your hands that spot which rightfully should be mine. You must completely and absolutely abstain from manual labor. There is absolutely no giving in, not for one single moment. We both must fulfill our part of the bargain. I have very good reasons for this wager. I leave it up to you. If you don't want to do it, then no more books, no more pictures."

I did not hesitate at all and gladly promised abstinence for a mere two weeks.

"But," you continued, "that is not everything. Our mutual obligations should be of a similar value. It would be unreasonable to expect from you such a sacrifice just to view some pictures, or scan a stack of books. Let's make a wager which you are sure to win. I bet you my entire library and my complete collection of pictures against your virginity that you will be unable to stick it out for fourteen days as you promised."

"Really, dear sir," I retorted extremely irritated, "you have unmitigated gall to think so lowly about my willpower and to overrate my passions so grossly."

"Please, Miss Therese," you exclaimed, "please, no trial! I cannot argue with a woman who is losing her temper. Besides, I have the feeling that you have no idea what I am aiming at. Listen to me. Is it not true that your self-esteem is slightly damaged every time I make you a present, because you receive it from a man whom you are not satisfying the way you know you could? Well, my dearest Therese, you don't have to have that guilt feeling when you get the books and the pictures, because you will have earned them honestly."

"My dear count," I retorted haughtily, "I realize that you are setting a trap for me, but I warn you that it is you who will be caught in it. I accept your bet and, what is more, I will take it upon myself to spend my days doing nothing else but viewing the pictures and reading the books. And I will start right this morning."

You ordered the entire library to be transferred to my rooms. I devoured, so to speak, in the first four days, a great number of books. I only looked up from them to view the paintings whose voluptuous compositions were portrayed with a beauty of coloration and forcefulness of expression which made my blood boil through my veins. The fourth day a sort of ecstasy came over me after I had read for about an hour. I was still in bed and my bed curtains had been removed so that I had a full view of two particularly beautiful paintings. One was *The Festival of Priapus* and the other *The Love of Mars and Venus*. My imagination became overheated at the mere sight of those positions. I threw away my blankets and bedsheets. Without giving any thought to whether or not the doors to my apartments were locked, I began to imitate all the positions that were pictured on those two marvelous paintings. Every position I assumed gave me the sensation the painter had intended. A loving couple to the left of *The Festival of Priapus* picture excited me particularly, because the taste of the young woman coincided with my own. Mechanically my hand went to that spot where the hands of the young man were resting, and I was just about to stick my finger in my hole when I remembered the conditions of our bet. I stopped just in time.

I did not have the slightest inkling that you were a witness to my weakness, if you can call this delightful natural passion by that name. But, good God, what an idiot I was to resist the incredible delights of true ecstasy. But that is the power of a prejudice which had been pounded into my mind. It makes us blind, it is a tyrant. Other couples in this picture caused my admiration and some of them I felt downright sorry for.

Finally my gaze rested upon the second picture. What incredible voluptuous delight in the position of Venus. I stretched myself, like her, comfortably out on my bed. My thighs were opened slightly, my arms spread out wide. I admired the splendid position of the god Mars. The fire that sparkled in his eyes, and the power of his enormous member, made itself felt deep in my insides. My heart trembled. I thrashed around upon the bed, my buttocks moving lasciviously.

"What?" I exclaimed. "The gods themselves are enjoying a happiness which I stupidly keep denying myself! Oh, lover, I cannot resist any longer. Count, please, come in, I am no longer afraid of your prick. You can stick it into your love, you can select any opening you want, only don't let me wait any longer! Everything is all right with me. I will enjoy your thrusts and to prove to you that you have won, here . . . look . . . !" And I shoved my finger deep into my hot pussy.

What a surprise. The happy moment. Suddenly you were there. More shining than Mars in the picture, more proud, more powerful! The light nightshirt you wore was thrown off in no time.

"You are too sensitive," you said to me. "I do not want to use the first opportunity. I have watched your struggle, I have seen everything. I do not wish to taste victory because of a trick. I only appear, dear Therese, because you have called me. Now I want to hear it again, from your own lips. Do you want me?"

"Oh, yes, I do!" I exclaimed. "I am all yours. Shove it in and push as deeply as you can. Please, please, I beg of you! I am no longer afraid of your thick Peter!"

You sank into my arms and without hesitation I grabbed the lance which was quivering in front of my little hole, and I helped your enormous tool disappear into my cunt. You pushed it in deeply and your repeated shoving did not make me whimper once. I was completely engulfed by a delicious feeling and did not even think about pain.

Suddenly you said to me with a choking voice, "I shall not use my full rights, Therese. You are too much afraid to become a mother. I will be considerate. But my climax is near. Clasp your hand around my prick the moment I pull it out of you, and help it with a few jerking movements . . . it is time, my love . . . I am dying with lust and pleasure . . ."

"Aah, so . . . am . . . I . . . I . . . am . . . dying . . . I . . . don't . . . feel . . . any . . . thing . . .!" I groaned, moaned and whimpered, all at the same time, shuddering in delight as I had never known before.

At the same time I grabbed your tool, squeezed it lightly with my hand which served as its new scabbard. In my hand you reached the peak of your ecstasy. Then we started all over again and our joys have now lasted for more than ten years. Always in the same manner, no children, no fear.

This, my dear benefactor, may have been what you wanted from me when you asked me to describe the story of my life as faithfully as I possibly could. If this manuscript is ever going to appear in print, an enormous amount of blockheads and stupid prejudiced little souls will raise an outcry of disgust. They will criticize and scream about the metaphysical thoughts and they will pretend to be outraged at some of the descriptions. But they will also have missed the point of this book. The better for them, because I would not like to have it on my conscience to upset these stupid automatons. These are the people who act like pieces of machinery, who are used to thinking with the brains of others and who are petrified in their nightmares at the tiny fragments of original thoughts which once in a while come up in their minds. These people will be with us, I am afraid, throughout the ages, fighting a losing battle, but fighting nevertheless, because their stupidity, their prejudices and their ignorance prevent them from enjoying life as it could and should be enjoyed. The mere thought that others could find enjoyment out of life makes them vicious in their stupidity, and they will seek out little words to stumble upon, and they will try to wreak their vengeance, and impose their moronic little wills.

Once more I will try to answer them. Everything I have written down is the result of my own experiences which I have tried to treat as intelligently as possible and, to my knowledge, as free from prejudice as possible.

Yes, you poor ignorant people. The concept of Mother Nature is a many-headed imaginary monster. Everything is the work of God. He gave us the need for food and drink, and also for the enjoyment of pleasures. Why, therefore should we blush and crawl away in shame, if we fulfill His intentions. Why shouldn't we contribute to the happiness of Mankind by serving many dishes, each of which is spiced with a varitey of condiments and spices to serve and satisfy the many different tastes? Should I truly be afraid to displease God, or to incur the condemnation of certain people because I proclaim a truth which can only clarify and which could never do any harm? I repeat once more, you black-thinking judges of so-called morality: We do not think the way we want. The soul has not a will of its own. It merely reacts through the sensations of our senses which are caused by the matter surrounding us. Intelligence will explain this to us, but does not guide us. Self-love, the hope to experience pleasure or the desire to avoid misery are the mainsprings of our decisions. Our happiness depends upon the conditions of our organs, upon our education, and upon outside influences. If the human laws would be correct, they would be designed in such a manner that we could enjoy ourselves, by giving pleasure and by leading an honest life.

Yes, there is a God. We cannot help but love Him, because He is a being of infinite goodness and perfection. The intelligent human, the philosopher, should contribute to the well-being of society by His morally correct example.

There should be no religion. God is enough onto Himself. Knee-bending exercises and other contortions, the imaginations of other human beings, cannot possibly contribute one iota to His glory. Moral good and evil can only be an idea of Man, not of God.

The laws, enforced in great variety by every country, keep the communities together, and they should be obeyed. The ones who violate those laws, and who get caught, must be punished. The good example which is set by many so that those who are weaker can follow it, is as necessary as the punishment of those whose example tends to disrupt the happiness of society. If a king and his government want to be loved by their people, they should act only to the greater good of the people in their charge.

ANGELICA

Nothing about the grounds of the Abbey caused me the slightest horror, on the contrary, everything around me breathed abundance and gaiety, and as my relatives, whose companion I was, let me have my own way and never crossed me in any of my desires, you can imagine that I found this mode of living entirely to my liking.

Until my first communion the time passed easily and without the slightest care and though I was aware of the fact that the monks from a neighboring Monastery were frequent visitors, I paid but little heed to the comedy that was daily enacted about me.

It is true they tried to keep me in ignorance of what was going on, from motives known to themselves, so that when I saw them caressing each other, I innocently attributed it to mere friendship.

As I often went into the garden with the sisters and their company, I became gradually attached to a young Bernardine monk who had always been kind and agreeable to me and to whom I owed my friendship out of pure gratitude.

In the course of time, changes took place with me, which filled me with mingled wonder and fear, and which my cousin strove to allay. I reached the age of puberty, I noticed with pleasure the appearance of two little alabaster globes, ornaments of which all women are proud, but what interested me more was the fine down that began to show itself at a certain spot on my body and, wishing to know if my cousin had the same on hers, I managed to get a look one night when she was changing her undergarments, I saw then enough to convince me that mine was only a starter.

The next day after dinner we had company and I went with a party of them into the park. Dom Delabrise, the young Bernardine I have spoken of, after being absent for nearly six months, was with us and I confess I was very glad to see him again and he, too, seemed favorably impressed with my appearance.

A strange light glimmered in his eyes as he directed his glances towards me and while taking all kinds of sweet and tender liberties with my person, but without over-stepping the rules of propriety.

When I left him it was with a feeling that I cannot describe, love and regret mingled with one another, a feeling which only those who have themselves experienced it can understand.

I became pensive.

At this time an epidemic of smallpox appeared in the neighborhood and I was one of those who first contracted this dread disease and this put for the time being, an end to my awakening love. For three long months I was confined to my bed, during which time I asked my cousin again and again if she thought that I would become pitted, for I was afraid of becoming ugly.

Dom Delabrise came three times to see me during my illness. The little attentions he showed me during this time contributed to increase the tender affection I began to feel for him. I was overjoyed one day when I heard him say that my beauty was not going to be marred in any way by the disease. Though quite young, yet my childhood had passed and my mind became wholly occupied with him whom I had learned to love.

Whenever I caught sight of him my whole body began to tremble as if it wanted to go to pieces. One day he came and asked me into the parlor and after kissing my hand, he told me that he had come expressly to see me, and as the sisters were busy that afternoon, he would be glad to entertain me alone, if I was willing. I told him that I was delighted and that I would be ready for him by two o'clock. He appeared punctually at the appointed time.

Kissing me tenderly and, as I thought, with more passion than usual, he took hold of my hands and began to pour into my willing ears many warm words of affection.

I was extremely green and answered only in monosyllables, although under the circumstances I was glad to play the listener.

Pretending to examine my collar, he touched my throat and I even scolded him for it. Judging from this that I was not inclined to be severe with him, he returned to the attack and kissed me most passionately, following up his advantage by running his hand up under my clothes.

I made some sort of resistance owing to that innate prudery that is found in every woman. As he did not give up the struggle, however, I let him go ahead and do as he pleased. The touching and tickling of his licentious fingers caused me the most peculiar sensations. Hearing someone coming, he made haste to escape. It proved to be my maid and the prior.

"We must part," he said. His eyes showed

his exasperation and disappointment. I myself was vexed, for I was just experiencing a certain pleasure that I did not wish to cut short in such an abrupt manner.

It was surprising what ease one could approach without being noticed, especially in a *Paloir grille*, as this was. The room was partitioned off by a screen made of lattice work with two wings, which on being opened formed a little square closet, which was used to satisfy the demands of nature.

The rest of the day I was morose, thinking only of Dom Delabrise. The sisters noticed it and after supper, my maid asked me what was ailing me.

I replied: "Oh, nothing."

She then replied with a knowing look at the others: "She is only growing and it is making her a little anxious." I laughed with the rest, then got up and went to bed. I lost no time in falling asleep but awoke about midnight, after dreaming some of the strangest dreams.

I dreamt that my friend was at my side caressing me and that he had made me take hold of a certain thing, which I could not recall, having at that time no acquaintance with that part of man's anatomy. I awoke with an agreeable thrill and with my hand on my pussy, which I found to be slightly wet.

But that was not the first time this had happened to me; the difference was that I had not before taken much notice of it. I sighed instinctively, as any girl would under the circumstances. I also began to frig myself, confining my attentions to a little protuberance which was so sensitive as to put me beside myself with pleasure.

After playing with myself for a few moments I fainted from sheer pleasure and once again the sweet, dewy fluid put me under its balmy influence. Again I fell asleep, not to awake until my cousin returned from prayer.

Quite satisfied with my discovery, not a day passed that I did not repeat the operation, always thinking of my lover, whom I would have liked to have with me but he rarely came, as he was too much occupied with his studies.

A week passed during which I was more left alone than usual. My cousin absented herself more frequently, but being used to this I never inquired where she was or what she was doing. But wishing to finish a piece of work, she stayed with me one whole day and it did not displease me at all to have her company for she loved me a great deal, but at the same time it annoyed me, for I had to pretend a certain thing, to get a chance to enjoy with ease the little exercise I made my pussy undergo, and which I practiced in the toilet room.

She suspected something, however, and watched me, taking care though to slip away from her point of observation before I came out again. Having no idea of being watched, I satisfied my lustful desires and frigged my pussy until the desired spasmodic thrill overcame me and then I returned to my work, and on entering, my cousin asked me: "Angelica, where have you been?"

"Why, cousin, I have been to the toilet."

"There is more than one thing that takes one to the toilet, I see," my cousin said. "I saw everything. Who in the name of mercy taught you to do it? It's nice, I must say."

I was dumb with confusion, I threw myself on her neck and she did not repulse me but merely scolded me a little and left the room.

I suspected that she would go and inform the prior of what she had seen and I followed her and saw her enter the room. I quickly got up to the door and on her telling about the occurrence, I heard them laugh, I then looked through the keyhole. Rosa was present, too. After indulging for a while in laughter, my cousin said to the other two:

"I believe you both would be tickled to death to have yours pulled."

"Yes," said the prior, "I would for one; will you join us?"

"No," she returned, "I am not in the humor today, just amuse yourselves while I take a look at this book."

A small vessel was placed over a flame and while Rosa prepared an instrument about as long and thick as three of my fingers, the prior, who was a fine looking fellow, sat in his easy chair and amused himself in tucking up his robe and rubbing his penis. Then he called the other nun and made her kneel in front of him and take his stiff tool in her mouth, on which, to my astonishment, she began to suck just as a babe sucks at his mother's breast. In the meantime Rosa had taken the vessel from the flame and poured its contents, which I now saw consisted of milk, into the instrument; this she fastened round her loins and, getting behind my cousin, shoved it up her cunt and began to work it back and forth. After a few thrusts, my sensual cousin closed her eyes, uttered a few sighs and then suddenly cried out: "Let it shoot; let it come!"

Rosa pressed the bulb and the warm liquid was forced into her at the moment when the final spend or spasm overcame her.

At the same time I saw the prior stretch his legs and I was surprised to see some white fluid run down the side of my cousin's mouth. Rosa then took my cousin's place and she, too, received the same treatment.

When the erotic excitement gave way to calm and they all began to converse quietly together, I stole away to my room. I began to think over what I had seen and concluded that I had found the road to pleasure and that all I now lacked was acquaintances, and just at the moment that I thought of the warm milk that the sisters had used, my cousin entered.

"Well, Angelica, you have become more sensible, I hope."

I did not answer but hung my head and appeared penitent, so she continued: "Listen to me, my dear little friend, perhaps you do not know that it is a mortal sin to touch yourself in those parts; therefore you ought to confess and resolve never to do so again. Do not be angry, my dear child, because I tell you this. It may be a joke, but nevertheless, do your duty."

"I am not angry," I said, "I will go to confession, but not to the Reverend Director."

He was a hypocrite for whom I had acquired a singular aversion, not that he was over strict, for he had been gay enough in his younger days and interfered very little with the sisters and their visitors. I abhorred him, however, so I shall not refer to him again in my story.

"Confessions are free," was my cousin's response. "Father Anselmo will be here on Monday and you may go to him." I consented to this, though I felt very much like laughing in my cousin's face after what I had witnessed, but what would have been the use? We take things as we find them, you know. My worthy cousin feared that when I left the convent I might reproach her for not having first put me on my guard against the awakening of my sexual instinct.

I decided what course I would follow and I asked my cousin how I would best put the subject before the Reverend Father.

I awaited his arrival and began mortifying my flesh and only twice did I succumb to the temptation of employing my fingers to satisfy the burning lust of my slit, until the priest arrived.

Monday, I presented myself before the sacred tribunal. I began as others do, saving the most interesting part of my confession until the last. I nearly put my confessor to sleep with a lot of unimportant trifles before I came to the real sin. His eyes began to shoot fire when I commenced to touch on the best part of my confessions:

"Ah. Oh! Oh . . . what is that I hear?"

"Yes, Father, I have sinned against my own person, both with my eyes and my hands."

"And pray, against what part of your body have you sinned, my child?" This he asked in a soothing, fatherly voice.

"On that part that distinguishes the sexes!" I answered with downcast eyes.

He put several more questions of like nature to me and then having heard enough he said:

"Listen, child, I must hear the confessions of five sisters before dinner, I have not the time to hear the rest of your confession now but be in the parlor by one o'clock and we will talk the matter over." He then gave me a light penance and sent me away.

At the appointed time I found him in the parlor; our conversation at the start was trivial enough. It was interesting enough for him, however, for he kept his eyes fixed on me most of the time. After a moment's silence he began:

"Now let us speak about those things; I mean about those terrible things of which you accused yourself this morning. Was it not immediately after your interview with the young monk that you began?"

"Yes, Father."

"Not before that?"

"No, Father."

"Did you not feel an itching 'round about that part?"

"Nothing of the kind, Father."

"And you did not touch yourself until . . ."

"No, Father, I only rubbed it with my shirt."

"Be candid, did you not feel pleased with the discovery you had made? Come now, speak out, don't be afraid of me. I am not a bad fellow," he continued, taking me by the hand.

"To tell you frankly what I felt? Oh, I don't know how I could ever do it."

"Promise me not to reveal anything and I will tell you things, child, that will set your mind at rest."

I promised secrecy and he commenced thus:

"You have not done such terrible things as your little brain has imagined, for when nature makes known its wants, there is no wrong in resorting to those means to calm the violent feelings that overcome us poor mortals. But does it really give you pleasure to manipulate those parts?" he asked again, and eyeing me with fixed attention, he put a hand beneath his robe and I saw that he was fingering something.

The fact was that our conversation had excited the Reverend Father's sensuality.

He put his hand under my chin and kissed me and being too well pleased with his little discourse on ethics, I did not resist, besides he was a fine-looking man and still young, not over thirty at the most.

This little favor seemed to set him afire. He kissed me a second time and, undoing my neckband in spite of some resistance on my part, he gloated over the beauties hidden beneath, his eyes gleaming with passion.

"Oh, what a beautiful child you are! Why should I not be made as happy as that young Bernardino?" And coming over to where I was sitting, he grabbed one of my legs and with his knee against the other, he forced my legs apart, and then with his free hand he began to rub and finger my little pussy.

I bent forward, telling him all the time to quit, as somebody might come, but he pleaded with me so earnestly that I finally consented to let him have his way.

After feasting his eyes and fingers, he praised me most lavishly and then taking my hand, he placed it under his surplice. I withdrew hastily, thinking I had touched some venomous reptile.

"What ails thee child?" he asked. "Don't be afraid, come now, I want you to get acquainted with it, touch it, finger it, that's the way, my little sweetheart."

"And what is this thing, anyhow, Father Anselmo?" I asked as I began to handle it. "My, how hard and warm it is!"

He now took it out and showed it to me and my surprise was great to see the difference between him and me. The instrument that I now held in my hand appeared to be about a foot long and as thick as my wrist, below I noticed a wrinkled sack hanging, which seemed to contain two objects that might have been taken for large eggs, for all I know. I noticed also that it was surrounded by a bunch of light brown hair, which made it look like a white and red post sticking out of the tuft of moss.

He held my arm, begging me to have compassion on him and directed the movements of my hand and as he was of a strong and healthy constitution and easily wrought up to the spending point, he asked me to stop and then made me stretch myself at full length on the carpet, like a martyr that was going to be immolated. I made no resistance whatever. He admired my naked charms for a moment or two and then, with his right arm, he raised my posteriors. Hee fondled the fleecy covering of my pussy and then rubbing a licentious finger along the lips, back and forth, he tried to sound the depths.

I begged of him to stop, for it hurt me very much. He would not listen and softly forced his finger in and then worked it in such a manner that procured me more pleasure than I had ever before experienced, and seeing from the way that I was beginning to heave and sigh that I was about to discharge, he gave me a voluptuous kiss and I lost consciousness in his arms. When I came to again, he was caressing me, fondly congratulating me on the sensuality of my nature.

So it was my turn to amuse myself at his expense. I became familiar with his prick, as he told me to name it. He lay down on the altar, still bearing the traces of my sacrifice to Venus, while I sat down on a stool, placing myself in such a manner that the reverend gentleman could reach my grotto of pleasure with his lips, then I raised his staff and how he enjoyed it. How pleased he was when I began fingering and caressing his proud tool; he cried out with pleasure.

"Oh, you dear little sweetheart, kiss me, rub harder, press tighter. I'm coming, I'm coming!" And, drawing himself up, he finally collapsed in a spasm and sank on the floor.

I felt something warm filling my hand and, looking, I saw for the first time that matter from which we spring.

"Well, now, you see the shape you have put me in!"

He only laughed and began to dry me with his handkerchief. To satisfy my curiosity, I plied him with questions which he willingly answered, one and all. I started in as follows:

"I assure you, my Father, that I was very anxious to know how men were formed and I would have found out long ago if my cousin and the Princess had not come in on us, when myself and Dom Delabrise were together, for he would not have failed to have spread his merchandise out before me."

For all that I knew, the difference between one sex and the other was that one procures great pleasure from the other when they have connection. Still I did not know as much as I would like to know about it.

"Look here, child, here is a specimen that would soon enlighten you on that score and, although you are new at the business, if we were in a more convenient place, I would realize with you what you are looking for."

"I understand, Father, but I am afraid your attempts on me would be in vain, for I cannot believe that my small thing could accommodate such a dagger as yours. You would split me in two."

"It is true I would most likely hurt you at the start, but having it once lodged up to the hilt, you would experience a pleasure far superior to any that you have as yet enjoyed."

"That means that the part of man is made especially to have connection with ours?"

"Without a doubt, the great author of Nature has created man and woman of different sexual attributes to that very end."

"But what else besides pleasure results from this union of our parts?"

"Beings like ourselves."

"Good, so that is the history of the human fabric. That white juice that I saw coming out of your thing, there, I suppose, is the essence which produces this effect?"

"Yes, partly, for it takes a woman's seed, too, to complete the work. These two semen coming together produce the foetus, which in time develops, takes life and becomes a baby."

"I would like very much to have some fun with a man but I would not like to have it go so far as that. I would not like to have a baby, they say it hurts dreadfully."

"Depend upon me, I can manage that part of it first rate, for should I ever meet you in some convenient place, you will have nothing to fear on my part. Now, for a little advice; if any one has connection with you, exact a promise that he shall pull his prick out of your cunt when he is about to finish, so that the discharge will fall outside on your belly, and in this way you are certain to avoid babies. But it is not the pain alone that you should consider about bringing babies into the world, it is also the law which brands you as an outcast when you have the misfortune to become a mother.

"I maintain, however, that you are entitled to all the joys of concupiscence you can get, provided, of course, that you have some regard for appearances. Those men or women who are forced by circumstances to remain single, whether it be on account of lack of means or cupidity of their parents, who have forced them to adopt a life that condemns them to a state of celibacy, those people, I say, should not be obliged to forego the pleasures of sexual intercourse. Nature has supplied them with organs and Nature intends that they shall use them. So let me say, once more, one may amuse himself or herself under any conditions, taking only the precautions not to run afoul of our iniquitous laws, which seem to have been formed only to tyranize the weak."

"I will bear in mind what you have told me, but see, it is almost three o'clock. I am afraid my cousin will soon be looking for me."

"Don't be uneasy about your cousin, she is

very busy and will not bother her head about you for some time yet."

"Why, what in the world is she doing?"

"If you wish to know what she and the prioress are doing this very minute in the sacristy, go listen at the door, then come back and tell me what you hear."

"I have an inkling of what may be going on in there."

"You have? How is that?"

"A few days ago I saw the Mother Superior, my cousin and Rosa amusing themselves with some strange instruments."

"I think I know what you mean. It is what is called a dildo. Each one has a good friend who caresses her with it and I am sure you will be shortly initiated into the joys of dildo fucking. Now, do as I told you and if you cannot see anything, you will doubtless hear something."

I went off and, after finding what Father Anselmo had insinuated I would find, I returned and reported to him.

"You spoke the truth, Father Anselmo, I recognized the voice of the parish priest, and as near as I could judge, he was serving my cousin to a good piece, of this I was convinced from the way in which the Mother Superior addressed Dom Lamotte, the parish priest.

" 'You will fuck me once more, dear Father. The others have had their fill and I can stand a good deal more than they can, so give it to me once more.'

"Then everything became quiet for several minutes, only interrupted by an occasional kiss. Then I thought I heard the squeaking of the sofa."

"You see, Angelica, I was right, but what ails you now? Did it give you a funny feeling? Your cousin won't be back for some time yet, let us make use of the opportunity. Take up your dress and let me see that lovely cunt; how brown you are getting there. Now turn around. Oh, what a beautiful arse, so white and round; you are sighing! Now hold your legs apart and we will see if we cannot make this mossy love fountain spout forth again."

"Oh, oh, dear Father . . . I cannot . . . oh, I cannot speak . . ."

"Are you enjoying it, sweetheart?"

"Yes, and I am going to repay you if I can. But first let me look at it, your prick, I mean; is that the right word? It looks like a nutcracker about the head. That makes you laugh, and what are these two things in the pouch? What a lot of hair there is around here!"

"Those, my dear, are the testicles, or as you should call them, the 'balls.' All males, men as well as animals, have them and those that have them not are not able to fuck. Hold on, Angelica, I am coming. Here it comes, kiss me, child."

"Did I do it right?"

"Yes, you bet you did! Let us get up."

"Now tell me about the dildoes. Why do they put milk in them? That puzzles me."

"I will tell you why. You see, women are not provided with willing servants as the nuns here are, who lack nothing in this respect, as you have just seen. They are compelled to find solace with one another, and the hot milk which they inject produces almost the same effect as though they had connected with a man. Still there is a big difference, for, after all, a dildo is but a lifeless instrument and one can never give as much pleasure as a prick."

"Now let me look at it again. My, what a queer looking object it is, now what causes it to undergo such a change as that? Don't laugh, what in the world becomes of all the stiffness? And the head of it that looked so red and inflamed, what made it come down in such a short time? And it has not the same color at all, and the skin that nearly covers it now; I did not notice it at all before."

"This change that it seems surprises you so much is in reality its natural condition. If it were always in that state in which you saw it at first, it would be very inconvenient. Only occasionally it takes that form. The sight of a woman or even our imagination will cause it to stiffen and stand up proudly, which goes to prove that the man was made for the woman and the woman for the man."

"That is strange. See, it is getting hard!"

"It would have to be a stick or a stone if a hand like yours would not bring it to life again, but that is enough, it exhausts a person when carried to excess, and you ought to restrain yourself and only do it when your desires overpower you, for as you are not fully developed yet, excess would do great harm. Do not mention anything of what I have told you or of what has taken place. I will come to see you again and then I will bring you a dildo proportionate to your age, so that you can amuse yourself. Good-bye, sweetheart."

I will ask the reader not to criticize the poor Franciscan monk too severely; I, for my part, bore him no ill will for having taken advantage of my youth and inexperience.

After the Franciscan left me, I retired to my room, very well satisfied indeed; my cousin putting in her appearance shortly after, her face flushed, seemingly suffered from the heart. "When did Father Anselmo leave?" she asked.

"At two o'clock, my cousin."

"And what did he say to you when you confessed your little pranks?"

"He forbid me to do it again."

"Very good, but you do not look as if you had followed his advice."

"Why, dear cousin?"

"Because your eyes pronounce the contrary."

I smiled and threw myself on her neck.

"Don't hang on me so, my little friend, for I am terribly warm. Let us work together until supper time," she said, giving me a motherly kiss.

Then while we were working she regaled me with an account of the beauties of a religious life, although I had already told her that I would embrace it, if for no other reason than to be always near her. I repeated my promise, taking a most solemn oath to that effect. From that time the most cordial relations, which exist even to the present time, date. Mamma, who came to see me quite often, was well pleased with my final resolutions and announced it with greater amiability than usual.

The following day at eleven o'clock in the morning, Dom de la Platier and Panza came to the Abbey. One was the lover of Rosa and the other was Agatha's. As I wished to see them together and judging that they would make use of the same room in which I had seen my cousin, I skirmished around a little and found an old entrance to an unused hallway, which ran along the back part of the building. I examined the wall and discovered that it was broken in a place where I had only to pull aside a piece of tapestry to gain a full view of the room.

My cousin had told me that she would spend the afternoon with the Abbess, so I went and took my place at the peephole in the wall. I was waiting some time, when finally they arrived. Agatha locked the door behind them and put the key into her pocket. Veils and skirts were soon cast aside, instruments of war were displayed and seemed in good condition. All four threw themselves on the bed, where after an exchange of a few sweet phrases they placed themselves in position for the sacrifice.

I had a full view of the posteriors of the reverend gentlemen, which were going like steam engines, while my ears caught the sounds of disjointed words and exclamations, such as: "Fuck . . . ah . . . deeper . . . quicker. I could d-i-e . . . fuck; keep on, you dear f-u-c-k-e-r."

But then there is a limit to everything and this sport of pleasure is no exception. Dom Panza was the first to roll off, exposing as he did so the cunt of the slender blonde, and if cunts shed tears, hers certainly was doing so. Flowing down the crack of her splendid arse, they formed a pool on the towel they had so thoughtfully placed there. The other two came in a close second.

They were still in the act of drying their parts when my cousin, who I thought was still with the Abbess, happened to pass close by the corridor in which I was stationed, caught sight of me and, coming up softly, beckoned me to follow her. My confusion was too great to describe. I ran hurriedly away and was the first to reach our room.

"That is very nice, I must say, to play the spy like that!" she said in a low tone. "If the sisters knew that you had spied on them, they would never forgive you."

I must have looked very downcast, for my cousin came and threw her arms about me and, bursting into laughter, she began to reassure me. "Come now, Angelica, don't be afraid," she said. "Truly, I would not have them know it for anything in the world, but tell me how you came to peep at them?"

Mustering a little courage, I answered:

"I was on my way to the park and while passing through the corridor, I heard queer noises to my right, so I looked to see what it was. I hadn't been there more than a second when you came along." She eyed me steadily for a moment and began: "What you have seen prompts me to tell you sooner than I had wanted to of many things that are being done here. Of course, you have been kept in ignorance until now, but I must exact a promise from you never to divulge either what you have just seen or what I am going to tell you now. Since you have made up your mind to stay with us, I will reveal all to you this evening, keeping nothing back."

"Oh, cousin," I replied, "I shall be very discreet; depend upon it."

Then we embraced each other and went to the apartments of the Abbess. We had supper with her, after which we returned to our apartments and as soon as we were in bed, we resumed the conversation. My cousin—Felicity was her name—began thus:

"Because I wished to have you always with me, I induced you to embrace the life of a nun, but I swear that if I had been unhappy, I would have warned you not to take this step. But as it is, I consider myself happier here than I could ever hope to be in the world.

"Here we have all the enjoyment of life without its inconveniences. Women were made as companions to men, and this maxim is practiced, if not openly preached, in this convent, and you have seen how pleasant it is to have one's arms and legs twined about a man capable of satisfying one's wants, you will learn more of this later.

"I noticed with pleasure how you were growing and, better still, how sensible a mind you had. Onion peddlers know each other even in the dark, so you need not be surprised when I tell you that your little prank with Dom Delabrise did not escape my attention when I surprised you in the parlor together. One look was enough; I knew as well as if you had told me what had taken place. I am delighted that you have taken a liking to him and, far from putting any obstruction in the way of your lovemaking, I will do all I can to bring you two together as often as possible."

"Oh, how much I am obliged to you, dear Felicity. Yes, I do love him. I conceived an affection for him even before I knew why, but really I feel a tenderness towards him that I cannot explain. I might say that I love him through some kind of present that he can contribute to my happiness and I am never happy when I am not in his company. The day you surprised us in the parlor was a cruel intrusion for me, for I enjoyed myself with him."

"Had you already accomplished the act? You know what I mean?"

"No, but his hands were feeling all over and the sweet kisses he was showering on me gave me so much enjoyment that I have ever since had a longing for his company."

"No doubt he did not fail to show you what he had?"

"No, I am sorry to say, you came in on us too soon but I have been doubly repaid by the splendid view I had of Dom Panza and Dom Platierre."

"And what did you think of their tools and the manner in which they used them."

"I saw that they were strangely made and of enormous size and capabilities, and I wondered greatly how such big things could disappear in the bushy depths between the sisters' outstretched legs and also at the ever quickening in-and-out motion and movements of the sisters' arses, who seemed to want to follow the retreating tools. All this seemed to give general contentment, both to the attacked and the attackers."

"And what did you do all this time, Angelica?"

"I was all on fire and I wished to be treated in the same manner, and this being out of the question I decided that if this could not be a duet than I must content myself with a solo."

"Never mind the solos, some day you will play duets and quartets, too, only do not rush things, just keep cool and wait. Dom Delabrise suits you. He is a handsome young fellow, I congratulate you on the choice, but listen to my advice.

"We all make mistakes and you made one when you let him take so many liberties with you on so short an acquaintance. You never should throw yourself at a man's feet like that, nor let him guess that you are as passionate or even more so than himself.

"It is only after a great deal of attention and perseverance on their part and after giving an undeniable proof of their regard by an assiduous courtship that we should accord them a small favor. This makes them more ardent lovers, more devout worshippers at the shrine of our charms. It is in this way that we must lead them on. Now, take me, for instance: I have a good friend in the parish priest, you must have seen us often together.

"Now, do you imagine that I abandoned myself to him all at once? I should say not. Many a time I have heard him plead and sigh, many a time I have seen him on his knees begging me to have pity on him, assuring me with heartrending sighs that he could never live through his martyrdom, so whatever favors he now receives, he paid for dearly.

"And when your friend comes, I promise he shall be yours on condition that you keep him in suspense for quite awhile before you grant him the last favor."

"I understand now, my dear Felicity, I have been so easy."

"No doubt you have."

"You can leave it to me. I will bear in mind what you have told me, only I think I am taking a great risk. I might lose him because . . ."

"Because your sensuous nature torments you, that's it. We all have passed through the same trying process but rather than lay down my arms, I'd sooner use a candle. It is always that way with people who do not wish to listen to good advice and let their passions get the best of them, and it usually ends disastrously. I do not feel like saying any more tonight. Let us sleep now; some other time, more on the subject."

Before going to sleep, I reflected on what my relative had told me. I was overjoyed at the thought that from now on I could see Dom Delabrise without trouble, and I formed plans how to act when in his company. My little intrigue with Father Anselmo had taught me many things, and he, too, would not meet with the same complaisance on my part as heretofore.

The following day my cousin completed her revelations as to the amorous life the sisters were living and I renewed my promise to take the veil as soon as I was of proper age.

After dinner I took my work and went to the Mother Superior. She received me in a cold, reserved manner. I responded in the same way. I also called on several of the sisters, who received me with more cordiality. But the one who pleased me the most was Suzanne, whose acquaintance the reader will make in the course of my history.

What I longed for, for a long time, finally arrived in the shape of a letter from Dom Delabrise and it tended to rouse my drooping spirits more than anything else that could have happened; he wrote:

"Dear Angelica:

"I was in hopes of seeing you yesterday but an unhappy chance deprived me of that pleasure. I hope, however, soon to be able to tell you with word of mouth what my pen cannot explain in a proper manner.

"If ever a man fully appreciated his good fortune it is myself, your humble servant, I assure you, entrance into the convent was the beginning; and you were at that age when you couldn't understand what love is. I was drawn to you by some invisible force. I thank my good fortune that I enjoy seeing the little flower which I might say I planted with my own hands blossoming out into a beautiful rose, which I flatter myself is for me to pluck.

"Dear Angelica, twenty times a day I leave my most serious occupation just to let my mind dwell on thoughts of you. I can hardly wait for the time when I can tell you how worthy you are of my deep and sincere love; it is my hope that our superiors will not again break up our sweet tête-à-tête.

"With a love that cannot be written, I have the honor to be,

"Your most humble servant,

DOM DELABRISE."

Showing this letter to my cousin, she made me promise to treat him with more reserve than before, so I answered him in the manner indicated below:

"Dear Sir:

"Your letter is full of kind expressions, but kindliness on your part is not new to me, so I assure you of my heartfelt gratitude.

"I invite you to come whenever you wish, you will always be well received, provided you keep yourself well in check and do not become too enterprising.

"My cousin, who is a very farsighted person, reproached me severely and you know I had reason to reproach myself. You have lost my esteem but you may regain it again by never placing me in the same embarrassing position, which would force me to withdraw it.

"Yours truly,

ANGELICA."

After dinner the same day, the parish priest, Dom Panza and Dom de la Notte, came into the Abbey. Their lady loves joined them after dinner and I went to call on Suzanne. I would have much preferred to spy on the three amorous couples, but it was expressly forbidden and what really prevented my spying the most was that they had chosen a room that was tightly closed.

At night my cousin had as usual her confidential chat. I started in:

"I have passed a long and tiresome afternoon, though Suzanne is a charming girl, I was not at ease with her and consequently our conversation was uninteresting."

"You know, Angelica, what I told you, don't

precipitate anything with the sisters, let them make advances first. None, besides the prioress, know that you are aware of our amours, and Suzanne is not yet one among us. She has been struggling against Dom Bigot for nearly a year and has not surrendered yet, but I think nevertheless she will soon come into our dove cote."

"Did you not enjoy yourself very much this afternoon?"

"My admirer proved his love four times."

"And the prioress?"

"Just as much, with this difference, that she has not got to adopt the precautions that we do; so there is nothing wanting in her enjoyment, which is therefore much greater."

"Then she runs no risk of getting knocked up?"

"She has been going through this performance for ten years and nothing has happened to her yet. There are lots of sterile women and she is one of them. I am not fool enough to take any chances, and I advise you to look out for your own little affair. Now let us sleep, but where are your hands?"

My cousin was not mistaken for during our conversation I had been rubbing and fingering myself until I brought on the crisis just when she ended her admonition.

"There on my breast."

"Come now, don't do that too often, it is harmful."

The prioress called on us the next day, bestowing upon me more than the usual attention and consideration.

"Now, Angelica," she said, "don't fib, why did you not say your devotion today?"

I reddened and looked helplessly at my cousin.

"Speak up, now, do not be afraid of me, I am one of the girls myself." She gave me a kiss and I returned it warmly and allowed her to examine me very thoroughly.

"There is a little down sprouting on it already," she said, addressing my cousin. "It is already beginning to darken this fluffy spot here, what do you think Felicity, is she not fit soon to be on the peg?"

In return I said many funny things; among others, I asked her why moss was growing on such funny things. She answered saying that all she knew about it was that it was natural for one's cunt to wear tresses.

We went for a walk and while passing a small cabinet in the park, I saw Suzanne with a Franciscan monk, who was looking very downcast. I made my thoughts known to my companions, who enlightened me on his history.

The next day the lovesick monk returned to the charge but in vain; he finally decided to let Agatha plead his cause for him. In the following I will endeavor to give part of the conversation that I overheard between Dom Bigot and Suzanne.

"How can you be so severe with me, Suzanne? Have compassion on me and reward my faithful love and grant me the favor you crave yourself."

"It is of no use; it can never be. Why can we not love each other without . . . no. No . . . it cannot be, I tell you."

"You torment me beyond all description, if you were less beautiful, my suffering would be less; pray have pity on me. Why do you wish to avoid me? Can nothing that I say have any effect upon your obstinate will?"

"It cannot be. I repeat it, no. Be done with it."

"Oh, Suzanne, by all that I hold dear in this world, I promise . . ."

"Come, come now, my fine gentleman, so that is what you wish, is it? Well, make your mind easy; no man yet got the best of a woman against her will. You are an ungrateful wretch. Now leave me; I never want to see you again."

Our fair one tore herself from his grasp and seemed greatly exasperated.

Agatha, following a sign from Dom Bigot, appeared upon the scene to lend her assistance to overcome the scruples of the fair nun. Addressing Suzanne, she said:

"How are you? What on earth ails you, you look so cross. Is it because Dom Bigot is leaving so soon?"

"Please don't mention his name in my presence again. I don't like him, and if you have come to talk about him, you will do me a favor to retire."

"Calm yourself, dear friend, and try to bring back the cheerful smile that is becoming to you, yes, I can speak to you about him, and what is more, I want you to listen. If you had only seen him as he went out, he was not the same man anymore. He begged me with tears streaming down his face to set him right with you and I am confident that had I not promised to intercede with you in his behalf, he would be tempted to do something rash. Such love, Suzanne, deserves a better fate."

"Actions speak louder than words with me, dear Agatha. When one loves, he conforms to the loved one's wishes. He knows what my thoughts are on certain things and he has promised me a hundred times never to give offense to them, and just as often he has failed to keep his word."

"His conduct is a proof of the love he bears you. He has only had eyes and ears for you and no one else but you. Now if his love was not sincere, he would have tried to get even by making love to one of us. I give you credit for that but I think it would have done him a better service with you if he had been less attentive and had made you a little jealous by paying attention to one of us, but he is altogether too honest for that; he never even gave us a pleasant word or a smile. There was no one for him but Suzanne. I for my part think him a very handsome and attractive young man, and if I did not like you so much, I would set my cap for him."

"And what does that signify; have you not one already?"

"Good. Good. I could just hug you for those words; your heart betrays you. You are being moved to pity; you love him, you cannot deny it. It was not today that I found this out. Now, why don't you accord him that supreme happiness?"

"Since you have discovered my secret, I will make a clean breast of it to you. I have confidence in you and will tell you all, keeping nothing back. I love Dom Bigot as well as he ever loved me and I am sure my pleasure would equal his own if I let him have his way. But the fate of poor Richardierre is still fresh in my memory and I dread to undergo the same terrible ordeal.

"When I pulled away so suddenly, it was through fear that I would succumb. I did violence to my own desires in doing so, I assure you. If I pretended to disdain his lance it was not because I feared to have it pierce me, but I kept on repeating all the time to myself: Dom Bigot is a young and vigorous man and as soon as a free passage was offered him, he would stretch and tear me unmercifully, and then he would lose all self-control and my poor body would be the sufferer. This is the reason why I do not give in."

"Your fears are ill founded, my dear Suzanne. It is as much to his interest as to yours, that he should spare you, and he would therefore never think of causing you unnecessary pain. He is to return in three days; now tell me what I am going to tell him when he returns?"

"Oh, you are terrible; unawares you lead me on. He may come, however, he will never dare to make proposals, and you may be sure I will not make any advances."

"Don't trouble yourself on that score, I will give him the necessary hint."

"What is it you say? Now don't let him hope for it."

"All right, let us go for a walk."

La Richardierre, whom Suzanne referred to, was a young woman who had an affair with a rash devil-may-care fellow who knocked her up. Her worry and remorse were so great that she died before she gave birth to the fruit of her womb.

My cousin told me that Suzanne's affair was

as well as settled and she would soon be initiated with all due formalities into the society. My curiosity being aroused, she promised to satisfy it in some other way, arranging it so that I might be a spectator at the ceremony, taking care to place me where my presence would not be known to the priests or nuns.

After dinner, Dom Delabrise asked to see me in the parlor. I was a little embarrassed at the meeting but recovered myself. I answered his questions as easily as I could. My answers for a while kept him in respect, but soon his passion got the best of him and he became daring. I soon gave him to understand that if he did not behave I would leave the room.

"How coldly you treat me!" he said. "My unfortunate absence has worked a great wrong, I see."

"There is no coldness on my part," I answered. "I am delighted to see you, but remember what I told you in my letter."

"Only too well for my peace of mind; I greatly fear someone has supplanted me in your affections."

"You have a strange opinion of me, Dom Delabrise; I know no other than you. Gratitude or something deeper draws me to you and my ears are forevermore opposed to the pleadings of others. Now, stop, that will do, you are smothering me . . . take your hand away."

"Don't run away from me, you wicked girl."

"It is time for me to go," I said, as I rose to join the company in the park. He assented and I amused myself, romping with the sisters. Dom Delabrise, however, followed me whereever I went, now and then sighing, which told me he rather wished that we were alone.

I was with him for a few minutes before he left and allowed him to embrace me but once. My cousin was well pleased with my conduct and she exacted another promise that I would lead him on a little longer.

I will describe here the park, as it will be the scene of a number of actions, which will be described later.

It was rather a spacious park, with a lot of shady trees and bushes, grape arbors and a kitchen garden, so nicely distributed that any fancy would be suited.

Directly behind the vineyard was a pavilion. Its only apartment was one large room which derived its light from two windows. A large double door made the lattice work; for furniture it had two sofas and a few armchairs. The armchairs were so constructed that by lowering their backs they formed two beds of comfortable size; the springs were rather the worse for wear but still they were not so bad, considering the wear they were put to.

At each corner of the room was a small closet and in each closet a cot, strong and durable. The latticed door led to a terrace at each end of which was a pond with fresh, clear water. Trees surrounded this pond, giving bathers protection from the hot rays of the sun.

Back of the porch was a meadow surrounded by a thick hedge of elm trees. This was the favorite retreat of the loving couples and many were the sacrifices offered to Venus, the insatiable goddess. There was hardly a tree which could not tell of the homages paid to the frail goddesses under its shade.

I for one was enchanted with this retreat and I explored it over and over. When we were about to leave it, my cousin pointed out to me the place where I was to conceal myself the day on which Suzanne was to be initiated.

Dom Bigot returned the following day and immediately sought Agatha to find out from her how she had succeeded in appeasing the wrath of his beloved.

"May I ask what success you had in conducting my case with Suzanne?"

"I suceeded far beyond my expectations."

"What is that you say? Can it be possible that Suzanne will receive me?"

"She will receive you with pleasure, and you have everything to hope."

"Oh, tell me all, I pray of you, do not deceive me."

"Directly after your departure, I went to Suzanne and reasoned and pleaded with her. I made her see that her conduct towards you was harsh in the extreme and that any other in your place would have ended it right there. She received my words in a way that surprised me beyond doubt that she loves you, and if she has not yielded to you it is because she fears that you might lose control of yourself and would not be sufficiently able to protect her against conception."

"How much I am indebted to you! How can I ever repay you for your kindness? I have a new lease on life."

"She will probably enter a few objections, but push your cause and she will be yours."

"Suzanne will yield! I can no longer contain myself!"

"Contain yourself nevertheless and do not make any proposals before dinner; you would not have sufficient time and you might hurt your chances. Present yourself to the Abbess and do not let anyone see by your actions that you are up to something; after dinner, I will take Suzanne to the room under some pretext and then you may come in and I will retire. It is time for us to part now, so goodbye. I am glad to have been of service to you."

After dinner I did not fail to station myself where I could see and hear everything and, shortly after, I was delighted to see Suzanne and Agatha make their appearance.

"Why have you brought me here, Agatha?" said Suzanne. "I did not take notice where you were taking me to, I will not stay here, he can see me in the parlor or the park."

"Under the circumstances, when you are to become reconciled, nothing should trouble you."

"You are a wicked girl. Well, what did he say? Is his love still so warm?"

"He accosted me like a man who is swaying between love and despair, but no sooner had I told him that you were willing to see him again than he became a different man; he could hardly hold himself for joy."

"I will meet him with pleasure. He was in my thoughts all night long, and now I have nothing to fear, for here I know I cannot escape him. You make me laugh with your reasoning.

"To speak sincerely, I think I am going to yield and I fear, you know what. I dread he may be too large for me."

"Oh, you simpleton, do you not know that in coition the woman's part usually assumes a size large enough to take in the man's without any great suffering. I was equally struck with the size of Dom de la Platierre's instrument, but I suffered ever so little when he took my maidenhead and I felt so good when he was pushing it in that I was grieved beyond measure when he took it out again, and the only regret that I have today is that it is not twice its size, for the tighter the fit, the greater the pleasure."

"You will tell me all about it; I hear someone coming. Dear me, it is him . . ."

"Good-bye, I will leave you."

Dom Bigot entered and, going up to Suzanne said: "Ah, Suzanne, have I the happiness of meeting you again?"

"Please arise; I do not like to see you this way, kneeling before me."

"What do I hear, my pardon is assured? I must kiss those charming lips for it."

"I cannot breathe; my, you are terrible."

"No, I am not, my angel, I am as gentle as a lamb."

"That will do, you crush my skirts."

"How white and well starched!"

"Oh, you naughty man, where are you putting your hand now; stop it, I won't have it."

"Why not, my dear; why do you oppose our mutual enjoyment? Let go my hand." And with this, he opened his robe and pulled out a very large staff and taking her hand, said: "See here, touch this."

"No. No." But at the same time he tightly held her hand on his fine prick.

"How cruel you are, I am crazy with impatience."

"How are you going to . . ."

"I will take into consideration your fears,

and you shall not suffer in the least, come . . . now let me . . . I cannot wait."

"Oh, how hard you throw me on the bed; leave my skirts down, I tell you."

"Oh, what thighs, so white and firm. Did mortal ever see such a beautiful cunt? Oh, why have you made me wait so long."

"Oh, it is too big. You hurt me, you tear me apart, it will never go in. Oh! Oh! How you hurt . . . oh!"

"A little patience, it must go in and it . . . goes . . . in . . . at . . . last . . . at l-a-s-t!"

"Oh, Bigot, my dear friend—I am c-o-m-i-n-g . . . oh . . . how nice. Oh, Bigot, I, I . . . love you."

"Oh, Suzanne, kiss me, hold me tight, move your arse faster . . . faster, oh, ah, ah . . ."

"Now, look what you have done, I am all wet."

"Give me a kiss, Suzanne, dear, you see I have been careful not to deposit my semen where it might cause trouble."

"I have been a goose to deprive myself so long of so much pleasure. I will never refuse you any more, but let us rest a while now. Let me look at that queer tool of yours. Let me examine how it is made, but do you know that at the start it hurts like fury and only my love for you made me submit to the pain your lance was putting me to?"

"And afterwards?"

"Towards the last it gave me a great deal of pleasure, well compensating me for what I had suffered at the start."

"Come, lay down again and spread your legs apart, so, that's right. Your cunt is wide open now and from now on, only pleasure will be your share in copulating, otherwise called fucking."

"Now, easy . . . slowly . . . it hurts a little when your prick enters, now it is all right."

"Ah, dear little Suzanne, your tight little cunt feels heavenly around my prick."

"Hold me a minute, Bigot, my leg is cramped . . . all right, now."

"How do you like it, now? Do I fuck you right, love?"

"Yes, dear; but how pressed you must be, you fucked too fast. I cannot keep pace with you . . . there . . . you have done already, could you not hold out a little longer?"

"I did not hurt you very much that time?"

"No, my pleasure was greater than I ever dreamt it could be, only you left me behind this time, another time try and be slow until you see that it also overcomes me, or better still, let me tell you when to increase the tempo of your stroke. We can make it last longer then, but your prick is shrinking up, hold on; I will stiffen him again."

"Oh, you are an adorable girl; how your cunt works that prick of mine, your muscles inside are just playing with it, it feels as if a hand was frigging it, oh, glory, hallelujah, it is stiffening up, do you feel it, dear?"

"Yes, it is living again, that big snake inside of me, but you lecherous fellow, your hands are roaming everywhere, what do you think of that backside of mine for a pair of cymbals; there is plenty to get hold of, is there not? Oh, you cochon, but it feels fine to have your finger in my arsehole."

"You beat Venus as regards the beauty and size of your arse and you certainly will make a worthy priestess of Venus, an expert performer in all the differnt ways of making love, my pet."

"Enough talking; now act, you are in condition again, so let us do it once more and then we will rest."

Dom Bigot, to prolong his own as well as his partner's ecstasy, kept himself well in control, he treated her to long, strong, but slow, pushes and managed to make Suzanne spend several times without losing his own seed, working up the naturally lascivious nature of his partner to an erotic fury which found expression in the wanton movements of her arse and the obscene words she continually uttered to the intense delight of Dom Bigot.

Finally, after several spasms of delight, they glued their lips together and now Bigot let go at her with all his might and after a number of very rapid strokes, they both spent and then for a few minutes lay motionless and still. Then, after indulging in several glasses of wine, they fell asleep in each other's arms.

This refreshment was of great benefit to them. The attitude they assumed in going to sleep, pleased me greatly. Their legs were entwined, her hand was holding his staff of life, his hand was on her grotto of love, their partly opened mouths were near together, they seemed to breathe but one breath.

Never was a more beautiful pair than Suzanne, who was not yet twenty, and Dom Bigot, who was barely five and twenty.

Watching them, I cursed the lawmakers here below who could so cruelly make laws against a sensible and real pleasure as this was.

I left them sweetly sleeping in each other's

arms and started to go into the park, when an unforseen event made a sudden change in my plans.

Just at the entrance of the park I heard the sound of voices, I stopped to listen and looking towards the spot whence the voices came from, I saw the Abbess' chambermaid and a strange manservant. Soon I became aware of what was going to be done. The show had just commenced when I became an interested spectator.

The aforesaid manservant had his one hand under Rosalie's skirts and with the other hand he was hugging her for further orders. Rosalie was not slow in doing her best to repay the compliment. I heard him ask her to come into the park. It would be better there, he said, they would be more comfortable in one of the shady bowers. "There is no convenience here and I do not like to fuck standing up."

"Oh, no," said Rosalie, "someone might see us; wait, I will get into a position that will enable you to get at me in fine shape." So saying, she put her head against the wall and jutted out her rump in a most advantageous manner.

There was no delay on his part. He quickly divested himself of everything but his white vest and shirt, which he tucked up around his waist, showing the lower part of his body and his battery ready for the attack.

He got at her from behind and soon his rammer was sheathed up to the hilt. After treating her for a few minutes to slow, deliberate strokes his movement began to slacken.

"Hold back a little, Rosalie," he whispered. "Let us try to get through together."

He stopped a moment or two but soon began again with redoubled vigor.

"I am coming," cried out Rosalie. "And here it is from me," cried the footman, as he was getting into the short digs, then a few spasmodic jerks, one long shove and all was over.

I could see by the twitching of their thighs and legs that they were enjoying the supreme pleasure as she felt herself backed up tight against the belly of her stallion.

They rested, letting their instruments soak in the plentiful spendings of each other. Master Jacques unsheathed his tool covered with spunk. He seemed to have lost confidence in his copulating powers, for when Rosalie showed by unmistakable signs that her appetite was not yet appeased, he cried for quarter, saying:

"Wait until evening. I am tired now; tonight in the park we will be more at our ease." After putting themselves in order they again took a stroll in the park. I did likewise, staying there nearly an hour. Then I went back to take a look at the two lovers. They were still in nearly the same attitude that I had left them. Agatha entered a few minutes later and slapped Suzanne's arse and pulled the Reverend Father's nose.

"It is you, is it?" she said, as she awoke, and the amusing part of it was that the fair lady, feeling ashamed, hid her face in her hands and at the same time made a grand display of her arse and cunt. Bigot threw his arms around her and embraced her warmly.

"What do you say to it now?" asked Agatha.

"Look," replied Suzanne, "what havoc he has caused, but I don't fear him any longer. He can fuck me whenever and as often as he pleases, the more the better."

"Ah, how you excite me!" put in the brave priest. He began to finger her but soon thinking of something better, he pulled her to the edge of the bed and putting her legs on his shoulders, he took straight aim and drove his dagger home. She withstood the onslaught most admiringly, not in the least abashed by the presence of Agatha, who was applauding and urging him on with cries like:

"That is the way ... get there! Lively ... harder ... fuck that fresh cunt with might, let her have it strong and hard ... that's right ... drive it into her up to the womb, fuck her, Bigot, you are all right."

And Suzanne, whether it was to please her companion or her salacious self, paid him back tit for tat, move for move. Then, taking him by the chin, she pulled his face towards her, letting her tongue protrude far between his lips, inviting him to suck it. Both would have liked to prolong the struggle, but the crisis came too soon, amidst spasmodic heaves and long-drawn sighs.

Agatha, after giving them time to regain their breaths, announced that there was company in the abbey.

"Who is there?" asked Suzanne.

"Cimbreau, the canon, and two officers of dragons. Felicity has made the acquaintance of the canon and the prioress and Rosa have taken charge of the officers. Last year they were very intimate, so arrange your clothing and come; you will be interested."

As soon as I heard this, I went to see the prioress and her friends. I was made the recipient of much attention on the part of the three gentlemen. Especially was this the case with the canon, whose compliments were profuse.

Agatha and Suzanne, after getting Dom Bigot away, came and joined us. My cousin drew me aside and asked me to get Suzanne to share her bed with me, which she agreed to without hesitation. I knew what this meant.

We all supped together and, after supper, we arranged a party for the benefit of the good old lady.

Rosa and one of the officers left the room together; it was then about eleven o'clock. I suspected they were up to something, so in an offhand way I told Suzanne that I had something to do and if she would kindly wait for me I would be back shortly.

The chamber that served for these gallant tête-à-têtes was not far off, and although it was now dark, it would serve their purpose better than the park; I was not mistaken and quietly drew near and overheard their conversation.

"Do not scold me, sweetheart," said the officer. "I did not think it would be so long before I could see you again. I counted the days until the order came for us to return home with our regiment."

"You are great rovers, you soldiers. You roam about from place to place, all the time. At least you might let me hear from you, if you cannot come to see me."

"What about you. I would also like to hear from you when I am away, but let us make better use of the time that we can be together, than to reproach each other. I want to gaze on your hidden charms and give the poor thing between my legs a chance to revel in your hermitage, so small and cute. How silky is the moss that grows along these avenues. Oh, how I love to feel the quivering flesh of a woman."

"You ought to know my heart, Byron. Remember last year when you told me my rump was like the canon of the holy church."

"Exactly, you have a beautiful rump and your neck has no equal in form. Yes, you were very kind and obliging to me last year, and I hope you enjoyed yourself as well as I did."

"I certainly showed by my behavior that I did."

They exchanged a few more kisses and then Rosa invited him to take coffee with her next morning in that very room.

I hastened away and rejoined the company.

I slept that night with Suzanne, who was very pleasant company till we fell asleep. The next morning I went to see how Rosa and her soldier were getting along with their coffee. I judged by the state of their clothing that one combat had already been fought. Rosa was sitting on the foot of the bed, arms and shoulders bare, while the baron drank out of her cup. I noticed that the baron's tool was standing forth in all its glory.

The coffee down, his ever-ready hand began to play on her instrument, then he upset the fair nun and examined, to his own as well as her satisfaction, the abode of carnal pleasure.

Then, begging her to remain in that position, he rammed his prick into the willing cunt of the salacious nun.

It surprised me with what vigor and abandon they finished the act and I feared the consequences for Rosa, but I have found out since that when such love encounters follow themselves in succession, they are entirely harmless, for the discharge after the third assault is but thin water, incapable of producing a germ.

These two fortunate lovers did not give up the combat till both had a surfeit of pleasure. I had seen enough. I went in search of my cousin, I found her still in bed and was questioning her how she had spent the previous night when the prioress entered.

"What, still in bed, little woman?"

"Yes, I am very tired; that horrid canon would not let me close an eye all night. Did you come after me; wait a moment, I will be ready."

Two Franciscans had arrived at the abbey, Dom de la Platierre and another strange monk. It was a happy event for Agatha. She found occasion to absent herself before dinner and in the afternoon had the complaisance to entertain her lover and his friend, one after the other and then both together, one taking the legitimate road and the other occupying the neighboring premises in her arsehole.

Dom de la Platierre, as a matter of courtesy, took the sodomitic quarters. I devoted a part of the afternoon to answering a letter which I received from Dom Delabrise; his letter follows:

"Mademoiselle:

"You cannot imagine my feelings since I

have last seen you. I do not know what to make or think of it. A thousand different thoughts are crossing my mind. What have I done to be treated thus. Everything I said was treated by you as a huge joke; I am suffering.

"Now, if you really do not disdain me, why do you act so? I am not entirely ignorant of what has taken place between my confreres and the sisters and I am as interested as they are to keep the secret. I know that they are happy. Why should I be the unhappy one?

"If you were not going to embrace a religious life, like myself, I would be obliged to take some kind of action. I do not know myself. But we will both soon be members of the same religious order, so why not make our hearts one?

"When my studies are over I will attach myself to the same monastery where I am now and I will be able to give you frequent proofs of my love and devotion. For heavens sake, take pity on me. I am waiting impatiently for your answer and I am and always will be,

"Your slave,

DOM DELABRISE."

This letter really touched my heart and I answered as follows:

"Monsieur:

"I cannot persuade myself that you conceived the idea that I ridiculed all those gracious things that you said to me.

"Why were you so greedy? If I avoided you, it was because you were arousing in me the same passions that were consuming you and I well knew that if I did not flee, I would lose all my self-control. You are welcome to come any time and be convinced.

"Adieu, till we meet again,

ANGELICA."

I read my letter over and saw I was giving him a pretty good hold on me, but considering everything, I decided to let it go.

All that I had seen had made such an impression on me that I could not wait. Our guests remained for three days at the abbey and nothing was spared to make their stay agreeable.

The day of their departure the younger Franciscan handed me a letter and box from Father Anselmo. Quickly withdrawing, I found the very thing he had promised me, a medium sized dildo covered with skin and mounted with silver, and containing everything for its operation. His letter stated his regret that he was obliged to depart without seeing me once more and his hope to be more fortunate on his return.

Felicity and myself retired to our room. As soon as we were seated she asked how I was progressing with my love affair. I showed her the last letter I had received from Dom Delabrise and told her what I had answered.

"Yes, my child, it is as I expected. The scenes which you have witnessed in the last few weeks have ripened you and you are longing for the delights of copulation and your health will suffer if the sacrifice of your maidenhead is delayed much longer. And as you seem to have Dom Delabrise well in hand and he is devoted to you, it has been decided by the prioress and myself that Dom Delabrise, who will be here tomorrow, shall have the pleasure of plucking your maidenhead and introducing you to the joys of being well fucked; does that meet with your approval?"

"Yes, dear cousin, I cannot wait the time. I have been suffering from the want of consolation a strong man can give a poor woman. I thank you very much for procuring me this bliss so soon."

"Good. Then hold yourself in readiness to receive him tomorrow afternoon, but do not think that all will be smooth sailing. You will have to undergo some pain, but of course, you know that; bear it bravely and joy will soon reward your suffering.

"Remember, too, that you must not let him spend inside of you for at least the first three times. I will caution him myself to take care of that."

The following day my cousin pointed out to me that it would be best to rest up well before the final actions were taken. I would experience more satisfaction and be in better condition to undergo the operation without the least trouble.

Finally evening came and with it Dom Delabrise. We greeted each other in a formal way, as everybody was watching us. We sat down to supper and after supper we had a stroll in the park, during which he managed to rouse my feelings to the highest pitch of erotic excitement. He led me to a seat and, kneeling down in front of me, he put his hand under my clothes. My legs spread to give his fingers room to explore all my hidden charms. Soon he made me take up my dresses. Drawers I had already taken off on the advice of Felicity.

"Oh, dear Angelica," he said, "you have such a beautiful little cunt. I must kiss it." I felt his tongue licking and sucking at the top of the love chink. He soon had me afire. I pressed his head with one hand and, leaning down, tried to find his tool.

He took notice and managed to get it out of his trousers and put it into my eager hand. It felt as big as my arm. I pressed and fingered it and this excited me so that I paid my tribute in a plentiful shower.

After letting me rest for a while, my lover jumped to his feet and said: "Come, dear, let us go to your rooms, I must possess you now or I shall waste what by right belongs to you."

I was only too eager and we hastened as fast as we could to reach my room. My cousin greeted us there with a smile and said: "I will only help you undress and then I will withdraw until tomorrow morning. I hope by that time you will have been made a woman," She began to undress me and after having stripped me to the skin, she rendered my lover the same service. Going to the wardrobe, she brought out a perfumed bottle of vaseline and, taking his tool in her hand, applied a generous dose all over it. Then, turning to me, she greased the holy of holies and with the words: "Dom Delabrise, I have done all I could to make your path smooth and slippery, get into her and do not spare her salacious little cunt," she retired.

Hardly had the door closed when my lover placed me in the position he thought best for the work in hand. He laid me across the bed, with my arse on the edge, then he put one pillow under me, spread my legs as far apart as possible and, getting between them, he placed his prick at the entrance and tried to force his way in. He got his head in and stuck; he gently moved back and forwards, steadily pressing inwards and gaining ground slowly but surely, while I suffered immense pain under the stretching that my cunt had to undergo. But I suppressed as much as I could all signs of suffering.

Dom Delabrise said: "Dear, only a little patience, you will soon feel only pleasure, your pain will vanish. I will draw back a little ... now in again. Ah, delicious! I feel your hymen; I must go through that, then you know only pleasure will be your share. I am swelling up more; the thought of taking a maidenhead is too exciting; I must go in now or I will spend before I have ravished you, you little angel." And with this he began to push with all his might and, drawing his tool nearly entirely out of me, he returned to the attack with a mighty shove. I felt something tear within me and his big prick was in to the hilt. I fainted and when I came to again, I found Dom Delabrise busy inspecting my lacerated cunt and applying some water to it, washing off the bloody traces of my virginity.

He looked up and, seeing me smile, he jumped up and kissed me rapturously. Then laying me lengthwise on the bed, he got in beside me and sucked the nipples of my bosoms and soon the amorous desires overcame all fear of pain. Getting hold of his ever ready prick, I pulled him on top of me.

He was soon in me and treated me at first to slow, then ever-quickening movements, which soon brought on a plentiful spend of my love-juice; he followed suit, but when he felt it coming he pulled out his prick and spurted it all over me from my cunt to my neck. As soon as the last drop was out, he drove the still stiff prick in again, so as to get the cunt used to its visitor, as he expressed himself. He repeated the same action twice more in succession and finally, overpowered from sheer exhaustion, we both fell asleep.

In the morning, I was all ready for poking again and my lover set to work with a vim that made me sigh with pleasure. This time we—at least I—really enjoyed to the full the delightful actions and experienced an entire feeling of satisfaction and contentment.

I was plied with all kinds of questions and everyone wanted to hear a complete account of my defloration.

Sunday evening we all repaired to the pavilion to prepare for the formal initiation of Suzanne. The actors, to the number of six, met in the parlor at seven o'clock; they were soon joined by their mistresses. The door was locked and bolted and, after embracing one another, we drank some spiced chocolate. We were ordered to disrobe and were soon in a state of complete nakedness, during which we all regarded each other.

Suzanne was led in. The two little mounds of her breasts were firm as ivory and white as alabaster, and the two crimson buttons a feast for the eyes.

We were all sworn to the rules of the order; never to divulge anything we may see, hear or do in the meetings.

A bed was then brought forth and Suzanne was placed on it. Then we were each instructed to take a partner and arrange ourselves on cots close by and await the word of the prioress.

This soon come. "Get ready, Dom Bigot, and do your duty by Suzanne and we will follow suit." No sooner said than done. Suzanne suffered the introduction of the big prick of her lover without a murmur and soon the rocking and poking became general.

Suzanne and Dom Bigot got out of their bed and received the congratulations of their confreres.

After a little rest, each chose a partner for the second act of this lustful drama. They wished to offer, all at the same time, their noble sacrifice, to the goddess who presided over all their pleasures and they finally drowned their instruments in streams of spunk.

The prioress, while being fucked, amused herself by handling the two pricks of two fathers standing on each side of her, to give more ardor to the champion screwers. Each held across his lap one of the nuns, as one would hold a child about to be chastised.

Suzanne was stationed between these two batteries, belly to the front, thighs apart, two fingers holding open her pretty little snatch. Agnes and the parish priest were doing it dog fashion.

The prioress was far from satiated, for she

called de la Platierre to lie on his back. She mounted him and then called to de la Motte, offering him her arsehole to bugger, and, calling the Franciscan, she made him stand in front of her while she licked and sucked his prick.

After this sweet enjoyment, at which I had shed my love juice times without number, we all returned to our rooms for much needed rest.

* * *

I leave you to imagine what must have been my feelings after witnessing the scenes before described, being very young and possessing strong sexual passions.

Reaching my room, I threw myself on the bed and fell asleep. I cannot say how many stiff pricks I saw in my dreams. They were of all sizes and shapes and they made such an impression upon me that I awoke with a start, burning with sexual desire. Involuntarily I began to rub and press and finger my itching cunt, until a discharge brought relief.

Then, getting up, I partook of some light refreshments and went to the park again. It was about six o'clock. I saw the Society approaching and went to meet them; the ladies smiled pleasantly and the gentlemen passed some complimentary remarks.

I asked my cousin to tell the professor that I wished to speak to him and he hastened to my side. We entered one of the stalls and he asked me kindly what he could do for me. I asked him as a favor to let Dom Delabrise come over on the following Wednesday.

"With all my heart, my dear girl," he replied, "your wish will be granted. Who on earth could refuse anything to such a charming girl? You have the privilege of seeing him as often as you wish, but for the sake of appearance you must be cautious. However, you won't have to reproach me on that score.

"And will you promise me something in return? That you will meet me in some quiet corner and I will come expressly to see you. Try and have the key to the pavilion and I will write and let you know on what day I can be at your service. Now be sure and don't disappoint me."

He embraced me again and then, hearing the bell calling us to supper, we went in. All our guests had departed save Dom de la Platierre.

We remained at table much longer than usual in order to amuse the Abbess but as the conversation ran along very dull subjects, everybody was glad to retire when the sign was given.

On finding ourselves alone in our room, my cousin asked me if I had seen everything that had taken place.

I told her that I had not, for I had left about the time that Dom Bigot had finished. "Then you missed the best part of it," she said.

"What in the name of God could you have done more?" I asked.

She described other parts of the ceremony of taking the vows of chastity with which I was about to become acquainted at my own initiation and which I will describe then.

Until the arrival of my lover, I passed most

of the time in the company of the ladies, who now gave me their full confidence. At last the long looked-for day arrived.

Dom Delabrise came straight to my room. Very little time was lost in cooing and loving; he upset me and had my skirts up in less time than it takes to describe it. He pushed his noble prick with one shove up to the hilt and fucked me beautifully twice in succession.

The night passed in a way you may imagine and we did not leave the bed until late the next day.

At about three o'clock in the afternoon we repaired to the garden, I having possessed myself of a key.

The day being very warm, we made our way to the fountain, which seemed so cool and nice that we soon divested ourselves of our clothing and proceeded to take a bath. After the bath we concluded that an offering to the god of love would be just the thing.

I had told him of the various postures that the ladies had assumed at the reception given to Suzanne and we tried a few. For instance, I made him fuck me dog fashion, which I enjoyed very much, as it seemed to me that his prick was penetrating me further than ever before; then we tried a St. George and finally the wheelbarrow act was given a trial.

However, as pain follows pleasure, we finally were forced to part. A messenger came to inform me that I was wanted in the parlor, so, kissing my lover, I hurried off to see what was wanted of me. On reaching the parlor, a woman handed me a letter. I broke the seal and read as follows:

"Sweetheart:

"I will meet you in the pavilion this evening at nine o'clock. Try to bring Suzanne with you. The strange Bernardino is very much in love with her and cannot make up his mind to leave without seeing her once more. I know she will come when she knows who is there. Take care to conceal this from everybody else. In pleasant anticipation, I am,

"Your humble servant,

P——"

I showed the letter to Suzanne and she seemed quite surprised. Then, recovering herself, she whispered:

"Ah, Father Grignolet, just what I want. You shall fuck me to your heart's content. He has such a fearful big tool; I was already longing to have it shoved into me at the reception."

We agreed to meet then at the appointed place. I then took my cousin into the secret, as I kept nothing from her.

After throwing on a few light wraps we went to the place. Hearing a rap, I motioned to Suzanne to conceal herself, just to make the other gentleman a little anxious, then I went and opened the door. They entered eagerly and Dom Grignolet, casting an eager glance around the room and not seeing Suzanne, asked with every sign of disappointment:

"Where is she?"

"She could not come," I answered, but Suzanne burst out laughing and was soon discovered.

"So this is the way you two tease people!" he cried, as he gave her a warm hug.

It was a lovely night, so we went and sat down on the edge of the meadow. I soon held the royal baton in my hand but I raised some objection to submitting to the principal object of our meeting, so he proceeded to calm my fears by kissing me and assuring me that it was not so monstrous after all.

"See," said he, "I will go nice and easy, and it will not hurt you a bit."

With a few words of encouragement from Suzanne, I let him have his way. He began by pushing lightly at the entrance, which invisibly opened, letting it slip in clear to the hilt, then making no further effort to control himself, he gave himself up to the fullest enjoyment of a passionate fucking. His movements, becoming faster and faster, were nearly equaled by my own and the supreme crisis came to us at nearly the same moment.

"See," he said as he treated my cunt to another vigorous lunge, "I got through in great shape and you also, little one. You know how to wriggle your arse to get there. Ah, that's the way. Squeeze tight. Oh, that's nice. I'm stuck on that juicy cunt of yours."

Grignolet and his companion were not so quick as we were, and they were making desperate efforts to catch up.

"Look," I said to the professor, "see the full moon bobbing up and down," referring of course to the big white arse of Grignolet, which trembled with suppressed emotion, so to speak.

Catching sight of an apple lying in the grass I made a dive for it, and, taking straight aim, I hit the bull's eye between the two fat cheeks of Grignolet's arse. This made us laugh but he, without stopping or losing a stroke, cried: "Stop your nonsense!"

After a few more strokes they came to a finish. Hours are but minutes when one is making love of this sort, and midnight was upon us before we knew it. So we proposed to the two gentlemen to make use of the two beds that were in the pavilion and that we would keep them company until morning.

They readily agreed to this and, the night being warm, we stripped. As the professor showed inclinations to take another turn, I took a kneeling position on the bed and he, understanding what was wanted, mounted me and drove his long prick into my hungry cunt from behind. I felt it pushing against my womb and this was decidedly the best fuck yet, though it tired me, and as soon as we both had spent, we fell asleep with the agreement of repeating the same performance in the morning.

The sun was already high when we awoke and the first thing that we did was to make an all around examination of our genitals, which naturally fired us to a repetition of the previous night's deeds. While the professor was engaged in doing it to me in the same fashion as the night before, Grignolet entered the room and said:

"Ah, my brother, you seem to be very well served by this young girl."

"Yes indeed, and how is it with your partner?"

"Fine, very fine; it could not be better. They say that enjoyment kills desire, but with me it seems to be born over again right away. I have no doubt that you are in accord with me, for your sweetheart is also most charming. Now that I think of it, I must make her pay for that prank of throwing the apple at my arsehole. I am sure I have another charge left." As the professor just then ejected his seed all over my buttocks and withdrew, he quickly took his place and treated me to a vigorous fucking, which I enjoyed to the utmost.

But I called to the professor and Suzanne to come to my assistance and slap this impudent arse while he was fucking me, which they did, thereby increasing the force of his strokes which formed a delightful diversion for the onlookers. This ended, we sent our friends away well satisfied.

The following Monday the Society gave another reception. I remained in my room and put Dom Delabrise through his paces.

A few days later the young Franciscan kept his word with Agatha. His return was the signal for launching into some new and varied amusements. She kept him in her own room during the first day of his arrival, in order that her companions might not see him and also that she might carry out the scheme that she had planned for just such an occasion.

The next day she sought me and said:

"Listen, Angelica, you must help me to disguise my young Franciscan, the one who gave you a letter for me about a month ago. You remember? He is in my room now and I want to pass him off for my niece. I will bet anything the ladies will not know the difference. Oh, what a lot of fun we will have.

"He is just light and nice enough to pass for a cute young miss of eighteen or twenty. Your clothes will just about fit him and everything will pass off all right, if you will only promise to hold your tongue."

"Don't worry about me, I will play my part all right. I think my cousin is not there now so I will run down to my room and bring up the dresses. Just wait a moment for me."

I soon returned, loaded down with petticoats, waists, skirts and chemises, drawers; everything, even shoes and stockings. The young Franciscan was there and hurried to relieve me of my burden, thanking me at the same time most graciously.

"I know I shall do something that will betray me," he said.

"Do exactly as we tell you," said Agatha, "and there will be no chance for it; your voice is soft and sweet and there is not a sign of hair on your face, so I do not see why . . ."

"I won't be able to keep from laughing and admiring at the same time."

I pretended to leave, but Agatha told me to come back as she would have need of my assistance, so I left the room noiselessly, retraced my steps, stooping down in front of the door, and listening to what was going on between the two.

First I heard the voice of Agatha saying: "Take off everything, why don't you?"

"What! My shirt too?"

"Why certainly; here is one for you to put on. Oh, the poor dear, how odd he looks, it is just too comical, oh, my . . . oh, my . . ."

"What do you mean, me or John Thomas? If you mean the latter all I have to say is, he is quiet now but it will not do to arouse him. I will not answer for anything he does then, for he has a head of his own."

"Never mind that, I have had my fill. Well, how awkward you are, here, not that way ... there, that is better ... hold on ... straighten the skirt a little, now the sleeve, so. Your breast is too flat, we have to puff it out that way. Now for the hair, I wish Angelica were here to help me."

"So her name is Angelica. She seemed to be a very nice, sociable young lady."

"You seem to take to her."

"Your kind favors are quite enough for me as long as you condescend to bestow them upon me. There is small chance of my looking elsewhere for them. Does she intend to become a nun?"

"Yes, and that before very long, too. Well, the devil take the bonnet, I cannot manage it. Ah, there you are, Angelica, just in time, I cannot manage this young lady's hair; a little more and I would be tempted to swear."

"My clothes fit him to perfection; give me that switch. Ah, there, that is it. Just too sweet for anything. How pretty you look, to be sure!"

"Hold on a minute."

"What is the matter? Have you the colic?"

"No, but I have the cramps."

"Oh, I see, you are not used to having such a pretty maid to dress you; it seems to upset you somewhat.

"Well, Agatha, you had better treat him for the cramps. I will be back presently." And with that I went out, running in again in about half an hour.

"Well, how is our young miss feeling now? From the condition of your clothing you two must have been working with might and main to effect a cure for the cramps." I helped them again to put themselves into a presentable shape.

A quarter of an hour afterwards the prioress entered with my cousin. Our strange young lady returned their salutations with the best of grace.

"Tell her to be seated," said the prioress, addressing Agatha. "Your niece seems to have caught a cold; how or when did she come? You have not told me that you expected her." A question like this would have embarrassed an ordinary person, but not one with such a ready wit as Agatha, and the Franciscan supported her nicely in everything she said.

"I did not expect the dear," said Agatha. "She was in deep trouble and I being her nearest relative, she came here for consolation and I am delighted that she did, even if she dropped in on me so suddenly and unannounced; she got here this morning."

While Agatha was thus pulling the wool over the eyes of her companions, the Franciscan cast down his eyes and assumed an air of deep distress and even went so far as to shed a few crocodile tears.

I had to turn my head to keep from laughing outright while the prioress consoled to the best of her ability, putting a multitude of questions to him all of which he answered in a way that would be creditable to the most accomplished liar.

"Do not grieve so, sweetheart. I know your mother will be very anxious about your sudden departure but she will feel better when she hears that you have come to this place. Tell me without concealing anything; what caused your sudden flight? I am a friend and adviser of your aunt and will be the same to you if you will let me. All I can do shall be done to make life pleasant for you while you remain here, so unburden yourself with the fullest confidence."

"Just because a young officer called on me several times, my mother imagined . . ."

"Ah, your mother imagined that all was not right between you two?"

"Yes, and she forbid him to enter the house."

"And that grieved you sorely?"

"Words cannot express my emotion, I cannot give you any idea of the extent of my suffering."

"But your mother did not raise any objection until you had done something to rouse her suspicion; perhaps he acted somewhat familiarly without meaning any harm. You know mothers are very jealous of the virtue of their daughters, so perhaps she was justified in acting as she did."

"Yes, it is true, she caught him as he was about to kiss my hand after he had whispered a lot of sweet words in my ears."

"Yes, yes, my suspicions were true, and when he had gone, she scolded you, I suppose."

"Yes, a great deal; from that time on my life was made a burden to me. It nearly drove me insane when I could no longer see him; his absence was insupportable. He was ever uppermost in my mind, his many acts of kindness, his pleasant and entertaining little stories . . ."

"And I suppose you devised a way of seeing him secretly?"

"Yes, that is true. Although my mother was very strict, she was not however so blind to her own pleasures that she did not leave me alone occasionally; times which I took occasion of to smuggle him into the house. I took one of the maids into the secret and was thus able to carry on our meetings for quite a while without being discovered.

"One day we thought she was at devotions when she came upon us; I concealed him as best I could but there were always gossipers about and the report soon spread that he was seen to issue from our garden at eight o'clock in the morning."

"I suppose that it was in your bedroom that you used to hide him from prying eyes?"

"How queer you are!" interposed my cousin, "asking such strange questions. It does not concern us where she hid him, just let her tell us what her mother said."

"She paid me a visit while I was still in bed and pounced upon me like a tigress. I thought she was going to tear my limbs from my body. She threatened me with placing me in a neighboring convent of which it was known that the inmates were treated in a very severe manner.

"I got up and dressed myself; I took only the clothes that I have on my back; I made my way to the hut of one of our tenants, which was not very distant. I remained there for the rest of the day and then made my way here to my aunt. So that is why I am here, enjoying the good fortune of your acquaintance and hospitality."

I now had to leave the room in order to relieve my pent up mirth, which done, I returned to help along the comedy.

"You must take your niece to pay her respects to the Abbess," the prioress advised Agatha.

"Not yet, I want first to write to my sister and I think it best to wait till I receive her answer."

"Well, as you think best; we must take her however, to see the house and the garden after dinner, and make the acquaintance of our friends. And you, my dear child," she added, turning to the Franciscan, "be at your ease and everything will come out all right."

My cousin heartily approved, only adding that she would be pleased to have me act as companion to the newcomer. Then, bidding us adieu, they retired.

No sooner were their backs turned than we had to burst into a violent fit of laughter. Agatha congratulated the Franciscan on the excellence of his acting and the better to show her appreciation, she gave him several impulsive hugs. I felt like doing likewise but he saved me the trouble and gave me a few hearty kisses, which I most graciously accepted. Then we went to dinner, bidding him come along and make himself at home.

As there were no other visitors at the abbey this afternoon, all the ladies came to visit us, as much out of curiosity to see the niece, so-called, of Agatha, as to pass the time away.

The Franciscan had to answer a thousand questions, which he did in such a clever manner that none suspected his sex. The reader will wonder at this and so would I, had I not been present to see it.

After vespers we went for a stroll in the park and by and by we found ourselves in the pavilion. The Franciscan was greatly pleased with it. Then all proceeded to go in bathing, a proposition which greatly embarrassed the Franciscan but he got out of it by pleading sickness, saying he feared taking more cold.

"Let them bathe without you," said the prioress. "Come over here and sit by my side to keep me company."

We retained our chemises in order to not scandalize the pretended young miss and I noticed that his gaze was principally fixed on Suzanne and myself. I was giving full play to the round globes of my posterior so that he could observe them at his ease and out of pure vanity, on entering the water, I raised my linen so that he could see that what I had concealed there was not to be sneezed at either.

The others who entered the water showed nearly as much as I did. He was evidently not used to such sights for they soon had their effect on his masculine nature.

Agatha perceived this and whispered in my ear: "We should at least have put drawers on him. I am sure he cannot help betraying himself." Sure enough, the prioress, seeing how uneasy he acted, asked him if he still felt indisposed and turning, he answered: "No." But the one thin skirt was ill-suited to hide the cause of his uneasiness and the prioress, accidentlly putting her hand down, felt something thick and rigid.

"Ah, what is this!" she exclaimed. "I believe if I am not mistaken, that . . . come here and see what a comical young lady we have here."

He made a comical effort to rise but she held him fast. "Oh, oh, girls, come here and see what a comical young lady we have here."

Three of them ran to see, their wet chemises drawn tight about their rumps. Agatha and I remained where we were, writhing in veritable spasms of mirth.

"Well, if this is not a nice how do you do; no wonder they were so careful of him."

My cousin came and asked me who he was and went back to tell the others.

"Ah, ah, my gay rooster! That is how you disguise yourself, so to pursue our young pullets; we will have to cut your *Corpus Delicti.*"

"Pardon him," said Rosa. "I pray thee, it would be too bad to deprive him of his cordon."

"Let me catch my breath, ladies, and I will perform any penance you may impose on me."

"Well, really," said Suzanne, "did you have to perform such very disagreeable ones during your apprenticeship, whenever you made some slight infractions on your saintly obligations?"

"I object to further questioning; I saw him first, so he belongs to me," said Agatha.

"You have no longer any claim on him," cried my cousin. "You ought to be satisfied with the slick game you put up on us, and take it in your turn, the same as the rest of us."

"For your sake, ladies, I wish that he was supplied with half a dozen good stiff ones," was the comment I had to make.

"See, you were in the plot, too, my pretty miss, and I have a mind to make you pay for it all. The more I think of it, the more it surprises me, and still, who wouldn't be deceived by that sweet countenance, those childish airs and those large, innocent blue eyes, and to better deceive us he made up a well constructed story of a supposed love affair, told with such an air of remorse and shame, I will never wonder at anything again."

"Embarrass me, my friend; oh, what a white skin he has and this that I hold in my hand is no trifle, either. Believe me, Agatha, I see here a choice morsel for you which I know you will certainly appreciate."

"Take some of it yourself while you are dressing, just to satisfy yourself of what he can do in that line."

"That is very well," said Suzanne, "but are you not afraid that it will tax his strength too much. He does not look rugged, so you ought to be as sparing with him as possible."

"True, but the young should work; it does them good. See the motion of his hind quarters, isn't it just splendid? Why, both of them are dying with rapture."

"Yes, but not in the same condition in which you took him. It will be some time before I furnish another bird for that bush of yours, seeing how you have treated this one."

Just then Rosa called: "I hear some noise in the pavilion. See, there is Dom Bigot, the Vicar and Dom de Platierre."

"Angelica, hurry quick into the shade of the elms with our young friend here and when you have rearranged his clothes, come back here again, both of you . . . good evening, gentlemen, you are welcome, have you just arrived?"

"I should say not, we have been rapping on all the doors for the past hour without a response. We began to believe you were not here. And how are you Suzanne, you have just bathed, I presume?"

"Yes, their skins look fresh and rosy."

"Pray be on your good behavior, for we have with us a young lady who would be greatly shocked at the least show of impropriety."

"Who is she?"

"She is Agatha's niece; see, here she comes with Angelica."

"She is a beauty, no doubt about it. I would rather have her tumble into my bed than many other things that I can mention."

"You talk as if everything was made for your especial benefit. You rascal, you cannot see a girl but what you want to get between her legs then and there."

The two monks greeted the Franciscan most cordially and made desperate attempts at gallantry, mistaking him all the while for a pretty young maid yet in her teens, and he acted the part to perfection.

The monks and most of the ladies finally departed, the prioress and Agatha remaining behind for a moment to bid me take good care of him, and to have him sleep in my cousin's room. My cousin being aware of this arrangement, slept elsewhere in order, as she said, not to discommode me and spoil our fun.

She also thoughtfully asked Agnes to bring our supper. I then returned to my young man, who said, as he greeted me with a kiss:

"I am to sleep with you?"

"Oh, no," I said, "you are to sleep in my cousin's room. I will have some clean linen put on her bed so that you may sleep comfortably."

"Oh, then I am to sleep without you?"

"After all that you have been through today, and what the other ladies have accorded you, I do not wish to be too exacting. I can wait for some other time, you must be in need of a good rest."

"I am not so tired but that I can fire a few more shots; you do not know the prowess of a votary of St. Francis."

"Well, I do not think you have any strength left, for you had to meet a woman today who well knows how to take the starch out of a thing like that, but if you insist, you rogue, let me see if there is any life in it."

"Yes, if you let me see that little cunt of yours. I had only a glimpse of it today as you were entering the water. My, but this is a dandy one."

"That will do; someone is coming. Oh, it is Sister Agnes."

"Here, I have brought you some supper. Ah, what a pretty companion you have, Angelica, and if I am not mistaken she is concealing something about her person that is against the rules."

"Ah, I see my cousin has let you into the secret, now tell me, wouldn't you wish to have a niece like that?"

"You certainly have made a nice catch, but I do not envy you your good fortune. I wish you every enjoyment. Here, this is to restore your failing energies, so excuse me: I must be off. Good-bye."

"That sister is a nice girl, to be sure."

"Sit over there and let us begin our supper."

"No, let us sit close together, but first let me take off this kerchief. You will be more comfortable. Let me uncover those beautiful titties; tell me all about them. Oh, how I long to kiss the dear little treasures."

I made him eat a great deal of celery roots, cooked in the broth of tender spring chickens and many other delicacies.

After supper we took a stroll in the park to aid digestion. During our walk he kept up his foolishness and I did not have the heart to enter any objection. We saw the two monks and some of the sisters approaching, so we turned and went inside. We sat up a little while and then went to bed. I pretended that I did not want to sleep with him and said:

"Listen, I am as fond of this pleasure as you are, but I know that men tire themselves sooner than we do, so do not tease me. I will give you all you want in the morning."

"Well, I am here now, so let us talk, laugh and enjoy ourselves. Since I came stark-naked into this world, I have been blessed with a goodly share of personal charms."

"Yes, your skin is white and very soft for a boy."

"Perhaps it is because I am so young yet and, like yourself, the only hair I have is on the top of my head or below on my belly, or maybe like a cat's a little round the tail, but as to tails, I have one of the nicest that you ever laid eyes on."

"Yes, but I do not want to see anything so nice. Hug me again and you can feel and play with what you think will amuse you the most. I won't object, but let me sleep now and I will promise you all you want tomorrow morning."

So we fell asleep and did not awake until ten o'clock the next morning. He was refreshed and was giving me a proof of it, when my cousin, the prioress and Agatha came in.

"Good morning, children. Just look at that young rogue, say, doesn't he seem to enjoy himself!"

"You ought to be grateful to us for getting you this lovely maid."

"I appreciate my happiness and your kindness as also that of the other ladies here, which calls for the most sincere gratitude. My satisfaction can but change to deep sorrow when a cruel fate compels me to part from so charming a place and from such friends."

"You are a good young man and we thank you, but listen, pet, remember it is because you are in holy orders and your companionship is agreeable, that we have accorded you this little diversion, but no indiscretions, you understand?"

"Your words do not please me. I am young, that is true, but I know when to hold my tongue. And besides, I am an interested party and I think you are right in not denying yourself the pleasures so dear to all the world, so have no fear of what I may say or do.

"We can well say that such and such has smothered all those desires that nature has given him, I have my own opinions about the matter and I am not simple enough to follow their lead. If I had embraced this calling, I have done what many others have done before me. One must hitch onto something or other, if he doesn't know how to make the most of it, that is his fault. Therefore, ladies, I hope to be able to give you now and then a proof of my gratitude."

"You have spoken so nicely that I am tempted to embrace you myself. You must come and see us often; you will always be welcome. Now, don't you think it is time to get up?"

I expect the reader to form anything but a good opinion of me for being unfaithful to Dom Delabrise so soon. And scanning over my conduct I must admit there are sufficient grounds for it. But I plead my youth for an excuse; I saw Dom Delabrise but once a week, so my passions, fanned by example, got the best of me.

That does not mean that the sentiments he had inspired in me have grown the least colder. If chance had thrown other lovers in my way, he remained always the most dearly beloved as the continuation of this story will prove.

The young Franciscan stayed four days longer and performed his penance to our entire satisfaction, promising before he left to return as soon as possible to what he termed an enchanting island. The ladies spoke frequently of him but other objects came to claim their attention, so they gradually began to forget him.

The following day I received a letter from my true love, which ran as follows:

"Dearest Angelica:

"We must depart tomorrow to our orders,

and I cannot have the supreme pleasure of seeing you this week. It is useless to describe the pain it gives me to leave thus without seeing you, for you well know what the state of my feelings must be.

"One thing consoles me, however. I will only be absent for seven or eight days at the most and then I will repay myself for what I have missed this while.

"The prior promised us a vacation of three days and you can imagine with whom I will spend them, but there is a string tied to it. Although everyone is to have a vacation, we will not all have it at the same time. We are to take it by twos and one of my friends named Vernier has asked leave to accompany me and I didn't have the heart to refuse him.

"It is the same Vernier that you met last year; Rosa knows him well. He, and he only, knows what has been going on at the convent; the rest know absolutely nothing about it and the prior did not grant them permission to visit it. His coming need not worry us in the least; he can amuse himself to his heart's content. As for us, we can take care of that little matter to the king's taste.

"So until we meet again, take good care of your health and I will husband my forces so that when we meet, our mutual pleasure shall be greater than ever.

"Good-bye, my queen, a thousand kisses for you.

"Your ever faithful and sincere friend,

    DOM DELABRISE"

I was glad to hear from him but I thought it most untimely and was therefore somewhat vexed. Somehow I felt that he could never be the same to me. To draw my mind from these thoughts, I went in search of Suzanne, whom I found alone.

This was a surprise to her, as she believed I was yet with my new lover; I stated the object of my visit and she asked me to take a seat and help her with some embroidery she was engaged upon, so we could talk at our leisure.

"Well, Suzanne, what is your opinion of the young Franciscan?"

"He is perfectly charming; we passed two hours together and I was delighted."

"He is the innocent cause of much sorrow for me tonight."

"And how so?"

"I dreamt of Dom Delabrise the other night and he reproached me most bitterly for bestowing my affections upon another, and the truth is, I have come to blame myself for my conduct."

"Never mind what I tell you, you ought to hold Dom Delabrise dearer than any other man in the whole world, but that does not mean that he must have a monopoly.

"Take me and Dom Bigot, for instance. I love him dearly but I do not pass my pleasure on account of him. No, whenever the opportunity presents itself of getting some extra fucks, I take it, as I am sure he does too, with other women. Liberty is a beautiful thing in itself. Besides, variety is the spice of life. There are pleasures that I derive from Dom

Bigot that I never would from another, because I really love him.

"By and by you will experience the same feeling with Dom Delabrise, but that should not prevent us from taking another prick into our cunts once in a while. If it does not give entire satisfaction, it always cools, at least for a time, the heat of our burning slits. Besides, situated as we are, we could hardly do otherwise. It would not be good policy for us to give ourselves up entirely to one man and run the risk of jealousy. When you swear fidelity, you put shackles on your conduct."

"Your advice is most sensible and has quieted my scruples with regard to Dom Delabrise, but he shall always have the warmest place in my heart, just the same."

"And I suppose you are not so awfully sorry that he has not come today after all."

"Don't let us speak about it any longer; I feel as if I were going to . . ."

"Tut-tut, it is always best to talk about what we love most, but when we have finished this strand, we will quit, and do what we can to console each other."

She then came over and sat near me, and throwing her arms around me, she gave me an impetuous hug, then, taking my face between her hands, she kissed me several times; then, drawing my hand over her shoulders, she began to work her nimble fingers through my waist until they reached my titties, an operation that sent a thrill of pleasure through my whole body.

She lingered, fondling first one nipple and then the other. I could feel her knees shaking from excitement as she tried to force her hand down on my belly, but a tight waistband prevented her from going that far. Suddenly, as if beside herself with desire, she pulled me down till I lay almost across her lap and before I knew what she wanted, I felt her hand beneath my skirts and another spasm of delight overcame me.

Her magnetic fingers were soon playing up and down, to and fro around my secret parts, now and then finding their way along the crack that divided my arse.

I became weak from sheer pleasure and rolled off her lap onto the floor, she falling on top of me; my skirts were clear up to my waist and the sight of my limbs seemed to excite her still more, if such a thing was possible.

She almost sank her teeth into the flesh of my legs and body. I rolled over on my stomach to avoid her bites, and she drove her face between the cheeks of my arse and I could feel her tongue forcing its way into my enchanted little arsehole.

I had caught the fever from her and was now subjecting her person to the same treatment.

We had wriggled into the position that knowing ones well call "69"—that is, our heads were buried between each other's thighs and we were licking and sucking each other's cunts so that soon the supreme spasm of spending overcame us.

I felt it flowing from me at the moment when Suzanne's slit squirted a shower of whitish liquid all over my face. The reaction now came, our muscles relaxed, our heads dropped and we held each other for a while in a limp embrace.

Then I made my cousin acquainted with the contents of the letter from Dom Delabrise. She did not seem to be much put out about the fact of Vernier coming. She, on the contrary, seemed highly pleased.

One day while rummaging in her bureau, I came across a small article of a peculiar shape, covered with fine hair, the same as that which ornamented my dildo.

"Say, cousin, what is this?"

"What is what, my dear?"

"This, what is it used for?"

"Oh, that is what men use when they have connection with women, to guard against children."

"How is it that our friends never made use of them?"

"I'll tell you why. They do not use them except when they have had no fucking for some time and they fear that they cannot control themselves. At the moment of spending and to prevent any serious consequences, they put on these preventatives."

"Has it ever been used in you?"

"Yes, but I don't mind."

"I will put it into my pocket, to satisfy my curiosity."

"It serves also another purpose, you know. There are women called whores, who sell their charms to the first comer. Well, the most prudent of these make use of it to guard against contagion of some sexual disease which men are sometimes afflicted with."

"As I see, the one wears it to prevent getting knocked up and the other to ward off disease."

"Precisely!!"

Until the arrival of Dom Delabrise, I did the best I knew how under the circumstances. Rosa, Suzanne and myself were strolling in the park when he and his friend arrived at the convent. They immediately came out in search of us, not even taking off their traveling boots.

The preliminary civilities were hardly over when Suzanne, under some pretext, hurried off in spite of our entreaties to make her stay. Rosa took charge of Vernier.

"Well, Blondy, it is a rare treat to see you!" she said, addressing him in the most familiar way. "Don't be such a stranger after this; you must accompany your friend every time he comes."

We paid very little attention to their lovemaking and cooing—we were too busy with our own—but when they entered one of the rooms in the pavilion, I called my lover's attention to it.

He immediately expressed a desire to do likewise, so we lost no time in getting inside. As we entered we heard the other two talking and, according to what we heard, they were just then busily engaged in inspecting each other's secret charms. Rosa was saying:

"I like your prick, because your hair and mine are of the same color; see, there is no difference between them."

We did not take time to amuse ourselves in the same manner. Dom Delabrise was in too much of a hurry. I had his long, stiff dart in my hands and my burning cunt was consumed with a desire to sheath it.

He made me kneel down on the bed and at once shoved his prick from behind into my hot cunt. He worked slowly and succeeded in making me come three times before he pulled out to squirt his spunk all over my arse.

I was delighted with this new way of fucking, for I felt his dear prick go in much further than before and I made up my mind that in the future I would practice this mode oftener. I told my lover so, who informed me that there were many more ways of making love, which in time he would teach me.

It being near supper time, there was just time enough for the two monks to put themselves into a respectable state to go and make their bow to the Lady Superior.

After supper I brought forth the little object of which I have spoken, wishing to try it and satisfy my curiosity. It did not take me long to make up my mind that it was of little value. I felt no agreeable sensations of it working in and out.

I managed to have Dom Delabrise with me that night and made him fuck me six times before he went to sleep. I awoke first in the morning, ready for more deeds of love, and I therefore lost no time in uncovering my lover and inspecting his sweet prick. I began to finger it and had the satisfaction of getting it into working condition, when my lover awoke. I turned and offered him my altar from behind. He understood and gave me another dose dog-fashion, as he called it.

Just then my lover's chum entered and, seeing how we were employed, wanted to retire, but my lover as well as myself, as if calling from one mouth, called to him to stay.

"Don't be bashful," said Dom Delabrise. "You will enjoy this picture. Angelica dear, frig his prick while I keep on fucking you and then you may have him in your cunt after I am done."

I pulled the prick of Vernier out of his trousers. I found it already stiff and the sight excited me to the highest pitch of lasciviousness. I felt myself coming but instead of causing my excitement to abate, the lewd proceedings kept me in fighting trim. Delabrise shot his spunk all over my arms and made room for his friend, who entered me in the same position. He managed to make me come twice before he let his load fly. I, in the meantime, fingered my lover's prick and stiffened it up again.

I treated him to a furious frigging, which caused him to spend all over my hand and face. Then we got up, satisfied for the time, and went to recover ourselves with a rich breakfast.

My cousin received company in the parlor that day and I had the room all to myself and was able to make my lover's stay a continued round of pleasure.

I had Suzanne in with me and Vernier was also of the party, and between myself and Suzanne, we succeeded in keeping the two monks in continuous excitement. We made them perform wonders of fucking and when they had finally to leave us, they did so with the knowledge that they had spent a delightful vacation, even though we had completely drained them.

The following Thursday, Dom Delabrise returned and it was, as far as I was concerned, the worst possible time he could have chosen, for I was very much indisposed, as my monthly period had just come around.

I informed him of the matter, which ill-fitted the special purpose he had come for. He was very much put out by this mischance. No sooner were we in our bedroom than he renewed his lamentations. I tried to reason with him but it was of no avail. He even went so far as to try to take the fortress by storm and did not desist until I had promised to do my best to quench his passions in some other way.

"Ah, my poor man, how you must suffer, let me put my hand into your trousers and see what is the matter—hm—but it is hard. I think I know a cure for it, though. Lie on the bed . . . that's it . . . you know that I do not mean to be unkind. There, how do you like this? Does my tongue tickle it nicely? Now I will take it into my mouth and suck it like a baby sucks the mother's breast. Tell me, pet, does it make you feel good?"

"Yes, yes, darling, keep on, don't stop, dear. You were always kind to me, I love you more than ever, you sweet little sucker . . . keep . . . keep on . . . let me move it in your sweet mouth . . . ah! that is nice . . . a little more . . . oh! oh! I am c-o-m-i-n-g."

I swallowed the cream and found it delicious. Then I made him button up, as I expected my cousin to enter any moment.

We had supper and then I proposed to share my bed with him. He was still thanking me for the pleasure I had given him when my cousin entered and I told her in whispers about my indisposition and that he would like to have her in my stead, but didn't dare to ask her.

"Willingly. Did he think I would refuse? I would indeed be hard to please if I did not accept an offer like this."

She ate supper with a particular relish that evening. I left them to themselves. Finally they stripped and went to bed. I bid them good night and wished them all kinds of pleasure, then I went to bed.

I prepared breakfast and served it to them while yet in bed. During the afternoon we found ourselves entirely alone. I suggested that Dom Delabrise should tell us how old he was and under what circumstances he had had his first connection with a woman.

"I was seventeen and had already entered our order when I gave up my maidenhead to a girl of fourteen and she made me a present of hers, and it happened in this way:

"The young girl was my cousin. She was left an orphan while still very young. My mother took and raised her with us. I left home at the age of twelve to enter the order of White Monks. While there, I learned many things from my young companions and among other things was a knowledge of the relation of the sexes, so that in case a girl fell into my power, I could fuck her without further instructions, even with as much skill as Brother Luce performed on Sister Agnes.

"After being formally enrolled, I was permitted to pay a visit to my home. My brother was away studying and my sister was married, so I found nobody at home but my parents and my cousin.

"I hardly knew her, so much had she changed, but it was a change decidedly to her advantage. I noticed from the fullness of her bust that she was no longer a child and I resolved then and there that I would deflower her.

"My mother furnished me the chance I was looking for by giving me a bedroom which opened into the one occupied by my young cousin. I did not dare pay her a visit the first night. I wished to feel my way first and see how she would take my advances. She had given me a friendly embrace on my arrival, but that was not enough to encourage me to take any more serious liberties with her.

"In the morning I rose before she did; it was already broad daylight. I softly opened the door and peeped in; she was still asleep, but her bust was entirely bare.

"I tiptoed near to see if I could catch a glimpse of her sweet grotto of love, and succeeded in seeing the whole of her fine little cunt as she just then made a movement, giving me a full exhibition of the works I was determined to penetrate before night had passed.

"I tumbled back into bed again and jerked myself off. Chance brought us together a short while before dinner and I took occasion to compliment her upon her appearance and she returned the compliment.

" 'But I have not got such pretty things as you have on your breast.'

" 'There is nothing strange about that, you would have it if you were a girl.'

" 'Then I wish I were one. I have never seen anything nicer.'

" 'Hush, Aunt is coming; she will scold us. Besides, you who are ordained should not talk like this.'

" 'There is nothing in my vows that prevents me from admiring anything beautiful, especially for the gratification of His chosen servants, like myself, and there is nothing sinful for me to admire His creations in any form in which I may find them.'

" 'Oh my God! If my aunt heard you! She who has thanked the Lord for having a saint in the family.'

"We were still talking when a servant entered. She immediately changed the subject of our conversation and a stray smile that I observed gave me an idea that I would be successful. Girls mature early, you know, Angelica, and they could give us men pointers on such matters."

"The men have always those opinions of us and they are the very ones to start and awaken our early maturity. I suppose you found occasion to have another little private talk with her."

"Yes, that very afternoon, about four o'clock we went together to visit some relatives of ours living a little distance out of the city. We did not stay very long and returning, took our way thru the woods skirting the banks of the river.

"As a boy, I knew a hidden place and I intended to take my cousin there to continue the conversation we had had in the morning. I found the place and, saying that it was too early yet to return home, I prepared to sit down in this secluded spot and have a chat.

"She blushed and trembled but, without hesitation, she agreed. We sat down and, coming close to her, I put my arm about her waist and started to unbutton her dress, saying:

"'Cousin dear, do you remember what we were talking about this morning? You know it is no sin to admire the work of God, so let me see your titties; instead of sinning, you will be doing a very commendable thing by allowing one of His servants to admire the beauties given you by Him.'

"'Oh, cousin dear, do not deceive me, it is surely not wrong to expose myself thus?'

"'Oh, you innocent, if you feel pleasure in showing me that which no one else has yet seen, it must be a good work, you are performing, for otherwise God would prevent you from feeling pleasure.'

"'Yes, I think you are right. It gives me pleasure, especially when you are handling them as you are doing now. I have a feeling creeping over me, the like of which I have never felt before.'

"'Do you like that feeling?' I asked her, while I pressed hot kisses on her titties and, taking the nipples between my lips, I began to tickle them with the tip of my tongue.

"I produced the effect I intended. Her hand stole down and pressed the point above the junction of her thighs.

"'Cousin dear,' said I, 'if you feel pleasure where your hand is now, I must see that place too. You will do me a great favor and by doing me this favor, you will be doing something very laudable.' With this, I put my hand beneath her skirts and began to feel for her little cunt, which was quivering with excitement under my lewd touches. She let me do as I liked and, pushing up, I feasted my eyes on her treasures.

"My hands wandered all over her mound, which was just beginning to show a little fine fleece. I pushed my finger between the half-open lips but soon her hymen hindered my getting deeper into her and, to make her still more willing, I knelt down in front of her and began to kiss and suck her clitoris; her naturally lascivious temper now began to assert itself. Her arse began to move under my proceedings and sighs of pleasure escaped her; she was ready to receive the final lesson in venery. Getting up, I released my now impatient prick, which longed to make the acquaintance of the fine little temple of love, which I continued to finger.

" 'Look here, cousin, you may as well admire my hidden beauties and caress them too, if you wish.' With this, I felt her little hand already feeling my delighted prick; I showed her how to pull the skin back and expose the purple head, which evidently pleased her very much.

" 'What do you call this?' she asked.

" 'This is my prick and what I am feeling is called a cunt; and these two parts are made for each other and there is no greater pleasure in this world for man and woman than putting the prick into the cunt. This action is called fucking, and if you will let me, I will fuck you for our mutual pleasure.'

" 'But, cousin, is that not sinful? But no, it cannot be, for I know that it would give me pleasure to feel this beautiful thing in here.'

" 'Now it is no sin if you do it with me, at least, but if it should be I can absolve you, but as you have remarked, it can be no sin as those parts have been made for that purpose, only we must keep this a secret between us, as there are always people who are envious of being not able to obtain any heavenly enjoyments and twist things in such a manner as to make it appear that the most innocent pleasures are sins.'

" 'That is all right, cousin. As long as you and I know we are doing nothing wrong, it is nobody else's business, and as I am sure that you only want to teach me laudable and commendable things, you may instruct me how to fuck. I am longing for that enlightment; just tell me what to do and I am sure that I will prove an apt scholar.'

" 'No doubt, my dear. I will instruct you in this right off, but before proceeding I must tell you that you will experience at first intense pain, until your little cunt has been stretched sufficiently to accommodate my prick but this will be immediately followed by the most exquisite pleasures, so if you are willing to bear those pains, say so, and I will offer my prick to celebrate the first fuck in your narrow slit.'

" 'Well, I am ready, so do not lose any more time, but fuck me.'

" 'Lay back . . . take off your drawers . . . good . . . now spread your legs as much as you can.' I then topped her, put my prick to the exceedingly small opening and began a steady pressure; after quite a while I succeeded in lodging the head between the lips.

The little one cried out with pain, but this, instead of making me more tender, only increased my passion and keeping up a steady pressure I was buried in her halfway. Then, pulling back again, I asked her to buck up against me. She did so, and putting my whole force to it, I pushed at the same time, and while she cried aloud I felt my prick breaking down all obstacles and sinking into her up to the roots.

"The long sustained excitement caused me to spend now and my spunk ran in a stream from me, oiling her splendidly and soothing the torn and lacerated parts of my young relative.

"My prick never lost any of its stiffness and I remained lodged in the sweet cunt, motionless until my little girl came to again, when she pressed me with all her might, saying:

"'You have hurt me fearfully, but it now begins to feel good.'

"'Well, shall I begin to move again?'

"'Yes, but slowly at first . . . that is nice. Now a little faster . . . tell me what to do, shall I move up as before . . . yes, that is nice . . . faster now . . . faster . . . oh! this is the best ever. I thank you for having taught me this. Ah, I must cross my legs over your back, oh, now it is going in deeper. Ah, I feel something flowing from me . . . do not . . . pull out . . . leave it . . . where it is.'

"She had spent for the first time, but her desires were not satisfied yet for she treated my prick to a series of pressures, making me feel that I did not want to leave this enchanted place, so I took another turn out of her, then we got up and hurried home. On the way thither I told her that I intended to sleep with her the coming night and she was delighted with it.

"So when I retired I went directly to her room and found my cousin already in bed, waiting for me, and during that night and all the following ones of my stay, I gave her instructions in the art of fucking and she certainly proved an apt scholar. She was, and is today, one of the hottest pieces of cunt that I ever met with, excepting you, my dear Angelica, and this is the story of the loss of my maidenhead."

"What became of your cousin?"

"She is today my sister-in-law and, as I return every year for a few weeks at the old home, we repeat the lessons, and if I had to embrace the priesthood to please my mother for the purpose of leaving most of the estate to my older brother, I have taken the task upon myself to make the children for him and, as I am a good deal better furnished than he is, my sister-in-law is delighted to help me all she can. Out of four that she bore him, I can with right claim to be the father of three of them, among whom was the first born.

"I fucked her the night before the wedding continuously from ten in the evening till six in the morning. She tried to outdo me and succeeded in stiffening my prick nine times before I would cry for quarter.

"Before the ceremony I had to hear her confession in the sacristy and instead of doing this, I fingered her cunt and she my prick, till she had me stiff again, then kneeling down on the floor, she made me fuck her dog fashion twice; oh she is certainly a hot piece, for she asked me to get the chaplain to look after her ailings in my absence, and he, being a friend of mine, is helping her out with his prick."

This story had made my cousin so hot that she asked Dom Delabrise if he could not quench the fire he had kindled. I took pity on Felicity, made her kneel where she was, uncovered her from behind and made Delabrise mount and give her a good poking.

The time had now come for Delabrise to leave and, after taking me in his arms, he expressed the hope of meeting me well the next time. Then he left.

A few days after this I received word that I would be permitted to take the black veil and that in consideration, therefore, I should employ the intervening time in visiting my people. In consequence, my mother called at the convent to take me home.

My companions exacted a promise from me that I would write frequently and let them know how I was getting along. How I kept my promise may be seen from the following letters:

"My dear Felicity:

"I arrived Thursday at my parents' home; no one could have had a grander reception. One glance told me that many changes had taken place since I had left. I understand that the Bishop of — is responsible for most of these changes and that he has furnished the funds to fit out the house in its present luxurious style.

"I have not had the pleasure of making his

acquaintance but we expect him in a few days and then I shall be able to tell you what he looks like. My sister treats me with genuine sisterly affection.

"One afternoon, while we were together doing some work, she told me the life in the convent was the best that a woman could adopt and she said that she would one day most likely follow my example.

"Now, knowing that her cunt had earned all the wealth surrounding me, I had a time to suppress my mirth at this hypocritical talk. I pretend to be very innocent and I had to bite my lips more than once to keep from bursting out.

"I expect to keep on playing the guileless innocent until I have succeeded in getting behind the secret of this little whore, my sister, and the Bishop.

"I am desirous of seeing you and my lover again. Remember me to him and to the ladies whom we consider our intimate friends.

"I am your loving cousin,

ANGELICA."

"Dear Felicity:

"I cried with joy on reading your letter, I have had the pleasure of meeting the Bishop and of dining with him. He is a handsome man and was politeness personified. He even offered me his services should I have need of them. I do not doubt but he would be willing to contribute to an increase of my income.

"He has for a servant a young lackey, quite good looking, who, if I am not mistaken, takes more than an ordinary interest in my sister's maid, to which she is not at all indifferent. His Excellency acted with the utmost reserve towards his lady love while I was present, but in spite of all their precautions I noticed that their eyes, whenever they met, talked most eloquently the language of love and I believe that they repaid themselves for their compulsory restraint the very next night, for they slept together.

"This is all the information I can give you this time, but I have devised a plan whereby I can spy on them without being seen and, in my next letter, I may be able to give some interesting news.

"I have not yet made the acquaintance of the Bishop's nephew, but if he tries to make love to me, he will receive a cold reception, for if he is as handsome as Adonis, I will not love him.

"Preserve your strength, so that when I return, I may show you that I am as ever,

"Your most affectionate cousin,

ANGELICA."

"Dear Angelica:

"I enclose a letter from Dom Delabrise. He begged me to explain to you how it came about that this letter was so long delayed, and I assured him that you would not be angry with him. We talked about you a great deal and, knowing that you would be thankful for anything that would console him, I took your place and had him fuck me four times, so that he could enjoy your embrace by proxy, so to speak. Adieu, pet.

"Yours,

FELICITY."

"Dear Felicity:

"I am delighted to hear that you saw fit to console my poor Delabrise with your own charms and, when you see him again, tell him that I am longing to be with him again.

"I have finally caught our lovers at some of their amatory combats and will tell you how I managed it.

"Having examined the garret directly over my sister's room, I employed the better part of three days that my sister was away from home to make an opening in the floor of the garret so that I could get a good view of her room, taking care to make it so that nothing could be seen in the ceiling.

"On the same day that my sister returned home, the Bishop called to see her. That was about four o'clock in the afternoon. After supper I took leave of the company, saying that I wished to retire. So I went to bed early and was up again at five in the morning, ready for all emergencies.

"I dressed myself immediately and stole softly to the garret, leaving my shoes at the door which I closed after me. On tiptoes, I slipped over to the hole in the floor and put my eye to it, stretching myself at full length on the floor; this gave me an easy and comfortable position and I could observe all that took place in the room below, which I believed was the temple where my sister sacrificed to Venus.

"It was already broad daylight and the blinds and curtains were thrown back. The lovers, still asleep, were partly uncovered. My mouth watered at the sight of the long and big prick lying so nicely between the Bishop's thighs. I had held my post nearly an hour before they began to stir and finally they woke up.

"The first move my sister made was to put her hand on the still limber prick. She evidently was experienced in handling this dart. She began with shoving the skin back and forth, uncovering the head and then pulling the skin over it again, while with the other hand she played with the bag underneath. Then she took the prick between her two hands, rolling it between. Seeing that her work was about to be crowned with success, she got up and knelt well over the Bishop in such a manner that her cunt was just above his face and her face above his prick. No sooner was she in this position than the Bishop began to kiss her cunt and suck it, while she reciprocated in the same manner on his prick; no sooner had she succeeded in getting it entirely stiff than she jumped up and bringing her gaping bijou over his prick, she let herself slowly down upon it, burying it to the root in her happy cunt.

"I could see that she was well educated in all the refined ways of making love, for she rode her lover with consummate skill. He must have been on the verge of spending when I heard him mutter the word 'arsehole,' and my sister, understanding his wishes, allowed the stately prick to slip out of her cunt and, taking hold of it, she lodged it in the neighboring hole and made it disappear between the big cheeks. The Bishop grunted with satisfaction and, reaching under the pillow, he handed a big dildo to my sister. She quickly inserted it in her cunt and kept working it there, while she at the same time flew up and down on the Bishop's prick, who shouted:

"'Ah, my dear, you kill me with pleasure! You are the best little whore I ever had the luck to possess. You never leave anything to wish for; you always know how to please my most lascivious ideas; I do not think that there is anything for you to learn in the way of whoring!'

"'Oh yes, I think there is, but I have learned all that I know from you; you have been fingering my cunt since I was barely nine years old and at that time you made me suck your prick and a year later you buggered me; and when I succeed in giving you satisfaction now, it is because you taught me and I know what your wishes are and try to anticipate them because I am grateful for all that you have taught me and because I love you for that.

"'But I really think there is yet more to learn in the way of lechery and I know where I could learn some new ideas, that is, in the fine brothels of Paris, and understand me well, for your sake, I would stay in one of them for a few weeks only, to be still better able to satisfy your licentious cravings."

"'You are a jewel to propose what I had not dared to propose to you, fearing you might be offended, but now as you have proposed it, you will do as you said. I will foot the bill and to show my gratitude I will buy a country estate for you and settle enough on you to make you independent, should I die suddenly; but enough of that now; I am coming—do you feel it squirting into you, pet?'

"'Yes, your hot spunk fills my whole entrails, but finish me off, please, work the dildo for me. That is right! Shove it up as far as it goes . . . ah I am spending!'

"She got up now and went to the bidet to cleanse herself, then, returning to the bed, she performed the same operation on the prick of her lover.

"I had seen enough and heard enough, so I left my place of concealment, went to my room and had to take my finger to quiet my lewd feelings caused by the spectacle which I had witnessed. In the afternoon the Bishop's nephew called. I had very little conversation with him. I could see by the way he eyed me that I would suit his lustful purpose very well, but he displeased me and I will give him such a send-off the first time that he speaks of love that he will lose all hope of ever possessing me then and there.

"Please hand the enclosed letter to Dom Delabrise, it may draw him out of the deep gloom. Let me hear from you often and rest assured that I am,

"Your affectionate cousin,

ANGELICA."

"Dear Felicity,

"I am glad to know that I will find a new

companion when I return to you. I have been treated to another view of two lovers, but before I begin to tell you what I saw, I must tell you about myself and how I was treated by my cousin and the Bishop's nephew.

"Sunday afternoon I was sitting in my room, writing to Dom De'abrise, when my cousin entered and signified a desire to speak to me privately. I hastily covered the letter I was writing and invited him to take a seat near me.

"He was quite agitated, his face was paler than usual and I thought I could detect the odor of liquor on his breath. He began by telling me his troubles and his ambitions, how he would like to be a lieutenant in the army and that the Bishop's nephew was the one to procure the appointment for him, and how he was deeply in debt and that the Bishop's nephew held nearly all his notes and that he would surely be ruined if the aforesaid nephew was not appeased.

"I listened till he had finished and then I told him how I felt about the matter. My life was devoted to the Church and God, I would do all I possibly could for him, even go to the Bishop in his behalf, but as for the nephew, he was out of the question.

"I tried in every way to calm him, but all my efforts had directly the opposite effect. He was becoming more and more excited; he pleaded and threatened in turn. I was becoming alarmed and made a move to leave the room. My crazy cousin got between me and the door and would not let me pass.

" 'No, you can't leave here,' he said between his teeth, 'till you listen to reason; my future depends upon it.'

"The Bishop's nephew then came in and added his entreaties to those of my cousin. I was now thoroughly aroused. I flew at him like a tigress and commanded them to let me pass. I rushed at my cousin and tried to push him aside. He grabbed me roughly around the waist and held me. I attempted to scream, but he placed his hand over my mouth and would not let me.

"He made some motion with his head to the Bishop's nephew and, as if prearranged, the latter bolted and shut the door from the inside and then drew the blinds.

"I was struggling all the time to free myself and in the scuffle was thrown to the floor. The Bishop's nephew now knelt down and tried to turn my head so that he could kiss me. I scratched his hands and spit in his face, but in spite of all that I could do, he managed to put his mouth to mine. Then he began to fumble under my skirts.

"I did my best to kick him, but he caught me by the ankles and raised my legs up so that my petticoats fell down off them and my whole lower parts were exposed to the lascivious glances of the cur. I could struggle no longer. I was completely exhausted. My cousin saw that and let go of my head.

"The nephew then threw himself full length upon me and forced my legs with his knees. By wriggling my hips first one way, then another, I kept him from getting his prick into me for some time, but at last I felt it slip in.

"The excitement of the struggle had nearly done the work for him, for he had not given half a dozen passionate shoves before he finished. I could feel that he had a much larger and thicker prick than my cunt had ever felt before and I was beginning to feel good when he stopped. He then rolled off and held me while my cousin took his place.

"After a few moments the pleasure became too much for me, I could not contain myself any longer. I threw my legs over my cousin's back in the heat of passion and glued my lips to his, while I shoved my arse to meet him halfway, to heighten the pleasure. The Bishop's nephew was frigging my arsehole and my fully aroused clitoris.

"I have found pleasure with Dom Delabrise, I have found pleasure with the Franciscan and with one of my own sex, but the pleasure I experienced now was never equaled before, the most exquisite of delights: rape!

"My cousin finished and got off me, but the Bishop's nephew was not yet satisified, so he mounted me again. This time he treated me to slow and deliberate shoves. At first I made some pretense of repelling him, but his shaft had not worked out and in a dozen times when I surrendered unconditionally and when he asked me if I would like a change of positions, I was more than willing.

"He got up, made my cousin lie down on his back. I had to kneel over my cousin, one knee on each side of his head, then the Bishop's nephew mounted me from behind, driving his stallion's prick into me with one mighty shove. I felt it touch way up at the entrance of my womb. At the same time I felt my cousin's tongue tickling my clitoris and with one finger he was buried in my arsehole. It was more pleasure than I had ever had before.

"I bent over and took the now stiff prick of my cousin into my mouth and paid back his efforts in my behalf. Before long the sexual spasm overcame me and the Bishop's nephew, but he was a prudent man, so pulling out, he forced the entrance next and deposited there his burning spunk.

"We now repeated this performance, only the men changed places. Both now had all they wanted for a little while at least, so they assisted me to rise and allowed me to sit on a chair.

"They both asked my forgiveness for what they had done to me and as I was not hurt, it was easy to forgive, after the intense delight they had given me. They next brought out some wine and plied me with it and I soon became half-drunk.

"I got frolicsome, talked and laughed; they exchanged lewd glances and I didn't resist in the least when they began to put me into a complete state of nakedness.

"I was fast getting drunk and I only dimly remember that the two men, one in the front and the other behind, violated me from both sides at the same time. I know I felt a sharp pain in my rectum and I heard a voice give an exclamation of satisfaction and that is all I remember till I awoke some three hours later, none the worse for my experience.

"My cousin got his commission in the army and his debts were paid. To compensate myself in a measure, I made my cousin sleep with me for the few nights he is to stay at home and he has taught me a few new tricks in the way of procuring sexual pleasure.

"A few nights ago he told me that if I would consent to meet him and the Bishop's nephew in my bedroom and submit to their assaults, the Bishop's nephew would settle two thousand livres a year on me and as I have noticed that the political situation is such a one that it is quite possible that all the convents will be suppressed, I have consented as well for your, Dom Delabrise and my own sake, for that will give us the means to stay together even if such calamities should happen to religious orders.

"Last night, I being alone at home with my cousin, the Bishop's nephew took me to my sister's room, where they both seemed to be well acquainted; for they got out of the hidden drawers all sorts of contrivances to be used to commit various kinds of sexual excesses; dildos of all kinds and sizes, switches, whip books and lewd scenes.

"In the course of the night all these things came into use and I must say that what those two devils do not know about increasing the delights of love is not worth knowing; they used or rather misused me in every possible way, but I could not expect to get off so easy when such a price had been given me, and, really, I was thankful for the experience. Besides, I found out that my sister deceives the Bishop and that his nephew as well as my cousin come in for a share of her favors.

"To return to the Bishop, he spent a week in the country with my sister, who returned alone, saying that the Bishop would follow her in a few days. On the eve of her return I heard my sister give some rather strange instructions to her maid: to wake her at a very early hour the next morning, as she wished to be ready by eight o'clock.

"I determined to be up as early as she. I hurried to take up my station at the peephole, but what was my astonishment to see my sister already up, standing there stark-naked, the hair of her grotto of love all done up in curl papers and her maid kneeling before her, comb in hand. I had to push my handkerchief into my mouth to keep from laughing right out.

"My sister then sat down and spread her legs apart; then the maid proceeded to take the papers out, leaving a nice little curl where the papers had been; then some dark brown powder was thrown on the curls to make the surrounding flesh look whiter and then they were trimmed so that not a single hair stood out further than its neighbor.

"The maid now rubbed her body with essences, after which she threw on a light wrapper, neatly made.

"A delicate pink shirt with delicate embroidery, a skirt of the same which covered only half of one leg, completed her apparel. Then my sister, thus dressed, stretched herself unconcernedly on the sofa, awaiting the arrival of the Bishop. The maid, also stark-naked, stood in a position that exposed her cunt to advantage.

"The Bishop entered. He wore a long trailing robe, whose train was carried by his lackey, and looked for all the world like the Great Mogul entering the harem quarters.

"He stood for a moment admiring the two Venuses, he praised the maid for the taste she showed in dressing cunts and the maid fell on her knees before him and, taking the exposed prick into her mouth, gave it a hearty suck, this being done in place of the customary kiss on the hand.

"He now gave free reign to his passions. He swooped down upon my sister and attacked her with passionate vigor. As for me, I pushed a dildo into my burning cunt and soon brought down a plentiful spend.

"After relieving myself I went back to my post and saw my sister being fucked in the front by the lackey and in the rear by the Bishop, while the maid was licking the latter's arsehole and working an enormous dildo in and out of her cunt. They finally finished, all four at the one time.

"There, my dear cousin, is what I have been up to. Next week I will return and then we will try to imitate some of these actions with the aid of some of our gentlemen friends. In the meantime, I am,

"Affectionately yours,

ANGELICA."

* * *

Angelica returned to the Abbey and took the veil, but a few weeks afterwards the government confiscated the property of the convents and then Angelica, Felicity and Suzanne and some others emigrated together with their lovers to America, where they married and founded a little colony and prospered and continued at their old games.

CARROLL & GRAF

GREAT EROTIC FICTION, ART BOOKS AND SEXUALITY TITLES FROM CARROLL & GRAF

EROTIC FICTION

- ❏ Banks, Carolyn/TART TALES 8.95
- ❏ Berliner, Janet (ed.)/DESIRE BURN 9.95
- ❏ Hill, Charlotte and William Wallace (eds.)/
  EROTICA: AN ILLUSTRATED ANTHOLOGY OF
  SEXUAL ART AND LITERATURE 18.95
- ❏ Hill, Charlotte and William Wallace (eds.)/
  EROTICA 2 18.95
- ❏ Hill, Charlotte and William Wallace (eds.)/
  EROTICA 3 18.95
- ❏ Hiller, Catherine/SKIN 8.95
- ❏ Hurford, Christopher (ed.)/EROTIC VERSE 10.95
- ❏ Jakubowski, Maxim (ed.)/THE MAMMOTH
  BOOK OF EROTICA 10.95
- ❏ Jakubowski, Maxim (ed)/THE MAMMOTH BOOK
  OF INTERNATIONAL EROTICA 10.95
- ❏ Lloyd, Joan/BLACK SATIN 8.95
- ❏ Lloyd, Joan/THE PLEASURES OF JESSICA LYNN 8.95
- ❏ Lloyd, Joan/SLOW DANCING 9.95
- ❏ Scott, G.C./THE PASSIVE VOICE 8.95
- ❏ Scott, G.C./HIS MISTRESS'S VOICE 9.95
- ❏ Selsdon, Esther (ed.)/LOVE'S THEATER 10.95

SEXUALITY/SELF-HELP

- ❏ Devlin, Dr. David/THE GOOD SEX GUIDE 17.95

- ❏ Hayman, Suzie/THE GOOD SEX GUIDE 2   16.95
- ❏ Hertford, Jane/ENJOYING SEX (POCKET GUIDE) 9.95
- ❏ Hertford, Jane/LOVING SEX (POCKET GUIDE)   9.95
- ❏ Hertford, Jane SENSATIONAL SEX (POCKET GUIDE)   9.95
- ❏ McCarthy, Barry and Emily/SEXUAL AWARENESS…10TH ANNIV.   11.95
- ❏ Quilliam, Susan/SEXUAL BODY TALK   15.95
- ❏ Rey, Caroline (ed)/THE MAMMOTH BOOK OF LOVE & SENSUALITY   10.95
- ❏ Stanway, Dr. Andrew/THE ART OF SENSUAL LOVING   16.95
- ❏ Stanway, Dr. Andrew/THE JOY OF SEXUAL FANTASY   16.95
- ❏ Stanway, Dr. Andrew/THE LOVING TOUCH   17.95
- ❏ Swift, Rachel/HOW TO HAVE AN ORGASM…AS OFTEN AS YOU WANT   10.95
- ❏ Wilson, Dr. Glenn/CREATIVE LOVING   17.95
- ❏ Wilson, Dr. Glenn/CREATIVE LOVEPLAY   17.95
- ❏ Wilson, Dr. Glenn/THE PERSONAL TOUCH   17.95
- ❏ Wilson, Dr. Glenn/THE SENSUAL TOUCH   17.95

Available from fine bookstores everywhere or use this coupon for ordering.

Carroll & Graf Publishers, Inc., 19 West 21st Street, Suite 601, New York, NY 10010-6805

Please send me the books I have checked above. I am enclosing $ (please add $2.50 per title to cover postage and handling). Send check or money order—no cash or C.O.D.'s please. New York residents please add 8 1/4% sales tax.

Mr. / Mrs. / Ms. _____

Address: _____

City: _____ State / Zip: _____

Please allow four to six weeks for delivery.